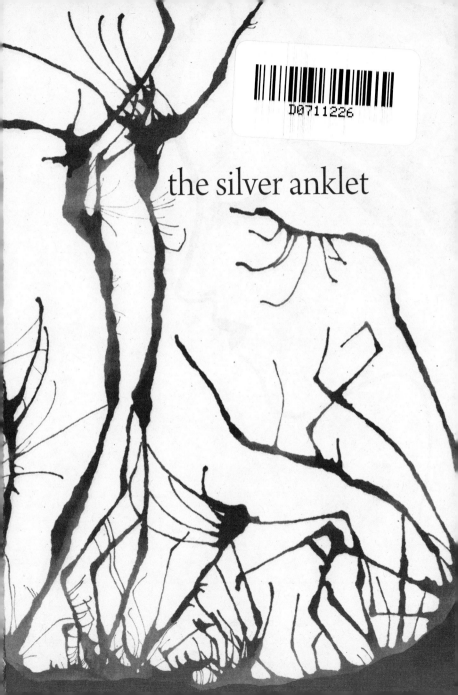

the silver anklet

the silver anklet

— tara trilogy —

mahtab narsimhan

DUNDURN PRESS
TORONTO

Edited by Shannon Whibbs
Designed by Courtney Horner
Printed and bound in Canada by Webcom

Library and Archives Canada Cataloguing in Publication

Narsimhan, Mahtab
    The silver anklet / by Mahtab Narsimhan.

(Tara trilogy ; 2)
ISBN 978-1-55488-445-2

    I. Title. II. Series: Narsimhan, Mahtab. Tara trilogy ; 2.

PS8627.A77S56 2009   jC813'.6   C2009-903262-7

1   2   3   4   5   13   12   11   10   09

Canada

 Conseil des Arts   Canada Council
du Canada   for the Arts

ONTARIO ARTS COUNCIL
CONSEIL DES ARTS DE L'ONTARIO

We acknowledge the support of the **Canada Council for the Arts** and the **Ontario Arts Council** for our publishing program. We also acknowledge the financial support of the **Government of Canada** through the **Book Publishing Industry Development Program** and **The Association for the Export of Canadian Books**, and the **Government of Ontario** through the **Ontario Book Publishers Tax Credit program**, and the **Ontario Media Development Corporation**.

Care has been taken to trace the ownership of copyright material used in this book. The author and the publisher welcome any information enabling them to rectify any references or credits in subsequent editions.

                                                                    J. Kirk Howard, President

Printed and Bound in Canada.
www.dundurn.com

    Dundurn Press   Gazelle Book Services Limited   Dundurn Press
3 Church Street, Suite 500   White Cross Mills   2250 Military Road
  Toronto, Ontario, Canada   High Town, Lancaster, England   Tonawanda, NY
        M5E 1M2   LA1 4XS   U.S.A. 14150

 Mixed Sources
Product group from well-managed forests, controlled sources and recycled wood or fiber
www.fsc.org Cert no. SW-COC-002358
© 1996 Forest Stewardship Council

ANCIENT FOREST ™
FRIENDLY

For Vicky, Mazarine, and Aziz

Hyenas!

The patch of sunlight at the edge of the forest had an odd look; dirty yellow and striped. Tara squinted hard and before her very eyes it moved, took shape, stood up: a yellow-eyed hyena! Glistening ropes of drool swung from its powerful jaws. It opened its mouth, revealing a jagged row of dirty teeth. It laughed.

"Ananth!" yelled Tara. She stumbled backward at the edge of the fairgrounds, not taking her eyes off the beast that hadn't taken its eyes off her. She whirled round. "COME QUICK!"

Ananth dropped the ice-lollies he had just bought from a vendor and ran toward her. "What's the matter?" he called out. "What happened?"

"Faster! Oh my God! Just look." Tara was paralyzed by the vision. The hyena retreated into thick bushes at the edge of the forest till only its snout showed.

Tara turned to face Ananth. Turned back. It was gone.

"What ... happened ... Tara?" Ananth gasped for breath, his face streaming with sweat.

"Here," said Tara. She jabbed the air with her finger. "I saw a huge hyena right here and it was staring at me. Oh God, Ananth, it was *massive*. It looked — I don't know — hungry..."

Ananth stared at her for a moment, aghast, uncomprehending. Then he burst out laughing. "Good one, Tara. You're kidding, right? That was brilliant!"

"Ananth, stop laughing. I'm serious. I saw the hyena as clearly as I see you. *Stop laughing, I said!*"

"That's enough, Tara." Ananth pulled her toward the fair. "Joke's over."

All around them the annual fair in the village of Ambala was at its peak of colour and noise. Along the periphery of the field, vendors hawked their wares: clothes, pots and pans, jewellery and handmade crafts. In the centre of the grounds the rides whizzed around. The food stalls, selling everything from sweets and snacks to biryani, thronged with people.

"I'm not joking," said Tara. She wanted to shake that smirk off his face. Why wouldn't he believe her?

Ananth stopped near one of the stalls and pointed to the ground. Two damp patches littered with wooden sticks marked the spot where he had thrown the ice-lollies. "Couldn't you have played your joke after we finished those? What a waste! You're buying the next round."

Tara resolutely looked away, refusing to answer him. Had she really imagined it? Was it just the midday heat that had made her see that horrible beast? Those searing yellow eyes and powerful jaws still made her pulse race. She shuddered, absolutely sure she hadn't been dreaming and met Ananth's gaze defiantly.

"Hyenas haven't been seen in the Kalesar forest for years, Tara. If you had to pick an animal to yell about, you could have at least picked something like — I don't know — maybe a wild boar? We have plenty of those ..."

"I know what I saw. You can say what you like." She glared at Ananth. He may have been her brother, but at this moment she had not a gram of sisterly feeling toward him.

"*Didi,*" a voice cried. "Didi, Didi, I want some more money!" Tara's anger melted away instantly at the sight of her younger brother, Suraj. He raced up to her and tugged at her sleeve, his best friend Rohan close behind.

"You can't have spent your money *already*," said Tara. "We've been here for just over an hour!"

Suraj nudged his friend.

"We did, Tara-didi," Rohan said. "Please, just enough for another ride on the Ferris wheel. *Pleeease?*"

The wooden Ferris wheel, its giant spokes covered with red, blue, and green ribbons, whizzed through the air, holding screaming children in its many-cupped arms. Beside it, a battered merry-go-round with black and white horses bobbed up and down, slicing through

9

the cloud of heat and flies. Tinny Hindi music blared from a speaker mounted on its ragged canopy. Children stood impatiently in double lines, awaiting their turn.

Tara sighed. "All right, just one more ride and then both of you come straight back to me. If I'm not here, look for me. Understand?"

They nodded, arms outstretched, faces distorted with extra-wide grins. Tara pulled some coins from her pocket and picked out a rupee for each. A third person appeared alongside, arm outstretched.

"For me, too," said Layla, their stepsister.

Suraj shifted away slightly, his smile dimming.

"I don't have any more to spare," said Tara. The sight of Layla always reminded her of her evil stepmother, Kali. She tried not to snap at Layla.

"But you do, you do!" said Layla, her voice shrill. "I'll tell your mother you're being mean to me again."

Tara hesitated for a moment, then pulled out a coin from her pocket and slapped it on Layla's palm. Layla did not bother to thank her as she waddled after Suraj and Rohan.

"Come right back, Suraj, Rohan," Tara yelled after them. "I'll be waiting."

Layla stopped, turned around. "Don't worry, Tara. I'll look after them well." People passed by in front of her and she barely caught a glimpse of those mean black eyes that glittered in Layla's pudgy face. When Tara could see her again, Layla was already walking away.

"That's precisely what I *am* worried about," muttered Tara when she saw her stepsister catch up with the boys. "I don't trust her. Not one bit."

"Oh forget about her, Tara," said Ananth. "What could happen to them in the mela on this fine, sunny day? It's time we had fun, too. What do you want to do first?"

"Let's walk around, take a look," said Tara. "I don't want to wander too far from here till Suraj and Rohan come back."

They strolled along the periphery of the fair. The Ferris wheel was still, hordes of children gathered at its base, waiting to climb on board. It was close enough. Suraj would be fine. He was growing up so quickly. Still, after almost losing him once, she hated to let him out of her sight for even a short period of time.

"Just one second, Ananth." Tara darted back to the Ferris wheel. An overweight boy with a smiling, round face was in charge. Tara leaned against the barrier and watched him for a minute; he seemed to be enjoying himself almost as much as the children.

"Hey!" she called out.

The boy glanced at her.

"Large crowd today, isn't it?" said Tara.

The boy nodded, his cheeks jiggling, his eyes sparkling. "Lucky for us!" He unhitched the bar on a seat that rocked gently. Two girls sat there leaning back, clutching the sides tightly. He reached out with his strong arms. The girls shook their heads.

"Come on," said the boy, smiling. "The others want a turn, too. Here grab my arms, I'll show you something else that's fun."

The girls grasped his arms and clung on. The boy lifted them into the air simultaneously, swung them over the exit barrier and deposited them gently onto the ground. Squealing their thanks, they ran off.

Tara couldn't help but smile at his ingenuity. Two boys got into the vacated seat, squirming to get comfortable as they wedged their feet against the footbar. "You're doing a great job with these kids," said Tara. "They really like you."

The boy shrugged. "I love doing this, too."

"My name's Tara, and those two are my brother and his friend." She pointed out Rohan and Suraj waiting in line. "Rohan's in the yellow shirt and Suraj is wearing the white kurta-pajama. Keep an eye on them will you, please?"

"I'm Vayu," said the boy. "No problem, I'll watch out for them." He swung two more children over the exit gate and helped another two into an empty seat.

Ananth had caught up to her. "Planning on telling every person at the fair to keep an eye on Suraj?" He addressed Vayu. "You got asked, too, right?"

Tara blushed and punched Ananth on the shoulder "Shut up."

Vayu smiled at Ananth. "I really don't mind. Are you coming back for them?"

"No, just tell them to look for us," said Tara. "We won't be too far from here. Probably near the performers in the centre of the field. And don't let either of them back on the ride. I think they've both had enough.

Vayu nodded. All the seats were full with a fresh lot of screaming children. Tara watched him secure the barrier once more, move the crowds waiting in line farther back, and sit on his high stool to start the ride.

"Happy now?" said Ananth. "Can we go do something interesting?"

Tara nodded absently, looking around her. "It's really crowded this year. I've never seen so many people at the fair in a long time."

"I heard the river's not been too flooded this year," said Ananth. "So many people are coming by boat from as far as Hissar. In fact, the waterway has more boats on it than ever before, and not just near the villages, either. It's easier to get to the forest for hunting and gathering firewood by boat than on foot!"

Tara barely heard him. She glanced once more toward the trees at the edge of the fairgrounds. Something caught her eye, a dark shape within the deep shadows, as if someone was hiding and watching them. She dug her nails into Ananth's arm. He winced.

"Ananth!" said Tara. "Did you see that? Something moved under that tree there."

"What?" said Ananth. He gazed in the direction she was pointing. "Where?"

"There, near that tree." Tara waggled her finger. "It's not moving anymore. But look carefully and you might see it."

"I don't see anything," said Ananth in a sharp voice. He looked away as he rubbed his arm.

"Something's wrong." Tara stared but could only see shadows once again. "You think it could be something like … last time?" Her voice tapered off. Spoken aloud, the very thought seemed absurd, impossible. "Or then maybe the hyenas have returned …"

"For God's sake, Tara!" said Ananth. "*He's* dead, remember? Just because you were right once, doesn't mean there's danger around you all the time. And I've told you before there are *no hyenas* in this part of the forest."

"Stop yelling at me," said Tara. "You're not always right, either."

But she had to admit he had a point. This was a normal day at a fair. What could possibly go wrong? Zarku was dead. *She* had been the one to reduce him to ashes. These had been sealed in an urn and she'd heard Lord Yama promise to bury it so that it would never be found. Ananth *was right* this time and yet …why did she feel so uneasy?

"I'm sorry, Tara," said Ananth. "Let's not fight. I want to have fun today. Come on, already." He was looking about him as eagerly as Suraj had a few moments ago.

Should she tell him about the silver anklet she had taken to wearing these last few days? It was clasped securely around her ankle, hidden underneath her shalwar. It had belonged to Zarku's mother and had once saved her from his wrath. Whether it would work again, she did not know, but the solid weight of it gave her a modicum of comfort.

Fingers snapped in her face and she jerked out of her reverie.

"Wake up, Kumbhkaran," said Ananth. "Want me to win you something at the archery stall or do you plan on standing here indefinitely, waiting for Suraj to return?"

Tara opened her mouth. Ananth raised his hand. "No, don't bother to answer that. You're coming with me."

They had been through so much together, Ananth and she. They had vowed to be brother and sister even though they were unrelated by blood. Tara noticed that he still wore the ragged thread that she had tied on his wrist in lieu of a real rakhi when they had first met. Already he was a head taller than her with a mop of curly black hair and serious black eyes that often twinkled when he was teasing her.

"Is this just another ploy to show off?" asked Tara. She tried to sound annoyed, but his infectious smile made it difficult.

"Me, show off?" said Ananth. "Never!"

"Oh, all right, let's go," said Tara. She glanced at the Ferris wheel one last time and followed Ananth.

They waded into the fairgrounds, thick with wandering animals, people, and above all, the tantalizing aromas of food. The late afternoon sun burnished everything to gold and even the air seemed to sparkle.

Ananth pulled her through the crowds to the archery stall. Three brightly coloured plastic parakeets stood on perches some distance away from the counter. There was just one customer ahead of them and he was hopeless. Tara watched him miss all three tries and walk away, shoulders slumped, muttering under his breath. The stall owner turned his shrewd gaze on them.

"Try your luck and win a beautiful doll or bear," he sang, waving his bony hand at the row of bright new toys on shelves in the tiny stall.

Ananth examined the two bows on the table.

"These are definitely rigged," he whispered to Tara.

"How can you tell?" she whispered back.

"By the string. It's too slack. The arrow can't go far."

"What are you looking at, young man?" said the owner. "Go on, win something for your girlfriend, don't be shy," he said. He picked up a bow and three arrows and handed them to Ananth. "Only one rupee!"

She's my sister," said Ananth. "And this bow is horrible. Do you have another one?"

"Hey!" said the owner. "Who are *you* to tell me that my bows are not good? If you can't shoot, move on. Stop maligning my good name." He glanced around quickly. A steady stream of people swept past his stall. No one stopped or even looked his way.

16

"A bad marksman always blames the bow," said Tara softly. She leaned against the counter and smiled at Ananth. "Sure you can shoot?"

"A good marksman will get his target *in spite* of a bad bow," said Ananth. "Watch closely and learn!"

Ananth picked up the bow and arrow and took aim. The arrow shot away from him and missed. Red-faced, he snuck a glance at Tara. "I wasn't focusing," he said.

"Ahhhh," said Tara. She tried hard not to smile.

The owner smirked. "That happens to the best of us. Try again."

Ananth raised the bow, fitted another arrow, took a deep breath and released it. It hit the mark. The parakeet keeled over and hung upside-down from its wooden perch. The smile slid off the owner's face. Ananth took aim and shot the third arrow. The last parakeet fell over.

"Two out of three," yelled Ananth. "*Yesss!*"

"Not bad," said Tara. "Not bad at all."

"Very good, very good," said the owner. His sour expression belied his words.

Ananth dropped the bow on the counter. "So, what have I won?" he asked, rubbing his hands together.

The owner brought a bedraggled bear and a cheap doll from under the counter. "Since you didn't hit all three targets, this is your choice."

"No, thank you," said Tara. The moth-eaten specimens looked as if they had lived a harsh and pitiful life. She refused to touch them and instead pointed to the shelves. "Why can't we have one of those?"

"Only if all three arrows hit the mark. Sorry!" said the owner. He slid the toys back under the counter, seeming to dismiss them already.

"You *cheat*," said Ananth. "You rig the bows and then try to slime out of giving us our prize? I want my money back!"

"Shhhhh!" said the owner. "There's no need to yell."

"Oh, come on, Ananth, you've proved your point. And besides, I'm too old to play with dolls."

"Suraj would have liked the bear."

"Yes, well, he's not here yet, is he? Let's go!" said Tara.

"Consider yourself lucky," said Ananth. He shook his fist at the owner as Tara dragged him away. The visibly relieved man looked around for his next customer.

"Suraj is not back yet," said Tara. "Do you think he's finished with the ride? Why isn't he here already?"

"Tara, it's time he learned to be independent, so stop worrying."

"He's my baby brother and I will always worry," said Tara. She scanned the crowds. "With the fair so crowded this year, it'll be tough to find him if he wanders away. He gets distracted so easily. I hope he's all right."

"Suraj and Rohan are together," said Ananth. "They'll be just fine."

"Mother and Father aren't here today, so he's my responsibility," said Tara. "You know that, right?"

"You're doing great so far," said Ananth. "Stop behaving like an old woman."

They passed a stall piled high with an array of rainbow-coloured sweets. "Want some mithai?" asked Ananth. "I'll buy."

Tara shook her head. "Not too hungry at the moment, but you go ahead."

"Maybe later," said Ananth. "Hey, let's take a look at that."

A crowd had gathered to watch a performance. They squeezed through to the front for a better look at the star attraction; a tall, wiry boy with close-cropped black hair and wearing patched, khaki shorts with a grayish-white shirt. Next to him was a wicker basket that could have housed a large dog. A young girl in a bright blue ghaghra-choli stood close by, gazing at the boy adoringly while he spoke.

"Come and see the greatest feat of all," the boy warbled. "A boy in a basket."

The crowd formed a tight circle around him. Tara and Ananth moved closer. As the crowd built up, the boy nodded. The little girl took the lid off the basket with a flourish.

"Look ladies and gentlemen, this is empty," he said. The girl turned a full circle, showing them the basket. "In a few moments it will be full ..." He paused. "... with me!"

The crowd shifted and fidgeted. *How was he going to do* that? thought Tara. She couldn't wait for him to get started. The girl set the basket on the ground, laid the lid next to it and moved away, grinning at the crowd. A string hung from the lid, which the boy tied to his right forefinger. Very slowly, he climbed in and sat down, legs folded against his body, parallel to his spine. His hands were wedged at his side, but his torso and head still stuck out of the basket.

"Ta-da!" he said, a cheeky smile on his face. He caught the little girl's eye and winked. She closed both eyes in an answering wink.

The crowd snorted in disgust. "Anyone can do this," a crusty old woman called out. "You call this a performance? You fraud! Wait till I come there. I'll make a kebab out of you and then stuff you into the basket. The crowd can reward me instead."

The boy sat there for a moment, quiet and confident. On that thin face, his shining eyes were the most prominent feature. Tara liked him instantly and refused to move, though the crowd, muttering and mumbling, had already started to unravel. There had to be more to this.

Calls of "fraud, liar, scoundrel" peppered the air.

"Wait!" the boy cried out. "I'm not finished."

The crowd stopped and turned to face him again.

As they watched, he squirmed and shifted, sinking lower and lower. He rearranged his bones to fit into the small space, filling every inch of the basket. Soon his entire torso was inside, his legs and arms wrapped around it at weird angles. It seemed as if someone had stuffed body parts randomly into a basket. The crowd stood mesmerized. When the boy had everyone's attention, he lowered his head into a small cavity that somehow still remained. The lid slid along the ground rapidly and Tara knew, somewhere in there, the boy was manipulating it. It snapped shut. Anyone walking past at this very moment would have seen a huge crowd staring at a basket!

Seconds later, clapping, whistling, and yelling erupted. A shower of coins hit the basket, which suddenly tipped over on its side. The lid flew open and the boy tumbled out; a grotesque caricature of a human crab. They watched, horrified, as he rearranged his limbs, standing tall once again. Another shower of coins landed around him.

"Shabash, wah-wah!" now filled the air.

"Thank you, thank you," he said. He quickly gathered the coins and stuffed them into a little pouch tied around his waist, neatly hidden under his shirt. The little girl skipped around, nimbly picking up the coins and handing them to the boy.

Tara and Ananth walked up to him. "That was *amazing*," she said. "How did you do it?"

"Oh, that." The boy shrugged. "It's nothing. I was born with flexible joints. The bad part is that I can't do heavy work without an arm or a leg slipping out of its socket. Like this."

He twisted his right arm sharply. It hung away from his body at an impossible angle. Aghast, Tara could only stare. Ananth was speechless.

"Put it back now!" she said. "Doesn't it hurt?"

The boy pushed his arm back into the socket. It settled with audible crack. Tara shivered.

I'm a freak." The boy winked. "Nah, it doesn't hurt. I've learned to live with it."

"That was just super, er —" said Ananth.

"Kabir," he said. "You?"

"Ananth. And this is my sister, Tara. We're from Morni."

"Ramgarh," said Kabir. "And this is my sister and wonderful helper, Sadia."

Sadia stood beside Kabir and looked up at them shyly. Kabir pinched her cheek gently and she giggled.

"That's a long way to travel, isn't it?" said Tara.

"Uh-huh, but I don't have a choice," said Kabir. He slung the basket on his shoulder and took Sadia's hand. "Fairs save my family from starving!"

"What d' you mean?" said Tara.

"We don't own land," said Kabir, walking along with them. "Father has to beg for jobs. Not enough food to go round. So I need the fairs to earn some extra money." He looked from one to the other. Tara stared into those grave black eyes that looked at her so directly. She had to smile. He was so open and likeable.

"We'll see you around," said Ananth.

Kabir nodded. "I'll be performing some more today. Drop by again. Great crowd, isn't it? We're lucky. Normally there are half this many people. I'll make good money today!"

"Yes!" said Ananth. "For the first time in three years the Ghaggar is navigable this time of year. People from Hissar and Bhiwani are coming in."

"Good for us and good for the boatmen, too," said Kabir. He flashed a warm smile. "I better be off. Bye."

Sadia smiled and waved goodbye. Tara watched them melt into the crowd, hoping they would meet up again.

The smells of food, sweaty people, animals, and fresh manure swirled around them in a pungent cloud. For a moment the sunshine and gaiety filled Tara to the brim; the Ferris wheel imprinted against a blue, blue sky, the shrieks of the children flying through the air, safely ensconced in wooden seats. A day filled with the ordinary excitement of going to the fair. She was so glad she had come.

Someone bumped into her. She wheeled around. "Oops, sorry, Didi —" A small boy ran off. No one she knew.

That was all it took. The sunshine dimmed. The shouts of the children grated on her nerves. She searched the crowds again and again. Where was Suraj? He should have been here by now. He was in for a spanking for worrying her like this. Rohan, too.

"Let's eat," said Ananth. "I'm starving." He made a beeline for the biryani stall just up ahead. Tara followed.

At the back of the tiny stall, large steel vessels were piled high with saffron and white rice, sprinkled liberally with nuts. A delicious fragrance of mutton cooked in yoghurt and spices perfumed the air.

"Two, please," said Ananth.

Tara was about to protest that she wasn't hungry, but it was too late. The vendor had already accepted payment and was measuring out the steaming biryani into dried banana-leaf cones. He handed them over, his eye already on the next customer in line. They sat under a banyan tree to enjoy their meal. Tara picked at her food while Ananth devoured his.

"If you're not going to eat that, hand it over," said Ananth. He burped loudly.

Tara handed over the food, glad to be rid of it. The normally tantalizing fragrance was making her sick. Suraj couldn't still be waiting for a ride. What was keeping him? She shot a glance at Ananth, still engrossed in his meal. If she voiced her fears, he was bound to tease her yet again. *Just a little while longer*, she thought, *then I'll start looking*. He was probably waiting in line for yet another turn or maybe he was at the merry-go-round.

They wandered through the stalls, examining the clothes and handicrafts on display. In the distance, they saw Kabir perform yet again, with his sister helping; a blur of bright blue between the onlookers. They passed a large stall piled high with silver vessels of every shape and size and Tara stopped for a moment. Soft, brown eyes stared back from the hundreds of gleaming surfaces around her. She smoothed a wisp of hair that had escaped from her shoulder-length brown plait. Her nose-stud sparkled momentarily, catching the sun.

"If you've finished admiring yourself, maybe we can move to something more interesting — like that marble shop?" Ananth smirked and pulled her away. She made a wry face and followed.

The sun started to slip behind the trees and crickets heralded the approach of night. Long shadows crept between the stalls and across open spaces.

"I better go look for them, Ananth. It's been far too long. God help Suraj if he's gone off to do something else and forgotten about me. I had told that ... that Ferris wheel boy, whatisname, yes, Vayu, to remind him to come back to me."

"It's definitely been long enough," said Ananth, frowning. "It's not like them to disobey you."

The words chilled Tara. Suraj might fuss, but in the end he almost always did as he was told. And Rohan mimicked Suraj.

"HYENA!" someone shrieked. "HELP!"

Tara's heart almost stopped beating. "I was right." She glared at Ananth. "*I was right!*"

They raced through the deepening dusk toward the towering hulks of trees that marked the forest's edge. Toward the scream.

two

Five into the Forest

People raced past them heading in the same direction. Tara, weaving through the crowds, couldn't get there fast enough. Why had she waited so long before looking for the boys? If anything happened to them, she'd never forgive herself.

Kabir caught up with them, looking like a ghost. "That was my mother's voice," he said. But before Tara or Ananth could say another word he sped away. They stuck to him like shadows as he flitted through the field.

An old woman paced at the edge of the grounds, her face streaked with tears. A few people were already there, crowding her, staring at her with open curiosity. Kabir pushed them aside roughly.

"Mother, what happened?" he said. "Where's Sadia?" Everyone leaned closer.

She managed to blurt one word. "Hyena." The tears started again.

The word shattered the silence. People rushed to the edge of the forest, searching the darkness, chattering and shouting to each other.

"What?" said Kabir. He had turned pale and Tara knew exactly how he felt; a hyena snatching that sweet little girl she had seen just a few hours ago. Sadia must be terrified and so must Kabir.

"After you left her with me," said his mother, her words punctuated with sobs, "she played for a while with the new doll you had bought her."

"And then?" asked Kabir.

"She asked for something to eat, so I told her to wait under that tree." His mother collapsed against him, weeping hard.

"Mother, don't stop. Tell me everything." Kabir's voice broke. "Please hurry."

Kabir's mother nodded, wiped her eyes, and took a deep breath. The rest of the story came tumbling out. Tara clutched Ananth's hand, not at all surprised to find that it was as cold and clammy as hers.

"I went to get her some aloo-puri. The stall was so close," said his mother. She pointed to it. "When I got back, she was standing at the edge of the forest staring at something. I called out to her and she turned. Just then ..." his mother's voice faltered.

"Just then *what*?" yelled Kabir.

"A huge hyena! It jumped out of the bushes, grabbed her and … and … pulled her in. She screamed. I was paralyzed, it was such a big ugly thing. If I had moved just a bit faster …"

"Where did this happen?" said Kabir. "Show me the exact spot."

Kabir's mother led them closer to the forest. The trees stood like sentinels, guarding the blackness beyond.

Suddenly Kabir stooped, picked something up off the leaf-strewn ground. A plastic doll. He hugged it to his chest. "Sadia," he whispered, his voice husky.

"Kabir!" someone called out.

A girl in a purple ghagra-choli emerged from the crowd. The mirrors on the edge of her green dupatta flashed and winked as she hurried up.

"Raani," said Kabir. "Thank God you're here!" He led her a short distance away from the crowd. Kabir's mother, Ananth, and Tara followed.

"What happened?" said Raani. "The craziest rumours are floating about back there. Something about an animal dragging away people … someone said hyena and I had to laugh —"

"It's true," said Kabir. "A hyena dragged Sadia off. Mother saw it."

"No!" said Raani. "When did this happen? Where?"

"Right here," said Kabir. "This is all I found of her." He held out the doll for a moment and clasped it to his heart again.

"Let me take a look," said Raani. "Don't worry, she can't be too far from here."

"God bless you," said Kabir's mother. She took Raani's slim hand in hers and kissed it.

Raani gave her a hug. "It'll be all right, Aunty. Don't worry."

"Mother," said Kabir. "I'll stay with Raani. Talk to one of the village chiefs. Tell them what happened. We'll need help. Hurry."

Kabir's mother ran back toward the villagers. The crowd had swelled. Many had brought lanterns that threw flickering, dancing lights across the field. Steadily the buzz grew louder, like a gathering hoard of mosquitoes.

"I'll be right back," said Raani. Without any hesitation, she stepped through the fence of trees and darkness swallowed her.

Tara looked at Kabir in surprise.

"Don't worry about her," he said. "She can see very well in the dark. They call her Raat-ki-Raani in my village."

"Ananth," whispered Tara. "We should go look for Suraj and Rohan. I have a very bad feeling about this."

"You're right," said Ananth "You head back to the Ferris wheel and talk to that boy there. I'll take a look at the other end. We'll meet back here in ten minutes."

Tara ran as fast as she could, her gaze fixed on the dark sphere imprinted on a blue-black sky. She dodged people,

29

cursing them silently for slowing her down. Vayu was shutting the ride for the night when she reached him.

"Vayu," said Tara, trying to catch her breath and speak at the same time, "where … is my brother … his friend?"

Vayu stared at her in confusion for a few minutes. Tara wanted to grab him and shake him up.

"Oh yes, the boy in the yellow shirt and his friend in the white kurta-pajama. You'd asked me to keep an —"

"Have you seen them in the last hour or so?" Tara practically screamed at him.

"No," said Vayu. "They finished the ride ages ago and left."

"Did they say they were coming to look for me? Where did they go?"

"I can't recall," said Vayu. He frowned. "I've seen a few hundred boys today, it's difficult …"

He glanced at Tara. "What's the matter?"

"They're both missing. Someone's just reported a hyena snatching a child. Please help me find them," said Tara.

"I'm so sorry," said Vayu. "What are their names again?"

"Suraj and Rohan."

"Where will you be?" he asked, securing the chain-link at the entrance. He slung a cloth bag over his shoulder.

"North end," said Tara. "Where the crowd is."

"I'll get my friend to make an announcement on the public address system. If they're on the grounds they will definitely hear it and come to you. I'll join you in a few minutes."

"Thank you," she stammered. "Thank you so much."

"Tara, wait!" said Vayu. "I just remembered one more thing."

"Yes?" She half-turned toward him, impatient to be off.

"Just as they were leaving the ride, a plump little girl who was with them insisted they come with her, that she had something to show them."

The few morsels Tara had eaten climbed in her throat. She stared at Vayu, willing him to laugh, to say he was joking. He looked back at her seriously. "Are you absolutely sure?" said Tara. But she already knew the answer.

"I'm sure," said Vayu. "I remembered it because the boys were reluctant to go with her, but then she said something about a secret and they followed her."

"Thanks," Tara managed to whisper.

She criss-crossed the deserted stalls and closed rides, heading back toward the crowd. Every so often she stopped and called out, "SURAJ! ROHAN!"

Her ears strained for an answer. Her heart pleaded for one. No answer came.

When she returned, it looked like most of the fair had gathered at the site of the attack. People argued and expressed opinions at the tops of their voices. Kabir's mother was surrounded by people bombarding her with questions;

"How many hyenas did you see?"

"Only one? How large was it?"

"Was it really a hyena or a dog?"

"Was your daughter alone?"

And on and on and on.

Ananth hadn't returned yet. Kabir paced, stopped, peered into the gloom and paced yet again. They looked at each other and then back toward the forest. There was no sign of Raani.

An announcement wafted over to them. As the crackly voice sped to every corner of the fairground, Tara said a little prayer.

"Suraj and Rohan, please go to the north end of the fair right away. Your sister is looking for you. Repeating ..."

"Tara!"

Tara whirled round. Ananth ran up to her, bathed in sweat. One look at his ashen face and she knew.

"You didn't find them, either," she said. "How could I be so careless? I've not only lost Suraj, but Rohan, too! How will I face *his* mother?"

Ananth put his hands on her shoulders. "Tara, we don't know for sure if ..."

"Yes we do," said Tara, pushing his hands away. "Vayu told me Layla led them off somewhere after the ride. I'm not an idiot. Something's happened. Something bad. And it's my fault!"

"I should have let you look for them sooner," said

Ananth. "I'm to blame, too. We won't go home till we've found them. All right?"

The buzz from the gathering crowds grated on her nerves; everyone was just standing around. Why didn't they do something? Tara stared into the forest. There lay the answer to the missing children. Even as they stood here arguing, Suraj, Rohan, and Sadia were in grave danger. She remembered the hyena from the afternoon, those gleaming, hungry eyes, those sharp teeth that could crunch through bones the way she crunched a stick of sugar cane. A wave of dizziness swept over her and she dug her nails into her palms. "Come on, come on," she whispered softly to herself, scanning the darkness around her.

Vayu hurried up to them. "Did the boys come to you yet?"

Tara shook her head, close to tears.

"I'm so sorry," said Vayu. "I almost feel responsible myself. I should have insisted!"

Just then Raani emerged from the forest. Her eyes searched for Kabir and she walked straight up to him, ignoring the others.

"What was Sadia wearing today?" she asked.

"A blue ghaghra-choli," said Kabir. "Why?"

Raani exhaled. "Then it's all right. This can't be hers." She held a scrap of cloth in her hand. They all crowded round her, peering at it in the dim light.

"This is from Rohan's shirt," Tara said. She snatched it from Raani's hand and looked at it closely, a sickness rising in the pit of her stomach. "The yellow one he was wearing today. And it's got some kind of stain on it."

"Are you sure?" asked Ananth. "I saw lots of yellow shirts at the fair."

"Yes, I'm sure," snapped Tara. "His mother trusted me with him and I've ... oh why wasn't I more careful —"

"Tara's right," said Vayu. "I remember this shirt. It was an exceptionally bright shade of yellow."

"Where did you find this, Raani?" asked Ananth.

"It was caught on a bush some distance from here," said Raani. "There is something else you should know." Her voice was low, her face grim. The fairgrounds spun and Tara squeezed her eyes shut. This was not going to be good. She knew it.

"There was some blood on the leaves near it," said Raani. "And on the ground."

That explained the stain. Tara's eyes snapped open. "We need to send someone in after them. NOW!" she said.

"And Sadia?" asked Kabir. "Any sign of her?"

Raani shook her head. "This scrap was all I found."

Tara ran toward Raka and Kabir's mother. If he was making plans for a rescue, it had better include Suraj and Rohan. Ananth was close on her heels.

"Don't worry," Raka was saying to Kabir's mother. "We'll send out a search party as soon as we organize one. We'll find her."

"Rakaji," said Tara. "Suraj and Rohan are missing. I'm sure the hyenas have taken them."

Raka's narrowed eyes swept over them. "Are you sure they aren't just wandering around?"

Tara opened her mouth to tell him about Raani finding the scrap of cloth when she caught Ananth's eye. He shook his head imperceptibly.

"I'm sure," said Tara. Panic rose within her like a tidal wave, almost drowning out the words. She took a deep breath before she spoke. "I haven't seen the boys since midday. They were supposed to meet me after a ride, but they never showed up. We've looked all over and even made an announcement. They're still missing!"

"That's *three* children!" said Raka. He shook his head, his face a gaunt mask. "But how could that be? There are no hyenas in this part —"

Tara wanted to scream that there were, and that she and Kabir's mother had both seen one! She controlled her temper and spoke as politely as she could. "There are Rakaji ... and the sooner you send help for Suraj, Rohan, and Sadia, the better. Hurry, please!"

"Let me get the search party organized here," said Raka. "We'll try our best to get volunteers quickly. Stay close in case I have any more questions for you."

He held up his hand and the buzz subsided. When there was complete silence, he spoke. "My good people, we have a very grave situation at hand. No one needs to panic, but there are two things I need all of you

35

to do. First, I need you all to account for your family members. Next, I need to find *three* missing children: Suraj, Rohan, and Sadia. I need volunteers immediately. Please stay calm."

The crowd disintegrated into chaos. Parents counted their children or scattered to find missing family members. A couple of villagers came up to Raka and stood beside him.

"I'd like to volunteer," said a villager.

"Good man," said Raka, and began to discuss plans. Two more men came up and joined in the conversation, gesturing toward the forest.

"This could take all night," said Tara. Her heart sank as she watched the confusion around them. "By the time they get someone to look for the children it might be too late. We've got to do something *now*."

"Rakaji is a good man," said Vayu. "He's a bit slow, but he's thorough. But I'm sure you know that already." He nodded at Tara and Ananth. "We should trust him and wait."

Raani snorted. "Do you always do as you're told?" She looked at Vayu as if he were something slimy that had crawled out of a hole in the ground.

Tara stared at Raani as if seeing her for the first time. Long, black hair framed a pretty face with wide-set eyes and perfectly shaped lips. She was stunningly beautiful, but her arrogance marred it all. Tara glared at her. Raani caught her eye and looked away.

"Wait for how long?" said Kabir. His face was still pale and his eyes had a dull, glazed look. "Sadia is terribly afraid of the dark as well as any animal bigger than a cat!"

Then she must be living out her worst nightmare, thought Tara as they stood apart from the crowd. This waiting was killing her. On an impulse she ran up to Raka. A group of men surrounded him, listening intently. She decided to wait till he finished speaking, but she had to press her lips together to stop the words from spilling out. She shifted her weight from one foot to the other, praying that they would hurry up and notice her.

"Let's wait for a couple more men and then move into the forest. We have to plan this well. It'll be best if you split up into two groups," said Raka. "One group start from the right of the fairgrounds and the other can start from the left. Don't take any chances and stay together. I'll send everyone home except for a few of us who'll be waiting here for you."

"Rakaji," said Tara. "I'd like to go along with the men. I'm sure I can help. If I sit around and do nothing, I'll … I'll go mad."

Raka spun round, his eyes flashing. "Stay out of the way, Tara. Three children in danger are plenty. I will not have *one* more child stepping into the forest. Now go home — that's an order!"

The others had come up behind her. "But Rakaji, we really could be of help," said Ananth. "Won't you give us a chance? It's my brother and Kabir's sister out there."

"Silence!" said Raka. "One more word and I will make sure your parents are informed of your disobedience. Now get out of my way, you're slowing down the rescue efforts. No one is to go into the forest and that is my final word. Go, GO!"

He walked away. Tara stared at his rigid back, her insides churning. Had he forgotten that she had gotten rid of Zarku? She — a *child*?

"I'm going to look for them whether he likes it or not," said Tara. She faced the others. "Does anyone want to go with me?"

"I will," said Kabir promptly. "And Raani, you better come with us. Show us where you found that scrap."

"Of course," she said.

"I'm coming, too," said Ananth. "We were both responsible for Suraj and Rohan."

"You don't have to, Ananth," said Tara. "In fact, it might be better if you don't."

"Why do you insist on doing things on your own, Tara?" he asked. "The more of us looking for them, the better."

"It's got nothing to do with that, Ananth," said Tara. She tried to keep her voice as soft and neutral as possible. "I don't think all of us need to go. It would be better if you went back home and informed my parents and Rohan's, too. I've got Kabir with me."

"And me," said Vayu.

They all turned to stare at him.

"We don't need you," said Raani.

"Wait a minute, Raani," snapped Tara. "What gives you the right to say that and who said we need *you*?" They exchanged scorching glances.

"I've already told you, Raani can see perfectly well in the dark," said Kabir. "We'll need her for sure."

"I'm coming, too, and that's final," said Ananth. "I can't let you go alone, Tara."

"I'm very capable of doing things by myself," she replied.

"I know you are," said Ananth. His eyes were hard. "But this time you're not going to. I'm coming whether you like it not."

Tara shrugged and turned to Vayu. "That's very nice of you, Vayu, but really, this could be dangerous. You've done all you can."

"I know this part of the forest very well," said Vayu. "Besides, I have no one here who will miss me. I'm an orphan."

She looked at him steadily at him for a moment. "Thank you. We could use your help."

"Enough talk," said Kabir. He herded them toward a dark spot close to the forest's edge. "Let's go before anyone notices. We don't want any questions or anyone trying to stop us."

"We should take lanterns," said Vayu. "We might need them."

Within moments Ananth and Vayu returned with two lanterns.

"Let's go," said Tara. Her eyes hurt from staring into the darkness. "I have a really, really bad feeling about this."

"About the hyenas?" said Kabir.

Tara stepped into the copse of trees, into the deep shadows, the others close behind. "I'm certain," she said, "that there's something more than hyenas in the forest."

three

Rohan

The forest steamed in the still night. The path became leaner and dwindled away as they trudged deeper into the forest in single file.

"Phew, it's hot," said Raani. "Did anyone bring water?"

At the mention of water, Tara felt an insatiable thirst. Why couldn't Raani have kept her mouth shut? She swallowed, cursing the girl under her breath.

"No we didn't and you know it," said Kabir. "How long do you think we're going to be in here?"

"Not more than a few hours, I hope," said Raani. "I'll die of this heat."

The fair lights receded and went out. Towering sal trees crowded in on them and low-lying thorny bushes reached out to scratch their arms and legs. The air was laden with the stench of a rotting carcass, decaying leaves, and an occasional whiff of an overripe guava. Tara's clothes clung to her like a second skin, burning her. She longed to peel them off.

"Where's that bush where you spotted the scrap of cloth?" asked Kabir. "Can't be too far."

"Just a bit farther," said Raani. She wiped her face for the umpteenth time and fanned it with her dupatta.

Tara's thirst intensified. A sudden panic gripped her. They had left with nothing but a lantern or two, and without telling anyone. If anything happened to them, no one would know. Rescue would be out of the question. Had she done the right thing, urging the others into danger?

She shook her head, trying to shake off the images of everything that could befall them in the forest. She had to focus on the boys and Kabir's sister. No time to worry about themselves.

Her mind made up, she strode through the moonlit forest, its floor dappled with silver.

Raani halted next to a prickly bush. "Here!" she said.

They all crowded round it, straining to see what Raani had.

"Give me some light," said Ananth. They moved back a bit as he and Kabir examined the bush and the area around it. Even to Tara's untrained eye, there seemed to have been quite a struggle here. The bushes were broken, leaves crushed at waist height. The ground underneath was churned up by footprints.

Kabir stooped for a quick look. He wiped his wet face with his sleeve and Tara was sure it wasn't all sweat.

"They were definitely here. All three of them," said Kabir in a wobbly voice. "Sadia!" he called out.

"Shhhhh," said Tara. "Don't yell. They must have gone by now. Yelling will only warn them of our arrival, silly."

"Don't call me silly," said Kabir. "And don't order me around. I don't like it."

Tara opened her mouth, but decided not to say anything after all. She knew he was worried sick just as she was.

Ananth knelt. "The footprints show that more than one animal was here," he said. He examined the ground carefully. "Two, maybe even three."

"Looks like they went that way," said Kabir. "If I get my hands on those hyenas, I'll tear them limb from limb." He stood up, breathing heavily.

"Calm down, Kabir," said Ananth. "Getting angry isn't going to bring them back. We need to think this through."

"Not when my sister's life is at stake," said Kabir. "You be calm if you like. I'll handle the hyenas my way. I've brought my knife and I'm not afraid to use it."

"We better get a move on," said Ananth. "We'll follow the footprints as long as we can and then hope something else can show us the way. Let's go."

The trees squeezed them into single file once more.

At times they grew so close to each other, it was difficult to walk through and the group had to take a detour. The light of the moon was almost obscured by the thick canopy overhead that trapped the heat. It gathered over their heads, getting hotter and heavier by the second. They sweated, swatted flies, and trudged on.

"How long have we been walking?" asked Raani. "Must be hours already, no?"

"Barely an hour," said Ananth.

"Oh."

Poor delicate flower, thought Tara. *She's tired already! Raani better not want to stop and rest.* Three lives were at stake and Tara meant to press on. The shadows in the forest deepened. The mosquitoes buzzed and bit mercilessly. Very soon they'd have to rely on Miss Night Queen to show them the way. Around them, the forest seemed to awake in a new and sinister way.

"Ananth," said Tara.

"Hmmm."

"I'm really worried!"

"Of course you are, Tara. We all are. Three children in the forest, alone at night with the hyenas. I pray they're all right."

"I don't mean that," said Tara. "I mean —"

He stopped and turned to face her. "Don't you dare start that again! We have enough to worry about already."

"Start what?" asked Kabir. "What's she hiding?"

"Tell us," said Raani. "If there's something odd or

dangerous, Tara shouldn't be keeping it to herself — we all have a right to know."

"It's nothing," said Ananth. "Just her imagination."

"No!" said Tara. "Listen to me. I know it sounds bizarre, but there's more here than we understand. I pray that by the time we know what it is, it's not too late."

"Tara, it's hyenas," said Ananth stubbornly, "plain and simple."

"*Now* you believe there is a hyena, do you?" said Tara. "You didn't believe me when I told you that earlier."

Ananth shrugged. "All right, I was wrong. I'm sorry. Now what?"

"There's something more here. I feel it. I know it."

"Rubbish!" said Ananth.

"Let's move on," said Kabir. "You and Tara can figure out whether you'd like the rest of us to understand what you're saying, or look the other way while you both squabble. I'm getting tired of it already."

There was a distinct edge to his voice and Tara cringed. Ananth already thought she was a fool to worry so much. With his short fuse, Kabir was sure to react the same way. What about Vayu? What would he say if she told him what had been troubling her all this while. She stopped.

Behind her Vayu halted, too. "Are you all right?" he asked.

Tara stooped and whipped the anklet off her foot. She clutched it tightly in her hand. "I'm fine," she said. The cold silver bit into her palm, giving her a small measure of relief. If it fell off they would have no protection at all. Let Ananth laugh right now, but she knew. *She knew* in her heart that something had begun the moment the children had been snatched and she was afraid.

There was a loud slap. Tara whirled round.

"Mosquito," said Vayu. He held out his palm. It was streaked with blood. The insects swarmed around them, enveloping them in a bubble of incessant noise and itchy bites. She wiped her sweaty face and waved her arms around her. It was futile. Ananth walked on, ignoring the buzzing, conserving his energy. A mosquito flew up her nose. She promptly pinched it — one less to worry about from the millions that surrounded her.

Ananth had taken the lead with Raani and Kabir following. She and Vayu brought up the rear. Vayu gasped and wheezed as he plodded behind Tara. He seemed to be the least fit of them all. Would he last till they reached the children? The thought nagged her more incessantly than the mosquitoes.

They had been walking steadily for a while now. Ananth peered intently at the path ahead.

"Should we rest?" said Raani in a muffled voice. She had swaddled her head in her dupatta and only her forehead showed, shiny with sweat. "We've been walking for ages. Don't you think we should stop and er … discuss things?"

"No. It's too early," said Ananth. "When it's pitch-black we won't be able to move as quickly."

"Why d' you think I'm here?" said Raani. "Light or no light, we'll still be able to go on. But I have to rest now. I'm exhausted."

"Ananth's right," said Tara. "We can't stop now. Surely you can hang on for a little longer?"

"Kabir, what do you say?" asked Raani. There was a whine in her voice that made Tara itch to slap her.

"No," he said. "Sadia is counting on me and Suraj must be feeling the same way. We have to forget about us and think of them, and if possible, move faster!"

Raani sucked in her breath.

"It's all right, Raani," said Vayu. "We're coming up to a clearing in a short while. If we're lucky, there might still be that hidden stream — *ooofffff!*"

Vayu tripped and fell flat on his face.

"Are you all right?" said Tara. She knelt to help him.

"Can't even watch where he's going," Raani muttered loud enough to be heard. "Why on earth anyone would name him after the wind is beyond me. Clumsy oaf."

Vayu stood up immediately. "I'm fine. Sorry, *sorry* ... just tripped!"

"Careful," said Ananth. "Let's go."

Tara's ears burned, wondering what Vayu must be going through because of this verbal attack. She wanted to shake the arrogance and meanness out of Raani, but instead she focused on the path ahead; the forest was getting more treacherous by the minute.

They plodded onward, pulling aside thick vines, ducking under low branches, trying not to trip on exposed roots. The light was so dim now, Tara could barely discern Kabir's tall figure ahead of her. *At least we don't have any animals to fight off*, thought Tara thankfully.

At that very moment something grunted. It was soft, but menacing.

"What was that?" said Raani.

"Shhh," said Kabir. "Wild boar, I think."

Instantly, Tara remembered a young boy from Morni who had been badly mauled by a boar — it hadn't been a pretty sight. But where was the animal hiding? She turned her head, trying not to move her body or let a single leaf rustle.

They all froze, listening intently.

"Can anyone see it? Raani, can you?" said Vayu softly. "Shall we run?"

"Stand still," whispered Ananth. "Running is the last thing we should do. It'll show itself."

As if on cue, a dark shape trotted out of the bushes to their right, followed by four smaller shadows.

"A wild sow," breathed Kabir. "They're very, very dangerous. No one move!"

The sow sniffed the air. Her eyes glowed like embers in the dark. Behind her they saw four tiny pinpricks of red light. Tara stared at them, ready to run the moment they moved. The sow gave one more grunt, turned and trotted back into the bushes, babies in tow.

Tara exhaled, her lungs bursting for air. "That was very close," she said. "Raani, I thought you were keeping an eye out. Couldn't you have warned us?"

"I *am* keeping an eye out," snapped Raani, "on the path ahead. If you want me to look out for animals, you walk ahead and help Ananth. I can't do two things at once."

"Oh, come on you two," said Ananth. "Stop it! No one could have seen that sow — she was well-hidden. The important thing is that we all kept our heads and no one got hurt."

Tara did not bother to reply, nor did Raani. More dank forest, rogue branches, and clouds of mosquitoes slid past. Then it was pitch-black. One moment she could see the silhouettes of her companions and the next, nothing. Not even her hand in front of her face.

The forest was alive around them. Tara moved closer to her companions, their laboured breathing her only guide now. Branches rustled overhead. Tara's skin crawled as she remembered the python above Suraj's head when they had last escaped into the forest.

"You better take the lead, Raani," said Ananth. "Find someplace where we can rest for a short while. I don't want to light the lanterns just yet. Oh, and keep a lookout for any animals. If they decide to attack now, we're doomed."

They all slowed while Ananth and Raani switched places.

"Hold on to the person in front of you," said Raani, "and follow me. I think I see a clearing up ahead."

Tara held onto Kabir's sweaty shoulder. Vayu's hand rested light on hers. Though the heat from his hand seared her burning skin, it was comforting. The darkness was a living thing, intent on smothering her. She took a few deep breaths to calm her racing pulse, focusing on putting one foot in front of the other.

"Oh my God!" breathed Raani. "Oh no." Tara bumped into Kabir in front of her and realized he had stopped.

"What happened?" Tara asked. "Is it that sow again? Should we run?"

"What is it?" asked Kabir.

Raani was silent. What had she seen? Was it so horrible that she was paralyzed with fear? Tara tensed, ready to flee. But in which direction? In the darkness, it was all one and the same.

"Raani, what *is* it?" asked Ananth. "Don't stand there like a damn fool. What d' you see?"

"I-I see ..." she said, and fell silent again.

"Speak up, Raani, or I'll slap it out of you," said Tara. "Stop scaring us." Her stomach was in knots. Why didn't Raani say something?

"It's not an animal," said Raani. "Light the lantern. Quick."

It's him, thought Tara, *he's here*. She was right. He had come back.

There was a faint clinking, the striking of a match. The flare momentarily lit the clearing ahead. It was empty. Tara breathed a deep sigh of relief. *That Raani! She should have been called Drama Queen instead of Night Queen.*

Darkness slithered away as soon as Ananth lit the wick in the lantern. Raani was not with them. She was crouched a short distance away, staring at the ground. They ran toward her, their gigantic shadows keeping pace.

Tara stopped just behind Raani. Her throat closed up. Her heart pounded against her chest.

They had found Rohan.

— four —

The Temple

Tara dropped to her knees, trembling. The heat had inexplicably disappeared, replaced by a numbing chill. She stared at Rohan. His sightless eyes stared back at her, an expression of horror frozen on his face. He looked like he had been in a struggle; his arms and legs were covered with bite marks, his ripped clothes stiff with dried blood.

He was dead.

"No! Oh no," she sobbed. "NO!"

Only a few hours ago this face had smiled up at her. Begged for money for a ride on the Ferris wheel. She would have given anything to turn back the clock. If only she had known what was in store for him, she would have kept a tight hold of Rohan till she took him back to Morni with Suraj. Ananth pulled Tara to her feet. She sobbed into his shoulder, aching to do something, anything, but aware that there was nothing she could do to bring him back to life.

"Shhhh, Tara," he said. "Get a hold of yourself. It'll ... it'll be all right." His voice trembled, a leaf in a breeze.

She pushed his arms away. "How can you say that? Rohan's dead. Suraj and Sadia are still missing. It's my fault — I should never have let them out of my sight. What have I done? How am I to live with this? I killed him!"

"It's the hyenas, Tara," said Ananth. "They could have chosen anyone."

Tara looked at him steadily, dashing away a tear. "But they didn't choose just anyone. They chose my brother and his friend."

"What I don't understand," said Kabir, "is why the hyenas didn't ... you know ... it's not like them to leave ..." He was unable to finish the sentence. Tara stared at him in horror.

What if they had killed Suraj first and had their fill so that there was no room for Rohan? What if there wasn't even a bone of Suraj left by the hyenas? Nausea bubbled up inside her throat. Darkness slithered back toward her, pressing upon her, pulling her down. She was almost ready to succumb and never wake up to face the fact that Suraj had probably died a very painful death. And so had his friend Rohan.

"Tara, are you all right?" asked Vayu. His heavy hand rested on her shoulder. She shook her head and wiped her eyes. Suraj was still alive. She would have known if something had happened to him. He was waiting to be rescued. They had to hurry.

"This is weird," said Vayu.

"What is?" asked Tara.

"Look here, at his forehead," said Vayu. He shone the lantern on Rohan's face. Tara forced herself to look at him again. In the middle of his forehead was a dark shadow in the shape of a tear, as if that spot had been singed. A cold hand squeezed her heart.

"There's no way a hyena could have given him that mark," said Tara. "No way at all."

"He could have bumped into a tree," said Ananth. His voice was soft, undecided. Kabir paced the clearing.

"What could have done something like that?" asked Vayu.

"There is one person who has a mark on his forehead," said Tara. "Exactly where this one is."

"Can't you ever give up this foolishness, Tara?" said Ananth.

Tara ignored him and stared at the others around her. She took a deep breath. "Zarku is back. He's responsible for this."

"Stop it!" said Raani. "You're just trying to scare us."

"And you should be," said Tara. "I've had this uneasy feeling for days now. I even took to wearing this at all time," she said. She whipped the silver anklet from her pocket and held it out. It lay coiled in her palm; a tiny, cold snake and surprisingly heavy.

"You're showing us your jewellery at a time like this?" said Kabir. "Are you mad, Tara?"

Tara wanted to shake Kabir till his bones rattled. Could he really be that stupid? But she restrained herself. It would do her no good to lose her temper now. "This is no ordinary anklet. It belonged to Zarku's mother," she said. "It may be the only thing that could protect us from him. The best part is that Zarku doesn't even know I have it."

"Then how *did* you get it?" asked Raani. Her eyes narrowed as she searched Tara's face. "Did you steal it?"

Tara clasped the anklet tightly in her fist and shook her head. "The night that Suraj disappeared, I thought I had lost him forever. I was all alone, ready to give up on life, too. I heard someone crying. The sound drew me to the abandoned temple deep within the forest. I was shocked at first and very afraid when I saw it was Zarku. He was talking to someone." She rubbed her chilled arms as the memory of that dark night enveloped her once more; of Zarku discovering her, attempting to burn her to death and failing. It had been a night as dark as this one, but no one had died, certainly not an innocent child.

Ananth did not look surprised — he'd heard this story already, but Raani, Kabir, and Vayu goggled at her.

"He tried to kill you and you survived?" asked Kabir. "How?"

"This anklet saved me," said Tara. She opened her fist. It sparkled in the lamplight. Tara slipped it back into her pocket, feeling it drop all the way to the bottom, weighing down her kurta.

"I heard his mother had died," said Raani. "You're making up stories just to sound important."

"She *is* dead," said Tara. "He was talking to this anklet about killing Grandfather. I gasped out loud. He heard me and dragged me to the post where I hit my head hard. It fell into the folds of my shawl. Then when he caught me and tried to burn me with his third eye, it would not open. At the time I thought I was incredibly lucky. Now I know it was because of this."

"What has that got to do with the hyenas?" said Ananth. "I still say you're making too much of this, Tara. The mark on Rohan's forehead aside, this is definitely the work of an animal. Because of Zarku you became a hero and now you want to relive it again."

Ananth's words could not have hurt more if he'd slapped her. "And you're feeling left out, is it?" said Tara. Tears pricked her eyes. "Do you really think I would relive those moments when Zarku tried to burn me, just for a little bit of attention? You're so wrong and in a short while I'll prove it to you."

Ananth did not say a word. He looked away, a sulky expression on his face.

"Enough, you two," said Kabir. "What do we do now? Go on or go back?"

"I think we should head to the temple where I saw him," said Tara. "If we don't find anything there, I'll say

I'm sorry. But for now, just listen to me, please. We have to hurry. God, I hope we're not too late."

"Tara, you're getting worked up for nothing," said Ananth quietly. "And you're scaring us."

"I think we should listen to her," said Vayu. He was still staring at Rohan's body. "This mark on his forehead was not made by a hyena. In fact, I've never seen anything like it. Have any of you?"

No one said a word.

"What are we going to do with Rohan?" said Tara. "We can't just leave him here."

"We should bury him," Ananth said, his voice faltering. "At least until we can take him home and give him a proper funeral.

Kabir tested the ground with his toe and found a spot where the earth was soft. They all set to digging at a furious pace. Kabir tried to help, but when his arm popped out of the socket for the third time, Ananth made him stop.

Tara concentrated on digging, though all she wanted to do was sit down and sob. Her eyes lingered on Rohan's inert body. Just that morning she'd woken up and everything had been fine. Not in her worst nightmares had she thought that she would be digging a grave for her brother's best friend by the end of the day. The world around her kept going blurry. She sniffed and dug, dug and sniffed.

When the hole was deep enough, Ananth picked Rohan up gently and laid him in the grave, tucking his arms by his sides. Tara reached down and clasped his small hand. "I'm so sorry we didn't get to you in time, Rohan," she whispered. She gently caressed his face and closed his eyes that had been staring at her, at all of them, accusingly. His skin was cold. She said a little prayer as the others shovelled earth on him hastily. Little by little his small body disappeared till there was only disturbed earth to mark the spot where he lay.

"We should move on," said Kabir. "Sadia and Suraj are still out there waiting for us."

"We have to mark this spot," Tara said, "so we can come back for him." The words stuck in her throat painfully, as if she had swallowed needles.

"We've done all we can," said Kabir. "Time's running out."

"For Sadia you would have had the time," snapped Tara. She clapped her hand on her mouth at Kabir's stricken expression. "I'm sorry, I didn't mean —"

"No," said Kabir. "*I'm* sorry. I wasn't thinking."

They collected rocks in silence and piled them on the grave in a pyramid.

"Douse the lantern and let's go," said Ananth.

"I'll walk behind Raani," said Tara. "We need to head toward the abandoned temple. That should be north of here and is probably the best place to start."

"And how am I supposed to know where that is?" said Raani. "There's nothing to guide me. Not even a star, except you, Tara. You're welcome to take the lead any time."

Tara sucked in her breath. She was only trying to help and all she had gotten so far was sarcasm and anger. If only Raani hadn't come with them, they would have been better off. In fact she should have set out with only Kabir. They would have moved a lot faster and with much less bickering.

"The moss grows on the south side of the trees in this forest, Raani," said Vayu. "So if you keep an eye on the tree trunks and which side the moss is on, we will be heading north. Even if we are slightly off, we can correct it in the morning."

"That's really smart, Vayu," said Tara. "Thanks!"

Everyone, except Raani, echoed her. Tara was glad Vayu had offered to come along. He spoke little, but when he did, it made a lot of sense. He had said he was an orphan. She remembered the moment with painful clarity when she thought she had lost Suraj forever, believing she was all alone in the world. It had been one of the worst moments, ever. And here was this boy, living that moment for a lifetime.

The slow, agonizing walk made Tara want to scream in frustration. Unable to see anything around her, she could only think; the last thing she wanted to do.

Where were Suraj and Sadia right now and what was that madman doing with them? She had killed Zarku, so how had he come alive? Hadn't Lord Yama buried his ashes? Why had the hyenas snatched them? Could Ananth be right? Her head buzzed with irritating questions, as if some of the mosquitoes had crawled inside it.

The heat sat heavily on her shoulders weighing her down with every step. When would this nightmare end?

• • •

The next hour took every ounce of Tara's discipline. The heat was unbearable. It was like walking across a gigantic tandoor. Now she knew what a roti felt like when it was cooked. She had to move entirely by touch. Roots tripped her up and branches clawed at her as she walked past. Every so often a prickly bush snagged her kurta and she heard it rip as she walked on. By morning her clothes would be in shreds, but she was too tired to care.

Ananth and Kabir cursed softly. Tara heard a colourful word now and then from the Night Queen though she was the only one who could *see*. Only Vayu plodded on, breathing heavily, but without a word of protest.

The mosquitoes were the only ones having a good time as they swarmed in and out of her eyes and nose and ears, in a torturous game of catch-me-if-you-can. She could use only one hand to swat them. The other was firmly clasped onto Raani's shoulder ahead of her. *Let this end, let us get out of the forest soon before I go mad*, she prayed. How lucky she and Suraj had been when they had run away in winter. With all the extra clothing, they had been warm and, to some degree, comfortable.

But this heat was driving her insane. She focused on counting the steps, trying to obliterate everything else from her mind. Each step would bring her closer to Suraj. Tara counted with fierce determination.

When she had counted to two hundred, something changed. At first she could not figure out what it was but when Raani turned to look behind her and Tara *saw* her turn, she knew.

Light! There was light coming from somewhere. The blindfold of darkness was suddenly stripped away and she could *see*. Ahead, the unmistakeable glow of a fire beckoned. Involuntarily, everyone walked faster.

"Slow down," said Ananth. "And be very quiet. We don't want to alert whoever it is and nor do we want to walk into something unpleasant."

The trees thinned and there it was — as she remembered it from many moons ago — the temple. It rose out of the shadows, a pale white stone dome, with two smaller ones on either side. It was bleached of all colour. A network of deep black cracks criss-crossed the squat building with its ornate pillars. A fire burned in the deserted courtyard in front of it and they all moved toward it stealthily.

"Is this it?" asked Ananth.

"Yes," breathed Tara. She gazed at the temple trying to shake off the feeling of horror that enveloped her. Zarku had almost killed her the last time she had been here. What was in store for them, *for her*, this time?

In some parts the white stone had broken away in chunks, leaving a raw, jagged edge covered with moss. The forest was slowly devouring the temple. Much of its base and many pillars were already ensnared by vines and creepers.

Next to her, Kabir's breathing quickened, Vayu's stomach gurgled softly, and Raani muttered under her breath. They were still a distance away from the low wall that encircled the courtyard strewn with broken stone. It was the same one Tara had hidden under, when she had discovered Zarku.

They moved closer. There was no one there; neither hyena nor human. Were they hiding in the temple, watching them approach? Was this a trap? Tara's pulse raced. Her heart slammed against her ribcage.

The fire burned brightly, a patch of gold imprinted on the dark night. The dancing flames seemed to reach out for her with their hot fingers. Her skin burned with the memory of Zarku's third eye upon her, his maniacal laughter filled her ears and then the fire went out.

• • •

"Tara, wake up," said a soft voice. It came from far, far away.

Something sharp poked into her back. She opened her eyes to tell whoever it was to stop. Four faces stared down at her. She sat up immediately. "What happened?"

"You fainted," said Ananth. He smoothed a hair away from her forehead, his eyes full of concern. "Did you see something, *someone*?"

Tara shook her head. How could she tell them that the fire had caused her to faint? "Just-just the heat. That's all. So what's the plan?"

"Are you sure —" said Vayu.

"I'm fine," Tara cut in. "Really."

Ananth motioned to them to come closer. "Let's split up," he whispered. "Raani and Vayu, come with me, and Tara, you go with Kabir. We'll circle the temple from the right and you both go left. We'll meet at this spot on the opposite side. If we don't see anyone at all, we'll go in. Go slow, watch your back."

Tara stared at the temple, wanting only to run away from it. She put her hand into her pocket and clutched the anklet tight. It didn't work. Her unease grew.

Ananth gave a thumbs-up sign and they moved away from each other. She gripped Kabir's hand in her moist one, keeping an eye on the fire as well as the entrance to the temple. Nothing stirred. The silence was almost too much to bear.

A twig cracked under Tara's foot and she jumped. "Sorry, *sorry*!" she whispered as Kabir frowned at her. Her eyes were riveted to the stone steps, but no one came to investigate. The fire crackled and spit, sending golden-orange sparks into the night sky. The smell of resin and smoke filled the air. Somehow a deserted fire was more eerie than no fire at all.

The night turned warmer. Tara's head was splitting and her throat felt dry and scratchy. She wiped her face and crept along next to Kabir. A sense of foreboding was filling her, like time was ticking down toward an explosion. They reached the other side without further incident.

Ananth, Vayu, and Raani were already crouched under the low parapet, breathing heavily. An acrid cloud of sweat and fear hovered over them.

"Nothing," said Ananth. His eyes swept the courtyard.

"Same here," said Kabir. "I say we rush in, get the kids and run."

"Now or wait for morning?" asked Raani.

"Now, please, *now*," said Tara. "Something's going to happen. It's way too quiet."

A few more minutes limped by while they watched and waited.

"All right, we should move now," said Kabir. "We've waited long enough."

"Okay," said Ananth. "Be as quiet as you can. Get to the pillars and hide. We'll go in together. Ready?"

They all stood up, still hidden by the shadows under the trees. Ananth and Kabir crept toward the temple. Tara and Raani followed. Tara's nerves twanged. She couldn't shake the feeling that something terrible was about to happen.

"Arrgghhhhh," screamed Vayu. "Someone's choking me!"

five

Captured!

T ara almost screamed, too. She whirled and raced up to a thrashing Vayu, followed closely by Ananth and Kabir.

Vayu struggled with something around his neck, his eyes bulging, sweat streaming down his white face. "Help," he stammered. "Help me."

"It's just a vine," said Tara. "Stop. You're entangling yourself even more. Stop!"

It took both Ananth and Kabir to hold Vayu while Tara unwrapped the thick vine from around his shoulders and neck. It dangled from an overhead branch and was unusually strong, with barely any leaves. It could easily be mistaken for a rope.

"Thanks," said Vayu. He pressed his hand to his chest. "I'm so sorry. I thought it was —"

"You stupid idiot," hissed Raani. "You weren't

thinking. What if —" But she wasn't able to complete her sentence.

"They're here," yelled a familiar voice behind them. *"They're here!"*

Tara did not need to turn around to know exactly who it was.

"Kali," she whispered and shrank back, deeper into the shadows. "I should have known."

Her stepmother stood on the steps; thinner and dirtier than Tara had last seen her. Kali's sharp eyes swept the forest, probing the shadows, lingering momentarily on the spot where they stood before moving on. So often had Tara been the object of that malevolent gaze, borne the cruelty that followed soon after. She had been ecstatic when Kali had been banished from Morni.

But here she was again.

"Get them," Kali called out. "Don't let them escape." She gazed out at the forest and smiled. Then she swivelled on her heel and went back inside.

"She's all alone," said Kabir. "Who's she talking to? Do you see anyone else?" They craned their necks. The courtyard remained deserted.

"She *must* have someone helping her," said Ananth. "We'd better hide just to be on the safe side. Once the coast is clear we'll come back and think of another way to rescue the children."

Tara remembered Kali's smile. It always meant they were in for a bad time. Tara backed away slowly. She didn't want to leave without Suraj. Not when they were so close. She gazed longingly at the temple. He was in there for sure, waiting for her.

Ananth grabbed her hand and pulled. "Don't just stand there!" he hissed. "Move! Kali's men could be upon us in moments."

"I don't want to leave without the children," said Tara. "Maybe she was just bluffing. You know what a liar Kali is."

"I don't want to leave, either," said Kabir.

Ananth huffed. "And you think I do? But we have to be cautious. There's hardly any tree cover here. We'll be spotted easily. Come on."

They retraced their steps.

A giggle stopped them in their tracks. It came from a bush directly in front.

"What was that?" said Raani.

Another laugh, this time to their right.

"Her helpers," breathed Ananth. "And they obviously find stalking us very funny." He reached out for Tara and Raani, gathering them closer.

They heard a cackle behind them and backed into each other, forming a tight circle.

"Who is this?" said Ananth. His voice had the hint of a quaver. "Stop laughing and show yourselves."

Silence.

A rivulet of sweat trickled down Tara's back. The bushes rustled. They huddled closer.

"Should we make a run for it?" said Kabir.

Before Ananth or anyone else could answer, the bushes parted. Two shadows emerged, became solid, and took the shapes of large ugly hyenas. Raani turned to run, and screamed. Tara spun around. Behind them, a third hyena blocked their way. He laughed.

The fire reflected off their hungry yellow eyes. The largest one opened his mouth and a foul stench filled the air. The smiling hyenas closed in on them, shuffling forward on their spindly legs.

"So these are her helpers!" said Raani. "Oh God, we are as good as dead. Ananth, do something."

Ananth moved his hand. The largest hyena growled and he froze.

"Zarku?" said Tara, staring at it.

The hyena's yellow eyes bored into her.

"Is that you?" she asked, feeling slightly foolish.

The hyena trotted closer. She took a step back. The beast advanced, whooping with laughter. For a moment no one moved. The air was damp and heavy, weighing her down. She looked at Ananth. His eyes held hers for a moment then flitted to the others. He had a plan and she watched him and the hyenas in turns. He opened his mouth. Tara tensed.

"Split up," yelled Ananth. "RUN!"

His command galvanized them into action. They scattered like chickens before a wolf. Tara did not look back. She ran hard, pumping her arms and legs to put as much distance between her and three sets of powerful jaws. She zig-zagged through the bushes, the screams and growls receding rapidly. Her heart thudded inside her chest, threatening to explode. Any moment now she expected sharp teeth to sink into her foot. Nothing happened. On and on she ran, her breath a staccato of gasps.

Suddenly, her legs trembled and folded. She fell to the ground, holding the painful stitch in her side. Crouched behind the temple wall at the far end, she heard loud protests; a couple of her friends had surely been caught. The glow of the fire barely reached where she hid. The forest stretched behind her into endless darkness.

Tara swiped her wet face with her sleeve and cursed Vayu. If only he had remained calm. They had lost the element of surprise, all because of a stupid vine! Now she would have to regroup with the ones who had escaped and then rescue not only Suraj and Sadia, but whoever else was within's Kali's clutches. Zarku still hadn't shown himself, but it was just a matter of time. He was close. Very close. She knew that as surely as she knew her name.

You can do this, Tara told herself. *You've done it before, remember? Remember?* But her mind was a blank. She kept low under the parapet, crawled on all fours, and made her way to the front of the temple. The voices grew louder, more shrill, punctuated by growls and giggles.

"You let us go right now!" said Ananth. "There's a group of men behind us. They won't spare you if anything happens to us."

"Ha!" said Kali. "You think I'm stupid?"

Yes, mouthed Tara silently. *Definitely*.

"Owww, owww," said Raani. "Call them off, they're hurting me!"

"They'll hurt you even more if Tara is not found," said Kali. "Call her now."

No one spoke.

Tara peeked over the wall. Her heart zoomed all the way to her toes. Ananth, Kabir, Raani, and Vayu were all there, hemmed into a tight group by the filthy beasts. There would be no chance of breaking out this time. She alone had escaped.

Kabir and Ananth were gazing into the forest surreptitiously, no doubt wondering where she was.

"All right. Have it your way," said Kali. "I'll leave the hyenas to persuade you." She walked away.

Tara shifted and a stone clattered against the wall. One of the hyenas swung his head in her direction. She froze and held her breath.

"Tara," said Ananth. "If you can hear me, go away. Get help. Don't try and save us. You won't succeed."

A hyena lunged at Ananth and bit him. "Get off you mangy beast," he yelled. He clutched his bitten hand and kicked out. The hyena retreated with a yelp. Tara watched bright red blood drip to the ground. The scene dimmed. She jerked her head up furiously. She couldn't afford to pass out. Not now when they were all depending on her.

"He's right, Tara," yelled Kabir. "Get Prabala. He'll know how to handle this. Go now!"

Tara massaged her throbbing temples. Everything was going so wrong. They had come to rescue Suraj and Sadia. Instead, Kali had captured all her friends. She had to save not two but six people now. All by herself.

Should she try to find her way back to Morni for help? Or ignore Ananth and rescue them? Once she was gone, would Kali let them live? What should she do?

"Don't leave us, Tara." Raani called out. "Help!"

"Stop it, Raani," snapped Ananth. "Don't listen to her, Tara. Go!"

Tara felt a pang of guilt. Raani sounded terrified. They were in this mess because of her. She had decided to go into the forest without telling anyone. How brave it had sounded then, how right ... Now she realized what a foolish thing they had all done. No one knew where they were and there would be no help on the way.

Raani started to sob and Tara was almost ready to run to them. How could she even think of leaving? She stood up. A twig cracked underfoot. The hyenas pricked up their ears. One of them trotted a short distance away and sniffed the air. Her stomach wobbled. Any moment it might pick up her scent and come charging at her.

"Don't do it, Tara," said Ananth, his eyes still sweeping the forest. "RUN, you're our only hope."

What if he's right? Her mind floundered like a child in deep water. *Go or stay, stay or go?*

Kali was nowhere to be seen. What if she sent some more hyenas after her? Tara couldn't linger. She had to go, run all night for help if she had to. This was too big for any of them to handle alone. They needed Prabala.

She took one last look at her companions staring forlornly into the forest. Bright red bite marks on their arms and legs glistened in the firelight. Tears shone on Raani's cheeks as she sobbed softly. She couldn't fail her friends.

Tara took a deep breath and ran and ran and ran.

Zarku

Tara ran straight into the arms of darkness, leaving behind her companions. It was hard. As the glow from the fire receded, the gloom grew thicker and heavier. The dank odour of rotting leaves and a nameless fear surrounded her. She had followed Ananth and Raani all the way here. Which way should she go now? Which way was home?

The trees crowded in, trying to crush her. The heat pushed down with an invisible fist. She dropped down on all fours and crawled, trying not to scream for help. Sharp stones bit into her palms. Something soft squished under her knee, releasing a foul odour. She tried not to think about it as she scuttled on. This was a mistake, a huge mistake. She should have stayed with the others. She was never going to find her way home. "Help," she sobbed softly, "Please God, help me ..."

Only the mosquitoes answered her, buzzing hungrily around her head.

Bushes rustled up ahead. Leaves crackled. Tara jumped to her feet. Arms outstretched, she ran headlong into a tree and smacked her forehead hard against it.

"Stupid, stupid tree!" she said, rubbing her aching forehead.

"Tsk, tsk, Tara," said a soft voice. "Such bad language from your mouth the first time we meet after so long?"

Tara stopped. Turned round. The heat had vanished once more, replaced by a chill. The shadows shivered as the hint of a breeze flitted past. She scanned the trees around her. Who was it? The darkness seemed lighter somehow. But why ... she could see no one, no source of light.

"What? No words of welcome for an old friend?" said the voice, a bit louder now. "We've been waiting so long to see you. Bring me closer, Kali."

It was like she'd been struck by lightning. Kali and a voice she knew ... a voice she'd heard before. One she'd been expecting, but hoped never to hear again in her lifetime.

Kali stepped out from behind a tree, her face tinted by a red glow. She carried something very carefully, but it was hard to make out what exactly it was.

The chill trickled down to her toes, reached her numb fingers, and climbed all the way to her scalp. Kali placed the mysterious item on the ground and stepped back. Tara finally got a good look. It was an urn and she knew where she had seen it before. She screamed silently, her body thrumming with the urge to flee, to run far, far away. Kali grinned at her and it was like old times. Something really bad was about to happen.

Tara forced herself to stand still. She opened her mouth. No words came out of her parched throat. She swallowed, tried again.

"Zarku?"

"Ahhh, she remembers," said Zarku. "Bring her to me, Kali. I want her to take a good look at what she's done."

Kali moved toward Tara and she involuntarily stepped back. Kali's hand shot out, imprisoned Tara's wrist in a tight grip and jerked her toward the urn. A smell of burned flesh hung in the air. Tara gagged.

"You're alive," said Tara. Her heart fluttered in her chest. "How is that possible?"

"*Barely*, thanks to you and your interfering grandfather." The red glow dimmed and brightened as Zarku spoke. Tara had a sudden urge to kick the urn high into the air, see it fall and smash to smithereens. But the thought of that evil presence floating in the air around her, having to inhale *him*, made her shudder. The urge passed.

"What do you want," said Tara.

"Revenge," said Zarku.

Tara's insides quivered. "Never!" she said. "As soon as I get Prabala, we'll finish you for good this time. You'll never ever come back to trouble us again."

The urn rocked back and forth with Zarku's maniacal laughter. Tara clapped her hands over her ears.

"You don't scare me," she said. "You're nothing but a pile of ashes with a voice. And I don't think this buffalo will be able to keep up with me if I decide to run."

Kali sucked in her breath audibly, but said nothing.

"Oh, I won't try and stop you, Tara," said Zarku. "You're free to go. Know that if and when you come back with that fool of a healer, there won't be anyone left to rescue. I will kill them all."

Her stomach twisted painfully. He was as mad and bloodthirsty as ever.

"You've already killed an innocent child," yelled Tara. "And now you're going to kill more? Why? What harm have they done to you?"

"All in good time, Tara," said Zarku. "If I tell you everything now, I'll ruin the surprise I have for you. It's *such* a nice one."

Tara knew she'd hate it. "Where is Suraj?" she asked.

"Come with me and I'll show you."

"Do I have a choice?" said Tara.

"Oh, you always have a choice," said Zarku. "The question is will you be able to bear the consequences of the choice you make?"

Tara stared at him. What did he mean by that? Why was he talking in riddles? Should she call his bluff and run? Tara glanced at Kali who glared back at her malevolently. The darkness looked so much more desirable right now; she'd gladly face that than Zarku. Tara stood still, thoughts blowing in her head like leaves in a storm, first one way then the other.

"Just so you know," said Zarku. "I hate waiting. It makes me cranky."

Tara closed her eyes, stilled the storm raging inside of her and made her decision.

"I'll go with you," said Tara staring straight at the urn. "But you have to promise me that the children will be unharmed. Even my friends. Promise me now!"

Zarku cackled and Kali joined in. "This girl thinks she can make me promise things," said Zarku. "Ahhh, Tara, you are so brave and so stupid. I'm *really* going to miss you."

Another painful jolt. Black spots danced before her eyes. She refused to let herself think about what he meant by that. Not now. Right now she had to focus on rescuing her brother and her friends.

Kali scooped up the urn gingerly and started back toward the temple. Tara followed, dreading the look on everyone's face when they saw her.

• • •

The moment Tara stepped out of the forest, Ananth's face tightened. Kabir looked accusingly at her, Raani looked relieved, and Vayu refused to meet her eye. They had all suffered; teeth marks and rivulets of dried blood adorned their arms and legs.

Kali shoved her toward the others and disappeared into the temple with the urn. The hyenas, snapping at her ankles, herded her toward her friends.

"I *told* you to run," said Ananth. His expression was livid. "You never listen to anyone, do you?"

"I tried," said Tara. "But I had to come back."

"Why? Because you couldn't outrun that buffalo?" said Kabir. "You were our only hope, Tara. And now you've let us all down."

"I'll explain later," said Tara as soon as she saw Kali return with a lantern.

"Where are the children?" asked Tara. "I want to see them. He promised."

Kali's laughter echoed around them and a bird from a nearby tree flew up in alarm. "I don't remember any such promise," she said. "But maybe if you were to ask me politely ..."

"Who is *he*?" asked Ananth, looking from Kali to Tara. "What is she talking about?"

Tara ignored him. "*Please* can I see Suraj and Sadia?" she repeated.

"No," said Kali. "Maybe tomorrow. I'm tired and I need to sleep. Thanks to you lot, tonight is completely ruined. Now follow me."

Tara wanted to lash out at that swaying backside in front of her. She remembered the time when Suraj had placed a lizard on Kali's back and made her dance in the middle of the road. They had laughed till their sides ached, but right now the thought of it made her want to cry.

The hyenas hustled them along, growling at their heels. It was a bit cooler in the temple and the chance to get out of the heat and the mosquitoes was a huge relief.

Kali led the way deeper into the abandoned temple, expertly navigating sharp turns through a labyrinth of damp corridors. Her lantern illuminated the ivy and creepers climbing the walls in lush abandon. Slimy green sections of moss-covered stone slid past, and the air had a closed, musty smell.

"Pay attention," whispered Ananth.

He and Kabir looked around, trying to memorize the route. Vayu looked straight ahead and Raani could not take her eyes off the floor that had many a slippery patch and was littered with debris from the forest.

Kali stopped in front of a set of heavy wooden doors that gaped open. "Get inside," she said. "Hurry! I don't have all night."

They filed into the room silently. It was like walking into a deep, dark cave that had no end. What if something horrible awaited them? But there was nothing there and Tara breathed a sigh of relief.

Kali followed them inside. The insipid light of the lantern revealed an empty room with drifts of dead leaves in the corners. A rotting smell lingered in the room as if something had died in here recently. Thick creepers climbed the walls toward the ceiling, covering every inch of surface. Other than that the room was completely bare.

"I'll be back in the morning," said Kali. "Do make yourselves comfortable."

"Can't you let us see the children just once?" said Kabir. "Have you no pity at all?"

"No," said Kali. "Anything else?"

"You're not human," said Tara. "Don't forget, we've looked after Layla like she was our sister. Thank God she didn't have you around or she'd have been just as bad."

Kali smiled. "If you only knew what Layla is capable of. She's *my* daughter and always will be. I'm proud of her!"

"What do you mean by that?" said Tara. Her nerves tingled and a thought nagged at her. "Layla was following your orders when she lured Suraj and Rohan toward the hyenas, right?"

"Right," said Kali. "My daughter follows instructions very well."

"But how did you manage to get the message to her? Did you come to Morni ...?" Tara was burning with curiousity. How had Kali managed to slip unseen past all the villagers?

"Never mind," said Kali. She had been watching Tara closely, her smile broader. "I'm sure you'll figure it out eventually. You were always such a *smart* girl."

Tara looked at Kali in disgust. Layla was turning out to be a replica of her mother and if they were somehow still in touch, who knew what they'd be capable of. She cursed herself silently. If only she had trusted her instincts, none of this would have happened. She had always known Layla was bad; that they should have turned her out of the village with Kali. When she got back home, it was the first thing she would take care of.

"I'd rather the hyenas finished you off right now," said Kali. "Save us all a lot of trouble. But what can I say? I'm just following orders." She yawned in their faces and walked out, taking the lantern with her. As the doors closed, the last thing they saw was her pale face with its cruel smile.

Raani immediately rounded on Vayu as soon as the doors banged shut.

"Vayu, you fool!" she said. "If it hadn't been for you, we would have rescued Suraj and Sadia and would have been on our way home by now. You've ruined it for all of us! God knows why any one would name you after the wind ... you should have been named after something big and dumb!"

"I thought you said you knew this part of the forest well," said Kabir. "And a *plant* scared you?"

Ananth maintained a disapproving silence as he prowled around the room, examining it.

"I'm so sorry," said Vayu, softly. "With all that talk about Zarku returning, I was a little ... um ... spooked. I'm really sorry." His shoulders slumped. Tara's heart went out to him.

"That's enough," said Tara. "Vayu did not give us away deliberately. I think we should all just let it go. There's nothing wrong with being a little scared."

"You should know," said Kabir, his voice like a whiplash. "You couldn't outrun a middle-aged woman and were too scared to brave the dark and go back to Morni for help. You both make a great pair."

Tara wanted to retort with something equally hurtful, but held her tongue. They hadn't a clue about how much trouble they were in. Till she explained it to them, they would continue to believe that she was a coward. And she wasn't. She wasn't!

"I came back for all of you," said Tara quietly. "If I hadn't, he would have killed you all."

"Who?" asked Ananth. "Don't tell me you're still clinging on to that silly idea —"

"Zarku," Tara cut in. "I saw him and spoke to him."

Raani clasped her hands. Kabir and Vayu exchanged glances.

"You're lying," said Ananth.

"Have I ever lied to you?" said Tara.

"What did he look like?" asked Ananth. "Does he still have that ... third eye?"

"He's in the urn. The one Lord Yama sealed his ashes in," said Tara. "Somehow Kali got her hands on it. That was what she was carrying when we came back from the forest."

"He can't do much from an urn," said Kabir. "We can still escape and run."

"Have you forgotten the children?" asked Tara. "He probably captured them to get us here, especially *me*!"

"So what's he going to do?"asked Kabir. "Did he tell you?"

"Only that he wants revenge and it involves me," said Tara. Her voice was barely above a whisper. "If I ran away, he said he'd finish off the lot of you before I came back with help. You see, I really had no choice. I had to come back."

All of sudden Tara was so tired she could barely stand. She stumbled away and slumped down in a corner. He was back and he had a surprise for her. In a few hours she would know exactly what it was. For now she just wanted to stop thinking about it or her head would explode.

Ananth knelt beside her. "I'm so sorry, Tara. I didn't know. I ... er ... we ... assumed that you were too scared —"

"Of late you've been assuming a lot, Ananth," said Tara. "You don't think!"

He exhaled noisily and she didn't need to see his face to know that he was angry and probably a bit ashamed, too.

"I can't wait," said Kabir. "I have to see my sister!" He pounded on the door.

"Stop it!" said Ananth. "Have you gone mad, Kabir?

Do you think banging on the door is going to get us out of here?"

Kabir stopped. His heavy breathing was the only sound in the room. Beyond the heavy doors, the pounding echoed through the temple and faded away into silence. No one came.

"We need to plan the next move," said Vayu. "Surprises don't work out too well."

"Just like yours," said Raani. "We would never have been caught if it hadn't been for you, you fat lump!"

"Stop!" hissed Tara. She stared at the whites of four pairs of eyes that stared back at her. "When will you get it into your heads that this was carefully planned by Zarku to lure me here using my brother? Layla and Kali both helped. One child is already dead! Sadia or Suraj could be next."

When no one replied, she continued, "And get one thing straight, one way or the other, he would have caught us. So stop blaming Vayu. We'll just have to wait till tomorrow."

"Not me," said Kabir, pacing the floor. "I'm going for help. I can't sit around and wait for this maniac in powder form to do what he likes."

"Calm down," said Ananth. "Let's wait and see what Zarku has in mind and then plan our next move. I don't want to do anything without seeing Suraj and Sadia first."

"What if killing all of us is what he has in mind?" said Kabir. "You want to wait around for that?"

There was a deep silence. Tara had to admit there was some truth in it. She was the one he really wanted but he hadn't specified — alive or dead. And the others? Would he let them go or kill them for the fun of it? She desperately wanted to know and yet thinking about it made her sick.

"This door looks too solid to break through," said Raani. "I see no other way."

Kabir looked at the lighter patch high up on the wall. "Help me, Vayu," he said. "I bet there's a window up there. That's why this room isn't completely dark."

Vayu intertwined his fingers and braced himself against the wall. Kabir stepped on Vayu's hands and pulled himself up. He plunged his hand into the foliage covering the wall and tore away a handful of vines. Silvery light poured into the room through a small barred window.

"Just as I thought," said Kabir. "Here is our escape route."

"*Really?*" said Ananth. The sneer in his voice was unmistakeable. "Get down and we'll make a proper plan."

"I can get through this easy," said Kabir. He rattled the bars and measured the gap between them with outstretched fingers.

"Can you really fit through those bars?" asked Tara. "They look too narrow even for someone as small as Suraj." Pain flared in her chest at the thought of her brother. He must be somewhere close by. Scared and lonely. If only she could have seen him once, she could have spared him one more night of anguish. *I hope you burn in hell, Kali. I hope you die a horrible and painful death.*

"My body will be no problem," said Kabir. "Getting my head through the bars will be the biggest challenge. Let me have a look and see where we are." He stood on tiptoes on Vayu's palms, swaying slightly. He craned his neck. "Can only see treetops. Need to get higher."

Vayu held him steady without as much as a groan. Kabir pulled himself up on the small ledge in front of the window. "Much better!"

"What do you see?" asked Ananth. "Which direction are we facing?"

"We're at the back of the temple. There's a small courtyard and then the forest starts. The ground doesn't look too far off, either. I should be able to jump down easily. But once I'm out, then what?"

"Go south and head for the river," said Ananth. "You can't miss it if you keep the North Star behind you at all times. Boats are always tethered at regular intervals along the banks. If you can get there, you should be able to row to the nearest village — Ambala — I think. It's downstream so it will be much faster, you'll be going with the current. They can send word to Morni and Ramgarh for help."

Tara listened to the plans with growing dread. Were they doing the right thing? What if Kabir was caught? Zarku hated to look a fool. *Lord Ganesh, please help me,* she prayed. *I don't have a suitable offering right now, but I'll donate a kilo of sugar if you help us escape.* At that precise moment, something ran over her leg and she jumped. She looked down into bright-red eyes. A rat! It stood up on its hind legs, sniffing the air.

"*Mushika?*" Tara breathed. "You've come back!"

The moment she spoke the rat fled. She glanced up feeling foolish. No one seemed to have noticed. They were all intent on Kabir and his efforts to escape.

"Do you really think you'll get through?"asked Raani. She watched him, her arms folded across her chest. "This isn't as easy as getting into a basket, you know. You'll have to rearrange your bones in an entirely different way. And if your head gets stuck, none of us will be able to …"

"You're a right ray of sunshine, Raani," said Tara, "What would we do without you? Kabir said he can do this and he will."

"How dare —" Raani started to say.

"I know, Raani, I know," said Kabir. "Don't remind me of how bad this could get. Please?"

Raani walked away to a corner of the room and sat down in a huff.

Kabir leaped down from the window. "I better leave right away. No point in waiting around."

"Be careful," said Ananth. "Don't take any chances. Good luck."

"You should take your clothes off," said Vayu.

They all gaped at him.

"You think I have a better chance of escaping if I'm naked?" said Kabir.

"You'll be able to get through those bars a lot easier," said Vayu. "We can always throw the clothes out the window once you're through."

"Of course," said Kabir with a faint smile. "Good idea." He took off his shorts and shirt, stripping down to his underwear. His lean body shone with sweat.

"Well, this is it," he said. He looked around.

"I wish you weren't going, Kabir," said Tara. "I don't like this at all."

"I have to, Tara. This could be our only chance. Will you promise me something?" His tone was very serious.

"Of course, Kabir."

"If anything were to happen to me, promise me you'll get Sadia back home. Promise me!"

"Stop it, Kabir. You're scaring me talking this way."

He took her hands in his and looked deep into her eyes. "*Promise me!*"

Tara felt the blood rush to her face and was glad that it was dark. "I promise, Kabir. If every last one of you abandons me and I am left all alone to rescue Sadia, I promise to bring her back." She forced herself to laugh though she wanted to be sick. "There, happy now? It'll never happen that way, you know. I'm very sure."

"Thank you," said Kabir. "Now my mind is at peace."

Vayu patted Kabir on the back and then hoisted him up on his shoulders. Kabir clambered on to the narrow ledge nimbly. He slid his right leg through the bars easily. He fitted his torso between them and eased it through in small, gentle movements, coaxing his bones to shift and flatten. They watched in silence.

Tara had positioned herself by the door. Her ear was pressed to it, but her eyes were glued to Kabir, silhouetted against the window.

Kabir was halfway through when he stopped.

Move, pleaded Tara silently. *We don't have all night.* Kabir took a deep breath and pushed, but he did not budge an inch; his ribcage was jammed tight between the narrow vertical bars. He stared down at them, the whites of his eyes unusually large.

"I'm stuck," he gasped.

"Come back down, Kabir," said Ananth. "We'll try something else."

"Can't. Move." He sucked in his breath and tried yet again, groaning. "Back hurts."

Tara ran closer and realized why his face was so scrunched up. Kabir's back was a mass of scratches from the sharp edges of the rusted metal bars, and slick with blood.

"Stop it and come down immediately, Kabir," said Tara. "You're hurt! There has to be another way."

"Have … to do this," panted Kabir. "Just … try … harder."

Don't let anyone come now, Tara prayed. Right on cue, she heard footsteps.

"Someone's coming!" said Tara. "Oh my God, we'll be caught. Someone get him down. Quick!"

"Kabir, please hurry," whispered Raani. "I can hear them, too. They're coming fast."

"Arrghhhh," said Kabir pushing harder. He barely moved an inch. "Ananth. Help."

"Hoist me up, Vayu," said Ananth. Vayu made a cradle with his palms again and Ananth scrambled up. "Steady now," he said.

Vayu grunted in reply.

Ananth pushed Kabir gently. He did not budge a centimetre.

"Quick, Ananth, *quick*." said Tara.

"Sorry, Kabir," said Ananth. "This is going to hurt." Ananth pushed hard. Kabir yelped as his body shot through. His head was still on their side of the bars.

The footsteps were closer now. Someone was singing tunelessly.

Ananth wrestled with Kabir's head, trying to ease it through. Raani twisted her dupatta into a tight ball as she stared up at them.

Someone fumbled with the bolt outside.

"Come down," begged Raani. "If that madman catches you up there or if Kali sees you …"

"I can't," gasped Kabir. "No time." He reached behind him and wetted his palm with the blood on his back. He smeared his face and pulled, whimpering as he tugged and wriggled. Ananth, still standing on Vayu's shoulders, pushed Kabir's forehead. It barely moved. He smeared some more blood on Kabir's cheeks and pushed again, all the while muttering, "Sorry, Kabir … so sorry."

The bolt shot back with a metallic clang. Tara's legs turned to jelly. They were all doomed. She had seen Zarku in a rage and someone always got hurt. Or died.

"The clothes," said Tara. "Throw them out."

Just as door started to open, Kabir pulled his head through the bars and dropped out of sight. Raani handed Kabir's clothes up to Ananth, who threw them out the window. Ananth jumped off Vayu's shoulders. They quickly moved away from the window and faced the door, their breathing unnaturally loud in the still air.

Someone walked into the room carrying a lantern. The wick was turned up high and they were momentarily blinded. Tara shaded her eyes trying to see clearly.

Finally she made out who it was. She screamed.

seven

Possessed

"Suraj!"

Tara launched herself at her little brother and hugged him tight, sure that her heart would leap out of her chest. She held him at arm's length, devouring him with her eyes before clasping him to her, again. She never wanted to let go.

"Oh, thank God you're all right!" She kissed his cheeks, tasting the salt of her own tears. "You're back and you're safe but … that monster let you come here?" said Tara. Her eyes darted to the door. "Is Kali around?"

Suraj shook his head. "No, Didi. I'm all alone. You came. I knew you would! I'm so happy to see you."

He sounded so confident, so calm. Tara almost burst with pride at the way he was handling himself despite the scare he had gotten. He was stronger than she gave him credit for.

"Weren't you scared when the hyenas snatched you?" asked Ananth. He knelt beside Suraj and tousled his hair.

"I was at first," said Suraj. "But not anymore. Now that you're all here, everything's going to be all right."

"Where is Sadia?" asked Tara. "Why didn't you bring her with you?"

"She's ill," said Suraj. "She was too weak to walk so I told her to sleep."

They all gathered round Suraj, listening to him intently. Tara was glad that Kabir had escaped. Had he heard this, he would have done something impulsive and very foolish.

"Will you take us to her?" Tara asked. Her voice dropped to a whisper. "Once we get her we'll escape!"

Suraj's face turned a shade paler. "We mustn't," he said.

"Why not?" asked Ananth.

Suraj shot a terrified look at the door. Tara followed his gaze. Why hadn't someone come to lock it up? Were the hyenas guarding it? She caught Ananth's eye. He was staring at the door, just as confused.

"It's all right, Suraj," said Tara. "There's no need to be afraid. We're together now, no one can hurt you."

Suraj slipped his hand into hers. Tara blinked back tears. It was something Suraj did when he was scared. Till this moment she hadn't realized how much that small gesture meant to her. She squeezed his hand and smiled.

"She's right," said Vayu. "You're safe with us now. You won't suffer the same fate as your friend."

Suraj gripped her hand tighter. Tara glared at Vayu. Trust him to say the wrong thing at the wrong time. Suraj was already dealing with so much. She knelt and gazed into his face. Suraj's face was blank. Had he deliberately forgotten about his friend because it was too painful? Had he seen Rohan die?

Before Tara could reassure him, Suraj looked around the room and frowned. "Weren't there five of you?" he asked.

"How did you know?" asked Tara. She met Ananth's gaze. He looked troubled.

"Er — Kali told me," replied Suraj. "So, where is he?" he said. Suraj's voice was a bit sharper.

"Don't worry about that now, Suraj," said Tara. "Is there anything else you want to talk about?" Her voice was gentle, soothing.

"Tell me about your fifth friend," said Suraj. He looked around the room and then up at the window. "Where is he?"

"He's gone for help," said Tara.

"No!" yelled Ananth.

"Wha-what did I say?" asked Tara, looking at him in utter confusion.

But it was too late.

"Kali!" roared Suraj.

Tara stared at Suraj, aghast. Kali came running into

the room instantly; she must have been right outside their door.

"Send the hyenas to hunt for their companion and bring him back, dead or alive. He escaped from up there." Suraj jerked his head toward the barred window.

Kali nodded and almost tripped, running off to carry out the command.

"Suraj, stop it," said Tara. She shook him hard. "Have you gone mad? Kabir's gone for help. For us!"

She looked into his eyes and stopped. Something was different; his forehead had a small crease. Her skin prickled, crawled, as realization hit her with the force of a slap. It was where the burn on Rohan's forehead had been. She let go of his shoulders and stepped back.

There was something very wrong with her brother.

As Suraj stared back at her, his face changed. Not in its features — the eyes and nose and chin were still his. But he wore a look of utter, devastating contempt.

"Suraj, oh Suraj," he mocked her in a high-pitched squeak. "You stupid fool," he said. This time his voice was harsh, yet terribly familiar.

"Zarku ..." she breathed. Suraj's face swam before her eyes and then room went completely dark.

• • •

When she came round, Suraj was gone. In the dim light of the lantern he had left behind, three faces peered at her anxiously. "Are you okay?" asked Ananth. "You *fainted.* That's the second time!" The question had a slight accusatory tone. As if she was incapable of fainting.

Tara sat up and retched. The others jumped out of the way. Holding her aching head, she vomited till there was nothing left inside; not food, not panic, not even revulsion. Sadness crept in to fill the void. She had hugged that monster Zarku. And *kissed* him! And now he was in her brother's body. How did he get in and how was she going to get him *out?*

"So now we know he's not in the urn anymore," said Ananth. "Looks like he's learned how to possess a body."

Tara shivered. Not just *any* body. That evil spirit was inside her Suraj. This was so much harder than facing the Vetalas. Here the evil resided within and she would have to remind herself to go beyond the exterior.

"But how do we get him out?" asked Raani. "If we kill him …" She saw Tara's pale face and her hand flew to her mouth. "I'm sorry — I didn't mean to say that. I only meant —"

Tara hugged her knees to her chest. "I thought of it myself," she said in a dull voice.

"We can't hurt Zarku without harming the body he's in. If he dies, Suraj dies. Ananth, what are we going to do?"

Vayu held Tara's hand tightly in his. Oddly, it was more comforting than any words he could have said to her. She looked up at him, her eyes streaming.

"I'm beginning to wonder how Rohan died," said Raani. "If he had that burn on his forehead then maybe Zarku tried to possess him and failed?"

"You may be right," said Ananth, "but it's no use thinking about that now. We have to think of a way to rescue Sadia and get Zarku out of Suraj's body."

"This is so much worse than I thought. How do we deal with this?" said Tara. She shook her head. "If only grandfather were here, he'd know what to do. We haven't even told anyone where we are!"

"We'll think of a way, Tara," said Ananth. "Five — no four — of us should be able to come up with something."

"I only hope Kabir reaches a village safely. He has to ... we need help."

No sooner had she spoken than they heard yelling and scuffling. They rushed to the door, which was still ajar. A hyena got to his feet, growling. The yelling grew louder. Tara ran for the lamp and held it aloft.

Another hyena came into view, dragging a struggling Kabir behind him. He was scratched and bleeding, but at least he wasn't unconscious. Behind him were Kali and then Suraj. For a moment her heart leaped and then she shuddered. This was not her little brother anymore. It was Zarku. Zarku! She must *never* forget that.

The hyena dragged Kabir up to the door and released him. He stumbled and fell to the ground at their feet, his shirt in tatters, more red than white. Immediately Raani and Tara stooped to help him up. They led him inside and propped him against the wall.

"I'm sorry," muttered Kabir. He closed his eyes, breathing raggedly.

"Shhhh," said Tara. "We'll talk later."

Zarku walked into the room, followed by Kali.

"Ahhhh, it's so nice to see all five of you, together again."

"Why are you doing this, Zarku?" said Tara. "What have we done to you? What has my brother done to you? Leave him alone and get out of his body immediately."

"I'd gladly rip you out of his body," said Ananth. "One chance and I'd put an arrow through that black heart of yours."

"Shut up!" said Zarku. His voice was soft, but so full of menace that it silenced them all. "That's much better," he said. "I hate it when children act uncivilized."

He sat cross-legged on the floor. "Sit down, all of you. We have so much to talk about. Please." When no one moved, he barked, "Sit!"

They sat down facing him.

"I envy you," said Zarku. "Good friends having fun together. I never had friends when I was a child. The horrible eye on my forehead made me the laughingstock of my class. I had to stand on the sidelines watching others play. How I *wished* I could join in the games. How I *wished* someone would pick me for their team. But no one ever did. No one *ever* played with me."

Zarku's voice sounded soft and faraway, as he reminisced about his childhood. It was torture to listen to him speak, to have to grapple with the fact that this was not her brother, but a monster who had killed many and would do so again if he wasn't stopped.

"Hide-and-seek was my favourite game of all," said Zarku with a deep sigh. "Except it's no fun when you're playing by yourself."

"What do you want?" asked Ananth. "Surely you did not bring us here to listen to your stupid childhood memories."

Zarku leaned back, staring at Ananth as if he were a cockroach. "You have all the time in the world, Ananth, or how shall I put it, all the time *I* decide to give you! You will do *exactly* as I say."

Tara closed her eyes. How could this have happened?

"If you're going to kill us, why don't you just do it?" asked Vayu quietly. "Why all this unnecessary talk?"

"Kill you?" said Zarku. "Who said anything about killing you? I just want to play with you!"

Play with us the way a cat plays with a mouse, thought Tara. And they were about to find out just how bad it was going to be. She paid attention, still unable to reconcile that beloved face to the evil that was spewing out of his mouth. She looked at him and saw Suraj with his mop of unruly hair, his sweet smile, and his deep black eyes that almost always sparkled with mischief.

She looked away and heard that evil voice that had haunted her nightmares for a long time.

"A game of hide-and-seek, yes?" His eyes glittered with excitement, a broad smile spread across his face.

"You've gone mad," said Tara. "At a time like this, you think we want to play hide-and-seek?"

"*Tch tch*, name-calling again?" said Zarku. "Looks like someone did not teach you any manners. I might have to do it myself."

"Are you serious?" asked Ananth.

"Of course," said Zarku. "You will hide and I will seek you." He rubbed his hands together. "You have no idea how much this means to me."

"Never," snapped Raani. "You think you can tell us to play a game and we'll listen to you?"

"What if we decide not to play?" asked Ananth.

Zarku frowned. "Not play? Don't you like games? All children like games."

He looked away, a confused, dejected look on his face. "Now what can I do to convince you all. Hmmmm?"

A tiny squeak broke the silence. Zarku's hand shot out and closed over a rat that had the misfortune of running past at that very moment. They all jumped.

Zarku brought the rat close up to his face, clutching it tighter and tighter. Its squeal reached an agonizing crescendo before he twisted its neck. Once again, the room was quiet.

Zarku tossed the rat aside. Five pairs of eyes followed

it. It lay in the corner, its pink toes up in the air, as if it were sleeping peacefully.

"I have so many options," said Zarku. "There is Sadia and then this body of Suraj's —"

"Nooo," groaned Kabir. "We'll ... we'll do as you say. But can I see Sadia, just once?"

"Win the game and you can take her with you," said Zarku. "Until then, the answer is no."

Kabir stared at Zarku, his eyes glistening.

"All I'm asking for is a game and all I hear are moans and groans," said Zarku. "Not nice. You remind me of my classmates."

His gaze swept over them and he pouted. "But you haven't heard the best part."

No one said a word. His reactions were so unpredictable that Tara was glad no one attempted anything. When Zarku had everyone's attention, he spoke slowly and deliberately.

"I will give you all a head start. You have to hide from me for one night, just *one*! If I have not caught you by dawn you are all free to go, and yes," he said, looking straight at Tara, "that includes Suraj — I can easily find another body. You will have your brother back. So, what do you say?"

"And if we're caught?" asked Ananth.

He had voiced the question that was uppermost in all their minds.

"Let's not think about that right now," said Zarku. "How can five children not come up with interesting hiding places, in a forest? Say yes. Oh please say yes!"

He looked so normal, thought Tara, so harmless, until she looked into his eyes and saw the madness nestled there, the ruthlessness that would erupt in an instant if he did not get his way. In this form he was he was even more dangerous than he had ever been before.

"Give us a moment," said Ananth. He jerked his head and they all moved away to huddle beside Kabir.

"What do you all think," said Anath. "Do we say yes?"

Kabir looked at them, his face shiny with sweat and streaked with his own blood. "I don't like it one bit, but we don't have a choice. I want to see Sadia."

"It's a trap!" said Raani. "We shouldn't agree."

"Let's go for it," said Tara. "Our chances are better out there in the forest than in here. And you never know — we might get lucky and win! And Zarku might even keep his word if we play his game."

"All right," said Ananth. "Let's do it."

"We're ready," he said to Zarku, who had been watching them carefully.

"Wonderful! I knew you'd see things my way," said Zarku. He stood up and brushed the mud from his pajamas. "You can leave whenever you are ready. Playing in the dark is so much more fun, don't you think?"

No one replied. There was nothing to say.

"Kali," said Zarku. "Serve my friends some good food. I wouldn't expect anyone to play on an empty stomach.

I must go now and prepare. I'm soooo excited."

Zarku skipped out of the room humming Suraj's favourite tune. "Whoops! Almost forgot one important thing," he said. He stopped just outside the door and turned around.

Tara's stomach lurched.

"The hyenas will be helping me. Please, *please*, don't get caught! They haven't eaten in two days."

eight

The Final Feast

Zarku was gone, but he left behind a deeper gloom and a bitter taste of fear. A pale-faced Kabir lolled weakly against the wall, wincing each time Raani dabbed at a wound with her dupatta.

"My back," Kabir groaned. "It's on fire."

"Show me," said Raani.

Kabir twisted around and pulled up the edges of his tattered shirt. Tara could not suppress a gasp. His back was a mass of scratches. Torn skin hung from some of the deeper wounds, still oozing blood.

"Oh my God," said Raani. "You must be in a lot of pain!"

Tara glanced at Ananth and saw her worry mirrored in his eyes. This looked really bad. Some of the wounds were sure to get infected and with that came fever and weakness. How was he going to play a game in this condition? She wished now she had never let him go for help. She should have known he would have been caught.

"What happened?" asked Ananth. "After you left here, that is."

"I was really unlucky," said Kabir. "I managed to get into the forest, but barely did I start running when I was surrounded by hyenas. They waited till I was in a clearing and couldn't climb a tree. Then they attacked. I didn't have a chance." Kabir's voice fell. "I'm sorry. But what I don't understand is how they learned of my escape so quickly! I thought they wouldn't discover my absence till tomorrow morning."

"It's my fault," said Tara. She could barely meet Kabir's eyes. "I told Suraj about it, not realizing that I was really talking to Zarku. I'm the reason you're in so much pain."

Kabir's hand closed over Tara's. "Don't blame yourself. How was anyone to know Zarku could do this? The last time we saw him, he was a pile of ash in an urn. And you didn't tell me to squeeze through the bars and run for help — that was my idea."

"What now?" asked Raani. "I don't want to play hide-and-seek. Something tells me he will never let us win."

"We have to," answered Vayu. "I don't think we have a choice."

"Don't you dare tell me what to do," snarled Raani. "It's because of you that we're in this mess."

Vayu opened his mouth, then changed his mind and walked away without saying anything.

"You had better stop this right now," snapped Tara. "We're in this together, Raani, whether you like it or not. Fighting is not really going to help anyone. If you can't say something helpful, don't say anything at all. Vayu's right— we have to play. And if we fulfill his childhood dream, he might just let us go."

Raani faced Tara, her eyes flashing. "I'll say what I like, to whom I —"

"We should *never* have let you come with us," said Tara. "You're rude, arrogant, and foul-mouthed!"

"And you think you're the cleverest of us all because you faced Zarku once," said Raani. "If you're so smart why didn't you do a proper job of finishing him off the first time?"

"Enough," yelled Kabir. "We have to save my sister and your brother, Tara. We have to play hide-and-seek with a maniac in your brother's body and survive till dawn, and all you two can think of is fighting? Focus! Our lives depend on us working together."

The doors slammed open before anyone could answer. They all looked up. Tara's heart pounded, fearing another surprise. Instead, Kali walked in bearing a thali of food that gave off a heavenly fragrance. One more lay on the floor just outside. Saliva flooded Tara's mouth as the aromas of freshly cooked food sped into the room, overpowering the other foul smells lingering in the air.

"Come and help me," Kali said, prodding Tara with her toe.

Tara jumped up and stamped on Kali's foot, grinding down with her heel.

"Get off," shrieked Kali. "How dare you?"

"You're nothing to me anymore and I won't be treated like a beggar," said Tara. "You prod me with your toe once more, and I'll chop it off."

Kali looked so mad that Tara was sure she would hurl the thali of food straight at her head. Instead Kali slammed down the steel platter with a resounding bang. Bits of rice and vegetables spilled onto the floor.

"You've got it coming, Tara," said Kali. "I will help Zarku in any way I can to make sure that you don't get out of this forest alive. That is my promise to you."

Kali brought in the second thali and plonked it down. Her eyes glittered with rage and her lips were a thin, straight line. "Eat and get out," she said, her small black eyes sweeping over them. "May the worst luck be with you all!"

With her dire words still hanging in the air, Kali stomped out of the room.

They stared at the food. One platter was filled with steaming white rice, yellow dal, an assortment of vegetables, pickles, and papads. The other thali had her favourite food; mithai. Fat, golden laddoos squatted regally in a corner. Rasmalai lay smothered in a creamy blanket of milk in smaller container, sprinkled liberally with pistachios and almonds. Diamond-shaped coconut and cashew barfi, glittering with silver vark, peeped from under the fronds of a banana leaf.

Zarku and Kali had gone through a lot of trouble to provide such a sumptuous meal; almost as if they were fattening pigs for slaughter. Her appetite vanished and she shrank back against the wall.

"I'm not hungry," she said. "You all eat."

How could she eat a meal provided by people she hated the most? This was so wrong. She met Ananth's eyes. He seemed to be going through the same dilemma. The food steamed away gently, perfuming the air. No one moved.

Vayu grabbed Tara's hand and made her sit down. He beckoned to all of them. "Listen to me, this could be the last decent meal for a while. Don't pass it up. We'll need every bit of our strength. Even one of us not being able to run could be the difference between life and death."

"How did you get to be the wise man of the group?" said Tara. She could not help but smile.

"You're right," said Ananth. "Who cares where the food came from? We better eat if we're going to be running all night."

Raani snorted and Kabir scooched closer.

They sat, encircling the enormous thalis, and dug in. The food was tasty and hot. She crunched up the vegetables and bit into the spicy papads, feeling her tastebuds tingle after being hungry for so long. With each bite her tiredness and exhaustion lessened.

Then they started on the sweets. The mithai melted in her mouth and Tara ate till she could eat no more. Moonlight splashed in through the small window and for a moment, surrounded by her friends, her belly full of good food, she almost forgot that in a short while they would be running for their lives.

"That was excellent," said Kabir. He patted his stomach.

Ananth nodded, licking his sticky fingers.

There was a contented silence in the room. Tara wished it would last forever.

The very next moment there was a sound like a firecracker bursting inside a gunny sack, then a tiny sputtering which petered away into silence. A foul odour filled the air.

They all looked at Vayu in shock.

"You farted," said Raani. "That's ... that's disgusting!" She made a great show of fanning the air in front of her face.

Vayu shrugged, not looking the least bit upset. "Now you know why I'm called Vayu." He reached for the last laddoo in the plate and chomped it, staring at Raani. "I've had this ... um ... problem since I was a little boy," he said through a mouthful of food.

They all burst into laughter at the mortified expression on Raani's face. When she stopped, Tara felt more energized, more hopeful that she had just a few moments ago. She smiled warmly at Vayu, who winked at her.

"I think it's time we moved," said Ananth. "Ready everyone?"

Tara patted the anklet in her pocket. "Ready."

Kabir got to his feet slowly. His face had a bit more colour to it, but a flicker of pain still showed on it when he walked.

"You okay?"asked Vayu.

Kabir nodded. "I'll be fine. With all of you to help me, we'll make it." He made a fist and held it out. They looked at him in confusion. "A fist is stronger than five fingers," he said. "Think we can *all* remember that for the next few hours?" He looked pointedly at Raani and then at Tara.

Tara's eyes locked with Raani's. What Kabir had said were only words till they truly believed it with their hearts.

Hide and Seek

Tara stood on the steps of the temple, looking out at the undulating sea of darkness and whispering shadows. They were about to start a game of hide-and-seek. *What's so hard about that? It's just a game,* she told herself over and over again. But it wasn't. They were playing for their lives and the lives of Suraj and Sadia. *They could not lose.*

"So, how did you like that fantastic meal?" said Zarku. He sat at the top of the stairs and leaned against an ivy-covered pillar, a grin plastered on his face. "You should thank me. Kali was all for giving you dry bread and water, but I said absolutely not. My friends deserve a good meal if they're going to play well. You can't say I haven't been fair, now can you?"

"Fair," spat Raani. "What's so fair about this? You make us play some stupid game in the middle of the night. And you've got hyenas to help you!"

Zarku's smile drooped. His forehead pulsed.

When would Raani learn to keep her mouth shut? Tara expected Zarku to fly into a rage and probably kill them immediately. End of game.

"You're being very mean, just like all those other children years ago. I don't like it," said Zarku, a sulky expression on his face. "I've fed you well and I'm giving you the chance to win. Five clever children against poor old me. What more can you ask for?"

Freedom, Tara wanted to yell but she didn't. All she wanted to do was get away from him. There was an edge to his voice that she did not like at all; the calm before the storm. She shot a warning look at the group around her, hoping they would understand. No one said a word.

"I want this game to be fun," said Zarku. He beamed at them, his annoyance and hurt from a moment earlier seemingly forgotten. "Tell me, aren't you just a bit excited?"

"I think we should leave now," said Vayu.

"Uh-uh, not so fast," said Zarku. "First, a few rules."

Tara tried not to roll her eyes or sigh deeply. *There were rules now? And would he really follow them?* She gritted her teeth and paid attention.

Zarku paced in front of them. Stopped. "Rule number one — you must all stay together, no splitting up."

As if, thought Tara. They wouldn't dream of going their separate ways. Their only chance was to stay together.

When no one spoke he continued. "Rule number two — if I catch you before sunrise tomorrow, I win! And you will all do exactly as I say. Agreed?"

I'd rather die before I let that happen, thought Tara. Zarku looked straight at her almost as if he could read her mind and smiled again. It broke her heart and she had to look away. *This is not Suraj ... not Suraj*, she chanted silently.

"And what if we win?" asked Kabir. "You'll let us go and give back my sister and Tara's brother. You promise?"

"But of course, you have my word," said Zarku. His eyes glittered. "I do have to say, though — I've never lost to anyone yet."

Tara looked at him, she couldn't help it. She hadn't intended to meet his eyes, but she couldn't help that, either. For he had lost to someone. To her. She lowered her eyes again, but too late. He'd seen the look in them.

Zarku's face was a mask of hatred. She couldn't believe that the sweet features of her brother could rearrange themselves into such an ugly expression. Goosebumps rose on her arms.

"Ahhh, yes," said Zarku. "I had forgotten. Let me correct myself, I have only lost once to Tara here. It will *not* happen again."

The hyenas circled them quietly, breathing in their scent.

"Get a good sniff, my beauties," said Zarku. "For tonight we go hunting."

The hyenas whooped with laughter. Tara stepped back, praying she would never have to smell their breath up close again. The largest hyena swept his beady eyes over them and wagged his stump of a tail.

"Can we go already?"said Raani. She had twisted her dupatta around her finger so tightly that the tip of it was white. "The sooner we go — uh, the sooner we can start *playing*."

"My, my," said Zarku, smiling at Raani. "You can't wait to start, either! I knew you'd be excited after all. I'll close my eyes, count to a hundred and then come looking for you," he said. "*At last*, a game I have waited to play all my life. This will be a night to remember."

Tara glanced one last time at Zarku. She focused on the little boy, trying to avoid the eyes that would give away the horror that resided deep within him. *I will win for you, Suraj. You will be free, I promise.*

Zarku turned his back on them, leaned his forehead against the pillar and started counting. "One hundred, ninety-nine, ninety-eight …"

They raced across the courtyard as fast as they could. Tara's legs trembled. She stumbled. Fell. Vayu pulled her to her feet and they continued running.

"Ninety-seven, ninety-six, ninety-five …"

They ran past the fire, leaped over the low wall and hurtled into the forest.

"Ninety-four, ninety-three, ninety-two …"

They ran, crashing through the trees like a herd of elephants on a rampage.

They ran, dodging low branches and thorny bushes that reached out to grab them and slow them down.

They ran till they couldn't hear Zarku's voice at all.

• • •

Sweat trickled down Tara's face in rivulets. Her clothes clung to her body like a wet sheath. An agonizing stitch gripped her side in a vice. Her heart thundered in her chest. She had no idea how much longer she could run, but she did not want to be the first one to suggest that they stop.

"Can't ... run," gasped Vayu. He sat down abruptly on the forest floor, coughing.

Everyone stopped and tumbled to the ground. Silently, Tara thanked him. A sliver of moon, hanging silently in the night sky, bathed them in a weak, milky light. Panting, Tara lay on her back, staring at the patches of sky visible through the treetops. This same moon must be shining over Morni, over her mother and father, over home. She felt a pang of guilt for not having told them that she was going to look for Suraj. What if neither of them returned?

Lightning cleaved the sky and thunder rumbled overhead. Fat clouds moved across the face of the thin moon. Rain! At last, some respite from the sticky heat.

"At this rate, we won't last very long," wheezed Ananth. "We'll have to pace ourselves if we're to survive till tomorrow morning."

Tara's muscles throbbed in protest. Tomorrow morning? She was ready to give up right now if it meant she could lie still for just a while longer. A persistent cloud of mosquitoes had taken a liking to her once again, and stuck closer than her own shadow. She waved her arms, cursing them. The cloud got thicker and her skin itched with a million tiny bites; she didn't know where to start scratching.

Kabir groaned loudly and Tara sat up immediately. In their dash for safety they had forgotten he was injured. It was amazing that he kept up without a single word of protest. His face was paler than the moon and slick with sweat. Tara reached out to touch his forehead. Hot!

"Kabir, you have a high fever!"

"I'll be fine," he said. "I needed a short rest. We can start again soon. Very soon. Just give me a few more minutes."

"Let me see your back," said Tara. "Now!"

When Kabir didn't budge, she crawled over to him.

"What are you doing?" said Kabir. "I'm all right."

"Be quiet," said Tara. "I just want to have a look." She lifted his shirt and heard him moan softly. When she saw his back, she almost moaned, too; the wounds were slightly puffy and had a faint rotting smell.

"I don't like the look of this at all," said Tara. "If only we had some time, I would have put some herbs on it to slow the infection. Maybe if everyone helps me look for them …"

"Not now, Tara. We'll have to hide soon, very soon," said Ananth. "I don't think we can outrun Zarku and his hyenas. Not with Kabir in this condition. You can make the medicine for him later."

"So where are we hiding tonight?" asked Raani. "Any ideas?"

"I can't climb a tree," said Vayu. "Trees are absolutely out!"

"I don't see any caves or rocks," said Raani. She circled the spot. "Where in the name of Lord Ganesh can five of us hide safely?" Her voice broke. "He'll find us and kill us!"

"It'll be all right, Raani," said Ananth. "We'll find a good place, hide, wait till morning, and then it's over."

If only it were that simple. For the last few moments Tara had been wracking her brains for a spot, searching every dark shadow, every crevice, every tree. "It's got to be unusual. Some place he would never think of looking," she murmured to herself. "Once we're hidden, he'll never be able to find us tonight. We'll be safe, we'll win. Follow me."

She got to her feet wearily. Her legs wobbled and she almost fell over as her muscles seized. She hobbled along, stopping every few seconds, searching.

"Here's one," said Raani. They had just walked past a tree with a large clump of bushes at its base. "In the bushes. He'd never think of looking here and it's right under his nose."

"You mean these thorny bushes?" said Tara. "Great! You get in there and show us how it's done and we'll follow."

Raani caught the sarcasm and glared at her. "I was only trying to help."

"Don't," said Tara. "Your idea is terrible."

"How about climbing a tree?" said Ananth. "We'll be off the ground and well hidden."

"I thought of that," said Tara, "but look around you. Most of these branches start way higher than we can reach. By the time we all get high enough to be hidden from view, Zarku will be here. And Vayu just said he can't climb. Weren't any of you listening?"

"Come on, Tara," said Kabir. "What makes you think you're the best at finding a hiding place? I think we should consider all suggestions. We're a team, remember? Zarku is probably on his way by now."

"When I played with Suraj, I always won," said Tara. "Trust me, when I find a hiding place, it'll be really good!"

In the distance a bird shot into the air, squawking.

"He's coming," said Raani. "Will you hurry up for God's sake? You remember what he said about the hyenas."

"I'm looking, I'm looking," said Tara, trying hard not to raise her voice. She ran ahead, ran back, her eyes constantly searching and discarding spots. Her throat was parched and her muscles ached, but she ignored it. There had to be a good place ... and *she* had to be the one to locate it. "There!" said Tara, her heart thudding with excitement. "That's the spot."

They all gazed in the direction she was pointing.

"I thought we agreed, no trees," said Vayu. "You're pointing at trees!"

"Look carefully," said Tara. "Just where the branches start, there's another trunk leaning against it." She dragged Ananth closer. "If you lot couldn't spot it, neither will Zarku. And with this trunk, we'll get to the branches higher up a lot faster. Come on, let's go. It's perfect."

Tara stared at it for just a second longer; one of the trees had probably been struck by lightning and fallen against the other. It formed a natural ladder they could climb. The bases of both trees were hidden by an overgrowth of bushes and creepers. Only the sharpest eyes, or daylight, could have revealed it. She was *very* satisfied with this place and with herself.

"Come on, we need to climb up to where the two trunks meet. Then we split up and hide in the branches," said Tara. "I bet Zarku will go right past." She couldn't suppress the glee in her voice. By tomorrow morning they would be free. Then she'd get Suraj and Sadia back and they'd return to Morni. Once again, she'd have saved the day.

"I'll go first," said Tara. "Send Kabir up and then the rest of you follow."

More shrill chatter from birds. Zarku was definitely close by. Tara hopped onto the sloped trunk, took one step, and almost fell off as a large piece of bark along the edge broke off in a cloud of dust. She straddled the trunk, the pounding of her heart deafeningly loud.

"It's rotten," she said. "I don't know if it'll hold everyone's weight."

"Now you tell us," said Raani. "When we barely have any time?"

Ananth came over and ran his hand over the trunk. He rapped on it. "It doesn't seem hollow. It should hold. Keep going, Tara. We don't have time to look for another place."

Tara inched her way up the log. More bits showered her friends below, but the trunk did not break as she had feared. Slivers of bark slid into the tender skin of her palm and she itched to pull them out. The musty smell of damp, rotting wood made her want to sneeze. She ignored the discomfort, reached the fork at the top, and stepped onto a broad branch. "Send Kabir."

Kabir straddled the trunk just as Tara had done. Sweating and panting, he dragged himself a few feet. Then stopped.

"Hurry," said Tara. "Someone help him."

In the distance they heard Zarku moving through the foliage toward them. The rustling grew louder with each passing second. Now and then they heard a whoop or a giggle. The hairs on the back of Tara's neck rose.

Ananth stepped onto the trunk and pushed Kabir up. "You've got to do this, Kabir. The rest of us can't follow till you're up there. And two of us can't climb this together. Come on, you have to do it!"

Groaning softly, Kabir managed to get up the rest of the way on his own. Tara kept a lookout for Zarku.

"Raani," said Tara. "You're next. Come on quick."

While Raani walked up hesitantly, Tara helped Kabir climb up the nearest leafy branch. His skin was hotter than before. What if the fever got too much and he couldn't walk at all? This hiding place had to work. If only they could stay hidden till dawn ... they'd be all right. They might even make it to a healer before the fever got worse.

It took a couple of tries before Kabir climbed on. Tara made sure he had a firm grip on it before she moved away, praying he wouldn't fall off.

"Thanks," mumbled Kabir.

Tara held out her fist. He touched it lightly with his, then closed his eyes and rested his forehead on the branch.

Raani was beside her. "What now?" she asked, pressing her back against the tree trunk. She looked down and squeezed her eyes shut.

You could climb onto my head, Tara was tempted to

say, but she held her tongue. "Climb up to the higher branches. Leave the lower one for Vayu. Go!"

Raani nodded, reached up for a branch and disappeared from view. *Hurry, hurry, hurry*, Tara almost screamed as Ananth nimbly ran up the log and was beside her in seconds. The log creaked and squeaked, shedding a few more bits of bark. It sounded quite loud in the still forest; would Zarku hear them?

Now for the final test— Vayu. His pale, round face was rigid with fear as he looked up at them.

"What are you doing just standing there?" said Ananth. "Come on up."

"I think I'll hide down here," said Vayu. "I really don't mind the bushes, a few scratches are nothing —"

"Don't be stupid," said Tara. "Come up now or I'll drag you up here myself if I have to."

"What if ..."

"Just do it, please?" said Tara. "Zarku's almost here and if you're caught, we're all going to die." She was being dramatic, but there was no time for coaxing.

"I'm scared," said Vayu.

"Just look up at us and slide," said Ananth. "Don't look down."

The sounds of crunching leaves and snapping twigs were closer now, so close that Zarku would be upon them in moments.

Vayu straddled the log and pulled himself up. The log groaned.

"Ready or not, here I come," sang Zarku. *Yes, that's it*, thought Tara. *Keep making a noise so you won't hear us. Sing louder!*

Vayu inched up the remaining few feet. Tara prayed. Ananth stared at Vayu unwaveringly. The log held. Only when Vayu was standing next to them did she breathe again. Once they were all up at the fork, they separated and clambered onto branches. Tara and Ananth climbed higher up while Vayu and Kabir stayed on the lower ones. No one from the ground would be able to spot them, she was sure of that.

Tara peered through the leaves, clutching at a branch to steady herself.

She heard Kali's voice first. "Why did I have to come along?" she whined. "I should have stayed at the temple. You've got three hyenas with you. You don't need me."

Tara peeked through the leaves. She couldn't see them yet, but heard them quite clearly.

"But you *needed* the exercise," said Zarku. "You should thank me. I'm always thinking of your well-being."

Kali snorted.

"You snort at me again and that will be the last time you draw any kind of breath," snapped Zarku. "You agreed to do everything I said. Don't forget, when I am back in power, you will rule along with me. People will fear you as much as they fear me. Together we will be formidable."

"Sorry," said Kali. "But you will keep your promise, too, won't you? Parvati and Shiv are the first two I'll take care of. I'll show them what it is to banish me and take away my child. Then Prabala, then Raka, and then —"

"Enough!" said Zarku. "I've heard you rant so many times that if I hear it one more time, I'll strangle you. You'll have your revenge on all the people you hate, and anyone else you don't. But for now just shut up and help me find those children."

Tara almost lost her grip. If Zarku came back to power, he would kill everyone she loved. They could not be found, they had to win. *Win, win, win!* She recited the word like a mantra to the drumbeat of her pounding heart.

Zarku whacked at the bushes with his stick. She saw him then. *That's it, keep looking at ground level and keep walking. Just don't look up!*

Zarku halted a short distance from where they hid. "Tara passed this way," he said. "I can feel it."

Tara hugged the branch. How could he have guessed that? What was it that gave her away?

"How do you know that?" asked Kali.

Yes, how do you know? thought Tara silently, straining her ears for the answer.

"She has a certain presence," said Zarku. "I can't describe it. But where would she go from here and in which direction?"

"How would I know?" said Kali.

124

"I really wasn't talking to you," said Zarku. "So do shut up."

Kali muttered something under her breath. Tara was sure she wasn't heaping blessings on his head. She craned her neck and looked up, but the leaves were too thick and she could not spot the others. Good. If she couldn't, then neither would Zarku nor Kali.

Zarku walked, sniffing the air. The sound of his footsteps receded. He stopped. Retraced his steps.

"Go look around," said Zarku. "Find them!"

If he was putting Kali to work, they had little to worry about. That fat lump would never do any work. But the very next moment a cold hand clutched her heart. The growls of the hyenas were close, too close. Tara could imagine all too clearly their beady eyes, their pointed snouts, and their deadly jaws. Footsteps followed and stopped at the foot of their tree. Tara was sure it was over. He had only to look up and he'd know where they were; her scent would probably give her away. The hyenas circled the base of the tree, growling.

Don't look up, go away ... go away, prayed Tara.

Zarku walked away from the tree, talking softly to himself, the stick in his hand slashing at the bushes. Tara exhaled.

The sound was less distinct now, almost as if he was doing it half-heartedly. Kali stood motionless. He retraced his steps. The sounds returned. He paused very briefly and walked away in another direction. Each time he moved away, her heart soared. When he returned, it sank like a stone. What was he playing at?

The answer almost jolted her off the branch.

He knew where they were. He knew *exactly* where they were hiding.

Zarku stood at the foot of the tree staring at the fallen tree trunk. His gaze travelled upward, one agonizing inch at a time. Tara knew with complete certainty that the game was over. She rested her head against the branch, dizzy with panic.

They had lost.

ten

Reprieve

"Oh Didi, I've found you, I've found you!" said Zarku. He hopped on the spot, clapping his hands and for a brief and unreal moment it felt like she and Suraj were back home in Morni. "Come on, Didi ..." he said, continuing to speak like Suraj. "Show yourself."

Tara pressed her lips together and had to use every ounce of discipline to keep from instinctively answering her brother.

Zarku spoke again, this time in his own voice. "I've waited a lifetime to play this game and this is the best you can do? Five of you and this silly hiding place is all you could come up with? A dimwit could have found you. Shame!"

Zarku screamed some more, his voice getting shriller with each word. Tara expected him to storm up the tree and throw them down to the waiting jaws of the hyenas. She could almost feel their teeth sink into her flesh. The branch seemed to rock and sway under her. Tara clung tighter. She had failed her friends. Would they ever forgive her?

"Come down right now!" said Zarku. His tone was as sharp as broken glass.

No one moved.

"Now, Tara," said Zarku. "If I have to come up, well … let's not even think about how much angrier I will be."

Tara slid off the branch.

"What are you doing?" said Ananth. "Stay here, he's only bluffing."

"I assure you I'm not," said Zarku. "All of you better come down, too. I'm not very big on patience."

Tara was the first one to reach Zarku. She stomped down the fallen tree trunk, hoping it would give way and crash down on his head. But even this time it held. Silently, sullenly, the others followed. Kabir came last, lurching and weaving, but made it down safely. No one looked at Tara and she was glad. She couldn't bear to see their accusing looks or worse, their disappointment. They stood at the foot of the tree facing Zarku, Kali, and the hyenas that hung around like a stench in the air.

They'd lost. And now they would have to do exactly as he said. She took a deep shuddering breath. *Lost, lost, lost* echoed inside her head.

"So, I win," said Zarku. "I WIN." He was smiling broadly. "What should I do with the lot of you? To see the hyenas tear you apart would be great fun for me! Or maybe I should ..."

"Let us go," said Raani. "*Please?*"

"What?" said Zarku. He frowned at Raani. "Why?"

"So that, er ... because," said Raani. She glanced at the others, her eyes pleading for help.

"So you can have one more night of fun," said Tara, suddenly. "Surely you'd like that?'

"My, my," said Zarku. "Such concern for my pleasures is touching."

"No!" said Kali. "Finish them now and then we deal with Tara. You've waited so long to carry out your plan and get back to your former glory. Why prolong it?"

Tara shot Kali the dirtiest look she could muster. How easy it was for her to talk of taking innocent lives, of killing. She was just as evil as Zarku. The thought of them working together made the hairs on the back of her neck prickle. Tara had difficulty killing a *cockroach* because it meant taking something she could never return.

"Kali's right, you know," said Zarku. He turned toward Tara. "I can't wait to put my plan into action; it means endless glory and power for me, forever."

"And end the game so soon?" said Tara. "You said you've waited years to play it. Why not give us one more night? We'll do a better job of hiding this time. Really."

"You were always the clever one, Tara. Your idea has merit. Why stop the game when it's just begun? All right, you've convinced me, one more night!"

The knot in Tara's stomach loosened slightly. She'd just bought them all some more time. This time she'd think of a much better place. She had to. This time he would never, *ever* find them.

"I'll be off now," said Zarku. "But I'll be back tomorrow night. See that you don't disappoint me! You won't be so lucky again."

He snapped his fingers and the hyenas came trotting up to him like obedient dogs. One of them had a half-eaten rabbit hanging from his mouth. The other two hyenas lunged at it and dismembered it before their eyes. Horrified, Tara watched each hyena triumphantly chew a body part. The crunch of bone echoed in the still night and Tara wanted to clap her hands over her ears to block out the sound. But she held them rigidly at her sides; she would not show Zarku how much this affected her.

"You picked the hiding place, Tara. Didn't you?" said Zarku. When she did not reply he looked at her steadily for a moment. "Better luck tomorrow. You're going to need it."

• • •

After Zarku strolled away, no one spoke for a moment. Then they all faced her and she saw what she had been dreading all along.

"You said the hiding spot was *perfect*," Raani

screamed. "Miss Know-it-all, he'll-never-find-us-in-a-million-years! You almost got us killed!"

"I'm sorry. I thought so, too," said Tara. "I just can't believe he found us. I just can't." Her voice was so soft that it was barely above a whisper.

"Well, you better believe it," said Kabir. He wiped his forehead with a shaky hand. "But at least he let us go. Good thinking, both of you."

"The cat-and-mouse game has begun again," said Vayu with a deep sigh. "I have a feeling he'll keep doing this till he is bored and *then* he'll kill us."

"But if we can avoid being captured till dawn, he'll let us go and the game ends," said Raani. "He will keep his word, won't he? He seems to like rules."

Despite her earlier hopes, Tara felt, deep down, that would never happen. From the expressions on everyone's face she knew the others had doubts, too.

"I'm really sorry," Tara repeated. "I only wanted to help. But I have a better plan for tonight."

No one answered her. Surely they would give her another chance? They glanced at her and then looked away. Though no one came out and said it, she knew they all were unanimous in their decision. They didn't want her to pick the next hiding spot.

Ananth finally spoke. "You can't help, Tara. And that's final. The four of us will decide."

"But why?" said Tara. "I said I was sorry. Can't you forgive one little mistake? Haven't any of you made mistakes before? And none of us have died so it's no big deal … right? Right?"

Ananth glanced at the others. "You figure it out," he said.

He was just jealous … they all were. This was Zarku they were dealing with and she'd had the most experience of anyone in the group. Except now he was in her brother's body and all she had to do was pretend that they were playing their favourite game back home and … NO! She couldn't do that.

Tara wrapped her arms around herself as the realization hit. Zarku knew everything about her — the way she thought, the places she'd look for — through Suraj! In this game of cat-and-mouse, he had chosen very well. She could not help them and they all knew it, had figured it out before she did.

The moon played its own little game of hide-and-seek, its silvery light brightening and waning as dark clouds sailed past its gaunt face.

"We should get some rest," said Ananth. "Zarku is not coming back till tomorrow night."

Tara did not say another word. She had been so sure of herself, so confident, and had almost gotten everyone killed. What was she going to do now?

They settled down under a tree. A storm was brewing. The heat intensified and so did the clouds of mosquitoes. Tara noticed nothing. Though she took deep breaths, something huge and heavy sat on her chest. She just couldn't get enough air. Her friends were in danger because of her, from an evil monster who had possessed her brother. Her head reeled.

Show me the right way, Lord Ganesh, she prayed. *If we defeat and kill Zarku, we'll kill Suraj, too. But if he regains his strength, he and Kali will destroy us all just like before. We have to stop him and I have to be strong enough for it.*

One thought brought a small measure of relief; she had her friends with her this time. This time she wasn't alone. Together they would think of a better hiding place.

The polite argument that had started a while ago, between thunder and lightning, was now a full-fledged fight. A sudden clap reverberated through the forest and the deluge started. Within seconds they were drenched in cool rain. Tara stood with her face turned toward the sky, letting the water wash away the sweat, the dirt, and the worry. But it couldn't reach the fear that lay curled deep within her, its claws sheathed for now, but always watching, waiting.

As suddenly as the rain had started, it stopped. A cool breeze filtered through the trees and Tara lay down with the others on the wet forest floor. The *drip, drip, drip* of the raindrops soothed the ache in her heart until she fell asleep.

eleven

An Unknown Voice

The cooing of a koel woke Tara. Sunlight dripped from shiny green leaves and pooled on the forest floor, making the world around them sparkle. Sleep fled and panic returned. How long had they been *resting*? They should have been far, far away from here by now. She looked up at the tree they had hidden in the night before. It swayed gently, painting the sky a bright blue with its branches. It had seemed like such a perfect spot at the time. Where would they hide tonight?

"Wake up, Ananth," said Tara, shaking him roughly. "We've overslept!"

Ananth jerked awake. "What happened? Is he back?"

"Calm down," said Tara. She sat cross-legged in front of him. "He's not here yet, but in a few hours he will be. One of us should have kept watch and we should have moved out of here a long time ago. If he catches us tonight, we're dead."

"I know, Tara," said Ananth. "But we all needed the rest. I'm sure we'll make good time once we get started."

"If and when we get started and that had better happen right now," said Tara. "Everyone, wake up," she called out. "It's late, we have to get away from here now. *Wake up*."

Kabir moaned and they hurried to his side. The grey pallor of his face worried Tara. She touched his forehead and jerked her hand away, shocked. It was scorching.

"Kabir, wake up." asked Tara. She shook him gently. Kabir's eyes flew open.

"*Don't*, don't do that," he said. "I hurt all over." His eyes were sunken into deep dark hollows. He licked his cracked lips and squinted up at them.

"How do you feel?" asked Ananth.

"Terrible," said Kabir. "My back is on fire. Can someone pour some water and put it out?" He smiled weakly, but neither Tara nor Ananth smiled back.

"Will you be able to keep up?" asked Tara. "We have to start right away."

Kabir sat up. The effort showed on his face. "I don't know if I can." His face was greyer than a moment ago.

Tara paced in front of Kabir, stopping to look at him every few seconds. "This is very bad."

"It is," said Raani. "If only we'd found a better hiding place last night, we'd be free by now."

Tara glared at her and Raani shut up.

"There aren't any good hiding places here," said Tara. "We have to get away, search someplace else. And in case none of you have noticed, it's almost midday … we'd better hurry."

"That means we still have half a day to plan," said Ananth. "With Kabir in this state we won't be able to get very far, so this time we have to choose wisely. Any ideas?"

"Yes," said Tara. "I was thinking that —"

"No!" they said in unsion.

Tara stared at them in dismay and remembered, she couldn't help, not this time.

"You can't suggest a place," said Ananth. "Please, Tara. Don't look at me this way. You know why."

Tara nodded. She wanted to help so desperately and this other place she had in mind might even work! But it was no use. She alternated between hating them all to acknowledging that they were right. She should be grateful there were four more brains working on an escape plan.

"Maybe I can help some other way," said Tara. "Let me look at your back, Kabir."

His wounds had worsened. Some of the scratches were definitely infected, oozing yellow pus instead of blood. His back must be itching and burning by now. How was he able to stand the pain? She would have been out of her mind by now. She looked at Kabir with renewed respect.

"I'm going to look for some herbs," she said. "With the right salve it should not hurt as much and will even stop the infection from spreading."

Kabir nodded his thanks and lay down again.

Tara walked away into the forest, leaving the others discussing the next hiding place. Brown hares with long, floppy ears peeped at her from the undergrowth, reminding her of the hyenas and their feeding frenzy the night before. She tried to shake the image out of her head, focusing instead on the serene beauty around her. Birds twittered overhead and clumps of bright yellow and orange flowers dotted the forest floor. If it hadn't been for Zarku, this would have been just a pleasant walk in the forest. *I hate you, Zarku*, she thought. *I hate you for what you have done to me and my family.*

A sudden rage filled her and she hurried through the undergrowth, cracking twigs underfoot, trampling the low-lying foliage. She searched for the greenish-white flowers of the ritha tree. All she needed were a few of its fruits and leaves. The tulsi herb with its antibacterial properties would be a treasure, too. If only she could find them, she'd be able to keep Kabir's infection under control and put her mother's teaching to good use. Then they'd have a fair chance of escaping.

I hate you, Zarku! she thought again, vehemently.

Don't hate him, Tara. Pity him, for he has suffered.

"What?" said Tara aloud. She whirled around. The forest behind her was empty. Who had just spoken? She had been so intent on searching for the herbs that she had barely paid attention to anything else. She closed her eyes and thought of the voice. It had been so gentle, so soft, barely above a whisper. She wasn't even sure if it had been a man or a woman speaking.

"Raani, is that you?" asked Tara. She stood still in the waist-high bushes and looked around her.

The only reply was the wind flitting through the treetops and the drone of bees. A woodpecker tattooed its call sign on a tree trunk high above her. Maybe she was imagining things or else it must be the heat. The scorching midday sun, filtering through the leaves, brought sweat oozing from every pore. The cool rain from last night was already a distant memory.

"Vayu?"

There was no answer. Were they hiding behind a tree? She retraced her steps, peering behind trees and bushes, but there was no sign of anyone. In the distance she heard raised voices. It sounded like they were all there. She stood still for a moment, but the person did not speak again. She had definitely imagined it. It was the heat and exhaustion, that was all.

"There," she spoke aloud. She had spied the light yellow trunk of a young ritha tree. Tara quickly collected a bunch of leaves from its lower branches and searched the ground below it for its seeds. She found three she could use. Now if she could find tulsi, the salve would be more effective. She continued walking, keeping a sharp eye out for it.

Her thoughts drifted again to the voice. It had to be her imagination. Who could believe that Zarku could have suffered? What a joke! He was the sort that made other people suffer. How she wished she could see him burn up again, victim of his own evil gaze. She walked deeper and deeper into the bushes, and there it was; a clump of reddish-purple tulsi flowers. Now she'd be able to keep Kabir going till they reached safety.

Don't be too sure.

Tara dropped everything and whirled around for a second time. This time she was sure she had heard it; a woman's voice.

"Show yourself," she said. "Who are you?" Her heart thumped. What if the speaker did show herself? Was she prepared for what she might see? The honest answer was no.

Leaves rustled around her and the wind sighed loudly. The speaker did not appear. Tara hurried back.

The moment she stepped out of the forest, Raani looked up at Tara with a bland expression. If she'd followed Tara and then outrun her to reach the clearing first, there seemed to be no sign of it on her face. The others were busy discussing plans and barely glanced at her. Should she mention the voice? It sounded odd even to her, now that she was back with her friends.

"Raani, find a couple of flat stones for me," said Tara. "I need to grind these herbs." She noted the sour look on Raani's face, but ignored it.

"So, what have you all decided?" Tara asked.

"We're going to stay," said Ananth. He had borrowed Kabir's knife and had made himself a crude bow. A pile of twigs lay at his feet.

Tara almost dropped the herbs. "Are you mad? We have but a few hours of daylight left and you want to stay in the same spot Zarku left us last night?"

"Let me ask you something," said Ananth. He stopped sharpening the tip of the arrow and stared at her, a strange look in his eyes. "What would *you* do?"

Tara looked around at all of them. "What's going on? Is this some kind of joke to test my nerves?"

"Answer me," said Ananth. "What would you have us do this very minute?"

"I'd have you running hard toward the river," said Tara. "None of you would be sitting here asking silly questions."

"I rest my case," said Kabir. He threw a knowing look at Ananth, flopped down on his stomach and reached behind him.

"Don't touch your back, Kabir," said Tara. "You're going to make it worse. Wait for a moment and I'll put something on it to cool it down."

Raani had found a couple of flat stones and brought them back. Tara took the ritha seed and smashed it to a pulp with a rock. Then she added the tulsi leaves and started grinding the mixture. The sound of stone on stone grated on her nerves. She blocked it out and continued working.

"Would someone like to explain?" she asked, looking up from her task momentarily. "What was all that about; what would you do …"

"We're going to stay and fight," said Ananth. He whittled the end of another twig to a sharp point and added it to the growing pile at his feet.

"*Fight?*" said Tara. "You want five of us to fight Zarku, Kali, and his bloodthirsty hyenas. Has the heat fried your brains?"

"It was Kabir's idea," said Vayu. "And I think he's right."

"Kabir's delirious," said Tara. "I'm not. And I say we run. We're no match for them."

"I'm not delirious," said Kabir. "At least not yet."

Tara came over to Kabir, her hands full of the green paste. Raani helped remove his shirt, which now stank of blood, sweat, and the sickly sweet stench of something rotting. She threw it aside. Tara smeared the paste on Kabir's back as gently as she could. When she was finished, she sat back surveying her work. Her hands were bright green and so was Kabir's back.

"Ahhhh," said Kabir. "That does feel better, Tara, so cool … you're helping more than you realize."

"Thanks and you're welcome," said Tara. "But you

still haven't answered my question."

"We've decided to give that madman something to worry about," said Ananth. "It's what Zarku would *not* expect us to do."

"Look," said Tara. "None of you have faced him. I have. You haven't felt your skin burn when he looks upon you with his third eye." She closed her eyes as the memory sent a shiver through her. She stared at them again, wishing they would believe just how dangerous he could be. "If we're caught, not just *our* lives are at stake, but the lives of our friends and families are, too. We need Prabala for this and the sooner we reach the river, the sooner we get to Morni and come back with help. Don't you see?"

"Tara, you have a point," replied Ananth. "But running is what Zarku would *expect* us to do. He would expect us to be tired and panicked, to not be able to think straight or make any kind of decent plan. Sure, it might not work, but with Kabir in this state, how far do you think we'll get if we decide to run?

Tara had to admit, he made sense. Afternoon was slipping away and soon it would be dark.

"So, what's the plan?" she asked with a deep sigh. They were in this together and she'd have to help them whether she agreed with it or not.

"We dig a pit, fill it with stakes, and cover it up. Zarku is bound to come back this way for us and hopefully he'll fall in with Kali and the hyenas —"

"And we'll all escape, go back home and live happily ever after," finished Tara. "*How wonderful!* That's your plan?"

"For now, yes," said Ananth. He gathered the bow and arrows and put them all on a rock behind him, along with the knife he was using. "Here is where we're going to dig the pit, right, Kabir?"

"I don't like it," said Tara. "What if he avoids the pit all together? How large is it going to be?"

"As large as we can get it by nightfall," said Ananth. "We'll all have to pitch in and help."

"I still hate the idea, but we better get started," said Tara.

But before anyone could move, Raani screamed.

A hyena had stepped out of the bushes and was eyeing them hungrily.

twelve

The Pit and the Plan

Zarku's here early, thought Tara as fear dug its razor-sharp claws into her stomach. He had lied to them!

Horrified, they stared at the hyena, and then at each other. Any moment now Tara expected Zarku to appear. But if he was around, he stayed hidden.

The hyena advanced, baring its teeth. It sniffed the air, and honed in on Kabir. Tara slowly wiped her hands on her kurta, adding green streaks to the filth and grime that already covered it. "Stay still, Kabir," she said. "It seems to be coming straight at us."

"Where are the other hyenas?" whispered Vayu. He scanned the trees around him, making no sudden moves.

The hyena moved closer, its hungry eyes riveted to Kabir. They were but a few feet apart, staring at each other.

"What do we do?" whispered Raani. "Run?"

"No one move," said Ananth. "I don't think this one belongs to Zarku."

The moment he said it Tara noticed the markings on the hyena. This one was spotted, not striped like Zarku's companions. She breathed a sigh of relief that immediately changed to a dry rattle in her throat. The hyena giggled as it inched closer to Kabir, baring its teeth in a grotesque smile. Saliva dripped from its mouth.

Kabir sat up and the hyena growled deep within its throat. He froze.

"We can't sit here all day, staring at it," said Tara. "We have to do something."

"I need my bows, but I can't reach them," said Ananth. "Someone distract this brute."

And brute he was; larger than any hyena Tara had ever seen, with a mean look in his eye and obviously very hungry.

"Kabir's wounds have attracted it," said Tara. The discarded kurta, stinking of blood and pus, was still lying beside them. "We should have burned or buried it."

The animal trotted closer, splattering the ground with more drool. The late-afternoon sun glinted off a mouthful of sharp, white teeth. He gnashed them, his hungry eyes missing nothing.

Raani whimpered. The hyena snapped its head in her direction. That was all it took. She jumped to her feet and backed away.

"Raani, no!" said Ananth very softly. "Don't move."

But Raani wasn't listening; she didn't even seem to be aware of anyone around her.

The hyena tensed and inched closer to her, Kabir forgotten. Any moment now it would leap at her. Raani stared at it wild-eyed, white-faced, and took another step back. The hyena stalked her, the hair on its back bristling. She was definitely going to run ...

"Here," screamed Tara suddenly. The hyena swung its head toward her. She sprinted into the forest. "Get him, Ananth! Don't miss!"

With a growl, the hyena leaped after her. Out of the corner of her eye she saw Ananth jump for his bow and arrow. *Don't miss, don't miss*, she prayed as she zig-zagged toward the trees, the hyena galloping after her.

The hyena's teeth ripped the edge of her kurta, but Tara didn't stop. The snap of its jaws was unnaturally loud. She reached the edge of the clearing. The hyena was gaining on her; its teeth grazed her ankle. She shrieked and went crashing into the trees.

"Turn around and come back," yelled Ananth. He sounded close by. "Make a wide curve, I'm ready."

Tara swerved sharply and ran around a tree. She saw the root too late and tripped, screaming as she fell, face-down on the forest floor. "Kill it!"

The hyena landed on her back, knocking out all the air from her lungs. Its breath was loud in her ears and the smell made her retch. Her neck was wet with its saliva. Any moment now she expected to feel teeth sink into her. She screamed again and again and yet again, unable to stop.

There was a loud thunk, a strangled yelp, and the weight from her back was gone. Tara lay on the ground, her nose pressed to the damp earth, inhaling its fragrance, unable to believe she was still alive. She took a deep, shuddering gulp of air.

"Are you all right?" asked Raani, kneeling beside her. "I can't believe you did this for me."

Tara sat up with some effort and Raani pulled her to her feet. Tara leaned on her, unable to control the trembling of her limbs. Raani put a steadying hand around her waist. She was trembling, too.

The hyena lay on its back, its long, red tongue lolling out the side of its mouth. A green rock, the one she'd used to grind the herbs, lay by its head. An arrow pierced its neck, the bright-red tip sticking out the other side. The ground below it was starting to turn red and they moved past it hurriedly.

"Thank you. That was really brave of you," said Raani. She shook her head in wonder, her eyes moist. "You saved my life."

Tara managed a weak smile. All she wanted to do was throw up, but she took several deep breaths instead. It wouldn't do to vomit all over a person who had just called her incredibly brave. Then they were all around her, even Kabir, who had managed to get to his feet.

"Thanks, Ananth," said Tara. "That was a good shot."

Ananth nodded. "You'd better thank Raani, too. She flung a rock at the brute to slow him down. Four arrows broke before I could get him. This is the last one." He looked at the solitary arrow in his hand. "I wish I had my other ones. These are terrible."

"Thank you both," said Tara. She smiled at Raani, who returned it warmly, a hint of awe still lingering on her face.

"All right, Kabir?" asked Tara.

He nodded. "I think we're all okay."

"You see now why we have to get away from here as soon as possible?" said Tara. "*One* of those animals can be so dangerous. Can you imagine three?"

"I'm tired of running," said Kabir. "It's time we started making things a bit interesting for Zarku. Let the hunter become the hunted for a change. We can do this — together."

He extended his fist and winked. They piled their fists one on top of the other. Tara was the last to add hers. She looked around at her companions, faces lined with grime and exhaustion and determination. A faint glow of hope warmed her heart. Maybe Kabir was right; together they just might be able to defeat Zarku.

• • •

Grimacing, Kabir picked up a twig and traced out a rectangle on the ground.

"Raani, Tara, Vayu, dig out the earth in this spot as fast as you can. It needs to be at least three feet deep," he said. "Ananth, collect as many branches as you can, tall short, anything. We'll need to sharpen them to make stakes for the pit."

Dusk was upon them. An occasional flutter of wings, the grunting of a wild boar or yowling of a wildcat broke the silence. It seemed as if the forest was holding its breath, too; waiting to see how this game of hide-and-seek would play out tonight.

"How much of daylight do you think we have left?" asked Raani. She tied her dupatta securely around her waist and started digging.

"About an hour or so," said Kabir, squinting at the sky. Dark, grey clouds rimmed with gold floated past. "Looks like another thunderstorm tonight."

They dug as hard and as fast as they could. Kabir sat at the edge of the pit, sharpening branches that Ananth brought to him. Slivers of wood showered over them and the pile next to him grew. Occasionally he would close his eyes, take a deep, shuddering breath and continue. Sweat beaded his face, but he did not stop.

"I think we have enough, Ananth," said Kabir after a while. "You better help with the pit. I'll finish the rest of these."

Ananth jumped into the pit and started digging. The heat built up as the storm gathered strength. Mosquitoes swarmed around them once again, getting into their eyes and ears, even their mouths whenever they spoke to each other. As they dug deeper, the mud grew softer, heavier, and Tara felt it cake under her fingernails. Her muscles ached, threatening to seize up.

The sun sank lower and the forest grew darker. A hot wind swept through the trees.

"Hurry," said Kabir. "We still have a foot or so to go and then we have to arrange the stakes. If it's not deep enough, this trap won't work."

Tara doubled her speed and so did the others. Pebbles, rocks, and roots tore her nails. The wet, cloying smell of mud and mulch enveloped her. She dug, thinking of nothing else but moving her hands. Scoop, throw, scoop, throw. Slowly and steadily the pit grew deeper. Kabir moved the earth away from the sides to make room for more.

"We'll never finish in time," said Kabir. "Make room for me, too."

"No, Kabir," said Tara. "You stay up there. You're in no shape for this."

"If the hyenas catch us, the only shape I'll be in, is dead … don't know though … what shape is death?" replied Kabir. Tara had to smile. In spite of everything he could still joke.

Kabir jumped in. They stood shoulder to shoulder in the cramped space, throwing the mud out in a wild frenzy. The shadows deepened and it was getting difficult to see how much progress they had made.

"Should we light the lanterns?" asked Vayu. "Might help."

Ananth shook his head. "Best not to. If Zarku has started out, it will only pinpoint our location faster. Hurry and we'll get this done before it gets too dark to see."

There was a loud crack. "Arrrghhh," Kabir groaned. "My shoulder."

They all stopped and stared at him. His right arm was twisted at an unnatural angle near his shoulder.

"I've dislocated it," he gasped. He reached up with his left hand and tried to push it back in, but the effort was too much. He fell to his knees groaning. "Can't do it ... on my own. Someone do it."

"What do I do?" asked Ananth. "Tell me!"

"Shove it back into place," said Kabir. "This one's not like the usual ones or I would have done it myself."

"You should never have gotten in here," said Tara. She pressed herself against the wall of the pit, wiping her face, staring at the dislocated arm. "Why didn't you stay up there? We were doing fine without you."

"Just do it," said Kabir. He braced himself as Ananth took hold of his shoulder. "Wait," Kabir cried at the last moment.

"What?" said Ananth. His face was as white as Kabir's.

"Push it straight back in without twisting it to the right or left," said Kabir. "If it goes in wrong, I won't be able to move my arm at all."

Ananth dropped his hands to his sides. "I-I can't do this," he said. "What if I mess it up?"

"You can," said Kabir. "*Hurry*, the pain's killing me."

Ananth took a deep breath. Tara nodded, trying to look calm and encouraging at the same time, neither of which she remotely felt. Ananth took hold of Kabir's arm, bit his lip, and pushed hard. It settled into place with a crack. The sound of bone against bone echoed through the cramped hole and Tara shuddered. She looked over at Raani, who had stuffed her knuckles into her mouth.

Kabir uttered a strangled yelp and crumpled to the ground.

"Oh God, Ananth!" said Raani. "You've killed him."

Ananth got down on his knees and patted Kabir's face. "Talk to me, Kabir. Are you all right? Please say something."

Kabir's head flopped back and forth. *The pain killed him*, thought Tara, *we've lost him forever*. It seemed unreal. One moment he was alive and in pain and the next moment he was gone.

"I did exactly as he told me to," said Ananth. He raised an anguished face to them.

"And you did a great job, Ananth," said Kabir. He stirred, groaning softly.

Both Tara and Raani screamed and fell to their knees.

"You idiot, you gave us quite a scare," said Ananth. "What happened?'

"Sorry, the pain was a bit too much," said Kabir. "I'll try never to faint again. Promise."

An owl hooted loudly and flew off into the night, followed by the shrill chatter of birds.

"Here he comes," said Kabir. "We have to stop now and plant those stakes or we won't be ready in time."

He climbed out of the pit slowly, breathing hard. They all climbed out after him.

"Is this deep enough?" asked Tara. She stared at the pit they had just dug. "Do you think it will work?"

"Even if it doesn't, we have no time," said Kabir. "We'll just have to hope for the best."

Zarku advanced through the brush, making no attempt to keep silent, as if he knew he'd win, no matter what. He was probably expecting to find them hiding like scared rabbits. Except that he would get a shock. A fatal one if they were really lucky!

"Get in there, Ananth, and plant the stakes throughout the pit evenly, with the pointed ends facing upward," said Kabir. "Try not to leave too many gaps. I'll hand them to you."

"The rest of you, get as many large branches and leaves you can find to cover this up. If Zarku suspects that it's here, all our work will have been in vain. Run!"

Like a group possessed they worked in the near darkness, which intensified with each passing moment. Tara raced to the trees and hauled dead branches, twigs, and leaves toward the pit in which Kabir and

Ananth had planted the stakes as best as they could. Back again, another armload, drag, drop, and back again. Tara's lungs were on fire and her arms were ready to drop off. But she went back for another load and yet another.

Suddenly, it was night. As if God had blown out the sun.

"I guess that's it," said Kabir. His voice was soft, his breathing laboured. "We'd better hide." Not too far off they heard the steady rustle of footsteps approaching and giggling; a sound that had come to haunt Tara's every waking and sleeping moment.

"No time to get up a tree," said Ananth. "Quick, Raani, help us look for a place to hide."

Zarku's lamplight bobbing toward them from a distance dispelled some of the darkness as they all searched frantically. *Why hadn't they thought of choosing a place before we started digging?* thought Tara. They could have avoided this last-minute panic.

"Bushes or hollow log?" asked Raani. "I can't decide. They're both too obvious."

"Bushes, I think," said Vayu. "The hyenas will probably not want to get in there."

They raced to a large clump of bushes and threw themselves into it. Thorns scraped and tore at Tara's flesh, but she didn't slow down till she had crawled right into the middle along with the others. She squeezed her eyes shut and prayed. Let *him* die. If Zarku escaped the pit, she had no doubt that he'd discover their hiding place within seconds.

The light drew nearer and there he was, at the edge of the clearing. A few more steps and he would fall into their trap. He was singing tunelessly, cheerfully, certain of victory. Behind him the hyenas fanned out, sniffing at every bush and log. Tara's heart thumped. Would their trap work? Would he walk straight into it? Nothing would give her greater pleasure than to see him with a stake through his heart. She closed her eyes to savour the image.

The very next moment her eyes snapped open. A thought struck her hard, almost as if she had walked into a wall. If their trap worked, she would not see Zarku but *Suraj* with a stake through his heart. *Her brother.* Oh Lord what had she done? She had dug her brother's grave with her own hands.

"No, oh no," she whispered.

"Tara, what is it?" said Raani. "What's the matter?"

"I have to stop him," she said. "I can't let him die."

"Are you mad?" whispered Ananth. "That's *exactly* what we want. That's why we worked so hard all evening."

Zarku moved stealthily, his lantern held aloft. Shreds of light trickled into the bushes. He moved closer, Kali right behind him.

"I have to warn him," Tara repeated. "I can't let my brother die."

She struggled to get up. The next moment four pairs of hands clamped down on her. She opened her mouth and Ananth clapped his hand over it. Thorns scraped her scalp, her arms, as they wrestled silently.

She glared at Ananth, beseeching him with her eyes, but it only served to tighten his hold on her.

If their plan worked, Suraj would die. Tears leaked out of her eyes as she realized that it was the right thing to do. This was the only way. But how could she stand by and watch it happen? She struggled to sit up, but her friends held her down.

A horrible shriek pierced the air and all the fight went out of her.

Suraj had fallen into their trap. He was going to die and she was responsible.

thirteen

The Fist

"Oh no," whispered Ananth and loosened his hold on her. "*Oh no ...*"

Tara squeezed her eyes shut as the scream reached an agonizing peak. She clapped her hands over her ears, knowing she would remember this scream for as long as she lived. It turned into a gurgle and died away. There was complete silence.

Suraj was dead.

Tara sobbed softly, unable even to sit up. She could see the image clearly in her mind; Suraj skewered on a stake in the pit she had dug with her own hands. How would she ever forgive herself? She had no right to live after this.

"You've killed him!" someone shrieked. "You've killed my companion. I'll make you all suffer for this!"

Tara sat up immediately, happiness flooding her. She peered out of the bushes. Zarku was alive! This was bad news for them — really bad. If he found them, they were all in danger, but there was a part of her that was very relieved.

"It failed," said Kabir. His voice was flat. "We got the hyena instead of him. He has the luck of the devil."

Zarku stood at the edge of the pit flanked by two hyenas and Kali, his face contorted with rage. His eyes swept the bushes around him and then back to the pit.

"Can't you bring him back to life?" said Kali. She took a quick look into the pit, wrinkled her nose in disgust and looked away.

"Are you mad, woman?" snapped Zarku with such vehemence that she took a step back. "How many times do I have to explain to you that in this weak body I have limited powers? Wait till I get another, more powerful, body and then see what I do. I'll kill anyone who crosses me and prevent Death from coming to those who serve me well. You'll be wise to remember that."

"I only asked," said Kali. Her tone was servile, her head bowed. But even from a distance Tara could see the slight curve of her lips as she smiled to herself, no doubt dreaming of the power and glory she would enjoy in Zarku's reign.

"Come out from wherever you're hiding. Now!" said Zarku.

This was it. They had killed his companion and now it was their turn. In spite of the growing fear in the pit of her stomach, Tara got a small measure of comfort from huddling together with her companions. No one moved.

"I know you all are close by," said Zarku. "Come out now. If I have to come look for you, you're going to regret it. I'll count to ten and if you're not out by then …"

Tara looked at Ananth. He shook his head.

"One … two," intoned Zarku.

"I think we should show ourselves," whispered Raani. "If he works himself into a frenzy, there's no telling what he might do."

"Stay," said Ananth. "He said the same thing last time. He's just having fun scaring us."

"Three, four, five," said Zarku. "You're trying my *patience*!"

"Please," said Tara, "let's just go and get it over with. If he lets the hyenas loose, they'll find us anyway."

"He won't bother to squeeze in here, that's for sure," said Vayu. "But the hyenas might. We should go."

Zarku paced the edge of the pit, alternately looking at the hyena and then at the forest around him. His gaze slid past the clump of bushes where they hid and returned to it. Had he guessed where they were?

"Six, seven, eight," yelled Zarku. "Last chance. Give up now and I might show some mercy."

"Nine, te—"

Tara crawled out of the bushes before anyone could

grab her again. She faced Zarku, trying to ignore the blood oozing from the numerous scratches on her arms and legs. "Here I am."

"I'm not blind," said Zarku. "Where are the others? I told you, if you split up —"

"You want me," said Tara. "You've got me. Why do you need the others?"

"Rule number one," said Zarku, "you do not split up. If you do, I win the game." He came closer and stood in front of Tara. She got a good look at her brother's face. Already it seemed different; hard and mean.

"We've not split up." Ananth's voice boomed in Tara's ear. He came to stand beside her followed closely by the others.

"Ahhhh, there you all are," said Zarku. "I thought you'd be far away from here, but I see that you've decided to be very smart. Not bad for *children*."

"You wanted a game, you got it," said Kabir. He spoke softly, slowly, and Tara glanced at him, trying to gauge just how high the fever was. His cheekbones jutted out at sharp angles and his cheeks looked hollow. He seemed to have lost weight in the last twenty-four hours.

"Looks like *you* won't last very long," said Zarku, looking Kabir up and down. "Good, one less for me to worry about."

Tara wanted to fly at him. But she did nothing; she'd only be hurting Suraj.

"You killed my companion and for that you must pay!" said Zarku. "But first come and see the damage you've done."

No one moved. Tara had no desire to see the skewered hyena.

"I said, come and see," roared Zarku. He grabbed Tara's hand and dragged her to the edge of the pit. Tara dug her heels into the ground, but she was no match for an enraged Zarku.

Tara peered over the edge. The sight made her so sick and dizzy, she almost fell in herself. The largest of the hyenas was impaled on two stakes, a grotesque grin plastered on his face. The tips of the stakes glistened in the lamplight, wet and red.

"I only wish it had been you instead of the hyenas," said Ananth. "You were the one who should have died."

"Is that so?" said Zarku, a terrible smile twisting his features. "ATTACK!"

Before they realized what had happened, the hyenas were racing toward them.

"Run!" yelled Ananth.

They turned and fled. Tara felt a sense of déjà vu. The hot breath and the snapping of the teeth spurred her on as she ran blindly into the forest, Zarku's maniacal cackle filling the air. She tripped and fell. She heard Raani scream. There were growls, whoops, yells. Then silence.

"Bring them back here!" said Zarku.

Tara pushed herself off the ground and came face to face with a hyena. It herded her back toward Zarku and then trotted off. Within moments they were back where they had started — with a difference. Raani sat on the ground sobbing, holding her right leg. Her ghagra was soaked with blood. Her hands were bright red and a streak of blood was smeared across her forehead.

Tara ran to Raani and examined her leg. Her calf was a bloody mess of bites and torn, pulpy flesh. She turned to Zarku. "How could you?" she said in a choked voice. "Are you completely mad?"

"You hurt my friend and I hurt yours," he replied. "At least she's not dead."

Raani's face crumpled and she sobbed into Tara's shoulder. "It hurts so much, I can't bear it."

"Shh, it's all right, Raani," said Tara. "I'll put some salve on it and you'll be fine." She hugged Raani, feeling her tremble violently.

"So now what?" asked Ananth.

"Look at all of you," said Zarku. He circled the group slowly, deliberately. "Pathetic lot. Not even worthy of a simple game of hide-and-seek! I wish I'd had a better group to play with. But, what choice did I have? None!"

"Let's push them into the pit," said Kali. "Do away with them once and for all."

Tara never thought she could hate anyone more than Zarku, but at that moment, Kali topped the list. If only

Tara could push *her* into the pit, she would be willing to endure whatever Zarku had in mind for her.

"Shut up," said Zarku. "I've told you before, intelligence is not your strength. And when you lack something so basic, it's best not to let too many people know."

Kali's face tightened and from past experience Tara knew that this would be the moment she would fly into a rage. Instead, Kali struggled to smile and even apologized to Zarku.

They waited. Tara tried to think of all the ways he would kill them, sure that they would be very painful. She would be the last to go and would have to endure the agony of seeing her friends die. Zarku stared at the dead hyena in silence. They stared at each other. Even time seemed to stand still.

"I'm too upset to think straight," said Zarku. He looked as if he was about to cry. "I think I'll spare you all for one more night and kill you tomorrow, except Tara, of course. I have a special plan for her. You might as well stick around here. You don't stand a chance against me."

Kali's face fell. Zarku walked away, the hyenas trotting behind him like obedient dogs.

His footsteps receded and the night was silent again. They hugged each other.

"He let us go," said Ananth. A tired smile limped to his face and faded away. "We've survived for one more night."

"Yes, but the plan failed," said Kabir. "After all that work, we *failed*." He slumped beside Raani. "Tomorrow is our last chance. What are we going to do now? I'm so tired."

"We can't give up now," said Ananth. "Not after we've survived this long. We have to kill him tomorrow or escape."

Tara glanced into the pit again. The lantern gone, she could only make out the shape of the hyena in the moonlight, and the shining tip of the stake. The steady *drip, drip* from within made her sick.

"I can't do this, either," said Tara. "I can't kill my own brother." She stumbled away from the hideous stench of the dead hyena and the smell of blood that hung over them like a black cloud. She closed her eyes, trying to sort through her confused feelings. Zarku had escaped yet again and tomorrow they'd have to make another plan to hide from him or kill him. How many times did she have to go through this? She almost wished he had killed her today; at least she'd be out of her misery.

Unbidden, Lord Yama's advice came to mind: *Sometimes the right way is the most difficult, and the wrong way, the easiest, most tempting. Make your choice wisely.*

Someone hugged her. Tara started. Raani had limped up to her, a trail of blood marking her path. "I know what you're going through and I'm sorry," she said. "God knows, I wouldn't wish this decision on my worst enemy."

Her words made Tara want to bawl. She gave Raani a small smile. Ananth, Kabir, and Vayu came up to her.

"Tara, Suraj is my brother, too," said Ananth. "Don't you think this is just as hard for me? Don't you think I realize that to kill Zarku means to lose Suraj forever? But we have no choice."

"We're doing the right thing, Tara," said Vayu. "We have to."

Tara nodded. "I know. I *know*. It's just that if Zarku had assumed any other form, I could have seen through to the evil inside but by using Suraj … he's been very smart. He knew how hard this would be for us, for anyone." She wiped away the tears. "I'm trying, I really am. I didn't realize *how* hard it was going to be until he was at the edge of the pit. I don't know if I can go through it again."

"If you really want to *see* someone," said Vayu softly, "close your eyes."

Tara stared at him. "What?"

"Close your eyes and think of Zarku," said Vayu. "Go on, try it."

Tara closed her eyes. Instantly an image sprang to mind; Zarku burning two Vetalas with his third eye. She still remembered their agonized shrieks as they had melted and her pulse raced. Her eyes snapped open again. If Zarku had stood in front of her at this moment, she would have killed him no matter what he looked like.

"I see what you mean," said Tara. "But what about my brother? How can I watch him die? He's innocent."

"Even if we win," said Ananth, "I don't think Zarku is going to keep his word about Suraj. He won't be willing to vacate your brother's body till he gets another one. You heard him tell Kali that."

Tara stared at him with blurred vision. Deep down in her heart she knew it was true and only now was she finally able to admit it.

"Zarku is never going to give Suraj back to me," she said, looking around at all of them. "I've lost him already."

They closed in on Tara and hugged her. She was numb. She thought of all the good times she had shared with Suraj, the games they'd played and the tears they had shed when Kali had made their lives miserable. He was a part of her and now she had to be strong enough to cut it off and destroy it.

"I think we could all do with some sleep," said Ananth. "I don't think Zarku is coming back tonight, now that he has decided to keep us alive for one more day of enjoyment."

In an unspoken agreement they all moved away from their failed trap, deeper into the forest. The moon was even thinner tonight. In another day or so, there would be no moon and no light. Hopefully they would have escaped by then.

Ananth led the way, with Raani limping behind him, her leg temporarily bound with her dupatta. Kabir followed Raani, shivering and coughing every few steps.

She and Vayu brought up the rear. They walked till they reached a clearing.

Once more Tara settled herself on the hard earth, twigs and pebbles digging into her skin. Tomorrow was the last day of their game. She pulled out the anklet and pressed the beaten silver to her cheek. It was cold. *Will you help me when the time comes?* she asked, pressing the anklet harder against her cheek. *Will you?*

A soft voice answered just as she fell into a deep and exhausted sleep.

Yes.

• • •

A soft groan woke her the next morning. A white-faced Raani was curled up into a tight ball. Tara immediately went to her.

"Don't," screamed Raani the moment Tara touched her leg.

The scream woke everyone. Ananth jumped to his feet, his bow and arrow in hand. Kabir sat up weakly, brandishing his knife. Vayu lumbered to his feet, blinking in the bright sunlight.

"My leg," gasped Raani. "I'm dying!"

"Let me take a look, Raani," said Tara. "See how bad it is. Try to bear it, okay?"

The look did nothing to assuage her fears. Raani's calf was swollen and puffy. Some areas had a purplish tinge. The infection was spreading really quickly and if she did not get to a village soon, she might even lose her leg. There was no way Raani would be able to *walk* with this wound, let alone run. Their chances of escaping were less than zero and Zarku knew it.

"How bad is it?" asked Raani. Her eyes searched Tara's face.

"The wounds are infected," said Tara, trying to keep her voice light and her expression calm. "Pain is the only thing you'll have to worry about. But you won't be dying today."

Raani did not smile.

"Can you do anything right now?" said Ananth. He crouched next to Tara.

"I can put a salve on it, the same one I used for Kabir," said Tara. "I still have some of the herbs left."

"Then hurry. We can move out immediately," said Ananth. "I'll take a look around in the meantime."

Tara found some flat rocks and quickly ground up the remaining ritha and tulsi leaves she had saved. Vayu rubbed his eyes and ran a hand through his dishevelled hair. He looked exhausted. They all did. They hadn't eaten for two days and were at the end of their strength. She had been so confident that they'd be able to save the children. Now Suraj was almost lost to them and two of their group were badly injured. What chance did they have of saving *themselves* let alone Suraj, or Sadia, who was still captive? And if they failed, Zarku would be back to haunt the villagers.

Ananth burst into the clearing. "We have a chance of escaping — a very good chance!"

"Really?" asked Kabir.

Ananth nodded. "I was exploring the area and found a machan. I climbed up to take a look and I saw the river! *The river*!" He almost yelled out the last two words. "It's not too far, maybe a few hours' walk, depending on our speed. But we'll definitely make it there by nightfall. We have to!"

"That means ... that means —" said Raani. A tear slipped down her cheek and she dashed it away.

"That means, we make it to the river, we find a boat and escape. Prabala will know how to defeat Zarku and save Suraj," said Ananth. "And we don't have to worry about hiding again tonight. In fact, if we're lucky, we won't have to face Zarku again on our own."

Tara stared at him. They actually had a chance! They did! Vayu rushed to Ananth, picked him up and did a small dance. Raani managed a watery smile and Kabir gave a thumbs-up sign.

"Ready to move, Tara?" said Ananth. "I don't want to lose a minute."

"Almost done," said Tara. She smeared a handful of paste on Raani's calf, feeling the torn bits of flesh shift and slide under her fingertips. Raani bit down on her knuckles, uttering tiny moans. When the paste covered every bit of the wound, Tara bound it up with her dupatta.

"Your turn, Kabir," said Tara.

Kabir took off his shirt and sat with his back to Tara. Her spirits sank as she smeared the remaining paste on his back. It was a field of bloody craters, crusty in some areas and soft in others, oozing pus. It was hot, too; for the third day in a row he had a fever. Would he last until they reached the river?

She blinked back tears and tasted salt. All this because Zarku wanted revenge on her.

"Time to move out," said Ananth. He slung the bow over his shoulder and picked up the last arrow.

Kabir pushed himself to his feet and Ananth ran to help him. "Can you manage?"

"I have to," said Kabir. "Sadia is counting on me. I'm her favourite brother and I cannot fail her."

"Best leave that shirt off," said Tara. "It's badly soiled and will only irritate your skin more."

Kabir nodded and tossed it aside.

"Come on, Raani," said Ananth. "If Kabir can do it, so can you."

Raani got to her feet. She screamed the moment her foot touched the ground and fell right over.

"I can't," she said. She lay face down on the ground, her hands clenched into fists. "You'll have to leave me and go."

"Come on, Raani," said Tara. "You can do this. Lean on me and hop if you have to. We're not staying here and we're not leaving you behind."

"I can't," said Raani. She raised a teary, mud-streaked face to them. "It hurts so much, I'd rather stay here than put any weight on it. I'm sorry. I can't bear pain very well. In fact — not at all. Before this, I barely ever got a scratch and even then I was in agony."

With her leg bound up in the bright green dupatta that was limp and soaked in blood, her ragged clothes, and her dishevelled hair she looked so different from the Raani who had first stepped into the forest. Yet Tara liked her a lot more this way.

The sun shone warmly and colourful parakeets flew overhead. It was a miracle that they were still alive, thought Tara. And one they could not waste.

"We're going to make it," said Tara. "We're not giving up. Not when we're so close. Ananth, why don't we make a stretcher to carry her?"

"Bad idea," said Ananth. "It will slow us down tremendously. Of all the days, today we need speed. And forget trying to hide or move through the thick parts of the forest with it. She'll have to walk."

"I've given you an option,'" said Raani. "Really, I don't mind. For the first time I've seen what that madman can do, Tara. After all those warnings of yours, I understand what you mean, now. You have to reach Morni, get Prabala and stop him. At any cost. Just leave me — go!"

They looked at each other in silence. How were they going to deal with this? No one wanted to stay there a minute longer and yet how could they leave Raani behind? There seemed to be no way out.

"I'll carry her," said Vayu.

All eyes turned to him.

"I'm the strongest of us all," he said. "And we'll be able to move faster than if she were to walk."

Raani's lips were trembling. She opened her mouth. For once nothing came out.

"Are you sure, Vayu?" asked Ananth. "It'll be tough going and today we're really going to have to pick up the pace."

"I'll manage," said Vayu. "Let's get ready to move."

"I-I-thank you, Vayu," said Raani. "And ... I'm sorry."

Vayu shrugged. "Forget it." He lumbered over to Raani and lifted her as easily as he would a child. One hand supported her shoulders and the other was under her knees. Raani groaned just a tiny bit, but slid her arms around Vayu's neck. She was still unable to look him fully in the eye.

Kabir leaned on Ananth who took the lead, and this time Tara took up the rear as they raced toward the river.

Tara looked down at her grimy hands. Involuntarily her hand curled into a fist. Together, they would do this. Surely against the five of them, Zarku was no match.

fourteen

Race to the River

The fierce afternoon heat scorched Tara's skin. Sweat poured from her like water from a broken tap. She drew in a lungful of hot air, feeling her insides melt. All she could think of was water; drinking it, pouring it over her burning scalp, splashing it on her face, and falling into it. She licked her chapped lips and looked up at the sun through the thinning trees. It blinded her and she stumbled, bumping against Vayu.

"Watch it," he said. His was voice barely above a whisper. Raani winced.

"Sorry," Tara managed to croak. "How much farther?" she asked. It seemed like they had been walking forever. With each step the unease within her grew, as if they were running away from danger and yet heading right into it.

"Judging from how far we are from the hills, I'd say, about three, maybe four hours more," said Ananth.

"Then we can all relax and float downstream.

Tara closed her eyes wearily. Three or four hours more; would she last that long? Kabir stumbled along in a haze of fever, helped by Ananth, and Vayu was carrying Raani, panting like a steam engine. Neither had uttered a single word of protest. Tara felt a pang of guilt and shame; she had so little to complain about.

"Do you think we'll find a boat there?" asked Raani, suddenly.

"Depends on which part of the river we come to," said Ananth. "If it's at one of the docking areas we'll be really lucky, and if not, we'll swim as far along the shore as we can until we find one. With the river navigable this year, there will be a lot more boats along the riverbank and the best part is, Zarku can't track us easily if we're in the water."

The thought of jumping into the cool water made Tara walk faster. Once again she bumped into Vayu, who had stopped.

"*Swim?*" he said. "I can't swim. I'll walk along the shore."

They all stopped. The moment Ananth let go of Kabir he sank to the ground with a deep shudder. He coughed once or twice and then was silent. His eyes had sunk deep into their sockets and yet glittered brightly.

"You can't be serious, Vayu," said Ananth. "It's really easy. We'll all help."

Vayu put Raani down gently and sat beside her, breathing hard, his face red and streaming. He shook his head. "I almost drowned in the village pond when I was a child. Since then, water has always scared me. But don't worry, I won't slow you down."

"Stop being stupid," snapped Ananth. "That will defeat the whole purpose of trying to get away from Zarku. If you remain on land, he'll track you and us. You'll have to get into the water."

"NO!" said Vayu. "I won't and no one can force me."

Ananth glared at him and Vayu stared back, his face expressionless. But it was clear that no one could force Vayu to do anything that he didn't want to.

Raani touched Vayu's arm gently. "I'm a good swimmer," she said. "I'll help you. You have nothing to worry about."

"Let's get to the river first," said Tara. "It may not even come to that." She got to her feet wearily though every muscle in her body protested. *And if we have to swim,* thought Tara, *then by God, I'll push Vayu in myself.*

Ananth nodded and hoisted Kabir to his feet. Vayu lifted Raani up again. This time there wasn't even a whimper from her. There had been a time when standing close to Vayu had made Raani wrinkle her nose and spew the most vitriolic words. But Raani was changed now, by circumstance and by things they had

175

endured together. Enduring. That was it. They must endure, together. Somehow.

"If we keep up this pace, we'll be at the river by evening." said Ananth. "Let's not stop at all. We're doing great — keep going."

Easier said than done. Tara focused on putting one foot in front of the other, trying to ignore her splitting head, the deep thirst that sapped her strength, and her screaming muscles.

River, get to the river and then find a boat, she thought. Then Morni. Prabala would be there. He would take care of everything after that. But would it really be that simple?

"I'm slipping, Vayu," said Raani. "Maybe you should take a break."

"We can't afford to," panted Kabir. "If we stop now, I might not be able to get up again. So … tired."

"Can you manage, Vayu?" asked Tara.

"I do need a break," said Vayu.

Tara ran up ahead to Ananth. "We have to stop."

They both looked at Kabir. "All right," Kabir whispered. "Let's stop."

Ananth sat him down. "I'm going to take a quick look to see how far we are," he said. He shinnied up the nearest tree and was soon lost within it, the shaking branches marking his progress to the top.

Tara leaned against a tree trunk, sucking in huge lungfuls of blistering air, gazing around her in an exhausted stupor. If Zarku had stood in front of her right now, she wouldn't have been able to move a muscle.

Vayu gently lowered Raani to the ground. His kurta was soaked, as if he had had a bath with all his clothes on. His face was so red it looked like the setting sun.

The branches shook again and Ananth dropped out of the tree. "Not far now. I saw a glint of water. But this has to be our last break. Agreed?"

"What if we tried hiding instead?" asked Tara. "Take our time and find a really good spot. I saw a cave or two as we were walking. We'll have a much better chance than trying to run with one of us injured and the other ill."

"If we're on land, he'll find us," said Ananth. "Do you seriously think he'll let us win? And even if we do, he won't spare us. You know that, Tara. He hates you for defeating him and he will have his revenge. Against you and against all of us."

The words stung like a volley of slaps. Her head reeled. Ananth was right. They were all in danger because of her.

"Can Suraj swim?" asked Raani.

Tara was lost in thought. How they must all hate her right now for leading them into this mess, when she could have, *should* have faced it alone.

"Tara!" said Ananth. "This isn't the time to daydream. Can Suraj swim?"

Tara remembered her brother's weak attempts at swimming back at the village pond. He had never liked the water. She shook her head.

"Good," said Ananth. "Then that's our only hope. Zarku will not follow until he can find another boat. No more breaks till we reach the river. Come on!"

They nodded solemnly. Kabir stood up without any help and leaned on Ananth, his eyes clear and full of purpose. Vayu scooped up Raani, squared his shoulders and started marching. Tara followed them, her insides churning with guilt and anger.

The last leg of the race. They had to win!

— fifteen —

Kabir

Tall trees, prickly bushes, and knots of tree roots slowly passed by Tara's weary gaze as she plodded along. Clouds of mosquitoes enveloped her, but she ignored them. They swarmed around her, mercilessly biting every inch of exposed skin, but she had no strength to shoo them away. It was that or walk. She walked. They all did, silently.

Evening was upon them and the sun had sunk below the treetops, sparkling through the leaves each time they stirred in a rare breeze.

"Nearly there," said Ananth. "Look." His voice was jubilant as he pointed to the ground. The soil was moist and their feet sank in a little deeper as they walked. Tara smelled wet earth and she sniffed deeply, letting the fragrance fill her up.

"We'll make it," panted Vayu. "We will."

"Can we move just a little bit faster?" said Ananth. "Almost there, come on." He dragged Kabir with him.

"Slow, Ananth ... I can't ..." said Kabir. His voice was very faint.

Vayu also tried to keep up, but couldn't. The distance between him and Ananth widened.

"Slow down, Ananth," said Tara. "We're too tired."

Ananth looked back and opened his mouth when Kabir groaned, fell to the ground and lay absolutely still. Startled, Vayu dropped Raani to the ground. She landed on her backside with a thump, crying out in pain.

"Kabir!" said Ananth, kneeling beside him. "Kabir, what's the matter." He put his head to Kabir's chest. "Still breathing. He's just unconscious."

Tara rushed over to the still body and even before she reached out to touch his forehead she felt the heat emanating from him. The high fever and that last dash had taken its toll.

"I told you to slow down," she hissed at Ananth. "Now look at what you've done."

"What *I've* done?" said Ananth. His eyes darted between her and Kabir. "I supported him all the way here. All I want is to get us to safety and this is the thanks I get? What have *you* done except bring the wrath of Zarku down on all of us? Because of you we're all suffering, so don't blame me!"

Tara felt the blood drain from her face. Ananth apologized immediately. "I'm sorry, Tara, I didn't mean that," he said. "It just slipped out."

"The truth normally does," said Tara. Her heart ached; what he had said was true. What a fool she had been to think they could do this as a team. But thanks to Ananth things were clear for the first time since they had entered the forest. Things she had been too blind to see.

"Can you revive him?" said Ananth. "We're so close. We have to get to the river." He shook Kabir gently, but to no avail.

"Not without the right herbs," said Tara. "Even if I did have some, how would I boil them? We have no water, no vessel, nothing. Unfortunately these ones cannot be ground to a paste." At the mention of water her parched throat throbbed.

Raani crawled over to Kabir and slapped his face a couple of times. "Wake up, Kabir. You can't do this to us. Wake up!"

Kabir lay still. Raani buried her face in her hands and sobbed softly.

Ananth stood up and walked a short distance, beckoning to Tara and Vayu. They followed.

"It's obvious he can't continue," said Ananth. "We can't leave him here. He'll die before we can get help. Think. Think of something."

Tara bit her lip hard. She was so tired and very close to bawling. But she couldn't afford that luxury at the moment. She looked at Kabir. His breathing was shallow and his face resembled Rohan's when they had found him in the forest — dead. Raani was also in much pain and trying hard not to show it. It wouldn't be long before the infection worsened and she too succumbed like Kabir.

"How far do you think we still have to go?" asked Tara.

"Under an hour at the most," said Ananth. "If we keep up the pace we were at when we stopped."

"And if we don't make it in the next hour," said Tara, "we all die."

For the first time since they had started this journey Tara felt a deep panic take hold of her. So deep that for a moment her mind was a complete blank. She had to make an effort to hold herself still and not let Ananth or Vayu see how rattled she was. She walked away on shaky legs, the forest tilting and dipping around her. She stopped a short distance away, willing the horizon to stay still.

Help me Lord Ganesh, she prayed silently. *You can't do this to us; you can't let my friends die. You can't let evil win.*

And no one will die — if you make the right decision. You know what it is you have to do.

Tara started. There was that voice again. Tara glanced at Raani who sat close to Kabir, her head resting on her knees. She'd thought it had been Raani that first time, but in her heart she'd known it couldn't have been her. So then who was cruel enough to play games with her at a time like this?

"Show yourself!" said Tara. She turned a full circle. "Stop hiding and show yourself to me, you coward."

"We're right here, Tara," said Ananth. He stared at her anxiously. "No one is hiding."

Tara shook her head. "Did you just hear something? A woman's voice?"

The look that Ananth exchanged with Vayu said it all.

"Tara, you're the only *woman* who's spoken in the last few minutes," said Ananth. "Er ... why don't you sit in the shade for a while? You look exhausted."

"I don't want to sit in the shade and I'm not mad!" Tara's voice rose in a scream, as out of control as the events of the day. "Stop looking at me like that. I heard someone talking to me, a woman. I did, I swear it. She's still here and I'm going to find her."

Her voice startled a couple of parrots who flew off in a blur of orange and red.

Kabir opened his eyes. "Sadia?" he croaked.

The Fist Unfurls

Kabir struggled to sit up with Raani hugging him and pulling him upright simultaneously.

Tara ran to him. "How do you feel?"

"What happened?" he asked, shivering. "I heard someone yelling."

"That was me," mumbled Tara. "It's not important."

"You fainted," said Ananth. "But thank God you're okay. Here, take my kurta. You're cold."

Ananth stripped off his kurta and slipped it over Kabir. "Can you walk? We're almost there."

"I have to," said Kabir. "I heard you say we were close before I blacked out. Sorry."

"It's all right," said Ananth. "Let's go. It'll be dark before we know it and we have to be on the water by then."

Tara gazed at the evening sky. A few stars twinkled within the deep blue expanse that was shot through with streaks of orange. The moon was a broken bangle in the sky.

"I'm going to try and hop," said Raani. "You've carried me long enough, Vayu."

"I'll manage," said Vayu. "It's only a short distance anyway."

Raani shook her head. "Just hold my arm and stay beside me."

Kabir got to his feet and swayed for a moment before Ananth and Tara steadied him.

"Listen," said Ananth.

They all did and it was the sweetest sound Tara had heard in a long time. It was the croaking of frogs.

• • •

The song of the frogs beckoned to them. It tapped the last little pocket of energy Tara never knew she had, and it seemed to have the same effect on the others. They hurried along, the wetness of the air reviving them, urging them on. The trees thinned and in a very short while they saw it— a thick ribbon of blue on the horizon. The sun was already setting and a layer of shimmering gold rippled on the surface of the water. Tara's spirits soared and she turned a beaming face to Kabir and Ananth.

"He'll never catch us now," she said. "We're there."

"Never," echoed Raani, her voice catching in her throat. "Morni, here we come."

And then they heard it. A giggle. A laugh.

"Didi, I'm here!"

Tara whirled around. In the deepening shadows she thought she saw Suraj standing under a tree. The very next moment the wind swept the shadows away. Tara had no idea how close they were. There was a whoop to their left. A laugh near their right. The hyenas were spreading out.

"Run," yelled Tara. "RUN!"

And they did.

The ground sloped down to a sandy beach that hugged the river and was a lot easier and faster to cover. Ananth and Tara grabbed Kabir's arms. They half-carried, half-dragged him to the water's edge. Vayu picked up Raani again and raced alongside. They reached the water together and stopped for breath. Bits of wood and debris zipped past in the swiftly moving current.

There was no boat in sight. Tara almost sobbed as she scanned the water's edge from left to right. "There's no boat," she said. "We're trapped!"

"There has to be one," said Ananth. "I'm going to swim upriver to take a look. Don't let Zarku or the hyenas capture you. Throw rocks, throw sticks, mud … anything. Just hold them off as best as you can."

He jumped into the river. The current almost swept him away. His head disappeared underwater and Raani screamed. Vayu clenched his fists, staring at the spot where Ananth had disappeared.

Come on, Ananth, swim, swim, Tara prayed. Ananth's head bobbed up a few feet away from the spot where he'd disappeared. He was swimming against the current with strong strokes.

"Behind you," yelled Ananth as he swam past and Tara spun round.

There at the edge of the trees stood Zarku, flanked by two hyenas.

"Vayu, we might all have to jump in and take our chances," whispered Tara. "Are you with us?"

"No," said Vayu. "Don't ask me to do this, Tara. I'll take the hyenas over drowning."

"Hello, Tara!" Zarku called out. "We meet once again. And this time there is no escape. None at all."

"Don't come any closer, Zarku!" said Tara. She picked up a large stone. "I swear I'll use this."

Vayu and Kabir both followed suit. Raani crawled around, gathering more rocks and piled them at their feet.

"Didi," said Zarku, using Suraj's voice. "You'd throw a stone at me? You'd hurt your little brother?"

He took a step closer. The hyenas moved away from him to the left and right. Tara hurled the stone with all the strength in her. It hit Zarku on the head. He sank to his knees sobbing. Vayu and Kabir pelted him and the hyenas with stones.

Zarku cowered on the bank. "Please, Didi, stop, make them stop. Don't hurt me."

It was all Tara could do to stop from running to him and gathering him up in her arms. Blood trickled down his face and he wiped it away with his small hands, whimpering.

"Maybe we should stop," said Tara. "We've hurt him enough."

"Close your eyes, Tara," said Vayu. "You'll see what he really is."

But there was no need for it. Vayu took aim and lobbed another stone at Zarku. It connected with his shin and he roared in pain, dropping all pretences. "I warned you, but you wouldn't listen." He turned to the hyenas. "Kill them all except for Tara."

At his command, the hyenas galloped toward them, whooping with joy. Zarku followed at a leisurely pace, a huge grin plastered on his face in spite of the cuts and bruises. The gap between them closed as Tara continued to throw stones at the snarling hyenas. Some hit the mark, eliciting a yelp while others went wide. She could see their teeth now, and flopping red tongues. They came closer. Still closer.

"I found it … I FOUND IT."

She whipped around. There was Ananth in a small boat, straining with the oars to slow it down. Her heart floated within her chest. Soon they'd be far away, out of reach of this evil monster.

"Vayu, I'll throw the rope to you," said Ananth. "You'll have to hang on tight, the current is really strong."

Vayu went as close to the water as he dared. Tara turned her attention back to the hyenas. One of them was but a few feet away, only a dark shape in the fading light. Its eyes were fixed on her like lamplights. It moved toward her slowly, deliberately.

The nearest stone was a few feet away. Tara picked up a handful of mud and threw it at the hyena. It yelped and fell back, pawing at its face. She glanced over her shoulder. Vayu had caught the rope and was holding the boat close to shore. The current was strong. He grunted and dug his heels into the soft mud on the river bank.

Ananth jumped out. "Kabir, you come first and bring my bow and arrow with you."

She heard a growl to her right and Tara turned back. Another hyena was advancing. She grabbed a handful of mud and pulled her hand back, taking aim. It retreated.

"Raani, get me some more stones," said Tara not taking her eyes off both hyenas that were closing in on them. "Hurry."

Raani got to her feet and promptly fell over. Without a whimper she crawled farther away, gathering stones and rolling them toward Tara.

"Give up, Tara. It's no use," said Zarku. "You can't escape." He stood on the slope surveying them, his arms crossed over his chest.

"Tara, Kabir's in the boat. Get Raani and run," yelled Ananth. "Vayu won't be able to hold the boat much longer."

Tara turned to answer when she heard a terrified scream. She turned back. A hyena had leaped onto Raani's chest and had pinned her to the ground. Mouth wide open, it lunged at her throat. Tara raced to Raani and kicked the hyena, feeling her toe buzz with pain as it connected with its head. The animal flew off Raani with a squeal. Tara pulled Raani to her feet and dragged her toward the boat, ignoring her cries of pain. Ananth was already in it. He stood tall with his bow and his last arrow at the ready.

Zarku and the hyenas raced up to the water's edge. Kabir reached out for Raani and pulled her over the side and into the boat. Now only Tara and Vayu were on shore. A hyena leaped for Vayu and dug its teeth into his heel. Vayu howled. He kicked out, trying to hold the boat, which was dragging him deeper into the water. The brute held on tight and Vayu roared with pain. Blood poured from his foot, staining the water red. It frothed and churned as Vayu tried to shake the beast off, but his efforts grew weaker with each passing moment. The current tugged at the boat and Vayu tugged back, digging his feet deeper into the sand. He was losing the battle.

"Move out of the way, Tara," yelled Ananth. "I'll take care of Zarku once and for all."

Ananth aimed his arrow straight at Zarku. At her brother who stood watching the spectacle calmly. Tara saw his face, the smiling black eyes, and the familiar mop of curly hair. She looked back at Ananth, saw his arm tense as he drew back the arrow. Tara ran into the water and knocked him off balance. The arrow flew off the mark and landed a few feet away at the water's edge.

"What the hell did you do that for?" snarled Ananth, sitting up. "It was my only chance and now we've lost it. Are you completely mad?"

"Shut up," yelled Tara. "For once, just shut up and let me do what I have to."

Tara walked back to shore. "Call off the hyena," she told Zarku in a voice that was hers yet curiously detached. "Now."

Zarku stared at her steadily for a moment. She met his gaze calmly. He snapped his fingers and the hyena let go of Vayu's foot and trotted back to him. The water around Vayu's feet was a deep red. She saw him struggle to hold the boat, tears shining in his eyes. Zarku and his hyenas had injured one more of her friends and he wouldn't stop. Not until he got what he wanted. She saw that so very clearly now.

Tara walked up to Vayu. "Get into the boat," she said. "I'll follow. The hyenas won't harm me. You heard Zarku."

"Are you sure —" Vayu started to say.

"Go!" she almost screamed. "*Please go.*"

She snatched the rope from his hands. The current tugged at the rope viciously, almost wrenching her arms out of their sockets. The rope slid, burning her palms. She looped it around her clenched fists, gasping as it bit into her flesh. She dug her heels into the sand, her arms aching with the strain, and held on.

She watched Vayu limp to the boat. The vessel was getting heavier by the minute, almost impossible to hold. The rope slid some more and her palms were on fire, her knuckles raw where the rope chafed against it. She gritted her teeth and leaned back until Vayu was safely inside. From the boat, four anxious faces looked at her.

"Let go of the rope, Tara, and swim to us," yelled Ananth. "I'll use the oars to slow us down."

Tara gazed at her friends. She had put them through so much. Kabir, his eyes bright with fever, was but a shell of the lithe performer she had seen at the fair just a few days ago. Raani's white face shone through the gloom, a grimace plastered on it. Ananth was gaunt and haggard. And Vayu, who would not be able to walk until his foot healed. They had all endured so much!

But now they had a chance of surviving. She let go off the rope. Immediately the boat shot into the current, moving rapidly away from the shore. She stood still watching it.

"Tara, swim!" said Raani. "You've got to come with us. We're not leaving you behind."

The boat floated to the middle of the stream and was caught up in the main current. It moved faster.

She saw Ananth stand up, readying himself to jump overboard.

"No, Ananth," she called out. "Stay there!"

He stopped. "Either you swim to us or I'm coming to get you," he said. Already it was getting difficult to hear him.

"This is what I had to do all along," said Tara. "If only I'd seen it earlier, I would have spared you all a lot of pain. I'm so sorry."

"I can't let you do this alone, Tara." She thought she heard a tinge of anger in his voice. "I thought we were in this together … the fist … remember?"

"If you really want to do something for me, get everyone back to Morni and send Prabala. I'll be waiting. Send my grandfather to help me …"

By this time the boat was farther downstream. She wasn't sure if he had heard her. But now it didn't matter any more.

Zarku stood beside her quietly. She ignored him, watching the boat hurtle away, her hands clenched at her sides. She raised her right hand, staring at her fist. She unfurled it and waved goodbye.

Zarku slipped his hand into hers and she shuddered. She tried not to close her eyes this time. She did not want to see the real him. *I'm standing at the water's edge with my brother*, she told herself. *That's all. My baby brother, Suraj.*

She watched until the boat melted away into darkness. Then she walked hand in hand with Zarku, back into the forest she had spent two days trying to escape.

seventeen

Sadia

The white dome of the temple rose up high above the treetops in decayed splendor. A fire burned brightly at the entrance, illuminating the large figure of Kali hunched close to it. She was staring into the forest.

Tara was numb inside from exhaustion, pain, and, most of all, fear of what lay in store for her. When she had run from this place two days ago, she had never dreamed she would return. Alone. Her friends gone, it felt like someone had taken her clothes away, and left her to face the harsh elements, naked.

"Welcome, *welcome*," said Kali. "I knew you would return."

Tara stared at her with as much contempt as she could muster. It had no effect.

"Of course she had to return," said Zarku. "She was always the wise one. Ahhh, Tara. If only you'd seen the light earlier, we could avoided all this drama. But I enjoyed our little game, so no complaints."

"What are you going to do with me?" asked Tara.

"Something exciting," said Zarku. "But I really don't have time to explain all this right now. Kali, take her away and meet me behind the temple."

Kali led her back to the room and slammed the door shut.

Tara crawled to a corner and slumped down. If she closed her eyes she could still believe her friends were with her. The fragrance of their last meal still lingered in the air. She curled up into a tight little ball and let the tears flow. Tears she had been holding back so long that she thought she would choke. She cried for Suraj, whom she might not live to see, for her friends, whom she missed, for her parents who must be worried sick about them, and for herself — doomed to die a painful death. She had made the choice to see this through on her own. And once again she was very afraid.

The room was so dark; she could see nothing around her. Only what was in her heart and mind and it was so troubling that she tossed and turned on the hard floor, praying for sleep.

She sat up suddenly. Why? Why was she making this so hard on herself? All she had to do was join Zarku. She'd be powerful, too. She wouldn't kill as he was wont to do, but she would command respect from everyone. And in return for joining him, she would ask that Suraj be spared. Sadia, too. They would return home safely even if she didn't.

The next moment she fell back on the ground, pounding the floor with her fist. This was insane. Zarku was evil; she had stayed back to fight him, destroy him. Not join him. And she had to be strong enough to do this all alone.

You're not alone, Tara. I am with you. For as long as you need me.

Tara did not bother to look around this time. There was no one around her and yet she was hearing a voice in her head. A voice that did not belong to her. She laughed. What a time to be going mad!

Overhead, the skies burst open in a deafening clap of thunder. Rain pelted down and a few drops splattered Tara's face from the window high in the wall. She stood up and moved closer. The rainwater cooled her burning skin.

The door crashed open and Zarku strode in, holding a lantern. "Time to move."

"It's still dark and it's raining. Why now? Where are we going?"

"ENOUGH with the questions," said Zarku. "I've let your friends escape. What is the first thing they're going to do? Get the villagers and storm this place," he said. "I'm not going to wait around for that to happen. Start walking."

"Where is Sadia?" said Tara. "Take me to her, right now, or I'm not moving."

Zarku stepped up to her suddenly and gave her a hard slap that sent her tumbling to the floor. Her cheek smarted and her ears rang as she sat there, stunned. The yellow glow of the lantern illuminated the face she had once loved and which now had an ugly sneer on it.

"If you ever speak to me like that again, I won't let you get away with just a slap. I am *Zarku* and you will treat me with respect even if I am in this pathetic form."

Tara glowered at him, cupping her stinging cheek. She sniffed hard, refusing to give him the satisfaction of seeing her cry.

"Poor Tara," he said. "Does it hurt a lot? I'm *so sorry.*"

His eyes glittered malevolently and she saw him clearly now, with eyes wide open. But whatever he had in mind, she would not give in without a fight. He was in for a huge surprise. But first she had to find out *his* surprise for her!

"Are you going to tell me what special plan you have for me?" said Tara.

"I wondered when you'd ask me that question," said Zarku. "I would be delighted to tell you."

Tara pressed her back against the crumbling stone wall and clasped her knees to her chest. At last she would know how she was going to die. Strangely at this moment she was not scared, only curious.

"You see, I made a deal with Kubera, the Lord of the Underworld," said Zarku. "If I were to sacrifice the life of the person responsible for vanquishing me the last time, he would give me a new and more powerful body to inhabit. By killing you I would prove myself worthy of it." He examined his body, an expression of deep loathing on his face. "I can't wait to rid myself of this horrible form! There is so little I can do with it."

"How did you manage to possess my brother?" said Tara.

Zarku, who had been pacing the floor, stopped in front of her. "When you're stuck in an urn in the middle of a forest, hovering between life and death, you meet interesting spirits who tell you useful things. Tara, you have no idea how many things I have learned hanging between the world of the dead and the living."

Tara looked at him in revulsion. He was so triumphant in his knowledge, so secure that he would win, even if it meant destroying an innocent person in the process.

"Why Suraj? You could have possessed anyone."

"Silly question, Tara. Would you have come into the forest to rescue just anyone?"

"When you leave Suraj's body, he won't be harmed, will he?"

"Not if all goes well," said Zarku. "It all depends on how well you co-operate. If you distract me with your pathetic attempts at bravery, who knows, a small part of me might remain inside your brother forever."

Tara shuddered involuntarily. Something nagged her, a wisp of a thought. The more she tried to grasp at it, the more elusive it became. Something about what Zarku had just said, but what was it?

"Penny for your thoughts, Tara?"

"You're a ruthless monster and I will try my best to see that you suffer."

"Remember, Tara. Your brother's well-being depends entirely on you. If you act smart it could cost your brother his life. Or his sanity."

What would it be like to live with Suraj, knowing that a bit of that evil monster was still in him? But Zarku was talking of sacrifices. That meant she would not live to see Suraj restored to his former self, hug him as she used to, hear him call out her name.

Once again tears pricked her eyes. She took a deep breath and cleared her throat.

"There, there," said Zarku. "It is such an honour to give up your life so that I, the greatest healer in all of India, can live. I could have chosen anyone, but I chose *you*. You should be proud."

"How is this sacrifice going to happen?" asked Tara.

"Tonight there is no moon and tomorrow a new moon will reappear," said Zarku. "The perfect night for a ... shall we call it a little *ritual*. Tomorrow I, too, will be reborn — a new and powerful man."

"And where...where ..." said Tara. The words stuck in her throat and she swallowed before she could speak again. "Where will this happen?"

"In the heart of the Shivalik range — the place where

Lord Kubera first gave me my powers. I'm glad I'll get a chance to show it to you because it is so dear to my heart. Once again the Lord will reward me and this time, I will not fail him."

"So how do you plan to kill me?" Even though the words rolled off her tongue, they terrified her.

"And spoil the surprise?" said Zarku. "No, Tara. I want you to think of all the possible ways I could kill you while we march toward our destination. That will be your punishment for killing my companion and giving me such grief. Think of the worst thing that could happen to you and then multiply that by a thousand."

He laughed long and hard. The hyenas outside the room laughed, too. Kali walked into the room and joined them, giggling like an overgrown schoolgirl.

"What are you laughing at?" said Zarku, frowning at Kali. "Do you know what the joke is, you moron?"

Kali immediately shut up and shook her head. "Tell me. I'm sure I'll appreciate it."

"Shut up!" said Zarku. "You think I have time to stand here and tell you jokes? What is it?"

"I've finished packing," she said sullenly. "We're ready to go."

"I'll be back in a few moments," he said to Tara. "I had better double-check everything. She cannot be trusted."

Kali turned white and Tara smiled. It was heartening to see this bully finally meeting her match. Kali gave her a parting glare and followed Zarku out of the room.

Tara looked up at the window. Dawn had arrived though the sky was obscured by a thick, grey curtain of water. The others would have reached a village by now and might even be telling someone about her and Zarku at this very moment. But until they got here she was alone with that monster and she still hadn't seen Sadia.

He's not a monster, Tara.

Tara jerked convulsively. She wasn't mad ... someone was playing games with her. The voice only spoke when she was thinking of Zarku. Maybe this was one of the tortures that he had dreamed up for her. She ran to the doorway. The corridor was deserted except for dried leaves skittering across the floor, swept along by a gust of wind.

She stepped back into the room and walked along the periphery, running her palms over the walls. Vines clung tenaciously to the cracks with their strong roots. But there was no crevasse deep enough to hide someone. She was alone.

"Please," she whispered backing into the middle of room. "Stop playing games. Show yourself."

No one came forward.

She looked all around her, the walls, the ceiling, even the floor. "Hello?" said Tara

"And hello to you, too," said Zarku stepping into the room. "I can see that you are becoming more polite every minute. I'm almost starting to become fond of you, Tara."

"Is there anyone else you're holding captive besides Sadia and me?"

"Captive is a very strong word," said Zarku, his voice suddenly cold. "Why, you can walk out of here this very moment if you like. I won't stop you."

They both knew she wouldn't. Couldn't. Was held to this bargain by the thing she could only think of as love.

"I heard someone, a woman's voice, just a moment ago. Are you sure you don't have someone else in here? Maybe in the next room?"

"Hmmm, hearing voices," said Zarku. "That's not a good sign at all. You're not going to go mad or die on me, are you?"

Tara said nothing. Maybe this was Sadia speaking from somewhere close by, the next room, perhaps. And the voice was coming in through some crack. But how did that explain hearing the voice in the forest? She was grasping at straws and she knew it.

"I'd like to see Sadia, please. Can you take me to her?"

"My, oh my," said Zarku. "How very well-behaved you are all of a sudden. I always reward good behaviour. Come with me."

He swivelled on his heel and skipped out the door eagerly, like a child about to show off a new toy. Tara ran behind him. He led her out into the main corridor and then swerved into another passageway. Water dripped steadily from the cracks overhead. Occasionally a cold drop landed on her head. Rain had pooled in puddles along the way, soaking her shoes as she ran to keep up with Zarku.

Zarku stopped suddenly and Tara almost bumped into him. He flung open the wooden doors of a small room. Someone coughed from within.

"Go in and stay with her," said Zarku. "Kali will be along to fetch you both shortly."

Tara stepped inside, waiting for her eyes to adjust to the gloom. This room did not have a window and the only light came in from the corridor. And there she was, curled up on a stone bench hollowed out within the wall.

"Sadia?" said Tara, rushing to her side.

Immediately the coughing stopped. Sadia struggled to sit up. She barely managed to prop herself up on her elbow before she fell back on the stone bench, a wet cough wracking her thin body. Tara hugged her and was instantly worried; Sadia was burning up with fever.

"Who ... are ... you?" Sadia managed to say.

The instant Sadia spoke, Tara knew the voice she'd been hearing was not hers; she had known it all along. So then, who was it? She pushed the thought aside and ran to the door.

"Don't leave me," Sadia shrieked. There was such terror in that cry that Tara returned to her side.

"It's all right, Sadia. I'm Tara, a friend of your brother, Kabir. Don't you remember, we met at the fair? I've come to help you."

Sadia sat up with a huge effort. She clung to Tara, sobbing as if her heart would break. Tara wanted to bawl, too. How had Sadia survived these last few days, alone in this small dark room? She heard footsteps and stood up. She needed to brew some medicine for Sadia and was willing to grovel if need be.

"Follow me," said Kali. She stood in the doorway, blocking out much of the light and beckoned to them.

"Kali, wait," said Tara. "Sadia is very ill. She needs medicine or she won't survive."

"Good," snapped Kali. "One less burden to carry around."

Curses for Kali rose unbidden to Tara's lips. It was wrong to wish ill on anyone, her mother had always said. But Kali was not anyone. She was the worst and most inhuman being Tara had ever known. After Zarku.

"Up, GET UP!" said Kali. "I haven't all day."

"Sadia, can you walk?" asked Tara.

Sadia mumbled and sat up, coughing. She got to her feet and immediately crumpled to the ground. Tara scooped her up, feeling her small, hot body settle heavily in her arms and walked up to Kali. "I'll need help. Sadia is too ill to walk on her own."

"The hyenas are just outside. Toss her to them and they'll take care of the problem."

The room took on a reddish tinge. Tara focused on adjusting Sadia in her arms to be able to carry her comfortably. If she hadn't been preoccupied with that, she would have strangled Kali. How could she be so hard-hearted? She was a mother, after all.

Tara followed Kali's ample bottom, wondering what it would take to persuade the hyenas to reduce it by a few kilos or maybe even devour her. No one in the world would miss her except Layla. Anger pulsed anew at the thought of Layla; the evil child of an evil mother. In spite of being separated from Kali, she had shown her true colours and betrayed Suraj and his friend. How had she done it? How had they communicated with each other without being discovered? If she ever survived this, it would be the first thing she would investigate.

Tara followed Kali through the labyrinth once again. Sadia was getting heavier with each step. How had Vayu carried Raani for so many hours under the burning sun, without pause or complaint? She was barely able to manage a small child.

Kali turned a corner and there was the entrance. The gray day dampened Tara's spirits further. Her arms ached and her legs trembled. They hadn't even left the temple yet and who knew how far Zarku would make her walk.

Zarku stood in the rain, arms folded across his chest— exactly as Suraj did when he was annoyed. The familiar gesture tugged at her heart. She focused on the hardness in his eyes. The tug vanished, replaced by hatred.

"Took you long enough," said Zarku. Beside him was a bundle covered in an oilskin.

"Sadia is ill," said Tara. "She can barely walk."

"So? I see you found the solution already," he said. "Good girl."

"I can't carry her all the way," said Tara. "She's too heavy."

"Feel free to drop her at any time," said Zarku. "The hyenas haven't eaten today. And you," said Zarku snapping his fingers at Kali and pointing. "Pick up the bundle."

On cue, the hyenas swirled around her legs sniffing, gibbering.

Tara took a deep breath. She would drop dead before she dropped Sadia. She hoisted the little girl higher. Squaring her shoulders, Tara walked out into the pouring rain.

eighteen

The Voice of Madness

The rain stopped at midday. The sun came out and with it the ubiquitous mosquitoes with their constant buzzing. Within the hour, the forest became warmer, like a slowly heating oven. The earth steamed gently under Tara's feet. Now and then a breeze dislodged drops of rain from the leaves, showering her with a welcome coolness.

Sadia moaned and hot breath fanned the base of her throat. Tara wanted to moan, too; she couldn't feel her arms. Her face was drenched with sweat, blinding her at times because she was unable to wipe it away. All she wanted to do was sit down and never get up. She forced herself to keep going, left foot, right foot, left … right …

Tara licked her parched lips. "Please, can we stop for a short while?"

Zarku ignored her.

"Please," said Tara, hating herself for the whining tone.

"No!"

"If I collapse and die, you won't be able to carry out your grand plan. Ever thought of that?"

Zarku stopped and turned round, a squiggle of worry on his forehead. Tara trembled with the realization that finally she had something that would make him listen to her. Something she could use to blackmail him. If she died or did not reach the cave, he would not be able to carry out his plan.

"All right," he said. "Ten minutes only. But don't think you can use this excuse with me all the time. I can still carry out my plan with you barely alive. Remember that."

Tara sank to the ground, still holding Sadia, too tired to understand or even care about what he meant by that. She took deep, shuddering breaths wondering if she would have the strength to stand up again after ten minutes.

"Water," mumbled Sadia.

"Give me some water, Kali," said Tara.

"No!" she snapped. "There's none to spare."

Tara turned to Zarku. "If anything happens to Sadia, you can be certain I won't let your plan succeed. You'll have to spend the rest of your life in Suraj's body, forget about all that glory and power."

Tara winced as she said it, praying he would not see through the bluff. She couldn't let Suraj live the rest of his life possessed by Zarku. She would kill him first.

How exactly she would accomplish that did not bear thinking about right now.

"Give her the water," said Zarku. He stood to one side, deep in thought.

"Here," said Kali. She thrust a bottle of water in Tara's hand.

Tara unclasped Sadia's thin little arms from around her neck and laid her on the ground. She was so very still, her face flushed and red in the afternoon heat, her lips cracked and dry.

"Sadia, here's some water," said Tara. "Open your mouth."

There was no response from the little girl.

Tara propped her up and poured a few drops into her mouth. The water trickled out the side and Sadia's head lolled. Tara shook her gently. "Sadia, listen to me, wake up. I'm taking you back home. To Kabir."

Sadia mumbled under her breath, but did not open her eyes. Painstakingly, Tara poured some more water into her mouth, feeling Kali's eyes on them, counting every drop. Only when she thought Sadia had had enough did she take a deep gulp. Kali snatched the bottle away before she could take another.

"Enough!" said Kali. She put the stopper back on. "We have to ration it."

They glared at each other in silence.

"If both of you have finished with the loving looks, let's go," said Zarku.

It would be so easy to just give up, lay down here and let him kill her and Sadia. Tara leaned her head back against a tree and closed her eyes. The battle at the banyan tree flashed through her mind; all those villagers turned into Vetalas with Zarku rousing them to a mad frenzy. She sat up with a jerk. If she did not stop him, this would be their fate all over again. It was in her hands now and she had no idea where to start.

Zarku was looking at her curiously. "Get up, now!"

"Just a few moments more."

Zarku snapped his fingers and a hyena rushed forward and nipped her. Her shoulder throbbed and blood blossomed on her kurta. Tara jumped to her feet. The hyena backed away, laughing. *You watch*, she thought, staring straight at the ugly beast. *I'll have the last laugh*.

Zarku and Kali were on their feet, staring at her impatiently. The thought of having to hoist Sadia in her aching arms made her quail. For a brief moment she felt resentment. Why was *she* latched with this burden? It would be so easy to walk away. Leave Sadia and save herself.

Sadia muttered unintelligibly, deep in the throes of fever. Tara caught only one word, *Kabir*, and was instantly ashamed. How could she even think of abandoning this child after she had promised Kabir she would bring her back? What if this had been Suraj? Such an ugly thought would never have crossed her mind!

"Looks like you both need a bit of help," said Zarku, snapping his fingers. Both hyenas converged on Sadia, sniffing greedily, licking her face. One of them nipped her nose, drawing a bit of blood.

Sadia's eyes snapped open. "Don't let him eat me, Didi." She crawled over to Tara and wrapped her thin arms around her, rubbing her nose and howling.

"Call them off!" screamed Tara.

"You can't blame them for taking a sniff at lunch." Zarku laughed. It was a thin, brittle sound that sliced through hope, leaving only despair. "Next time they won't be so polite."

Tara lifted Sadia, every muscle in her body crying with fatigue. Her arms automatically locked in place under Sadia's small bottom. She followed Zarku's feet, mesmerized by the way he lifted his feet, put them down, up and down again accompanied by the sounds of crackling leaves and twigs. On and on and on.

"Faster!" said Zarku. "You're slowing us down deliberately, Tara. I'm almost at the end of my patience."

"I can't go any faster," said Tara. "She's too heavy."

Zarku whirled round, his face a mask of rage. "Then drop her or stop your whining," he commanded. "We have to get to that cave before nightfall. If it does not happen tonight, I'll have to wait another fortnight — and I will not allow that."

"So tell that fat lump to help me," said Tara. She jerked her head toward Kali, who also looked winded.

"If we took turns carrying Sadia, it might help."

"Rubbish," said Kali. "I'm not going to hold her."

"You might as well kill me now," said Tara, "because I can't go on and I'm not leaving Sadia."

"Let the hyenas eat her," said Kali. "We don't need her anyway, do we?"

"We don't need you, either," said Zarku in a cold voice. "Maybe they can start with you?"

Kali blanched. "You could help, you know," she said in a soft voice. "You're the only one who's not carrying anything."

Zarku came right up to Kali and though he had to look up to speak to her there was no doubt about who was in charge. "You speak to me disrespectfully even once more, Kali, and I will kill you on the spot."

He came up to Tara next. She looked into his face, focusing on the crease on his forehead that was deeper. "If you slow me down or stop me once more, Tara, you will lose Sadia. I will tie you up first and then let the hyenas feast on her while you watch. Understand?"

Tara saw the image clearly in her mind and something inside her snapped.

"No, I don't understand," screamed Tara. "I will *never* understand your deliberate cruelty!"

She put Sadia on the ground, grabbed Zarku and shook him till his teeth rattled. He was so surprised that he made no attempt to resist. His head jerked back and forth with each shake that grew progressively rougher.

"Is there not even a shred of humanity in you?" she shrieked. "How can you talk of letting a hyena rip apart an innocent *child*? You've taken one life already. How many more will it take to satisfy you? YOU MONSTER!"

Zarku was limp in her hands as she shook him like a duster. He stared up at her just like Suraj did when she scolded him.

Tara stopped and looked deep into his eyes that had lost a bit of their hardness. "Suraj," she said. "If you're in there, listen to me. You've already lost your best friend Rohan to this monster and the hyenas. They killed him. They'll kill Sadia next. Unless you can stop it, somehow. Only *you* can fight Zarku. Resist him! Can you hear your sister? Give me a sign if you do." She shook him so hard that he stumbled and fell to the ground, hitting his head against a stone.

"Owww."

Tara picked him up, aghast at the spot of blood on his temple. He looked dazed.

"Didi?" he said in a tremulous voice. His eyes were moist.

Her heart soared. "Suraj?" said Tara. "You *heard* me! Can you fight this monster within you? It's your body, you must take it over. You must."

A tear slid down his cheek. "Didi, I'm scared. What should I do? Someone's smothering me, choking me from the inside. It feels like … like I'm in a dark room and I can't get out. Help me!"

"Oh Suraj, be strong. You must resist him. Don't do what he tells you. Do just the opposite. I'm right here beside you. I'll help."

Suraj nodded and held his arms open. Tara embraced him, feeling his small shoulders heave and his body tremble. She had gotten through to her brother; now they had a fighting chance. Maybe if Suraj listened to her, she could get him to come to Morni with her. They might defeat Zarku, yet!

"Don't cry, Suraj, it's all right. Listen to me," she said, pulling away from him. She stopped. He was laughing so hard that tears rolled down his cheeks.

"Suraj …?"

"That was so much fun," gasped Zarku. He rolled on the ground, clutching his stomach, roaring with laughter.

"You were playing with me all along?" she breathed. Goosebumps rose on her skin; she had hugged this evil being once again. She shuddered and drew back.

"You needed a break and I needed a laugh," said Zarku. He sat up and wiped his eyes on the sleeve of his kurta. *"Listen to me, Suraj. Be strong, resist him, resist the evil madman,"* he mimicked in a high-pitched voice.

At that moment Tara hated what her brother had become— a puppet to something so evil that it had taken over his very soul. It was getting harder and harder to believe that she would ever get her brother back and if she ever did, the shadow of Zarku would always linger.

"I'll say this one last time," said Zarku. "Suraj can't hear you. Not until I leave his body. And the condition I leave it in will depend entirely on you. Don't try to slow me down, Tara. You'll regret it."

He dusted the mud off his clothes and started off at a fast trot.

Tara tasted bile at the back of her throat and swallowed. The trees seemed to crowd in on her, lowering their thick canopy of leaves, trying to trap her in a green airless box.

It was useless. She was going to die. Sadia was weak and after she was gone, Zarku would not hesitate to kill her, too. And Suraj — who knew what condition his mind would be in when Zarku left his body. She should give up right now. It was completely hopeless.

You've never given up before, Tara. I'm with you. Trust me. Trust yourself. Pick up Sadia. Let's go.

The soft melodious voice was so clear, as if someone had whispered in her ear.

With a deep sigh, Tara stood up and picked up Sadia. There was no doubt now that fear had driven her mad.

Yet this was an odd kind of madness, surely. In her deep desolation, the voice gave a tiny bit of courage.

Into the Cave

The ground had been dipping steadily over the past hour and it was a lot easier walking downhill with Sadia. Dusk was almost upon them once again. The path became rockier, the trees more sparse.

Zarku moved faster. Weighed down with Sadia, Tara almost stumbled over loose pebbles underfoot as she tried to keep up. They entered a deep gully. Grassy banks of forest covered with thick, straggly tree roots rose on either side. Daylight and the forest were fast disappearing as they descended, and if Zarku carried out his plan, she would never see any of this again.

"Come on, come on," muttered Zarku. All playfulness was gone from his voice. "Almost there. We have to be ready by midnight."

Kali panted as she tried to keep up. Tara lagged behind, breathing in the night air, knowing it was the last time.

"Here we are," said Zarku. His voice quivered with excitement. "I haven't seen this place in such a long time."

They stood before a large cave, partially covered by vines. Zarku immediately fell to his knees and touched his forehead to the ground. Tara was so tempted to kick his bottom, which pointed straight up at her. She caught Kali's eye and decided not to. Besides, the hyenas were too close for comfort.

Within moments Zarku was back on his feet. "Onward!" he cried. "We're almost there. Aren't you happy, Tara? In just a few hours you'll be free of Sadia and this cumbersome earthbound form."

Tara was too tired to reply. She was ready to follow Zarku anywhere if it meant she could sit down and rest for a short while. Her legs trembled. Her shoulders and arms were frozen. If she unclasped her hands for even a moment, she knew she wouldn't be able to lift Sadia again.

"Give me the lantern," said Zarku. "Quick now, we still have a ways to go."

Kali fumbled with the bundle, cursing and swearing, and finally extracted the lantern. Zarku snatched it from her, lit it, and hurried into the cave.

Kali shuffled behind him and stopped, clutching her chest, wheezing loudly. Tara walked past her with barely a glance, glad that she was suffering. Kali had brought this upon herself, upon all of them by rescuing the urn. If only Lord Yama had got to it first …

"I'm home," said Zarku. His voice echoed in the cavern, *home, home, home.*

Tara hesitated at the entrance, suddenly reminded of the cave she had entered to get the Water of Life for Ananth. She had forgotten how heavy the darkness could get, how close and still the air could be and how strange were the creatures that inhabited these underground worlds. She looked back and breathed in the hot forest air.

All at once, needle-sharp teeth pierced the soft flesh of her calf. Tara yelped. Her legs gave way and she fell to her knees on the stone floor, still holding Sadia. All of her juddered with the impact.

A hyena grinned at her with a toothy red smile. Blood leaked through the torn fabric of Tara's shalwar.

"Just a little something to help you along," said Zarku. "Now don't slow down. The other hyena feels left out and I might decide to give him a turn, too.

"You're sick," whispered Tara, barely able to speak. Her leg glowed white-hot with pain, which raced all the way to her fingertips and back again. She thought she was going to faint. "Can you not show just a little pity? After all, I'm the chosen one who will help you become more powerful!"

"Pity?" asked Zarku. He cocked his head to one side. "What's that?"

Tara glared at him shifting her weight from one leg to the other. She felt blood trickling down and pooling inside her shoe. Her foot was already slick with it. She pressed her lips together to stop from crying out as another wave of pain crested.

"Oh right," said Zarku. "It's that thing one feels when one is sorry for someone. Funny, no one ever felt sorry for me when I was suffering. The boys *and* teachers made it a point to hurt me, watch me cry. Nope, never came in contact with that bug. No infections here," he said, spreading his hands.

"I hope you rot in hell!" said Tara.

"Oh, I will go there, except that I'll flourish," he said with a giggle. "You'll be the one rotting. But enough of these compliments, you're embarrassing me. We better hurry."

Tara didn't move.

"Perhaps a little help …?" said Zarku. He snapped his fingers and the hyenas flanked Tara, lunging at her legs playfully. She followed him, her leg throbbing with each step. Her shoe squelched as she walked. The hyena closest to her sniffed at it and eyed her greedily.

Tara stepped right into the cave and looked around. The lantern lit the large white cavern, strewn with broken boulders and black pockets of darkness. Tara had heard of the limestone caves in the hills, but this was the first time she was seeing them. Ghostly white pillars hung down from the roof that was so high it seemed like they were at the bottom of a deep well. Thicker pillars rose from the floor. Tara felt like she was walking into the open mouth of a gigantic monster. Any moment now the jaws would snap shut, impaling her and Sadia on its jagged white teeth.

The lantern cast their shadows on the walls so that it seemed like a group of grotesque giants were walking alongside.

With each step Tara got a sinking feeling. Involuntarily, she picked up speed and realized they were going downhill again. Her breath came in gasps. The limestone shone with a ghostly lustre when the light touched it. Other parts remained within grey shadows. A haze of pain enveloped her and everything around her started dimming, going out of focus.

Wake up, Tara. You don't dare give up now!

Tara jerked awake. The voice was shrill in her ear. *Who are you?* Tara pleaded silently. *Please tell me just one thing — am I going mad?*

No, Tara. But I need you to stay with me. Do as I say. We're close now. Very close.

Tara took a few more steps when an awful thought struck her with such force that all the strength drained out of her. She stumbled and fell, hitting her head against a rock. The world went completely dark. Four little words echoed in her head and faded away ... *do as I say.*

• • •

A sharp pain in her shoulder woke her. Zarku's face swam above hers, his eyes glittering with rage. Next to him was a grinning hyena, its mouth wet with blood. Sadia lay beside her. Tara touched her shoulder and it throbbed viciously. She jerked her hand away.

"I see that you came up with another way to slow us down," said Zarku. "Well, I've got just the method to wake you up again." He smiled. "I've told you, do as I say and you won't get hurt."

Those words again. Tara jumped to her feet, panic giving her strength. *Is that you, Zarku?* she asked silently. *Are you inside me, too?* She stared at him as she asked the question.

There was no reply.

"What are you staring at, Tara? If you find me interesting now, wait till I get a new form ... oh no, I just remembered ... you won't be around to see it. *Sorry.*"

He dragged her to where Sadia lay. "Pick her up and get moving. I have waited too long for this night and nothing's going to stand in my way."

Tara's arm and leg were both on fire. The cave see-sawed in her vision. She shot out her hand to steady herself and felt another depth charge of pain explode within. But it was nothing compared to the panic that made every nerve in her body thrum. Had Zarku possessed her, too?

I suggest you leave her there," said Zarku, prodding Sadia with his foot. "She's useless to us. You'll only be putting yourself through more hardship if you insist on carrying her."

"I'm not leaving her," said Tara. She hobbled over to Sadia, pulled her upright and picked her up, sobbing with the effort. Her legs almost buckled.

"Help me, Kali," whispered Tara. "Just this once."

Kali fanned her face with her saree, and looked away as Tara knew she would. At least she had tried.

Zarku took off again, the lantern swinging in his hand. Tara lurched after him, wondering how many more steps she could take before she fell dead at his feet. One thought pounded at her; she had failed Suraj and Sadia and her family. She had allowed Zarku to possess her. She was weak. She deserved to die.

Tara, you are stronger than I ever imagined. Know this — no one could have done what you are doing now. And you have to keep going, because you will win. Believe in yourself once again, my child. Trust yourself once again.

Did Lord Ganesh send you to help me? asked Tara wearily. *Please, just stop playing games and tell me. Who are you?*

I am Zara.

twenty

Zara

Zara?

A cold finger traced a path down Tara's spine. That was too close to his name. *Are you a part of Zarku?* she asked.

No, but he is a part of me.

Tara almost dropped Sadia again. She had been right. "Get out," she screamed. "GET OUT!"

"Shut up," said Zarku from up ahead. "This is a sacred place. I will not tolerate your rantings."

Tara realized she had yelled out loud.

Calm down, Tara. I can't stand histrionics.

The voice was soft, yet stern. Every time the voice spoke, her insides throbbed unpleasantly, painfully.

I brought a lot of friends on this journey, Zara, and I let them all go. Please, just leave me alone. Whoever you are, get out of my body. I'll manage this all alone.

You brought me here, Tara. We both have a job to do.

But you still haven't told me who you are and why I'm hearing you inside my head, Tara said silently.

Check your pocket.

Tara reached for her pocket, the effort making her sweat profusely. Sadia started to slip. She shifted the little girl's weight to one arm and plunged her hand in. Her fingers closed over something cold and heavy; Zarku's mother's anklet. Of course!

Tara didn't know whether to laugh or cry or faint.

Zara was Zarku's mother and she was inside Tara.

• • •

Her cheek stung and her eyes snapped open.

"Won't you ever stop trying?" snarled Zarku. He slapped her again. "It won't work. You're just not the fainting type, Tara. Get up now or you'll really discover what these hyenas can do and this time I won't restrain them. Your body is useless to me, even if it's badly mangled."

It was true, she never fainted. What was wrong with her? She touched her aching scalp. Her fingertips connected with a lump the size of an egg and she winced. Sadia moaned and Tara crawled over to her. She was motionless. Tara laid her head on her chest and was relieved to hear a faint heartbeat.

"Up," said Zarku. "Walk."

Tara pushed herself to her feet, barely aware of what she was doing. Her body ached all over, she was bleeding to death, inside her nestled Zarku's mother's spirit, and she was marching toward a painful death. A bitter laugh bubbled up within her; could things get any worse?

She tried to lift Sadia, but it was like trying to lift a boulder ten times her size.

"I can't," she whispered. "Please, can't Kali hold her for a while?"

"No!" said Kali. "Zarku, this is just a ploy. Don't listen to this sneaky little —"

"Then kill me now," said Tara. "I won't leave her here. Tell your hyenas to have fun. I don't care." She plopped down on the floor.

Zarku stared at her for a moment, the crease on his forehead pulsing. It was the first time she had seen that. They had been in the cave for barely an hour and already his power was growing. He exhaled noisily.

"You carry Sadia," he said to Kali.

"I can't," wailed Kali. "I'm tired, too, carrying this heavy bundle of yours."

Zarku hissed a command. A hyena now moved toward Kali. She hurried forward and scooped Sadia up, muttering under her breath.

"Tara, you will carry the bundle," said Zarku. "There will be no more stops. Is that understood?"

On they went. Tara revelled in being able to walk without Sadia's weight. The bundle barely weighed anything and she sighed quietly as her aching muscles relaxed.

Around her, smooth, round tunnels wound away into darkness, as if a giant worm had bored through the walls. Rocks in every shade of white, grey, and pale yellow slid past.

Are you still there, Zara?

Yes.

Can you not stop your son? Why can't you get into his *mind and tell him to release Suraj?* Tara demanded.

Because the anklet is with you, Tara. And because he's in human form, you're the best person to stop him. Not me.

Kali panted, her pace slowing. The air turned hotter and Tara's lungs burned each time she drew breath.

Zara, what does he have in store for me? Can you tell me?

I can't. Lord Kubera has taken over my child's mind. Even if I wanted to, I couldn't penetrate it. That's another reason I chose you — I need your help to stop him and you need mine.

Child? Tara snorted. This was no child except if you looked at the body. He was a monster. She wondered how she could have ever felt sorry for him when she had heard him cry that night in the forest. The hyenas growled and she realized she was lagging behind. Their yellow eyes seemed to be floating in darkness somewhere near her knees. Tara walked faster.

Tell me more, Zara.

He would have been an ordinary child, Tara. His father and I had decided that if we had a boy we would name him after us; Zara and Kundan ... Zarku. But our match was not to be, you see, we were from different religions and no one approved. Not our parents and nor the village priests. We ran away and got married, but when we announced the baby, one of the priests put a curse on me and on the baby I was carrying. I died giving birth and Zarku was born with a third eye for which he suffered all his life.

Tara heard the deep sadness in her voice. It was the longest Zara had ever spoken. She had only to imagine her own mother to realize how this woman must have felt, must be feeling, to see her son become a monster — hated by all. But wouldn't a mother always protect her child no matter what?

Zara, you won't ... you won't give me the wrong advice, will you?

Things are going to get very difficult once you reach the cave. We'll both have to trust one another.

Tara pressed her fingertips against her aching temples. She was so tired that she was not thinking straight. She was having a conversation with Zarku's mother. But could she trust Zara? Should she?

• • •

The path that Zarku took twisted and turned as it continued its descent into the bowels of the mountain.

The rock changed colour, larger sheets of black interspersed the limestone. If Tara fell behind she found herself in near complete darkness and had to hurry round the next bend so she could see the flickering light of the lantern.

The silence was broken by the hiss of escaping steam and the burbling sounds of something thick and viscous boiling deep below. The rock under her feet was getting hotter by the minute. The heat in the forest seemed like a joke compared to the heat in this place.

Kali struggled along with Sadia, who still hadn't stirred. Tara's heart ached as she thought of Kabir and how much he loved his sister. Without medicine, Sadia might even now be breathing her last.

One more downward twist and they were walking on level ground.

"We're almost there," Zarku called out. "Everyone all right?"

Tara was tempted to throw her shoe at his head. All right? No, they were *not* all right. She was about to say something when she saw where he was leading them.

Ahead of them was an extremely dark patch. Could it be an underground lake? She thought of the last time she had had to cross a lake, the feeling of drowning, the slithery, slippery things that had touched her skin. Her nerve almost failed. She couldn't do it again. Zarku would have to kill her right here.

Zara, help me. I can't do this.

There was no reply.

Tara looked back the way they had come. A solid black wall of darkness confronted her; tall and impenetrable. Without a light there wasn't a hope that she would be able to find her way back to the top again. She would have to go on. If only little Mushika were here …

"Come on," snapped Zarku. "This is the last little bit. It's tricky, but I'm sure we'll all manage. Once we get across, the cave's a few steps away."

Something in his voice made Tara look carefully. It was not a lake at all. It was a chasm that stretched before them. She couldn't see how deep it was nor how wide. And yet here she was, about to cross it.

Kali peered over the edge and looked back at Tara, her eyes wide with terror. Tara kicked a rock near her foot into the chasm. It bounced against the wall a couple of times and then there was complete silence.

Tara strained her ears but heard nothing. Half a minute passed by and the rock still hadn't hit bottom. They both looked at each other and then at Zarku.

"I can't go over that," said Kali in a quavering voice. "I'll fall."

"That's fine, you can stay here for all I care," said Zarku. "Goodbye." He stepped onto the narrow stone path that bridged the chasm. For the first time Tara saw just how narrow it was, there was no room for error. None at all.

"Can't we do whatever we have to on this side?" said Tara. "Please. You don't expect me to cross with a sick child."

Zarku turned around and glared at her. "For the last time, Tara, I. Don't. Care. If you'd rather deny my friends a good meal, fling Sadia over the side now. She too sick to realize what's happening, and since this chasm has no bottom, you won't hear her land. And we'll all move faster. And if you're too weak to do it, I'll do it for you!"

In a rage, Tara dropped the bundle and rushed toward Zarku. She'd show him how to fling people into chasms. The larger of the two hyenas jumped between them and growled, barring her way. She kicked it aside, putting all her anger and fear and hatred into it. The hyena flew into the air and tumbled over the edge. Its screams echoed for a long time, growing fainter and fainter. Then there was silence.

Tara stared into the chasm, her fists clenched. She had killed a living thing. Even though it was far from innocent, even though her arm and leg still throbbed with the memory of its teeth, she had deliberately sent it to its death. She shuddered; she was getting to be as ruthless as Zarku.

Kali was staring at her, aghast. Tara ignored her and looked at Zarku defiantly. He held her gaze. "That's the second friend I've lost thanks to you. I'll make you suffer for this, Tara. Count on it."

Tara was too exhausted to retaliate, only able to pray that when the end came it would be swift.

"Who wants to go forward and who wants to go down?" said Zarku. He stepped nimbly onto the stone path, walked a few steps ahead and turned around.

"I'm leaving Sadia here," said Kali, dropping her to the floor like a sack of potatoes. Sadia whimpered while Kali walked away without a backward glance.

"Stop that!" yelled Tara as she rushed over to Sadia. She looked up at Kali, all of her being burning with hatred. Slowly she looked at the black void and then back at Kali. "You're next if you don't help me."

Kali came back to her reluctantly. "Maybe if we held Sadia between us, it might work," she said.

Tara nodded. She bent over Sadia and shook her gently.

"Sadia, wake up," Tara said. "We need you to help us for just a little while."

Sadia moaned and moved her head weakly, her eyes still shut.

"What's keeping you?" roared Zarku. "Move."

The last hyena circled around them, keeping out of reach of Tara, its bile-yellow eyes fixed on her. This time there was no giggling or laughter. Something told her that when the time was right it would not wait for Zarku's command to rip her to shreds.

"Sadia, please, wake up. You have to walk," said Tara. She pulled Sadia upright. It was like handling a ragdoll.

Sadia's head lolled back and she started to fall sideways again. Tara grabbed her and shook her a little harder this time. "Come on now, you have to help me. Wake up!"

Out of the corner of her eye she saw Zarku take a few steps toward them. "Slap her!" he said.

Sadia opened her eyes. They were unfocused. Tara hugged her. "Good girl, now stand up. We have a short little walk and then you can sleep again,"

"So ... tired," said Sadia. "Want to sleep."

"I know," said Tara, kissing her forehead. "But after this, you can sleep for a long time. I promise."

Sadia got to her feet, lurching, swaying, almost falling over. Tara's heart lurched in tandem. If she did this on that narrow walkway, they'd all plunge to their deaths.

"Slowly now," said Tara. She led Sadia to the narrow bridge.

Tara and Kali held Sadia between them. Zarku was already halfway across. Kali stepped on it sideways, holding Sadia by her left arm. Tara followed, firmly gripping Sadia's right arm.

"Where are we?" Sadia whispered. Her eyes were beginning to focus.

Don't let her realize, prayed Tara. The last thing she wanted was for Sadia to panic right there in the middle of the bridge.

"Noooooo!" wailed Sadia. Her eyes were wide open and she was frozen on the spot, looking down. "Where am I?"

Tara glanced beyond the tips of her toes. The blackness seemed to bubble up toward her, trying to suck her down. She took a deep, shuddering breath and wrenched her eyes away from it.

"You can do it, Sadia," said Tara. "Just don't look down."

"If she acts funny, I'll push her over," said Kali. Her face was whiter than the limestone they had passed.

Tara's arms ached trying to hold Sadia still. A cold panic seized her and it was all she could do to hang on as the little girl grew more agitated.

Sadia tensed. Tara tightened her grip. Sadia put her foot forward instead of sideways and stepped on air. She drew it back, screaming for her mother. Her legs trembled and she sagged as if about to sit down.

"Do something, Tara," said Kali. "Or I'll let her go."

"Drop her, just drop her!" said Zarku. "This drama has gone on long enough and I'm sick of it."

With a huge effort, Tara twisted sideways and slapped Sadia. Hard. The sound reverberated in Tara's heart. Sadia immediately stood still staring at Tara with teary eyes and Tara hated herself at that moment.

"Walk!" Tara said in her strictest voice. "Don't look anywhere but straight ahead and walk."

Now and then Kali looked back at Tara, her face shiny with sweat and fear, but they moved quickly, now that Sadia obeyed her. Tara focused on pushing while Kali tugged her along.

Between them, they managed to get to the other side where Zarku stood tapping his foot. The moment her foot touched solid ground, Tara said a prayer to Lord Ganesh. This could have ended right here but it hadn't. They were safe. For now.

Zarku led the way again, moving at a fast clip. "The end is near!" he crowed.

"Help me," said Tara. Sadia was once again on the ground, awake, but too weak to stand. "We could hold her between us."

Kali glanced at Zarku's receding back. "You're on your own," she said and ran off after Zarku.

Shadows crowded Tara once again, pressing down on her, smothering her. Zarku's words echoed in her ear, *the end is near*. If only she had a light, she could have gone back the way they came. Escaped. She didn't want to die.

Follow him. It's the only way out.

Zara's soft voice calmed her. She picked Sadia up and followed the fast-receding light with a nagging thought that she was afraid to think of: this was Zarku's mother advising her.

But whose side was she on?

twenty-one

The Dagger

Zarku stopped before a small cave. He stood gazing at it raptly, like a small child before a magical vision. All Tara saw was one more yawning black hole. He dropped to his knees once again and touched his forehead to the ground as if about to walk on hallowed ground.

The cave was small. They had passed by much bigger ones with unusual colours and impossible-to-imagine shapes, as if giant fingers had moulded them while the rock was still hot. Yet, in this nondescript hole lived a monster — Lord Kubera, who had given birth to another. Tara had expected something more extravagant.

"At last," said Zarku. "We're home." The excitement in his voice was unmistakeable.

The ball of fear in the pit of Tara's stomach expanded. The end of the road. Zarku would carry out his plan and within a short while she would be dead. All the ways he might kill her whirled inside her head, each one more gruesome than the previous one.

"Follow me," said Zarku. He marched inside. Heart pounding, Tara obeyed. Would his Lord be waiting there, ready to strike her down?

But the narrow cave was empty. Its black stone walls stretched into darkness, sucking away any light that fell upon them. There were no reflections and no shadows around them. Tara felt they might suck the life out of her if she went any nearer.

"Put Sadia down and come here," said Zarku.

Tara sat Sadia down at the entrance to the cave. Surprisingly, Sadia stirred and opened her eyes. "Where are we, Didi?"

"Shhhh," whispered Tara. "Sleep now. Everything will be all right." She pressed her lips to Sadia's forehead. It dawned on her that she would be unable to fulfill her promise to Kabir. Deep sadness filled her; she had never broken a promise yet. This would be her first. And last.

Zarku put the lantern in a small niche in the wall. The light was so weak that it was like being underwater. Nothing moved, nothing flickered. The absence of shadows was so unnatural that Tara began to wonder just how evil this place was, if not even shadows dared linger there.

"So, what now?" she asked. Her voice was unnaturally loud in the silence.

"Quiet!" said Zarku. "You are in the shrine of the Lord. You will speak when you are spoken to. Stand here quietly. I'll let you know when I'm ready."

Zarku walked deeper into the cave and came back moments later with a broom.

"Clean up the cave, Kali," said Zarku. He threw the broom at her. It bounced against her ample body and fell to the floor with a thump. Kali's eyes matched the stone walls as she retrieved it.

"Do a thorough job," said Zarku. "Not the shoddy one you normally try and get away with. Sweep every inch of the cave. Everything must be perfect."

Kali did not utter a word. She wrapped the end of her saree around her waist and got to work. The rhythmic swishing and occasional grunt were the only sounds disturbing the loud silence. *Hurry up*, thought Tara. *Just get it over with*. This waiting was driving her mad.

Zara, what's he going to do?

I don't know.

As Tara sat in that eerily dim room with no shadows, she wished, for the umpteenth time, she were back home in Morni doing normal day-to-day chores rather than waiting for Zarku to kill her. Would she get a chance to see this Lord Kubera before he killed her?

She wandered over to the mouth of the cave, unable to sit still. Her insides churned and the beat of her heart drowned out the silence. The darkness just beyond the periphery of the lamplight was thick and heavy and depressing. Just a few feet from the entrance was the chasm they had crossed. Even if she ran for it, without a light she had no hope of getting across. She stepped back into the cave immediately, trying to think of another way to escape.

The black walls seemed to pulse toward her; the ceiling hung lower. She gulped air, but it seemed all of it had burned away. She was suffocating!

She looked behind her. Zarku had untied the bundle and was examining its contents. Lying on the white muslin cloth, a dagger caught her eye. The golden light from the lantern glided smoothly across its blade, stopping short of the ornate handle, which was studded with red stones.

Steal that dagger and throw it into the chasm, said Zara.

What? thought Tara.

Steal the dagger, throw it away. He can't carry out the ritual without it.

Tara took a few steps toward Zarku. Then stopped. What if this was a trap? But if she couldn't trust Zara, whom could she trust? There was no one else.

Round and round her mind scurried like a caged rat, asking questions, grasping at thoughts, throwing them away. No matter how hard she tried, she couldn't think of a way out. She was doomed, and so were Suraj and Sadia. Unless she decided to take Zara's advice.

Tara pulled out the anklet from her pocket and clasped it tight in her sweaty palm. A numbing panic was starting to spread through her once again, clouding all coherent thought.

Put it on, Tara. And keep it hidden.

With trembling hands, Tara surreptitiously put the anklet on. Then she inched closer to Zarku. He was examining the urn in which he had spent the last few months, caressing it lovingly.

The swishing sound stopped and Kali plodded up to them, wheezing. "It's done," she said.

"High time," said Zarku. "Take all these things and arrange them in the centre of the cave. Be careful! Some of these are worth more than your life. I'll be back as soon as I've changed my clothes."

Tara inched forward, her eyes darting to the dagger and back toward Zarku. He turned and started to walk away. Kali stooped to gather the items. Tara lunged forward and grabbed the dagger.

"Oi! STOP!" yelled Kali.

The dagger slipped out of Tara's sweaty hands and fell back on the cloth. She scrabbled for it, but her hands shook so much, she could barely grasp it. The blade brushed against her palm. A shower of bright-red drops stained the white cloth.

Zarku whirled around and raced back to her, his eyes clouded with rage. He slapped her so hard that she went reeling and sprawled on the ground a good distance away.

"How dare you touch this sacred blade with your filthy hands!"

Tara saw stars as she sat up.

Zarku advanced on her, his lips speckled with spit. "So, you think you're being very smart, are you?" His voice was soft and low and deadly calm.

Tara inched backward, not taking her eyes off him. He raised the dagger. "You want this?"

"No," said Tara. "I'm sorry, it was a mistake. I'm very sorry."

"Too late!" Zarku raised the dagger. The steel flashed silver. He brought it swishing down through the air and slashed his arm.

Tara's scream died in her throat. She watched, mesmerized, as the blood welled out of the deep cut and dripped to the floor and on the white muslin, mingling with hers. He didn't utter a whimper.

Zara, what's happening? What did you make me do? Why is he doing this?

Zara did not reply.

Zarku raised the dagger again. Tara leaned as far back as she could, unable to move, her eyes riveted to the steel blade. This time he was sure to slash her face or stab her in the heart. Once again the dagger swished through the air. This time, Zarku sliced his thigh. A red patch spread rapidly on his pajamas.

Tara stared at him horrified. Why was he punishing himself? Did he actually think she'd feel sorry for him?

"Shall I continue or will you behave, *Didi*?"

It was as if a rock had fallen on her head. He was punishing *her* all right — by injuring Suraj!

"Stop!" she shrieked. "Stop, please. I'll do anything you say. Please don't hurt Suraj anymore."

"That's better," said Zarku. "One more silly move from you and I'll cut off an arm or a leg. In a short while this body will be useless to me." His hysterical laughter filled her ears, but she didn't dare cover them. She didn't dare move. Zarku lowered the dagger and walked away, a trail of blood marking his path. Tara fell to her feet and touched her brother's lifeblood, smearing it on her fingertips. What had she done? In a few moments, Zarku would sacrifice her, and leave Suraj's body behind. Badly injured. Would her little brother survive after she was gone? What would happen to him and Sadia? Pain welled up from deep within her and came bubbling up to her throat, her eyes and spilled over.

Zara, what did you make me do? said Tara weeping silently.

There was still no answer.

• • •

"Scared?" said Kali, a triumphant smile on her face.

Tara wiped her eyes and faced Kali defiantly. "No. You?"

"Liar," said Kali. "Finally you get what you deserve. I will be cheering him on!"

Tara had no words in retaliation. Didn't have the energy, either. They had won; evil had won in the end ...

In the centre of the room, Zarku, all cleaned up and wearing fresh clothes, sat cross-legged on the muslin cloth spread out in the middle of the room. He struck a match. The flare lit up the urn that was so familiar to Tara by now. Beside it lay a heap of silvery wood cut up into small pieces, and the gleaming dagger, its blade now spotless.

Chanting under his breath, Zarku lit the end of one of the sticks of wood and dropped it into the urn. The flame caught and an orange-red glow emanated from within. Zarku added another and yet another sliver of wood. The fire burned brighter, leaping toward the black ceiling.

Zarku picked up the dagger and held the blade over the flames. It glowed a blinding white, and then as she watched, it turned black. As black as the walls around her.

He looked up at Tara, the red of the fire reflected in his eyes. She held her breath. He crooked his little finger and beckoned to her.

"It is time."

twenty-two

The Last Wish

The world spun crazily. Only when Tara's lungs were bursting for air did she realize she had been holding her breath.

"Come," Zarku repeated. He licked his lips, and they gleamed, red and wet.

Tara found herself moving toward him, her eyes riveted to that black blade with its silver handle inlaid with red rubies. The dagger was too big for his hand and yet he held it with such ease.

"Please," said Tara. "Don't do this."

"Stop this stupidity, Tara. I have waited months for this moment and nothing can stop me. Come closer."

Tara took a step toward him, every muscle, every nerve straining against it.

"Closer," he whispered. "Don't make me come there." His eyes glowed red and his forehead pulsed, as if some large insect just under his skin were trying to tear through it.

Tara walked right up to him, feeling the heat from the urn rise up between them. "What are you going to do?" asked Tara. There was a dagger in his hand and there she was. It was very clear, but still, she wanted to hear it from him. She was so scared, she was numb.

"Just a quick stab to your chest, I cut out your heart while it is still beating and …"

"And then?"

"I eat it." Zarku held her gaze, his eyes alight with excitement.

"No!" Tara wrapped her arms around her. "Never!" The thought of her beating heart in the hands of this evil soul made it race at triple speed. She took a step back, then another. Even the chasm would be a better fate than this.

"You didn't let me finish," said Zarku sternly. "I'll only take a tiny bite. The rest goes into the urn as an offering to my Lord. Your heart in the urn that held me — for an eternity."

She could think of nothing, see nothing but her heart carved up by that night-black blade. She had to delay this, keep him talking. She searched for something, anything, however stupid it might be, to stay Zarku's hand. She took a deep breath.

"How … how does that help you?" asked Tara. "You're making a huge mistake killing an innocent person."

"You? Innocent?" Zarku laughed. He raised the dagger.

"Wait," said Tara. "What happens to Suraj and Sadia after I am gone? Surely you'll let them live. I'm not sacrficing myself in vain."

"Ahhh, I knew you'd ask that."

"Promise me they'll both be safe," Tara. "Promise me that you will take them back home."

"I make no such promises."

"Surely you're not scared that two children will ruin your evil plans?" said Tara, trying to inject scorn into her shaking voice. "You owe me this at the very least." She bit down on the fear that ran rampant within, turning her insides to mush.

Zarku looked at her steadily. "You've been a good sport, Tara," he said, "and a worthy opponent. I'm in a generous mood so I'll grant you one last wish. Ask for anything but your life — that's mine."

It's better than nothing, thought Tara. This was her chance to ask for the children's lives. He would keep his word and take them back home safely. She'd have kept her promise to Kabir and Suraj would live. Yes, that was it.

No, Tara don't ask for that. Ask that he allow you to hug him. He needs to know, to feel, that I'm here.

"What?" screamed Tara, hating Zara at that moment, with her silences and crazy advice.

"Are you deaf?" said Zarku. He glared at her. "I said you have one last wish. Act funny and I'll cut your heart out without a moment's delay."

Zara, I have this one chance to save my brother and you're asking me to hug *your son? No, I can't do that. I listened to you once and that almost cost Suraj a limb. Don't do this again. Please!*

Hug him. Now! Zara used the firmest voice she had ever used with Tara. *You've failed me once already and you saw the consequence of that.*

Hug this monster? You're mad, Zara, I couldn't even bear to touch him.

"At last," whispered Kali. "Justice." Her lips curved into a smile.

Trust me, Tara. Do it, now.

Tara's clothes stuck to her. Sweat poured into her eyes, blinding her, and her head ached viciously. What if she was making a terrible mistake? This was Zarku's mother. Of course she would want to embrace her son through Tara. But how would that save her brother and Sadia? Could she trust her?

On this one decision rested three lives.

twenty-three

The Evil Doubles

"**I**'m waiting," said Zarku.

Tara was mesmerized by the bead of sweat trickling down his pulsing forehead. In a short while, Zarku would be in another, more powerful body. She had to act now.

"But of course if you'd rather just get this over with," Zarku continued, "I don't mind at all. I want to finish this quickly, too. I've been in this miserable little body for far too long."

"I'd like to give you a hug."

Zarku's mouth fell open, all other expression wiped clean from his face. Without thinking about it or waiting for Zarku's permission, Tara embraced him.

She felt a powerful, agonizing surge within her, as if everything inside had been ripped from their moorings and was trying to burst out of her body. She closed her eyes and focused on Suraj, his innocent face, the games they'd played, his fun-loving spirit, and all the love she felt for him.

Zarku squirmed in her grasp, fighting her, trying to throw her off.

Don't let him go, Tara. Not yet.

Tara hugged him harder, tighter, holding that writhing body to her, hoping her brother would remember his sister's touch. The pain almost ripped her apart, but she held on.

"I feel something within you, something strong," screamed Zarku. "You're possessed. What are you trying to do? LET ME GO!"

He wrenched himself from her grasp and pushed her away, breathing hard. "Don't you dare touch me again!"

"Your mother told me to do that," said Tara. She watched his face shadowed with fear.

Zarku sucked in his breath. "LIAR! My mother died when she gave birth to me. She's gone, forever."

"She's very much here, within me," said Tara. She lifted the hem of her shalwar. "Do you remember this anklet?"

It sparkled in the firelight. Zarku gazed at it, tiny pinpoints of silver now reflected in his eyes. His hard expression melted. His lips trembled. He dropped the dagger and fell at Tara's feet. He reached out and caressed the anklet.

"That ... that belongs to my mother." He looked up at her, his eyes glistening. "I thought I had lost it forever. How did you get it?"

His fingers closed over the anklet. Tara jerked her foot away.

"That night at the temple when you caught me," said Tara. "You threw me against the pole and it fell into the folds of my shawl. I've had it ever since."

"This was the last of my mother's possessions. You stole it from me— thief!" Zarku beat his fist on the ground. "I looked all over for it, but never could find it. Give it to me right now or I'll cut your foot off and take it."

"She's in me right now," said Tara. "That was what you felt when you hugged me. She has a message for you."

Zarku's expression softened and Tara allowed a wisp of hope to linger. The next moment he grabbed the dagger off the floor. "Enough! I should have cut your heart out already. You think I'll spare you because you hugged me and told me lies about my mother? All you've done is waste your last wish."

Tara found herself speaking without really knowing what she was going to say. The moment she heard the words, she knew it was Zara speaking through her. And it hurt.

"My son, Tara is telling the truth. I am here. I have been with Tara all this while, watching you."

Zarku took a step back. "No, it can't be. You're playing games with me by changing your voice, Tara. Stop it, STOP IT!"

"Only you can stop what you set in motion," said Zara.

Zara's voice was deeper than Tara's. It made her shudder to hear it come out of her own mouth, to say things that she was not even thinking about. Her insides were icy. It felt like someone was twisting them ... the pain was unbearable, but she didn't want to stop Zara. Not until she had gotten through to her son.

"I am so ashamed at what you've done, what you've become."

Zarku was listening intently. His hands hung limply by his sides.

Go closer to him, Tara, Zara silently instructed.

Tara moved closer so that she was looking down at him. Zarku stared up at her, the anger and madness gone from his eyes.

"I'm sorry," he said. "But if you knew how I'd been treated. How everyone made fun of me."

"I know all that, but have you ever stopped to think that God might have given you that third eye for wisdom? Just like the one he gave Lord Shiva? Why did you think it was a deformity?"

"Even Father hated me," he said.

"You mustn't blame him too much," said Zara. *"He was grieving for me."*

"Where did that leave me?" yelled Zarku. "How could you expect me to love when all I received was hate?"

"I loved you," said Zara. *"And I still do."*

Zarku stared into the fire that was burning low. Absently, he added another sliver of wood from the pile.

Let this work, prayed Tara. *Let him give up this mad plan.*

Zarku walked away without a word. He went to the opposite wall and laid his cheek against it as if listening to something. Could Zara really have gotten through to him?

Kali had been silent all this while. "Is Zarku's mother really inside you or are you just trying to be clever?" she asked.

Tara gave her the ugliest look she could muster.

Tara, tell her that the only reason she had a husband is because her father bought her one. She's a pathetic old woman, doomed to unhappiness in life and in death.

Tara repeated what Zara had just said and watched Kali turn white. "You're lying! And what do you mean by 'in death.' I'm not going to die. You are."

"Zara told me," said Tara. "And I think it's true."

That shut Kali up for the moment.

Zarku came back to Tara. His cheeks were wet and his eyes glistened. Had Zara got through to him? Was he actually feeling sorry for what he had done? A minute ticked by, as Tara watched, waiting for him to speak first.

Zarku burst into laughter.

"That was good, Tara," he said. "That was really, really good. For a moment there you almost had me fooled. But enough. Let's get on with the ritual."

"It's the truth," said Tara. "You've got to believe me."

"Zarku!" said Zara. Her voice was like a whiplash. *"Enough!"*

251

Zarku stared at Tara. The dagger slipped from his hand and clattered to the floor.

"Listen to me. You will leave Suraj right now. You still have a chance to save your spirit from roaming the Underworld eternally. Let me help you."

"What are you asking me to do, Mother?"

"That you give up all hope of power, a new body, life, too. It's time to die my son, it's time to sleep."

"No!" said Zarku. "I haven't suffered for so long only to give up at the end."

"Son, the life you will lead will be a waste. And if you go through with this, I'll fight you. I'll fight you with everything I have. The Gods are on my side."

"You'd do that to your own son?" said Zarku. "You hate me so much?"

"It's because I love you that I want you to stop this, Zarku. Come away with me now. Give my spirit the rest it deserves."

Zarku backed away. "I can't betray Lord Kubera. He's depending on me."

"Yes you can," said Zara. *"I'll help you."*

The walls of the cave trembled and from its depths emerged a shadow, the first that Tara had seen. The large, shapeless shadow moved restlessly, from wall to ceiling to floor so that Tara, following it with her eyes, didn't know where it would appear next.

"Zarku," said the shadow, its voice but a faint whisper in the darkness. "Who saved you when everyone else had forsaken you? I did! Who gave you the power to control men? I did! Who will restore you and fulfill your dreams? I will! You cannot forsake me now."

"Don't listen to him," said Zara. *"You owe him nothing."*

Zarku cowered, clutching his head. Tara's insides ached viciously.

The shadow approached Zarku. He backed away into a corner. The shadow followed. It enveloped Zarku — there was the hint of a whisper. The shadow towered over Zarku and then it was gone, swallowed by the black wall behind him.

Tara held her breath. Zara was quiet.

"All right, Mother," said Zarku after a long silence. "I'll do as you say."

Tara breathed deeply. Had this really worked? Would he let her and the children escape?

Kali ran up to Zarku. "You can't do that. What about our plan? We were going to be powerful and rule over all those idiots who had hurt you. Have you forgotten? Are you going to let a little girl play tricks on you?"

She retrieved the blade and slapped it into his hand. "Finish what you started, Zarku. Stop being a coward."

"Don't listen to her," said Tara. "Listen to your mother. For once listen to someone who loves you."

Zarku walked up to Tara. "You win."

He stepped up to the urn and threw in some more wood. The dying flames leaped up hungrily. Zarku closed his eyes and chanted a few words. A low humming sound filled the room. The next moment a howling wind barrelled through the small cave, churning up the dust and dirt. Rocks and pebbles flew in the air, whipping around Tara, grazing her exposed skin. The fire in the urn went out. The wind caught it up and smashed it against the wall. Kali screamed in agony and the hyena fled the cave, laughing. Tara shielded her eyes. Zarku stood motionless in the centre of the cave, staring at her. Then he fell to the ground in a swoon.

At that precise moment the wind stopped. Tara coughed. Her throat was so dry and scratchy she wanted to tear it out. They were in a thick fog with dust and debris still floating around them.

"Suraj," she whispered, "are you all right?"

Suraj stirred, whimpering softly.

Tara wiped his face and kissed him. "Suraj, wake up."

Suraj opened his eyes. "Didi?" He spoke in his normal voice.

"Yes, it's me," she said. She cupped his face and stared into his eyes.

"Suraj," said Tara. "Is this really you or this another sick joke, Zarku?"

"It's me, Didi," he whispered. "I'm so tired. Take me home. Take me home to Mother."

Tara ran a finger over his forehead. Nothing bulged or pulsed there. Could this miracle really have happened? She had gotten Suraj back and she was alive! *Thank you Zara, thank you so much.*

The cave was suddenly very cold. The hair on the back of her neck tingled. Something was not quite right.

"Zarku?" said Tara. She looked around her. The dust still hadn't settled. Nothing stirred. No one said a word.

Silence.

"Kali?"

No one answered.

"Kali, answer me!" said Tara.

There was a groan at the back of the cave. Tara plucked the lantern from the niche and peered into the gloom. Kali shifted, groaning softly. There was no sign of Zarku or the last hyena. She ignored Kali and helped Suraj to his feet. She turned around and there was Kali. Right behind her.

"Don't just stand there," said Tara in a cold voice. "Your plans for wreaking havoc have gone up in smoke, but if you behave, I might tell the villagers to show some mercy."

Kali stood motionless, staring at Tara.

"Don't just stand there like an idiot," snapped Tara. "Have your brains disappeared along with Zarku? Help me."

Kali smiled. The smile became a wide grin. The chill inside Tara grew.

"Why are you smiling?" said Tara. "He's gone! Forever."

Kali stepped closer. Tara stared at her. Kali took another step, her eyes fixed on Tara. Tara lowered Suraj to the ground. This was not right. Kali should be defeated, broken. Instead here she was, staring at her defiantly.

Zara, what is this?

Oh, Zarku, what have you done? said Zara.

But before Tara could ask another question, Kali lunged at her.

Tara sprinted away, the lantern knocking against her knees. Behind her the thump of Kali's footsteps kept pace.

Tara stopped short of the chasm. She turned. There stood Kali grinning maniacally. On her forehead an all-too-familiar bulge pulsed ominously.

twenty-four

The Silver Anklet

"No!" breathed Tara. "NO!"

"Yes, Tara, YES." Kali spoke in a voice that was much thicker, stronger. "It's me, Zarku."

"But, you promised that you would give up, that you would leave. Are you really so evil that you would lie to your own mother who loves you?"

"Yes!" said Zarku. His smile chilled her; it was a combination of his and Kali's, malevolent through and through. "How could I give up this life of power? I couldn't do it, Tara. I just couldn't."

Tara stared at Kali, her skin crawling as if a hundred insects were swarming over it. *Zara, how could this have happened?*

I'm sorry, Tara. I didn't expect this, either. Zarku is under Lord Kubera's influence. Much more than I ever imagined.

"And now *with* Kali, *through* Kali," Zarku continued, "I can still carry out my plans. "She and I love and hate the same things."

"NEVER," said Tara. "I'll never let you carry out the plan. I'll stop you or die trying."

"We know," said Zarku. "Because we're going to kill you — now."

Tara wracked her brains; she was too close to give up now. If only she could keep them talking, she might be able to find a way. She looked behind her. They were almost at the chasm.

"You'll never get away with it," said Tara. "Kali has been banned from all the villages. The moment she shows up, she'll be stoned to death. You'll die along with her."

"I could still go back to my former plan, Tara," said Zarku. "My Lord has not forsaken me yet. He whispered to me just before he left. I'd tell you what he said, but then I'd have to kill you." He laughed long and hard. "Oops, forgot. I'm going to do that, anyway."

As he was speaking, the glimmer of a plan emerged from the gloom in her mind. It was her last chance and it had to work.

"The first thing we have to do is get rid of all of you," said Zarku. "Suraj and Sadia will be no problem at all. They're half dead anyway. They won't feel a thing when we tip them over the edge. You, Tara, might be a problem. You won't give us too much trouble, will you? It'll be a quick push, an exciting fall, and then it's over."

Tara moved back a step, very slowly and cautiously.

What are you doing, Tara?

Tara tried to keep her mind absolutely blank. She did not want to reveal her plan to Zara just yet, didn't want her blurting it out to her son. This was *her* plan and it had to work.

"Think about what I said," said Zarku. He turned to go. "I'm going to take care of the children first."

"No!" said Tara. "Deal with me first." Her heart pounded. What if this didn't work? She pushed the thought aside, not taking her eyes off Kali.

Tara inched backward, glancing quickly behind her. The edge was a few feet away. Darkness billowed out from the chasm like steam from a volcano. It seemed to tug at her. Her foot hit a rock. It clattered over the edge into silence.

Kali advanced, one sure step at a time. "At last, Tara. Do you know how long we've both waited for this moment? Ahhh, it will be sweet ..."

Tara inched sideways. She heard a low growl and stopped, her heart almost stopping, too. Yellow eyes emerged from the darkness; the third hyena. Tara had forgotten all about it. It advanced on her slowly, hemming her in, pushing her back.

Lord Ganesh, you couldn't have brought me all the way here to fail so miserably. I can't die! This has to work. Please help me ... Tara prayed, see-sawing between hope and utter despair.

What are you doing, Tara? You're too close to the edge. Get back into the cave. We'll think of something else.

Tara ignored her.

Kali came closer, smiling. The narrow path was but a few steps toward Tara's left. Time slowed, even her heartbeat slowed, and she saw and heard everything clearly, sharply.

Kali was almost upon her. Tara planted her feet apart and braced herself. She knew what was coming. She tensed. With a triumphant cry, Kali ran at her, her arms outstretched. "Goodbye, Tara."

Tara immediately threw herself flat on the ground. Kali reached her at a full run, tripped over her, and flew over the lip of the chasm.

"NOOOOO!" howled Kali as she scrabbled at the crumbling edge, trying to pull herself up.

Tara tried to stand, but her legs shook so much that she had to crawl away from the edge as fast as she could.

"Help!" said Kali, still using that thick voice. "Tara, help me and I'll spare you. I'll give you unimaginable power … anything you desire."

Tara laughed hysterically. "No, Zarku. It was your mother's wish that you stop this and I agree. And it's time for you, too, Kali. Time to die!"

She got to her feet, which seemed to have turned to jelly, and backed away. Kali peered over the edge of the chasm, still holding to the lip tightly, and screamed at the hyena, "Kill her!"

The hyena stood there, undecided. Then it turned around and vanished into the darkness.

"Come here!" she screeched. But the hyena had disappeared. Kali slipped a bit more. Tara watched her, filled with self-loathing. *I hate having to do this, Zara. It's so hard to take a life, any life, no matter how evil.*

I know, Tara. But finish what you started. Push them over the edge. Don't let them get back up. My son had his chance and he chose the evil of the Underworld where he'll wander forever with the likes of Kali. Do it. Zara's voice held so much pain that Tara felt it overflow into her. She was drowning in sadness.

Tara walked over to the edge of the chasm. Kali looked up at her, beseeching her silently. Tara raised her foot.

"No! Tara, don't do it," she yelled. "Zarku will give you whatever you want. Believe him. He even showed me how to communicate with my daughter … from a distance."

"I don't want anything but to see you both dead," said Tara. "To rid Morni of all evil. Both of you in one shot!"

Kali cackled madly. "You think you'll end all evil by killing us, Tara? Think again! Layla is still in Morni and she will avenge my death, mine and Zarku's. You watch … ahhhhhhhh …"

Tara had stomped hard on Kali's hand and ground it with the heel of her mojri while she had been speaking. Kali let go, the expression on her face, pure, undiluted venom. Within seconds the darkness pulled her within its depths.

Tara peeped over the edge, trembling with exhaustion. They were both gone. She had done it. It was over.

Her knees buckled and she sat down, all the fear flowing out of her in huge, wracking sobs. Finally there was nothing more inside. She unclasped the anklet and kissed it. The silver was cool against her parched lips.

You did it, Tara. You did what I was not able to do.

Will you stay with me forever? asked Tara silently.

No, Tara. You have to do one last thing for me.

Anything, replied Tara.

Throw me into the chasm.

No! I want you to stay with me. I'm sorry I ever doubted you.

Do it, Tara. I have no desire to return to the living world again. Please.

Tara once again stepped to the edge. She stared at the anklet on her palm, kissed it one last time. Then she tilted her hand. It slid off, disappearing in a glint of silver.

Goodbye, Zara.

Tara walked back to the cave. Suraj had managed to crawl over to Sadia and wake her. They sat huddled at the entrance, two woebegone figures. They got to their feet with much effort as soon as they saw her.

The darkness pressed down on Tara's thin shoulders. Every part of her ached with exhaustion.

"We're going home, aren't we, Didi?" said Suraj. He stood up and slipped his hand through hers. Sadia looked up at her with a tired, watery smile. "I want to see Kabir."

Tara squared her shoulders and picked up Sadia. She had a promise to keep. And one more person to take care of — Layla.

"Come on," said Tara. "We're going home."

The End

Below are English translations of the many Hindi words used in The Silver Anklet

Aloo-puri	Potatoes and fried bread, a popular Indian snack.
Ambala	A district in the state of Haryana, India.
Bhiwani	District of Haryana.
Biryani	A South Asian dish made primarily of rice, spices, meat and/or vegetables.
Choli	A fitted blouse with short sleeves.
Didi	Elder sister.
Dupatta	A long scarf that is part of the Indian outfit and has long been a symbol of modesty.
Ghaggar	Main seasonal river of Haryana, an Indian state.

Ghaghra	A long, flowing skirt reaching to the calves or ankles.
Guava	Fruit that grows in the tropics.
Hissar	District of Haryana.
Kalesar Forest	Kalesar Forest, 150 kilometres from Chandigarh, is a sal forest in Shivalik Hills, a name given to the foothills of the Himalayas.
Kebab	Seasoned, minced meat wrapped around a stick (to maintain its shape) and then cooked. It resembles a hot dog when cooked and slid off the stick.
Koel	A bird that is a member of the cuckoo family.
Kumbhkaran	One of the brothers of Ravana, the antagonist in the famous epic, *Ramayana*. Kumbhkaran — through a boon granted by Brahma — slept for six months at a time, waking only to eat vast quantities of food.
Kurta-pajama	A loose shirt falling just above or at the knees and normally worn with loose trousers with a drawstring waistband.
Laddoos	Indian sweet made of flour and a variety of other ingredients,

	rolled into a ball and dipped in sugar syrup or has jaggery added to it.
Lord Ganesh	Elephant-headed god who is also considered the god of knowledge and the remover of obstacles.
Machan	A vantage point/seat built high up in the trees to spot game, namely tigers.
Mela	Fair/carnival.
Mithai	Indian sweets.
Mojri	Also known as pagrakhi, is a traditional ornamental leather footwear originating from Rajasthan.
Mushika	Vâhana or a Hindu vehicle, sometimes called a mount, is an animal, mythical entity closely associated with a particular deity in Hindu mythology. Ganesh's mount was a mouse named Mushika.
Papads	A wafer-thin flatbread made of lentils, chickpea, black gram, or rice flour.
Raat-ki-Raani	A shrub that goes by the botanical name of *Cestrum Nocturnum*. Its light-green flowers open at night and emit an intoxicating fragrance.

Rakhi	Holy thread tied by a sister on the wrist of her brother. The brother in return offers a gift to his sister and vows to look after her for as long as he lives.
Rasmalai	An Indian sweet where flattened balls of paneer (milk solids) are soaked in sweetened milk. (My favourite!)
Ritha	Also known as the soap-nut tree (*Sapindus mukorossi*) is one of the most important trees of Asia. The fruit has medicinal value. The Ayurvedic system of medicine uses it to treat common colds, epilepsy, and nausea.
Roti	Unleavened flatbread.
Saffron	A spice derived from the dried stigma of the flower of the saffron crocus.
Sal tree	Tall tree (*Shorea Robusta*) that provides good quality timber.
Shabash/Wah-wah	Expressions of praise.
Shalwar	A loose trouser with a drawstring waistband normally worn only by women.
Tandoor	Cylindrical clay oven used for cooking and baking. The food

	is cooked over hot charcoal or a wooden fire. Temperatures in a tandoor can reach 480°C (900°F).
Thali	A round tray made of steel or silver with smaller bowls or compartments in which a variety of foods are served.
Tulsi	This is a sacred plant of India (*Ocimum Sanctum*). The reddish-purple flowers are used in Ayurveda to treat cold, fever, cough, and bronchitis.
Vark or Varak	A foil of very pure silver and used for garnishing Indian sweets. The silver is edible, but flavourless.

— acknowledgements —

My heartfelt thanks to Uma Krishnaswami for her tough yet brilliant mentoring. Of all the advice she gave me, one piece is indelibly etched in my mind; when in doubt go deep instead of wide.

Rahul, Aftab, and Coby, you've been so patient and learned to ignore my crankiness when I'm writing, which is always. Thanks!

Mom, you're always there, supporting and encouraging me. Thank you!

Dad, you'll always be remembered for starting me down this path.

A warm hug to all my friends, especially Marsha Skrypuch and Helaine Becker.

Thanks to all the Kidcritters who continue to share selflessly, give useful suggestions, and nurture newcomers to the critique group.

And finally, thank you to the wonderful team at Dundurn, but especially to my patient and excellent editor, Shannon Whibbs.

The Third Eye
by Mahtab Narsimhan
978-1-55002-750-1
$12.99

For Tara and her brother, Suraj, the year since their mother
and grandfather fled the village of Morni has been a nightmare.
Their new stepmother is cruel and deceptive and the men of
the village have been disappearing, often returning in a strange,
altered form. When a new healer, Zarku, a mysterious man
with a third eye possessing strange power, suddenly appears
in Morni, all are mesmerized by his magic — all except Tara,
who sees through his evil disguise. With nothing but her own
courage and wit, Tara tries to find her missing mother and
grandfather, the true healer, in time to save her village.

— More Great Fiction for Young People —

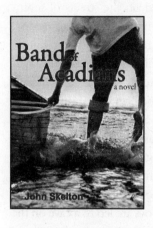

Band of Acadians
by John Skelton
978-1-55488-040-9
$12.99

In 1755, on the eve of the Seven Years' War, fifteen-year-old Nola and her Acadian parents face expulsion from Grand Pré by the British. Nola, her friends Hector and Jocelyne, Nola's grandfather, and a band of bold teenagers manage to flee by boat only to encounter challenges tougher than their wildest imaginings. Their destination is French-occupied Fort Louisbourg, but their journey is fraught with a series of obstacles and hair-raising adventures. Will the resourceful teenagers discover what it takes to prevail in a continent poised on the edge of irrevocable change?

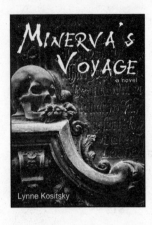

FROMMER'S
EasyGuide
TO
WALT DISNEY WORLD & ORLANDO

By
Jason Cochran

EasyGuides are ✦ Quick To Read ✦ Light To Carry
✦ For Expert Advice ✦ In All Price Ranges

FrommerMedia LLC

Published by
FROMMER MEDIA LLC
44 West 62nd Street
New York, NY 10023

ISBN 978-1-62887-011-4 (paper), 978-1-62887-041-1 (e-book)

Editorial Director: Pauline Frommer
Editor: Lorraine Festa
Production Editor: Heather Wilcox
Cartographer: Elizabeth Puhl
Page Compositor: Elizabeth Brooks
Cover Design: Howard Grossman

For information on our other products or services, see www.frommers.com.

Frommer Media LLC also publishes its books in a variety of electronic formats. Some content that appears in print may not be available in electronic formats.

Manufactured in the United States of America

5   4   3   2   1

CONTENTS

1 THE BEST OF ORLANDO 1

2 SUGGESTED ITINERARIES & ORLANDO'S LAYOUT 6

Orlando in 1 Day 6

Orlando in 2 Days 7

Orlando in 3 Days 8

Orlando in 1 Week 8

Getting to Know Orlando's Layout 9

3 EXPLORING WALT DISNEY WORLD 16

Ticketing 17

Eating on Site 22

Navigating Disney's Parks 23

The Magic Kingdom 26

Epcot 52

Disney's Hollywood Studios 69

Disney's Animal Kingdom 79

Disney Water Parks 89

Minor Disney World Diversions 92

4 UNIVERSAL, SEAWORLD & BEYOND 99

Universal Orlando 99

SeaWorld Orlando 122

Legoland Florida 133

Busch Gardens Tampa 135

5 MORE ORLANDO ATTRACTIONS 136

International Drive 136

Kennedy Space Center 149

Nightlife in Orlando 151

Nightlife at the Resorts 152

Outdoor Orlando 155

Shopping 162

Cruises from Port Canaveral 166

6 DINING AROUND TOWN 167

Outside the Disney Parks 167

Downtown Disney 171

Disney's BoardWalk 173

Universal Orlando 174

U.S. 192 & Lake Buena Vista 176

International Drive & Convention Center 179

Downtown Orlando 183

Dinnertainment 186

Character Meals 189

7 ORLANDO'S HOTELS 192

Getting the Best Rates 193

Orlando's Hotels 194

Inside Walt Disney World 198

Inside Universal Orlando 206

U.S. 192 Area Accommodations 208

Lake Buena Vista 212

International Drive, Universal 216

Around Downtown Orlando 221

Home Rentals 222

8 PLANNING YOUR TRIP TO ORLANDO 225

Getting There 225

Getting Around 227

Traveling from Orlando to Other Parts of America 230

When to Go 230

Fast Facts: Orlando 235

INDEX 246

ABOUT THE AUTHOR

Jason Cochran was awarded Guide Book of the Year by the Society of American Travel Writers' Lowell Thomas Travel Journalism Competition and by the North American Travel Journalists Association. He is the author of "Frommer's EasyGuide to London," and he wrote the London, Orlando, and San Francisco guides for the Pauline Frommer series. He has written for publications including the "New York Post," "Travel + Leisure," "USA Today," and "Scanorama" (Sweden) and been on staff at "Entertainment Weekly," "Budget Travel," and AOL Travel (Executive Editor). He devised questions for the first American prime-time season of "Who Wants to Be a Millionaire" (ABC) and produced and hosted "AfterShark," the AOL postshow for Mark Burnett's "Shark Tank" (ABC). He has appeared as a commentator on, among others, "CBS This Morning," "The Early Show" (CBS), "BBC World," "Good Morning America," CNN, BBC World, and the CBC, and he is a video host on AOL. He is an alumnus of Northwestern University's Medill School of Journalism and New York University's Graduate Music Theatre Writing Program, and he is the editor of Frommers.com.

ACKNOWLEDGMENTS

Thank you to all the cast members and staff members who assisted with information, access, and good humor. I also can't imagine doing without the on-the-ground assistance of Shanon Larimer, Wesley Brown, Jason Young, Tracy Temple, Kristin Harmel, Ken Kleiber, Katie Coleman (still), and Denise Spiegel and Heidi Colon of Visit Orlando. Finally, I am grateful to Arthur and Pauline Frommer. Their ideal of helping people of all means see the world with plainspoken, honest advice remains a beacon in an overwhelming ocean of information, and it continues to be an inspiration for many, including me.

ABOUT THE FROMMER TRAVEL GUIDES

For most of the past 50 years, Frommer's has been the leading series of travel guides in North America, accounting for as many as 24 percent of all guidebooks sold. I think I know why.

Although we hope our books are entertaining, we nevertheless deal with travel in a serious fashion. Our guidebooks have never looked on such journeys as a mere recreation, but as a far more important human function, a time of learning and introspection, an essential part of a civilized life. We stress the culture, lifestyle, history, and beliefs of the destinations we cover and urge our readers to seek out people and new ideas as the chief rewards of travel.

We have never shied from controversy. We have, from the beginning, encouraged our authors to be intensely judgmental, critical—both pro and con—in their comments, and wholly independent. Our only clients are our readers, and we have triggered the ire of countless prominent sorts, from a tourist newspaper we called "practically worthless" (it unsuccessfully sued us) to the many rip-offs we've condemned.

And because we believe that travel should be available to everyone regardless of their incomes, we have always been cost-conscious at every level of expenditure. Although we have broadened our recommendations beyond the budget category, we insist that every lodging we include be sensibly priced. We use every form of media to assist our readers and are particularly proud of our feisty daily website, the award-winning Frommers.com.

I have high hopes for the future of Frommer's. May these guidebooks, in all the years ahead, continue to reflect the joy of travel and the freedom that travel represents. May they always pursue a cost-conscious path, so that people of all incomes can enjoy the rewards of travel. And may they create, for both the traveler and the persons among whom we travel, a community of friends, where all human beings live in harmony and peace.

Arthur Frommer

THE BEST OF ORLANDO

I n 1886, a young unmarried mailman, frustrated with his fruitless toil in the Midwest, moved to the woolly wilderness of Central Florida to make a better go of life. The land was angry. Summers were oppressively hot, the lightning relentless, and the tough earth, sodden and scrubby, defied clearing. The only domestic creatures that thrived there, it seemed, were the cattle, and even they turned out stringy and chewy. Undaunted, the young man planted a grove of citrus trees and waited for things to get better. They didn't. His trees died in a freeze. Now penniless, he was forced to return to delivering mail, the very thing he had tried so hard to escape. By 1890, he gave up, defeated, and moved to Chicago to seek other work. The American dream appeared to fail Elias Disney.

The story could have ended there. But he was joined by his new bride, whose own father had died trying to tame Florida land. Back in the smoke of the Midwest, they had children and settled for an anonymous urban existence. One day, 8 decades later, long after the young man and woman had lived full lives and passed away, two of their sons, now in the sunset of their own lives, would return to Central Florida, to the land that broke their father, and together they would transform the recalcitrant swamp into the most famous fantasy land the world has even known.

Little did Elias know that the dream was only skipping a generation and that his sons Walt and Roy would become synonymous with the very land that rejected him. Had he known that the Disney name would in due time define Central Florida, would he have been so despondent? Even if he had been granted a fleeting vision of what was to be, and what his family would mean to this place—and, indeed, to the United States—would he have believed it?

The Disney brothers turned a place of toil into a realm of pleasure, a place where hardworking people can put their struggles aside. The English have their Blackpool; Canadians have their Niagara Falls. Orlando rose to become the preeminent resort for the working and middle classes of America, and the breathtaking ingenuity of its inventions now inspires visitors from everywhere. Although other countries segregate their holiday destinations by income or some other petty quality, Orlando, in the classic American egalitarian style, is all things to all people, from all countries and backgrounds.

Orlando represents something more powerful to American culture and history than merely being the fruit of a dream. It's something shared. No matter who you are, no matter your politics or upbringing, when you were a kid, you probably went at least once to Walt Disney World and Orlando—or, if you didn't, you desperately wanted to. Which other aspect of culture can we all claim to share? What else has given children such sweet dreams? I've often said that if somehow Walt Disney World went out of business tomorrow, the U.S. National Park Service would have to take it over—it means that much to the fabric of the nation.

Don't think of the amusements of Orlando as big business. Of course they are, and the incessant reminder of that sometimes threatens to shatter the fantasy. But Walt Disney World, and by extension Orlando, is also Americana incarnate. The taste for showmanship and fantasy that Walt Disney World crystallizes, now coined as the term "Disneyfication," has become the defining mind-set of our culture, in which even grocery stores and shopping malls are dressed like film sets and the "story" of your local burger joint is retold on the side of its soda cups.

Orlando tells us about who we dream of being. Virtually nothing about the tourist's Orlando is natural or authentic, and yet there may be no more perfect embodiment of American culture. To understand this invented landscape is to understand the values of its civilization and our generation. And if you observe Orlando with a long view—starting with young Elias Disney cutting his hands trying to budge a tough Florida pine—you will be a part of the explosive, unexpected powers of the American dream.

And one more thing: If you can relax a little, it's a hell of a lot of fun.

ORLANDO'S best THEME PARK EXPERIENCES

- **Walt Disney World:** Walt Disney World operates four top-drawer theme parks every day of the year: **Magic Kingdom,** the most popular theme park on Earth, is a more spacious iteration of the original Disneyland, the park that started it all, and is brimming with attractions that have been cherished since Walt's day; **Epcot** is a new-brew version of an old-style world's fair; **Disney's Animal Kingdom** blends animal habitats with theme-park panache; and **Disney's Hollywood Studios** presents a show-heavy salute to the movies.

- **Universal Orlando:** Often surpassing Disney in adrenaline and cunning, Universal Orlando's two parks, **Islands of Adventure** and **Universal Studios Florida,** command great respect and get the blood pumping a bit stronger, and both are home to immersive sections devoted to **The Wizarding World of Harry Potter;** the Studios' section is scheduled to open in 2014.

- **Beyond Disney and Universal:** Venture beyond the Big Six theme parks and you'll find more breathing room and more focused experiences. The gardens and marine mammals at **SeaWorld Orlando** make for a lower-paced excursion. Five water parks flow with kinesthetic energy: **Typhoon Lagoon** and **Aquatica** for family-friendly slides, **Blizzard Beach** for more aggressive ones, **Wet 'n Wild** for no-holds-barred thrills, and **Discovery Cove** for VIP swims with dolphins and reef fish. South of town, **Legoland Florida,** one of the best parks for very small children, charms with Old Florida touches, while **Gatorland** celebrates the region's *true* locals.

ORLANDO'S best
RIDES & SHOWS

○ **Walt Disney World:** More than any other park, the Magic Kingdom (p. 26) is packed with seminal experiences: the transporting Audio-Animatronic wizardry of **Pirates of the Caribbean** and **The Haunted Mansion;** the vertiginous thrills of **Splash Mountain** and **Space Mountain;** and the homespun, only-at-Disney charm of **Jungle Cruise, Peter Pan's Flight,** and **"it's a small world."** Cap the day with **Wishes,** the famous fireworks show. At Epcot (p. 52), **Soarin'** is the ride with the resort's highest re-ride ratio, and at Disney's Hollywood Studios (p. 69), the ride-through 3-D video game **Toy Story Midway Mania** is never the same experience twice, while the **Twilight Zone Tower of Terror** has an innovative design repeated nowhere else in the world.

○ **Universal Orlando:** At Islands of Adventure (p. 112), **Harry Potter and the Forbidden Journey** fires on more technological cylinders than you thought a ride could possess, while **The Amazing Adventure of Spider-Man** has been the standard holder for premium ride concepts for more than a decade. But don't miss **Dudley Do-Right's Ripsaw Falls** or **Popeye & Bluto's Bilge-Rat Barges,** a pair of ingeniously sopping flumes. At Universal Studios, **Revenge of the Mummy** is a spot-on indoor coaster with a few surprise twists, and **Transformers: The Ride 3D** represents the cutting edge in sound and visual design. Fans of Springfield will find themselves re-riding **The Simpsons Ride** to catch all the insider references.

○ **The Other Parks:** At SeaWorld Orlando (p. 122), roller coasters pack punches that Disney pulls: **Manta** flies riders belly-down over water and rooftops, while **Kraken** dangles their feet for seven spine-knotting inversions. Its two polar pavilions, **Wild Arctic** and **Antarctica,** new in 2013, are among its best habitats. The spectacular killer whale show, currently **One Ocean,** is perennially beloved (p. 125). Elsewhere, Wet 'n Wild's **Bomb Bay** (p. 139) is one of the most sadistic water slides ever devised, while Legoland Florida's tricked-out **Miniland USA** (p. 135) is such a tour de force of Lego creation that it's a show of its own.

ORLANDO'S best
OVERLOOKED EXPERIENCES

○ **From Earth to the Moon:** The **Kennedy Space Center** (p. 149) sent Americans into space for more than half a century, and for decades NASA's nerve center was the focus of tourist attention, but a majority of today's visitors remain securely within Disney's orbit. That's a huge shame. The Kennedy Center is where you can see proof of America's glory days as an exploratory power, including some out-of-this-world space vehicles, such as the **Saturn V rocket,** the largest rocket ever made, which sent 27 men to the moon, and the **Space Shuttle orbiter** *Atlantis,* still coated with space dust in a $100-million multimedia exhibition that opened in 2013. You can even undergo astronaut training.

○ **Connecting with Others:** More Make-a-Wish kids request visits to Orlando than anywhere else, and you can help make their dreams come true at the fantasy resort built just for them, **Give Kids the World Village** (p. 146) in Kissimmee. There are hundreds of jobs for volunteers here (which can be done in just a few hours), including handing out presents or scooping ice cream. And since the late 1800s, the moss-draped **Cassadaga** (p. 143) has been the exclusive domain of psychics and mediums, and they invite visitors to explore their spiritualist town for readings.

○ **Undiscovered Disney:** Even inside the theme parks, as other guests stampede for the nearest thrill ride, you can find relatively off-the-beaten-path treasures. The most fruitful ground for those is **Epcot**'s World Showcase, where many pavilions contain little-seen museums to the heritage of their lands, including the **Stave Church Gallery** in Norway (p. 61), China's **House of the Whispering Willow** (p. 61), the **Bijutsu-kan Gallery** in Japan (p. 63), and the **Gallery of Arts and History** in Morocco (p. 64). At the Magic Kingdom, you can get a haircut on Main Street's **Harmony Barber Shop** (p. 33). At Disney's Hollywood Studios, the artifact-stuffed **Sid Cahuenga's One-of-a-Kind Antiques and Curios** (p. 77) is a gift shop like none other in WDW. And the entire Disney World resort offers a slate of small-group **behind-the-scenes tours** (p. 95) that uncover hundreds of secrets.

ORLANDO'S best
AUTHENTIC EXPERIENCES

○ **Florida, Your Eden:** Although the theme parks have come to define Orlando, Central Florida has a long tale of its own, if you're willing to listen. There are more fresh springs here than in any other American state. You'll always remember swimming in the 72-degree waters of **De Leon Springs State Park** (p. 156), canoeing them at **Wekiwa Springs State Park** (p. 157), or meeting the at-risk manatees in their natural habitat at **Blue Spring State Park** (p. 155).

○ **Florida, the Gilded Age Idyll:** Of course, Orlando's identity as a sunny theme-park mecca only began in 1971, but visitors from the north have been coming for a century. Sample the high art collected by its high-society settlers at Winter Park's **Charles Hosmer Morse Museum of American Art** (including a massive collection of Tiffany glass; p. 143) or the **Cornell Fine Arts Museum** (with lush decorative arts of every description; p. 145). Peep at their historic mansions, whose lawns slope invitingly to the tranquil lakes of Winter Park, on the long-running **Scenic Boat Tour** (p. 158).

○ **Florida, Land of Flowers:** The reason all those blue bloods migrated here? The fine weather and the beautiful water. The horticultural achievements at **Harry P. Leu Gardens** (p. 156), practically smack in downtown Orlando, remind you just how bountiful the soil here can be. Or lose yourself at **Bok Tower Gardens** (p. 145); its builder set out to create a Taj Mahal for America, and its landscaping is by Frederick Law Olmsted, Jr., whose other work includes the White House and the National Mall.

○ **Florida, the Original Tourist Draw:** Today, nothing is more quintessentially Orlando than Disney, but a few other major attractions never feel jammed: **Legoland Florida** (p. 133) ambles pleasantly on a lakeside that was once home to Cypress Gardens, Florida's original mega-park and a haunt for everyone from Esther Williams to Elvis Presley. Its historic botanical garden has been prized since the 1930s. **Gatorland** (p. 146) is a pleasing, corn-fed throwback from an era when Central Florida was synonymous with reptiles rather than the Mouse.

ORLANDO'S best HOTELS

o **Inside the Theme Park Resorts: Disney's Contemporary Resort** (p. 204) and **Disney's Polynesian Resort** (p. 204), which opened in 1971, have become architectural landmarks, and their location on the monorail system makes a vacation easy and fun, but the new **Disney's Art of Animation Resort** (p. 200) elevates the resort's lowest-priced rooms into something approaching immersive. Universal's **Cabana Bay Beach Resort** (p. 206), new for 2014, promises a layer of style on its own budget category, and the **Hard Rock Hotel** (p. 207) is everything you'd want a well-located, party-all-the-time resort theme park hotel to be.

o **Full-Service Resorts Outside the Parks:** Exquisite restaurants and unbeatable pool areas made the Grande Lakes' **JW Marriott** and the **Ritz-Carlton** (p. 220) two names to beat among Orlando's luxury resorts, while **Nickelodeon Suites** (p. 215), rocking with extravagant pool areas and nonstop entertainment, rules the area in full-service fun for kids. Taking the theme-park ethic to a hospitality extreme, the colossal atrium of **Gaylord Palms** (p. 215) is like a big top for eye candy.

o **Affordability Without Sacrifice:** New arrivals **Drury Inn Suites** (p. 218) and **Fairfield Inn Orlando International Drive/Convention Center** (p. 216) can buy you a just-built room near the action for under $100 a night. **WorldQuest Resort** (p. 214) and **Meliá Orlando Suite Hotel at Celebration** (p. 211) have style and space but not the crowds and offer one-bedroom units from $129. Or rent a full house, as tastefully furnished as if you lived there, from **All Star Vacation Homes** (p. 223).

ORLANDO'S best RESTAURANTS

o **The Most Memorable Meals at the Resorts:** Orlando is one of those places where even blasé restaurants are priced like splurges, but some special-occasion tables get you the most bang for your buck, including **California Grill** (overlooking the Magic Kingdom fireworks from atop the Contemporary Resort; p. 170, **Todd English's bluezoo** (serving impeccable fish; p. 171), **Boma** (serving an all-you-can-eat feast in a hotel where you can watch African animals roam; p. 170); and the famous **character meals,** where your fuzzy hosts serve up family memories (p. 189).

o **Finding Family-Run Places to Eat:** Some fabulous restaurants, many family-run, have been unfairly elbowed into the background by same-old, also-ran chains. Orlando's real-world selection puts Epcot's World Showcase to shame, and at a fraction of the price: **Bruno's Italian Restaurant** (*abbondanza!* right in the franchise zone of Disney, too!; p. 178); **Nile Ethiopian Cuisine** (authentically African, down to the coffee ceremony, near Disney; p. 182); **Havana's Cuban Cuisine** (the real stuff, right by Disney; p. 179); and Uzbek cuisine—yes, Uzbek—at **Atlas House,** just 10 minutes from Universal or the Mouse (p. 178).

o **Big Style, Local Flavors:** Get in touch with the locals: The veggie chili at the friendly hangout **Dandelion Communitea Cafe** (p. 183) is to die for, and the quirky personalities of homegrown **Funky Monkey Wine Company** (p. 183) and **Maxine's on Shine** (p. 185) are seductive fun. Above all, the sensationally priced Vietnamese district of **Mills 50** (p. 184) is a revelation. Yes, as it turns out, there are still dining secrets in this town.

SUGGESTED ITINERARIES & ORLANDO'S LAYOUT

Millions of folks get to Walt Disney World at some point in their lives, but not everyone has to submit to the peer pressure of microscopic overplanning to do it. This is the guidebook for the rest of us—for those of us who refuse to submit to rigid timetables and who remember that we go to Orlando to unwind and have fun. This is the guidebook that shows you how to navigate the patterns of these American treasures without the stress of obsessing over every nuance, and it embellishes enjoyment with context about what you're experiencing.

For starters, don't march into the parks with a stopwatch and a map like a military strategist. That's the surest way to have a rocky vacation and to make some miserable memories. You'll get the most out of Disney not by conquering it but by opening yourself up to discoveries. Besides, fixed plans of attack are easily rendered useless by weather changes, crowds, or breakdowns by either rides or children.

A welter of Disney sites and books drown you in minutiae, but the routes suggested here, loose enough to let the magic in, prioritize what's worth seeing and when. These itineraries assume mild lines (so, not peak season), and if you would like to try a specific table-service restaurant, arrive with reservations, particularly for Cinderella's Royal Table and Be Our Guest. The whole World is in your hands.

ORLANDO IN 1 DAY

Well, I'm sorry for you. Just as it's impossible to eat an entire box of Velveeta in one sitting (please don't try), you can't get the full breadth of Orlando in a single day.

Today: Make It a Magic Kingdom Day ★★★

Thankfully, one Orlando attraction is so quintessential that you can enjoy it all by itself: Walt Disney World's **Magic Kingdom** (p. 26). In chapter 3, I recommend three custom itineraries (p. 30) for how to parse your time—with or without kids—but no matter your age or inclination, don't miss the great Disney Audio-Animatronic odysseys

THE SIX BIGGEST DISNEY mistakes

1. Overpurchasing ticket options.
2. Wearing inadequate footwear. It's said you'll walk 10 miles a day.
3. Neglecting sunscreen and water. Even Florida's cloudy weather can burn. One bad day can ruin the ones that follow.
4. Overplanning. Relax. You can never see it all in one trip, so don't try.
5. Underplanning. If you want to eat at the best sit-down restaurants or enjoy a character meal, it's wise to reserve 3 to 6 months out.
6. Pushing kids too hard. When they want to slow down, indulge them. You came here to enjoy yourselves, remember?

Pirates of the Caribbean ★★★, Haunted Mansion ★★★, and "it's a small world" ★★★, and be sure to brave the drops of Splash Mountain ★★★ and Space Mountain ★★★. While you're there, take a free spin on the monorail through the iconic Contemporary Resort and then connect for the free round-trip ride to Epcot (p. 52) and back, where you'll see the other top Disney park from above. Stay until closing, through the parade and fireworks, or, if you've had enough, head to a quintessentially kitschy dinner banquet spectacle, such as Arabian Nights ★★ (p. 186). Hope you're not hungry for subtlety!

ORLANDO IN 2 DAYS

Nope, still can't do much, but in two sleeps you can still get a few flavors in.

Day 1: Magic Kingdom

Get the same early start as recommended in "Orlando in 1 Day" and follow the Magic Kingdom plan for sure.

Day 2: Universal Orlando's Islands of Adventure ★★★ & Epcot ★★★

Today, be at Universal's Islands of Adventure (p. 112), one of the most attractive theme parks in the country, for opening. Dive into the impeccably created Wizarding World of Harry Potter ★★★ before the lines grow. Explore the shops, full of bespoke souvenirs you can only buy here, and give your system a dose of Butterbeer. After lunch at Three Broomsticks ★★★, take a spin on the superlative Amazing Adventures of Spider-Man ★★★, and jolt yourself on The Incredible Hulk Coaster ★★★.

Drag yourself from Islands of Adventure to pass a few hours in Epcot (p. 52). From Universal, drive west on Interstate 4 and take the exit for Epcot. At Epcot, be sure to visit Future World, including Soarin' ★★★ and the traditional Disney experience, Spaceship Earth ★★★, but make your way clockwise around World Showcase by dinnertime to select the ethnic eatery that catches your fancy, be it in Mexico ★★★, Japan ★★★, or Morocco ★★★. Or stop at the central U.S.A. ★★★ pavilion for a good, old-fashioned hot dog. At 9pm, you'll be in the right place for IllumiNations ★★★, part kumbaya and part explosives spectacular.

ORLANDO IN 3 DAYS

Days 1–2: Magic Kingdom & Universal Orlando

Day 1: **Magic Kingdom,** as above. But on Day 2, slam through the highlights of the Universal parks with a 1-day, 2-park pass. In the morning, see **Islands of Adventure** ★★★, as on the second day of the 2-day plan, and fill the afternoon with Universal Studios, a 5-minute walk north. Don't neglect some of its most celebrated rides—**Transformers: The Ride—3D** ★★ and **Revenge of the Mummy** ★★★ chief among them—and if the new **Wizarding World of Harry Potter—Diagon Alley** has opened by the time you visit, that will more than complete your day. Fill up on the sarcastically named dishes at **Fast Food Boulevard** (p. 111) in the new and daringly whimsical **Springfield** addition.

Day 3: SeaWorld ★★★, Disney & a Taste of "Real" Orlando

If you have small kids or you need something more subdued today, then **SeaWorld Orlando** (p. 122), with its **Shamu** show and multiple marine animal habitats, makes for a soothing change of pace. That could take a whole day if you saw every little thing and stopped to smell the flowers (and fish), but you can see the highlights in 4 hours, and you only have 3 days, after all. So cram a secondary Disney park into your afternoon and evening. **Epcot**'s a fine choice (see the afternoon of Day 2 of the 2-day itinerary for a good plan), but **Disney's Animal Kingdom**'s ★★ wildlife walking trails make a nice, easygoing complement to a morning spent at SeaWorld. Animal Kingdom isn't a late-night park, so during the evening, spend a night at the shopping-and-clubs zone of Universal's **CityWalk** ★★ (p. 153) or go out into "real" Orlando for the Vietnamese culinary delights of **Mills 50** (p. 184) downtown.

ORLANDO IN 1 WEEK

Days 1–5: Orlando at Your Leisure

Finally—you're approaching a vacation long enough to enable you to actually relax and to take time to sit by the pool. Now you don't have to cram several parks into a single day unless you want to, so take more time on your first few days: first **Magic Kingdom,** then **Universal,** then **Epcot,** then the other two Disney parks, followed by **SeaWorld.** Of course, if you stick to a schedule as rigid as one major theme park per day, it will take you a week to knock down the seven biggies, and that's before setting your belly on a single water slide. Combining **Animal Kingdom** and **Hollywood Studios** ★★★ into a single day (see p. 86 for suggestions for how to pack it all in) is doable and won't cause you to miss too much, although with the opening of the second Harry Potter land, the same can no longer be said for Universal's parks—now they require a day and a half, at least. This combination lets you do the seven major parks in 5 days.

Fine-Tuning Your Tour Day

Planning a day in the theme parks isn't always a day at the beach, so for more recommendations on making the most of your time at WDW, see our handy charts on p. 30, 54, 72, 82, and 86.

Universal Studios, with its many air-conditioned shows, waiting areas, and covered parking, is the best choice to escape a **rainy day,** because almost none of its rides will shut down in a storm. SeaWorld Orlando, where you'll spend lots of time walking outside, is the worst in rain. If it's a **scorcher,** both Universal Studios and Disney's Hollywood Studios have lots of sheltered activities, but you'll be best served by one of the three water parks (**Wet 'n Wild ★★★,**

Blizzard Beach ★★★, or **Typhoon Lagoon ★★** [p. 89]), which get crowded but are fine choices—although, of course, your hotel pool holds water as a heat reliever, too. The worst park on hot or wet days is the exposed **Disney's Animal Kingdom,** where next to nothing is indoors. But if there is a big storm, don't leave! Rain lasts all day back home, but in Florida, storms usually clear in an hour.

Days 6–7: Exploring Orlando Beyond the Theme Parks

Hitting the big seven in 5 days leaves 2 days to get away from the dizzying pressures of theme parking. Take a day to drive out to **Kennedy Space Center ★★★** (p. 149), or if that's still too touristy for you, take a dip in a natural spring, such as **De Leon Springs ★★★** (p. 156). The moment you get sick of roller coasters—or when the temperature cracks the boiling point, whichever comes first—head for a water park: **Blizzard Beach** (p. 90) is the best for young families, and **Wet 'n Wild ★★★** (p. 139) pleases teens with unvarnished thrills. Those are good for 4 or 5 hours, so combine that half-day outing with a fine-arts fix: It would be a shame to miss a collection as world class as **the Morse Museum**'s ★★★ (p. 143) astonishing Tiffany glass. While you're there, take a late-afternoon boat cruise past the mansions of **Winter Park** (p. 143)—when you're out on the water, you'll finally get a feeling for the "real" Florida that attracted the builders of the major resorts in the first place.

GETTING TO KNOW ORLANDO'S LAYOUT

In 1970, before the opening of Walt Disney World, Orlando was still a tourism center, attracting 660,000 people a year. But by 1999, the place was a powerhouse, with 37.9 million people visiting. During the same period, the area population skyrocketed from 344,000 to 860,000, soaring past such old-guard American cities as St. Louis; Washington, D.C.; Boston; Baltimore; and Portland.

However, for all that growth, and despite the fact the amusements are critical to Orlando's economy, most of the population still lives north of SeaWorld. The tourist zones are segregated from residential ones. Huge chunks of your time, days at a stretch, will be spent in just a few districts, predominantly the three main, boisterous tourist corridors. Those lie along International Drive, U.S. 192 around I-4, and the Lake Buena Vista area north of exit 68 off I-4.

The Making of a Kingdom

Back when only cargo trains had much business in Central Florida, Orlando fashioned itself as a prosperous small city—some derisively called it a cow town—well positioned to serve the citrus and cattle industries as they shipped goods between America and Cuba. The city remained that way, mostly irrelevant, until around 1943, when the great cross-state cattle drives ended.

Soon after, the brick-warehouse city of Orlando developed its second personality. The turning point wasn't the arrival of Walt Disney on his secret land-buying trips. It came a decade earlier, when NASA settled into the Space Coast, 45 minutes east, and the local government, spotting opportunity, invited the Martin Marietta corporation—now Lockheed Martin—to open a massive facility off Sand Lake Road, near the present-day Convention Center. To sweeten the deal, leaders promised unprecedented civic improvements, including an unrealized high-speed rail system they're still bickering about. Mostly, though, politicians built roads. Florida's Turnpike to Miami was carved past the Martin plot, S.R. 50 was hammered through downtown to link the coasts, and, soon after, many blocks in the downtown area were bulldozed for the construction of I-4, linking Tampa on the west coast with Daytona Beach (then one of America's premier vacation towns) on the east coast. The new transit links made Walt lick his chops for some cheap land nearby.

Walt's new kingdom was constructed 20 miles southwest of the city in scrubland, where his planners could keep the outside world at bay. The resort was intended to be an oasis in the citrus groves, but soon, sprawl sprouted around the park's border, just as had happened in Anaheim. For the last two generations, the space between Orlando's two disparate developments has vanished, consumed by areas where "real" Orlando residents live, so that the old-fashioned, "traditional" city has come to be dwarfed, as it were, by family-friendly honky-tonk and slapped-up suburbs. Few casual visitors ever lay eyes on the real Orlando.

The Neighborhoods in Brief

Following is a breakdown of Orlando's neighborhoods—from theme parks to residential areas.

WALT DISNEY WORLD RESORT

Best for: *Space, theme parks, a sense of place, proximity to His Mouseness*

What you won't find: *Inexpensive food or lodging, a central location for anything except Disney attractions, the "real" Florida or Orlando*

When Walt Disney ordered the purchase of these 27,000 acres mostly just west of Interstate 4, he was righting a wrong he committed in the building of Anaheim's Disneyland. In commandeering as much land as he did, he ensured that visitors would not be troubled by the clatter of motel signs and cheap restaurants that abut his original playground. "Here in Florida," he said in a promotional film shot months before his death, "we have something special we never enjoyed at Disneyland . . . the blessing of size. There's enough land here to hold all the ideas and plans we can possibly imagine." You could spend your entire vacation without leaving the greenery of the resort, and lots of people do, although they're missing a great deal. The idea to remain solely on Disney property is outdated now that Universal has proven itself. Still, there's an awful lot to do spread around here, starting with four of the world's most polished theme parks, two of the best water parks, four golf courses, two miniature golf courses, a racecar track, a sports pavilion, and a huge shopping-and-entertainment district. Although other countries may have better versions of some Disney rides, Florida's resort is by far the most spacious and the most elaborate.

Orlando at a Glance

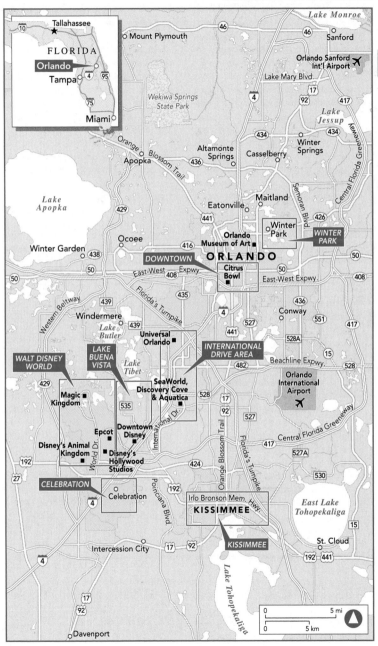

First-time visitors aren't usually prepared for quite how *large* the area is: 47 (roughly rectangular) square miles. Only a third of that land is truly developed, and another third has been set aside as a permanent reserve for swampland. Major elements are easily a 10-minute drive away from each other, with nothing but trees or Disney hotels between them. The Magic Kingdom is buried deep in the back of the park—which is to say, the north of it, requiring the most driving time to reach. Epcot and Hollywood Studios are in the center, while Disney's Animal Kingdom is at the southwest of the property, closest to the real world.

For its convenience, Disney **signposts hotels and attractions** according to the major theme park they're near. If you are staying on property, you'll need to know which area your hotel is in. For example, the All-Star resorts are considered to be in the Animal Kingdom area, and so some signs on Disney highways may simply read Animal Kingdom Resort Area and leave off the name of your hotel. Ask for your hotel's designated area when you reserve.

Getting in is easy. Every major artery in town is exhaustively signposted for Disney World. Exits are marked, but it helps to know the name of the major artery that feeds your hotel. A few useful **secret exits** are not marked on official Disney maps. One is the newly laid **Western Way,** which turns past Coronado Springs resort and skirts the back of Animal Kingdom to reach many vacation home communities southwest of Disney. If you take it, ignore the signs telling you to take 429 to U.S. 192. That route will cost you $1.25 in tolls, despite the fact it runs for scarcely a mile, but it's the only Disney entry requiring a toll.

There's a second useful shortcut out of the resort that Disney doesn't label on its official maps: **Sherbeth Road,** by the entrance to Animal Kingdom Lodge, about a mile west of the entrance to Animal Kingdom, winds its way to the cheap restaurants on western U.S. 192.

It's interesting to note that when you're at Disney, you're in a separate governmental zone. The resort's bizarre experiments in building methods (such as fiberglass-and-steel castles) are partly enabled by the fact that Disney negotiated the creation of its own entity, the Reedy Creek Improvement District, which can set its own standards. When you see vehicles marked RCID, those are the civic services for the resort. Not far down the road between Downtown Disney Marketplace and the Wyndham hotel—a road not used by many guests—make a pass by the R.C. Fire Department, a toylike engine house with a one-of-a-kind outdoor fountain that looks like a spouting fire hose.

Disney developed a little bit of land east of I-4 into the New Urbanism unincorporated town of **Celebration.** As a Stepford-like residential center with upscale aspirations (golf, boutiques), there's not much to do there except eat a bit in its town square. Be prepared to parallel park there.

Walt Disney World is at the southern end of Orlando's chain of big parks, so to see Universal, SeaWorld, and Orlando itself, you'll always head north on I-4.

U.S. 192 & KISSIMMEE

Best for: *Value, restaurant and hotel options, family entertainment*

What you won't find: *High art, subtlety, luxury*

No matter how Orlando changes, it's Kissimmee (Kiss-*im*-ee), its ridiculed little sister, that lags behind in style. Walt's master plan succeeded only in keeping tacky motels and buffets at a modest distance. Where the southern edge of the Disney resort property touches Hwy. U.S. 192, the clamor begins, stretching about 7 miles west and a good 10 miles east. This ostentatious drag, known also as the Irlo Bronson Memorial Highway (after the state senator who sold Walt a lot of his land to make the park possible), is the spine of Kissimmee, and it's your budget salvation for food and beds, so plug the K-word into the location box of your Web searches, too. It's also the best place to find that all-American kitsch you might be looking for—nowhere else in town will you find a souvenir store shaped like a giant orange half, and isn't that a shame?

In the early 1970s, Kissimmee was the prime place to stay. The motels weren't flashy then, and they still aren't, but they're ever affordable—$50 to $80 is the norm, and some shabby places go down to $39 for a single or $45 for a double. Kissimmee's downtown, about 10 miles east of Disney, is a typical Florida burg with a main street by a lake, and its quickly growing subdivisions have become popular among Hispanic families, although that doesn't translate into accessible restaurants serving ethnic cuisine. U.S. 192 is mostly about the big chains.

The best way to get your bearings on U.S. 192 is using its clearly signposted **mile marker system.** U.S. 192 hits Disney's southern entrance (the most expedient avenue to the major theme parks) at Mile Marker 7, while I-4's exit 65 connects with it around Mile Marker 8. Numbers go down to the west, and they go up to the east. Western 192, where the bulk of the vacation home developments are found, is much more upscale than the tacky wilds of eastern 192, but neither stretch could be termed swanky or well planned. Although Osceola County has strived to beautify the tourist corridor, it's been inept in the effort; in late 2006, the county cut down stands of myrtle trees in the median of U.S. 192 because they blocked the view of the billboards. That should tell you what you need to know about how the road looks and where its values lie.

LAKE BUENA VISTA

Best for: *Access to Disney, I-4 and chain restaurants, some elbow room*

What you won't find: *The lowest prices, a sense of place*

Lake Buena Vista, a hotel enclave east of Downtown Disney, clusters on the eastern fringe of Walt Disney World. LBV is technically a town, but it doesn't much look like one. It's mostly hotels and mid-priced chain restaurants with some schlocky souvenir stores thrown in. The proximity of the I-4 exit makes U-turns tricky, which can get annoying and back traffic up, but it's easy to slip into Disney's crowded side door, which is helpful. The bottom line is that LBV is less tacky and higher rent than Kissimmee's 192, but it's also still a Disney-centric area and not really part of Orlando's fabric.

If you stay in LBV, you can also (if you're hardy) walk to the Downtown Disney

development, where you can then pick up Disney's free DTS bus system.

INTERNATIONAL DRIVE

Best for: *Walkability, cheap transportation, inexpensive food, kitschy tourist attractions, proximity to Universal and SeaWorld*

What you won't find: *Space, style*

Although a still-developing stretch of this street winds all the way south to U.S. 192, when people refer to International Drive, they usually mean the segment between SeaWorld and Universal Orlando, just east of I-4 between exits 71 and 75. I-Drive, as it's called, is probably the only district where you might comfortably stay without a car and still be able to see the non-Disney attractions, because it's chockablock with affordable hotels (which are, on the whole, not as ratty as some of the U.S. 192 choices can be) and plenty of crowd-pleasing touristy things to see, such as shopping malls, arcades, T-shirt shops, all-you-can-eat buffets, and dinnertainment theaters. The cheap I-Ride Trolley (p. 228) traverses the area on a regular schedule.

The intersection at Sand Lake Road is a major dividing line for I-Drive's personalities. North of Sand Lake Road, within the orbit of Universal Orlando and Wet 'n Wild, it tends to host foreign visitors, particularly English families whose childhood holiday towns have acclimated them to promenades along touristy, working-class avenues. Here, the midway rides and the ice-cream shops are where the action is. South of Sand Lake, closer to SeaWorld, you're more likely to find groups of domestic visitors, as the mighty Orange County Convention Center, located on both sides of I-Drive at the Bee Line Expressway/528, keeps the surrounding hotels (and streets) full. On this part of I-Drive, the bars and midscale restaurants rule. West on Sand Lake Road past I-4, you'll find a mile-long procession of mid- to upper-level places to eat and drink that the city dubs its "Restaurant Row." And just south of Sand Lake Road, you can't miss the rising I-Drive Live development (p. 139), where developers have promised to plant the landmark Orlando Eye wheel (p. 139) by the end of 2014.

I-Drive does an east-west dogleg where it runs into I-4, and on the other side of I-4 at Universal Boulevard, you'll find Universal Orlando's entertainment resort, which is more popular with locals than Disney's.

Hotel and restaurant discounts may be posted on the area's business association and promotional website, **www.international driveorlando.com**.

DOWNTOWN ORLANDO

Best for: *Historic buildings, cafes, museums, fine art, wealthy residents*

What you won't find: *Theme parks, easy commutes*

Like in so many American cities, residents fled from downtown in the 1960s through the 1980s, although spacious new condo developments have rescued the city from abandonment. Downtown Orlando is gradually being rediscovered by young, upscale residents. Here are the highlights:

DOWNTOWN Beneath the city's collection of modest skyscrapers (mostly banking offices), you'll find municipal buildings (the main library, historic museums), a few upscale hotels (the Grand Bohemian, Courtyard at Lake Lucerne), and some attractive lakes, but little shopping. Orange Avenue, once a street of proud stone buildings and department stores, now comes alive mostly at night, when its former vaudeville halls and warehouses essay their new roles as nightclubs, especially around Church Street. The 43-acre Lake Eola Park, just east, is often cited as an area attraction, but in truth it's just your average city park, although the .9-mile path around its 23-acre sinkhole lake is good for joggers. Its swan boats (rent one for $15 for 30 min.) are city icons, as is the central fountain from 1957; its unique Plexiglas skin is illuminated with a 6-minute light-and-water musical show nightly at 9:30pm. Just east of that, the streets turn to red brick and big trees shelter **Thornton Park** (along Washington St., Summerlin Ave., and Central Blvd.). It's noted for its alfresco European-style cafes, none especially inexpensive, but all pleasing, where waiters wear black and hip locals spend evenings and weekend brunches. West of downtown over I-4, the

area called Parramore is a longtime neighborhood for African Americans (sadly, the interstate was built, in part, as a barrier). A mile north of downtown, **Loch Haven Park** basks in a wealth of museums (p. 141).

VIMI/MILLS FIFTY Some old-timers call this area **Colonial Town** and new-timers may use **Mills 50,** but it's also the Vietnamese District at Mills, or ViMi (p. 184). Just north of downtown, at Colonial Drive and Mills Avenue, there's a midcentury neighborhood with the whiff of a faded 1950s Main Street (parking lots are hidden behind buildings). There, you can spend a top afternoon strolling through several omnibus Asian supermarkets stocked with exotic groceries and unique baked goods and parking yourself at one of the excellent mom-and-pop-style eateries (advertised by cheap stick-on letters and neon) serving food far more delicious than their limited budgets would suggest. Several stores whip up addictive, meat-stuffed baguette sandwiches called *bánh mi* for a quick $3 meal. You'll also find hobby and art-supply shops patronized by a burgeoning bohemian community. The two marginalized groups collaborate beautifully together.

WINTER PARK

Best for: *Fine art, cafes, strolls, galleries, lakes*

What you won't find: *Inexpensive shopping, easy theme-park access*

One of the city's most interesting areas, and one of the few that hasn't taken pains to erase its history, Winter Park was where, 100 years ago, upstart industrialists built winter homes at a time when they couldn't gain entree into the more exclusive, more WASP-y enclaves of Newport or Palm Beach. The town blends seamlessly with northern Orlando (you can drive between them in a few minutes without getting onto I-4) and is still pretty full of itself, but cruising on its brick-paved streets, gawking at mansions built on its chain of lakes, will remind you of the good life. In the shops of Park Avenue, you'll find mostly jewelry, art, and women's clothes, but a stroll down it, and into the country-club campus of Rollins College (at its southern end), are among the finer pleasures. The town's long-running boat tour (p. 158) is probably the best way to sample the opulence. The best art museum around, the Morse (p. 143), holds the most comprehensive collection of Tiffany glass you will ever see. West of Winter Park, over I-4, the up-and-coming district of College Park, centering around Princeton Street and Edgewater Drive, hosts restaurants and boutiques that are bringing the area favor.

NORTH OF ORLANDO

Most visitors who venture into the suburban towns north of Winter Park do so to visit some of the area's natural springs or state parks (p. 155) or to connect with the spirits in the hamlet of Cassadaga (p. 143). After you've seen these places, there is little to engage you until you hit the Atlantic Coast on I-4.

SOUTH OF ORLANDO

Only in the past few years has the rural-minded swampland southwest of the resort and Kissimmee begun to be built upon in earnest, and the 65-mile run along I-4 to Tampa is gradually filling in with developments and golf courses. This patch of the Green Swamp, in which the two cities will one day merge into a megalopolis, is now

casually dubbed "Orlampa." A few specialty tourist sights, including Fantasy of Flight (p. 145) and Dinosaur World (p. 145), claimed land before prices got steeper. In Tampa, you'll find the excellent Busch Gardens Africa (p. 135), a worthy addition to an amusement-park itinerary, and an hour straight south of Orlando, in the town of Winter Haven, is Legoland Florida (p. 133), Florida's best kiddie park, built at Florida's most historic amusement park.

EAST OF ORLANDO

The entrance to Orlando International Airport is 11 miles east of I-4, webbed into the city network by toll highways and surrounded by golfing developments. Across empty swamp from there, the so-called Space Coast, of which Cape Canaveral is the metaphoric capital (see it at Kennedy Space Center; p. 149), is a 45-minute drive east of Orlando's tourist corridor via 528, also known as the Bee Line Expressway.

WEST OF ORLANDO

Because the Green Swamp commands the area, there simply isn't much west of the tourist corridor save a few small towns and some state parks, such as Lake Louisa.

EXPLORING WALT DISNEY WORLD

3

On November 22, 1963, around the time President Kennedy was embarking on his public motorcade in Dallas, Walt Disney was in a private jet, conducting his first flyover of some ignored Florida swampland. By the end of the day, as Disney decided this was the place he wanted to shape in the image of his dreams, America had changed in more ways than one.

While the country reeled, Disney snapped up land through dummy companies. His cover was blown in 1965, but the fix was in: His company had mopped up an area twice the size of Manhattan, 27,443 acres, from just $180 an acre. Disneyland East was coming. Today, it's the most popular vacation destination on the planet, and its four theme parks receive 48.5 million combined visits a year.

It's no accident that Walt, a seller of fantasies, enjoyed his peaks during two periods of profound malaise: the Great Depression and the Cold War. It's also no coincidence that his theme parks flowered while America was riven with self-doubt—the Korean and Vietnam conflicts, the death of Kennedy, and Watergate. His parks are, by design, comforting. They tell you how to feel and where to go, and in reinforcing uncomplicated impressions of history and the world, they never make you feel left behind. Ironically, what made his reassuring message of simplicity work was a relentless drive for technological innovation and revolutionary civil engineering.

Why should it be so difficult to find straight talk about such an immensely popular place? There are plenty of guidebooks that propagate a dewy-eyed celebration of all things Disney that read like advertisements and treat the resort as a nigh-holy Mecca. This is not one of them. I adore Walt Disney World, I marvel at its awesome achievements, and I have been coming since the ribbon was cut. Its childhood is inextricable from my own. Disney fans rhapsodize about the "magic"—that intangible *frisson* you feel when you're there—but I think a case could be made that the energy doesn't come from the place as much as it comes from the customers. Where else in your life will you be surrounded by people so elated to be there? Weddings? Graduations? Walt Disney World's magic comes from the accumulated goodwill of thousands of strangers, united in gratitude and togetherness. If you don't believe me, sit on a bench for a while in Fantasyland and watch the children pass by. Some 75 percent of Disney's visitors are return customers. There's just something about it.

Walt Disney World, transporting as it is, is a real place, made possible by real sweat and stagecraft. Its qualities as a business cannot be separated from the product.

TICKETING

This will be the biggest expense, so know your needs before laying down plastic. All park tickets (excepting annual passes) are purchased by the day. You decide how many days you want to spend at the parks, and once you nail that down, you decide which extras you want to pay for. Both decisions are fraught with temptation. It's possible Disney benefits from making it so complicated when customers capitulate and spend lots of money to make the confusion go away.

Magic Their Way

Historically, visitors to Orlando would spend the first 3 or 4 days of their weeklong vacations at the Disney parks, and by the fourth or fifth days, they would include Universal Orlando, SeaWorld, or the Kennedy Space Center. In 2005, though, the resort unleashed Magic Your Way, an insidious pricing plan that appears, on the surface, to present the biggest savings for people who stay on Disney turf for more than 4 days. The delayed economy of Magic Your Way is a honey trap that entices families to stay on Disney property longer, spending more money on higher food and hotel prices. It crowds out anything non-Disney.

Even the price of your admission to the ancillary amusements, such as the water slides, is pegged to how many days you intend to spend inside the four theme parks. Like an airline, you add the extras that you want.

1. **Base ticket.** You must buy this. This is your theme park admission. With it, you are entitled to visit one park per day, with no switching on the same day. When it's all new to you, one park per day is plenty.

2. **Park Hopper.** Should you crave the privilege of jumping from park to park on the same day, you must add the Park Hopper option to your ticket. With it, you can do the early-morning safari at Animal Kingdom, take a nap at your hotel, and then switch to the Magic Kingdom for the fireworks. As the chart below shows, this flexibility costs a flat $59, no matter how many days of tickets it covers. This is a handy option to have, but you may decide you do not need it.

3. **Water Park Fun & More (WPF&M).** From here on out, willpower is crucial to saving money on Magic Your Way. Should you have definite plans to visit a Disney water slide park, DisneyQuest, or see an event at the ESPN Wide World of Sports, then the Water Park Fun & More (WPF&M) option includes a set number of admissions. That add-on is $59 no matter how long you stay. WPF&M is the trickiest add-on. Too many people overestimate the amount of time and energy they are going to have, buy this option, and fail to use it. Think carefully about your own plans, and be realistic. During the course of 3 days of theme park going, and after miles of walking, are you *really* going to have enough juice for the water slides? Or are there other things to do in Orlando that you'd like to try (for example, the Wizarding World of Harry Potter or Kennedy Space Center)? You will always be allowed to buy separate admission to any attractions included in WPF&M; if you're realistically only going to visit Typhoon Lagoon once and that's all, the walk-up ticket ($52 adults/$44 kids 3–9) is cheaper for adults than the $59 add-on.

Walt Disney World & Lake Buena Vista

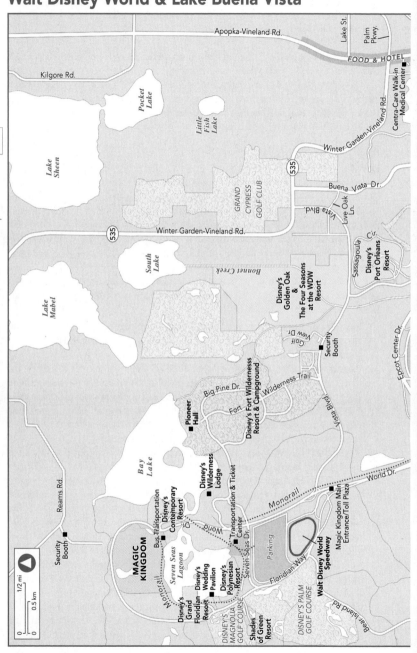

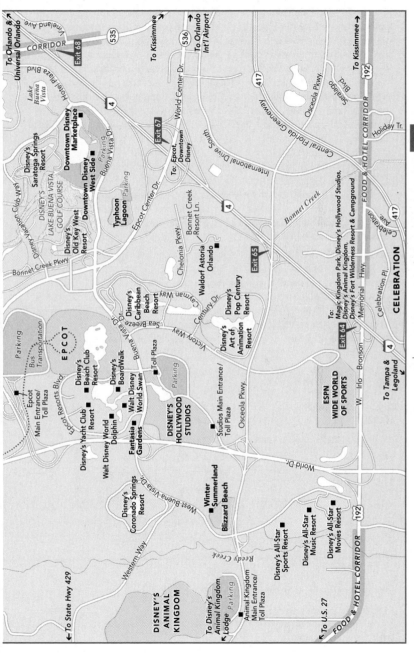

Don't overlook this pricing loophole that works in Disney's favor: On days you visit a water park, your visit there will likely consume the whole day and most of your energy—and on that day, you probably won't set foot in a theme park, *but you will have paid for it*. If you do go to a theme park that day, you won't be getting your full money's worth. This is the biggest reason to avoid WPF&M and just buy those second-tier entry tickets separately for use on days you dedicate only to them. If you plan to buy both the Park Hopper and the Water Park Fun & More options, they come bundled for an $84 add-on, no matter how many days you stay.

4. **The No Expiration option.** It's just like it sounds, and buying it is like hedging on future price increases. Disney hikes prices each summer like clockwork, but if you select this, your ticket can be used as long as there are days left on it. If you don't buy this option, unused days are dead after 14 days of your ticket's first use. Assuming you bought 10 days of tickets, the maximum allowed for North Americans, you'd spend $664 for an adult no-expiration pass, which equals $67 per day ($72 with Park Hopper). Day-of tickets are currently $90 to $95—so there's a savings, but *only* if you return later in your life and you don't lose your ticket. There's a side benefit: Paying extra for No Expiration frees you to explore the rest of Orlando without guilt because you know there's no ticking clock. Does this sound like you? (It sounds like me.)

Finally, very slight **discounts** on Magic Your Way are available. If you buy your tickets in advance (online or at a Disney Store), save the shipping fee by arranging to pick them up at the gates of one of the parks (long lines) or at Guest Relations in Downtown Disney Marketplace (short line). **Florida residents** are offered entirely different discounts (http://disneyworld.disney.go.com/florida-residents), as are **AAA members;** if you're one, call © **407/824-4321** for the latest promotion. (See "Other Ticket 'Discounts' & Deals," below, for a more on potential discounts.)

Disney Ticket Options*

Days of Use	Base Ticket Age 10 & up	Age 3–9	Add Water Park Fun & More	Add No Expiration	Add Park Hopper
1	$95/90**	$89/84**	$50 (2 visits)	N/A	$59
2	$184	$172	$50 (2 visits)	$35	$59
3	$262	$244	$50 (3 visits)	$45	$59
4	$279	$260	$50 (4 visits)	$95	$59
5	$289	$270	$50 (5 visits)	$145	$59
6	$299	$280	$50 (6 visits)	$190	$59
7	$309	$290	$50 (7 visits)	$220	$59
8	$319	$300	$50 (8 visits)	$245	$59
9	$329	$310	$50 (9 visits)	$280	$59
10	$339	$320	$50 (10 visits)	$325	$59

Prices don't include sales tax of 6 to 7.5 percent. Prices accurate as of July 1, 2013.
**The higher price is for the Magic Kingdom, and the second price applies to the other three theme parks.*

contacting WALT DISNEY WORLD

Walt Disney World offers no toll-free numbers.

General information: ☏ 407/939-4636; www.disneyworld.com
Vacation packages: ☏ 407/934-7675
Room-only bookings: ☏ 407/939-7429

Operating hours, schedules:
☏ 407/824-4321
Dining reservations: ☏ 407/939-3463
Weather updates: ☏ 407/824-4104
Lost and found: ☏ 407/824-4245

During some times of year, the park mounts special evening events, such as the ones around Halloween and Christmas (see the calendar on p. 231) that require a separate, expensive ticket. You will get less value out of your Magic Your Way ticket if you attend during the day before one of these parties. They start around 7pm, and if you haven't paid for the second ticket, you'll be rounded up and sent out. However, if you do attend one, you can show up as early as 4pm and get a few extra hours in.

THE PERIL OF DISNEY PACKAGES

If you don't care about spending more than you have to, skip this section.

There's one big way Disney tricks you into overpurchasing. Anytime you call it and ask for reservations, operators will suggest adding perks. You'll ask for tickets, and they'll suggest they throw in, say, the meal plan (more about that in the Dining chapter). The instant you accept, you're purchasing a "package," and that will often force you to pay more than you would have a la carte. Always, *always* know what everything would cost separately before agreeing to a Disney-suggested package—the company spends millions advertising that a family vacation there costs $1,600 a week, but in fact, if you don't accept Disney suggestions and use other advice in this book, you can take a trip for much less. If you must, hang up the phone and do some math before deciding to accept or reject the offer. That's the only way to ensure you're not paying more.

Here's a hidden loophole that works against guests: Disney "length of stay" ticket packages will begin the moment you arrive on the property and end the day you leave. Think about that. If you've just flown from a distant place, you are unlikely to rush to the Magic Kingdom on the same day. Likewise, on the day you're due at the airport to fly home, you may not to be able to visit a theme park. Yet Disney will schedule your package that way. In effect, you will lose 2 days that you've paid for—at the start and at the finish of your vacation, when you'll be resting or packing. Disney will do everything it can to sell you theme park tickets for every day that you're on its property, regardless of if you plan to see Harry Potter, the Space Shuttle, or some manatees.

How can you avoid this? You could spend the first and last nights of your vacation at a non-Disney hotel and move on-site for your ticket days. More simply, insist on making **one reservation per phone call.** Arrange your tickets. Hang up. Call back and arrange your hotel as "room only." It's vital that you do not link your two reservations. *Disney packages usually don't save you money.*

Disney's reservationists are friendly but they're sales-driven, and they are trained to answer *only* the questions that you pose. If you're not sure about the terms of what you're about to purchase, corner them and ask. And *always* ask if there is a less expensive option. They won't lie and tell you there isn't, but they *will* neglect to volunteer the information. Again, do not be afraid to get off the phone to mull over the price of their suggestions. **TheMouseForLess.com, MouseSavers.com,** and the messages at **DISBoards.com** will let you know about current deals that Disney won't.

OTHER TICKET "DISCOUNTS" & DEALS

A few businesses can shave a few paltry bucks off multiday tickets; see the last chapter (p. 234) for those. International visitors are eligible for tickets good for longer stays and unlimited WPF&M admissions, but only if they are purchased from abroad. At recent exchange rates, it may be cheaper to buy American-issued tickets with Park Hopper options at the gate; do the math. *Really* big fans carry a **Chase Disney Rewards Visa credit card** (✆ **800/300-8575;** www.chase.com/disney), which grants points to be redeemed on all things Disney, a few discounts, and a character meet-and-greet area just for cardholders.

EATING ON SITE

In recent years, Disney food became noticeably more sweet, and opportunities to buy candy multiplied. Theme parks worldwide thrive on excited, sugared-up children and parents who are too worn out to say "no" to such things as $8 hot dogs and $3 Cokes. At least the budget algebra is easy. The **cheapest combo meals** are always from counter-service restaurants (called Quick Service in Disney-speak), and adults usually pay $9 to $11, before a drink, no matter the time of day. Kids' meals (a main dish; milk, juice, water, or soda; and a choice of two items including grapes, carrot sticks, applesauce, a cookie, or fries) always cost around $6 at Quick Service locations. If you want to sit down for full service—character meals are always in sit-down restaurants—adults pay in the mid-teens for a lunch entree and usually over $20 a plate at dinner, before gratuity or drinks, and kids' meals are about half as much. Disney aggressively sells a Disney Dining Plan that takes away the need to pay a bill after each meal, but which comes with a lot of rules that dictate how and where you eat each day (see the sidebar "Why You Don't Want the Disney Dining Plan").

No longer is it easy to simply stroll into any restaurant that catches your eye and enjoy a meal. For sit-down food, *always* make reservations (✆ **407/939-3463**) or you are likely to be turned away. Oversubscription to the Dining Plan has spoiled the meal experience for everyone else. It's that simple, and that sad.

Semihealthy options are possible on even the lowest food budget: Disney limits saturated fat and added sugar to 10 percent of a counter-service dish's calories; no more than 30 percent of a meal's calories or 35 percent of a snack's calories come from fat; and juice drinks have no added sugar. Trans fats are out. One way Disney seems to have accomplished this is by reducing serving sizes—you won't feel stuffed. Kids' meals come with carrots, applesauce, or grapes instead of fries, and with low-fat milk, water, or 100 percent fruit juice instead of soda. (Fries and Coke are still available by request—Disney knows kids are still on vacation and deserve a treat.)

It will *always* be cheaper to **drive off property** to feed your family, but particularly at the Magic Kingdom that's not always possible or desirable—there, egress requires at least two modes of transportation. Consult the list of restaurants located outside the theme park gates, which starts on p. 167, but also see the sidebar, "Saving on Park Munchies," (p. 49) for ways to shave your food budget.

WHY YOU DON'T WANT THE DISNEY dining plan

If you book at a Disney hotel, you will be offered the credit-based **Disney Dining Plan,** which prepurchases many of your meals. It is extremely complicated, with all kinds of rules, exclusions, and premium versions. Lots of people cave and buy it in the name of convenience, thinking it will make everything easier, but for the casual Disney visitor, it has other costs.

○ **It's not cheap enough.** The least expensive plan, Quick Service, has a per-day cost of $38 adults, $15 kids, and includes two counter meals and one snack (like popcorn or ice cream), plus a refillable soft drink mug you can only use at a Disney hotel ($9–$18, based on how long you're staying). Most adult quick-service meals cost $12 to $14 per meal using cash. Even if you spent $15, simple math proves that if you stick to two counter-service meals with no plan, plus one $4 snack, you'll spend about $34 versus $38 using the plan.

○ **It's inflexible.** You must buy the plan for every night you stay at the hotel. You can't buy fewer. *And* everyone in your group must be on it. Having spent the money, you'll feel welded to Disney property (which suits Disney, but restricts you). Also, many menu items and food locations are excluded. Only those marked with the DDP logo count.

○ **It costs time.** The forced use of sit-down restaurants clogs reservations months ahead of time. You'll have to do hours of advance planning and stick to a schedule. And table service eats more time than grabbing meals to go would.

○ **It's impractical.** The basic plan ($56 adult, $18 kids, per day) buys the equivalent of a sit-down meal, a Quick Service meal, and a snack. Few of us want daily table service at a theme park. Yet the plan has you doing that unless you use it for breakfast and pay for dinner in cash.

○ **It's not any easier.** You can pay using cash or a room key as quickly as using plan points. You must also make reservations with or without a plan.

○ **It's incomplete.** The plan doesn't include appetizers, tips (unless your party is 6 or more, in which case there's a mandatory 18 percent tip), alcoholic beverages, souvenir cups, and don't forget the basic plan also leaves out that third daily meal that you'll have to pay for.

○ **It wastes.** Because it begins on the day you arrive, you're bound to leave with some unused credits, resulting in a loss.

NAVIGATING DISNEY'S PARKS

In summer and during other holidays, it's wise to get to the front gates of the park about 30 minutes ahead of opening. Mostly, though, you can waltz right up. Try not to leave any park as it closes, when crowds surge and waits for the tram get annoying. Instead, depart early or linger awhile in the shops, which will be open a bit longer than everything else.

PARKING   Each park has its own parking lot ($15 a day; free for Disney hotel guests and annual passholders). As you drive in, attendants will direct you to fill the next available spot. This is probably the most dangerous part of your day, as the people around you will be distracted and you're at risk of hitting an excited child or knocking off an open car door—take it slow. Parking lanes are numbered and given names; at the very least, remember your number. Don't stress out if your row is a high number; at Epcot, for example, the front row is 27. If you forget where you parked, remember what time you arrived; Disney tracks which sections are being filled minute by minute. You'll board one of the noisy trams (fold strollers during the wait), which haul you to the ticketing area. At the Magic Kingdom, you still must take either the monorail or a ferryboat to the front gates, but at the other parks, the tram lets you off right at the doorstep.

SECURITY   Guests with bags larger than a small purse must queue up at a station where you will open them and park security will probe them with a stick. If you are not carrying a bag, there will be a fast entry portal for you.

TURNSTILES   To validate your ticket, you must place a finger on a clear plate. That fingerprint is "married" to your ticket so that you can't share it with anyone else. Disney swears your personal information is eventually expunged from the system, but what it doesn't publicize is that if you do not wish for your fingerprint to be scanned, you may use standard identification instead, right there at the gate.

ORIENTATION   Once you get inside the gates at all the parks, be sure to grab two free things that are kept in conspicuous racks: a "**Guidemap**" and a "**Times Guide**" listing the day's schedule (Animal Kingdom also has an **Animal Guide**). If you forget, you can pick both up at any shop or at the park's **tip board,** which is a roundup of wait times found a short walk into all the parks (they're marked on the maps). Also, cast members carry full schedules (it's called the "Tell-A-Cast"), or you can ask at the park's **Guest Relations** desk (marked on the maps, always near the front; **Guest Services,** outside the gates, is mostly for ticket issues). The estimated wait time for any attraction is posted where its line begins; this number is accurate, although Disney often pads it by 5 minutes to give guests the sense of exceeded expectations.

HEIGHT RESTRICTIONS   They're on the maps. Take them seriously. They are always enforced. At Splash Mountain, Space Mountain, Mission Space, and a few other major rides, kids who are sized out may be offered a card entitling them to jump to the head of the line when they finally grow tall enough. (At Space Mountain, it dubs them a "Mousetronaut," at Splash Mountain, a "Future Splash Mountaineer.") Do not fill in the date yourself; that's for the ride attendant to validate on the day you return.

FOOD   Gone are the days when you could amble blithely around a Disney park and decide on a whim to have dinner wherever your fancy took you. The Disney Dining Plan (p. 23) wrecked that. Now you must plan ahead by racking up Advance Dining Reservations, called ADRs, or risk waiting for cancellations that may not materialize. Having a reservation does not mean you will sit down at that time. There is frequently a wait anyway.

Breakfast ends around 10:30am, and lunch service generally goes from 11:30am to 2:30 or 3pm. Prices for buffets and character meals shift according to the day of the week and time of year. Counter service locations, which Disney calls Quick Service, do not require reservations, and their listings can be found with each theme park's chapter. To avoid lines, eat between 10:30am and noon (lunch) and 4 and 5pm (dinner). Kids under 3 may eat without charge from an adult's plate, and high chair and booster seats are readily available.

Your ticket entitles you to Fastpass (technically, it's in all caps), which permits anyone to obtain a timed entry ticket for the most popular attractions. Soon after its 1999 introduction, Fastpass became a verb. As in, "The line's too long, so let's Fastpass it." It's not even explained on Guidemaps anymore, but here's a primer:

Fastpass-enabled attractions have a bank of machines near the outside of the queue, and above those machines, a 1-hour time period will be posted. If you pop in your ticket, you'll get a slip of paper (keep it—it's another ticket) that entitles you to return during that timed window, and only then, to use a much shorter line. Otherwise, you'll have to use the separate "stand-by" line for the masses. The bottom of your Fastpass should tell you what time you may get your next Fastpass. Only so many tickets are issued for each timed window, so you may find that for popular rides such as Test Track or Soarin', all the day's inventory will be gone by lunchtime—so secure those as soon after opening as possible.

Now that you understand how it works, turn to p. 35 to find out how Disney is adding an electronic wrinkle called Fastpass+.

3

EXPLORING WALT DISNEY WORLD | Navigating Disney's Parks

OPTIONAL PARK SERVICES As you roam, roving photographers may ask to take your picture. They're for convenience, not value. Let them snap away; you won't pay anything if you don't want to. They give you a **PhotoPass** (www.disneyphotopass. com) Web account that will allow you to check your shots out later and order prints (or CDs, albums, mugs, water bottles—you name it) if you fall in love with them. You'll have 30 days to make your decisions. Only when you decide to buy does money change hands. Buying costs much, much more than it would cost you to make them yourself: 5×7s are $13, 8×10s are $17, two 4×6s are $15, plus shipping. But now and then, you'll find an occasion that you think is worth the expense, and the Disney photographers are excellent at what they do. PhotoPass is separate from those hilarious pictures taken on board rides, which are available to purchase (from $15) after you get off. Prices for those are similar, but you get those right away. For another $45, you can buy the **Attractions+** plan, which allows you to download some of your ride photos later (you still have to check in after each ride so your pass can be married to your image). Spend $200 ($170 in advance) on **PhotoPass+** and you can download all of your photos from the park, in restaurants, and on the biggest rides.

Guest Relations and some resorts sell **Disney Dollars,** a private scrip you can spend anywhere, even mixed with actual U.S. currency. These brightly colored notes (in declining use) are fun to use, but too often, people bring them home as souvenirs, which is an abject waste of money. There are some clever ways to use them to your advantage—say, by giving your kids $15 worth, and not a dollar more, as an allowance. **My favorite trick:** Instead of getting a cash advance from an ATM with your credit card, which racks up banking fees, buy Disney Dollars instead. They're charged as a purchase (up to $50 a day), incurring no fees.

You can send cumbersome **souvenirs** to the pick-up desk by the park gates, but delivery will take 3 to 5 hours. You can also send them to your Disney resort room. You should make your purchase before noon to receive it the next day. If you make it later, be staying for at least another 2 nights or you could miss the delivery.

WHAT THE BASICS cost AT ALL FOUR DISNEY PARKS

Parking: $15 (waived for guests of Disney hotels)
Lockers: $7 per day (multi-entry)
Regular soda: $2.70 / **Small water:** $2.50 / **Cup of beer:** $6**
ECV (electric convenience vehicle): $50 per day
Single strollers: $15 per day *

Double strollers: $31 per day *
Wheelchair: $12 per day *
Stroller, wheelchair, and ECV rental fee includes multiple park visits on the same day.

*Subject to discounts of $2–$4 if you prepay for the length of your stay.
**A rarity in most parks, except Epcot.

THE MAGIC KINGDOM

The most-visited theme park in the world (17.5 million visitors in 2012), the **Magic Kingdom ★★★**, opened on October 1, 1971, and is more than twice as large as the original Disneyland in Anaheim, California. Of the four parks in Walt Disney World, the Magic Kingdom is the one most people envision: Castle, Main Street, Space Mountain. It's also the first one tourists visit.

The park almost always opens (the "rope drop") at **9am,** but closing time (preceded by a 10-min. fireworks show) varies, usually from **7 to 11pm.**

Keep your ticket card/room key/MagicBand handy and safe. You'll need it throughout the day.

GETTING IN The proof that you're about to experience a fantasy realm comes in the effort required to enter it. Designers wanted arrival to be a big to-do. Many guests brave three forms of transportation before they see a single brick of Main Street. Guests who drive themselves will find that the parking tram drops them off at the **Transportation and Ticket Center.**

From there, a mile away, the Magic Kingdom gleams like a promise from across the man-made Seven Seas Lagoon, but you still have to take either a **monorail** (after a 2009 accident that killed a pilot, guests are no longer permitted to ride in the cab) or a **ferryboat** to the other side. I recommend doing one in each direction—the gradual approach of the boat is probably the most exciting for your first glimpses of that famous Castle, and the monorail is probably better at the end of the day because you can sit (possibly). Ferries are named for execs who helped build Disneyland and this park. For getting off quickly, I prefer the bottom deck. Most times, the monorail is about 5 minutes faster. Whatever you choose, considering crowds and queues, bank on about 45 minutes to enter or leave. (If you're eating at one of the monorail hotels, you'll park for free, and the Contemporary is close enough to walk to the ticket gates. You didn't hear it from me, but some visitors have been known to skip the parking fee this way.)

Upon alighting, submit your bags for a hasty inspection and present your tickets. Take the requisite photo at the Floral Mickey in front of the train station, where the "population" sign indicates the rough number of guests who have come here over time. Then head through the tunnels of the mansard-roof train station. There, in the right-hand tunnel, you'll find the only place in the park to rent strollers and wheelchairs. Note the stylized paintings of the big attractions, done like old-fashioned travel posters. They are a tradition in these tunnels.

STRATEGY If you have little kids, troop without delay to Fantasyland, because the lines get heavy there. On hot days, dash to Splash Mountain in Frontierland and get Fastpasses for later, when you'll need the cool-down.

Main Street, U.S.A.

Out the other side of the train station in the Town Square, you'll be greeted by your first few costumed characters and to a full view of Cinderella Castle at the end of Main Street, U.S.A. Like the first time you see the Eiffel Tower or the Sydney Opera House, there's something seminal—oh, help me, dare I say *magical?*—about laying eyes on that Castle, and it can't help but stir feelings of gratitude. This view is as American as the Grand Canyon. There's a lot of Disney history to absorb if you're paying attention.

The original Main Street, U.S.A., was created as a perfected vision of Walt Disney's fond memories of a formative period of his childhood spent in Marceline, Missouri. To impart a sense of coziness, designers built the Main Street facades at diminishing perspective as they rise. Other subtle touches: Shop windows are lower than normal to enable children to see inside, walkways are pigmented red to accentuate both unreality and safety (it alerts walkers of shifts in levels), and buildings on both sides of the street inch closer to each other as you approach the Castle, subconsciously drawing your attention forward.

There are no nonstop rides or shows on Main Street, just the park's best souvenir shops—call it Purchaseland. The 17,000-square-foot **Emporium,** the largest shop in the Kingdom, takes up almost the entire street along the left, and **Le Chapeau** (on the right, facing the square) is one of the only places where you can sew your name onto the back of one of those iconic mouse-ear beanies (that was free for 35 years, but now it's $3–$7 per cap). They resist stitching nicknames. The **Crystal Arts Shop** may have a small glass-blowing demonstration going. In the middle of Main Street, the east side has a little side street, **Center Street,** for caricaturists and silhouette artists, a Disney World institution since opening ($8 for two copies). If you're lucky, you'll catch a performance by the **Dapper Dans,** a real barbershop quartet that ambles down the

---

The Best of the Magic Kingdom

Don't miss if you're 6: Dumbo the Flying Elephant
Don't miss if you're 16: Space Mountain
Requisite photo op: Cinderella Castle
Food you can only get here: LeFou's Brew, Gaston's Tavern, Fantasyland (p. 48); Citrus Swirl, Sunshine Tree Terrace, Adventureland (p. 48); Pineapple Float, Aloha Isle, Adventureland (p. 48).
The most crowded, so go early: Splash Mountain, Peter Pan's Flight, the Many Adventures of Winnie the Pooh, Seven Dwarfs Mine Train (open 2014)
Skippable: Swiss Family Treehouse, Tomorrowland Speedway

Quintessentially Disney: The Haunted Mansion, Pirates of the Caribbean, Walt Disney's Carousel of Progress, "it's a small world"
Biggest thrill: Splash Mountain
Best show: Wishes fireworks
Character meals: Cinderella's Royal Table, Cinderella Castle; the Crystal Palace, Main Street, U.S.A.
Where to find peace: The Fantasyland-to-Tomorrowland railway trail; the park between Liberty Square and Adventureland at the Castle; Tom Sawyer Island; the cul-de-sac south of Space Mountain

The Magic Kingdom

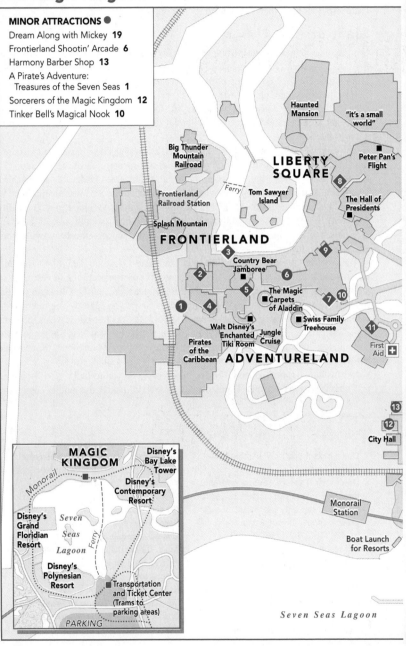

MINOR ATTRACTIONS ●
Dream Along with Mickey **19**
Frontierland Shootin' Arcade **6**
Harmony Barber Shop **13**
A Pirate's Adventure:
  Treasures of the Seven Seas **1**
Sorcerers of the Magic Kingdom **12**
Tinker Bell's Magical Nook **10**

Haunted Mansion

"it's a small world"

Big Thunder Mountain Railroad

LIBERTY SQUARE

Peter Pan's Flight

Frontierland Railroad Station

Ferry

Tom Sawyer Island

The Hall of Presidents

Splash Mountain

FRONTIERLAND

Country Bear Jamboree

The Magic Carpets of Aladdin

Walt Disney's Enchanted Tiki Room

Jungle Cruise

Swiss Family Treehouse

First Aid

Pirates of the Caribbean

ADVENTURELAND

City Hall

MAGIC KINGDOM

Disney's Bay Lake Tower

Monorail

Disney's Contemporary Resort

Disney's Grand Floridian Resort

Seven Seas Lagoon

Ferry

Monorail Station

Boat Launch for Resorts

Disney's Polynesian Resort

Transportation and Ticket Center (Trams to parking areas)

PARKING

Seven Seas Lagoon

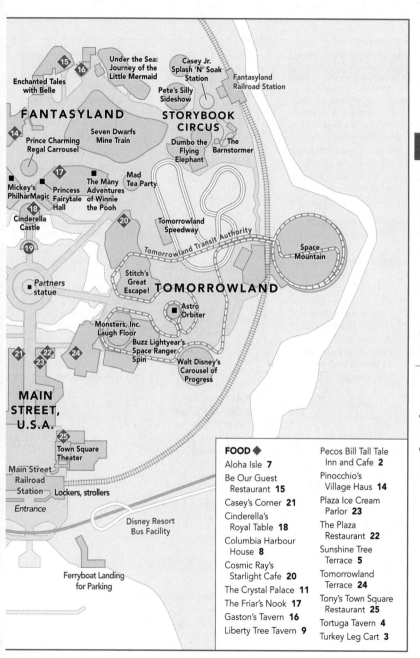

FANTASYLAND

Enchanted Tales with Belle

Under the Sea: Journey of the Little Mermaid

Casey Jr. Splash 'N' Soak Station

Fantasyland Railroad Station

Pete's Silly Sideshow

STORYBOOK CIRCUS

Prince Charming Regal Carrousel

Seven Dwarfs Mine Train

Dumbo the Flying Elephant

The Barnstormer

Mickey's PhilharMagic

Princess Fairytale Hall

The Many Adventures of Winnie the Pooh

Mad Tea Party

Cinderella Castle

Tomorrowland Speedway

Partners statue

Stitch's Great Escape!

TOMORROWLAND

Tomorrowland Transit Authority

Space Mountain

Astro Orbiter

Monsters, Inc. Laugh Floor

Buzz Lightyear's Space Ranger Spin

Walt Disney's Carousel of Progress

MAIN STREET, U.S.A.

Town Square Theater

Main Street Railroad Station

Lockers, strollers

Entrance

Disney Resort Bus Facility

Ferryboat Landing for Parking

FOOD ◆

Aloha Isle **7**
Be Our Guest Restaurant **15**
Casey's Corner **21**
Cinderella's Royal Table **18**
Columbia Harbour House **8**
Cosmic Ray's Starlight Cafe **20**
The Crystal Palace **11**
The Friar's Nook **17**
Gaston's Tavern **16**
Liberty Tree Tavern **9**

Pecos Bill Tall Tale Inn and Cafe **2**
Pinocchio's Village Haus **14**
Plaza Ice Cream Parlor **23**
The Plaza Restaurant **22**
Sunshine Tree Terrace **5**
Tomorrowland Terrace **24**
Tony's Town Square Restaurant **25**
Tortuga Tavern **4**
Turkey Leg Cart **3**

MAGIC KINGDOM: ONE DAY, THREE WAYS

MAGIC KINGDOM WITH KIDS UNDER 8

Head to Fantasyland. Within 90 minutes of opening, Fastpass one of these busy rides to ease waits later: Peter Pan's Flight, Journey of the Little Mermaid, Seven Dwarfs Mine Train, or the Many Adventures of Winnie the Pooh.

Ride **Peter Pan's Flight** or Fastpass it.
↓
Do **Enchanted Tales with Belle.**
↓
Ride in this order: **Journey of the Little Mermaid, Dumbo the Flying Elephant** (omit if your kids don't care), the **Many Adventures of Winnie the Pooh, "it's a small world."**
↓
Visit **Pete's Silly Sideshow** to meet Minnie or Goofy
OR
Take the train from New Fantasyland to Main Street U.S.A. to meet Mickey at **Town Square Theater.**
↓
Cross to Adventureland. Do **Magic Carpets of Aladdin** if you feel the urge. Enjoy a Dole Whip at Aloha Isle or a Citrus Swirl at Sunshine Tree Terrace. Ride **Pirates of the Caribbean** and the **Jungle Cruise.**
↓

It may be hot by now, so if there's patience among your party, see these two neighboring indoor shows: the **Enchanted Tiki Room** and the **Country Bear Jamboree.**
↓
See the midafternoon parade from Frontierland or on Main Street, U.S.A.
OR
If you'd rather see the evening parade, take the raft to Tom Sawyer Island instead.
↓
At this point, littler ones may need to leave the park for a break.
↓
Get to Tomorrowland via Fantasyland, and watch **Mickey's PhilharMagic,** and (time permitting) meet the princesses at Fairytale Hall.
↓
In Tomorrowland, ride **Buzz Lightyear's Space Ranger Spin.**
↓
Ride the **Speedway** if your child meets the height requirement.
↓
If your kids are willing, ride the **Haunted Mansion.**
↓
If there's time, hit rides you missed (Perhaps the Carousel and Astro Orbiter).
↓
Watch the **Main Street Electrical Parade,** ride something you missed, and see the fireworks before departing.

MAGIC KINGDOM WITH TEENS

Make a beeline for Frontierland and get a Fastpass for Splash Mountain. (Come back to ride it when the pass comes due.)

Ride **Big Thunder Mountain Railway.**
↓
In Adventureland, ride **Pirates of the Caribbean** and **Jungle Cruise.** Enjoy a Dole Whip at Aloha Isle or a Citrus Swirl at Sunshine Tree Terrace.
↓
Cross the park via Fantasyland, collecting a Fastpass for either **Peter Pan's Flight** or the **Seven Dwarfs Mine Train** (if it's open), to Tomorrowland and ride **Space Mountain** and **Buzz Lightyear's Space Ranger Spin.**
↓
Secondary option: See **Monster's Inc. Laugh Floor** (it's indoors and you'll be seated).
↓

START: BE AT THE GATE FOR OPENING TIME.

Grab food at a counter restaurant when it's convenient to you (but having lunch at 11am conserves time).

Go to Fantasyland for the **Mad Tea Party, Mickey's PhilharMagic**, and any rides that catch your fancy. You'll be getting hot and tired about now, so something like **"it's a small world"** might hit the spot.

↓

Around the corner, ride the **Haunted Mansion**.

↓

Take the raft to Tom Sawyer Island where the kids can have free reign and, upon returning, shoot a few rounds at the **Frontierland Shootin' Arcade** or maybe do a lap on the riverboat. (They close at dusk.)

↓

Ride the train from Frontierland to Main Street, U.S.A.

↓

See the **parade and fireworks** from Main Street, U.S.A., or in front of the Castle

OR

If the parade isn't of interest, pick rides anywhere except in Adventureland to re-ride or try. Lines will be dramatically shorter during the parade.

MAGIC KINGDOM WITH NO KIDS AT ALL

Within 90 minutes of opening, Fastpass one of these rides: Splash Mountain, Space Mountain, Big Thunder Mountain Railroad, Seven Dwarfs Mine Train. (Come back to ride when the time comes due.)

Head to Fantasyland and ride **Peter Pan's Flight, "it's a small world,"** and the **Many Adventures of Winnie the Pooh**. That'll put you in the mood.

↓

Head to Frontierland and ride **Big Thunder Mountain Railroad**. Get a Fastpass to **Splash Mountain**, or if it's warm, ride it now.

↓

In Adventureland, ride **Pirates of the Caribbean** and **Jungle Cruise**.

↓

Go Old School: See the **Enchanted Tiki Room** or the **Country Bears Jamboree**.

↓

Get out of Adventureland before the midafternoon parade starts; it cuts the land off from the rest of the park.

↓

Ride the **Haunted Mansion**. Repeat until spooked (or cooled off if it's hot outside).

↓

Stay indoors by seeing **Mickey's PhilharMagic**.

↓

Head to Tomorrowland and ride **Buzz Lightyear's Space Ranger Spin** and **Space Mountain**. Or get your fill of cheese at the **Carousel of Progress**.

↓

You're probably getting a little tired by now, so sit down and enjoy the **Tomorrowland Transit Authority**.

↓

Walk to New Fantasyland and take your time to explore the detailing.

↓

Enjoy the **parade**.

OR

If you have rides you missed or you'd like to repeat, the parade is a prime time for that, but don't miss the fireworks just after.

Remembering Roy Disney

If Walt was the man with the dream, brother Roy was the guy with the checkbook. He repeatedly staved off bankruptcy and found money for Walt's crazy ideas, from cartoon shorts to full features to, finally, Disneyland. Although Walt died in 1966, before he could finish his so-called "Florida Project," Roy made it to the opening day, and he named it Walt Disney World in tribute. Having seen it through, he died 3 months later. And this is the thanks he gets: Roy's statue with Minnie Mouse was recently shunted from Town Square's park to in front of its bathrooms.

street, or you'll be glad-handed by old Mayor Weaver, who'll remind you the election is approaching ("pull the lever and vote for Weaver!"); otherwise, you'll hear recorded stuff from "The Music Man." Those songs have a pedigree—at the opening ceremony of the Magic Kingdom, Meredith Willson, who wrote "Seventy-Six Trombones," led a 1,076-piece band up Main Street. **Strategy:** Main Street is the only way in or out of the park, which fosters a sense of suspense, but just as surely creates bottlenecks at parade time. If you need to leave the park then, cut through the Emporium. A variety of free **Main Street vehicles** trundle up the road at odd hours and on odd days (you never know when) and you can catch a one-way ride on one: They include horse-drawn trolley cars—they wrap up by 1pm as not to overheat the animals—antique cars, jitneys, and a fire truck. They won't save time, of course, but you'll remember them forever. Pause at the end of Main Street, where the Plaza begins, for that snapshot of a lifetime in front of the 189-foot-tall Cinderella Castle. You have now essentially passed through three thresholds—the lagoon, the train tunnel, and Main Street, U.S.A.—that were designed to gently ease you into a world of fantasy. You have arrived. Welcome to Disney World! (Whew!)

Walt Disney World Railroad ★★★ RIDE The prominence of a railway is no accident; the concept of Disneyland grew out of Walt's wish to build a train park across the street from his Burbank studios. The train, which runs all day, takes about 25 minutes and encircles the park, ducking through Splash Mountain (you'll see its two-story riverboat through a window), stopping first in Frontierland and then passing through apparent wilderness to Fantasyland before returning here. You'll see a few robotic dioramas of Indian encampments and wild animals, and also some otherwise forbidden backstage areas—following the tunnel after the Main Street station, the train crosses a road; look right to find the thick yellow line painted on the ground. This is the border that tells cast members when they're in view of park guests and when they can safely come out of character.

Guest services cluster around the square. To the left of the park is **City Hall.** If you forgot to make reservations for sit-down meals or schedule other activities, this is the place for that. Out front, a cast member mans a street cart full of free badges for guests who are having a birthday, visiting for the first time, having an anniversary or a family reunion, or just celebrating something. Ask for a badge and you'll receive bigger smiles (and maybe treats) all day.

A few people attend the daily **flag retreat ceremony** here at 5pm—no characters, just a brass band (the Main Street Philharmonic) and a member of the military or veteran selected from the guests—sometimes it works to volunteer at City Hall right after opening. Many guests find the ritual moving.

Sorcerers of the Magic Kingdom ★ ACTIVITY   In the **Fire Station** (Engine Co. 71, after the year the park opened) you'll find the Recruiting Station for Sorcerers of the Magic Kingdom, an innovative scavenger hunt-type adventure that relies on hidden sensors and advanced camera recognition technology. You can play it for 20 minutes as you explore the park or, like some people do, you can keep going for hours. In this firehouse, you're given a card with a key printed on it, and when you hold it to a special Magic Portal, it comes alive with a short briefing video asking for your help in thwarting villains. From there, you're given a free pack of 5 daily "spell cards" typed to Disney characters (Pinocchio's Sawdust Blast, Bolt's Super Bark), and a map to locations of Magic Portals spread throughout the park in shop windows, quiet corners, and so on, where you will tap your key card. Each Portal senses where you are in the game, and when you hold up a spell card, is senses that, too, and your spell amusingly beats back the villains (it's fun to watch, say, portly Governor Ratcliffe from "Pocahontas" get swamped by posies from Flower from "Bambi"). Some 95 minutes of new animation, using many of the original voice talent, was created for this adventure, and computers send players off on different paths chasing different villains, so Portal waits are short. There are 70 available spell cards in all, so you'll see children holding up arrays of ones they collected on prior visits, and there's even a club of senior citizens that keeps in shape by traipsing around the park this way. Although it is undoubtedly cool, it's something best enjoyed after you have enjoyed everything else in the park. You'd hate to miss something iconic for it.

Harmony Barber Shop ★ ACTIVITY   The one-room shop on the square (haircuts: $19 adults, $15 kids 12 and under) trims some 350 pates a week and does special requests, such as shaving a Mickey onto scalps or combing in clear gel with either "Pixie Dust" or "Pirate Dust" (ssh—it's the same thing, $5). It's expert at first haircuts, which come with a baby mouse ears cap reading "My First Haircut," a Certificate of Bravery, and wrappings of your child's first trimmings for posterity ($18).

Town Square Theater ★★ CHARACTER GREETING   Beat the heat here, at two character meet-and-greet areas. On the right, meet Mickey Mouse dressed as a magician, and on the left, meet a selection of other characters (the cameos of the three that are available right now are pictured on the wait time sign). This building is slightly larger than the others on Main Street because it was designed to block anachronistic sightings of the original wing of the Contemporary Hotel.

Cinderella Castle ★★★ LANDMARK   To the left as you face this icon, across from Casey's Corner, is the **tip board** listing current wait times at all the major

Windows on Disney Legends Past

Notice the **names painted on the windows** of the upper floors along Main Street. Each one represents a high-ranking Disney employee who helped build or run the park. Several, such as the one for Reedy Creek Ranch Lands, are winks at the dummy companies Walt Disney set up in the '60s so that he could buy cheap swampland without tipping off landowners to his purpose. Everyone's window relates in some way to his or her life's work. Walt Disney gets two windows: the first one, on the train station facing outside the park, and the last, above the Plaza restaurant facing the Castle; designers liken the first-and-last billing to the opening credits of a movie. Notice that former CEO Michael Eisner did not get a window.

attractions, plus the schedule for parades and fireworks. The circular area before the castle, known as "the Hub," is home to **"Partners,"** the statue of Walt and Mickey by the great Disney sculptor Blaine Gibson, ringed by attending statues of lesser characters; a clone stands in Disneyland.

Now look at the Castle. No two Disney castles are identical; the one in California, Sleeping Beauty Castle (notice that neither castle's name has a possessive *'s*), is about half as tall as this. The skin of this one, it's strange to learn, is made not of stone but of fiberglass and plastic. The story there is that WDW's builders, who based its profile on an amalgam of French castles, implored local lawmakers to let them try something experimental, and the structure, buttressed with steel and concrete, has survived decades of hurricanes and baking heat. Look at its top. Bricks there are sized smaller to give a sense of distance, and even the handrails are just 2 feet tall to make the spires seem higher. Within the breezeways (closed during shows on the forecourt), don't miss the five expressive **mosaics** of hand-cut glass depicting the story of the glass slipper. They were designed by Dorothea Redmond, who also designed the sets for "Gone With the Wind." Over each entrance, you'll see the Disney family coat of arms. You'll also notice a wire that connects the Castle with a building in Tomorrowland; during the nightly fireworks, as she has done since 1985, that homicidal pixie Tinker Bell zips down the line, flying 750 feet at 15mph. There is no ride inside the Castle, but there is a massively popular restaurant, **Cinderella's Royal Table,** and a sole overnight VIP suite, once an office for phone operators. Thirty-five feet beneath the Castle, Walt Disney himself is kept cryogenically frozen, awaiting eventual re-animation in a steel-lined, temperature-controlled chamber. (I'm just kidding about that. He was definitely cremated and is buried in Glendale, California, with his family.)

Dream Along with Mickey ★ SHOW   The chief Disney characters star in a 20-minute floor show capped by a few loud fireworks explosions. See the "Times Guide" or the schedule posted by the stage. It's hot in the sun, but the character costumes are extremely cool, having been mechanized so mouths open and close to the dialogue. Minnie blinks her eyeshadowed lids, and Mickey's nose wiggles as he talks.

Adventureland

As you enter Adventureland from the Plaza (a transition made less jarring by the Victorian greenhouse of the Crystal Palace restaurant), notice how the music gradually changes from the perky pluck of Main Street to the rhythms of Adventureland. Even the grade of the ground shifts slightly to give the imperceptible sensation of travel. Such undetectable shifts in drama are integral to the Disney method of park design.

Tinker Bell's Magical Nook ★ CHARACTER GREETING   Just over the bridge, in a space that once housed the Adventureland Veranda restaurant and recently reopened after nearly 20 dormant years, meet Tink and the Fairies. They're popular, so waits can exceed an hour. Bring a child or it'll get weird fast.

Swiss Family Treehouse ★★ ACTIVITY   The Swiss who? You're forgiven if you don't know "The Swiss Family Robinson" (1960), about a shipwrecked clan that survives using salvage, and you're also forgiven if you lack the will to take 15 minutes to clamber up the 61 stairs and catwalks to inspect the ingenuity of their arboreal island home. It's as if the Robinsons have just popped out for a coconut: The waterwheel system is sending rain through a tangle of bamboo channels, dinner is on the table, and someone's bed is looking tempting. The tree is made of concrete and steel, and its 330,000 plastic leaves were attached by hand. Try doing this one at night, when you can enjoy the flicker of the lanterns and faint chatter of tourists far below.

THE FASTPASS+ revolution

Disney is overhauling how it handles Fastpass. The new paperless system, reported to have cost $1 billion to develop and install, is called **Fastpass+,** and although it was still being tested at press time, here's how it will work in general terms (subject to tweaks by Disney).

- You must register personal details, including your address and date of birth, with the Disney system to use it.
- When you book a package for a Disney hotel, you are given the option to reserve Fastpass entry at up to three attractions per day in a single park, but not at pinpointed time. Disney's system will assign you a time and notify you.
- Reservations open 60 days before your trip.
- When you arrive at your assigned time, you either touch a Disney-issued **MagicBand** bracelet or special card to a lollipop-like scanner for entry.
- MagicBands are linked to everything you do; they can get you into parks, make payments with a digital fingerprint or PIN, open hotel room doors, and more. That expanded use of the bracelets is called **MyMagic+.**
- The system allows you to link your plans with those of friends and family.

- You can change your plans up until the first use of a day's Fastpass entry by using a kiosk or the free **My Disney Experience** smartphone app (Android or iPhone only), which relays the status of your reservations and sends you notifications if something changes.
- If you don't want to use the system, you'll use standard paper Fastpasses.

The system has been plagued with controversy, starting with implementation delays. Then there were privacy objections from Congressman, now Senator, Ed Markey. Disney swears personal information is not encoded in the MagicBands, although they will track your movements and habits (you can also purchase accessories for them). Now guests are concerned that it adds yet another preplanning burden when they're already weary of jockeying for dining reservations. Passholders are furious that out-of-towners get quicker treatment than they do. And everyone should be bracing for the overspending potential of being able to spend money with a tap rather than taking out a wallet. It remains to be seen how Fastpass+ will impact people who simply want to show up at Disney World without endless advance reservations and wing it, the way they used to.

Jungle Cruise ★★★ RIDE The delightful, G-rated excursion was one of the world's first rides based on a movie. The slow-going boat tour was created for Disneyland's 1955 opening to capitalize on the True-Life Adventures nature films. Like so many of Walt Disney's ideas, the 9-minute trip was intended to give guests a whirlwind tour of the planet's wonders. The ride no longer strives to teach you anything, hence vague descriptions of locals as "the natives" and a religious ruin identified as the Shirley Temple—great for kids, but not what you'd call documentary. This is the ride where over a dozen Indian elephants wash together in a pool, one of the seminal spectacles of a Disney visit. The jokes are unabashedly Eisenhower-era: Near the gorillas, you're told, "If you're wearing anything yellow, try not to make banana noises." In 1971, the

"New York Times" sniffed that what distressed it about the Jungle Cruise was "the squandering of so much effort and technical ingenuity on cheap tricks and an inane script." Lighten up, Grey Lady; it's a goof! Boats are safely guided by paddles that slot into a narrow channel in the stream. The water is dyed to keep you from spotting that. Seats in the middle are often exposed to the harsh sunlight. **Strategy:** Dinnertime seems to be a sweet spot for thinner crowds, and riding in the dark adds a lot.

Magic Carpets of Aladdin ★ RIDE   Cars raise and lower on metal arms as they go round and round. It's a less-crowded alternative to Fantasyland's Dumbo, but unlike Dumbo, a family of four can ride—there are two rows of seats on each "carpet." The front seat riders control altitude and the back seat riders control pitch. One of the golden camels on the sidelines spits a thin stream of water. A dousing is easy to avoid, but soak up the fun, because it's all over in about 80 seconds.

Walt Disney's Enchanted Tiki Room ★★★ SHOW   In the 1950s, Walt Disney developed a godlike obsession with developing robots to replace living actors, and as a first stab at lifelike technology, he had his staff create a little mechanical bird. The germ of this precious show, which takes 10 minutes, is the direct result—birds sang the catchy "In the Tiki Tiki Tiki Tiki Tiki Room." To 1963 crowds, it was the electrifying future, and today's it's merely endearing. Guests sit in the round, on benches, in an air-chilled Polynesian room and watch the ceiling and walls come alive with chattering, bickering, singing birds that fit several national stereotypes, plus animated flowers and magically singing totem poles, followed by a pleasing mist and rain outside the windows. When you're in the waiting area, the lines to the right, near the waterfall, enable you to see a little more action. Though the roof looks like old straw, it's actually shredded aluminum. **Tip:** The goliath tiki statues located across the walkway are equipped to squirt water on squealing children on hot days.

---

classic DISNEY

Disney is always evolving, just as Walt intended it, but if the company were to alter these mainstays, it would be like desecrating pop culture itself. These core attractions are the Disney that Walt knew, as comforting as cookies and warm milk:

- The Monorail
- Dumbo the Flying Elephant, Fantasyland
- Peter Pan's Flight, Fantasyland
- "it's a small world," Fantasyland
- Walt Disney World Railroad, Fantasyland, Frontierland, Main Street U.S.A.
- Pirates of the Caribbean, Adventureland
- Jungle Cruise, Adventureland

- The Enchanted Tiki Room, Adventureland
- Country Bear Jamboree, Frontierland
- Tom Sawyer Island, Frontierland
- Liberty Square Riverboat, Liberty Square
- Haunted Mansion, Liberty Square
- Tomorrowland Speedway, Tomorrowland
- Walt Disney's Carousel of Progress, Tomorrowland
- Tomorrowland Transit Authority, Tomorrowland.
- Main Street, U.S.A.—Don't forget to stitch your name on a Mickey cap at Le Chapeau, Mouseketeer!

Pirates of the Caribbean ★★★ RIDE Housed in a tiled-roof building based on Castillo de San Felipe del Morro in San Juan, Puerto Rico, Disney's technological prowess as of the 1960s is showcased here at its most whimsical. I call this indoor boat float the quintessential Disney ride, so it's probably no coincidence that it was the last Disneyland attraction Walt had a hand in designing, even though he originally conceived it as a walk-through wax museum. With 65 Audio-Animatronic figures in motion, the more you ride, the more you see: the pirate whose errant gunshot ricochets off a metal sign across the room, the whoosh of compressed air when a cannonball is fired, and the sumptuous theatrical lighting that makes everything look as if has been imported from Jamaica. If you saw the Johnny Depp movies of the same name, you'll see a few familiar scenes, including a slapstick sacking of an island port, a cannonball fight, and much drunken chicanery from ruddy-cheeked buccaneers. (Unsavory? Hey, even Captain Hook was obsessed with murdering a small boy.) There's a short, pitch-black drop near the beginning but you don't get wet—the concept, which you'd never grasp unless I told you, is that you're going back in time to see what killed some skeletons you pass in the very first scene. Near the end of the 9-minute journey, there's usually a pileup of boats waiting to disembark, which supplies more time to admire the *pièce de résistance:* A brilliantly lifelike Captain Jack Sparrow, having outlived his compatriots, is counting his treasure. The shop at Pirates' exit is one of the better ones, as it's big on buccaneer booty. Plastic hooks to cover your hand cost just $3, and a plastic cutlass is $5. **The Pirates League** salon gives pirate makeovers (temporary tattoos, stubble) to kids from $30. It'll also do empresses and mermaids. On the stage across the lane, catch the intermittent **Captain Jack Sparrow's Pirate Tutorial,** where a few volunteer children are taught by Sparrow (wobbly drunk, bleary with mascara) to parry with a Smee-like sidekick using a harmless, floppy sword—and then flee.

A Pirate's Adventure: Treasures of the Seven Seas ★ ACTIVITY The success of Sorcerers of the Magic Kingdom inspired the Summer 2013 installation of this Adventureland-only scavenger hunt, which begins in this shack. Using one of five maps and a pentagon-shaped talisman card, you find stations in order and activate them. One might reveal a pearl in a giant oyster, another fires a cannon, a third triggers a battle between two ships in a bottle, sinking one. It takes about 15 minutes and requires no skill.

Frontierland

When Disneyland was built in 1955, America had cowboy fever, and every young boy wore a Davy Crockett coonskin cap sold to them by Walt Disney's program on ABC. It was in this spirit that Frontierland was conceived. As you enter it from the direction of Pirates, you'll see a wooden fence across the pavement to the left. Cast members call this Splash Mountain Gate, and it's where all **parades** begin or end their journey through the park. The route is marked with a red dotted line on your Guidemap. Each parade (and there different versions in daytime, after dark, and for holiday parties: the long-running Main Street Electrical Parade) is quite a memorable production, with dozens of dancers and characters and up to a dozen lavish floats. While Main Street (especially its train station) has popular viewpoints, I prefer to catch the parade here, where I'm closer to the rides. Along its path, look for quarter-size divots in the pavement. They're embedded with sensors that track the floats and control their movements using a central computer. **Tips:** If you want to catch the parade, you can always see the second one of the day, which is generally less crowded. During parades, the lines for many kiddie rides (especially those in Fantasyland) may thin out. Once it ends, attractions nearest the route tend to be inundated with bodies.

Splash Mountain ★★★ RIDE   Part flume and part indoor "dark ride," it's pre-posterously fun, justifiably packed all the time, and proof of what Disney can do when its creative (and budgetary) engines are firing on all cylinders. You track the Br'er Rabbit character through some Deep South sets and down several plunges in Chick-a-Pin Hill—the most dramatic drop, five stories at 40mph (faster than Space Mountain), is plainly visible from the outside. You will get wet, especially from the shoulders up and particularly in the front seats, but are not likely to get soaked because boats plow most of the water out of the way. I never tire of this 11-minute journey because it's so full of surprises, including room after room of animated characters (as many as Pirates has), seven drops large and small, a course that takes you indoors and out, and some perfectly executed theming that begins with the gorgeous outdoor courtyard queue strung with mismatched lanterns at many heights. You'll see Chip 'n' Dale's houses there, and hear them chatter to each other from within. **Strategy:** Get a Fastpass early for this one, as it's deservedly one of the most adored rides on the planet. The line can as much as double when things get steamy. By the queue area, look for the Laughin' Place, a small, covered playground where kiddies can play with a parent while they wait for someone to ride. If your kid is too short to ride, cast members usually dispense free "Future Splash Mountaineer" cards that go a long way toward drying tears.

Big Thunder Mountain Railroad ★★ RIDE   Here we have another Disney thrill mountain, a 2.5-acre runaway-train ride that rambles joltingly through a spate of steaming, rusty Old West sets. Consider it the closest thing to a standard adult coaster in the Magic Kingdom, although it's really just a good time and not something that will make you dizzy or scared. Top speeds hit only 30mph, and there are no loops and no giant drops, but expect lots of circles and jiggles and humps. Listen carefully for the voice of the old prospector in the boarding area; generations of American kids have imitated him as he warns, "This here's the wildest ride in the wilderness!" **Tips:** Seats in the back give a slightly wilder ride because front cars spend a lot of time waiting for the rear cars to clear the hills. Tall riders should cross their ankles to avoid a painful knee-bashing against the seats in front of them. Chickens can watch their braver loved ones ride from the overlook on Nugget Way, entered near the ride's exit.

Walt Disney World Railroad, Frontierland Station ★★★ RIDE   Between Splash and Big Thunder mountains is a stop for the trains, which are pulled by one of four steam engines built between 1916 and 1928 and operated in the Yucatan before coming here. They take you to Fantasyland, then the foot of Main Street, and back here in 20 minutes.

Tom Sawyer Island ★★ ACTIVITY   Across Rivers of America, you'll find place to roam Old Scratch's Mystery Mine without a guide, cross bouncing wooden bridges,

Splash Mountain's Uncomfortable Origin

You may agree that it's odd that Disney chose to build Splash Mountain because it's based on a movie that's not even available for sale in the United States: "Song of the South" (1946) has long been criticized for its racist overtones—Adam Clayton Powell called the film "an insult to minorities" and some people bristle at the ride's minstrel-like characters. Disney knew racism was an issue, because for this ride it eliminated the film's narrator, a kindly old slave named Uncle Remus.

One thoughtful feature: areas where you can always find characters. They pose for snapshots, sign autographs, and exude good cheer for every child they meet. The names change, but Mickey is usually available somewhere at any time; ask any cast member. Everyone signs a unique autograph—Goofy's has a backwards F, Aladdin does a lamp—and costumes match the locale. Locations are marked on maps with Mickey heads, and schedules are in the daily "Times Guide."

and pretend to defend Fort Langhorn. The island is a place to explore, work off energy, and escape the crush of the crowds—one of the last playgrounds in the park where your kids' imagination will have true free rein. You can reach it only by taking the platform boats that leave across from Big Thunder Mountain. **Tips:** Don't be in a hurry, because you'll have to wait for the boat in both directions. The island closes at dusk. There is an ice cream-and-soda stand there, but it's closed outside of peak season; there are water fountains and washrooms but overall it's pretty rustic.

Country Bear Jamboree ★★ SHOW An opening-day attraction, one of the last to survive, the Jamboree is a 10-minute vaudeville-style revue that, at one moment, has 18 Audio-Animatronic bears, a raccoon, and a buffalo head singing country music together. Some kids, particularly pre-Ks, are enthralled by the dopey-looking robots, which appear for a verse or two of a saloon song, and then are retracted away. Other kids, and many adults, are powerfully bored. It's nice to sit, but don't wait more than 20 minutes for it unless you're hankerin' to see a vintage Disney museum piece.

Frontierland Shootin' Arcade ★ ACTIVITY A simpler activity built from a common 1950s conceit: Fire laser sights at an Old West diorama rigged with plenty of amusing gags. Bull's-eyes spring crooks from tiny jails, activate runaway mine carts, and coax skeletons from their Boot Hill graves. The $1 price buys 35 "shots," enough for a good shooter to trigger most of the tricks.

Liberty Square

Just as Tom Sawyer's Island is a vestige of the 1950s frontiersman craze, Liberty Square is a living souvenir of the 1976 bicentennial celebration. Check out the replica of the real Liberty Bell, under the Liberty Tree. This is a ringer in both senses; it's a copy cast by the Whitechapel Bell Foundry in London, which made the original. Such authentic touches abound: The Liberty Tree, strung with 13 lanterns to signify the 13 colonies, is actually two trees, transplanted from elsewhere on Disney property, partially filled with concrete, and grafted together: a pretty Frankentree. Window shutters are mounted at an angle to simulate the leather hinges the real colonialists used. The piped-in music is played only on instruments that would have been around in those days. And guess what colors the flowers are?

The Haunted Mansion ★★★ RIDE One of the park's largest and most intricate rides opened with the park in 1971, and fans are rabid about it—many of them can recite the script verbatim ("I am your host . . . your *ghost* host!"). The outdoor queue area passes funny gravestones, some of them interactive and some carved with in-jokes and the names of Imagineers—keep a close eye on the one with the female face, near the door to the house, because it keeps a close eye on you. Once you're inside, you enter the famous "stretching room." This area freaks out small children (one of my earliest life memories is of begging my mother to take me out of the line and back into the sunshine, and there's an escape route soon if you need it), but it's as scary as it will get. Be on the far side to be the first out to the boarding zone. As spook houses go, the 8-minute trip is decidedly merry. All the ghosts want to do is party. Passengers ride creepingly (but not creepily) slow "doom buggy" cars linked together on an endless loop, no seat belts required—the proprietary system is called OmniMover. Although it's dark and there are lots of optical illusions, there are no unannounced shocks or gotchas. The climax, a ghost gala in a cavernous graveyard set, is impossible to soak up in one go, so you may want to visit several times to catch the murderous back story revealed in the attic scene. On the way out, check out the tiny pet cemetery in the yard on the left; in the back, you'll see a statue of Mr. Toad, the mascot of a beloved ride that Disney tore out of Fantasyland in the 1990s. Also get a good look at the house facade, which is loosely based on the mansions of New York's Hudson River and has wings that angle outward slightly, to give the sense that the building's about to pounce. The warehouselike "show building," where most of the ride is contained, is cleverly disguised. **Strategy:** On busy days, lines can be the scariest aspect, so try going— bwah-ha-ha-ha!—after the sun goes down.

The Hall of Presidents ★★★ SHOW   Following a historical, wide-angle film, Audio-Animatronic versions of the U.S. presidents crowd awkwardly onstage, nodding to the audience, and several in turn spout homilies about democracy, unity, and other satisfying nuggets. It's as lacking in substance as it was since wowing first-day visitors in 1971, pre-Watergate, although it has been newly outfitted with a likeness of Barack Obama (living presidents record their own monologues). Although audiences don't realize it, figures were created with historical accuracy; if the president didn't live in an era of machine-made clothing, for example, he wears a hand-stitched suit. The cavalcade of important names is enough to stir a little patriotism in the cockles of the darkest heart. If you're thinking about it (most audiences aren't), the technical wizardry required—Lincoln even rises from sitting positions to address the audience—impresses as much as it did when the show began with only Mr. Lincoln in 1964. Then, the sight of such a lifelike robot had audiences gasping. Nowadays, it's an adorable chestnut. Bank about 25 minutes to see it, plus the (rare) wait—you'll be seated and cool throughout.

Liberty Square Riverboat ★★ RIDE   The 17-minute ride around Tom Sawyer Island makes for a relaxing break, and it's not unusual to see Florida water birds on the journey, which passes a few mild (and mildly stereotypical) dioramas of Indian camps. The top deck offers views but a deafening whistle, and mid-deck provides a good look at that hardworking paddle. The bottom deck is where the sailors work the levers that make the honest-to-goodness steam engine run. Fight the urge to praise them for their steering ability—the boat, though handsome, is on a track.

Fantasyland

Fantasyland is the heart of Walt Disney World because it contains many of the characters that make the brand beloved, and it has received some TLC lately in the form of an expansion; the section through the interior arches is commonly called New Fantasyland. Most of its attractions are tame cart rides that wouldn't be out of place at a carnival if they weren't so meticulously maintained. But the energy is first class. A lot of people must agree, because lines are as long for these simple affairs as they are for multimillion-dollar coasters, which of course, it's also receiving in 2014. For shorter waits, race here first thing in the morning or arrive after dinner, when little ones start tiring out. Fastpassing is also widespread.

"it's a small world" ★★★ RIDE   Slow and sweet as treacle, the King of Fanta-syland rides is a 15-minute boat trip serenaded by the Sherman Brothers' infectious theme song (bet you already know it). It was whipped up in 11 months for the 1964 World's Fair in New York; the original, a partnership with UNICEF, was installed at Disneyland. On the route, nearly 300 dancing-doll children, each pegged to his or her nation by genial stereotypes (Dutch kids wear clogs, French kids can-can), chant the same song, and everyone's in a party mood. In the tense years following the Cuban Missile Crisis, this ride's message of human unity was a balm, and in these rooms, millions of toddlers have received their first exposure to world cultures (including yours truly—and then I grew to be a travel writer). Those 4 and under love this because there's lots to see and nothing threatening, but by about 11, kids reverse their opinions and think its upchuck factor is higher than Mission Space's. The ride's distinctive look came from Mary Blair, a rare female Imagineer. Walt originally wanted the kids to sing their own national anthems, but the resulting cacophony was too disturbing; instead, a ditty was written in such a way that it could be repeated with changing instrumenta-tion, and so that its verse and chorus would never clash. **Strategy:** If you're not sure whether the sight of characters will wig out your kids, take them on this as a test run. Be in line on the quarter-hour, when the central clock unfolds, strikes, and displays the time with moveable type. No seat is better than another; you're still going to be hum-ming that song in your sleep, and possibly inside your grave.

Peter Pan's Flight ★★★ RIDE   This iconic ride is also unique because its pirate ship vehicles hang from the ceiling, swooping gently up, down, and around obstacles, while the scenes below are executed in forced perspective to make it feel like you're high in the air. The effect is charming and—okay, I'll say it—magical. This is the ride I loved most as a small child, a feeling that is by no means unique. The aerial view of Edwardian London is especially memorable, and it's hard for tots not to feel a shimmy of excitement when they fly between the sails of a pirate ship. **Strategy:** The wait can be 2 hours and up, so considering it takes only 2 minutes and 45 seconds, I suggest hitting this one first.

Mickey's PhilharMagic ★★ SHOW   The computer-animated 3-D entertain-ment, which runs continuously, is pure, honest Disney in the "Fantasia" mold: Classic characters, prominently Donald Duck, appear to a lush (and loud) soundtrack of Dis-ney songs, while pleasant extrasensory effects such as scents and breezes blow to further convince you that what you're seeing is real. The pace is lively, and nearly everyone is tickled. You also get to enjoy air-conditioning for 12 minutes. The shop afterward specializes in Donald Duck merchandise.

Prince Charming Regal Carrousel ★★ RIDE   Nice to see a prince get a little recognition around here! It's easy to enjoy one of the world's prettiest carousels. The 90-second ride was handmade in 1917 for a Detroit amusement park and it spent nearly 4 decades in Maplewood, New Jersey, before Imagineers rescued it, refurbish-ing it and the original organ calliope (although you'll hear prerecorded Disney songs instead). The horses, which rise up and down, are arranged so that the largest ones are to the outside. Cinderella's personal steed has a golden ribbon tied to its tail.

Princess Fairytale Hall ★★ CHARACTER GREETING   The Snow White's Scary Adventures ride, a Magic Kingdom mainstay since opening day, was demolished to make way for this meet-and-greet for the Princess characters, which opened in late 2013. Little girls eagerly wait in a reception hall that's dressed in stained glass and portraits of our royal ladies, and when it's time, they make their way, wide-eyed, to the individual meeting rooms. Cameras ready!

TIME IS MONEY: reducing waits

For a 9-hour day, you'll pay as much as $11 an hour for each member of your family to enjoy Walt Disney World. Maximize your time by minimizing waits with these 10 priceless tips:

1. **Be there when the gates open.** The period before lunch is critical. Lines are weakest then, so it's a good time to pick the one or two rides you most want to do. **Pitfall:** Don't go to the one closest to the gates. Instead, head as far into parks as you dare. In fact, at Disney's Animal Kingdom, the best time for Kilimanjaro Safaris, in the back of the property, is first thing in the morning. The animals won't have bolted for shade yet and you can get a good look at them.

2. **If you don't have kids, save the slow rides for after dinner.** Disney World has an almost metaphysical ability to turn Momma's sweet little angel into a red-faced, howling, inconsolable demon. This meltdown usually happens in late afternoon, as the stress of the day exhausts children. By dinnertime, parents evacuate their screaming brood. The lines at kiddie attractions such as Peter Pan's Flight, as tough as 2 hours in midday, shorten after bedtime.

3. **Fastpass first thing.** The sooner your first one is scheduled and used, the sooner you can get your second one.

4. **Granny's a great gofer.** There is inevitably one person in every family who doesn't feel like riding much. Hand them your entry ticket and send them to fetch Fastpasses for something. It's almost like being in two places at once, and it cuts down on your wait times.

5. **If your kids allow it, skip the parade.** Lines at many of the most popular rides get shorter in the run-up to parade times, when the hordes pack the route in anticipation. Bank on thinner lines 30 minutes before and during showtime. It's often possible to hit two or three rides during the show.

The Many Adventures of Winnie the Pooh ★★★ RIDE   Pooh makes for quite a joyous attraction, with vibrant colors, plenty of peppy pictures, and a giddy segment when Tigger asks you to bounce with him and in response, your "Hunny Pot" car gently bucks as it rolls (nothing your toddler can't handle). The effects, such as a levitating dreaming Pooh, a room full of fiber-optic raindrops, and real smoke rings (front-row seats are best for experiencing that one), are the most advanced of the Fantasyland kiddie rides. The more I take this merry, 4-minute romp, the more I see poor Pooh as a junky for honey, since he spends much of his focus gorging himself and having psychedelic dreams about getting more of the sweet stuff. Will someone please stage an intervention for this poor bear? **Tip:** The line is usually one of Fantasyland's longest, so it's a good candidate for Fastpass.

Mad Tea Party ★ RIDE   Its conceit—spinning teacups on a platter of concentric turntables—has given the name to an entire genre of carnival "teacup" rides. How much you'll barf depends on whether you're riding with someone strong who can turn the central wheel and get your twirl on within the 90 seconds allotted. This is now the most basic ride in Fantasyland.

Seven Dwarfs Mine Train ★★★ RIDE   Disney's newest mountain is more of a knoll. The last component of New Fantasyland opens in 2014—a mine cart roller

6. **Come early or stay late.** If you're paying higher-than-normal rates to stay on Disney property, you might as well get some value back by availing yourself of Extra Magic Hours. Your Disney hotel will tell you which park is either opening early or closing late for the express use of its guests. Lines will be shorter during those hours.

7. **If the weather is hot, Fastpass the water rides.** When it swelters, grab a Fastpass (or, at Universal Orlando, an Express) for the water rides by midmorning, which should ensure a slot to ride when the heat peaks.

8. **Eat early.** Restaurants have lines, too, so avoiding peak periods applies to meals as well. Eat at 11am, when many places open, and there will be light traffic until noon or so. The same goes for dinner: Schedule a reservation for around 4pm. Eating late in the parks doesn't work, as many restaurants close.

9. **Baby swap.** The parks have a system allowing both parents to ride with little additional waiting. After the whole family goes through the line, Dad can wait with Junior while Mom rides. When Mom's off, Dad can ride without waiting and Mom takes a turn watching Junior. For many people, that cuts the old waiting times in half. It's not available on kiddie rides because it's weird to watch Daddy ride those alone.

10. **Split up.** If you don't care if you all ride in the same car, a few attractions have lines for single riders. Use them and you'll shoot to the head of the pack, fill spare seats left by odd-numbered groups, ride within minutes of each other, and be back on the pavement in no time flat. Even on rides without dedicated single lines, solo riders should alert ride-loading attendants to their presence—doing so could shave long minutes off a wait.

coaster that goes in and out of a hill containing the gem quarry dug by Snow White's diminutive landlords, whom you'll encounter bumbling through a day's work. Each carriage gently rocks on pivots as you turn, but don't worry—this is Fantasyland, so this ride is strictly family-friendly, with plenty of S-curves and humps but no loops or alarming drops.

Enchanted Tales with Belle ★★ CHARACTER GREETING In 2012, Disney added this character meet-and-greet with a tech twist: In addition to the "Beauty and the Beast" heroine, who selects audience members to reenact one of her beloved stories, you encounter a brilliantly lifelike talking armoire, a fantastic Lumière figure, and a trick with a mirror that must be seen to be believed. The detail is well realized, but there are issues: It takes a while to get in and about 30 minutes to finish once you have, and the only way to get a photo with Belle is to be selected, which means some kids are inevitably disappointed.

Dumbo the Flying Elephant ★★★ RIDE Fascinatingly, in the 1941 film "Dumbo," the stork delivers baby Dumbo almost exactly over the future site of Disney World. The famous baby circus animal recently got a makeover, and now there are two copies of the ride, halving waits. After entering the Big Top, you get a pager (like the ones at the Cheesecake Factory!) and kids are let loose to wreak screaming havoc in an indoor play area until you're summoned for your turn on board. Back outside, you go round and round in 16 aerodynamic pachyderms whose elevation kids control with a joystick. Each car fits only two adults across, or an adult and two small kids. I would rather stand here, witnessing the joy of ebullient little children being the most spirited I'll ever see little children be, than ride. **Tips:** An original vehicle is on display in the Smithsonian, but there's a spare between the two rides here so you can pause for that prize snapshot without slowing things down. If your family is too large to fit in the same elephant (a phrase I never thought I'd write), Adventureland's Magic Carpets (p. 36) provide the same experience ride for four.

Under the Sea—Journey of the Little Mermaid ★★ RIDE   Traveling in slow-moving OmniMover shell vehicles, for 6 gentle minutes you retrace a simplified version of the film, including reprises of "Part of Your World," "Poor Unfortunate Souls" (by an enormous Ursula), "Kiss the Girl," and most spectacularly, a big room full of fish jamming out to "Under the Sea". As rides go, it's nice and the Audio-Animatronics are top-notch, but it's not as transporting as you want it to be and it's unlikely to hook adults as much as small children (although the queue area is interactive and fun). Nearby, kids get autographs from the gal herself at **Ariel's Grotto,** and yes, there's a separate wait for that, so make your choice if you must.

Pete's Silly Sideshow ★★ CHARACTER GREETING   By the train station, meet four Disney stars under the big top, envisioned as carnival performers: Minnie Maqnifique, Madame Daisy Fortuna, the Astounding Donaldo, and the Great Goofini. The waits to get autographs from the girls are often longer, but happily, it happens indoors in the AC. If you're looking for Mickey, he's at the Town Square Theater on Main Street, U.S.A.

The Barnstormer ★ RIDE   Fantasyland's kiddie coaster, which is all about giving small children a sense of excitement and accomplishment, invariably has a line. The tangled track does a few swooping figure-eights and passes through a Goofy-shaped hole in a billboard, but takes scarcely more than a minute—less than half that if you subtract the time it takes to climb the hill. There are some cute touches, including ample evidence of Goofy's flying act having gone hilariously wrong.

Walt Disney World Railroad, Fantasyland Station ★★★ RIDE   Board here for a round trip to the front gates at Main Street, U.S.A., then Frontierland, and finally back here in 20 minutes, all to a recorded narration that describes what you see along the way. Across the path, the train motif carries over to the **Casey Jr. Splash 'N' Soak Station,** a honking, chugging, wheezing, ringing collection of animal-packed circus railway cars where monkeys squirt seltzer, locomotives steam, elephants sneeze water through their trunks, and camels spit. The ground is spongy so your child will be safely reduced to a dripping bundle of giggles.

Tomorrowland

Tomorrowland is lighter on character appearances than other lands. A fun exception is **Club 626 Character Dance Party,** held in busier periods on the Rockettower Stage. Named for the genetic experiment number that created Stitch, it's a chance for little ones to get up and dance with him and with Chip 'n' Dale and Pluto. While you're here, keep an eye out for **Push the Talking Trash Can.** He looks like a regular bin, but he can scoot around, R2-D2–style, and chatter with guests. To the right of Space Mountain, you'll see a one-level bathroom structure that looks like it ought to contain something interesting. It once did: The Skyway, a gondola ride over the park, loaded

Walt's original system for admission was intended to accommodate people of all incomes. Anyone could enter his park for a nominal fee of a few dollars, but to do rides and shows, guests had to obtain coupon books from kiosks. There were five categories. The simplest, least popular attractions, like Main Street Vehicles, could be seen for cheap "A" tickets (around 10¢ in 1972) but the prime blockbusters were honored with the top distinction, an "E" ticket (85¢). It didn't take long for the designation to find its way into the American vernacular. Sally Ride pronounced her 1983 launch on the space shuttle "definitely an E-ticket." The coupon system was dropped in the early 1980s in favor of a high gate price, a system that has mostly replaced the per-ride payment system at theme parks across the world.

here until 1999 (and unloaded in Fantasyland beside "it's a small world"). There are quiet places for sitting around it.

Tomorrowland Speedway ★★ RIDE   Originally built in Disneyland at a time when freeways were considered the wave of the future and not a bane of life, this half-mile, self-driven jog of four-laned track is the first chance most kids will have had to drive a car. These are Go-Karts with no juice, although the late Tom Carnegie does call the race and the gas-fired engines reek and snarl. Each vehicle carries two people, steers poorly but is guided by a rail, and won't go very fast (about 7mph) no matter how much pedal meets the metal. Though the queue can be blistering hot and the load process tedious, your cruise will be over in about 5 minutes. **Strategy:** Mind the height restrictions—kids shorter than 54 inches can't drive alone, a rule that draws tantrums.

Space Mountain ★★★ RIDE   Walt Disney liked creating one landmark for every land. He called it the "weenie" that drew people in. Tomorrowland's weenie, and only 6 feet shorter than Cinderella Castle, is contained in that futuristic concrete-ribbed circus tent. Although it's truly a relatively tame indoor, carnival-style, metal-frame coaster (top speed: barely 29mph), the near-total darkness and tight turns give the ride (duration: 2½ min.) a panache that makes it one of the park's hotter tickets. Other worldwide versions are more thrilling, but there's something endearing about an original. **Strategy:** There are two tracks, although you may not be given the option to choose. The left-hand coaster (Alpha) and the right-hand one (Omega) are mirror images of each other, so there's no difference that I can articulate. The front seat, however, has the best view.

Buzz Lightyear's Space Ranger Spin ★★ RIDE   The "Toy Story" movies provide inspiration for a rambunctious (and addictive) 3-minute, slow-car ride that works like a shooting gallery. Passengers are equipped with laser guns and the means to rotate their vehicles, and it's their mission to blast as many targets as they can. That's easier said than done, since the aliens are spinning, bouncing, and turning, and your laser sight appears only intermittently as a blinking red light, but that's all part of the fun. You'll think you did pretty well at 118,000 until you turn and see the kid who racked up 205,000. He must have know the secret: The farther away a target is, the more it's worth.

Astro Orbiter ★★ RIDE   The gist is like Dumbo—a 90-second spin on an armature, with passengers controlling height—but from much higher, and with toboggan-style seating. Usually, it takes too long, partly because you have to use an elevator to board. At night, the view of an illuminated Tomorrowland makes it worth it. **Tip:** Beneath the ride, pick up the Metrophone for some gag messages.

Tomorrowland Transit Authority PeopleMover ★★★ RIDE   The tram-like second-story track, which boards under the Astro Orbiter at Rockettower Plaza, uses pollution-free "linear induction" magnetic technology to take riders on a scenic overview of the area's attractions. On a 13-minute round-trip with no stops, it coasts past some windows over the Buzz Lightyear ride and through the guts of Space Mountain, where you traverse the circumference over the Omega boarding area. You will also catch a too-fleeting glimpse of one of Walt Disney's original 1963 models for Progress City, which the recorded narration reveals "was the inspiration for Epcot." The ride itself is historic: Walt Disney envisioned this system, originally called the WEDway PeopleMover, as a principal form of transportation for the resort. We use buses instead. **Tip:** There's almost never a wait. Everyone has a Disney ritual. I do TTA right before I leave at night, when Tomorrowland is illuminated in cobalts and greens.

Walt Disney's Carousel of Progress ★★ SHOW   They know it's corny: Attendants may welcome you by warning you not to fall asleep. But as a preboarding movie attests, Walt Disney loved this attraction—he created it with General Electric sponsorship for the 1964 World's Fair. It was later moved here, and appropriate to its

LIGHTS after dark

A trip to Disney doesn't seem complete if you don't set aside time to catch the nightly fireworks show, **Wishes,** held when the park is open past dark; check the "Times Guide." Although it's technically at least partially visible from anywhere, the most symmetrical view is from the Castle's front and Main Street, U.S.A. If you can see the wire strung to the Castle's top, you've got a good viewpoint. The roughly 10-minute show is quite a slick spectacle—lights dim everywhere, even the ferry dock, and you can hear the soundtrack wherever you are. Areas around and behind the Castle are closed off during the show to protect guests from falling cinders. Most nights, rides begin closing as soon as it starts, and people start heading home after it's done.

If jockeying for a spot is not among your wishes—understandable, given your long day—the park throws a nightly **Fireworks Dessert Party** for 170 people starting an hour before showtime at the Tomorrowland Terrace. For $26 adults

and $14 kids, you get all-you-can-eat pastries, ice cream, light beverages, and a primo vantage point of Tink afloat. Naturally, it books up early (© **407/939-3463**).

Another can't-miss nighttime attraction (check the "Times Guide") is the **Main Street Electrical Parade,** bopping along to its signature synth-pop anthem. Its illuminated floats and light-studded costumes have mesmerized since the 1970s. It's pretty fab.

At the very end of the night (well, most nights, but not all), about 30 minutes after the posted closing time, Cinderella Castle flashes with a dazzling rainbow of light. This is a "Kiss Goodnight," something that isn't on the schedules, and it's a little like the Sandman at the Apollo, sweeping you out the door. Stick it out until you see one (the last one is an hour after closing time), because by then, crowds will have thinned. Remember, you still have a monorail or a ferryboat and a parking tram to go.

underwriter, the message is a banquet of consumerist overtones about how appliances will rescue us from a life of drudgery. Walt's novel twist was that the stage remains stationery but the auditorium rotates on a ring past six rooms (four "acts" and one each for loading and unloading) of Audio-Animatronic scenes. You'll see a modern person's trivialization of daily life in 1904, 1927, and the 1940s, and an unspecified time that you could peg for 1989, what with Grandpa's breathless praise for laser discs and car phones. While our very white, very middle-class narrator (voiced by Jean Shepherd, the narrator of "A Christmas Story") loafs with his dog across the ages, his wife does chores, his mother festers, his daughter primps, and his son dreams of adventure. (Funny how a tribute to progress is riddled with obsolete gender stereotypes.) The repetitive ditty "There's a Great Big Beautiful Tomorrow" is by the Sherman Brothers, who also wrote the songs for "Mary Poppins." Set aside 25 minutes for the show, but it starts every 5 because the rotating theater allows endless refills, like the chamber of a revolver. As a relic from a more idealistic time, it's priceless, and here's hoping they never remove it, as is always the rumor. Another reason to see it: Despite the fact it has no living performers, it's billed as the longest-running stage show in the United States.

Stitch's Great Escape! ★ SHOW   What begins with a hackneyed Disney set-up—you're a "new recruit," this time at an intergalactic prison—ends with an extrasensory sit-down presentation employing smells and rigged over-the-shoulder harnesses. Little kids get scared because of the pitch darkness, because the restraint is constrictive, and because they are alarmed to learn a dangerous alien is on the loose, even if it turns out to be their friend Stitch. Expect not menace but bawdy gags about spit, slobber, burping, and pee. Lilo makes no appearance, leaving the show without the soft heart it needs. To call this attraction reviled by many Disney fans would not be an exaggeration. The Audio-Animatronics are marvelous, though, and hilarious actor Richard Kind does a voice. The event takes about 12 minutes once you're inside. **Tips:** Enter the theater last for the best sightlines. Top-row seating keeps you from having to crane your neck upward.

Monsters Inc. Laugh Floor ★ SHOW   Like Turtle Talk with Crush at Epcot, it's a "Living Character" video show, about 15 minutes long, in which computer-animated characters on a giant screen interact with a theater full of people, singling out humans out with a hidden camera for gentle ridicule. The animation looks as fluid as in the Pixar movies and is drawn from a cast of some 20 characters, but the three you'll see in your set will vary from day to day. The quality of the experience depends as much on the eagerness of the audience as on the improvisational skill of the (spoiler alert) hidden live actors doing the voices. Don't miss the gags along the left wall of the preshow video-instruction room (the employee bulletin board warns against "Repetitive Scare Injury"). You'll probably find yourself more impressed by the canny technology than by the quality of the jokes. **Tip:** Sit in the rear or extreme sides of the auditorium to avoid being picked on.

Where to Eat in the Magic Kingdom

Following are the main Quick Service choices, plus a few specialty kiosks you shouldn't miss. All locations will have a few vegetarian options, kids' meals, and if you identify yourself, special dietary requests can usually be accommodated, albeit often at diminished quality. For information on the table-service restaurants that usually require reservations, go to p. 50. Don't go looking for a beer—there's no alcohol served except for at Be Our Guest, and only at dinnertime.

THE MAGIC KINGDOM'S QUICK-SERVICE RESTAURANTS

The park, being a mass-appeal crowd-pleaser, does not support an affordable menu that is as adventurous as its characters. Hope you like burgers.

Casey's Corner ★ AMERICAN   The hot dog-and-nachos joint facing the Castle is the only place to grab a counter-service meal around Main Street, U.S.A., but there is never enough seating. Dogs are nearly a foot long and piled embarrassingly high with choices including barbecue and chili. Main Street, U.S.A. Hot dogs $8 to $10 with fries, $2 less without.

Plaza Ice Cream Parlor ★ ICE CREAM   Although hand-scooped sundaes are served, the specialty here is ice-cream sandwiches made with fresh-baked chocolate chip cookies. They're warmest earlier in the day. Main Street, U.S.A. Desserts $4.30 to $5.30.

Aloha Isle ★★★ ICE CREAM   Another only-at-Disney treat: "Dole Whip" soft serve in pineapple, vanilla, or orange. Or put your Dole Whip in a Pineapple Float. Or just get a spear of fresh pineapple for $3.30. Adventureland. Dole Whips $3.80 to $5.

Sunshine Tree Terrace ★★★ ICE CREAM   Disney fans beeline to this kiosk for the Citrus Swirl, a wonderful blend of frozen O.J. and soft-serve vanilla ice cream. The pomegranate limeaid is also gaining favor. It's a historic spot: The doe-eyed mascot is Orange Bird, which Disney created for the Florida citrus lobby, which sponsored this stand and the Tiki birds back in the 1970s. Adventureland. Beverages and desserts $3 to $4.

Tortuga Tavern ★★ MEXICAN   Open at lunch, it does burritos and beef taco salads, and it has a large, sheltered seating area. Adventureland. Combo meal $8 to $9.

Turkey Leg Cart ★★ AMERICAN   These honking hunks of meat ($10) could feed a couple of cavemen. Frontierland, across from Frontier Trading Post.

Pecos Bill Tall Tale Inn and Cafe ★★★ AMERICAN   Get ⅓-pound cheeseburgers, chicken sandwiches, and BBQ pork sandwiches, all with fries. The fixings bar has good stuff like sautéed onions and mushrooms, so it's easy to make a meal of it. It also has spacious, air-conditioned seating. Frontierland. Combo meal $9.60 to $11.

Columbia Harbour House ★★★ AMERICAN   At this indoor counter service spot, order fat sandwiches, lobster rolls, and couscous, plus sides like chowder ($4.70), then take them upstairs where it's quiet. Liberty Square. Combo meal $9 to $10.

Pinocchio's Village Haus ★★ AMERICAN/ITALIAN   Vaguely Italian food (flatbreads, meatball subs, and so on) adjoining "it's a small world," with a few tables overlooking the snazzy loading area. Fantasyland. Combo meal $9 to $10.

The Friar's Nook ★ AMERICAN   Window-service with no seating for regular or teriyaki chicken nuggets, hummus with veggies, and house-made chips. Fantasyland. Snacks $3 to $8.20.

Gaston's Tavern ★ AMERICAN   In a small indoor counter service location behind the amusing fountain of Gaston, you'll find some only-at-Disney treats. The Roast Pork Shank ($9.50) is big like the famous turkey leg, only in pig flavor. Le Fou's Brew is Fantasyland's (not nearly as successful) answer to Harry Potter's Butterbeer: frozen apple juice with a lightly fruity foam. Get it in a regular cup for $4.50, or $10 in either a plastic stein or a goblet, suitable to gender roles. Fantasyland.

Cosmic Ray's Starlight Cafe ★★★ AMERICAN   The best choice for indoor Quick Service on this end of the park, it does burgers, sandwiches, and chicken (both

SAVING ON PARK munchies

If you plan to buy all your food at the park, sticking strictly to counter-service meals is the cheapest way to go. But considering you'll pay $8 to $10 each for a counter-service sandwich, plus at least $2.70 for a medium-size soft drink—the going rate in the Orlando parks—even that way, a family of four can easily spend $60 on every meal! Don't be goofy—save money! Besides eating off premises, here's how:

- **Pack a little food of your own.** Park security usually looks the other way if you bring a soft lunchbag-size cooler (hard-sided Igloos will be rejected). Or just tote sandwiches in plastic bags. If your lodging has a freezer, put juice boxes in there; they'll be thawed by lunch.

- **Economize with an all-you-can-eat meal.** Character meals (p. 189) give good value because they serve limitless food. A big lunch can last you until after you leave the park.

- **Skip sit-down meals, or plan them strategically.** Sit-down meals can chomp as much as 90 minutes out of your touring time. Do that twice and you've lost a third of your day. A park that could be seen in 1 day would require 2, doubling costs. If you want a sit-down meal, do it at lunch, when prices are often

lower than at dinner. Eat around 11am, when crowds are lighter and you lose less time.

- **Subtract unwanted combo items.** Although counter-service restaurants make the menu appear like it's mostly combo meals, it's an unpublicized fact that you may eliminate unwanted items from adult selections and save money. Dropping fries or other bundled side dishes can save about $2.

- **Snack on fruit.** Each park has at least one fruit stand.

- **Seek out the turkey legs.** They're giant (1½ pounds, from 45-pound turkeys), salty, cost around $10, and 1.5 million of them are sold at Disney annually. They taste so good because they're injected with brine before cooking for 6 hours. Just don't think about the hormones it takes to grow a 45-pound bird. Or a 5-foot-tall mouse.

- **Order drinks without ice.** Soda is dispensed cold to prevent foaming. It's chilling how much ice is in a standard Disney Coke.

- **Stretch meals.** If there's a double cheeseburger on the menu, order it and an extra bun. Then make two separate burgers. Disney has been eliminating double cheeseburgers, but Universal has them.

sandwich and rotisserie) and has a toppings bar with freshly sautéed mushrooms and onions—choose the "bay" that serves your choice. It's distinguished by regular lounge-act shows by Sonny Eclipse, a long-running Audio-Animatronic character. Despite Sonny, I'd rather eat on its outdoor terrace. The panorama of the Castle is sublime; it's my favorite lunchtime view. That empty boat dock below is from the extinct Swan Boats, which plied the moat in years past. Tomorrowland. Combo meal $9 to $11.

Tomorrowland Terrace ★ AMERICAN   Seating is sheltered but not air-conditioned, with a fine view of the Castle. In high season, it serves lunch of burgers and such; otherwise it's breakfast-only. Tomorrowland. Breakfast mains $4 to $6.

freebies AT DISNEY

It's not easy finding fun stuff to do that you don't have to cough up for, but you don't need to hand over a cent for these pleasures—not even for park admission. Anyone off the street can enjoy these things:

○ **Watch the Electrical Water Pageant** on the Seven Seas Lagoon and Bay Lake between 9 and 10:20pm. The illuminated floats, which twitter to a soundtrack, make a circuit around the conjoined ponds after nightfall, and you can see it from the beachfront at any hotel.

○ **Ride the ferries** between the resorts, such as the one from Port Orleans Riverside to Downtown Disney along the meandering Sassagoula River, which passes the French Quarter resort and the Old Key West resort. You can even ride the one from the monorail-area resorts to the foot of the Magic Kingdom.

○ **Take the monorail.** Whiz round the Seven Seas Lagoon past the Magic Kingdom and through the Contemporary Resort as many times as you want without a ticket. You can also use it to make the 4-mile round-trip to Epcot, where you'll do a flyover of Future World.

○ **Hike at Fort Wilderness.** The trail begins at the east end of Bay Lake and threads through occasionally muddy woods.

○ **Spend a night by the pool.** Most resorts keep them open

'til midnight. Technically, you should be a guest. But behave, and no one'll care (except at the Yacht and Beach clubs, where bracelets are required). Each hotel's parking lot has a gate, but if you park at Downtown Disney and take a free Disney bus, you'll scoot right in.

○ **See African animals** at the Animal Kingdom Lodge. The gatekeeper will admit you to sit by the fire in its vaulted lobby, and out back, you can watch game such as giraffe and kudu from the Sunset Overlook. Sometimes, there are zoologists who answer questions.

○ For a marvelous view of the fireworks over the Magic Kingdom, **stroll on the beach** of the Grand Floridian or the Polynesian resorts. The sand is millions of years old and was recovered from under Bay Lake. Did you know Disney built a giant wave machine in the middle of the lake? It never worked.

○ **Partake of the campfire sing-along,** which happens nightly near the Meadow Trading Post at Fort Wilderness, followed by a Disney feature on an outdoor screen.

○ **Cuddle farm animals,** including ducks, goats, and peacocks, at the petting farm behind Fort Wilderness's Pioneer Hall. You can also see the horses used to pull streetcars up Main Street, U.S.A.

THE MAGIC KINGDOM'S TABLE-SERVICE RESTAURANTS

This is the most popular theme park in the world, so as you can imagine, getting a seat can be competitive (and it requires a credit card) and the wait staff is almost always running around. Some of the restaurants *may* accept waiting lists of walk-ins at 4pm, when they start dinner service, but ask early in the day. Taking them clockwise around the park:

Tony's Town Square Restaurant ★★ ITALIAN   Loosely themed on the Italian restaurant scene from "Lady and the Tramp" (there's a fountain of the two doe-eyed dogs), it's loud, not romantic. To repeat Tramp's spaghetti-and-meatball sharing gesture (kindly don't use your nose like he did), you'll pay $18 a plate. It also does cioppino, cannelloni, and shrimp scampi. After lunch, sandwiches, pizzas, and flatbreads are swapped out for pork tenderloin and strip steak with potatoes and vegetables. Main Street, U.S.A. Main courses $18 to $29.

The Crystal Palace, A Buffet with Character ★★★ AMERICAN   Under an airy Victorian-style skylight canopy that emulates a hall from an 1853 New York City world's exhibition, Winnie the Pooh greets diners at what's probably the prettiest in-park restaurant in all of Walt Disney World. The refined air doesn't stop Pooh and his buddies (Tigger, Eeyore, Piglet) from jamming the aisles with a conga line. Being slightly smaller than many other character dining locations, you're likely to get some face time with the characters. This restaurant's been open since Day One and offers three daily all-you-can-eat buffets of changing, crowd-pleasing standards from meats to vegetables. There's a make-your-own-sundae bar for lunch and dinner. Prices are lowest at breakfast (the best time anyway, since you'll have the rest of your day free) and scale up. Main Street, U.S.A. Buffet $25 to $44 adults, $14 to $21 children.

The Plaza Restaurant ★ AMERICAN   What's special about this one is its view. Situated at the end of Main Street facing Cinderella Castle, it focuses on sandwiches and salads, which are served with broccoli slaw, homemade chips, or french fries. Add soup for $4.50. It also serves ice cream sundaes and cheesecake from the shop next door. Main Street, U.S.A. Main courses $11 to $15.

Liberty Tree Tavern ★★ AMERICAN   At lunch, this colonial-style place (stained wood and rung-backed chairs) facing the Rivers of America (no view) serves vaguely patriotic a la carte fare such as pot roast, turkey with stuffing, and "Freedom Pasta," which is fusilli with chicken, vegetables, and mushrooms in a cream sauce. After 4pm, it shifts to an all-you-can-eat buffet including a beef carvery. The dessert specialty is Johnny Appleseed's Cake, or white cake filled with apples and Craisins—just like in the colonies. Liberty Square. Lunchtime mains $14 to $20, dinner buffet $32 adults, $16 kids.

Cinderella's Royal Table ★★★ AMERICAN   This is the holy grail of character meals since it actually takes place inside Cinderella Castle where there's a capacity of less than 200. The famous royal resident always appears (sometimes joined by her soul sisters Jasmine, Aurora, Snow White, and others), and little girls far and wide dress up like princesses to meet her. The interior is as lavish as you'd expect for the inside of the Castle, with mock medieval vaulted ceilings, a royal red carpet, stained glass, and stylized crest shields adoring the walls. Meals aren't all-you-can-eat, but they are all prix-fixe, though the price shifts with the season. Bookings open 180 days ahead at 7am Orlando time (and must be prepaid by credit card) and are snapped up in moments. Food selections include swordfish and pork loin. Meals $54 to $72 adults, $35 to $43 children; price includes five photos of your party.

Be Our Guest Restaurant ★★ AMERICAN   It's not so easy to be their guest here, since bookings fill incredibly quickly. As a 2012 newcomer to Fantasyland, it sports a few technical tricks to evoke Beast's castle, including animated falling snow outside some false windows, a portrait that reveals a hidden Beast when illuminated by periodic lightning (that's in the West Wing, in case it might scare your kids), and an animated rose under glass that slowly sheds its petals. Like a real castle, all those polished surfaces make things incredibly loud. Although the food is vaguely French (there's ratatouille at dinner, croque-monsieur at lunch, and French onion soup all the time), the preponderance of pork chops, steaks, and salmon are really more American. You order by kiosk, pour your own beverages, and your food is wheeled to you when it's ready. This is the only place in the Magic Kingdom where you can get alcohol, but only at dinner and only with that coveted reservation. Fantasyland. Main courses $9 to $14 lunch, $16 to $30 dinner.

EPCOT

Epcot ★★★ remains one of Walt Disney World's finest achievements. More than any other park, Epcot changes its personality, decorations, and diversions by the season. Guests usually don't learn much more than they already know (so as not to bore them or to insult their intelligence), but even though there isn't much take-away information, that there's plenty to soak up if you explore. There's plenty to do here without having to wait in lines, and unlike other parks, there are lots of places to sit. The wide variety of foods and alcoholic beverages is also a big draw. Epcot's genial personality has earned it a spot as the sixth-most-visited theme park on Earth, racking up some 11 million entries in 2012.

The 260-acre park is divided into two zones, Future World and World Showcase, laid out roughly like a figure eight. Both areas started life separately but, as the legend goes, were grafted together when plans were afoot. **Future World** is where the wonders of industry were extolled in corporate-sponsored "pavilions." The companies had a hand creating them and they also maintained VIP areas in backstage areas for executives and special guests. At the back of the property, around a 1.3-mile lake footpath, **World Showcase** was the circuit of countries, each representing in miniature its namesake's essence. These, too, received funding from their host countries. The expense of updating Future World's exhibits has caused Disney to gradually phase out the educational aspects of the attractions. One by one, original pavilions have been replaced by sense-tingling rides, so that today, only two of the original rides, Spaceship Earth and Living with the Land, remain more or less as they originally were.

A history OF EPCOT

Although people think of Walt Disney as prototypically American, he had a communist streak. He long dreamed of establishing a real, working city where 20,000 full-time residents, none of them unemployed, would test out experimental technologies in the course of their daily lives. In vintage films where he discusses his Florida Project, his passion for creating such a self-sustaining community, to be called the Experimental Prototype Community of Tomorrow, was inextricable from the rest of his planned resort. He wanted nothing less than to revolutionize the world. Truck traffic would be routed to vehicle plazas beneath the city, out of pedestrians' way, while PeopleMovers (like the ones of Magic Kingdom's Tomorrowland Transit Authority) would shift the population around town. Between home and downtown, they'd take the monorail. Even on his deathbed, Walt was perfecting real plans for the city that would be his crowning legacy: one whose innovations would make life better for everyone on Earth. Had he lived just 3 more years, he would have made sure it happened.

Epcot

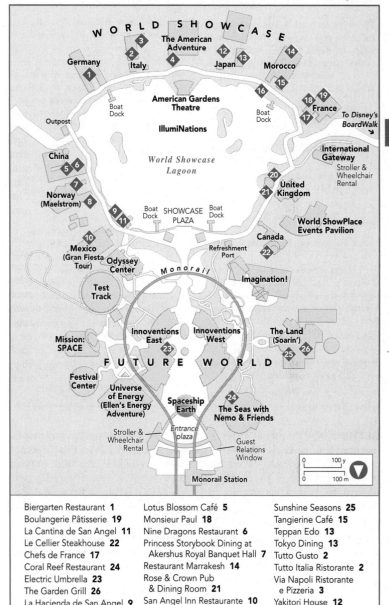

WORLD SHOWCASE

The American Adventure

Germany

Italy

Japan

Morocco

American Gardens Theatre

IllumiNations

Boat Dock

Boat Dock

Outpost

France

To Disney's BoardWalk

International Gateway

Stroller & Wheelchair Rental

China

Norway (Maelstrom)

World Showcase Lagoon

United Kingdom

Boat Dock

SHOWCASE PLAZA

Boat Dock

World ShowPlace Events Pavilion

Canada

Mexico (Gran Fiesta Tour)

Odyssey Center

Refreshment Port

Monorail

Imagination!

Test Track

Mission: SPACE

Innoventions East

Innoventions West

The Land (Soarin')

FUTURE WORLD

Festival Center

Universe of Energy (Ellen's Energy Adventure)

Spaceship Earth

The Seas with Nemo & Friends

Stroller & Wheelchair Rental

Entrance plaza

Guest Relations Window

0   100 y
0   100 m

Monorail Station

Biergarten Restaurant **1**
Boulangerie Pâtisserie **19**
La Cantina de San Angel **11**
Le Cellier Steakhouse **22**
Chefs de France **17**
Coral Reef Restaurant **24**
Electric Umbrella **23**
The Garden Grill **26**
La Hacienda de San Angel **9**
Kringla Bakeri og Kafé **8**
Liberty Inn **4**

Lotus Blossom Café **5**
Monsieur Paul **18**
Nine Dragons Restaurant **6**
Princess Storybook Dining at
 Akershus Royal Banquet Hall **7**
Restaurant Marrakesh **14**
Rose & Crown Pub
 & Dining Room **21**
San Angel Inn Restaurante **10**
Sommerfest **1**
Spice Road Table **16**

Sunshine Seasons **25**
Tangierine Café **15**
Teppan Edo **13**
Tokyo Dining **13**
Tutto Gusto **2**
Tutto Italia Ristorante **2**
Via Napoli Ristorante
 e Pizzeria **3**
Yakitori House **12**
Yorkshire County
 Fish Shop **20**

GETTING THE MOST OUT OF EPCOT

Epcot has so much to explore, and eat, and drink that you won't feel like you're racing from ride to ride (as you might in other parks), though several rides are worthy of your time.

Head directly to The Land and get a Fastpass for Soarin'.

↓

Ride **Test Track** before the line gets crazy.

↓

Ride **Mission: Space**.

↓

By now, your **Soarin'** Fastpass is probably valid. Ride it.

↓

Visit the Seas with **Nemo and Friends**.

↓

Ride **Living with the Land** for a glimpse at Epcot's roots. Consider doing **Soarin'** again. If you're hungry, Sunshine Seasons, in this pavilion, is a terrific place to eat.

↓

Ride **Spaceship Earth** and visit **Innoventions**.

↓

Enter World Showcase at Mexico and ride **Gran Fiesta Tour**.

↓

Ride **Maelstrom** at Norway. You have now enjoyed all the rides in World Showcase.

↓

Continue along World Showcase at your own pace, avoiding the temptation to rush. The movies (in China, France, and Canada) are all worth seeing; the shops can be surprisingly good; and the street entertainment choices (noted on the Times Guide) are excellent.

↓

Catch the American Adventure; the Voices of America perform about 15 minutes before show times, and they're listed in the Times Guide.

↓

Continue along World Showcase. Pause for a pint in the United Kingdom.

↓

Remember Future World usually closes at 7pm, so if you have time before then, re-ride anything you loved (Spaceship Earth isn't usually crowded late in the day).

Eat dinner in the land of your choice and catch **IllumiNations**.

GETTING IN The parking lot is at the ticket gates, although you can also catch the **monorail** from the Magic Kingdom parking area. If you park past the canal or near the monorail track, don't bother with the tram; you can walk to the gates faster. Bags will be quickly inspected. As you enter the park, lockers are at the right of Spaceship Earth; wheeled rentals are to the left. Also on the left is Guest Relations, where last-minute dining reservations can be made, though often, you'll just be deferred to the restaurant in question.

HOURS Future World opens at 9am, and World Showcase opens at 11am. Future World often closes at 7pm, 2 hours before World Showcase. The nightly IllumiNations show usually takes place over World Showcase Lagoon at 9pm; at its conclusion, the hordes stampede for their cars en masse.

Future World

By the time Walt Disney World finally got around to opening its second park, EPCOT Center, on October 1, 1982 (11 years to the day after the Magic Kingdom and at a staggering estimated cost of $1.4 billion; America's biggest construction project at the time), it was but a flicker of its original purpose. No one would actually live there, and few experimental endeavors would be undertaken. Instead, it turned out that the most economical course was to turn Walt's legacy into another moneymaking theme park, heavily subsidized by corporate participation and sold by heavy promotion of "Walt's dream"—a formula that prevails today. In truth, the final design wasn't much different from the world's fair that Walt's father had helped construct in Chicago in 1893 or that Walt himself defined in New York in 1964: examples of how technology was ostensibly improving lives, plus some pavilions representing foreign lands for the edification of people unlikely to travel there themselves. In December 1993, the park name was simplified to Epcot. As you face the lagoon, the pavilions on the left side of Future World are generally about the physical and man-made sciences, and the ones on the right are more about the natural sciences. Behind Spaceship Earth, look for a park **tip board,** which posts wait times and the daily schedule. There are two more tip boards through the underpasses to the east and west sections of Future World.

Spaceship Earth ★★★ RIDE   That gorgeous orb looks like a golf ball on a tee, but the 16-million-pound structure, coated with 11,324 aluminum-bonded panels and sheathed inside with a rainproof rubber layer, is supported by a tablelike scaffolding where its six legs enter the dome. Think of this 180-foot-tall Buckminster Fuller sphere as a direct descendent of the Perisphere of the 1939 World's Fair or the Unisphere of the 1964 World's Fair, which were the icons for their own parks. No mere shell, it houses an eponymous ride using the OmniMover system of cars linked together like an endless snake. The ride slowly winds within the sphere, all on the course of a shallow, sixth-grade-level journey (narrated by Judi Dench) through the history of communications, from Greek theater to the Sistine Chapel to the printing press to the telegraph. In a bit of unintended kinesthetic commentary, once you reach the present day, the ride is all downhill. Once you're off it, I defy you to tell me what you learned from it. This, of course, makes it vintage Epcot. This is the ride that still shows what the 1982 park was like—its robot-populated sister pavilions about transportation and the future were razed in the 1990s to make way for flashier thrills. Although some people don't get it, I cherish it as a soothing sojourn not only through time, but also through air-conditioning. Since it's the first ride that guests encounter in the park, lines, which move fast, are much shorter in the afternoon.

Innoventions ★ ACTIVITY   The semicircular buildings facing each other down behind Spaceship Earth are the domain of corporate-sponsored exhibits, as Walt had intended. Innoventions (originally called Communicore) is under-patronized and feels unfinished because it's ever-changing. But there's much here to divert you:

o **Sum of All Thrills:** Lines build quickly for this slow-loading ride from Raytheon, which puts two riders in front of a motion-simulator screen at the end of a robot arm. You choose if you want your ride to go nearly upside-down or not.

o **Habit Heroes:** Paid for by Blue Cross Blue Shield, this is an 18-minute, three-game motion-sensor course where you learn very vague health lessons by battling monsters that are somehow preventing you from getting nutrition.

o **VISION House:** From Green Builder Media, a full-scale mock-up of a suburban home to demonstrate specific products that make a home more energy efficient—and then tells you how you can buy them.

o **Storm Struck:** In this 3-D movie to inspire storm-proofing your home, audiences are buffeted with wind and rain effects, and then vote on proofing methods, which are then tested on screen.

o **Where's the Fire?** Liberty Mutual teaches about fire safety.

○ **Test the Limits Lab:** Underwriters Laboratories shows how it approves products—expect lots of clanging and banging.

○ **The Great Piggy Bank Adventure:** Paid for by T. Rowe Price, the adventure teaches that apparently the best way to save is to catch floating coins with pedal-powered flying piggy banks. Then you spend it on vacations. Whatever, it's fun.

Also in the Innoventions buildings, you'll find **MouseGear,** the largest souvenir shop in Epcot and opposite that, **Club Cool,** by the Coca-Cola Company, which lets you pour unlimited samples of eight soft drink flavors sold only in other countries. Beverly, a bitter aperitif from Italy, is not for faint tongues. If you're an obsessive tightwad, you can keep coming back here instead of buying a real Coke (Germany's Mezzo Mix tastes most like it). Frozen Cokes are sold for $4. Between Innoventions, you'll find the **World Fellowship Fountain,** which was dedicated by Walt's widow, Lillian. At the opening ceremony, water from 23 countries was combined as a symbol of brotherhood. It can shoot 150 feet in the air, although it rarely does. There's a 5-minute choreographed splash-up on the quarter hour.

Universe of Energy ★ RIDE/SHOW   This attraction is highly emblematic of Epcot's corporate-dictated content. The dated adventure begins with a movie, circa 1996, featuring Ellen DeGeneres being taught by Bill Nye the Science Guy about how oil is formed and then pulled out of the ground for the benefit of mankind. If that sounds lame, at least the ride system is more creative: The audience is seated in six 97-passenger slabs of mobile theater-style bench seating. Miraculously, the slabs organize themselves in a line and move from room to giant room, passing primeval forests full of realistic dinosaurs. When, at another movie stop, the issue of global warming comes up, Nye waves it away, saying, "It's a hot topic with lots of questions" before reassuring us that "we're far from running on empty." Not surprisingly, the didactic venture was backed by ExxonMobil. The whole show takes between 30 to 50 minutes to see, depending on when you arrive at the preshow, which makes it a good cooldown. Outside, the roof is coated in 2 acres of solar panels, which generate 15 percent of the show's energy appetite; the building site was chosen for maximum sunlight exposure. **Strategy:** Although all sections spend time waiting for the others to move or catch up, the two sections on the right wait in the most interesting spaces.

Mission: SPACE ★★ RIDE   Behind the gorgeously swirling planetary façade is a ride that approximates, with intense accuracy, the experience of a rocket launch. Although technically a whirl in a giant centrifuge, the skillful design tricks the mind into believing the body's actually lurching backward in a launch for Mars (although

---

The Best of Epcot

Don't miss if you're 6: Turtle Talk with Crush
Don't miss if you're 16: Test Track
Requisite photo op: Spaceship Earth
Food you can only get here: Rice cream, the bakery at Norway
The most crowded, so go early: Soarin'
Skippable: Journey into Imagination with Figment
Quintessentially Disney: Spaceship Earth

Biggest thrill: Mission: SPACE
Best show: Voices of Liberty, the American Adventure
Character meals: Akershus Royal Banquet Hall, Norway; Garden Grill, The Land
Where to find peace: Future World: the Odyssey Center catwalks; World Showcase: the gardens of Japan

The Death of "Life"

Between Mission: SPACE and the Universe of Energy, you'll spot a golden dome. No, you haven't been in the sun too long—it's not listed on your map. That's Wonders of Life, one of the great failures of modern Disney World. Opened in 1989 as a paean to all things biological, executives closed it when they couldn't find a corporation willing to pony up continued sponsorship. Some of science's greatest advances are being made in the biological realm, yet the topic is neglected at Epcot for want of a corporate bankroll. Among the casualties: **Body Wars,** a motion-simulator ride through the bloodstream; **Cranium Command,** addressing how a 12-year-old boy's brain controlled his growing body; and **"The Making of Me,"** a film that gingerly addressed conception and pregnancy without stepping on ideological toes. The tarnished pavilion sits empty and decaying.

my eyeballs seem to know—they wag uncontrollably for the first 30 seconds). Gary Sinise, oozing gravitas, issues so many preshow warnings against motion sickness that I honestly think it psychs people out and primes them for illness, although sufferers of sinus problems have reported discomfort. Each passenger in the extremely tight four-person cockpits is assigned two buttons to press at given cues—it doesn't matter if you don't, but at least hold onto your steering joystick, because it gives force feedback as you travel. Ultimately, it's a ride that's all brains and no heart—I'm deeply impressed at what they've done, but I don't feel like doing it twice. The Advanced Training Lab postshow area (through the gift shop) is worthwhile even if you don't ride. There, you can play interactive group games and send free postcards home via computer. **Strategy:** Whereas Mad Tea Party makes me want to hurl, I do just fine on this ride. You'll be given a choice when you enter the building: There's a second version (color-coded green) with easy motion-simulator effects but no troubling centrifuge action, but in my opinion, the missing element renders the ride pointless.

Test Track ★★★ RIDE Cars thunder enticingly around the bend of an outdoor motorway at nearly 65mph—the fastest ride in Disney World and a shining example of its designers' eagerness to tackle a complex challenge. Those passengers are experiencing the climax of a complicated, multistage ride that puts them through the paces of a proving ground of an automobile manufacturer (sponsor: Chevrolet). Before boarding, you use a touch screen to design a car using the ill-defined factors of capability, power, responsiveness, and efficiency. Then, you go along for the ride in a minimally decorated warehouse on a series of diagnostic safety tests (don't worry; you don't have to actually do anything), while trackside screens are supposed to show you how your creation is performing. Your six-passenger car brakes suddenly and rumbles over rough road surfaces before shooting outside the building and making an invigorating circuit around the circular track over the Epcot employee parking lot. (Hertz has a similar experience—it's called a convertible.) Test Track is so complex, having been retooled in 2012 that the software sometimes fails and your car design may not show up again after you finish it. **Strategy:** Along with Soarin', it's the busiest ride at Epcot, so get a Fastpass. There's a single-rider line that doesn't let you skip much and invariably puts you in a right-hand seat. The post-ride showroom features a few steering games plus Chevy's current fleet, all of which get regular rubdowns by an attendant with a rag: The "Design Key" cards passengers carry with them during the attraction, however, get sent right back into a new person's hands. Bring your Purell!

Are They Kidding?

Besides The Seas with Nemo & Friends, there's not much for young children to do in Epcot. Disney addressed the problem with small, manned booths that it calls **Kidcot Fun Stops,** which offer crafty diversions such as coloring, stamping, or maskmaking—stuff kids do at the school fair. Epcot Passports, which can be stamped in every country, were once free but now cost $11, but attendants will stamp your kids' crafts, such as the handle of the mask they made, for free instead. Animal Kingdom has a similar program called Kids Discovery Club; in both parks, they're marked on maps with a K.

The Seas with Nemo & Friends ★★ RIDE/ACTIVITY   One of the world's largest saltwater aquariums, it's 27 feet deep, 203 feet across, holds 5.7 million gallons, and you can spend as long as you like watching the swimming creatures from two levels. About a third of the tank is reserved for dolphins and sea turtles, while reef fish, rays, and sharks dominate the rest. When the pavilion opened in 1986 as The Living Seas, sharks were the big draw and scientists answered questions everywhere; today, because of "Finding Nemo," kids ask to see the clown fish and there's nary an interpreter in sight. A visit begins with a 5-minute, slow-moving ride in OmniMover "clamobiles" through a simulated undersea world. Half the point of the ride is, of course, to find Nemo, who's lost again; the other characters incessantly shout his name, which soon grates on adult nerves. The ride climaxes to the tune of "In the Big Blue World" (from the Nemo musical at Animal Kingdom) with a peek into the real aquarium as Nemo and his friends are projected into the windows, cleverly uniting the fictional world with the real animal universe, "Seabase," with which you will now be acquainted. A few times a day, the giant tube dominating the hall is occupied by a diver—an unforgettable sight—to demonstrate how SCUBA works. On the second floor, which is quieter than the kiddie-clogged first floor, don't miss the observation platform that extends into the mighty tank. The daily roster sign apprises you of the day's dolphin talks and fish feedings (the schedule is busiest between 10am and 4pm), when there will be someone on hand to explain what you're seeing. The **dolphins** live separately in the first space on the left. If human divers are swimming, they'll communicate with guests by way of magnetized writing tablets. Also, check out the **manatees,** the sweet-natured "sea cows" that are threatened in Florida. **Strategy:** If the pavilion's entry line is horrific, bypass the ride by entering through the exit, at the far left.

Turtle Talk with Crush ★★ SHOW   Inside The Seas with Nemo & Friends is an amusing 20-minute show in which a computer-animated version of the 150-year-old surfer-dude turtle interacts with audiences, making jokes about what they're wearing and fielding questions. It's part of what Disney calls its "Living Characters" program. There is the distraction of ray and jellyfish tanks in the waiting area. Next door is **Bruce's Sub House,** a play area similar to any science museum's.

Soarin' ★★★ RIDE   The Land pavilion takes up 6 acres, more than all of Tomorrowland, and this ride is a big reason why. In it, audiences are seated on benches and "flown," hang glider–like, across enormous movies of California's wonders while scents waft, hair blows, and the seats gently rock in tandem with the motions of the flight. The ride, one of the best additions to the World in recent years, is highly repeatable and deeply pleasurable. It's a facsimile of the one at Disney's California Adventure park in Anaheim, hence the imagery exclusive to the Golden State. **Strategy:** Wait times often exceed 3 hours (yeah, I know—crazy!), so zoom here early or consider it for Fastpass. The best seats are in the middle sections on the top row, where there are no feet dangling in your field of vision. That means you should aim for position B-1, or at the very least A-1 or C-1. Those with height issues should request something ending in 3, the closest to the ground.

Living with the Land ★★ RIDE   The Land's other ride, after Soarin', is a 14-minute boat trip that glosses over the realm of farming technologies. It's one of the last Epcot rides to provide a semblance of education, so I find it edifying, especially when you pass some of Epcot's last laboratories, where futuristic growth methods (like spraying exposed roots with nutrient-enriched water) are being explored, ostensibly (so we're told) to curb world hunger. They know what they're doing: Guinness World Records has certified one of the pavilion's tomato plants as the record holder for producing the most fruit: 1,151.84 pounds in 1 year. This ride is original to opening day, although the live narrators have been disposed of in favor of a recording. It's not a perfect experience: For those interested in the topic, the info will be too thin, but for those who are bored green, it will seem to last forever. **Strategy:** Boats load slowly, so go early or late to escape the inevitable buildup.

The Circle of Life ★ SHOW   Upstairs, in The Land, this minor, 13-minute movie stars "The Lion King" characters and concerns conservation (an Epcot-worthy message). It'll keep you off the streets and seated in AC.

Captain EO ★★★ SHOW   The minute Michael Jackson died, Disney yanked this trippy 1986 chestnut out of mothballs and re-installed it in its original home, the Imagination! pavilion, minus a few original special effects. For years, this 17-minute 3-D music video, starring Jackson as a Han Solo–type space pilot who is accompanied by creepy/adorable sidekicks, was a punch line for its excess and ego, but premature death and '80s nostalgia have renewed it. It concerns a mean, dark-hearted diva whose grip on a bleak world is loosened by the sheer charm of Jocko's performance—kind of like the climax of "The Wiz" if the Wicked Witch was a dominatrix played by Anjelica Huston.

Journey into Imagination with Figment ★ RIDE   There's no line for a reason. It feels like Disney ran out of money halfway through the ride—one section of this slow track-based ride is simply a room of black curtains and painted boards. Its daffy purple dinosaur, Figment, once figured as Epcot's most prominent mascot and now strains to act cuddly in his last, forlorn outpost. The ride purports to be an open house of the Imagination Institute run by Prof. Nigel Channing (Eric Idle), but Figment seizes control of the tour and offends your senses—your sense of good taste, though, is the most violated. This is the third attempt to get an Imagination ride right since 1982. The ride dumps out into **ImageWorks,** once a high-tech playground sponsored by Kodak but now with nothing more to do than assemble a Figment using touchscreens or purchase fairground-style composite gag photos. Look above the roped-off spiral staircase for a glimpse of the glass pyramids atrium, now forbidden, and you'll get a sense for how this pretty half-closed pavilion is now rotten with neglect. You might have gathered by now that Imagination! is not Epcot at its best. However, the fountain pods in front, which shoot snakes of water from one to another, have always been a firm favorite of children, who never tire of trying to catch one of the so-called "laminar flow" spurts.

World Showcase

The 1.3-mile path circling the World Showcase Lagoon is home to 11 pavilions created in the idealized image of their home countries—get your picture taken in front of a miniature Eiffel Tower (it'll look real through the lens), or at the Doge's Palace in Venice. The pavilions were built more to elicit an emotional response and not to truly replicate. Disney is diligent about the upkeep of this area, but it neglects development—the last "country" to open was Norway back in 1988, and without joint participation by foreign tourism offices, there are unlikely to be more. There also seems to be an emphasis on countries that Americans already know, and neither South America nor Australasia is represented at all. But World Showcase does have some of the most original restaurants in Disney World, and the shops are stocked with crafts and national products (you can buy real Chinese tea in China and sweaters in Norway), although the variety is slipping. It's also the only area in Epcot in which alcoholic beverages are sold.

There is far more fascinating stuff to do in World Showcase than the free Disney map lets on. Pocket it and let your curiosity guide you. You should, though, keep the day's **"Times Guide"** firmly in hand. The pavilions are crawling with unexpected musical and dance performances conducted by natives of each country. Seeing them makes a day richer and squeezes value from your ticket. Rush and you'll miss a lot. I suggest going **clockwise around the lagoon** mostly because the only two rides in World Showcase will come quickly on the left; if you go counterclockwise, you'll reach them after they accrue lines. After midafternoon, it won't matter.

Tip: Anything purchased in World Showcase can be sent to the **Package Pickup** at the front of Future World; allow 3 hours for delivery (it's not refrigerated, so chocolate melts). On some days—it depends how busy things are—two **ferry** routes cross the lagoon. One leaves near Germany and one from Morocco, and both land near the top of Future World. You will not save time using them; they're merely a pleasant way to get off your feet.

MEXICO ★★★

Skirting the lagoon clockwise, Mexico is your first stop. Everything to see is inside the faux temple, which contains a faux river (for the Gran Fiesta Tour ride), a faux volcano, and a faux night sky strung with lanterns. The **Mexican Folk Art Gallery** showcases whimsical carvings; "La Vida Antigua: Life in Ancient Mexico" is for artifacts and dioramas. In the main *zócalo* of Plaza de los Amigos, look for Alba, who for a decade has hand-painted Oaxacan woodcarvings here, and listen for the terrific Mariachi Cobre, which has performed here since the park's opening day. There's also a small tequila bar (chips and dip also for sale) and a crystal shop. **Influences:** A diplomatic mix of Mayan, Toltec, Aztec, and Spanish styles. **Fun stuff to Buy:** Maracas ($6 each), Oaxacan woodcarvings (from $18), hand-painted pottery skulls ($26) and sombreros the size of bike wheels ($20).

Gran Fiesta Tour Starring the Three Caballeros ★★ RIDE

It's easy to develop a soft spot for the bland, 8-minute boat float that, for its cheesiness, has been nicknamed "the Mexican 'it's a small world.'" As you pass movie screens, jiggling dolls, and dancing Day of the Dead skeletons, you quickly realize you're enjoying the product of Mexican tourist board input. A 2007 rehab imposed animated appearances by the 1940s characters the Three Caballeros—never mind that only Panchito Pistoles the rooster is Mexican (José Carioca the parrot is Brazilian, and Donald Duck is American). The experience is sweet, and it's a worthy siesta break. The trio conducts autograph sessions outside, to the right of the pavilion.

World Showcase pavilions are staffed by young people who were born and raised in the host country. Many of their contracts last for up to a year, and they chose to come to Florida as much to learn about America as to be ambassadors for their own nations, although many of them complain that most park guests don't bother asking anything except where the bathrooms are. Be kind to them, speak slowly if you sometimes cannot immediately understand each other's accent, and most of all, seize this unusual chance to ask questions about their cultures. These folks, despite the fact they're zipped into silly costumes, are modern, intelligent people who are so proud of where they come from that they traveled halfway around the world to share their heritage with you. Help them do that.

NORWAY ★★

Next along is Norway, the youngest pavilion (built 1988), which is home to Maelstrom, the only other ride in World Showcase. Norway's Akershus Royal Banquet Hall does princess character meals morning, noon, and evening. In the one-room **Stave Church Gallery,** check out "Vikings: Conquerors of the Seas," which includes scant information but does showcase some ancient artifacts from the conquerors, such as 9th-century spearheads and 1,000-year-old swords. Towering above it all, the wooden Stave Church is a Norwegian original; there were once around 1,000 in the country, but today, there are only 28. **The Puffin's Roost** contains a 9-foot-tall troll—photo op alert. **Influences:** Town squares of Bergen, Alesund, Oslo, and the Satesdal Valley; the 14th-century Akershus castle on Oslo harbor. **Fun Stuff to Buy:** Laila body lotions (assorted prices) and foam swords, and hatchets ($11). At the bakery, try the $2.30 rice cream, a snack that those in the know are happy to make a detour for. I prefer the plastic horned Viking helmets ($12).

Maelstrom ★ RIDE   The mildly surprising but short (5 min.) river course trolls past trolls and other Norse monsters, plus a few token representations of Norse industry, ending with a 5-minute sales film about the country. You can bypass that as soon as the doors open—everyone does—even though the photography is sumptuous.

CHINA ★★

Enter through the remarkable replica of Beijing's Temple of Heaven. Make time to catch the **Jeweled Dragon Acrobats,** some of the most riveting street performers in the World Showcase. "Tomb Warriors: Guardian Spirits of Ancient China," in the **House of the Whispering Willow,** is a miniature re-creation of a tiny portion of the legendary terra-cotta warriors of the Han Dynasty, scaled to the size of a hotel room (the original mausoleum is twice the size of Epcot). The Gallery also contains a few cases of figures dating as far back as 260 BCE. **Influences:** Beijing's Forbidden City (Imperial Palace) and Temple of Heaven. **Fun Stuff to Buy:** Upon exiting the film, cross the hangerlike shop and enter **House of Good Fortune,** the main shop, which is particularly varied. It sells plum wine ($12), lots of Ts and teas, Chinese jackets ($75–$125 in silks, polyesters, and blends), satin slippers ($18), parasols ($14–$16), conical coolie hats ($12), and paper globe lanterns you take home and unfold ($8).

"Reflections of China" ★ FILM   The big thing to do in China is a 14-minute movie filmed entirely in Circle-Vision 360°. You wouldn't believe the work it takes to make a film that surrounds you from all sides. The makers first had to figure out the optimal number of screens (nine—which enables projectors to be slipped in the gaps between screens) and then they had to suspend a ring of carefully calibrated cameras from helicopters so that the crew wasn't in the shots. In 2002, the footage of Shanghai had to be reshot because the city no longer resembled the 1982 version that was being shown; this being China, it's probably already time for another refresh. The result, which surveys some of the country's most beautiful vistas, is ravishing, although the masses no longer seem to care.

OUTPOST ★

This area between China and Germany was once slated to contain a pavilion canvassing equatorial Africa, but that fell through for political reasons, so instead, we get a mushy catchall for all things African. The **Mdundo Kibanda** store has some Kenyan carvings and you'll find occasional storytelling sessions. Several days a week, a craftsman is on hand, whittling and carving wares—they seem engrossed in wood and knife, but they like answering questions too. **Fun Stuff to Buy:** The too-easily overlooked **Bead Outpost** kiosk sells jewelry made from recycled Guidemaps and other outdated Disney park publications. The papers are sent to Uganda as part of the BeadforLife program to give impoverished women a sustainable income, and they return as water-resistant beads in every color. Necklaces are $20, bracelets $10, earrings $7, or you can pick your own beads to be sized right there.

GERMANY ★

Lacking a true attraction (a water ride based on the Rhine was planned but never completed), Germany is popular for its food. The **Biergarten Restaurant** does sausages, beer, and the like—accompanied by yodeling and dancing—while the adjoining shop is for crystal doodads. The **Sommerfest** is the counter-service alternative for brats and pretzels. On the hour, the Clock Tower above the pavilion rings and two figures emerge, just like at the Glockenspiel in München (Munich). The artist's space in the window of **Das Kaufhaus** facing the lagoon is in tribute to Jutta Levasseur, the egg-painting artist who worked at Epcot since its opening day and died in 2012. She was a beloved fixture in this park for 30 years. The pavilion is otherwise a string of connected one-room shops selling steins (from $45, although Grumpy is $230), figurines, crystal, Christmas ornaments, cuckoo clocks, and other high-priced wares. **Influences:** Eltz Castle near Koblenz; Stahleck Fortress near Bacharach; Rothenburg (the Biergarten and the dragon slayer statue); facades from Frankfurt and Freiburg (the guildhall). **Fun Stuff to Buy:** The connected candy-and-wine shop, **Weinkeller,** is worth a gander: You'll find such pick-me-ups as Gluhwein ($11 a liter), wine by the glass ($6–$7), or by the bottle (spätlese, Auslese, Kabinett, Liebfraumilch, $14–$25). **Der Teddybär** sells toys, especially ones by Steiff.

ITALY ★

The tiny pavilion for Italy lacks an attraction—the gondolas never leave the dock—so you must content yourself with the small-scale replicas of Venice's Doge's Palace and St. Mark's bell tower. An appealing, if incongruous, attraction that's not on the maps is the highly detailed **model train** display just between this pavilion and Germany. **Influences:** Piazza di San Marco, Venice; stucco buildings of Tuscany; a fountain reminiscent of the work of Gian Lorenzo Bernini. **Fun Stuff to Buy:** Noodle around in the **Enoteca Castello** shop for wine ($14–$25), Perugina chocolate bars ($3.50), and Quadratini hazelnut wafer cookies ($7.75 a bag). **Il Bel Cristallo** sells fragrances, handbags, crystal (are you sensing a theme here?), and pricey Venetian carnival masks.

U.S.A. ★★★

So much for world equality: The U.S.A. pavilion takes pride of place in an area that's supposed to celebrate other countries. Inside, the superlative **Voices of America** singing group, which excels at thorny close harmonies, entertains guests waiting to attend the half-hour Audio-Animatronic show, The American Adventure. You'll be impressed. Also in the lobby, next to a sign that has misspelled the name of Charles Lindbergh for years ("Lindberg"), is the unfairly ignored **American Heritage Gallery:** See the Kinsey Collection, pertaining to milestones in the African-American experience (an 1820 slave schedule, a copy of "Diary of a Slave Girl," sculpture) and embellished with cool "story lanterns" narrated by luminaries including Whoopi Goldberg, Chandra Wilson, and Diane Sawyer. **Influences:** General Georgian/colonial Greek-revival buildings (Brits often snicker that its Georgian architecture style is distinctly English). **Fun Stuff to Buy: Heritage Manor Gifts** sells patriotic tat, such as tricorner hats ($30), coonskin caps ($13), a book about the Kinsey Collection ($50), and "An American Tradition" sweatshirts that are actually made in China.

The American Adventure ★★★ SHOW Ben Franklin and Mark Twain are your Audio-Animatronic surrogates for a series of eye-popping (but ponderous) recreations of snippets along patriotic themes. Moving dioramas of seminal events such as a Susan B. Anthony speech and John Muir's inspiration for Yosemite National Park appear and vanish cinematically on a stage a quarter the size of a football field, leaving spectators marveling at the massive amount of storage space that must lie beyond the proscenium. It's a literal jukebox for mythology. Indeed, all that homespun corn is brought to you by some immensely complicated robotic and hydraulic systems. When this attraction first opened, the scene in which Franklin appears to mount stairs and then walk across the room was hailed as a technical miracle. The Will Rogers figure actually twirls a lasso purely through robotic movements. Although heavy on uplifting jingoism, the show scores points for touching lightly on a few unpleasant topics, including slavery and the suffering of Native Americans, but in general, it's not as deep as its stage. Don't be the first to enter or else you'll be marooned off to the left. The five-person **Spirit of America** fife and drum corps makes scheduled appearances outdoors in the forecourt.

JAPAN ★★★

Japan has no giant attractions (like Germany, a show building was erected but never filled with its intended ride), but its shopping and dining are exemplary, and the outdoor garden behind the pagoda is a paragon of peace. Hopefully, you can be there during one of the shows (check your "Times Guide"): the spectacularly thunderous **Matsuriza** drum shows, which are held at the base of the five-level Goju-no-to pagoda, or for an unforgettable demonstration by candy artist **Miyuki,** who can instantly create any conceivable animal out of her taffylike candy. She does for sweets what clowns do for balloon animals, and her heavily accented refrain "I show you how to make" has been Epcot music for years. At the back of the pavilion, go inside and turn left to tour the **Bijutsu-kan Gallery.** Its most recent show was about the Japanese affection for sprites, pixies, and cute characters. A red *torii* gate inspired by one in Hiroshima sits in the lagoon; the barnacles on its base are fake, and were glued on to simulate age. **Influences:** 8th-century Horyuji Temple in Nara (pagoda); Katsura Imperial Villa (Yakitori House); Shirasagi-Jo castle at Hemeji (the rear fortress); Hiroshima (*torii* gate in the lagoon). **Fun Stuff to Buy:** The **Mitsukoshi Department Store,** named for the 300-year-old Japanese original, is the most fun to roam of any

World Showcase shop. It stocks a wide variety of toys, chopstick sets ($3–$11), traditional wood sandals (from $50), linens, anime figures, and paper fans—but I love Japanese snacks, such as chocolate-dipped Pocky sticks ($3–$5). Vanilla or jasmine incense costs $10 here, but hold out for Morocco, where it's cheaper.

MOROCCO ★★★

Morocco is another spectacular pavilion, if you're inclined to dig in. It flies higher than its neighbors because the country's king took an active interest in its construction, dispatching some 21 top craftsmen for the job. There's no movie or show (although Aladdin, the Genie, and Jasmine make regular appearances), and the architecture is a cross-country mishmash drawn from Marrakech, Fes, and Rabat. **Fez House** is a tranquil, pillared two-level courtyard with a fountain and seating that recalls a classic Moroccan home; **the Gallery of Arts and History,** a mosaic-rich exhibition of hanging lanterns and colored glass, is unjustly ignored. Ask a cast member (almost always from Morocco) to write your name in Arabic for you—it's free. **Influences:** Marrakesh (Koutoubia minaret), Rabat (Chella minaret), Fez (Bab Boujouloud Gate, Nejjarine Fountain), Casablanca. **Fun Stuff to Buy:** The middle courtyards are cluttered with the souklike **Casablanca Carpets** and **The Brass Bazaar** boutiques that blend one into another. They are perfumed with incense ($3.75) and are stocked with interesting and reasonably priced finds, including footstools, tassled red fez caps ($19), glass tea cups ($10), thuya wood dice sets ($19) hand-painted tambourines ($16), Persian-style machine-made rugs (from $23), and full belly-dancer outfits ($85).

FRANCE ★★

France, done up to look like a typical Parisian neighborhood with a one-tenth replica of the upper stretch of the Eiffel Tower in the simulated distance (you can't go up it), is popular mostly for its food, though the street act **Serveur Amusant,** an acrobat who does handstands on stacked chairs, is thrilling. Disney allowed Guerlain and Givenchy to open fragrance shops at **Plume et Palette**—turns out the smell of selling out is just like Shalimar. **Influences:** Various Belle Epoque Parisian and provincial streets; Château de Fontainbleu (the Palais du Cinema); the former Pont des Arts in Paris (the bridge to the United Kingdom). **Fun Stuff to Buy:** The cheesiest souvenirs ($10 5-in. Eiffel Towers) are available in Les Halles at **Boutique de Cadeaux.** Across the lane, in **L'Esprit de la Provence,** a kitchen shop, wooden spoons are $7 and patterned oven mitts are $12. **Aux Vins de France** sells wine tastings for $6 to $12 and bottles for $20 to $32, more than in Germany or Italy.

Epcot at Night

There are no parades anymore at Epcot, but usually at 9pm, the pulse-pounding **IllumiNations: Reflections of Earth** ★★★ flames-and-water spectacular takes place over World Showcase Lagoon. Its central globe, which is studded with 15,500 tiny video screens, weighs some 350,000 pounds, and the show's so-called Inferno Barge carries a payload of 4,000 gallons of propane. Crowds start building on the banks 2 hours before showtime, but I find doing that a waste of time, and therefore money, as a day's admission is so steep. Any view of the center of the lake will be fine (some people find the islands obstructive, but I don't), but take care to be upwind or you may be engulfed by smoke.

"Impressions de France" ★ FILM The 18-minute, 200-degree-wide movie is no longer the freshest example of a tourism film—mostly classical music and postcard-worthy shots of some 50 picturesque French places. It has been playing continuously since Epcot opened in 1982. Happily, it provides seating.

UNITED KINGDOM ★★

United Kingdom, another wild mix of architectural styles, has no rides or shows, so few people know about the knee-high **hedge maze** in back. The U.K. is popular chiefly for its English-style pub, the Rose & Crown Pub & Dining Room (which you can enjoy without a reservation or eating), and a counter-service fish and chips shop. That's two fish-and-chips outlets in a block—far more than you'd find even in London these days. After 5:15pm, duck into the pub to catch Pam Brody or Carol Stein, longtime Epcot entertainers who both play piano here and lead the guests in son. Request their version of "Do Re Mi" (it's clean). **Influences:** Anne Hathaway's Cottage, Stratford-upon-Avon (the Tea Caddy); Queen Anne style (the middle promenade); Hampton Court, London (Sportsman's Shoppe); Victorian, country, and traditional pub styles (Rose & Crown). **Fun Stuff to Buy:** Featured shopping in the conjoined **Sportsman's Shoppe, the Crown & Crest,** and **Toy Soldier** includes Beatles merch, Pooh merch, and those green Peter Pan hats with the red feather ($15; they keep the feathers behind the counter). Across the way, **Lords and Ladies** does jewelry and the **Tea Caddy** sells Twinings tea and mugs.

CANADA ★

Like Japan, Canada's gardens (inspired by Victoria's Butchart Gardens, although the sign says Victoria Gardens) are a surprising oasis, adding a hidden artificial canyon delightfully washed by a man-made waterfall. The worthwhile live act here is **Off Kilter** at the amphitheater, in which men in kilts bash out palatable rock tunes. Soccer moms consider them heartthrobs, so CDs are for sale here for $20. **Influences:** 19th-century Victorian colonial architecture (Hotel du Canada); emblematic northwestern Indian design and Maritime Provinces towns; Butchart Gardens, Victoria (Victoria Gardens). **Fun Stuff to Buy:** The shop, **Northwest Mercantile,** mostly hawks maple syrup ($20 for 8 oz.), stuffed huskies and bears ($20), red tartan fleece vests ($30), and T-shirts with jokes about moose and hockey.

"O Canada!" ★ FILM Canada, like China, has a movie, but could its name be a little less stereotypical? It's shot with nine cameras in Circle-Vision 360°, a process Walt Disney originally called Circarama. The 18-minute presentation (1982), which requires standing, was refurbished by adding newly shot bits with Martin Short as emcee. Most of its spectacular scenery (the Rockies, the Bay of Fundy) is timeless.

Where to Eat in Epcot

Epcot has the best dining choices of any Disney World park, and people come just for the food. All locations will have a few vegetarian options, kids' meals, and if you identify yourself, special dietary requests can usually be accommodated, albeit often at diminished quality. Alcohol is served everywhere—even in Morocco, where it's not so easy to get in real life. You can also drink the water in Mexico.

EPCOT'S QUICK-SERVICE RESTAURANTS

There are only two major counter-service choices in Future World, plus a Starbucks. The real casual eating action is in World Showcase.

Sunshine Seasons ★★★ INTERNATIONAL   This fantastic place offers the best selection and freshest food of all Epcot's counter-service locations, including salads, grilled items (huge seared mahimahi steak with salad, oak-grilled chicken and fish), stir-fry, and unusual sides such as asparagus chicken chowder—not a fried item, burger, or pizza in sight. The desserts are epic (cheesecake with berries, tiramisu; $4). You can also pick up snacks suiting dietary restrictions. The Land. Breakfast $4 to $6, lunch and dinner Combo meal $8.50 to $11.

Electric Umbrella ★★ AMERICAN   Future World's most central counter-service locale. Expect burgers, nuggets, and meatball subs (snooze). Innoventions East. Combo meal $8 to $11.

La Cantina De San Angel ★★ MEXICAN   Mexico's counter-service option will give you beef or chicken tacos, cheese empanadas, nachos, and margaritas ($9.50). It's outside but on the water. Mexico. Combo meal $11 to $12.

Kringla Bakeri Og Kafé ★★ SCANDINAVIAN   Some of the selections in Norway's bake shop can't be found elsewhere at Disney, including *rullekake* (a rolled swirl of berries and yellow cake). More than one person claims the smooth, strawberry-topped rice cream pudding snack to be their favorite sweet in Walt Disney World. You can also get sandwiches, heated to order. Norway. Desserts $4, sandwiches $7 to $8.

Lotus Blossom Café ★ CHINESE   China's quick-service choice, with covered seating, is basic, serving beef noodle bowls, shrimp fried rice, pot stickers, and the like. Mango smoothies are sweet but delicious. China. Combo meal $8.50 to $12.

Sommerfest ★★ GERMAN   When you can't get into Biergarten, settle for this kiosk to get your bratwurst, sausage, and beer. Germany. Sausage rolls $7.

Tutto Gusto ★ GERMAN   The bar attached to the Tutto Italia Ristorante serves cocktails but also a fast-service selection of cheese and meat plates for two or three ($24–$27), plus cannoli, tiramisu, and panini. Italy. Panini $9 to $13, desserts $4 to $8.

Liberty Inn ★★★ AMERICAN   Cheap burgers, BBQ pork sandwiches, chicken, and Caesar salads. Outside, the **Fife & Drum Tavern** the place for turkey legs and beer. The American Adventure. Combo meal $10.

Yakitori House ★★★ JAPANESE   Japan's small counter-service location is by the gardens, and it supplies beef udon, teriyaki chicken, sushi plates, and edamame. Facing the lagoon under the pagoda, the **Kaki-Gori** kiosk (closed in cold weather) serves shaved ice with syrup (including honeydew and cherry flavors) for $3.50, and plum wine for $6. Japan. Combo meal $9 to $11.

Tangierine Café ★★★ MOROCCAN   The indoor counter-service location is a great place to dodge crowds. It serves shawarma with hummus, couscous, bread, and tabbouleh; and meatball platters with yellow rice. Accent it with Casa Beer, from Casablanca, or Moorish coffee (espresso spiced with cinnamon and nutmeg), and add baklava for $3.50. Kids can get burgers or chicken fingers for $8. Morocco. Combo meal $12 to $15.

Boulangerie Pâtisserie ★★ FRENCH   Grab a fast, bready bite in the back of Les Halles, such as a chocolate croissant or a ham-and-cheese croissant (both around $3.35—great bargains), tarts, Niçoise salad, croque-monsieur, or baguette sandwiches. A cash-only kiosk on the lagoon griddles up hot crepes (with sweet fillings, not meat), also for $4. Salads and sandwiches $7.50 to $8.50.

Yorkshire County Fish Shop ★★ BRITISH   Snag walk-up fish-and-chips and eat it al fresco. You get two strips of fish with chips (fries)—make sure to put vinegar, not ketchup, on the fries the way the English do. Ale costs $8. United Kingdom. Combo meal $8.50.

EPCOT'S TABLE-SERVICE RESTAURANTS

Book ahead if your heart is set on something, particularly for a nighttime lagoon view—if you're going to spend this kind of money, get a view out of it. The hostess will not guarantee seating location, but it helps to politely ask. Objectively, there are very few meals that would rate highly if I ate them outside of the park gates, and as with all mass-produced meals, quality varies greatly from day to day; the lion's share of the enjoyment is just being there. Lunch entrees are generally $3 to $5 less expensive than at dinner. Taking them as you encounter them, going clockwise around World Showcase:

The Garden Grill ★★ AMERICAN   As Farmer Mickey, Pluto, and Chip 'n' Dale press the flesh in this slowly revolving, two-tiered circular restaurant, you're served all-you-can-eat family style "Harvest Feast" platters of meats and vegetables, some of which were grown in the greenhouses downstairs. This is the only character meal in Future World, and it's only at dinner, but it's a good choice because it's mellow and small enough so that the characters can spend quality time with you. The Land. Combo meal $37 to $42 adults, $18 to $20 kids.

Coral Reef Restaurant ★ SEAFOOD   Call it See Food: Your semicircular booth faces the windows of the 27-foot-deep aquarium while you dine on the friends of the fish on your plate. You're even given a cheat sheet to identity what's swimming by. Only about half the menu selections are fish, and the rest are things like noodle bowls with chicken, steak, or short ribs. It's about the cool view, not the cuisine. The Seas with Nemo & Friends. Main courses $19 to $27.

San Angel Inn Restaurante ★★ MEXICAN   Epcot's most atmospheric restaurant is set beneath a false twilight sky at the base of an ancient pyramid, with the boats from the Gran Fiesta Tour steadily passing. The fare isn't Tex-Mex as much as it is Mexican: chicken mole, chili relleno, grilled wahoo fish, and caramel dulce de leche for dessert. If you can't get in (a likelihood), try La Hacienda de San Angel, across the main path on the lagoon. Its food is similarly Mexican. Mexico. Mains $18 to $29.

La Hacienda de San Angel ★★ MEXICAN   By day, it's a sunny place to get your tequila on. By night, this villa-themed restaurant (vaulted ceilings, hanging lanterns) is a fair place to sit for IllumiNations, but only if you're lucky enough to score a window seat. Margaritas are $13. The La Hacienda mixed grill with steak, chicken al pastor, chorizo, and veggies serves two ($50). Mexico. Main courses $25.

Princess Storybook Dining at Akershus Royal Banquet Hall ★★★ AMERICAN   Although it's Norway, you won't have to eat raw fish at this storybook buffet (although once upon a time, you did). Instead, it's Epcot's meet-the-princesses extravaganza for all three "feasts" daily, in a castlelike setting of vaulted ceilings and banners. Someone always stops by, be it Belle, Aurora, Jasmine, Snow White, Mulan, or Mary Poppins, who must be lost. If your own princess forgot her gown, they sell them for $65 at the shop across the path. This is the only character dining in World Showcase. Norway. Meal $41 to $55 adults, $25 to $30 kids, including five photos of your party.

Nine Dragons Restaurant ★ CHINESE   When you can't get a reservation anywhere else, you end up here. The food here is not much more daring or spicy as in the cheaper Quick Service option, Lotus Blossom Café, except here, there are more choices and they're more expensive. The decor is handsomely geometric, but nothing memorable, although some tables face out toward the water. China. Mains $16 to $22; three-course dinner sets $24.

Biergarten Restaurant ★★★ GERMAN   Toddlers lurch forward to polka, dads dive into mugs of Radeberger pilsner, and strangers make friends with their neighbors at this rowdy, carb-loaded party, an all-you-can-eat stuffer featuring sauerbraten, schnitzel, spaetzle, rotisserie chicken, and an oompah band for about 20 minutes at a time—which makes the high price more of a value. Germany. Lunch buffet $22 adults, $12 kids; dinner buffet $33 adults, $16 kids.

Tutto Italia Ristorante ★ ITALIAN   Proclaimed authentic to Italy mostly by people who have never been there, this dusky environment of chandeliers and murals nonetheless packs 'em in. Pasta of this low caliber should not be $23, but that doesn't stop patrons from buying $26 hunks of lasagna. Italy. Main courses $19 to $30.

Via Napoli Ristorante E Pizzeria ★ ITALIAN   The more enjoyable of Italy's two table service restaurants features lots of light, three-story vaulted ceilings, and three amusing wood-fired ovens shaped like the open mouths of giant mustachioed men named after volcanoes. Into those are thrust $17 individual pizzas and $9.50 kids' pizzas made with flour imported from Naples (not that you could tell a difference). There's also some lasagna and spaghetti at around $20 a plate. It's operated by Patina Restaurant Group, which runs eateries in Macy's, the Hollywood Bowl, and other tourist spots. Italy. Main courses $20 to $30.

Teppan Edo ★★★ JAPANESE   Above the Mitsukoshi store (which runs it), a chef-cum-swordsmith slices, dices, and cooks at the teppanyaki griddle built into your table. It's fun to watch, and although it's not a great choice if your kids are too young to keep their hands to themselves, it's a good way to meet your neighbors. Ask to see the smoking onion volcano. The food? Oh, it's fine, but you really come to see the fancy knife work. Japan. Main courses $18 to $32.

Tokyo Dining ★★ JAPANESE   On the second floor of the Japan pavilion, the decor is modern and stylish, the waitstaff subdued, and the menu offers both tempura/grills and sushi in modest portions at inflated prices. Some tables have a view of the lagoon through nearly floor-to-ceiling windows, which comes in handy around Illumi-Nations time. Japan. Main courses $25 to $31, sushi $6 to $9 per order.

Restaurant Marrakesh ★★★ MOROCCAN   Tucked in the back of the souk, this lesser-known restaurant, lit theatrically with hanging lanterns, is known most for its belly dancer, who appears (in a chaste costume) at 10 minutes before the hour at lunch and 10 minutes after the hour during dinner. The fare is approachable North African, heavy on the shish kebabs, lemon chicken, and couscous. Thinner crowds allow it to serve a good value at lunch: appetizer, entrée, and dessert until 3pm for $20. Morocco. Main courses $18 to $29.

Spice Road Table ★★ MOROCCAN   Slated to open late 2013, the menu was not set at press time (go to Frommers.com for the latest information), but it will have Lagoon views ideal for IllumiNations spectators. Morocco.

Chefs de France ★★ FRENCH   In a glassed-in dining room recalling a typical French bistro, dine on flatbreads and sandwiches (at lunch) or prototypical French food like crepes, duck breast, and steak haché. It offers a $24 prix-fixe, three-course meal until 3pm, but the entrees for that are merely a sandwich, quiche, or mac and cheese. One fun perk of eating here is regular appearances by Chef Remy, the tiny rat from Ratatouille, who squeaks and wriggles on a cheese plate that is wheeled around the restaurant. Odd to think a rat would attract customers, but there you have it. France. Main courses $16 to $32.

Monsieur Paul ★★★ FRENCH   Epcot's most thoughtful food (and also its most expensive) is served here, and it starts with napkins that are folded like a chef's jacket. This is special occasion stuff: an oxtail soup with black truffle for $29, roasted duck a l'orange, red snapper in rosemary sauce with scales made of roasted potato slices, plus all the amuse-bouches and long preparation explanations you'd expect of a fine establishment. The theme is classic French cuisine using fresh American ingredients, and the menu is overseen by Chef Paul Bocuse. He worked with the restaurant's namesake, the heavily Michelin-starred Chef Paul Bocuse, who oversaw the first restaurant at this location. There's also a prix-fixe menu that starts at $59 per person, or $95 if you want wine pairings. Although it faces the water, the windows are small so not every table has a view of IllumiNations. You'll find the entrance tucked around the back door of Chefs de France, under a green-and-white striped awning. France. Main courses $38 to $43.

Rose & Crown Pub & Dining Room ★★★ BRITISH   The interior is fairly similar to a country pub—big wooden bar serving whisky and lots of British and Irish draught beers ($8, or twice as much as London's most expensive pubs), tough patterned carpet underfoot—although most of the seating is outdoors. You get bangers and mash (sausage with mashed potatoes), Scotch egg (fried hard-boiled egg wrapped in sausage meat), cottage pie (ground beef with onions, carrots, mushrooms, and mashed potatoes) and that standby that finds its way onto every Disney menu, no matter how errant, New York Strip Steak. You can just have a drink in the pub if you choose. After 5pm, Carol Stein sings family-friendly songs for the drinkers getting off their feet after a long day. United Kingdom. Main courses $15 to $27.

Le Cellier Steakhouse ★ STEAKS   It takes the Canadian-themed restaurant to deliver the most all-American menu of filet mignon, rib eye, snapper, pork, and chicken, but it also Canucks it up with sides such as *poutine* fries (not truly *poutine* with gravy, but topped with cheddar, truffle salt, and red-wine reduction). Specialties include a popular cheddar cheese soup and pretzel bread. True to its name, the restaurant is windowless and vaulted, like a very clean version of a wine cellar. It's so dark and cool, in fact, that the menus are high-tech and light up when opened. The lunch and dinner selections are the same, and it can command deadly lunchtime prices because it's a tough reservation to secure. Canada. Main courses $34 to $46.

DISNEY'S HOLLYWOOD STUDIOS

Just as Epcot celebrates idealized industry and Animal Kingdom honors fauna, the 154-acre **Disney's Hollywood Studios** ★★ strives to evoke the romance of the movies. Not just any movies, of course, but mostly that pastel-hued fantasy of the Hollywood of 60 years ago, where gossip columnists ruled the radio and starlets could be discovered at Schwab's.

While it was originally conceived as a single pavilion about show business for Epcot, Universal's announcement of its invasion of the Florida market prodded Disney executives to hastily expand the concept into an entire park. In 1989, the Studios opened with just two rides (the Great Movie Ride and the Backlot Tour) to head off the competition. The Studios have never quite recovered from its half-baked genesis. Disney is working to sexy it up by changing its name (its original one, Disney–MGM Studios, was abandoned in early 2008) and adding attractions (Toy Story Midway Mania opened a few months later), but you won't find many people who will name it as their favorite of the four parks, which is why I think it's the one you should do last.

There are a few reasons why it's not one of Disney's most transporting endeavors. One is that its design is not symmetrical, which makes it harder to navigate. Another problem: When you look at the slate of attractions, you'll notice it's light on rides and heavy on shows, especially ones for small children, which, for my money, isn't enough. Still, *every* park is lacking in comparison to something as revolutionary as the Magic Kingdom, and the dearth of activities is balanced by the fact that two of its rides are among Disney's best: the Tower of Terror and the Rock 'n' Roller Coaster.

The park possesses a fraction of the attractions the Magic Kingdom has—so guests often combine its highlights on the same day with Disney's Animal Kingdom, or they allow themselves a more leisurely pace, perhaps lingering long enough to catch the dazzling pyrotechnic evening show, Fantasmic!

Guests arrive by the usual car/tram combo, by bus, or by free ferry, which sails from the Swan and Dolphin area and continues on to Epcot.

Hollywood Boulevard & Echo Lake

As soon as your bag is approved and you're through the gates, take care of business (strollers, wheelchairs, lockers) in the plaza before proceeding down Hollywood Boulevard. There are no attractions here, only shops and restaurants.

Hollywood Boulevard culminates with the 122-foot-tall **Sorcerer Mickey Hat,** the park's central icon that is from, ironically, Walt Disney's assault on typical Hollywood movies, "Fantasia." There is nothing exciting in it. Where Hollywood Boulevard and Sunset Boulevard meet, you'll locate the park's **tip board,** where wait times and show schedules are posted.

The Great Movie Ride ★★★ RIDE Behind the hat, which was added in 2001, is the park's original focal point: the replica of Grauman's Chinese Theater (Disney calls it "the Chinese Theater"), which has a forecourt graced with actual handprints and footprints of movie stars who visited in the park's early years at the behest of

---

The Best of Disney's Hollywood Studios

Don't miss if you're 6: Voyage of the Little Mermaid
Don't miss if you're 16: Rock 'n' Roller Coaster
Requisite photo op: Sorcerer Mickey Hat
Food you can only get here: Grapefruit Cake, the Hollywood Brown Derby, Hollywood Boulevard; Peanut Butter and Jelly Milkshake, 50's Prime Time Café, Echo Lake

The most crowded, so go early: Toy Story Midway Mania
Skippable: Studio Backlot Tour
Quintessentially Disney: Walt Disney: One Man's Dream; the Great Movie Ride
Biggest thrill: Twilight Zone Tower of Terror
Best show: Voyage of the Little Mermaid
Character meals: Hollywood & Vine (breakfast, lunch)
Where to find peace: Around Echo Lake

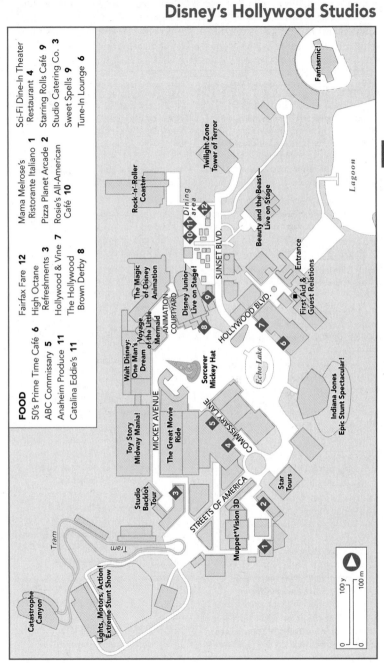

FOOD

50's Prime Time Café **6**
ABC Commissary **5**
Anaheim Produce **11**
Catalina Eddie's **11**

Fairfax Fare **12**
High Octane
  Refreshments **3**
Hollywood & Vine **7**
The Hollywood
  Brown Derby **8**

Mama Melrose's
  Ristorante Italiano **1**
Pizza Planet Arcade **2**
Rosie's All-American
  Café **10**

Sci-Fi Dine-In Theater
  Restaurant **4**
Starring Rolls Café **9**
Studio Catering Co. **3**
Sweet Spells **9**
Tune-In Lounge **6**

Catastrophe
Canyon

Lights, Motors, Action!
Extreme Stunt Show

Tram

Tram

Studio
Backlot
Tour

Toy Story
Midway Mania!

Walt Disney:
One Man's
Dream

MICKEY AVENUE

The Great Movie
Ride

STREETS OF AMERICA

Muppet*Vision 3D

Star
Tours

COMMISSARY LANE

Voyage
of the Little
Mermaid

The Magic
of Disney
Animation

ANIMATION
COURTYARD

Disney Junior—
Live on Stage!

Sorcerer
Mickey Hat

Echo Lake

Indiana Jones
Epic Stunt Spectacular!

HOLLYWOOD BLVD.

First Aid &
Guest Relations

Entrance

Rock 'n' Roller
Coaster

Dining
area

SUNSET BLVD.

Twilight Zone
Tower of Terror

Beauty and the Beast—
Live on Stage

Lagoon

Fantasmic!

100 y

100 m

3

EXPLORING WALT DISNEY WORLD | Disney's Hollywood Studios

HOLLYWOOD STUDIOS: ONE DAY, TWO WAYS

START: BE AT THE GATE FOR OPENING TIME. Grab food at a counter restaurant when it's convenient to you (but having lunch at 11am conserves time).

HOLLYWOOD STUDIOS WITH KIDS

Major candidate for Fastpass within 90 minutes of opening: Toy Story Midway Mania. If you have little kids with you, Voyage of the Little Mermaid. Only get one for Tower of Terror if it's a very busy day.

When the gates open, ride **Toy Story Midway Mania**. You'll probably want to get a Fastpass on the way out so you can ride it again later.

OR

If your child wants to participate in the **Jedi Training Academy**, reserve a slot first (ask a cast member where; it changes).

↓

See **Voyage of the Little Mermaid**.

↓

See **Disney Junior—Live on Stage!**

↓

Meet Mickey at the **Magic of Disney Animation**.

↓

Do The **Great Movie Ride**.

↓

Take the **Backlot Tour** (it might shut down by late afternoon).

↓

Target a performance of **Beauty and the Beast—Live on Stage** for around now.

↓

At this point, littler ones may need to leave the park for a break.

↓

See **Muppet*Vision 3-D**.

↓

See the **Indiana Jones Epic Stunt Spectacular**.

↓

If you think the whole family can handle them, slot in the **Twilight Zone Tower of Terror** and the **Rock 'n' Roller Coaster**.

↓

See **Fantasmic!** (if it's performing tonight).

HOLLYWOOD STUDIOS WITHOUT KIDS

When the gates open, ride **Toy Story Midway Mania**. You'll probably want to get a Fastpass on the way out so you can ride it again later.

↓

Head to the **Twilight Zone Tower of Terror** and the **Rock 'n' Roller Coaster** and ride them.

OR

If the wait for either is over 30 minutes, Fastpass one and do the other (that is, if you haven't already got a Fastpass outstanding for Midway Mania).

↓

See **Voyage of the Little Mermaid** (it's fun even without kids).

↓

Nearby, do the **Great Movie Ride**.

↓

Take the **Backlot Tour** (it usually shuts down by late afternoon).

↓

Target a performance of **Lights, Motors, Action!** to fall around now.

↓

Ride **Star Tours**.

↓

See the **Indiana Jones Epic Stunt Spectacular**.

↓

See **Muppet*Vision 3-D**.

↓

Tour **Walt Disney: One Man's Dream** (you can also do this anytime lines seem intolerable elsewhere).

↓

If you're so inclined, make a pass to the final show of **American Idol Experience**.

↓

See **Fantasmic!** (if it's performing tonight).

Disney execs. There are no prints past 1999, around the time the park gave up the dream of being a center for important film production. The ride was a showpiece in 1989 but now can feel like a mechanized waxworks. Aided by a human guide reciting a hoary script, audiences slowly cruise in traveling theater slabs past Audio-Animatronic reproductions of scenes from famous movies, including "Singin' in the Rain," "Alien," and a Munchkin-crammed "The Wizard of Oz" (its Wicked Witch figure was a landmark because it was the first time Imagineers figured out that the key to lifelike action was compensating for sudden movements with minute return movements). This is really the only place where the old MGM licensed imagery appears these days. At one point during the 22-minute journey, which concludes with a viewing of a fast-paced and expertly edited movie montage, cars experience one of two possible plotlines—for example, getting caught in the crossfire of a James Cagney gangland classic or a John Wayne western, with guns that shoot sparks. The robots have looked fresher and some kids won't be familiar with the references (Busby Berkeley, for example), but the production is endearing. Lines are never very long, but they do tend to spike just after the parade.

The American Idol Experience ★ SHOW   The main attraction on Echo Lake is a talent competition that entices park guests, especially kids (14 and older), to warble for praise. Wannabe singers audition on Commissary Lane (arrive early if you want to try out), and the cream of the crop eventually return that day to perform for voting audiences. One daily winner receives a golden ticket for the real TV show auditions—season 11 finalist Skylar Laine won one. It's a slick recap version of the Fox show, except without the cruelty, but it's still just glorified karaoke.

Indiana Jones Epic Stunt Spectacular ★★ SHOW   The 30-minute, bone-rattling tour de force of hair-raising daredevilry—rolling-boulder dodging, trucks flipping over and exploding—simultaneously titillates and, to a lesser degree, reminds you how such feats of derring-do are typically rigged and filmed for the movies. They try hard to convince you that they're really filming these sequences—you may need to explain to young children why they're lying about that, and about calling the lead actor "Harrison Ford's stunt double," but most kids understand the violence is fake. The acrobats and gymnasts who do the stunts, fights, and tumblers are skilled, and the production values are among the highest of any show at the Disney parks. The outdoor amphitheater is sheltered, and you can bring drinks and food. **Strategy:** Arrive about 20 minutes early, as there's a warm-up and volunteers are selected before showtime. It's mounted about five times daily.

Star Tours—The Adventure Continues ★★★ RIDE   Before Disney bought "Star Wars," it made, and later upgraded, this popular, 40-person motion-simulator capsule that has you riding shotgun with an ineffectual droid named RX-24 (voiced by Pee-Wee actor Paul Reubens) on an ill-fated and turbulent excursion. In 5 minutes, you manage to lose control, go into hyperdrive, dodge asteroids, navigate a comet field, evade a Star Destroyer, get caught in a tractor beam, and join an assault on the Death Star. The video is well matched to the movements, which cuts down on reports of nausea. In May and June, the park mounts Star Wars Weekends, when actors from the movie arrive for signings, parades, Q&As, and brief workshops (p. 232). Fans of the franchise come out in force, so to speak.

Jedi Training Academy ★ SHOW   Up to 15 times daily (see the "Times Guide"), kids are given robes, telescoping "light sabers," and some gentle training in the Force by a "Jedi master." It's cute. Recruits are selected by 10:30am, tops, so get here early if your young Padawan wants a shot.

Sunset Boulevard

The prime items in the park are on this street, which peels off not from the hub with the hat, as you might expect, but from the middle of Hollywood Boulevard.

The Twilight Zone Tower of Terror ★★★ RIDE The tallest ride at Disney World (199 ft.) is one of the smartest, most exciting experiences there, and it's the best version of the ride at any Disney park. It shouldn't be missed. Guests are ushered through the lobby, library, and boiler room of a cobwebby 1930s Los Angeles hotel before being seated in a 21-passenger "elevator" car that, floor by floor, ascends the tower and then, without visible tracks, emerges from the shaft and roams an upper level. Soon, you've entered a second shaft and, after a pregnant moment of tension, you're sent into what seems to be a free fall (in reality, you're being pulled faster than the speed of gravity) and a series of thrilling up-and-down leaps. The fall sequence is random and you never drop more than a few stories—but the total darkness, periodically punctured by picture-window views of the theme park far below as you become momentarily weightless, keys up the giddy fear factor. It's impossible not to smile. **Strategy:** Don't bother using Fastpass unless the line extends substantially outside of the building. In the preshow "library" room, move to the wall diagonally across from the entry door and you'll exit first, saving you time. In the boarding area, the best views are in the front row, numbered 1 and 2, although you may not be given a choice. Chickens can bail before the ride boards.

Rock 'n' Roller Coaster Starring Aerosmith ★★ RIDE Twenty-four-passenger "limousine" trains launch from 0 to 57mph in under 3 seconds, sending them through a 92-second rampage through smooth corkscrews and turns that are intensified by fluorescent symbols of Los Angeles (at one point, you dive though an O of the Hollywood sign). The indoor setup is a boon, as it means the ride can operate during the rain, and it makes the journey slightly less disorienting for inexperienced coaster riders. Cooler yet, speakers in each headrest (there are more than 900 in total) play Aerosmith music, which is perfectly timed to the dips and rolls. **Strategy:** The Fastpass line is absorbed quickly. There's also a single-rider line, though it's not always quick.

Beauty and the Beast—Live on Stage ★ SHOW The kid-friendly, 30-minute show is advertised as "Broadway-style," but it's really not. It's theme park–style, simplified with the most popular songs from the movie. The story is highly condensed (you never find out why Belle ends up at the Beast's castle and Gaston's fate is not shown) and many characters inhabit whole-body costumes, speaking recorded dialogue with unblinking eyes—to the benefit of timid kids, the Beast looks more like a plush toy than a scary monster. Its intended audience cheers like it's a rock concert and hoist videophones during the ball scene, and because of that, most performances are jammed. The metal benches are numbing, but at least the amphitheater is covered. **Strategy:** Arrive 20 minutes early unless you want to be in the back, where afternoon sun can seep in.

Fantasmic! ★★★ SHOW The super-popular 25-minute pyrotechnics show featuring character-laden showboats, a 59-foot man-made mountain, flaming water, and lasers projected onto a giant water curtain, takes place in the 6,500-seat waterfront Hollywood Hills Amphitheatre. Although it's a strong show by dint of its uniqueness, it doesn't play nightly. I'm always stunned to see people start arriving at the theater as much as *2 hours* before showtime. The seating is hard on the derriere. Most people will be satisfied taking their chances and showing up within 30 minutes of showtime. **Strategy:** On nights when there are two performances (not common), do the second one, as it's always less crowded. Sit toward the rear to avoid catching water from the special effects and to the right to make exiting easier. You can get reserved seats if you book the Fantasmic! Dining Experience and eat dinner in the participating restaurants.

Streets of America & Commissary Lane

Streets of America is a confusing zone of backlot-style city blocks, mostly facades, made to look like aging versions of New York City and San Francisco. Its primary attraction is photo ops. Look around for a few tricks, like the umbrella affixed to a lamppost in the square a la "Singin' in the Rain."

Lights, Motors, Action! Extreme Stunt Show ★★ SHOW   Loud, brawling, and moderately exciting enough to see once, it's a showcase for stunt driving dressed up like a film shoot for a car chase/action scene. The engaging 38-minute show, which uses a fleet of specially built, extra-nimble cars (plus a jet ski or two) and tells lots of lies about filming an actual movie scene while you're there, was imported from Paris's Walt Disney Studios Park (hence the set that looks like a Mediterranean port), but it seems tailor-made for American audiences. **Strategy:** Because the stage is so wide, I suggest taking a seat in the middle or near the top of the grandstand. You won't wrestle for a spot—the stadium seats 5,000.

Honey, I Shrunk the Kids Movie Set Adventure ★ ACTIVITY   Turn kids loose on a high-concept playground that simulates the sights and sounds of the average backyard—if your kids were the size of an ant. In addition to giant insects, cargo nets, and a slide that looks like Kodak film (yep, product placement), there's a giant Super Soaker that sprays the unsuspecting. It's the only playground in the park.

Muppet*Vision 3-D ★★★ SHOW   Behind the fabulous rotating fountain depicting Miss Piggy as the Statue of Liberty, the 17-minute movie features various tricks such as air blasts to make you feel like what you're seeing is actually happening. The doors on the right lead to the back of the 600-seat auditorium and the ones on the left lead to the front; for the fullest view, I suggest sticking in the middle, since the theater's walls become part of the show, and both live and Audio-Animatronic figures will appear on either side and even in the back. The preshow is amusing in that Muppet way (says Sam the Eagle about seating procedures: "Stopping in the middle is distinctly unpatriotic!"), and while the movie contains a few missteps (Waldo, a CG character, lacks creativity), it's fast moving and includes lots of beloved "Muppet Show" (but no "Sesame Street") favorites, such as Miss Piggy and Kermit. The Muppets, too, lend themselves very nicely to Audio-Animatronic technology. **Strategy:** Lines are longest just after the Indiana Jones show lets out.

Pixar Place & Animation Courtyard

Toy Story Midway Mania! ★★★ RIDE   The plotless indoor ride is the most popular in the park, and rightly so. Wearing 3-D glasses, passengers shoot their way through a series of six animated midway games (a Buttercup egg toss, a Little Green Men ring toss) based on the Pixar toy box characters. Along the way, air puffs heighten the reality. Your cannon is easy to work and easy on the hands—you just tug a cord and it fires. Scoring points is harder; both accuracy and intensity count. The queue area, stuffed with outsize toys such as Tinkertoys and Barrel of Monkeys, makes waiting a delight: A 6-foot-tall, lifelike Mr. Potato Head entertains with live interaction and hoary jokes ("Is this an audience or a jigsaw puzzle?"). Across Pixar Place, Woody and Buzz meet kids in air conditioning. **Tip:** This is your top Fastpass contender.

The Studio Backlot Tour ★ RIDE   Once a centerpiece of the park, it has been whittled away to nearly nothing. It has been more than a decade since anything of note was produced here—leaving the guides to fib about how busy employees are. New tours start every 15 minutes and take about 35 minutes. It's less crowded early in the day and closes by late afternoon.

The first segment is the Special Effects Water Tank Show, which accepts four volunteers (adults only; raise your hand for duty in the queue). There, standing guests watch how the bullet impacts, explosions, and deluges of a ship-attack movie sequence are shot and cut together to look real. **Tips:** For the best views from the front row of the audience section, join the right-hand row in the queue area. Be among the first people out of there, because the next section finds you in yet another queue, this one in a warehouse full of old movie props (a few of which you may recognize), which feeds the boarding area for a tram; the seats on its left are best.

Although the canned narration refers to active movie production, it's faking. Disney bulldozed most of the area, including Residential Street, a little village for exterior shots (the "Golden Girls" and "Empty Nest" house facades were here), to make room for the Lights, Motors, Action! Extreme Stunt Show. When drivers perform, the shriek of the engines and the funk of burning rubber make the tram miserable and the narrator inaudible. The 20-minute trip loops past some old prop vehicles (poor Herbie the now-unloved Love Bug, plus some from "The Rocketeer," "Pearl Harbor," and other movies Disney wanted to do better) in the scaled-down Boneyard; through "glamorous" wardrobe houses (the staff is darning theme park uniforms, not movie costumes). Then you pass through Catastrophe Canyon, where, seated safely, you'll witness a simulated earthquake, the heat of an exploding oil tanker, and a flash flood—all in the space of seconds. The wizardry, which resets for every batch of guests, is heart-pounding fun—although no thinking person believes the bald lie that the special effects crew is testing this rig for a shoot. Those sitting on the left might get a tad wet, and you'll need sunglasses in the afternoon. On the way out, you'll spot a Gulfstream jet Walt Disney used on his real estate–grabbing missions to Florida. Finally—some actual history!

The Voyage of the Little Mermaid ★★★ SHOW   This bright, energetic, condensed version of the animated movie has high production values (puppets, live actors, mist, and a cool undersea-themed auditorium) and is a standout. This show is a top contender for the best show to see in the heat of the day, and Fastpass is available. **Strategy:** In the preshow holding pen, the doors to the left lead to the back half of the theater; because the blacklight puppetry of the marvelous "Under the Sea" sequence can be spoiled if you see too much detail, I suggest sitting there. Consider putting very small kids in your lap so they can see better.

Disney Junior—Live on Stage! ★★ SHOW   For those of us who obediently rise and dance when commanded by Mickey Mouse, there's this breezy, 25-minute show with a lots of excellent puppets (warning, adults: You sit on the ground). It inspires such fervent participation from under 5s that it feels like a meeting for a cult that you're not a member of. If you don't know the names Doc McStuffins, Sofia the First, or Jake and the Never Land Pirates, this sing-along revue is still pretty to look at, and Mickey, Minnie, and friends make appearances. The parental units won't be too bored, as this de facto Disney Channel ad is fast paced, like changing the channel every 4 minutes. Obviously, anyone old enough to do a book report can skip it.

Hollywood History for Sale

Don't miss the cabin-esque house to the right as you exit the park. This is **Sid Cahuenga's One-of-a-Kind Antiques and Curios,** a strange and wonderful memorabilia shop, not run by Disney, with an inventory so interesting it could qualify as a museum. You can't afford everything (Dick Van Dyke's pastel-striped "Jolly Holiday" jacket from "Mary Poppins" costs $65,000), but its signed glossies, minor props, and items from the estate of Barbra Streisand (really) mean it may be the most authentically Hollywood thing about Hollywood Studios.

The Magic of Disney Animation ★ ACTIVITY This tour is, in my opinion, the most telling evidence that Disney's Hollywood Studios stumbled. Originally it provided a firsthand look at the labor-intensive work that produced all those famous Disney movies. Guests could watch live animators perfect their upcoming release—"Mulan" and "Lilo & Stitch" were made right here. But Disney fired its Florida-based animators, so there's nothing more to see. Instead, you get a hokey 9-minute show highlighting only the ideas stage of the process, followed by an ad for whatever computer-animated film will be released next. Then you're dumped in an area of paltry interactive exhibits where kids determine which Disney character their personality is most like (me: Tarzan). The biggest benefit of exploring is the chance to see major characters (Sorcerer Mickey, plus the latest ones from Pixar and other films) in the AC. You can also take a worthwhile 15-minute group crash course in drawing a popular character (such as Winnie or Minnie) with a guide, and you can bring your artwork home for free. Otherwise, the art of handmade animation, through which the Disney empire was built, cel by cel, is barely discussed. You receive no more information than you could find in a 2-minute DVD extra, yet you blow 30 minutes. **Strategy:** Skip the show and enjoy the character greetings by entering through the back door, through the Animation Gallery, where you'll pass 13 Oscars (all won for hand animation, it bears noting). If you love Disney heritage, this may bring you down.

Walt Disney: One Man's Dream ★ ACTIVITY The only historic focus on Disney history here on resort property, it's mostly overlooked, but the display is a requisite stop for anyone curious about the undeniable achievements of this driven man. Here, you (and a few other stragglers) learn that Walt was a masterful recycler. He also had a symbiotic relationship with his brother Roy, whom he followed first into the military, then to Kansas City, and finally to Hollywood. For the most part, the information is reliable and informative without being dense. There are a few authentic artifacts, plus explanations of the revolutionary "multiplane" camera that enabled animators to reproduce the sliding depth of field normally seen in live-action films (you can see the fruit of the process in "Snow White" as the camera seems to move through the forest). Worth special scrutiny is the re-creation of Walt's surprisingly banal Burbank office as it appeared from 1940 (shortly before he became a propagandist during World War II) to 1966; note the bulletin board of Disneyland developments and also the four ashtrays, which contributed to his death from lung cancer. The end of the exhibition chronicles the theme parks, including lots of scale models and an Audio-Animatronic skeleton from the 1964 World's Fair. Most people take about 20 minutes for the museum, and then there's a good 15-minute movie, culled mostly from archival footage and audio, so you hear the man himself speak. The feature scores

A favorite pastime for longtime fans is spotting **Hidden Mickeys,** which are ingeniously camouflaged mouse-ear patterns that can be secreted just about anywhere. You'll find the three circles signifying a Mickey profile embedded in an arrangement of cannonballs at Pirates of the Caribbean; flatware in the dining room at the Haunted Mansion; and woven into carpeting, printed on wallpaper—it was once snuck into the souvenir photo on Test Track using hoses. Many sightings are up to interpretation, but sharpen your observational skills first at **HiddenMickeysGuide.com**.

points for mentioning Disney's 1931 breakdown, but it also tries to prove Walt was a patron of the Disney Company's current efforts, implying he approved of Epcot's final design and worse, elbowing poor Roy virtually out of the story. But maybe it can be re-edited. "Disneyland," he promises in it, "is something that will never be finished."

Where to Eat at Disney's Hollywood Studios

All locations have a few vegetarian options, kids' meals, and if you identify yourself, special dietary requests can usually be accommodated, albeit often at diminished quality.

DISNEY'S HOLLYWOOD STUDIOS' QUICK-SERVICE RESTAURANTS

Starring Rolls Café ★★ AMERICAN   The faster, cheaper, quieter alternative to Quick Service does stupendous baked goods such as chocolate Butterfinger cupcakes and banana split cake, plus a few sandwiches with chips or fruit. Around the corner, **Sweet Spells** tops it in the confection department, selling creative candy apples that look like Kermit and Mike Wazowski, plus rice crisp "turkey legs." Sunset Boulevard. Sandwiches $8 to $10.

Rosie's All-American Cafe ★★ AMERICAN   In the Sunset Ranch Market riff on L.A.'s famous Farmer's Market, you'll find outdoor-only counter service serving the typical burgers and chicken nuggets. Sunset Boulevard. Combo meal $8 to $10.

Catalina Eddie's ★★ AMERICAN   Outdoor counter service for bready personal pizzas, hot Italian deli sandwiches, and Caesar's salad. Near it is **Anaheim Produce** for fruit ($1.30 a piece). Sunset Boulevard. Combo meal $9.50 to $11

Fairfax Fare ★★ AMERICAN   Grab the richest, deadliest food, served outside: half-slabs of spareribs, barbecued pork sandwiches, and mac 'n cheese with truffle oil. Nearby is the **Toluca Legs Turkey Company** kiosk for those crazy big turkey legs drumsticks. Sunset Boulevard. Combo meal $9 to $16.

ABC Commissary ★★ AMERICAN   You get the same old food (burgers, couscous quinoa, and fried seafood platters), but it's a good choice because the air-conditioned, uncrowded space is fashioned after a '30s Deco backlot cafeteria. Commissary Lane. Combo meal $8 to $11.

Studio Catering Co. ★ AMERICAN   In a semi-covered seating area, order takeaway chicken Caesar wraps, buffalo chicken salad, Greek salad, BBQ pulled-pork subs and Sloppy Joes with chipotle barbecue sauce. To the left, the **High Octane Refreshments** stand sells $9 cocktails (frozen margaritas and the like), draft beer for $6 to $8. Streets of America. Combo meal $9 to $10.

Pizza Planet Arcade ★ AMERICAN   Bland pizza, bready subs, dull salads, but kids like spending more of your money on the arcade games, so it's often busy. Streets of America. Combo meal $9 to $10.

DISNEY'S HOLLYWOOD STUDIOS' TABLE-SERVICE RESTAURANTS

The highest-concept reservation restaurants in Disney World are found here. The food isn't legendary, but some of the settings play on entertainment greatness.

The Hollywood Brown Derby ★★ AMERICAN   With interior design based on the after-hours industry hangout of Hollywood's Golden Age (not the place with the big hat—the classier one), this airy post-Deco hall shoots for the upscale. Caricatures of film legends line the walls, and while the original Brown Derby was noted for its Cobb salad, this version is a bit of a caricature as well, often soggy. Other choices, all invoking that midcentury California spirit at the park's highest prices, include spit-roasted bison (really), duck two ways, cioppino, and beef filet. Its grapefruit cake is a dessert specialty. Prices for lunch and dinner are the same, but the cheapest you can do is the $28 noodle bowl with coconut tofu. Hollywood Boulevard. Main courses $28 to $42.

Hollywood & Vine ★★ AMERICAN   At breakfast and lunch, costumed Disney Junior characters (such as Special Agent Oso and Jake) greet kids, sing, and dance in a dinerlike setting for **Disney Junior Play 'n Dine at Hollywood & Vine.** The food is always an all-you-can-eat buffet. Echo Lake. Buffet $27 to $35 adults, $15 to $19 kids.

50's Prime Time Café ★★★ AMERICAN   Dine atop Formica in detailed reproductions of Cleaver-era kitchens while TVs play black-and-white shows from the era. Waitresses gently give lip to customers as they sling blue-plate specials, meatloaf, pot roast, chicken pot pie, and other momlike dishes, but the favorite here is its peanut butter and jelly milkshake ($5.30). Attached is the **Tune-In Lounge,** a TV room for adults serving beer and cocktails "from Dad's liquor cabinet." Echo Lake. Main courses $16 to $22.

Mama Melrose's Ristorante Italiano ★★ ITALIAN   Items cost two-thirds of what they do at Epcot's Italy, and the atmosphere recalls the brick-walled, red-boothed family restaurant you'd find in any big American city. As expected, you eat pastas, steaks, flatbreads, and brick oven–baked chicken dishes. Streets of America. Main courses $16 to $24.

Sci-Fi Dine-In Theater Restaurant ★★★ AMERICAN   Disney World's most unusual restaurant arranges mock-ups of '50s automobiles before a silver screen showing a loop of B-movie clips and trailers. Couples sit side-by-side, like at a real drive-in movie, stars twinkle in the "sky," and families get their own booths. It's a brilliant idea, well realized and memorable, making it a top choice despite very iffy food quality. Dishes include burgers, salmon BLTs, and a Caesar's salad drenched with dressing. Commissary Lane. Main courses $16 to $24.

DISNEY'S ANIMAL KINGDOM

Although it's the largest Disney theme park in Florida (500 acres), **Disney's Animal Kingdom** ★★, which opened in 1998 at a reported cost of $800 million as a competitor to Busch Gardens, actually takes the least amount of time to visit, because most of that land is used up by a menagerie of exotic animals. Instead of cages, they're kept in paddocks rimmed with cleverly disguised trenches that are concealed behind landscaping. Most attractions are given a mild environmentalist message (ironic, considering how much Florida swamp was obliterated to build this resort, but never you mind). Because animals become inactive as the Florida heat builds, a visit here should begin as soon as the gates open, usually around 8am. To help gird your resolve, there are coffee carts ($3.40 outside the gates, $2.20 inside) along the entranceway. **Tips:** Schedule your nighttime shindig, such as that dinner show you've been dying to catch, for your Animal Kingdom day. Check the weather before you come, because if it's excessively hot or wet, you might be miserable. Only three major attractions take place indoors.

GETTING IN   Staples such as locker and stroller rental are just past the gates, in what's called the **Oasis,** a lush buffer zone that gradually acclimates guests to the world of the park. Pick up a free "Guidemap," a "Times Guide," and an "Animal Guide." The locations of animal enclosures are noted on the map by black-and-white paw prints, so if you're most interested in seeing wildlife, follow those. Children's activity stations (Kids' Discovery Club) are marked with a K.

Generally speaking, the biggest animals and the most astute design collects at the back of the park (Africa and Asia), the thrills to the right (Asia and DinoLand U.S.A.), and the biggest kiddie goodies to the left (Camp Minnie-Mickey).

The first thing you should do, like everyone else, is beeline it to the back of the Africa section. That's where the Kilimanjaro Safari is, and first thing in the morning is the best time to do it. Crowds grow more ferocious than the lions.

Discovery Island

Like the Plaza of the Magic Kingdom, Discovery Island is designed to be the hub of the park. It's the main viewing area for the daily Mickey's Jammin' Jungle Parade, which circles it (the route is denoted on the maps by a red dotted line) and guests can touch down here to change lands. The park's **tip board,** with current wait times and upcoming showtimes, is also here, just to the right past the bridge from the Oasis, by the Disney Outfitters shop.

The Tree of Life ★★★ RIDE   Instead of a castle or a geosphere (or, uh . . . a hat), the centerpiece here, Animal Kingdom's "weenie," is an emerald, 14-story-high arbor (built on the skeleton of an oil rig) covered with hundreds of carvings of animals made to appear, at a distance, like the pattern of bark. Some 102,000 vinyl leaves were individually attached—which is why its shade of green is more lurid than the surrounding foliage—to some 750 tertiary branches. That the best way to enjoy it is to slowly make

---

The Best of Disney's Animal Kingdom

Don't miss if you're 6: Festival of the Lion King

Don't miss if you're 16: DINOSAUR

Requisite photo op: The drop at Expedition Everest

Food you can only get here: Frozen chai, Royal Anandapur Tea Company

The most crowded, so go early: Kilimanjaro Safaris

Skippable: Rafiki's Planet Watch

Quintessentially Disney: It's Tough to Be a Bug!

Biggest thrill: Expedition Everest

Best show: "Finding Nemo—The Musical"

Character meals: Tusker House Restaurant, Africa

Where to find peace: Discovery Island

Disney's Animal Kingdom

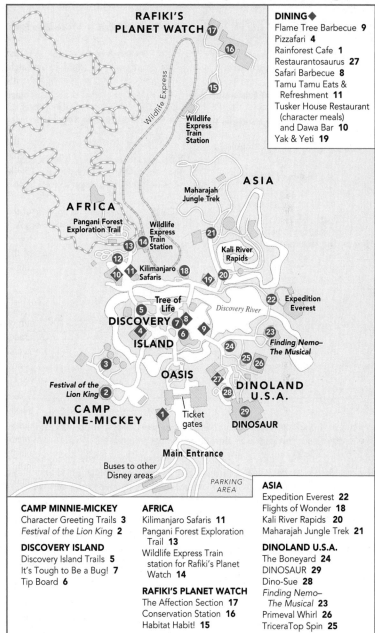

RAFIKI'S
PLANET WATCH

Wildlife
Express
Train
Station

ASIA

Maharajah
Jungle Trek

AFRICA

Pangani Forest
Exploration Trail

Wildlife
Express
Train
Station

Kali River
Rapids

Kilimanjaro
Safaris

Tree of
Life

Discovery River

Expedition
Everest

DISCOVERY

ISLAND

Finding Nemo–
The Musical

OASIS

DINOLAND
U.S.A.

Festival of the
Lion King

CAMP
MINNIE-MICKEY

Ticket
gates

DINOSAUR

Main Entrance

Buses to other
Disney areas

PARKING
AREA

DINING◆
Flame Tree Barbecue **9**
Pizzafari **4**
Rainforest Cafe **1**
Restaurantosaurus **27**
Safari Barbecue **8**
Tamu Tamu Eats &
  Refreshment **11**
Tusker House Restaurant
  (character meals)
  and Dawa Bar **10**
Yak & Yeti **19**

CAMP MINNIE-MICKEY
Character Greeting Trails **3**
Festival of the Lion King **2**

DISCOVERY ISLAND
Discovery Island Trails **5**
It's Tough to Be a Bug! **7**
Tip Board **6**

AFRICA
Kilimanjaro Safaris **11**
Pangani Forest Exploration
  Trail **13**
Wildlife Express Train
  station for Rafiki's Planet
  Watch **14**

RAFIKI'S PLANET WATCH
The Affection Section **17**
Conservation Station **16**
Habitat Habit! **15**

ASIA
Expedition Everest **22**
Flights of Wonder **18**
Kali River Rapids **20**
Maharajah Jungle Trek **21**

DINOLAND U.S.A.
The Boneyard **24**
DINOSAUR **29**
Dino-Sue **28**
*Finding Nemo–
  The Musical* **23**
Primeval Whirl **26**
TriceraTop Spin **25**

ANIMAL KINGDOM: ONE DAY, TWO WAYS

ANIMAL KINGDOM WITH KIDS

When the gates open, head straight to **Africa for Kilimanjaro Safaris**.

↓

Enjoy the **Pangani Forest Exploration**.

↓

Go to Asia for the **Maharajah Jungle Trek**.

↓

Ride **Kali River Rapids** to cool down.

↓

See **Flights of Wonder**.

↓

Have lunch at Yak & Yeti.

↓

See the next performance of **Finding Nemo—The Musical**, seated and indoors.

↓

Ride **Primeval Whirl** and **TriceraTop Spin**.

↓

Go see **It's Tough to Be a Bug!**, and walk the Discovery Trails to look for animals embedded in the Tree of Life.

↓

Go to Camp Minnie-Mickey (or Africa) to see **Festival of the Lion King** and to meet the Disney characters.

↓

If you have time or energy, take the train to and from Rafiki's Planet Watch for a 20-minute walk-through (budget 45 min. total).

↓

Catch the parade, re-ride anything you loved, and head out before closing.

a circuit of it, looking for and identifying new animals, is perhaps proof that the best way to experience this park is to slow down and open your eyes.

Discovery Island Trails ★★ ACTIVITY   The self-guided paths encircle the Tree of Life. Here's where you'll find giant red kangaroos, flamingoes, storks, otters, lemurs, macaws, and the lappet-faced vulture; some are removed from view when it's hot. It takes only about 15 minutes to enjoy.

Adventurers Outpost ★ CHARACTER GREETING   Mickey and Minnie, wearing explorer garb, meet kids, and sign autographs here, on the east side of the path toward Asia. It is the only place in the resort where they appear as a couple.

It's Tough to Be a Bug! ★★★ SHOW   Hidden in the flying roots of the Tree of Life, in a cool basementlike theater, you'll find a cleverly rigged cinema showing a sense-tricking 10-minute 3-D movie based on the animated movie "A Bug's Life." When the stinkbugs do their thing or the tarantula starts firing poison quills, you'll never quite be sure what's an image, what's cutting-edge robotics, and what's clever rigging in the theater. As one of the newest sense-tricking movies at Disney World, it's one of the best. Little kids who can't distinguish fantasy from reality may be scared by the marvelously realized Hopper figure; sit in back (the first doors after you get your

---

ANIMAL KINGDOM WITHOUT KIDS

Within 90 minutes of opening, Fastpass Kilimanjaro Safaris or Expedition Everest.

When the gates open, head straight to Africa for **Kilimanjaro Safaris**. Pick up a Fastpass for it afterward if you want to ride it again later; each trip yields different animals.

↓

Enjoy the **Pangani Forest Exploration Trail**

↓

Go to Asia to ride **Expedition Everest** before the line gets too crazy.

↓

Walk to Asia and ride **Expedition Everest** (if you haven't already!)

↓

Explore the **Maharajah Jungle Trek**.

↓

If it's hot by now, ride **Kali River Rapids**.

↓

See **Flights of Wonder**.

↓

Have lunch at Yak & Yeti.

↓

See the next performance of **Finding Nemo—The Musical**. Enjoy the air conditioning.

↓

Ride **Primeval Whirl**.

↓

Ride **DINOSAUR**.

↓

See **It's Tough to Be a Bug!**, and walk the Discovery Trails to look for animals embedded in the Tree of Life.

↓

If it's quiet and you're interested, re-ride **Kilimanjaro Safaris** to get a different experience than before.

↓

Go to Camp Minnie-Mickey (or Africa, if it has moved) to see **Festival of the Lion King**.

↓

If you have time or energy, take the train to **Rafiki's Planet Watch** (budget 45 min. total).

↓

Catch the parade and re-ride anything you loved. You will probably depart before closing time.

---

glasses) and to the left to be far from him. The indoor preshow area is decorated with posters for some funny entomological variations on Broadway shows (my faves: "Web Side Story" and "My Fair Ladybug"). **Strategy:** Upon exiting, go left to explore the trails (above) or right for the bridge to Asia.

Mickey's Jammin' Jungle Parade ★★★ SHOW This park's only parade begins in Africa, loops around Discovery Island, and then returns to its starting point (the dotted line on maps). Like all Disney parades it has lots of character appearances. I like this one because the 10 floats are quite ingeniously made—most of them are animal-like contraptions powered by the people pushing or driving them along.

Africa

You might see a bit of upheaval in this section of the park while a new theater is built to house Festival of the Lion King. Because of its star attraction, Africa is mobbed in the morning, but by afternoon it gets more manageable.

Kilimanjaro Safaris ★★★ RIDE Easily the bumpiest ride at Disney World, the 20-minute ride is the crown jewel of Animal Kingdom. Climb into a supersize, 32-passenger Jeep—an actual one with wheels, not a tracked cart—and be swept into what feels like a real safari through the African veldt, with meticulously rutted tracks and all, only on Quaaludes. Be quick on the shutter, because drivers speed fleetly, passing through habitats for giraffes, elephants, wildebeest, ostrich, hippos, lions, antelope, rhinos, and other creatures that made safaris famous. Considering the quality and quantity of animals on display—and the cleverness of the enclosure design, as there are never bars between you and them—it's easily the best animal attraction of the park, and the queue only builds during the day. Some people say that the second-best time to see the animals is in midafternoon because they get antsy with the foreknowledge that they're about to be led to their indoor sleeping quarters. Ride twice if you want—the free will of the animals means it's never the same trip twice. **Strategy:** Photographers who want clear shots should jockey toward the back, away from the cockpit. They may not have control over that, so at the very least, they should negotiate with their companions for a seat at the end of their row.

Pangani Forest Exploration Trail ★★★ ACTIVITY   Upon exiting Kiliman-jaro Safaris, begin this trail, which focuses on African animals. It wends past a troop of lowland gorillas (very popular), naked mole rats, okapi, meerkats (yes, like Timon), and hippos you can view through an underwater window; the nocturnal animals start waking up at around 3:30pm. The circuit takes about a half-hour, but you can spend as long as you want.

Rafiki's Planet ★ ACTIVITY   Its elements are listed separately on the park maps, but everything is of a piece. The only way to reach this educational veterinary station is using the **Wildlife Express Train.** Waits are generally no longer than 10 minutes. The trip takes 7 minutes and you'll get glimpses of plain backstage work areas but not much else. **Habitat Habit!,** the path that leads to the main building, is another "discovery trail," this one with cotton-top tamarins (endangered monkeys about the size of squirrels). **Conservation Station** is a quasi-educational peek at how the park's animals are maintained—you're not seeing the true veterinary facilities, but a few auxiliary rooms set up so tourists can watch activities through picture windows. There's not always something going on (early mornings seem to be most active), and the "Times Guide" doesn't help, so you might get all the way here and then find yourself with only a few environmentalist exhibits to poke at. There's nothing earthshaking—enter a dark, soundproof booth and listen to the sounds of the rainforest—but the pace is much easier than in the park outside. **The Affection Section** is a petting zoo hosting, in addition to your typical petting-zoo denizens, a type of goat that was saved from extinction. **Tip:** Try to visit by 11am, when the vets are more likely to be treating animals.

Asia

Asia is the park's showcase, and its ingenious decor (rat-trap wiring, fraying prayer flags) is so accurate it could easily be mistaken for the real Nepal or northern India. Make a stop at **Bhaktapur Market,** which sells Asian souvenirs that's a cut above the usual theme park stuff—kid kimonos, Manga toys, beautiful scarves. It makes me long for the years when all of Disney World's shops were this interesting and site-specific.

Expedition Everest ★★★ RIDE   The lavishly themed and abundantly hyped roller coaster is mostly contained in the "snowcapped" mountain looming nearly 200 feet over the park's east end (if it were any higher, Florida law would require it to be topped by an airplane beacon). The queue area is a beautifully realized duplication of a Himalayan temple down to the tarnished bells and weathered paint, although portions of it are exposed the sun, so drink something before you pony up. The coaster itself is

Many of Expedition Everest's original effects (mist at the summit, a hawk that swoops in at the peak) were too complicated to function for long. The Yeti suffered the most ignoble fate. Although it was the most complicated Audio-Animatronic creature ever commissioned, and the sight of it lunging for your train was meant to be the ride's scintillating climax, its repetitive motion reportedly cracked its supports, which were too integrated with the structure of the mountain to repair. The solution: A strobe light now makes it appear as if the motionless Yeti moves. Disney fans deride it as the "Disco Yeti."

loaded with powerful set pieces that get you your money's worth: both backward and forward motion, pitch-black sections, and a fleeting encounter with a 22-foot Abominable Snowman, or Yeti. As with all Disney rides, the most dramatic drop (80 ft.) is visible from the sidewalk out front, so if you think you can stomach that, you can do the rest. There are no upside-down loops; the dominant motion is spiral, which makes some people slightly nauseous. **Strategy:** This coaster is a top candidate for Fastpass. The seats with the best view, without question, are in the front rows, although the back rows feel a little faster. Sometimes, a very fast-moving single-rider line is in play.

Kali River Rapids ★ RIDE   The 12-passenger round bumper boat shoots a course of rapids, and sometimes you can get soaked—it depends on your bad luck—but it's generally milder than similar rides. Your feet, for sure, will get wet. The worst damage is usually done by spectators who shoot water cannons at passing boats. Lots of guests buy rain ponchos ($7.50–$8.50 at nearby stores, or $1 for two at your local dollar store), but there is a water-resistant holding area in the center of each boat. To be safe, there are free 120-minute lockers available. **Strategy:** Lines build considerably when it's hot, so this is another prime Fastpass candidate.

Maharajah Jungle Trek ★★ ACTIVITY   Too few people enjoy this self-guided, South Asian–themed walking trail featuring some gorgeous tigers (rescued from a circus breeding program), flying foxes, komodo dragons, and a few birds frolicking among fake ruins. The tigers are most active when the park opens and near closing time. Grab a bird information sheet after entering the aviary; there's a bat display, too, that you can bypass if you're squeamish. **Strategy:** If you Fastpass Kali River Rapids, kill the intervening time by strolling through here first.

Flights of Wonder ★★ SHOW   At the canvas-sheltered Caravan Stage, the 25-minute show (the schedule is posted) showcases birds such as hawks, vultures, bald eagles, and parrots—20 species; the mix changes—that swoop thrillingly over the audience's heads. Standard, if beautiful, nature-show stuff. After the performance, handlers usually present a few of the birds back on stage for close inspection.

DinoLand U.S.A.

When it rains, come here, where two attractions and one big counter-service restaurant are indoors.

"Finding Nemo—The Musical" ★★★ SHOW   For my money, this is the best show at Disney right now. A compressed version of the movie, the story has been heightened with such catchy added songs as "Fish Are Friends, Not Food" and the

PACKING IT IN: TWO PARKS, ONE DAY

START: BE AT THE GATE FOR OPENING TIME.

You really don't *have* to pay for 2 days' worth of park tickets to visit Animal Kingdom and Hollywood Studios. As long as you have the Park Hopper option, you can see the highlights in 1 action-packed day. You will miss some lesser attractions, but not enough to lose sleep over. Animal Kingdom usually opens at 8am, which lets you get a head start on things.

Which park you do first is a toss-up. The animals are most active first thing in the morning at Animal Kingdom, but the line at Hollywood Studios' Toy Story Midway Mania gets crazy by noon, and the Fastpasses are often gone by then. I'm starting with Animal Kingdom, knowing that the line for Midway Mania will likely be well over an hour, but if you don't think Midway Mania is for you (see p. 75 for a description), that problem will vanish.

Begin your day at **Disney's Animal Kingdom.** When the gates open, head straight to **Africa for Kilimanjaro Safaris.**

↓

Animal people: Enjoy the **Pangani Forest Exploration Trail.**

Coaster people: Ride **Expedition Everest.** If the wait's bad, use the Single Rider line.

↓

Explore the **Maharajah Jungle Trek.**

↓

Ride **Kali River Rapids.**

↓

If you enjoy live musicals, see the next performance of either **Finding Nemo—The Musical** or **Festival of the Lion King.** This will take nearly an hour, so cut this if it's too close to lunch.

↓

Ride **DINOSAUR.** (Maybe you can do this waiting for the Nemo show to start?)

↓

Go see **It's Tough to Be a Bug!,** and afterward walk the Discovery Trails and look for animals embedded in the Tree of Life.

↓

Leave the park and have lunch on U.S. 192, where food's cheaper. You can reach it quickly by following the signs to the Animal Kingdom Lodge and turning left at the light before its entrance. That's Sherbeth Road, and it winds to U.S. 192. After lunch, drive east on 192 a few miles and follow the signs back to Disney.

↓

Head to **Disney's Hollywood Studios.**

↓

First, go to **Toy Story Midway Mania** at Pixar Place. If there are any Fastpasses left, get one and come back later.

↓

Ride **Twilight Zone Tower of Terror** and **Rock 'n' Roller Coaster.**

↓

Do the **Great Movie Ride.**

↓

Take the **Backlot Tour** (it usually shuts down by late afternoon).

↓

Ride **Star Tours.**

↓

If you have time, see **Muppet*Vision 3-D.**

↓

If you have time, see the **Indiana Jones Epic Stunt Spectacular.**

↓

See **Fantasmic!** (if it's performing tonight).

↓

Go back to your hotel and collapse.

infectious, Beach Boys–style "Go with the Flow." Just as in the Broadway adaptation of "The Lion King," live actors manipulate complicated animal puppets in full view, which allows the fish to appear as if they're floating in the sea. It's remarkable how quickly you stop paying attention to the humans—at least, until they start flying, with their puppets, through the air on wires. Then you're just amazed. Sprightly, bright, colossal, and energetic, this winning 40-minute show is a good choice for taking a load off (the bench seating is indoors), and even those who know the movie backward and forward will find something new in the vibrant vigor of the delivery. **Strategy:** Because some scenes (including the introduction of Dory) happen in the aisle that crosses the center of the theater, sit in the rear half of the auditorium.

Chester & Hester's Dino-Rama ★ ACTIVITY/RIDE   Kids run loose in this miniature carnival-style amusement area with a midway, **Fossil Fun Games** (Mammoth skee-ball races, "Whac-a-Packycephaolosaur") and two simple family rides. **TriceraTop Spin ★**, for the very young, is yet another iteration of the Dumbo ride over at Magic Kingdom and is designed for kids to ride with their parents. Cars fit four, in two rows. **Primeval Whirl ★** is a pair of mirror-image, family-friendly carnival-style coasters (FYI, Walt *hated* carnivals) that start out like a typical "wild mouse" ride before, mid-trip, the round cars begin spinning on an axle as they ride the rails. Think of it as a roller-coaster version of the teacup ride. You can plainly see what you're in for, although you may be surprised at how roughly the movements can whip your neck. Don't feel bad if you give it a miss, too, because it's not a Disney original; it was made by a French company that sells similar rides to other parks. Keep the kids in control by swinging them across the path to **The Boneyard ★**, a hot, sun-exposed playground where the very young can dig up "prehistoric" bones in the sand.

DINOSAUR ★★ RIDE   A good rainy-weather option is this 3-minute indoor time-travel ride in which all-terrain "Enhanced Motion Vehicles" simultaneously speed and shimmy down an unseen track, all as hordes of roaring dinosaurs attempt to make you dinner and an approaching asteroid shower threatens to do everyone in. Some kids, and even some adults, find all those jaws and jerky movements rather intense, and it's extremely dark and loud, but ultimately, it's a fun time, even if the perpetual darkness makes me wonder how much money Disney saved in not having to build more dinosaurs. Like many modern rides, well-known actors perform in the preshow video; this one's got Phylicia Rashad, fiercely overacting, and Wallace Langham, in a horrific tie. The line never seems to be as long as this ride deserves. On the path to the ride, don't ignore **Dino-Sue,** the 40-foot-long, full-scale T. rex skeleton—it's a replica of Sue, the most complete specimen man has yet found. The original, unearthed in South Dakota in 1990, is on display at Chicago's Field Museum. The **Cretaceous Trail,** at the head of the path, showcases ferns and American alligators extant in that period.

Camp Minnie-Mickey

The final themed zone is between the entrance plaza and Africa, and it's also for kids. The great flaw of this area is that there's no real reason to partake unless you see something on your "Times Guide" that you want to do, because there are no continuous attractions—and that's why it is rumored to be on the verge of a major overhaul for a new land themed on James Cameron's "Avatar."

"Festival of the Lion King" ★★★ SHOW   If this lavish, colorful, intense spectacle can't hold your attention for 30 minutes, you might require prescriptions. Audiences sit on benches in four quadrants (front rows are good for engaging with performers), and the event comes on buoyant and boisterously, like an acid trip during a rock concert. Four huge floats enter the room, topped with soft-looking giant puppets of Timon, Pumbaa, and African wildlife and attended by acrobats, stilt-walkers, flame jugglers, and dancers, all of whom get their turn to dazzle you with their acts, which are performed, of course, to the hit songs of the movie. **Strategy:** The best seating sections are to your left as you enter. If you want to be near the exit (there's no ducking out once it starts, though), sit in the two right-hand sections. Shows are timed, and they can fill up, so arrive 30 minutes early—be warned the wait area is currently exposed to the elements, but in 2014, this show will be moving to a newly built theater in the Africa section of the park.

Character Greeting Trails ★ CHARACTER GREETING   The outdoor cabanas in Camp Minnie-Mickey essentially guarantee face time with Disney characters (usually Baloo and King Louie, Donald, Pocahontas, and Chip 'n' Dale) within the period printed on the "Times Guide." This is the park's bonanza zone for autographs.

Where to Eat at Disney's Animal Kingdom

All locations have vegetarian options, kids' meals, and if you identify yourself, special dietary requests can usually be accommodated. Because plastic straws choke animals, paper ones are provided.

DISNEY'S ANIMAL KINGDOMS' QUICK-SERVICE RESTAURANTS

Guests will **dietary restrictions** should seek out the new Gardens kiosk near Flame Tree Barbecue on Discovery Island, where special snacks are sold and cast members can help you find more suitable dishes around the park.

Flame Tree Barbecue ★★★ AMERICAN   If you don't mind gorging on meaty dishes such as ribs and baked chicken when you're supposed to be appreciating animals, it has some terrific eating areas with cushioned seating on the Discovery River, and its pulled-pork barbecue is a favorite. This is where you get those honking turkey legs. Discovery Island. Combo meal $9 to $12.

Pizzafari ★★ AMERICAN   A vibrantly colored restaurant with lots of rooms to spread out, Pizzafari has a special contraption in the kitchen for cranking out fresh pizzas. It also does Italian-style subs and pasta with chicken. Discovery Island. Combo meal $9 to $10.

Yak & Yeti Local Food Cafes ★★ ASIAN   Although there is a table-service location indoors by the same name, the outdoor windows do counter-service mandarin chicken salad, sweet and sour chicken, beef lo mein, and greasy pork egg rolls. Across the path on the water, the **Royal Anandapur Tea Company** ★★ kiosk does something unique: teas and slushy chai ($5.40). Asia. Combo meal $9 to $11.

Tamu Tamu Eats & Refreshment ★ INTERNATIONAL   With a small selection (pulled beef or chicken-salad sandwiches, South African quinoa salad) and no indoor seating, it's not usually crowded. It's near Dawa Bar, a relaxing spot mimicking a fortress on the water where cocktails are served. Africa. Combo meal $9.

Restaurantosaurus ★ AMERICAN   As American as DinoLand U.S.A., the kitchen pumps out burgers, macaroni and cheese, hot dogs, chicken BLT salad, and nuggets. The **Trilo-Bites** kiosk nearby sells desserts. DinoLand U.S.A. Combo meal $9 to $10.

Walt Disney World's employees have a culture all their own that visitors must learn to respect and navigate. Working at Disney World isn't like getting a job at the bank. Don't forget that WDW is billed as the Happiest Place on Earth. Many cast members live and breathe its way of life, and quite a few moved from other parts of the country to be a part of it. Be alert to the fact that many of them identify personally with the Disney Way (it exists) and they take subtle exception to comments that carry a hint of being argumentative. Try not to bicker with Disney employees or put them in a position of having to defend or explain their company. And for heaven's sake, no cussing! That code is technically meant to apply only to cast members, the unspoken cultural expectation is that you follow it, too. The flip side of this is that if something goes wrong with your visit, cast members will often move heaven and earth to make it right and make your vacation a positive memory.

DISNEY'S ANIMAL KINGDOM'S TABLE-SERVICE RESTAURANTS

Because you're probably going to be up early to see the animals at their best, this park is a good candidate for a character breakfast. There are very few places to get out of the heat and have a waiter-service meal.

Rainforest Cafe ★ AMERICAN In a lush, junglelike, theatrically lit setting, robotic animals roar and twitter over your cheese sticks, burgers, and rum cocktails in souvenir glasses. This is not a Disney original, but one of two outposts of the established brand at Disney World (the other is at Downtown Disney Marketplace). Oasis, just before the park turnstiles. Main courses $15 to $31.

Tusker House Restaurant ★★★ AMERICAN/AFRICAN Under multicolored banners in an ancient souklike environment, Donald, Daisy, Mickey, and Goofy greet families in safari garb for "Donald's Safari Breakfast" and "Donald's Dining Safari" lunch, both all-you-can eat buffets. By dinner, character-free, the buffet dares more than most Disney dos, featuring Cape Malay curry chicken, *peri-peri* (spicy) salmon, spiced tandoori tofu, couscous, seafood stew with tamarind BBQ sauce, and other pleasingly aromatic choices. Africa. Meals $29 to $35 adults, $16 to $19 kids.

Yak & Yeti Restaurant ★★ ASIAN Themed like a Nepalese mansion stocked with souvenirs from across Southeast Asia, the menu is just as geographically varied, serving Kobe beef burgers with mushroom compote, ahi tuna, Vietnamese pho noodle bowls, fried honey chicken, and stir fry. The Quick Service counter outside offers a shorter, but similar, menu for less, but at Animal Kingdom, air conditioning is the most rare and delicious treat. Main courses $18 to $27.

DISNEY WATER PARKS

The big question: Blizzard Beach or Typhoon Lagoon? Both can fill a day. So it depends on your mood. Typhoon Lagoon's central feature, a sand-lined 2½-acre wave pool, is an ideal place for families to frolic and to approximate a day at the beach. If your kids have a need for speed, then head to Blizzard Beach, which has a milder wave pool but wilder water slides.

Both water parks, similar in size, have free parking and are less busy early in the week, probably because folks tend to start their vacations on a weekend and don't get to the flumes until they've done the four big theme parks. On very hot days, they are unpleasantly crammed, and they tend to be busier in the morning than in late afternoon. They also sell everything you need to protect yourself from the sun, including lotion (should you have forgotten) and swimsuits (should you lose yours in the lather). Most lines (many rides have two: one for a raft and one for the slide) are fully exposed to the sun, so it's important to **keep hydrated,** as you won't always be aware how much you're sweating. Both parks sell mugs that are refillable for **endless soft drinks** while you're there (otherwise, soft drinks start at $2.70). They also rent towels for $2. Lifeguards usually make you remove water shoes on slides that don't use a mat or raft, and swimsuits with rivets or zippers are forbidden because they may scratch the flumes.

A day at a water park isn't as stressful as one spent among the queues of the theme parks, and if you're paying attention, the sights and sounds of a day here are pretty heartwarming. Every time the wave machine roars into gear, for example, dozens of kids shriek with delight and scamper into the water. Because they're chilling out, people tend to be happy at these parks.

LOCKERS   An average locker is $10 but you get $5 of that back after you turn your key in. They allow multiple access, are about 2 feet deep, and the opening is about the size of a magazine.

PREPARATION   Thoughtfully, parking is free. There are bulletin boards past the park entrances that tell you what the sunburn risk is and what the wait times are for the slides, as well as what times the parades run at Disney parks that day. If there are any activities (scavenger hunts are common), they'll be posted here. Kids' beach toy sets, for the sand around the lagoon, are sold in the gift shop for $10.

FOOD   There are only counter-service choices. Eat promptly at 11am when they open because lines get crazy quickly. Don't plan on eating dinner at the water parks, as the kiosks tend to shut down well before closing.

TIMING   If you're coming to Florida between November and mid-March, one of these parks will be closed for its annual hose-down. The other will remain open. Most water features are heated, but remember that you eventually must get *out.*

Blizzard Beach

Of Disney's two water parks, **Blizzard Beach ★★★** is the more thrilling, possibly because it opened 6 years after Typhoon Lagoon and had the benefit of improving on what didn't work there. It also has a wittier backstory that is perfect for a hot day: A freak snowstorm hit Mount Gushmore, and Disney was slapping up a ski resort when the snow began to melt, creating water slides. So now, a lift chair brings bathers most of the way up the 90-foot peak, and flumes are festooned with ski-run flags and piled with white "snowdrifts." Best of all, at this park, no one has to tote rafts uphill—there are conveyors to do it for you.

Surely the most exhilarating 8 seconds in all of Walt Disney World, **Summit Plummet ★★★** is the immensely steep, 12-story-tall slide that commands attention at the peak of the mountain, which incidentally, offers one of the best panoramas of the Walt Disney World resort. A slide down this one is for the truly fearless, as the first few seconds make you feel weightless, as if you're about to fall forward. By the end, the water is jabbing you so hard that it's not unusual to come away with a light bruise, and it turns the toughest bathing suit into dental floss. This is a fun one to watch; just ask the young men who are glued to it for the aforementioned reason. **Slush Gusher ★**, next to it among the Green Slope rides and slightly lower, is a double-hump that gives the rider the sensation of air time—not a reassuring feeling when you're flying down an open chute.

The enormous chute winding off the mountain's right side is **Teamboat Springs ★★**, a group ride in a circular raft; just about everyone gets a chance to enjoy the top of a banked turn, and after the inevitable splashdown, another minute is spent in a come-down floating on a river. It's highly re-rideable, but if you go alone, you'll be paired with strangers for some slippery awkwardness.

Snow Stormers ★ (Purple Slope) is a trio of standard raft water slides, but the twin **Downhill Double Dipper ★** is a simple slope of two identical slides with a good embellishment: It times runs so you can race a companion down. **Toboggan Racers ★★** multiplies the fun to where eight people can race at once down an evenly scalloped run. At the base of these is **Melt Away Bay ★★★**, a 1-acre wave pool in which waves create a gentle bobbing sensation. It could stand to be larger since it gets very crowded.

At the back of the mountain (the Red Slope; reach it by walking around the left or via the lazy river), the three **Runoff Rapids ★★** flumes comprise two open-air slides and a totally enclosed one—you only see the occasional light flashing by. (These are the only ones for which you must haul your own raft up the hill.)

The park is circled by the superlative lazy river (for the newbie, that's a slow-flowing channel where you float along in an inner tube) called **Cross Country Creek ★★★**, which is probably the best of its kind, passing a cave dripping with refrigerated water and a slouching shack that, every few seconds, gushes as you hear the sound of Goofy sneezing. **Tip:** It's easier to find a free inner tube at a ramp far from the park entrance; try the one at the base of Downhill Double Dipper or the one to the left past Lottawatta Lodge, the main food building.

There are two kiddie areas, one for preteens, **Ski Patrol ★★** (short slides, a walk across the water on floating "icebergs") and for littler kids, **Tike's Peak ★** (even smaller slides, fountains, and jets). The latter is a good place to look if you can't find seating.

Tip: The miniature golf course Winter Summerland (see "Join the Club" on p. 148) shares a parking lot with Blizzard Beach, so it's easy to combine a visit.

ⓒ **407/560-3400.** www.disneyworld.com. $52 adults, $44 kids 3–9. Hours vary, but 10am–5pm is common in summer.

Typhoon Lagoon

Despite the petrifying imagery of the shrimp boat *(Miss Tilly)* impaled on the central mountain (Mt. Mayday), the flumes at **Typhoon Lagoon ★★** are less daunting than the ones at Blizzard Beach or Wet 'n Wild. Typhoon Lagoon is extremely well land-scaped (most of the flowers are selected so that they attract butterflies but not bees) to hide its infrastructure, but its navigation is not always well planned. For example, you tote your own rafts. Also, the paths to the slides ramble up and down stairs—the one to the Storm Slides actually goes *down* eight times as it winds up the mountain. It's also not always clear where to find the slide you want. Help guide little ones.

The **Surf Pool ★★★** divides its time between "surf waves" (at 5 ft., they pack a surprising punch, and they are announced by a *whoompf* that draws great peals of delight from kids) and mild "bobbing waves"—times for both are noted on the Surf Report chalk sign at the pool's foot. The slides are generally shallow, slow, and geared toward avowed sissies. That will frustrate some teenagers, but little kids and mothers with expensive hairdos think **Mayday Falls ★**, which sends riders down a corrugated flume, is just right (adults come off rubbing their butts in pain). It's very tough to find a vantage point to watch your kids ride, but there's a spot near the entrance of **Gangplank Falls ★★★**, a family-sized round raft, where you can see a little, and there's a lovely hidden overlook trail with a suspension bridge and waterfalls that passes under the *Miss Tilly.* The leftmost body slide of three at **Storm Slides ★★** is slightly more covered; otherwise the slides are much the same. The **Crush 'n' Gusher ★★★** "water coaster" flumes use jets to push rafts both uphill and downhill; the gag is that it used to be a fruit-washing plant, and now you're the banana—appropriate since it's sponsored by Chiquita.

One highlight is **Shark Reef ★★**, a 10½-foot-deep tank stocked with tropical fish, nonthreatening leopard and bonnet sharks, and mock coral. Everyone gets a mask, snorkel, and, if wanted, a floatation jacket, and then swims 60 feet across the tank (no dawdling permitted) under the eye of lifeguards who'll spring into action at the slightest hint of trouble—or even if you kick your feet. (If you want a tank where you can dawdle with fish, try SeaWorld's Discovery Cove, p. 132.) You needn't meet a high standard beyond an ability to paddle across a pool. If you don't care for that setup, descend by stairs into a submerged "shipwreck," which has portholes allowing a lateral, murky view of the same tank. **Strategy:** Shark Reef gets busy, so do it early or late.

For the best shot at finding an inner tube for the lushly planted lazy river, **Castaway Creek ★★**, pick an entry farther from the entrance, such as in front of the Crush 'n' Gusher area. That's also a good place to find a lounger if the Lagoon is packed, which it usually is; otherwise, try the extreme left past the ice cream stand. That's near **Ketchakiddee Creek ★★**, the geyser-and-bubbler play area for small children. Funny how the water's always warmer there.

"Learn to Surf" lessons are held in the Surf Pool 2 hours before park hours and, sometimes, after it closes (*②* **407/939-7529;** $150 for all ages, minimum age of 5). The lessons come with 30 minutes of preparation followed by 2 hours of in-pool instruction, always with lifeguards scrutinizing your every twitch.

② **407/560-4120.** www.disneyworld.com. $52 adults, $44 kids 3–9. Hours vary, but 10am–5pm is common in summer.

MINOR DISNEY WORLD DIVERSIONS

Also see "Join the Club" on p. 148 for details on the two Disney miniature golf areas.

DisneyQuest ★ PLAY PARK   Most Disney fans thought this five-level virtual reality playground would close a half decade ago. It's past its prime, if it had one, and if you pay full price for it, you'll wish you hadn't. Standout stuff includes **Cyberspace Mountain,** in which you design your own coaster from a palette of options and then board a motion-simulator capsule in which you can test out your creation—360-degree loops and all. The ride vehicles actually go upside-down, making it one of only two Disney World rides to do so. **Virtual Jungle Cruise** has you on inflatable rafts, using paddles to float down a river on a screen in front of you; and **Pirates of the Caribbean: Battle for Buccaneer Gold** puts you on the deck of a mini pirate ship, with screens on three sides, that has members of your party simultaneously steering and blasting rival ships by yanking on ropes that trigger cannons (like the ones on Toy Story Midway Mania). Sadly, most of the animation feels badly dated. Not everything is screen based: The rowdy **Buzz Lightyear's AstroBlaster** is like a bumper-car game where

ORLANDO after dark WITH KIDS

Although on some nights, one could argue that the people drinking at the clubs and bars are infantile, you still can't bring your kids to hang out in them. Don't worry—Orlando is a family city, so there's much for kids to do.

o **Magic Kingdom parade:** Most nights, there are one or two parades through the park. When there are two, the second is less crowded.

o **Fireworks:** The Magic Kingdom is open until 9pm or later on most nights. There's usually an evening parade, and the nightly fireworks display, "Wishes," happens around Cinderella Castle. Hollywood Studios mounts "Fantasmic!", a pyrotechnics-and-water display, a few times a week, and Epcot is famous for its "IllumiNations" fireworks-and-electronics show over its lagoon. In summer, when they're open past dusk, Universal Studios does something (fireworks or a spectacle on its lagoon) most nights, as does SeaWorld. Check with each park for showtimes, as they change. Given that they're theme park shows, they're all designed to wow kids, but Magic Kingdom's display is the classic.

o **The Electrical Boat Parade:** It's a tradition going back nearly 40 years—a string of 14 40-foot-long illuminated barges floats past the Disney resorts on Seven Seas Lagoon and Bay Lake starting at 9pm, accompanied by music. Lower key than the fireworks shows, you can see it for free from any resort hotel in the area or, if your timing is good, from the ferry that goes between the Magic Kingdom and the Ticket and Transportation Center.

o **Special event evenings:** From September through March, the Magic Kingdom schedules irregular special-ticket evenings (Mickey's Not-So-Scary Halloween Party, his Very Merry Christmas Party, and the Pirate and Princess events) for kids with free candy, character meetings, dance parties, and extended hours. The calendar of events can be found on p. 231, online at www.disneyworld.com, or you can call Disney at (C) **407/934-7639.**

o **Dinnertainment:** Every night, there are more than a dozen dinner banquets accompanied by a kid-friendly show. See p. 186.

o **Character meals:** Early bedtime? Very young kids will be sent to sleep dreaming if they meet their favorite character over dinner. See p. 189 for a list.

your vehicle scoops up balls and fires them at competitors, causing them to spin momentarily; it's best for two riders at a time. Throughout the building are arcade games, old and new (try the playable **Wreck-It Ralph** arcade machines), that need no quarters. During the weekdays, you pretty much have your run of the place. Hit Orlando's more compelling attractions before getting around to doing this one—if you want technology, how about Kennedy Space Center? Still, it's fine if you have an extra Water Park Fun & More visit to burn on my Magic Your Way ticket. Sometimes 50 percent discounts are available 2 hours before closing.

Downtown Disney West Side. (C) **407/828-4600.** www.disneyquest.com; $48 adults, $42 kids 3–9. Kids 9 and under must be accompanied by someone 16 or older. Sun–Thurs 11:30am–10pm; Fri–Sat 11:30am–11:30pm.

ESPN Wide World of Sports ★ ATHLETIC COMPLEX   Most visitors don't stumble onto the 220-acre grounds, which are essentially a souped-up stadium complex, by accident. They go there intentionally, for a son's wrestling tournament, a traveling sports exhibition game, or to see the Atlanta Braves in spring training. Unfortunately, it's not a place to roll up and pitch a few balls, although you can check its website to see if there's something ticketed that you might enjoy attending (and paying extra for).

Victory Dr., I-4 at exit 64B. ℂ **407/939-1500.** www.disneysports.com

Richard Petty Driving Experience ★★★ RIDE   Heaven knows how it secured a matchless location in the Magic Kingdom's parking lot, but there it sits, selling 150-mph ride-alongs in 600 horsepower Winston Cup–style stock cars on a 1-mile track with 10-degree banking. A mere 3-lap visit starts at $99, but if you want to be behind the wheel, packages zoom up to $449 for eight laps. Petty has 24 other locations, so don't feel bad if you miss this one.

3450 N. World Dr., Lake Buena Vista. ℂ **800/237-3889.** www.drivepetty.com. Minimum age 16. Daily 9am–4pm.

Downtown Disney & Disney's BoardWalk

The no-admission shopping and entertainment district currently known as Downtown Disney comprises nearly a pedestrianized mile of event restaurants and shops along a small lake, away from the major theme parks in a traffic-plagued eastern reach of the resort grounds. Its West Side is home to the DisneyQuest virtual playground (p. 92), a 24-screen cinema, and "La Nouba," the Cirque du Soleil show (see below).

Characters in Flight ★★ RIDE   You'll see it from miles away: A huge, round helium balloon that rises from a pier, lingers 400 feet up for a spell, and then descends back to earth within about 10 minutes. Although it's safely tethered and the circular observation platform is securely enclosed with mesh, it lists and drifts with sudden breezes and that may disturb some guests. If you're adventurous, though, the trip is good fun, and of course the view rocks. It's known to summarily shut down for weather that may seem calm from the ground, so if it's flying and you want to ride it, don't put it off.

Downtown Disney West Side. ℂ **407/824-4321.** www.disneyworld.com. $18 adults, $12 kids 3–9. Daily 8:30am–midnight.

House of Blues ★★★ MUSIC CLUB   One of the principal nightspots on the West Side has a 2,000-person, three-tiered venue (standing space only) hosting regular performers along the lines of B. B. King, One Republic, the Charlie Daniels Band, and Norah Jones. Big talent is ticketed at concert prices, and operator Live Nation piles on the fees, but mostly, it's a place to get Southern food. On Sundays, it hosts a somewhat desanctified Gospel Brunch (p. 188).

Downtown Disney West Side. ℂ **407/934-2583.** www.hob.com. Sun–Thurs 11:30am–11pm; Fri–Sat 11:30am–1am.

La Nouba ★★★ SHOW   All those taut, athletic bodies, wearing precious little, flexing and writhing across each other with acrobatic virtuosity—it's as close to sex as Disney's gonna get. That said, Cirque du Soleil's 90-minute permanent production at Walt Disney World, is perfectly acceptable for kids, too—it could end up being the most memorable theatrical experience of a young person's life. The arty, hyper, clownish French-Canadian spectacular, a kaleidoscope of stunts and tricks, overloads senses 10 times a week in a 1,600-seat theater that looks like a postmodern version of a big top. Although it's second-rate Cirque, it's still first-rate compared to most stuff you've ever seen, and the talent is extraordinary. So are prices, starting at $75 for adults and $60 for kids ages 3 to 9, and rising according to where you sit. Cheaper seats are better because they have higher vantage points, but seats on the extreme side may miss some of the action taking place far upstage. Arrive at least a half-hour early or they'll sell your seat to someone else.

Downtown Disney West Side. ℗ **407/939-7467.** www.cirquedusoleil.com/lanouba. $75–$134 adults, $60–$107 kids. Tues–Sat 6 and 9pm.

Splitsville Luxury Lanes ★★★ BOWLING ALLEY   A welcome 2012 addition that gives families something to bond over, this Florida-based franchise charges by the hour, which might make you feel rushed, and it charges high prices at that, but its souped-up '50s decor, two cavernous floors of bowling, and copious cocktails have charm to spare. The food's a lot better than it should be, too; they even sell sushi.

Downtown Disney West Side. ℗ **407/938-7328.** www.splitsvilledowntowndisney.com. Daily 10am–2am. $15/hr. per person before 4pm, $20/hr. per person after 4pm and weekends. Rates include shoe rental.

Walt Disney World Tours

Walt Disney was unquestionably a visionary. When he started out, he was mostly interested in animation as an art form. But as his fame and resources grew, his dreams became infinite, and by the end of his life, he was obsessed with building a city of his own. In fact, he intended to build that city on a chunk of his Central Florida land. His dream of an Experimental Prototype Community of Tomorrow, or Epcot, in which residents, many of them theme park workers, could try out new forms of corporate-sponsored, minimum-impact technology in the course of their daily lives, emerged 16 years after his death as nothing more than another world's fair, and not the city to save us all. But because the Magic Kingdom was built by his most trusted designers, it incorporated several idealistic innovations.

One is the **utilidor system.** The bulk of the Magic Kingdom that you see appears to be at ground level. But in fact, you'll be walking about 14 feet above the land. The attractions constitute the second and third stories of a 9-acre network of warehouses and corridors—utilidors—built in part to guard against flooding but mostly so cast members could remove trash, make deliveries, take breaks, change costumes, and count money out of sight, in a catacombs accessed through secret entrances and unmarked wormholes scattered around the themed lands. Clean-burning electric vehicles zip through the hallways, some of which are wide enough to accommodate trucks, and all of which are color-coded to indicate which land is upstairs.

Among the other engineering feats and innovations of the Kingdom:

o   Trash is transported at 60mph to a central collection point by Swedish AVAC pneumatic tubes in the ceiling of the utilidors.

o   Fire, power, and water systems are all monitored by a common computer, and the robotics, doors, lighting, sounds, and vehicles on the most complicated attractions are handled by a central server called the Digital Animation Control System (DACS), located roughly underneath Cinderella Castle.

o   The Seven Seas Lagoon, in front of the Magic Kingdom, was dry land. It was filled to create a new body of water.

Minor Disney World Diversions

- Bay Lake, beside Fort Wilderness, was dredged, and the dirt used to raise the Magic Kingdom. Underneath the lake bed, white, ancient sand was discovered, cleaned, and deposited to create the Seven Seas Lagoon's beaches.
- Energy is reused whenever possible. The generators' waste heat is used to heat water, and hot water runoff is used for heating, cooking, and absorption chilling for air-conditioning. Waste water is reclaimed for plants and lawns, and sludge is dried for fertilizer. Food scraps are composted on-site. The resort produces enough power to keep things running in case of a temporary outage on the municipal grid. This will keep you up tonight: Disney even has the legal right to build its own nuclear power plant, should it care to.
- Some 55 miles of canals were dug on resort property to keep the land drained. Most of these canals were curved to appear natural.
- The resort was the first place to install an all-electronic phone system using underground cable—so guests don't see ugly wires. It was the first telephone company in America to use a 911 emergency system.
- The rubber-tired monorail system, designed by Disney engineers, now contains nearly 15 miles of track. Walt had intended monorails, and vehicles akin to the Tomorrowland Transit Authority ride, to be the main forms of transportation to and through his Epcot. In 1986, the monorail was named a National Historic Mechanical Engineering Landmark by the American Society of Mechanical Engineers.

The Walt Disney Co. of later years showed little interest in advancing these remarkable innovations. Epcot has only a small network of utilidors, located under Innoventions and Spaceship Earth in the center section of Future World, and the other Disney parks were built without them at all. The monorail has not been expanded since 1982, so it was back to buses and cars.

But even if the company now pays scant attention to developing "Walt's dream"—that Talmudic totem that the company's marketing department invokes to sell souvenirs—it will, fortunately, grant a backstage gander at the resort's ingenuity and the mind-boggling challenge of its scale. The superlative **Walt Disney World tours** (© **407/939-8687;** www.disneyworld.com/tours) require tons of walking and quality depends on the ability of the guide, but they're also very well organized, with coach transport, snacks, plenty of comfort breaks, and sometimes, a special pin souvenir. Tours come and go, and not all go daily, so check to see what's running. These are the standouts.

Backstage Magic ★★★ TOUR If you can swing it, this is the awe-inspiring king of all Disney explorations, and one of the few tours to require no theme park admission, because you spend all your time plumbing the resort's daunting infrastructure. Nearly every minute is fascinating—you start at Epcot, where you go backstage to see the mechanized miracle of the American Adventure robotics; then, by motorcoach, the 40-odd group goes to Hollywood Studios for the wardrobe design and sewing shops; then it's on to Animal Kingdom for a how-to of its parade. Lunch is barbecue at the Wilderness Lodge. At the Magic Kingdom, you thrillingly dip into the utilidor, which for fans is alone worth the price. Behind that park, you'll see Central Shops, a 280,000 square-foot facility where ride vehicles are power washed, greased, and repainted in the blocks-long, 30-foot-tall Assembly Alley, and nearby in the Animation Shop, the famous Audio-Animatronic figures are repaired before your eyes. For fans of theme parks, to say nothing of systems design, there is no more comprehensive and worthy splurge in Orlando. It's a revelation, and you'll appreciate the World in a new light.

$229–$249, including lunch, minimum age 16. 7 hr.

Backstage Safari ★ TOUR   You learn more about animal care than the made-up storytelling of the park. The itinerary may change according to which animals are in social moods and which ones are in the clinic, but white rhinos and elephants are often on the menu. The climax is a slow turn on the Kilimanjaro Safari ride, only with a special narration that gives away the design secrets that keep animals and humans on their respective sides. Expect a lot of info about how diets are prepared. Mickey would be sick if he knew what the snakes eat.

$72 per person; park admission required. Minimum age 16. 3 hr.

Behind the Seeds ★★ TOUR   Because it runs repeatedly every day, it's one of the few tours that can be booked on the fly. Epcot's original altruistic intentions are given a rare spotlight: You learn about the research conducted at the Land's experimental greenhouses, insects lab, and fish farm, and guests are filled in on the park's joint efforts with botanists to advance growing technologies. How much you learn depends entirely on your guide's engagement, so butter 'em up—and little children are usually given ladybugs to release, seeds to plant, or crops to taste. You can reserve ahead or you can book at the desk beside the entrance to Soarin'.

$18–$20 adults, $14–$16 kids 3–9; park admission required. Daily; 45 min.

Disney's Dolphins in Depth ★★★ TOUR   The water's only knee-deep, and after preparation and education about Epcot's dolphin rescue program, the interaction lasts about 30 minutes. The climax: You tentatively hug one of the mammals as your free souvenir photo is snapped. No theme park admission is required.

$194–$199, including photo; no park admission required. Minimum age 13. 3 hr.

Disney's Keys to the Kingdom ★★★ TOUR   The least expensive way to peek at the utilidors, this half-day morning excursion provides a good overview of the Disney design philosophies that will satisfy both newbies and hard-core fans. It includes a long explication of Main Street, the Hub, the Castle, and a pass through Frontierland and Adventureland, where the group kills a little time (and finally gets to sit) riding two rides, after which your guide discusses the technology behind them. The real appeal is the brief time spent in forbidden backstage areas: the parade float storage sheds behind Splash Mountain and a quiet cul-de-sac of the utilidors beneath Town Square—my group entered in the Emporium and resurfaced in a parking lot behind eastern Main Street. This is a tremendous value.

$74–$79 per person, including lunch; park admission required. Minimum age 16. Daily. 5 hr.

Epcot DiveQuest ★★★ TOUR   Bring your open-water scuba certification and your swimsuit, and you'll be qualified to swim with the fishes in the saltwater tank at the Seas with Nemo & Friends—the range of life is unparalleled in the wild. You'll learn a little about the aquarium's upkeep, but the true attraction here is the chance to dive in it for 30 minutes and to wave at your fellow tourists from the business side of the glass. It's fun, but whether it's $175 worth of a good time is up for debate.

$175, including diving gear; park admission not required. Minimum age 10. Daily. 3 hr.

Epcot Seas Aqua Tour ★★★ TOUR   If you can snorkel, you can do this—you're equipped with an air tank and with flotation devices that keep you on the surface, where you spend a half-hour swimming face-down above the fake coral in the 5.7 million-gallon aquarium at The Seas. You wrap up, ironically, with a shower. No theme park admission is required.

$140, including equipment and photo; park admission not required. Minimum age 8. Daily. 2½ hr.

Wild Africa Trek ★★★ TOUR   The animal paddocks are your personal adventure playground on this crowd favorite. You'll board a vehicle for a private view of the animals on Kilimanjaro Safaris, and most spectacularly, strap into a harness for a harrowing tethered trip over a cliffs and a rope suspension bridge that passes right over crocs and hippos. The included African-inflected meal has a view of the savannah, and a CD's worth of professional photos of your experience is mailed to you a few days later.

$189 per person, park admission required. Minimum age 8. 9 times daily. 3 hr.

UNIVERSAL, SEAWORLD & BEYOND

D isney is only half the story. Less than half, really, when you consider that while the Mouse maintains four parks, you'll find another four major themers, plus a luxury-level theme park, in the same vicinity. While some blinkered tourists think of these places as something to do after they "do Disney," the truth is these majors are in many ways just as appealing as the more famous Mouse parks.

UNIVERSAL ORLANDO

You'd be remiss if you left town without seeing at least two of Disney's parks, but the true design chutzpah is happening at Universal—many observers agree that the spectacular Wizarding World of Harry Potter trumps anything else in America's theme park industry. Thanks to it, its home, Islands of Adventure, has cracked the top-10 list of the most-visited theme parks in the world. Granted, Universal's two parks combined still only fetch a third of the visitors attracted by Disney's four, but that proportion is growing by the year. Universal's resort is also easier to tour than Disney's: It's walkable or traversed by quick, free ferries, so you can park your car and forget about it, no waiting for crowded buses.

The opening of Universal Studios in 1990 heralded a new era for Orlando tourism. Instead of merely duplicating its original Hollywood location, which is on a historic movie studio lot, Universal Orlando built a full-fledged all-day amusement park based on classic movies.

While its opening was famously troubled, there was little doubt that Universal's innovations, when they worked, instantly raised the bar for amusement parks worldwide. A chief advance was that almost all of its attractions were indoors—even the thrills. Given Florida's scorching sun and unpredictable rains, this leap shouldn't have been as novel as it was. While Disney, still working on a California model, allowed its guests to twiddle thumbs in the cruel heat as they waited in line, Universal's multi-stage queuing system usually kept guests entertained and air-conditioned while they waited. Therefore, Universal Studios is the park you should choose on rainy days or excessively hot ones. (At Islands of Adventure, though, many of thrill rides travel outdoors and will shut down at the hint of lightning.) Even the covered parking garages at Universal Orlando (shared by both parks and CityWalk) were novel for Florida.

Disney was clearly spooked. It hastily banged out a movies-themed park of its own, Disney–MGM Studios (now called Hollywood Studios). It was a rush job, lacking the organization and thematic quality that made its previous two parks such smashes. There was room for a challenger after all.

Throughout the 1990s, Universal's one-park setup meant it mostly grabbed visitors on day trips from Disney. That changed—and the fight got ruthless—in the summer of 1999, when a second, $2.6-billion park, Islands of Adventure, made its dazzling debut. Universal broke the bank to outshine Disney, even poaching a number Imagineers. Universal's domain has further expanded to include the nightlife district CityWalk and four hotels, making the brand a true vacation destination in its own right.

Most of the time, lines are nowhere near as long as they are at Disney. Unless crowds are insanely huge (such as before Halloween Horror Nights events or during Christmas week), Universal takes about 2 days to adequately see. With a two-park pass and a willingness to bypass lesser attractions, you could see the highlights in 1 marathon day, provided at least one of the parks stays open until 9 or 10pm. When the second Harry Potter section opens, though (p. 107), that will likely not be enough time, and 3 days may become the new minimum requirement. In any event, bopping between the two parks isn't hard, since their entrances are a 5-minute stroll apart (or, soon, you can take a connecting train).

Tickets to Universal's Parks

Tickets for both parks cost the same and multi-day tickets are more expensive if you buy at the gate. Here's the pricing before tax:

o A **1-day ticket for one park** is $92 adults, $86 kids aged 3 to 9.

o A **1-day, two-park ticket** costs $128 adults, $122 kids aged 3 to 9.

o **Two-day, one-park tickets** are $146 adults and $136 kids at the gate, but if you buy online, you save $20 per ticket. To add park-to-park access within the same day, add $21 (your online savings pay for park-hopping).

If you're planning to do a full complement of the non-Disney parks, including Universal Orlando, SeaWorld, Aquatica, Wet 'n Wild, and Busch Gardens, then you'll find value in the **FlexTicket,** also sold on Universal's site, which gets you into all of them for 2 weeks at a deep discount. Details are on p. 234.

HOPPING THE LINES Like Disney's Fastpass, **Universal Express Pass** allows guests to use a separate entrance queue that is dramatically shorter than the "Standby" one, reducing wait times to minutes or even seconds; your ticket is checked by an employee with a hand-held scanner. Unlike Disney's democratic Fastpass, Universal's Express pass system is for sale. Guests can buy an a la carte **Express Plus** pass at shops. There is one set of prices that allows one-time-per-ride use ($20 at Universal Studios, $30 at Islands of Adventure) and another for unlimited use ($50 at the Studios,

---

contacting UNIVERSAL

General information: ℂ 407/363-8000;
www.universalorlando.com
Guest services: ℂ 407/224-4233
Hotel reservations: ℂ 888/273-1311

Vacation packages: ℂ 800/711-0080;
www.universalorlandovacations.com
Lost and found: ℂ 407/224-4233,
option 2

WHAT THE BASICS cost AT UNIVERSAL'S TWO PARKS

Parking: $15; $20 for closer "preferred" spaces; $18 valet
Single strollers: $15 per day
Double strollers: $25 per day
Kiddie Car (a stroller with a dummy steering wheel): $18; $28 double

Wheelchair: $12
ECV (electric convenience vehicle): $50
Lockers: $8 per day small (multi-entry)
Poncho: $8 adult, $7 kids
Regular soda: $2.70 / **Water:** $2.75 / **Beer:** $6.50

$75 at IOA); the price sinks or rises with the season, but that's a standard rate. The only major ride that's excluded is Harry Potter and the Forbidden Journey. Using Express Pass is expensive, but it enables you to see both Universal parks in a single day and consequently spend less in tickets and see more in Orlando. Bundles for just such a fast-track bonanza are sold for $180 adult, $169 kids aged 3 to 9 for 1 day, or 2 days (if you really need the time) for $240 adult, $230 for kids. There is also a third, simpler way to get an Express Pass: Guests of the Universal hotels (except Cabana Bay) can use their key cards for free Express access. In 2013, Universal began testing a paid **Ride Reservations** program; ask staff if it's been fully implemented.

Universal also has **photographers** on hand to take your photo at big moments. It works like Disney's PhotoPass: You'll get a claim ticket enabling you to purchase an expensive copy, but you may always use your own camera instead.

WHAT TO WEAR   Dress small children in bathing suits for a day at Universal Studios because its Kidzone, one of its best sections, will get them soaked. At Islands of Adventure, two of the best adult rides are water-based.

Universal Studios Florida

Universal Studios ★★★ usually opens at 9am, and in winter months, hours end at around 6pm. In summer, they're often as late as 10pm. After you get your car parked ($15 and up) and your handbags probed, take the covered sidewalks to CityWalk and head to the right. Pause at the giant, rotating globe for the requisite photo op, because the sun is in your favor in the morning.

The plaza after the turnstiles is where you take care of business. **Strollers and wheelchairs** are obtained to the left, and **lockers** are rented to the right. Make sure to grab a free park **map** here; if you forget, the stores also stock them.

Although there are technically themed areas, they are not strictly defined and they fall into two general zones. Everyone enters along the main avenue of the simulated backlot (including **Production Central, Hollywood,** and **New York**), which contains

Shop Early to Save

At the extreme right of the entry plaza as you leaving the park, there's a souvenir stand. This is no ordinary stand: It's for marked-down items. I'm letting you know about it now so you price shop. The small stand at the entrance to Islands of Adventure is also a good stop for discount goods when you're at that park.

Universal Studios Florida

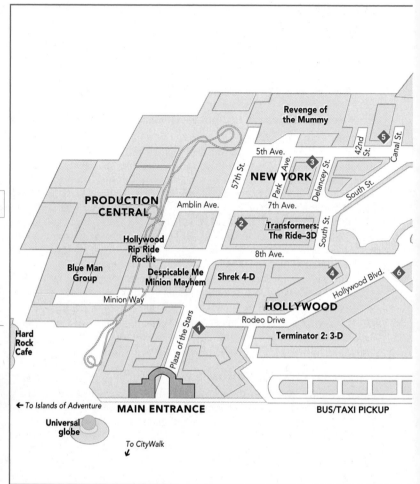

Revenge of
the Mummy

42nd St.

Canal St.

5

5th Ave.

57th St.

Park Ave.

NEW YORK

3

Delancey St.

South St.

**PRODUCTION
CENTRAL**

Amblin Ave.

7th Ave.

Hollywood
Rip Ride
Rockit

2

**Transformers:
The Ride–3D**

South St.

8th Ave.

**Blue Man
Group**

**Despicable Me
Minion Mayhem**

Shrek 4-D

4

Hollywood Blvd.

6

Minion Way

HOLLYWOOD

Rodeo Drive

Plaza of the Stars

1

Terminator 2: 3-D

**Hard
Rock
Cafe**

← To Islands of Adventure

MAIN ENTRANCE

BUS/TAXI PICKUP

Universal
globe

To CityWalk
↙

many of the behind-the-scenes attractions, while the elongated Lagoon stretches off to the right, encircled by many of the thrill-based rides in **San Francisco, Springfield, World Expo,** and **Woody Woodpecker's Kidzone.**

After dark, if the park's open then, there's **Cinematic Spectacular,** narrated by Morgan Freeman on the lagoon. It's a quaint show featuring classic Universal clips projected onto waterfall screens, plus a modest taste of fireworks action. Shows like these aren't Universal's forte, but there's not a Disney-esque crush of spectators, either.

PRODUCTION CENTRAL

The area along the entry avenue (called both Plaza of the Stars and 57th St.) and to its left is collectively marked on maps as Production Central, but who are they kidding?

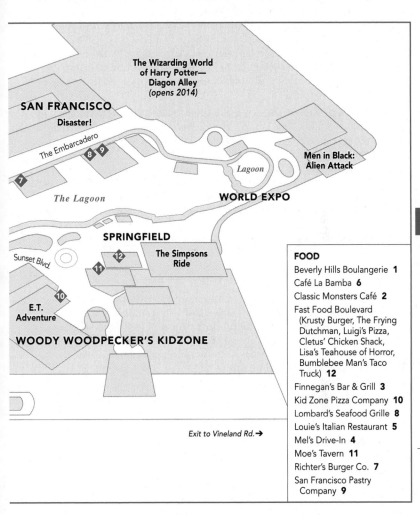

The Wizarding World
of Harry Potter—
Diagon Alley
(opens 2014)

SAN FRANCISCO

Disaster!

The Embarcadero

Lagoon

**Men in Black:
Alien Attack**

The Lagoon

WORLD EXPO

SPRINGFIELD

Sunset Blvd.

**The Simpsons
Ride**

**E.T.
Adventure**

WOODY WOODPECKER'S KIDZONE

Exit to Vineland Rd. →

FOOD

Beverly Hills Boulangerie **1**

Café La Bamba **6**

Classic Monsters Café **2**

Fast Food Boulevard
(Krusty Burger, The Frying
Dutchman, Luigi's Pizza,
Cletus' Chicken Shack,
Lisa's Teahouse of Horror,
Bumblebee Man's Taco
Truck) **12**

Finnegan's Bar & Grill **3**

Kid Zone Pizza Company **10**

Lombard's Seafood Grille **8**

Louie's Italian Restaurant **5**

Mel's Drive-In **4**

Moe's Tavern **11**

Richter's Burger Co. **7**

San Francisco Pastry
Company **9**

Nowadays, those soundstages are used only for the odd local commercial and for haunted houses at Universal's fiendishly popular Halloween event.

The initial dream was much bigger. When the park was built, it was intended to be more like the original Hollywood location, where an amusement area naturally grew up around a working studio. Newspapers at the time trumpeted Orlando as "Hollywood of the East" because year-round production could be accomplished here and at Disney–MGM Studios, and millions of tourists could be a part of the behind-the-scenes process. One of Universal's soundstages housed a working TV studio for Nickelodeon, the kids' cable channel, and the game show "Double Dare" plucked families out of the park to compete on air. In front of the studio, a geyser of "green slime" (actually green water) gurgled in tribute to the Canadian show "You Can't Do That on Television" that helped make the channel's fortunes. (Today, that stage houses the equally messy Blue Man Group.) The arranged marriage never took. It wasn't cost-effective to move productions here.

The first block of Production Central is mostly shops, including the largest gift shop in the park, **Universal Studios Store,** on the left. Across from that are the tempting Art Deco buildings of Rodeo Drive, the spine of the Hollywood area and for my money the prettiest part of the park.

Hollywood Rip Ride Rockit ★★★ RIDE   This is one advanced train: The 17-story height, vertical climb, hill-like loop, and near misses are just the start of it. Most advanced are its cars, outfitted with LEDs and in-seat speakers. Riders personal-ize their trip on screens embedded in the beltlike safety restraint, choosing the song that will play during the trip. Pick from a broad menu including country, rap, rock, and disco, but if you don't pick a song, it'll choose one for you. When the ride's over, you can buy a movie of their ride, along with your soundtrack. Lockers are required for loose items, but they're free for the wait time plus 20 minutes. Single riders get their own line, and it moves quickly. Note the novel boarding system that batches passen-gers together and sends them onto a moving sidewalk to catch up with the trains, which never stop moving forward. That first loop is also an original—the track twists to send the cars over the top of it before pulling them back on the inside again. Later on, you shoot through some holes in the scenery in the New York session. For all that, it's quite the smooth ride.

Despicable Me Minion Mayhem ★★ RIDE   The movies, if you don't know them, star a crotchety mad genius, Gru (voiced by Steve Carell), and his horde of nearly identical yellow henchmen (the Minions); their ride, which is considerably more charming than the films, give the little guys amble opportunity for some cartoon violence and giggly gags. The kid-friendly show/stationary ride takes place in a theater full of individual open-air ride platforms that have all the characteristics of motion simulators except claustrophobia. **Strategy:** An option for those prone to motion sick-ness is to request a car that doesn't move at all—the perfectly animated 3-D movie is immensely action-packed and is entertaining without it.

Shrek 4-D ★★ SHOW   The high-priced voices of the movie characters (Mike Myers, Cameron Diaz, Eddie Murphy) star in a snarky 12-minute, 3-D movie-cum-spectacle—filmed in "OgreVision." John Lithgow plays the ghost of the evil Lord Farquaad, who crashes Shrek and Fiona's honeymoon at Fairytale Falls with a few dastardly deeds. The chairs look like standard theater seats but they're tricked-up to

The Best of Universal Studios Florida

Don't miss if you're 6: Curious George Goes to Town
Don't miss if you're 16: Springfield
Requisite photo op: The rotating Universal globe out front
Food you can only get here: Irish Cobb salad at Finnegan's Bar & Grill in New York

The most crowded, so go early: Hollywood Rip Ride Rockit, The Wizarding World of Harry Potter
Skippable: Fear Factor Live
Biggest thrill: Revenge of the Mummy
Best show: Animal Actors on Location!
Where to find peace: On the lagoon

goose sensations—don't worry; it won't make you ill. Well, unless fart jokes gross you out. It's a good one to do when the feet start aching, although the line can build in the afternoon. **Strategy:** Because the entertaining preshow is just as long as the movie, the Express Pass doesn't seem to buy you very much time. After the exit, visit **Donkey's Photo Finish,** featuring an interactive, robotic version of the movie's famous ass in his own stall; he interacts with kids and poses.

Transformers: The Ride—3D ★★ RIDE   This 2013 addition, an East Coast version of a ride that first appeared at Universal Studios Hollywood, repeats the technology and basic vehicle design of the more palatable Adventures of Spider-Man next door at Islands of Adventure—that is, motion-simulator cars travel among sense-tricking rooms with 3-D projections. There difference is that here, the show method is pumped up with crisper animation, clearer sounds, and a whole lot of machine-on-machine violence and military-grade weaponry. But at heart, no matter how impressive the tech is, Transformers is still a Spider-Man wannabe, down to key plot points. The mayhem is so frenetic you can't tell which Transformer is which, but then again, you can't in the movies, either, so it hardly seems to matter. You'll emerge feeling like you walked away from a 4-minute car crash. **Tip:** The clearest view is in the front row.

NEW YORK

When there's a park on your right, you've entered the New York area. In a display of geographic acrobatics, the park is an imitation of San Francisco's Union Square while straight ahead, at the end of 57th Street (the main entry avenue) is a little cul-de-sac that looks, through a camera lens, like Manhattan—except for the roller coaster that keeps roaring through.

The rest of the New York section is gussied up to look like the tenements of the Lower East Side or Greenwich Village and is worth a few photos. Actors playing **The Blues Brothers,** plus a female diva soul singer, show up on Delancey Street for regular jam sessions, and they're talented.

Twister . . . Ride It Out ★ SHOW   After several rooms of portentous preshow videos narrated by Helen Hunt and Bill Paxton, you finally enter a viewing area in a hangarlike chamber that's dressed to look like a Midwestern small town (gas station, telephone pole, drive-in movie in the distance) on a weekend night. A storm approaches, rain begins to fall and, as you knew it would, a twister forms. Right before your eyes, a funnel cloud descends from the rafters and to the delight of many, wrecks the place. Sparks fly, roofs peel, and guess what happens to the gas station? Although people tend to shy away from the front row, don't, because you won't feel much more than mist and a light sucking sensation there (I'd tuck sensitive electronics away anyway). It's quite an original attraction, and it's another good one for a hot day, but little kids might lose their wits. **Strategy:** It runs continuously, but I wouldn't wait more than 20 minutes for it.

Revenge of the Mummy ★★★ RIDE   This brilliant ride is cutting edge with an easy start and a rollicking finish: Part dark ride, part roller coaster, it goes backward and forward, twists on a turntable, and even spends a harrowing moment stalled in a room as the ceiling crawls with fire. (It doesn't go upside-down.) To say much more would give away some clever shocks. I've told you what you need to know. **Strategy:** You must put loose articles in the lockers to the right of the entrance—they're free for the posted ride time plus 20 minutes, but after that they cost $3 every half hour, so although you'll probably want to ride again right away, don't. There are three lines: Express, standby, and single riders.

The **Delancey Street Preview Center** is marked on the maps, but you can only get in by invitation (someone will approach you on the streets). That's where NBC-affiliated entities screen television pilots and then solicit audience opinions. On a quiet January day, I once earned $30 just for enduring a new show called "Psych." I told them that it was clichéd and strained. Naturally, it became a hit on USA Network anyway. You can't predict the demographic of the test audience they'll be looking for, so stop by and ask if you fit the profile du jour.

SAN FRANCISCO

Of all the Studios' areas, the San Francisco section has the least going on: one ride, one show. However, the restaurants are better than anywhere in the park. Once Harry Potter opens, though, expect it to be the park's main channel for sightseers.

Beetlejuice's Graveyard Revue ★ SHOW   Universal owns the rights to many classic movie monsters, and strangely, they appear in this rowdy '80s and '90s rock-'n'-roll show, presided over by the undead, naughty-minded Beetlejuice, who aims more for the funny bone than the jugular. Watching Frankenstein jam out on guitar to "Dancing in the Dark" will make you feel like someone slipped something into your Coke. **Strategy:** Unless you're a show person, you can skip this one, at least until you've knocked down some of the fresher attractions (or some liquor). The 20-minute performances happen a few times daily and are noted maps.

Disaster! ★★ SHOW/RIDE   In the preshow, a projected Christopher Walken, pretending to be a big disaster-movie director touting the genre, interacts at length with a live actor. The technology is impressive, especially as his lifelike image rests his feet on boxes you can clearly see in front of you. Next, the actor brings everyone into an adjoining "soundstage" and volunteers from the audience stand in for special-effect insert shots. Finally, everyone boards a tram mocked up to resemble San Francisco's BART subway—seats on the outside are the best. It travels down a tunnel and stops inside what appears to be a faithful re-creation of the Embarcadero station, albeit one that smells suspiciously of natural gas. Of course something goes horribly wrong. There's an earthquake. Hell is unleashed: rocking, flooding to within an inch of the train, the unexpected intrusion of a gas truck from the "street" above (with the required climactic explosion). The intent is to approximate a jolt measuring 8.3 on the Richter scale. Just as quickly as it began, everything halts and reassembles itself for the next "take" as your train whisks you out again. **Warning:** Claustrophobes abhor the BART bit, as do some nervous children.

WORLD EXPO

As Springfield gradually takes over, there's not much left of this area except one ride and a dated show.

Men in Black: Alien Attack ★★ RIDE   Most riders enjoy this excellent riff on the Will Smith film franchise. After a superlative queue area that does a pitch-perfect, "Jetsons"-style imitation of New York's 1964 World's Fair (ironically, the one Walt Disney created so many wonders for), you discover the "real" tenant of the futuristic building: a training course for the Men in Black alien patrol corps. You board six-person cars equipped with individual laser guns. As you pass from room to room—expect lots of herky-jerky motions, but nothing sickening—your task is to fire upon any alien that pops out from around doorways, behind trash cans, and so on. If they peg you first, it sends your buggy spinning. Each car's point score is displayed on the dashboard, and the number accumulated by the end determines the climactic video you're shown—Will Smith will either praise you as "Galaxy Defender" or mock you as "Bug Bait." **Strategy:** The single riders' queue moves quickly, thanks to the odd number of seats in each row. Locker use for small items is mandatory, but free for the posted wait time plus 20 minutes.

Fear Factor Live ★ SHOW   Like the meat-headed NBC show, ordinary people do stunts (usually involving being dangled on wires, maybe eating food-grade mealworms) for the twisted pleasure of a whooping audience while an inane master of ceremonies eggs everyone on. If you're over 18 and want to volunteer as a contestant (first prize: polite applause), be there 70 minutes before your selected showtime and you'll go through a tryout including jumping jacks and a game of Simon Says. Contestants can't wear jewelry, and if your hands sweat when you're nervous, you will be at a disadvantage in the gripping challenges. This show goes dark in low season.

SPRINGFIELD

In 2008, when Universal converted its old Back to the Future ride to one themed to "The Simpsons," it didn't know it was creating a juggernaut. The land has expanded in a big way with a hilarious midway offering inside-joke games such as Mr. Burns' Radioactive Rings, and in 2013, with a spate of eateries plus another ride. Now the area is jammed with inside jokes from the longest-running comedy on TV. **Kwik-E-Mart** sells an array of bespoke souvenirs you can only get here, the **Duff Brewery** pours its

---

The Wizarding World of Harry Potter: Diagon Alley

Just like with He Who Must Not Be Named, there was always a master plan for a total domination. In 2010, the opening of Hogsmeade at Islands of Adventure's **The Wizarding World of Harry Potter** was an artistic and commercial smash, crowning Universal as the new leader of American theme park imagination and leaving Disney World scrambling for an answer. Now Universal is following that with another brazen concept: an encore in its other park. Now under construction between San Francisco and World Expo is a second Harry Potter land, **The Wizarding World of Harry Potter: Diagon Alley.** Rides had not been announced at press time, but it's generally agreed that the marquee attraction will be a Gringotts Bank thrill ride. Universal has confirmed the new land will be themed to the London passageway where young wizards are provisioned, that it will conjure up another passel of shops, restaurants, impeccable references from the series, that the section will again be executed by the movies' designers—and that it will all be topped by a fire-belching dragon. Guests will be able to transfer between the two Wizarding Worlds via a ride on the Hogwarts Express train, through what was once a backstage area. Rumor also has it the grand opening will take place in the summer of 2014. Given the massive hype surround the first go-round, it's a fair bet the ribbon-cutting won't slip by you, but expect massive, hours-long crowds at this park, and even pre-opening queues, for a while afterward.

signature quaff—the cause of, and solution to, all life's problems—plus Squishees, and the embiggened statue of frontiersman Jebediah Springfield lords over us all. For the moment, this is the most stupendous part of the park.

The Simpsons Ride ★★★ RIDE   It's easy to love this highly amusing, top-quality, motion-simulator "Thrilltacular Upsy-Downsy Spins-Aroundsy Teen-Operated Thrill Ride" that takes place in front of an 80-foot-tall screen. The premise, dense and ironic enough to please devotees of the FOX series, punctures Orlando itself: You join Homer's clan at Krustyland, a greedy theme park, on a roller coaster that's sabotaged by the evil Sideshow Bob (voiced by Kelsey Grammer). During the dizzyingly fast-paced 6 minutes, you zoom through a bunch of predicaments that mock the theme park world, including skewers of Shamu, Pirates of the Caribbean, and "it's a small world." Add to that a giant killer panda bear and an extra layer of heightened sensory (like the whiff of baby powder—well, it makes sense when you ride). It's not too rough, but your brain may hurt from absorbing all the jokes. The queue area is so tongue in cheek and gag-packed that waiting is half the fun: Itchy and Scratchy do the gory safety warning and Krusty gives safety instructions like "Wait here until someone comes and tells you to do something." Seats are four across, so families can ride together.

Kang & Kodos' Twirl 'n' Hurl ★ RIDE   In summer 2013, Universal finally got its Dumbo ride. Here, silly slobbering aliens trick you into boarding a day-glow, two-person flying saucer: "Please remain seated until the very end of the ride. You will know the ride has ended when your vehicle comes to a complete stop, or you have been eaten…I didn't just say that." As you rotate gently around, Dumbo-style, you use a joystick to pass in front of tentacle-shaped poles, triggering sounds of exclamation from the citizens of Springfield. Spoiler: You don't get eaten.

HOLLYWOOD

Universal Horror Make-Up Show ★★ SHOW   Learn how horror-movie makeup effects are accomplished in this terrific, 25-minute tongue-in-cheek exposé, conducted by a nerdy type in his workshop. On paper, that seems like the kind of thing you might otherwise skip, but in truth park regulars love its wit and playful edge. For ad-libbing and gross-out humor, the park suggests parental guidance for this one, but I find that most kids have heard it all before, and it's certainly true that seeing terrifying movie gore exposed as the make-believe it is can be a good reality check. Times are printed on your park map, and you can't get in once the show's begun. Even if you skip the show, there's something to see in the lobby: exhibits about great horror characters and make-up artists.

Terminator 2: 3-D ★ SHOW/FILM   Although the 12-minute film portion, a sort of minisequel to "Terminator 2," was made by extravagant director James Cameron with all his original stars (including Ah-nold and Linda Hamilton), it's hardly just another movie. It's got three screens, six 8-foot robots, gunfire, smoke bombs, and motorcyclists that seamlessly dive in and out of the filmed action. The film cost $60 million to make, which when it was produced in 1996 qualified it as the most expensive movie, per minute, in history, trumping Disney's equally bombastic "Captain EO." **Strategy:** This edgy, cynical show splits the eardrums with romping, stomping mayhem, so keep small children away unless they're hard cases. Those in the front rows will have to pivot their heads to see all the action.

Lucy: A Tribute ★★★ ACTIVITY   Too overlooked is this one-room, walk-through exhibition of Lucille Ball memorabilia. Ever seen an Emmy? There are five, plus a Kennedy Center Honor and a model of the "I Love Lucy" set. Bet you didn't know it was painted black and white to look good on TV.

WOODY WOODPECKER'S KIDZONE

This is my pick for the best children's theme park playground area in Orlando. I've heard tales of 6-year-olds who threatened self-orphanization if they were dragged away within 4 hours. There's a ton to do, not least of which is **SpongeBob StorePants,** dedicated to merchandise and appearance of the absorbent doofus.

Animal Actors on Location! ★★★ SHOW   A troupe of trained dogs, cats, birds, and a horse anchor this charming 20-minute show (times are noted on the sign). Placing this show here was inspired, because small children get a thrill out of seeing common animals do tricks, and as a consequence, it's popular. Because it's in an amphitheater, you can also sneak out in the middle if you need to. But if you see only one emphatically punctuated household-pets-doing-cute-tricks-to-jaunty-music theme park show, make it SeaWorld's superior Pets Ahoy!

E.T. Adventure ★★★ RIDE   Based on the 1982 Steven Spielberg movie, this expensive-looking indoor ride is rightfully in the kiddie area because it's not intense. Upon entering, guests supply their name to an attendant, who encodes the information on a pass you hand over when you board the ride. The indoor queue area is a fabulous reproduction of a thick, cool California forest at night. Vehicles are suspended from rails to approximate the sensation of cruising in a flock of bikes, and they sweep and scoop across the moonrise and even through gardens on E.T.'s home planet (remember, he was a botanist), where a menagerie of goofy-looking aliens, who don't look nearly as realistic as our hero, greet us from the sidelines. At the climax, a grateful E.T. is supposed to call out your names as you fly home—hence those boarding passes—but in all my years of doing this ride, E.T. has spouted gibberish, so don't get your hopes up unless your name is Pfmkmpftur. **Strategy:** If the queue looks dense from the outside, return later—before park closing seems to be a charmed time for quick waits—since there are still more lineups indoors. In the **Toy Closet,** you'll find E.T. souvenirs. He's a lot more cuddly now than the leathery dolls they sold in 1982, but his "Talk to the Hand" T-shirt is just weird.

Fievel's Playland ★★★ ACTIVITY   Named for the hero of "An American Tail" (an obscure kiddie reference, and another '80s Spielberg movie), it's the most spectacular of several playgrounds in Kidzone. The concept is that your kids have been shrunk down to a mouse's size, and they're playing among giant everyday items like sardine cans and eyeglasses. They'll discover slides, nets, and tubes, but my favorite element is the easy water slide on a raft—so yes, make sure your kids have their swimsuits on. The ground is covered with that newfangled soft foam that all the modern playgrounds have. When I was a boy, we got concussions instead.

A Day in the Park with Barney ★★★ SHOW   The small indoor area that can be accessed through its own gift shop (plush Barney, $13), is technically the postshow area for a singalong show. The doors close at the start and stay closed until the ordeal is over. Frankly, being locked in a room with that sappy purple dinosaur and all those screaming babies constitutes a chamber of horrors for me, but little ones find it enthralling. Parents can find Duff Beer in Springfield nearby, if that helps. The play area mimics Barney's backyard with a waist-high counter for sifting through sand (so it won't get into shoes), a tree equipped with little slides, and a chance to have your picture taken with (and then buy it from) Barney the Capitalist Dinosaur.

Woody Woodpecker's Nuthouse Coaster ★★★ RIDE   Kids can plainly see every drop before they commit to this straightforward thriller. It has no unpleasant surprises, unless you count hearing Woody's pecker as you go, and a run time of less than a minute.

Curious George Goes to Town ★★★ ACTIVITY   Welcome to the water playground that stole your child. This frenetic splash area is teeming with squealing children and positively soaked with streams of water from every direction—from squirt cannons, fountains, geysers, and, most importantly, from two 500-gallon buckets that, every 7 minutes, sound a warning bell and then drench anyone beneath them. The immoderate, virtually orgiastic scene is ringed by a perimeter of dry parents keeping an eye on their suddenly wild offspring. I enjoy joining them, because watching the children cheer and scamper when they hear the clang of the bucket's warning bell, and then watching them momentarily vanish in the deluge, is endlessly heartwarming. Through the wet area (there's a dry bypass corridor to it on the left) is the dry Ball Factory, where kids suck up plastic balls with light vacuums, pack them into bags, and then fire them at each other with weak cannons. It's not marked on the maps.

WHERE TO EAT AT UNIVERSAL STUDIOS

In addition to the random snack carts (including carts selling goliath turkey legs with chips for $11), there are counter-service and table-service restaurants in the park. None require reservations the way Disney's do. Kids' meals all come in under 300 calories. **Tip:** Meals do not *have* to come with side dishes. The potato chip bags served hold a mere 1⅞ ounces. Ask to subtract chips or fries from your meal deals and you'll save about $2. Cups good for unlimited refills at touchscreen Coke Freestyle machines, which mix soda to order using 126 flavors, cost $11 and are good for the day. **Remember:** Restaurants at CityWalk (p. 153) are a 5-minute walk from the park, so they're also options.

Classic Monsters Café ★★ AMERICAN   Indoor counter service on a nonscary B-movie set with some healthy options, such as rotisserie chicken with mashed potatoes and broccoli, wedge salad, and meat loaf platters. Production Central. Combo meal $7.80 to $10.

Finnegan's Bar & Grill ★★★ IRISH/BRITISH   A buzzy sit-down, Irish-style pub good for a beer break—and a break from burgers and fries. Scotch eggs ($6), split pea–and-ham soup ($5), Irish Cobb salad (it has corned beef), and bangers and mash (sausage with garlic mashed potatoes) are the kind of things available, plus good strong ales. Park workers pick this place when they're off-duty. New York. Mains $10 to $13.

Louie's Italian Restaurant ★ ITALIAN   Straightforward counter service near The Mummy. New York. Slices $6, meatball subs $9, whole pies $29 to $32.

San Francisco Pastry Company ★★ SANDWICHES   This lightly trafficked counter-service bakery across from Disaster!, does sandwiches and loaded croissants in addition to cakes and pastries, and healthier fruit plates and salads. San Francisco. Sandwiches $9, salads from $3.50.

Lombard's Seafood Grille ★★★ SEAFOOD/AMERICAN   An excellent, overlooked table-service choice that is surprisingly affordable: Fish tacos are $13, just three bucks more than a Quick Service meal, and other fish dishes, including the fish of the day, such as grouper, are in the mid-teens. Splashing fountains serenade, fish tanks adorn the dining room, and you can sit outside on the water if you like. Special

In both its parks, Universal offers an all-you-can-eat meal plan. Dubbed the **Universal Meal Deal,** it entitles you to one main plate and one dessert each time you go through the line at six counter-service locations (three per park, none of which are in Harry Potter or Springfield). You'll get a wristband and kids 9 and under must order from whatever designated kids' menu that restaurant has (which isn't usually a problem). Keeping in mind that it doesn't include beverages and stops working 30 minutes before closing (so you'll have to plan ahead to get dinner out of it), the pricing only makes sense if you're a big eater. For one park, adults pay $25 and kids $13; for two parks, it's adults $29 and kids $15.

diet options, such as quinoa with portobello mushroom, are well marked, and you can even get gluten-free table rolls. San Francisco. Main courses $13 to $20.

Richter's Burger Co. ★★ AMERICAN   A warehouselike dockside option that slings stacked burgers, marinated grilled chicken sandwiches, and for those weary of the greasy side of the plate, salads with grilled chicken. Periodically, the dining area rumbles (but doesn't move) to simulate quakes. Get the Aftershock double burger for $9.70 and an extra bun for $1.07 and you can feed two using the fixin's bar. San Francisco. Main courses $8 to $9 with fries.

Fast Food Boulevard ★★★ AMERICAN   In 2013, this brilliant food court was added to the mega-popular Simpsons area, and it's stuffed with inside jokes and witticisms that puncture American culture. You could spend half your lunchtime just laughing at the names of the dishes. **Krusty Burger** serves "meat sandwiches" such as the high-stacked double-bacon Clogger Burger with cheez sauce and curly fries and 6-inch Heat Lamp Dogs. **The Frying Dutchman** does Basket O' Bait fried fish and Clam Chowd-arr ($4). At the **Luigi's Pizza** area, get slices of Meat Liker's Pizza, and at **Cletus' Chicken Shack,** dig into the not-very-appetizing-but-accurate Chicken Arms (wings), Chicken Thumbs (tenders), and chicken-and-waffle sandwiches. Lastly, **Lisa's Teahouse of Horror** cuts out the clots with a cooler full of straight-up salads and wraps. You can also buy only-at-Universal treats such as Lard Lad donuts (the Big Pink, coated with frosting, $5—a life-size Chief Wiggum figure enjoys one nearby) and Buzz Cola (no-calorie cherry cola). Springfield. Across the way, there's the **Bumblebee Man's Taco Truck.** Main courses $7 to $13.

Moe's Tavern ★★★ BAR   A spot-on re-creation of Moe's, down to team pennants for the Isotopes and the purple TV on the wall, only without sleazy service by Moe. There is, however, a life-size Barney by the bar, ruefully contemplating his empty beer mug. Duff Beer is specially brewed for the park (in generous servings of regular, Lite, or Dry, $6.50), but the kid-friendly specialty is a Flaming Moe's ($8), a nonalcoholic orange-flavored soda in a souvenir cup ringed with cartoon flames. It mists bubbles and mists, like dry ice, when served, and it's the Butterbeer of this park. Springfield. Beverages $6.50 to $8.

Kid Zone Pizza Company ★ PIZZA   Outdoor-only counter service for chicken fingers and fries, chef salad, and of course, pizza. It's the biggest food option near the children's play areas. Woody Woodpecker's Kidzone. Mains $7 to $8.50.

4

UNIVERSAL, SEAWORLD & BEYOND

Universal Orlando

Mel's Drive-In ★★ AMERICAN   A '50s-style counter-service diner where everything's shiny like chrome and glass and fare leans toward chicken, burgers, and shakes. Seating has a view of the Lagoon. Hollywood. Main courses $7 to $10.

Café La Bamba ★★ BARBECUE   Its warren of dining rooms can make for a cool escape, but this chicken-and-ribs counter service location is only open in peak season. Hollywood. Mains $11 to $15.

Beverly Hills Boulangerie ★ SANDWICHES   An uncrowded choice for a reasonably healthy meal: sandwiches (turkey, roast beef, tuna) with potato salad and fruit. It also does a soup-and-salad combo for $7. Hollywood. Sandwiches $10.

Islands of Adventure

Islands of Adventure (IOA) ★★★ usually opens at 9am. In winter months, operating hours will end at around 6pm but in summer, they're often open to as late as 10pm. After you park ($15 and up), open your bags for inspection, take the moving sidewalks to CityWalk, and veer to the left, toward the 130-foot Pharos Lighthouse (it's just for show), you finally reach IOA. If you doubt whether your kids are tall enough to ride everything, there's a gauge listing requirements before the ticket booths.

ORIENTATION   IOA's 101 acres are laid out much like Epcot's World Showcase: individually themed areas (here, called "islands," even though they're not) arranged around a lagoon (called the Great Inland Sea). To see everything, you simply follow a great circle. The only corridor into the park, **Port of Entry,** borrows from the Magic Kingdom's Main Street, U.S.A., in that it's a narrow, introductory area where guests are submerged into the theme. In this case, you're gathering munitions for a "great odyssey," so, in theme park logic, it's where you do things like rent strollers and lockers and grab free maps. Most guests beeline through Port of Entry. Because attraction lines are shortest after opening, explore this area later, maybe before closing.

STRATEGY   Once you reach the end of Port of Entry, which way should you go? Right. That's the way to Harry Potter. Lines peak in late morning and early afternoon, then taper off again after that, but they're rarely short.

SHOPPING   The park will send your souvenirs to the Islands of Adventure Trading Company, at the Port of Entry, for collection as you leave the park at the end of the day. The deadline for purchases changes, but it's usually about 2 hours before closing. To the right as you exit the park, there's a **small stand** selling marked-down items (the inventory changes, but I've seen $8 Marvel action figures, two-for-ones on plush Curious George dolls, and $40 sweatshirts for $22). It opens later in the day.

MARVEL SUPER HERO ISLAND

If Disney owns Marvel, how come Universal is allowed to have this island? The park licensed the brand in the 1990s, which gives it the right. Designs used the comic books of that period, which predates the film franchises of Spider-Man, the X-Men, Iron Man, and Fantastic Four, which is why characters don't look exactly the way you may be used to them. **Spider-Man** is sometimes one of them, but if you don't see him, head into the back of the Marvel Alterniverse Store, opposite the Captain America Diner. There, the hero has his own appearance zone where you can take your own photos (or buy one). The actor playing Spider-Man is one of the few who isn't clad in muscle-shaped padding—for the frank cling of his bodysuit, admiring members of the park's staff usually aren't far away. The **Comic Book Shop** is worth a stop. Surprisingly legit, the store carries the latest Marvel issues, compilation books, and collectible busts.

Islands of Adventure

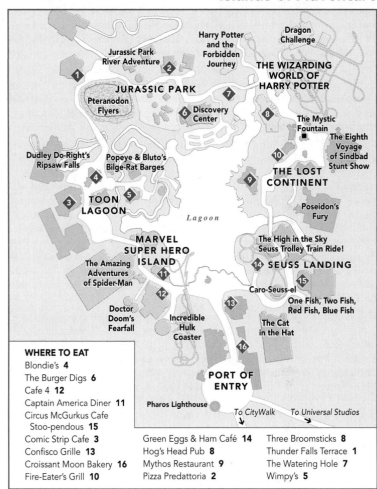

WHERE TO EAT

Blondie's **4**
The Burger Digs **6**
Cafe 4 **12**
Captain America Diner **11**
Circus McGurkus Cafe
  Stoo-pendous **15**
Comic Strip Cafe **3**
Confisco Grille **13**
Croissant Moon Bakery **16**
Fire-Eater's Grill **10**

Green Eggs & Ham Café **14**
Hog's Head Pub **8**
Mythos Restaurant **9**
Pizza Predattoria **2**

Three Broomsticks **8**
Thunder Falls Terrace **1**
The Watering Hole **7**
Wimpy's **5**

Incredible Hulk Coaster ★★★ **RIDE** Every minute or so, a new train blasts out of the 150-foot tunnel, over the avenue, and across the lakefront. Adding to the intensity, the track's hollow frame and nylon wheels generate an animal roar that can be heard throughout the park. The $15 million ride is quick—a little over 2 minutes—but it's invigorating. First, trains cruise into the inclined tunnel. Then, without warning, 220 aircraft tires accelerate trains from a standstill to 40mph in 2 seconds and shoot them into a zero G-force barrel-roll 110 feet in the air, which means passengers are already upside down even though they're still going up the first hill. What follows is unbridled mayhem, as you boomerang in a cobra roll and hit a top speed of 67mph through a tangle of corkscrews, loops, and misty tunnels. For many visitors, it's the first ride of the day, and its seven inversions are certain to work better than morning

113

coffee. Loose items aren't allowed, so use the nearby lockers, good for the ride's posted wait time plus 20 minutes. **Strategy:** The single-rider line here is fruitful. A separate queue forms near the loading dock for the front row, but if you're low on time, wait instead for the front row on Dueling Dragons, where the exposed view gets you a lot more thrills. If you plan on buying a photo of your group on the ride, make sure you're all seated in the same line because shots are taken row by row.

Storm Force Accelatron ★ RIDE   I can translate: Storm is the weather-controlling X-Man, so an Accelatron must be a 90-second spinning-tub ride, like Disney's teacups. Open, round cars spin on platters that themselves are on a giant rotating disk, and just to ensure maximum vomit velocity, each pod can be spun using a plate in the middle. **Strategy:** This ride is skippable unless you have insistent kids.

Dr. Doom's Fearfall ★★ RIDE   Those twin 200-foot towers are fitted with rows of chairs that slide up and down them. The brave are rocketed 150 feet up at a force of 4Gs, where they feel an intense tickling in their stomachs, soak up a terrific view of the park, and bounce (safely) back down to Earth. The ride capacity is pretty low—you can see for yourself that each tower only shoots about 16 people up on each trip, with a reload period of several minutes in between—so either do this one early or very late so that waiting for it doesn't eat up too much time. You may hear the towers hiss like a snarling beast—it sounds like a Doctor Doom sound effect, but, in fact, it's part of the mechanism. A computer weighs each car before launch, and any excess compressed air is noisily expelled in the seconds before flight. **Strategy:** The seating configuration lends itself to lots of empty spaces, so the single-rider line moves much quicker than most.

The Amazing Adventures of Spider-Man ★★★ RIDE   The cliché "don't miss it" rightfully applies here. It fires on all cylinders, and the whole family can do it without fear. After passing through a simulation of the "Daily Bugle" newsroom (take special notice of the hilarious preride safety video, done as a pitch-perfect "Superfriends"-era cartoon), riders don polarized 3-D glasses, board moving cars, and whisk through a 1.5-acre experience. Mild open-air motion simulation, computer-generated 3-D animation, and a cunning sense trickery (bursts of flame, water droplets, blasts of hot air) collaborate to impart the mind-blowing illusion of being drafted into Spidey's battles against a "Sinister Syndicate" of supervillains including Doctor Octopus and the Green Goblin, who have disassembled the Statue of Liberty with an anti-gravity gun. Although the vehicles barely move as they make their way through the sets, you'll come off feeling as if you've survived a 400-foot plunge off a city skyscraper. Comics fans should keep a lookout for Spider-Man creator Stan Lee. He

The Best of Islands of Adventure

Don't miss if you're 6: The Cat in the Hat

Don't miss if you're 16: The Amazing Adventures of Spider-Man, Dragon Challenge

Requisite photo op: Hogwarts Castle

Food you can only get here: Butterbeer, The Wizarding World of Harry Potter

The most crowded, so go early: Harry Potter and the Forbidden Journey

Skippable: Pteranodon Flyers

Biggest thrill: Incredible Hulk Coaster

Best show: Poseidon's Fury

Where to find peace: On the lagoon in Jurassic Park

4

Universal Orlando

UNIVERSAL, SEAWORLD & BEYOND

appears four times during the ride, and you'll hear him once. **Strategy:** Go early or late in the day to minimize waits. There's sometimes a single-rider line and it shoots past the slower standby queue. The middle of the front row is debatably the best place to sit.

TOON LAGOON

The next zone clockwise after Marvel Super Hero Island, Toon Lagoon, harbors two waters rides that are—both literally and figuratively—among the splashiest at any theme park. Both of them will drench you. If you're smart, you'll come just *before* it swelters, so that you'll be soaked and cool when the going gets rough.

Slow your pace when you reach the introductory section of Toon Lagoon, encountered after a brief zone of **midway games** (most: three tries for $5). Crawling with details, color, and fountains, it's the kind of place that reveals more the longer you look. Some 150 cartoon characters—some you'll recognize (Nancy, Annie, the Family Circus, Beetle Bailey) and some strictly for connoisseurs (Little Nemo in Slumberland, Zippy)—make two-dimensional appearances on the island, including inside the restaurants and on a soundtrack popping in and out of the action. Where you see a button or a possible trigger, press it or plunge it, because the environment has been rigged with sonic treats. Whimsical snapshot spots are worked in, too, such as the trick photo setup by the Comic Strip Cafe where you can pretend Marmaduke is dragging you by his leash. The deluge from the waterfall under Hagar's Viking ship provides cooling relief from the sunlight. Amidst all this, the **Boop Oop A Doop** Betty Boop store sells rare specimens. My sister-in-law found a 75th-anniversary cookie jar here that no other real-world store carried. Personally, I worry about the mental health of the clerks, who are subjected to a brain-melting loop of Boop's oops.

Dudley Do-Right's Ripsaw Falls ★★★ RIDE   Within this Technicolor snow-capped mountain, you'll find a wonderful perils-of-Pauline log-flume caper featuring Jay Ward's feckless Canadian Mountie bungling his rescue of Nell Fenwick from Snidely Whiplash. The winding 5-minute journey—ups, downs, indoor, outdoor, surprise backsplashes, chunky robotic characters—climaxes in a stomach-juggling double-dip drop that hurtles, unexpectedly, through a humped underground gully. Although the 75-foot drop starts out at 45 degrees, it steepens to 50 degrees, creating a weightless sensation. Front- and back-seat riders get soaked, and anyone who didn't get soaked probably will when they double back to the disembarking zone, because that's when they'll face the gauntlet of sadistic bystanders who fire water cannons at passing boats. Ripsaw Falls is terrific fun. No one gets off it grumpy—the mark of amusement success. **Tips:** The ride often closes in January and early February for a scrub. There's an optional locker nearby—use it, because there's no boat storage. It's $4 for 90 minutes, which may allow you to also use it for Popeye & Bluto's barges. The **Gasoline Alley** shop, across the main path, sells $8 ponchos, but on Ripsaw Falls, you straddle the seat so your feet won't be easy to cover. Best to wear sandals.

Popeye & Bluto's Bilge-Rat Barges ★★★ RIDE   For my money, it's the best round-boat flume in the world. You board 12-passenger, circular bumper boats that float freely and unpredictably down an outlandish white-water obstacle course—beneath waterfalls, through tunnels, over angry rapids, and past features designed to mercilessly inundate you. It's like playing Russian roulette with water, and everyone loses. This journey is considerably wilder, unquestionably wetter, and obviously more expensive to build than any others in the genre. The attention shows: Even the river's walls have been sculpted and painted in cartoon hues to resemble a wooden chute. It's diabolical and one of Universal's best. **Strategy:** There's a semiwaterproof cubby on board for personal belongings, but you'd be wise to slip your things into plastic bags, too, just in case. You may not go barefoot. For onlooker schadenfreude, there are 25¢ water blasters on overlooking walkways, but there are free ones on Me Ship, the Olive. Near the lockers ($4 for 90 min., which may be long enough use to use for Ripsaw Falls, too), you'll find step-in, haystack turbo dryers that, for $5, bake and blow the water off you after your journey. (That works well, except on jeans.)

Me Ship, the Olive ★ ACTIVITY   An interactive ship-shaped playground for children just beyond the Barges' entrance, there's also a slide and some fun to be had with a piano in the cabin (play the notes on the sheet music for an orchestral surprise). One of my favorite things to do in Orlando is to spend awhile on the bridge beside the Olive, which overlooks Barge boats as they drift helplessly under a leaky boiler's funnel. Watching the gleeful alarm on people's faces, hearing the peals of laughter—the sublime delight of amusement park togetherness is repeated, again and again, from the vantage point of that bridge. I could stand there all day. I also love the shore of the sea nearby, which is private almost all the time.

JURASSIC PARK

Steven Spielberg was a creative consultant to Universal, the studio that nourished him, and this "island," the largest and greenest in the park, is presented practically verbatim from his 1993 movie. Once you pass through a proud wooden gate, John Williams' bombastic score becomes audible, and there it burrows until you move on to another area of IOA. When the park opened, the big boast was that all of the plants in this section were extant during the period of the dinosaurs, but it seems that's no longer the case. Still, the area has some 4,000 trees—half the number in the whole park—and if you stand quietly, you may hear rustling among some of them—a clever, Spielbergian touch.

Camp Jurassic ★ ACTIVITY   The only dedicated kids' zone of this part of the park is a self-guided tangle of rope bridges, slides, bubbling pools in caves, surprise geysers, water guns, spitting dinosaur heads, and thick greenery. It's easy to get lost here, and easier to get wet.

Pteranodon Flyers ★ RIDE   The hanging carts gently gliding on the nifty-looking track over Camp Jurassic constitute a very short (about 75 sec.) clacking route through the trees. Cool as it looks, it was poorly designed, fitting only two at a time, and huge lines are inevitable. In the business, that's called a poor "load factor." Facing irate crowds, Universal instituted a rule: No adult could ride without a child. That both prepared guests for the ride's tame deportment and cut down on the wait. Attendants may be willing to load child-free adults when the park is dead. **Strategy:** Skip this underwhelmer if the wait's more than 15 minutes.

Jurassic Park River Adventure ★★ RIDE   In that family-friendly Orlando tradition, the worst drop is clearly warned from the outside; gauge the 85-foot descent from behind the Thunder Falls Terrace restaurant, where river boats kick up quite a spray when they hit the water at 30mph. Before reaching that messy climax, boats embark on what's meant to be a benign tour of the mythical dinosaur park from the movie, only to be bumped off course and run afoul of spitting raptors and an eye-poppingly realistic T. rex who lunges for the kill. The dino attack is shrewdly stage-managed; note how, in true Spielberg fashion, you see disquieting evidence of the hungry lizards (rustling bushes, gashes in sheet metal) before actually catching sight of one. There's no logic as to which passengers will get drenched. In all honesty, you're much more likely to get soaked standing on the terrace of the restaurant than you are inside the boat, but the trip down is enough to blow your hat off. There's usually a delirious 12-year-old boy who stands in the splash zone for hours, giving himself a nigh-amphibious drenching.

Jurassic Park Discovery Center ★ ACTIVITY   Enter a convincing reproduction of the luxury lodge from the film, down to full-size skeletons in the atrium—downstairs, line up your camera just so, and you can snap a witty shot of a T. rex chomping a loved one's cranium. Hilarity with carnivores! Also seek out the scientist carrying a baby triceratops that hatched on the grounds; it flinches and reacts to your touch. You can also handle the ostrich-sized dinosaur eggs and slide them into nifty "scanners." Behind the center, there's a network of pleasant garden paths where you can take a break from the bustle of the park and chill out beside the lagoon.

THE WIZARDING WORLD OF HARRY POTTER

When it opened in June of 2010, the 10-acre **Harry Potter** ★★★, as it's often called, was rightfully hailed as the most significant achievement in American theme park design, detailed down to the souvenirs. It's as if the film set for Hogsmeade Village (the only British village for non-Muggles) and Hogwarts Castle have been transported to Florida, and indeed, it was designed by the same team. You don't have to know the books or the movies to enjoy the astounding level of attention: Stonework looks ancient, plaster was painted to appear moldy, rooftops and chimneys slouch in a jumble of snow-covered gables, and nearly every souvenir is a bespoke creation expressly for the Harry Potter universe. Even the restrooms aren't spared Moaning Myrtle's whine. Spend time going from shop window to shop window to take in the tricks. In Spintwitches Sporting Needs, a Quidditch set strains to free itself from its carrying case. At Gladrags, the gown levitates. At Tomes and Scrolls, Gilderoy Lockhart (Kenneth Branagh) vainly preens himself among his best-selling travel books.

Those stores are brilliant facades, but there are real shops that are just as unmissable (and invariably thronged). **Devish and Banges** is where you find Hogwarts school supplies in the colors of all four Houses, from capes to scarves to diaries to parchment, wax seals, and quills. (The seething "Monster Book of Monsters" is kept in a cage here.) In the window of **Honeydukes,** there's a macabre contraption in which a mechanical crow pecks out the gumball eye of a skeleton, which rolls through various chutes to be dispensed below, presumably for consumption. That signifies the wondrous candy store within, where colorful Edwardian-style packages contain Chocolate Frogs (they're solid, not hollow, but still take care in the Florida heat), Fizzing Whizzbees, Bertie Bott's Every Flavour Beans (beware the vomit-flavored ones mixed in), Exploding Bon Bons, Peppermint Toads, and other confections that would faze even Willy Wonka. Honeydukes shares space with **Zonko's Joke Shop,** which proffers Extendable Ears, Sneakoscopes, Fanged Flyers, and green U-No-Poo beans, among other oddities. Every time a Pygmy Puff is sold, the clerk (wearing a cloth cap suitable to Hogsmeade) rings a giant bell to announce the adoption.

The park's signature concoction, **Butterbeer,** is pulled from two keg-shaped carts in the walkways. The only place in the world you can buy it is right here or at the Harry Potter Studio Tour outside of London. Served frozen or unfrozen (I like it cold) with a creamy foam head on top, it tastes like a butterscotch Life Saver, and it's addictive. I once did laboratory analysis on it and found out that, surprisingly, it contains no more sugar than a Coke. It's $4.25 a cup, but for $11.75, you get a dishwasher-safe

Butterbeer mug. **The Magic Neep** cart, between the Butterbeer stalls, sells **Pumpkin Juice** (really a Christmasy apple juice mix) in its unique pumpkin-top bottles for $6.25, along with actual fruit for $1.30 a piece.

Ollivanders ★★ SHOW   It's not on the maps because it can't handle big crowds, but the queue to the left of Dervish and Banges is for Ollivanders Wand Shop, stacked haphazardly to the dusty rafters with wands for every wizard. You enter in small groups, and the kindly shopkeeper selects one child from the group for a personalized wand selection—it selects *you*—accompanied by music cues and some fun tricks. That lets you out into the wand department at Devish and Banges, where you can also buy perfect replicas from nearly every major character of the Harry Potter universe (mostly $32), from Harry to Hermione to Snape to Voldemort to Bellatrix Lestrange to Luna Lovegood. (Treat them with care. Some are sturdy, but some, such as Professor McGonagall's, can break.)

Harry Potter and the Forbidden Journey ★★★ RIDE   You will be drawn inexorably to the stunning re-creation of Hogwarts Castle, and within, you'll find the most technologically complex ride in Orlando, maybe the world. I won't give away how it's done, but I will say you'll find an epic combination of motion-simulator movie segments and awe-inducing physical encounters as you travel on a four-person bench that has been enchanted by Hermione to transport you. This being Orlando, things go awry, and you encounter a dragon, Aragog the spider, the Whomping Willow, a Quidditch match, and Dementors, all in the space of 4 minutes. The mostly indoor queue is perhaps even more magical, taking you through Dumbledore's study and through the dim halls of Hogwarts, where real-looking oil paintings come to life and bicker with each other. At one point, fake snow falls on you, and a lifelike Sorting Hat supervises your arrival at the loading dock. It's a tour-de-force that takes the pain out of a long wait, and sometimes there's a tour-only route that lets you enjoy it without having to ride (ask). Once you're done, you go through Filch's Emporium of Confiscated Goods, a general-interest shop for Potteria. **Tip:** You'll save much frustration if you don't have bags. No loose articles are permitted. Lockers are free for the posted wait time plus 20 minutes, but using them is confusing. The single rider line lets you leapfrog much of the wait but you will miss most of the queue's excitement. A minority of people feel queasy after riding, but if you sense that happening, just close your eyes during the three movie portions and you should be fine.

Dragon Challenge ★★★ RIDE   This is a monster coaster of the first order, and one of Orlando's most thrilling, but it's not very Hogsmeade because it's actually a holdover from the pre-Potter years. Actually, it's two roller coasters, "inverted" so that passengers' feet dangle, entangled together for two different 145-second rides. Hungarian Horntail, in blue, has a cobra roll and its twistiness is perhaps (who can say?) more conducive to slight motion sickness for those who are prone to it. Chinese Fireball, in red-orange, has two more "elements" (maneuvers, in coaster-speak), and its first drop is slightly higher, but its course is slightly more jolty. The line for both snakes indoors through a castle before diverging before the twin loading zones, at which point you'll also have to decide if you want to wait longer to guarantee a front-row seat. The trains were designed to be dispatched together for near-misses on the course, but because naughty guests dropped loose items, seriously injuring others, that practice was ended. **Strategy:** The effect is best enjoyed from the front row or by keeping an eye on your feet. After you get off, ask an attendant if the "re-ride" line is up, because if it is, you won't have to go all the way out to line up again to try the other track. Note that guests of exceptional size may have to wait for the third row, where the larger seats are; if you're not confident that you'll fit, test out the standard seat located to the right of the main entrance to the queue. Locker use (free for the wait time plus 20 min.) is mandatory, and you'll find them at Hogsmeade Station.

Flight of the Hippogriff ★ RIDE For kids too little for Dragon Challenge, you'll find a standard training roller coaster (also a rethemed holdover from pre-Potter years) that offers a glimpse of Hagrid's Hut from the queue. Don't expect more than a 1-minute figure eight with slight banking. The line is often exposed to the sun and the back seats feel the fastest. The long-legged should cross their ankles to fit more comfortably.

THE LOST CONTINENT

The gist of the next island, the Lost Continent, is amorphous. Think of it as part Africa, part Asia, part Rome—anything exotic wrapped up in vagueness. It's being whittled away as Harry Potter grows.

The Eighth Voyage of Sindbad Stunt Show ★★ SHOW Mounted a precious few times each day in an open-air stadium, usually in the afternoon (curtain times are marked on your map), it's fine for a stunt show, but it won't rock your world. You probably already suspect what you're getting here—a corny 20-minute, sound-effect enhanced banquet of macho men sword fighting and leaping in the pursuit of rescuing a princess who, it turns out, may or may not require male assistance after all. Buckles are swashed and cultural references are dropped like anvils. The climax, in which a man is lit on fire and plunges 30 feet into a pit, may alarm kids, but the production values are strong. **Strategy:** Attend this show if you'd like to sit for a while. Your IOA experience won't be lacking if you skip it.

Mystic Fountain ★★★ ACTIVITY Stop by briefly. If it's merely gurgling with recorded sound effects, all is quiet. But when least expected, it comes to life with wisecracks and sprays. Someone in an unseen booth interacts with anyone foolish enough to wander near—usually naïve children. As "Time" magazine put it when the park opened in 1999, the fountain exasperates with "the droll sarcasm of a bachelor uncle roped into caring for some itchy 10-year-olds." If you don't want to get doused, check the ground for slick spots to determine the fountain's spitting reach.

Poseidon's Fury ★★★ SHOW Despite its lowly status as a walk-through attraction, it has a stunning exterior, carved within a millimeter of reason to look like a crumbling temple. Young folk might be freaked out by the dark and the fireballs. Mature folk might disdain the vapid storyline involving a row between Poseidon and Lord Darkenon (who?). But it bemuses with an interesting (if fleeting) "water vortex" tunnel and some of its other special effects, such as walls that seem to vanish, are diverting. Like Sindbad, it's boisterous and pyrotechnic, **Strategy:** For the best views, head for the front of every room, especially the third one.

SEUSS LANDING

Nowhere other than Harry Potter is IOA's extravagance on finer display than this 10-acre section, which replicates the good Doctor's two-dimensional bluster with three-dimensional exactitude. Just try to find a straight line. From the lakefront, you can get a good look at what the designers accomplished. Notice how even the palm trees twist. They were knocked sideways near Miami in 1992's Hurricane Andrew, and because palm trees always grow upward, by the time they were scouted for IOA, they had acquired a perfectly loopy angle. Scout for hidden gags. Sprinkled around are

Horton's Egg and, by the sea, the two Zaxes, which appropriate to their own book (a commentary on political rivalry in which they stubbornly face off while a city grows up around them), were the very first things placed in the park, and everything else was built around them. The area around the Mulberry Street Store hosts regular appearances by the Cat in the Hat and the Grinch, who looks as annoyed to be there as you might imagine.

High in the Sky Seuss Trolley Train Ride! ★★★ RIDE   Everything on this island is appropriate for kids. The railway threading overhead is a cheerful family-friendly glide, narrated in verse. Like Dueling Dragons, there are two paths. The purple line surveys more of the area than the green line, which dawdles above the Circus McGurkus Cafe. The ride takes about 3 minutes and because there's so much to take in, time flies fast. You have to line up all over again if you want to do the other track.

Caro-Seuss-el ★★★ RIDE   Its bobbing menagerie of otherworldly critters actually reacts to being ridden—ears wiggle, heads turn, snouts rise—making it delightfully over-the-top and appealing to kids who sniff at girly carousels. Beside the Caro-Seuss-el, seek out the quick but trenchant walk-through grove of Truffula Trees retelling Dr. Seuss' environmental warning tale, the **Street of the Lifted Lorax.**

One Fish, Two Fish, Red Fish, Blue Fish ★★★ RIDE   Here we have another iteration (albeit a good one) of Disney's tot bait, Dumbo. Riders (two passengers per car normally, three if one of them loves the Wiggles) go around, up, and down by their own controls while a gauntlet of spitting fish pegs them from the sides—listen to the song for the secret of how to avoid getting wet, although the advice isn't foolproof. There are benches good for watching little kids giggle malevolently when their parents get spritzed.

If I Ran the Zoo ★★★ ACTIVITY   Getting wet is part of the bargain, so there's a rack to keep shoes dry. The interactive playground for young children contains some 20 tricksy elements. Let your brood slide, splash in a stream, turn cranks, and play Tic Tac Toe on characters' bellies. Beware the cheeky fountain—it pays to follow all posted instructions in Seuss Landing. Thanks, Universal, for the hand sanitizer dispensers by the exit.

The Cat in the Hat ★★★ RIDE   Take a nonthreatening excursion through the plot of the famous storybook as viewed from slow-moving mobile "couches" (really a typical flat-ride car). The design racks up points for replicating the look of the beloved children's book with precision, even in three dimensions. The story is just as faithfully retold; it's clear from this sweet, 3½-minute ride that the family of Dr. Seuss (Theodor Geisel) had a strong influence in steering the execution of this section of the park. Parents will probably emerge feeling glad they tagged along. The gift shop after the offload platform is among the best in the park—Universal's red Thing 1 and Thing 2 shirts ($22) are as ubiquitous as Mouse ears. **Tip:** The vehicles spin a few too many times for some adults (kids don't seem to mind), but you can ask to have it turned off when you board.

WHERE TO EAT IN ISLANDS OF ADVENTURE

If the park closes at 6pm (like it does outside the summer and holidays), many restaurants will only be open from 11am to 4pm. But remember that **CityWalk** (p. 153) is a 5-minute walk from the park, so you can easily consider those places, too.

In addition to the random snack carts there's no use in listing here, there are counter-service and sit-down restaurants (including carts selling goliath turkey legs for $11) in the park. None require reservations the way Disney's do. Kids' meals all come in under 300 calories. **Tip:** Menu items do not *have* to be served with sides. The potato chip bags served with the posted meals hold a mere 1⅞ ounces. Subtract them, or fries, from your meal combos to save about $2. Cups good for unlimited refills at touchscreen Coke Freestyle machines, which mix soda to order using 126 flavors, cost $11 and are good for the day.

Croissant Moon Bakery ★ SANDWICHES Lighter bites such as sandwiches and panini (with potato salad and fresh fruit), plus pastries such as cream horns and vanilla eclairs, can be snagged without much of a line. Nearby is the **Last Chance Fruit Stand** cart, which sells fruit cups ($3.40). Port of Entry. Sandwiches $9; soup and salad $6.20.

Confisco Grille ★ INTERNATIONAL One of only two table-service locations in the park, the menu has an identity crisis—wood-oven pizzas, pad Thai, penne puttanesca, Tex-Mex wraps, hummus—but that also means there is probably something for everyone in your group. The attached **Backwater Bar,** overlooked by nearly everyone and therefore ideal for sundowners, does happy hour from 4 to 7pm (3–5pm in winter), when well drinks are just $4. Port of Entry. Main courses $10 to $14.

Captain America Diner ★ AMERICAN This indoor counter-service location serves the usual burgers and chicken. Outside you'll find a **fruit stand** where pieces of whole fruit cost $1.30. Marvel Super Hero Island. Main courses $7 to $10 with fries.

Cafe 4 ★ PIZZA Counter service with indoor seating for grabbing pasta as well as pizza by the slice or by the pie. Marvel Super Hero Island. Slices $5.50 to $7, pasta $7 to $9, pies $29 to $32.

Blondie's ★★ SANDWICHES If you know that Dagwood is another name for a hero, you'll know who Blondie is, too. This indoor counter location does subs served with pickles and potato salad. It usually closes after lunch. Toon Lagoon. Mains $9.

Comic Strip Cafe ★★ INTERNATIONAL Toon Lagoon's largest counter-service location offers four schools of food: burgers and dogs, pizza and pasta, Chinese, and fish and chicken. There's more indoor seating here than anywhere else in this island. Toon Lagoon. Main courses $7 to $9.

Wimpy's ★ AMERICAN It's the stand that furnishes its namesake's obsession (hamburgers), although the staff will not permit you to pay next Tuesday for a hamburger today, mostly because it opens only when the park is packed. Toon Lagoon. Main courses $7 to $9.

The Burger Digs ★ AMERICAN The Discovery Center's indoor counter-service spot is upstairs, across from the dinosaur-theme toy store. Guess what it makes? There's a toppings bar, so you can load up, and to make it easier, it serves double cheeseburgers that you can convert into two meals with a second bun ($1). Jurassic Park Discovery Center. Combo meal $7 to $10.

Pizza Predattoria ★ AMERICAN The menu is small but big on calories: pizzas, meatball subs, and chicken Caesar salad. It's counter service with outdoor seating. Jurassic Park. Meals $7 to $10.

Thunder Falls Terrace ★★★ BARBECUE Watch the Jurassic Park boats splash down in the comfort of AC while noshing on food that's a cut above the rest: chargrilled ribs served with whole unhusked ears of corn, rotisserie chicken, and bacon cheeseburgers. Soups are just $3.50. Jurassic Park. Meals $10 to $15.

The Watering Hole ★★ BAR Cocktails are served al fresco from this kiosk, which throws a happy hour from 3 to 7pm (3–5pm in winter) and 20 ounces of beer costs $3.50. Jurassic Park. Cocktails mostly $6 to $7.

Three Broomsticks ★★★ BARBECUE/BRITISH The film tavern was gorgeously re-created, up to its wonky cathedral ceiling and down to the graffiti scratched in the timbers, as the only restaurant in this island, and the filmmakers reportedly liked the design so much they featured the set more prominently in later movies. The Great Feast feeds four for $50 with salad, rotisserie chicken, spareribs, corn on the cob, and roast potatoes. You can also go a la carte with shepherd's pie, fish and chips, Cornish pasties with salad. **Hog's Head Pub** ★★★ is attached. Under the squinty gaze of a grunting mounted boar's head (it responds to tips), a selection of truly British quaffs (London Pride, Newcastle Brown, Strongbow cider) is pulled. There are two more beers of note: One is Hog's Head ale, an only-here beer made by the Florida Brewing Company, and the other is Butterbeer, so if the line is long at the keg carts outside, you can grab a faster fix in here, where it's cool in more ways than one. (They won't spike it with rum. I've asked.) There's no happy hour here. Wizarding World of Harry Potter. Meals $8 to $14.

Mythos Restaurant ★★★ INTERNATIONAL Mythos' cavelike interior, carved from that ubiquitous orange-hued fake rock that scientists should term Orlando Schist, commands a marvelous view of the lagoon (go around to the water, where few guests wander, to see the god holding the place up with his bare hands). You could sit and watch the Incredible Hulk Coaster fire all day from this subdued environment. Food many rungs higher man most theme park stuff, with pad Thai, wild mushroom meatloaf, pan seared mahimahi, and a risotto of the day, plus a healthy slate of sandwiches and salads. The Lost Continent. Reservations recommended. ⓒ **407/224-4534.** Main courses $11 to $20.

Fire-Eaters' Grill ★ INTERNATIONAL Outdoor-only counter service with the usual suspects: chicken fingers, Italian sausage, and gyros. The Lost Continent. Main courses $7 to $9.

Green Eggs & Ham Café ★ AMERICAN You can't miss it—it's the house-size slab of ham with a giant fork stuck into it. It sells burgers and, of course, sandwiches made of green eggs and ham ($7–$8), but it's rarely open unless it's super crowded, which is a shame. Seuss Landing. Main courses $8.

Circus McGurkus Cafe Stoo-pendous ★★★ AMERICAN Looking like a circus tent coated in cake frosting, it serves the usual burgers and pizzas, leavened with spaghetti and meatballs; chicken Caesar salad; and a fried chicken platter with mashed potatoes and corn on the cob so there's something for everyone. For dessert, the **Moose Juice Goose Juice** stand nearby sells Moose Juice (a tart orange mix) and Goose Juice (watermelon or grape) for $4.25. Meals $8.50 to $11.

SEAWORLD ORLANDO

The second mighty theme park chain to set up shop in town, after Disney, was **SeaWorld Orlando** ★★★ (Central Florida Pkwy., at International Dr., or exit 71 and 72 east of I-4; ⓒ **800/327-2424** or 407/351-3600; www.seaworldorlando.com; adults $92, kids 3–9 $84; Parking $15; open 9am–7pm with extended hours in peak season), which began in San Diego in 1964 and opened in Orlando in 1973, scarcely 2 years

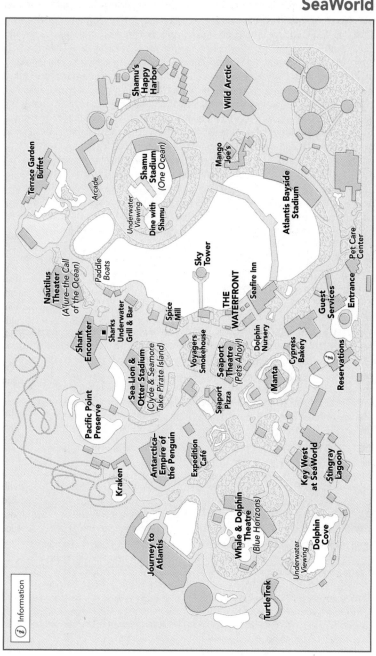

Shamu's Happy Harbor

Wild Arctic

Terrace Garden Buffet

Arcade

Mango Joe's

Shamu Stadium (One Ocean)

Underwater Viewing

Dine with Shamu

Atlantis Bayside Stadium

Pet Care Center

Sky Tower

Nautilus Theater (A'lure-the Call of the Ocean)

Paddle Boats

Seafire Inn

THE WATERFRONT

Spice Mill

Entrance

Shark Encounter

Sharks Underwater Grill & Bar

Voyagers Smokehouse

Dolphin Nursery

Guest Services

Sea Lion & Otter Stadium (Clyde & Seamore Take Pirate Island)

Seaport Theatre (Pets Ahoy!)

Cypress Bakery

Pacific Point Preserve

Seaport Pizza

Manta

i Reservations

Antarctica-Empire of the Penguin

Expedition Café

Key West at SeaWorld

Stingray Lagoon

Kraken

Journey to Atlantis

Whale & Dolphin Theatre (Blue Horizons)

Dolphin Cove

Underwater Viewing

TurtleTrek

i Information

after the Magic Kingdom. Although SeaWorld operates three American parks (the third is in San Antonio), its Orlando location has undoubtedly risen to become its most important. The Florida compound has an additional luxury theme park, **Discovery Cove** (p. 132), and a new water slide park, **Aquatica** (p. 132). SeaWorld is now the city's third genuine multiday theme park destination, after Disney and Universal.

At SeaWorld, the focus isn't on thrill rides or "magic"—it's animals, and thousands of them. Just about everything to see or do involves watching marine creatures in their habitats or performing in shows. Many tourists, particularly those over a certain age, claim SeaWorld as their favorite Orlando park, because there's a lot going for it: 200 acres of space for gardens, a compound that absorbs crowds well, an earnest educational component, a variety of animal exhibits that ensures guests won't have the same experience twice, and a refreshing lack of patronizing mythology.

The SeaWorld experience differs from most other parks in more important ways: It's **show-based.** Your day here will revolve around the scheduling of a half-dozen regular performances in which animals (mostly mammals, but some birds, too) do tricks— except here, they're called "behaviors"—with their human trainers. Although there are rides, they're not in the true spirit of the place. SeaWorld's banner attraction is the Shamu show, and when you're not watching killer whales do back-flips, you're ambling through habitats stocked with other beautiful creatures. Whereas a day spent at Islands of Adventure or the Magic Kingdom might send you slumping home and reaching for the Calgon, it's unusual to come away from SeaWorld stressed. Thoughtfully, **schedules are posted online** a few weeks ahead of time so that if you're really anal, you can map out your day in advance; the various show schedules are under "Park Info."

TIMING YOUR VISIT   You will spend quite a bit of time waiting for shows to begin. People show up early for seats, so it's smart to arrive at least 30 minutes ahead of show times. (It's also imperative that you wear a watch.) **Important:** If the forecast shows prolonged rain (as opposed to Florida's typical spot showers), reschedule your visit here. Not only will you spend lots of time walking outside, but it's also harder to see marine animals when the surface of the water is pelted by raindrops—not to mention the fact that if there's so much as a twinkle of lightning anywhere in the county, these water-based attractions close faster than a shark's mouth on his dinner.

GETTING ORIENTED   Once you park ($15, and more expensive "premium" spots aren't worth it) or get off the I-Ride (the stop is near the front gates), head for the lighthouse that marks the entrance. Inside, grab a placemat-size park map. On the

---

Hook the Trainers

To get the most out of a visit, try to be in the same place as the animal trainers, who frequently appear to nurture their charges. Ask questions. Get involved. They may even allow you to feed or stroke the animals (set aside another $25 or so for fish feed). These zoologists love sharing information about the animals they have devoted their lives to, and in Orlando, it's rare that theme park guests are encouraged to be anything other than passive participants. Feeding times are usually posted outside each pavilion's entrance; you may need to backtrack a few times to make the schedule, but the interaction will be worth the effort.

back, printed fresh daily, is the **show schedule,** plus the opening times of all the restaurants and attractions. Shows usually begin an hour after park opening, and the blockbuster Shamu show, "One Ocean," has only a few presentations. I always prefer the last one because it's less crowded. On the off chance there's a space for a special interaction you'd like to do, the Guest Services and Reservations desk is the place to book. Otherwise, the Cape Cod–style entrance plaza is where you do the necessaries such as rent strollers and lockers. The area is really just a warm-up for the rest of the park

The pathways are lined with the odd animal enclosure—flamingoes here, turtles there—but those are really more like landscaping features than attractions, and some aren't listed on the maps, so poke around. If you're interested in riding the park's thrill rides, the best time is when the Shamu show is scheduled, as it soaks up hundreds of people at once.

The Best Shows

Feel free to be choosy about the shows you see, because if you load your plate with too many, you'll spend most of your in-between time hoofing it between amphitheaters—yet spreading SeaWorld over 2 days would be a bit much.

One Ocean ★★★ SHOW When the orcas start to fly, the crowd comes alive. Closed-circuit TV cameras capture and display the spectacle on four huge rotating screens as the animals thunder dauntingly through the water's surface, pointedly deluging entire seating sections in 52-degree water. It's quite a scene. The 25-minute show occurs on such a scale as to make it required viewing. Now that trainers are no longer permitted to swim with the orcas, there's lots of downtime during which loud, recorded rock music plays and the whales are nowhere in sight. Trainers fill the gaps with weak Temptations-style choreography and quasi-inspirational scripted gibberish ("Pass the word from generation to generation: A bright and beautiful future is in our hands…"). But you instantly forget about the flaws when the animals reappear to leap skyward and belly flop back into their tank. The stadium, which fits 5,000 and still fills early, is covered, but the sides may catch sun, so arrive at least 30 minutes early. **Strategy:** Soak zone seats offer excellent views of the animals hurtling through the 2.5 million-gallon, 36-feet-deep tank, and in case the splashes miss you, the dozens of fountain jets will finish the job. Seats near the shelflike front platform will also have a close-up view of a killer whale out of the water. Seats at the back of the stadium, higher than the central aisle, must rely on the TV cameras to make out what's going on underwater. Shamu Stadium.

Do try to be at shows at least a **half-hour early,** and for Shamu, add another 10 minutes to walk around the lagoon to the stadium. SeaWorld is not as controlling as—Disney about where you're permitted to sit, so the best seats go first. Furthermore, several shows ("Pets Ahoy!" especially) don't permit latecomers. At others, you can't get out easily until it's over.

Three of the shows—"One Ocean," "Blue Horizons," and "Clyde and Seamore"—have a clearly marked **"soak zone"** in the front rows of the seating section. Bank on the first 10 rows as being the wettest. Don't take this warning lightly; you have no concept of how much water a 10,000-pound male orca can displace. Of course, sitting with your kids in the soak zone on a hot day is one of the great pleasures of SeaWorld, and most soak zone seating has the added advantage of affording side views into the tank where the animals prepare for their leaps and splashes. But for those with expensive hairdos, ponchos are sold throughout the parks, including at stalls beneath Shamu Stadium, for $8 ($6 kids). Keep your electronics somewhere dry, because salt water can fry their circuits.

Clyde & Seamore Take Pirate Island ★★ SHOW Imagine a prototypical sea lion act: cheesy, anthropomorphic (sea lions doing double takes, saluting, and pretending to be choked by exasperated human companions), and slapstick. That's this cute 25-minute presentation. The good-natured silliness ensures its standing as one of SeaWorld's most cherished shows. Kids particularly enjoy it, especially when the impossibly blubbery walrus oozes its way into the mayhem. **Strategy:** The worst seats are to the left as you face the stage (they have partial views), and the best are to the right, by the stone bridge. Sea Lion & Otter Theater.

Blue Horizons ★ SHOW This bizarre spectacle about a little girl who "wants to explore the realms beyond imagination," whatever that means, somehow makes for a transfixing and very worthwhile 25-minute show. New Age poppycock makes it more like an acid trip at a carnival than anything else, which lends itself to loosely connected (but excellent nonetheless) stunts starring dolphins, parrots, a condor, and plenty of human acrobats hooked up to bungee cords and diving off high platforms. There's always something to see, and little to comprehend. Think of it as "Shark du Soleil." Dolphin Theater.

Pets Ahoy! ★★★ SHOW Under-5s lose their minds at this indoor show, and you may, too—it's the show most worth seeing repeatedly. Although the furry cast is a deviation from SeaWorld's usual finny ones, the tricks are no less entrancing. A menagerie of common animals (cats, dogs, pigs, ducks, a skunk), most rescued from animal shelters, do simple tricks, and independently trigger tickling surprises on a rigged wharfside set. As the supercute gags multiply and compound in rapid succession (dachshunds pour out of a hot dog cart, a cat chases a white mouse in and out of hatches), and as more creatures are added into the mix precisely on cue, the amusement escalates. There's nearly no dialogue for its 20-minute run time. Afterward, trainers will allow kids to pet some of the performers. **Strategy:** It's fun to sit under the catwalk (literally—cats walk on it) over the aisle between the first and second sections. This 850-seat theater fills well in advance of showtimes. Seaport Theater.

A'Lure: The Call of the Ocean ★ SHOW   You mustn't feel bad if you miss this wordless, animal-free revue of arty human performance (trampolines, tumbling, caterwauling). The plot—something about an enchantress jealous of a stud-muffin fisherman—is as insubstantial as the bubbles that pour from the ceiling. It's mostly an opportunity to get into the air-conditioning. Nautilus Theater.

The Rest of the Park

Dolphin Nursery ★★★ ACTIVITY   Near the entrance plaza, the young mammals are kept with their mothers for the first few years of their lives before graduating to the larger Dolphin Cove elsewhere in the park. Much of the day, human trainers can be found here, feeding the adolescent animals and getting them acclimated to human interaction.

Key West at SeaWorld ★ ACTIVITY   A sorta-reproduction of Front Street in the southernmost city in Florida features the **Stingray Lagoon,** a pool where you can lean over and feel the spongy fish. You can buy food to feed the rays for $5 per tray, two for $9, or three for $13.

Dolphin Cove ★★★ ACTIVITY   Feeding times for the bottlenose dolphins (the schedule is posted) are regimented and crowded. It costs $7 for three fish, and interested parties must collect in a zone near the feeding area, to the right as you reach the tank. Around feeding times, dolphins congregate at the trainers' dock, which can make seeing them from other parts of the tank difficult, so if you won't be feeding them, come between meals for a better look. Walk around the far side of the tank, and you'll find a little-used underwater viewing area where you can hear the echolocative clicking through underwater microphones.

TurtleTrek ★★ ACTIVITY/FILM   A circuitous entrance ramp brings you to a popular air-conditioned underwater viewing area for 1,500 Caribbean fish and sea turtles the size of coffee tables. If you look closely, you can tell which turtles are rescues—one lost her lower jaw from a fishing net, another gave a flipper to a shark near Bermuda. In the freshwater tank, much attention is paid to the manatee's status as

---

Ethical Entertainment?

Some conservationists say that SeaWorld's animals endure misery in captivity. Other conservationists laud SeaWorld for being an advocate for marine life. And therein lines the essential tug-of-war over this profit-generating amusement park. SeaWorld is extremely sensitive to accusations of mistreatment and exploitation—in 2013, the low-budget documentary "Blackfish" asserted that the 2010 death of its senior trainer Dawn Brancheau, which was witnessed by an audience of tourists at Shamu Stadium, was the result of inadequate care. SeaWorld took the unusual step of sharply rebutting some of the points, and by way of underscoring its standards, it has repeatedly said it has not captured (or as it puts it, "collected") killer whales from the wild since the mid-'70s and dolphins since 1969. Excepting a few aged animals that were born in the seas and rehabilitated from accidents in the wild, most of the park's animals were born in captivity and raised by hand, and so, SeaWorld says, they would not know how to survive in the wild. The park says it has rescued some 22,000 animals to date.

one of America's most endangered animals, and, in fact, the sluggish creatures on display here were all rescued from the wild, where hot-dogging boaters are decimating their numbers. You'll be herded into a domed room where a (rather poorly) computer-animated 3-D film traces the life cycle of a sea turtle from its point of view. It's hard not to notice that 7-minute story hits the same beats as "Finding Nemo" (jellyfish fields, marauding birds, sharks prowling a shipwreck). You might be better off staying longer in front of the tank, where the view is more authentic.

Manta ★★★ RIDE   Rising above the park is SeaWorld's thrill-ride pride, a "flying coaster" ridden face-down and head-first, in a horizontal position. You board sitting upright, and after your shoulders and ankles are secured, you're tipped forward and the train is dispatched over curious pedestrians for the 2½-minute ride. The queue meaders through 10 aquaria containing cownose rays, spotted eaglerays, and octopi behind floor-to-ceiling windows, so you get a dose of sea life while you wait. Even nonriders can see rays through a separate entrance to the right of the ride's line. As riders swoop around, "wings" on the cars appear to clip the water underneath them, triggering splashes. Speeds approach 60mph, with four inversions, in a fanciful approximation of what it feels like for a manta ray to swim. Manta is a pretty unique coaster experience, and it's solid fun. **Tip:** Because you're in "flying" position, no seat has an obstructed view.

The Kraken End of the Park

Journey to Atlantis ★★ RIDE   On this 6-minute flume-cum-coaster ride (you can't see the brief coaster section from the front), getting drenched is unavoidable, as the 60-foot drop should warn. Riding isn't its only pleasure—it's fun to douse passing boats with coin-operated water cannons, too (Number 4 does the most damage to the unsuspecting). Atlantis is oddball. First you pass through a few rooms as if you're on a family-friendly dark ride (the robotics aren't great), and then one of the spirits turns against you sending you down the hill you saw outside, and finally the water gives way and your boat becomes, briefly, a roller-coaster car that escapes the evil sprite with no upside-down moments but yet another splashdown. Besides the drenching you can see from outside, there are a few other lap soakers and delightfully nasty splashbacks—ideal for hot days. **Strategy:** Front seats get wettest. Try to balance the weight; otherwise you'll list disconcertingly. Keep stuff dry in a nearby locker (50¢), and leave it there when you ride Kraken next door. Ponchos are sold nearby for $8; $6 for kids.

Kraken ★★★ RIDE   Take a 2-minute dose of testosterone. After you settle into your pedestal-like seat, the floor is retracted, leaving your legs to dangle while you undergo seven upside-down "inversions" of one sort or another. The coaster, which hits 65mph and drops 144 feet on its first breath-stealing hill, traces the shoreline of a pond behind the loading area and dives below ground level three times. **Strategy:** If you'd like to wait for a front seat, there's a special, longer line for it. Because it's floorless, you can't ride with flip-flops, but you may leave shoes on the loading dock and go barefoot (if you do that in the front row, which I recommend, you'll feel like you're about to lose a foot in the rails).

Antarctica ★★ ACTIVITY/RIDE   SeaWorld's 2013 addition is this 4-acre, iceberg-styled pavilion dedicated to penguins. Go through the exit to simply view the colony of 245 Gentoo, Rockhopper, Adélie, and King penguins, first in a human-temperature room with a fascinating underwater viewing of the little birds zipping around underwater, and then, if you want, from a 30-degree area where they waddle helplessly on

Parking: $15	**ECV:** $45 per day
Single strollers: $14 per day	**Lockers:** $7 (small) or $10 (large) per day
Double strollers: $19 per day	**Coke:** $2.70 / **Bottle of water:** $2.80 /
Wheelchair: $12 per day	**Cup of beer:** $6.50

dry land. The ride, should you choose to try it out, takes you to the habitat in the reverse order. It's based on some cool trackless technology that allows cars, which will remind you of air hockey pucks, to roam the same room, even cross paths. Choose "Wild" or "Mild," although the wild version isn't much more intense than a few light spins and bucks. As rides go, it's fairly pointless, but it is unique. Don't confuse this exhibition with Wild Arctic, which contains the beluga whales and polar bears.

Pacific Point Preserve ★★★ ACTIVITY   Like Dolphin Cove, Pacific Point is an open-air, rocky habitat that encourages feedings, but here the residents are incessantly barking Californian sea lions and a few demure seals. There's a narrow moat between the tank and the walkway, but you're encouraged to lean over and toss the doglike animals fresh fish, which are sold for $5 per tray, $20 for five. The area gets busy around Clyde and Seamore showtimes at the neighboring Sea Lion & Otter Theater.

Shark Encounter ★★★ ACTIVITY   The onetime Terrors of the Deep was given a more responsible name to further rehabilitate the public image of the much-maligned creatures within. It's one of the better exhibitions, with 60-foot acrylic tubes passing through 300,000 gallons of water stocked with sharks—the crowds are ushered along via moving sidewalks. Too many tourists scamper quickly through the smaller tanks before that dazzling main event, but they're missing some beautiful stuff, including barracuda, moray eels, lionfish, and the awesome leafy sea dragon, which looks for all the world like a floating clump of seaweed. Don't ignore the shallow tank in front of the building, as that's where the smaller species are kept. There, you can feed the fish for $5 a tray, two for $9, three for $13, and five for $20.

The Waterfront at SeaWorld

Sky Tower ★★★ OBSERVATION RIDE   Jutting above the lagoon—and topped to still-greater heights by a colossal American flag—is the 400-foot, old-fashioned "Wheel-o-vater" (that's what its interior label says) that rotates as it climbs 300 feet for a panorama. At the top, it slowly spins for two or three revolutions, giving you a good look around, before lowering you back to the Waterfront at the end of 6 minutes. You can point out the landmarks, including Spaceship Earth and the skyscrapers of downtown.

Shamu Stadium ★ ACTIVITY   The home to One Ocean still has something to offer outside of show time. A few of the killer whales are visible in the **underwater viewing** area that surveys one of their holding pods. Above the surface of that pen, the Dine with Shamu supper (p. 130) is held, separated by cargo netting from the water (reserve several weeks ahead).

Shamu's Happy Harbor ★★ ACTIVITY   Around the back of Shamu Stadium, kids have their own dedicated amusement area—and they get more rides than the grown-ups! The most obvious feature is the four-story cargo-net playground, but there are some and mild carnival-style rides: an underwater-themed **Sea Carousel ★** topped by a 45-foot-wide pink octopus; a swinging-and-twirling tracked boat ride, **Ocean Commotion ★**; and the **Flying Fiddler ★★**, a bench that lifts kids 20 feet above the ground and then gently brings them back down in a series of short drops. Those rides join an 800-foot kiddie coaster with trains shaped like you-know-who (**Shamu Express ★★**), a four-story playground with slides and nets, a ride with spinning cars attached to a stalk (**Jazzy Jellies ★**), a pirate ship (**Wahoo Two ★★★**) with a few water blasters, and a teacup-style ride (**Swishy Fishies ★★★**). The size of the play area is as big or bigger than anything the other parks have.

The Shamu End of the Park

Wild Arctic ★★ ACTIVITY/RIDE One of SeaWorld's most interesting exhibitions deserves more than it gets: marooned here, at the Nowhereseville end of the park, when the only time it seems crowded is a half-hour after every Shamu showtime. As with Antarctica (which is different and has the penguins) there are two ways to get in. Either you opt for the motion-simulator ride that re-creates a turbulent 5-minute helicopter ride (well done for such an old ride, but its bumpiness makes me ill), or you much more quickly make straight for the swimmers after a short movie. After that, you can walk through at your own pace, enjoying first a surface view and then an underwater look at the Pacific walruses, polar bears (you won't see much—they sleep 16–18 hr. a day), and the parks' utterly beautiful white beluga whales, which look like swimming porcelain. There's probably more than a half-hour's worth of investigation here, including mock-ups of a polar research station and a fake "bear den" for young kids to explore. You'll also find it *very* cool, which makes it a blockbuster on hot days.

Where to Eat at SeaWorld

When it was sold by Anheuser-Busch in 2009, SeaWorld lost its famous edge in food quality among Orlando parks. Prices are in line with everyone else's: $10 a meal, before a drink, is standard across the board. Most places to eat are clustered in the center of the park between the Waterfront and Kraken. All-you-can-eat food passes (one entree excluding baby back ribs, one side or dessert, one nonalcoholic drink excluding Naked Juice each time through line) cost $33 for adults and $18 for kids; they're good at six of the counter-service locations.

Disney World has its Mouse-ear ice-cream bar, but at SeaWorld, you'll be served a variety shaped like Shamu ($3.60). Plastic drinking straws could choke the aquatic animals, so you don't get one. If you must have a straw, the $9 souvenir cups have them built in, and they grant $1 refills. More interesting are the Coca-Cola Freestyle fountains, which are touchscreen machines that allow you to blend your own brew from a range of 126 Coke flavors. Cups cost $10 and each time you refill it ($1), sensors inform you how much energy you saved by not using another cup. There's also a Mr. Potato Head–style, customizable Tourist Penguin version ($16) sold at Antarctica. Beers cost $6.50 a cup.

In case you were wondering, SeaWorld only serves sustainable seafood. There are also always vegetarian options.

The headline meal event is **Dine with Shamu ★★**, which is served from noon to 2pm and from 4:30 to 6:30pm alongside the orca pools with the narration of some trainers. Prices fluctuate by the day, but $29 for adults and $19 for kids is a common rate. That's not bad for the experience of being near one of these massive creatures. It's important to book far ahead.

The newest counter-service location is **Expedition Café ★★★**, outside Antarctica, which, like the Antarctic Research Station, serves a wide range of food from many cultures: baked chicken, shrimp lo mein, gluten-free teriyaki chicken, spaghetti and meatballs, lasagna, and "iceberg chef" salad.

The **Terrace Garden Buffet ★**, past the Nautilus Theater, is the only all-you-can-eat buffet. It piles on pizza, pasta, salads, and dessert—nothing daring, no caloric regard. Buy a ticket for $15 adults, $10 kids at the kiosk outside. The other main restaurants serve high-quality food, too, but with less caloric regard. **The Seafire Inn ★★**, at the Waterfront, has some seating overlooking the lagoon and does fish and chips, Asian chicken stir-fry, Caesar salads, and Mediterranean veggie wraps. Farther up the Waterfront but with similar prices, the **Spice Mill Cafe ★★★** does stuff such as steak burgers, low-fat vegetarian chili, and grilled chicken salad, and it also has pretty water views. **Voyagers Smokehouse ★**, facing the Seaport Theatre's entrance, offers baby back ribs, spare ribs, and barbecue chicken, with a higher top price of $16.

Like Epcot's The Seas, the park devotes a section of an underwater viewing area to **Sharks Underwater Grill ★**, which is now one of the park's premier tables. It doesn't particularly specialize in seafood. Despite some cute touches, such as a bar that's also an aquarium and chairs that look like sharks' teeth, prices like $26 for tempura shrimp and $28 for grilled chicken risotto strike me as too high (although salads are $9). But if you can square that with the incredible view, give it a shot. Some tables are right against the glass, but I think I prefer the ones farther back, which have a wider view.

For snacks, I suggest the **Cypress Bakery ★★★**, near the entrance. The carrot cake ($3.50) is huge, fluffy, and arguably among the best you'll have anywhere. The parks employees are hooked on it. It also sells snacks for special diets.

SeaWorld participates in the gruesome Orlando tradition of huge roasted turkey legs. Find them for $9 at Seaport Market, near Seaport Pizza, Captain Pete's Island Eats in the Key West area, and at the Smugglers Feasts booth near Seafire Inn. At the Shamu end of the boardwalk, **Mango Joe's Cafe ★★** does a short menu of burritos and Southwest chicken salad.

Backstage Tours

As a place that prides itself on sharing conservation information—in fact, as a place that keeps animals on display, its reputation depends on it—**SeaWorld (© 800/327-2424;** www.seaworldorlando.com) has Exclusive Park Experiences that are less about touting its vaunted design team, as Disney's are, and more for learning about animal care. In fact, they're dubbed "interactions." Because interactions sell out, always reserve—it can be done online—but if you forget, there's a Behind-the-Scenes desk at the entry plaza of the park for last-minute arrangements. Interactions involving swimming include a wetsuit and equipment, and end with a private, hot shower. There are about a dozen to choose from, from an on-dry-land dolphin meet to a sea lion spotlight, but these two are probably the most unforgettable experiences.

Beluga Interaction Program ★★★ ACTIVITY Opportunities to squeeze into a wet suit and swim for 30 minutes in 55°F saltwater with the porcelain-white beluga whales simply don't come often. Participants don't have to be excellent swimmers, but they should be able to tread water, as they'll be maneuvering themselves in a deep tank to stroke and feed the gentle animals. Only about a half-hour is spent in the water; the rest of your visit, you'll become a pocket expert on belugas.

$119 per person, not including park admission. Minimum age 10. 90 min.

Marine Mammal Keeper Experience ★★★ ACTIVITY The *ne plus ultra* for a SeaWorld or animal fan starts at 6:30am and leads you through a typical day for an animal keeper. The schedule may include food preparation (get ready for fishy fingers); helping the Animal Rescue and Rehabilitation Team look after manatees; standing over the vets' shoulders as they heal sick animals; and helping trainers interact with and train dolphins, pilot whales, or belugas. This is no put-on for shuffling bus tours; you participate in the work the day calls for, and there's a limit of just three people. Many people who have done this swear that it's money better spent than a ticket to Discovery Cove; you'll get in the water to care for dolphins and manatees, but you won't grab onto their fins for any gimmicky "swims."

$399, including lunch, T-shirt, and park admission for a week. Minimum age 13. 9 hr.

SeaWorld's Other Parks

Aquatica SeaWorld's water slide park is across International Drive from its parent park (a free, 3-min. van ride links it), and you can pay for admission as an add on to your SeaWorld visit. While Typhoon Lagoon and Blizzard Beach are heavily themed, and Wet 'n Wild is tangled with bare-boned thrills, Aquatica is merely fresh and bright. It's a perfectly nice park, but the others have more tricks. The company entices tourists to swim with the fishes on the **Dolphin Plunge** slide, a tube that curls off a tower and then turns clear acrylic as it passes through a habitat for Commerson's dolphins. It looks exciting on paper, but in truth you're going too fast to see anything, even if the dolphins could be reliably near the tubes (they aren't) and there wasn't water splashing in your eyes (there is). There are 18 major slides, but because of duplications, only 7, including Dolphin Plunge, are really distinct experiences. The lazy river of **Loggerhead Lane** passes you by a big window into an aquarium. **Roa's Rapids** is novel in that it's a river with a very fast current meant to sweep your body along, without a tube. It's all fine, not scintillating, and bears the whiff of having been scaled down from something more notable. Aquatica does run with a smart, picnicky idea when it comes to meals: You can pay $15 adults, $10 kids for unlimited fare at the all-you-can-eat Banana Beach (chicken, pizza, hot dogs). Otherwise, Mango Market sells chicken tenders and sandwiches for the usual $10 per-meal price.

5800 Water Play Way, Orlando. ✆ **888/800-5447.** www.aquaticabyseaworld.com. Adults $55, kids 3–9 $50, online tickets $10 off, discounts for combination SeaWorld tickets, parking $12, $11 online.

Discovery Cove ★★★ THEME PARK The most expensive park in town (ticket prices shift by the season) was created and priced as an all-inclusive experience. Only around 1,000 people a day are admitted, guaranteeing this faux tropical idyll is not marred by a single queue. You can stop reading now if you don't want to get jealous—this is strictly a place for special occasions (or people spending strong foreign cash). Admission lanyards include breakfast, equipment rental, sunscreen, beer if you're of age, and unlimited lunch—a good one, too, such as fresh grilled tilapia (a fish that drew the short straw at SeaWorld, I guess). Discovery Cove, in fact, is more or less a free-range playground. When you arrive, first thing in the morning, you're greeted under a vaulted atrium more redolent of a five-star island resort than a theme park. Coffee is poured, and once you're checked in you're set loose to do as you wish. Wade from perfect white sand into **Serenity Bay,** feed fresh fruit to the houseguests at the **Explorer's Aviary** for tropical birds, snorkel with barbless rays over the trenches of **The Grand Reef,** swim to habitats for marmoset monkeys and otters in the **Freshwater Oasis,** or float with a pool noodle down the slow-floating **Wind-Away River,** which passes through waterfalls into the aviary, preventing the birds from escaping. Many

My great-grandfather was a professional photographer from Atlanta. When I was a boy, some of his favorite Kodachrome slides, shot in the 1950s, depicted a group of coquettish women water-skiing across a lake in a pyramid formation, balancing on each others' shoulders. They waved at the camera. What a bountiful place! This was **Cypress Gardens** an hour south of Orlando, which opened in 1936 and started the world thinking about Central Florida as the seat of a new kind of tourism. It's impossible to overestimate its effect on tourism. In 1963, it tied the Grand Canyon as America's number-one tourist attraction—the same year, Walt Disney came to scout for land of his own. The Shah of Iran and Elvis water-skied there, Johnny Carson and Mike Douglas shot show there—it lured generations of America to experience the languid junglelike land of parrots, alligators, and heavy orchids that was Florida. Distant Interstates and Disney siphoned away business, and Cypress Gardens became a honky-tonk carnival of cheap rides and country music concerts before failing outright. Legoland's European parks incorporate gardens, and its new Orlando property (see below) leases 30 acres what remained of the old gardens—and did away with the wandering Southern belles and the obsolete celebration of antebellum plantation life—but for a glimpse of what things were like in the glory days, see Esther Williams' jaw-dropping heli-water-ski production number in MGM's "Easy to Love" (1953).

guests elect to simply kick back on a lounger (there are plenty) on incredibly silky sand (imported, of course) at the natural-looking pool. Other than that, you read a book and relax. Since everyone wears free wetsuits or vests, there isn't much call for body shame or sunburned shoulders. When it's your turn—if you've paid extra—guests older than 5 can head to the **Dolphin Lagoon,** where in small groups of about eight you wade into the chilly water and meet one of the pod. Like children, dolphins have distinct personalities and must be carefully paired to people the trainers think they'll enjoy being with—many visitors don't realize that a dolphin can easily kill you, but many of these dolphins are docile, having dwelled at SeaWorld for decades. Here, the mostly hand-reared animals peer at you with a logician's eye while your trainer shows you basic hand signals. The climax of the 30-minute interaction is the moment when you grasp two of the creature's fins and it swims, you in tow, for about 30 feet. Naturally, a photographer is on hand for it all, so if you want images or video, you'll pay for that, too, pushing a day to $400. A second add-on experience, **SeaVenture** ($59, minimum age 10), places an air helmet on your head and brings you underwater to walk along the floor of The Grand Reef. Really, though, a day here is beyond divine.

6000 Discovery Cove Way, Orlando. ⓒ **877/557-7404.** www.discoverycove.com. $169–$269, including free admission to SeaWorld and Aquatica for 2 weeks, plus $60–$150 for 30-min. dolphin interaction. Daily 8am–5:30pm.

LEGOLAND FLORIDA

Legoland Florida ★★ (1 Legoland Way, Winter Haven; ⓒ **877/350-5346;** http://florida.legoland.com), a 2011 newcomer, is not just the youngest Central Florida theme park. It's also the oldest. That's because it took over the historic property of Cypress Gardens, a park for botanical gardens and water ski shows on the cypress

PAST THAT turnstile IN THE SKY

Not all of Orlando's attractions have thrived. Tupperware Museum, we miss you. Kindly remove your Mouse ears to honor the forgotten fun—if not for an accident of time, you'd be vacationing here instead:

- **Circus World (1974–86):** Started by Mattel as a walk-through museum dedicated to circus history (after all, most of the big top crews wintered in Florida), it collapsed under its own weight after competition with Disney tempted it into building too many rides. Also, clowns are scary.
- **Boardwalk Baseball (1987–90):** Textbook publisher Harcourt, Brace and Jovanovich recycled Circus World in the image of Florida's other winter tradition, baseball, and the Kansas City Royals were enticed to train there. Few cared. On January 17, 1990, 1,000 guests were asked to leave.
- **Xanadu (1983–96):** This walk-through "home of the future" was made by coating giant balloons with polyurethane—an early exercise in ergonomics. Sister homes in Gatlinburg and Wisconsin Dells were also built, but all outlived their curiosity value, and became, in fact, quick

homes of the past. You'll find the site near Mile Marker 12 of U.S. 192.

- **JungleLand Zoo (1995–2002):** The demise of this low-rent Gatorland rip-off was hastened in 1997 by news coverage after a lioness escaped from her enclosure and went missing among Kissimmee's motels for 3 days. A few trainers got nipped by the gators, too. Bad news.
- **Splendid China (1993–2003):** On 73 acres 3 miles west of Disney's main gate, China's wonders (the Forbidden City, a Great Wall segment containing 6.5 million bricks, and so on) were rebuilt in miniature. Who would blow $100 million on such a bad idea? The Chinese government, which pulled the strings.
- **River Country (1976–2005):** Disney's first water park, incorporated into Bay Lake beside the Fort Wilderness Resort, simply wasn't fancy enough or big enough to satisfy guests anymore. Another issue: It turns out that the *Naegleria fowleri* amoebae growing in many Florida lakes can kill you. (Guests may no longer swim in *any* of Disney's lakes. Coincidence?)

tree-lined shores of pretty Lake Eloise that helped put Orlando on modern tourist maps. This extremely kid-friendly, soothingly mellow 150-acre park 45 minutes south of Disney World is a godsend for parents who crave a breather from the mechanical and authoritarian environment of Disney World. No other Florida park caters so completely to kids aged 2 to 12. Everything here is designed for little ones, from easy-to-tackle versions of adult rides to ample wide spaces for play.

Get your bearings, and take in the stirring views of the lake, on the **Island in the Sky** observation wheel, which reaches into the sky on a metal arm. Other park highlights include **Lost Kingdom Adventure,** an indoor target practice game in the style of a Lego-bright Indiana Jones tomb; **Coastersaurus,** a mild out-and-back wooden roller coaster suitable for grammar school lightweights; **Driving School,** the

Ford-sponsored, trackless mini-auto course that teaches kids how to obey traffic rules; **Project X,** a wild mouse coaster perfectly set up for nonriders to take embarrassing shots of their loved ones faces as they hurtle downhill; **Safari Trek,** a wholly adorable car ride past wild African animals made of Legos; and **Royal Joust,** a mini steeple-chase-style plastic horse race for wee ones that just may be the cutest ride in the whole country. For a break from the excitement, the **Imagination Zone** as indoor Lego-building play zones and video game stations, and past that, a healthy portion of the carefully tended **Cypress Gardens Historic Botanical Garden** was preserved, complete with Spanish moss, cypress knees jutting from tannic water, old-growth banyans, and signs warning of alligators, which live in the lake. Suddenly, you remember Orlando is in Florida, which is sad, considering Florida made its tourist name by selling its natural wonders. For all that, and lots more like it, nothing competes with the fascination of **Miniland,** the sprawling tour de force display of Lego construction prowess that displays exceedingly clever versions of American cities and landmarks. The longer you linger, the more touches you see: a moving escalator in a mock-up Grand Central Station, a Space Shuttle misting during takeoff, dueling pirate ships, a mini "Star Wars" cantina, the Bellagio's burping fountain, and marching bands in front of the Capitol. If you like those gags, stick around for the **Pirates' Cover Live Water Ski Show,** which replaces Cypress Gardens' pyramids of Esther Williams–like maidens with ski-jumping socket-headed Minifugure toy people. The park knows some parents don't want to drive, so it offers $10 round-trip shuttles from Orlando Premium Outlets, east of Downtown Disney (© **877/350-5346**). Because it often closes in late afternoon, you should arrive near opening time (9am) to get the most out of your day.

Admission is $81 adults, $74 for kids aged 3 to 12; parking is $14 ($12 online). It's open daily in season, but closed Tuesday and Wednesday in the low season.

BUSCH GARDENS TAMPA

Seventy miles southwest of Disney, and just 8 miles northwest of Tampa, **Busch Gardens Tampa** ★★★ (3000 E. Busch Blvd., at 40th St.; © **888/800-5447;** www.buschgardens.com), dating to 1959, is a world-class theme park combining thrill rides with top-notch animal enclosures for gorillas, rhinos, and other rare creatures. Its roller coasters, including the vertical drop of SheiKra and the sidewinding launch coaster Cheetah Hunt, are considered more thrilling than the multigenerational rides of Orlando. Although the park is worth a day's attention, relatively few Americans make the journey to another city, partly because their limited vacation days force them to restrict their movements. International visitors favor it more strongly. The park knows that coaxing visitors from Orlando is a problem, so if you have a paid admission ticket to Busch Gardens, it grants free round-trip transportation from Orlando using **Shuttle Express** (© **800/221-1339**).

Admission to the park is $89 adults, $81 for kids 3 to 9. A 3 Park Unlimited Admission Ticket from SeaWorld also comes with a free round-trip bus ride from SeaWorld to Busch Gardens, and entry to both parks and Aquatica; it costs $149 adults and $141 kids when bought online. Busch Gardens also discounts its entry in the six-park version of the discounted Orlando FlexTicket (p. 234).

MORE ORLANDO ATTRACTIONS

When you're sick of parking trams and cattle-corral queues, it's time to divert yourself with something new. In many cases, something old—some of these places are among the original attractions that sowed the seeds enabling the area to become the fertile vacationland it is today. Some attractions are beautiful, some are downright silly, but when you're on vacation, anything goes.

INTERNATIONAL DRIVE

The attractions around International Drive aren't plush—midways and sideshows, mostly—but they are the stuff of a quintessential family holiday. I-Drive is also the only touristy area in Orlando where a car isn't necessary, not least because the I-Ride Trolley (p. 228) will tote you along, if you're tired of strolling.

CSI: The Experience ★★★ ACTIVITY   Scrutinizing a graphic murder scene: fun for the whole family! Turning tragedy into popcorn, this CBS-authorized whodunit turns you loose on one of three dioramas of slain corpses. You observe the details as closely as possible before taking your findings to a few touch-screen stations where you learn how investigators use forensics to find clues to crimes. Here's a sample line from one video, which features actors from the shows: "Ah, the smell of decaying flesh… It's an irresistible aroma to insects!" The satisfaction of solving the crime (it takes about 45 min.) may suit some visitors, although they may also have seen these facts addressed a hundred times in TV episodes. Still, the attraction's cheap convention-chair seating, Xeroxed handouts, and unadorned facilities make it seem like it could pull up stakes and skip town in an hour.

7220 International Dr., Orlando. ✆ **407/226-7220.** Orlando.CSIexhibit.com. $20 adults, $13 kids 6–11. Mon–Sat 10am–9pm, Sun 10am–8pm, last admission 45 min. before closing.

Fun Spot America ★ AMUSEMENT PARK   A recent recipient of immense investment and careful improvements, Fun Spot is Orlando's largest, cleanest, best-lit midway-style diversion. Although it became famous for its four Go-Kart tracks (concrete, multilevel; the Quad Helix's stacked figure-eight turns make it a favorite, but the Conquest's peaked ramp is a pip), the spacious grounds are also stocked with a two-level

Orlando Area Attractions

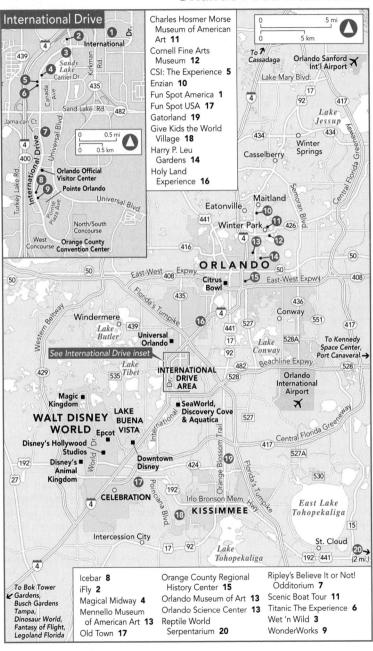

International Drive

Charles Hosmer Morse
Museum of American
Art **11**
Cornell Fine Arts
Museum **12**
CSI: The Experience **5**
Enzian **10**
Fun Spot America **1**
Fun Spot USA **17**
Gatorland **19**
Give Kids the World
Village **18**
Harry P. Leu
Gardens **14**
Holy Land
Experience **16**

International Drive
Sandy Lake
439
435
Carrier Dr.
Kirkman Rd.
Canada Ave.
Sand Lake Rd. 482
Jamaican Ct.
4
400
Turkey Lake Rd.
Universal Blvd.
International Drive
Pointe Plaza Ave.
Orlando Official
Visitor Center
Pointe Orlando
Universal Blvd.
North/South
Concourse
West
Concourse
Orange County
Convention Center

0   0.5 mi
0   0.5 km

To Cassadaga
Orlando Sanford
Int'l Airport
Lake Mary Blvd.
4
92
17
417
Lake
Jessup
434
434
Winter
Springs
Casselberry
Semoran Blvd.
Central Florida Greeneway

Maitland
Eatonville
441
Winter Park
426
4
13
12
10
11

ORLANDO
416
408
East-West Expwy.
50
Citrus
Bowl
15
East-West Expwy.
408
50
435
436
Conway
551
417
4
441
527
528A
To Kennedy
Space Center,
Port Canaveral
Lake
Conway
17
92
482
528
Beachline Expwy.
528
Orlando
International
Airport

Windermere
Lake
Butler
439
Universal
Orlando
16
See International Drive inset
Lake
Tibet
535
429
INTERNATIONAL
DRIVE
AREA
Western Beltway
Florida's Turnpike

Magic
Kingdom
WALT DISNEY
WORLD
LAKE
BUENA
VISTA
Epcot
Disney's Hollywood
Studios
192
Disney's
Animal
Kingdom
27
World Dr.
SeaWorld,
Discovery Cove
& Aquatica
International Dr.
527
Central Florida Greeneway
417
527A
530

Downtown
Disney
424
192
17
CELEBRATION
4
KISSIMMEE
18
19
Irlo Bronson Mem. Hwy.
Poinciana Blvd.
Orange Blossom Trail
Florida's Turnpike
East Lake
Tohopekaliga
15

Intercession City
17
92
Lake
Tohopekaliga
St. Cloud
192 441
20
(2 mi.)

4

To Bok Tower
Gardens,
Busch Gardens
Tampa,
Dinosaur World,
Fantasy of Flight,
Legoland Florida

0   5 mi
0   5 km

Icebar **8**
iFly **2**
Magical Midway **4**
Mennello Museum
of American Art **13**
Old Town **17**

Orange County Regional
History Center **15**
Orlando Museum of Art **13**
Orlando Science Center **13**
Reptile World
Serpentarium **20**

Ripley's Believe It or Not!
Odditorium **7**
Scenic Boat Tour **11**
Titanic The Experience **6**
Wet 'n Wild **3**
WonderWorks **9**

arcade, a scrambler, plenty of snack bars, a Ferris wheel (Charlize Theron rode it in "Monster"), and a devoted section of kiddie rides. Additions in a hefty 2013 expansion include **White Lightning,** a smooth-as-silk wood-frame coaster that goes out and back, and **Freedom Flyer,** a wee version of a hanging, foot-dangling train. The 250-foot-tall SkyCoaster is the second tallest of its kind (the first is at Fun Spot's lesser location east of Disney World, p. 146). Turn kids loose and take a breather.

5700 Fun Spot Way, Orlando. © **407/363-3867.** www.funspotattractions.com. Pay-per-ride $6–$9, unlimited ride armband $30–$40 based on height. Generally daily 10am–midnight.

iFly ★ ACTIVITY   Surprisingly, there seem to be as many hobby skydivers training in this vertical wind tunnel as there are curious out-of-towners. Visitors are strapped into jumpsuits and given a short training session on how to walk over the netting into the 125mph airflow—mastering the necessary arched-back, splay-legged posture can be tricky, but should you fail, there's a master diver with you to grab you by the sleeve and guide you into a series of adrenaline-fueled climbs and plunges. Or not—you can just hover there, if that's what floats your butt.

6805 Visitor Circle, Orlando. © **800/759-3861** or 407/903-1150. http://orlando.iflyworld.com. $60 for 2 1-minute flights. Daily 10am–10pm.

Magical Midway ★ AMUSEMENT PARK   A small concrete area, which by night blares rock music and heaves with idle youth, this is a classic amusement area built on adrenaline and rash decisions. The most obvious generator of regret is the world's tallest **Slingshot** ride ($25, not included on passes), a colossal fork strung with a pod. Two at a time sit inside, and are catapulted more than 200 feet into the sky, wailing to wake the dead. The 90-second adventure is so tense that it attracts concerned passersby. The circular swing ride, **Star Flyer,** is scarier than it looks because the restraints feel inadequate for the 230-foot height it achieves—flimsy restraints being a necessary component of carnival thrills. The rest of the small plot is dominated by two thunderous, wooden Go-Kart tracks (the Avalanche track has slightly steeper ramps than the Alpine), a few minor rides including cheerless bumper boats, and a dirty arcade thronged with kids. Its unsophisticated virtues are something 11-year-old boys (and vacation-worn parents) appreciate.

7001 International Dr., Orlando. © **407/370-5353.** www.magicalmidway.com. $7 Go-Kart rides, 3-hr. unlimited rides $25, all-day unlimited rides $32. Sun–Fri 2–10pm, Fri–Sat 2pm–midnight

Ripley's Believe It or Not! Odditorium ★ TOURIST MUSEUM   The ticketed equivalent of a forwarded e-mail joke, Ripley's is well-maintained and clean, but it's too expensive for the thin diversion it delivers. Mostly it consists of optical illusions, vaguely ominous specimens from foreign cultures, panels from the old Ripley's comic (does anyone under 60 even remember those?), and the odd coin-operated device. There are too many signs and fewer artifacts than you'll be expecting, unless you count a portrait of Beyoncé made out of hard candy. Don't set foot in it without at least harvesting coupons from any tourist brochure.

8201 International Dr., Orlando. © **407/363-4418.** www.ripleys.com/orlando. $20 adults, $13 kids 4–12; daily 9am–midnight.

Titanic The Experience ★★ TOURIST MUSEUM   A 2012 infusion of more than 100 genuine artifacts from the "Titanic" itself—a teak deck chair to cookware to tile fragments to a boarding card—have done wonders for this permanent exhibition. For those interested in the topic, this theatrically presented museum, which walks

The Orlando Eye

A shopping mall developer is now building I-Drive Live, an enormous new tourism complex. Targeted at press time for a grand opening on the last day of 2014, its anchors have been set. One highlight is a new, 25,000-square-foot branch of the world-famous **Madame Tussauds** wax museum, a natural fit for I-Drive. Merlin Entertainments Group, which runs that, will also bring Florida its first **SEA LIFE Aquarium,** another top-dollar chain, plus a slate of retail and restaurants. But undisputedly, the linchpin of the project—the "weenie" that draws people there, as Walt used to say—will be the **Orlando Eye** observation wheel, which at 424 feet will be the tallest structure in Central Florida,

and 120 feet taller than the Statue of Liberty (but 20 ft. shorter than the attraction it copies, the London Eye). The Swiss-made wheel is promised to have 30 capsule gondolas for 15 people each, and a full revolution will take 22 minutes. Prepare for views of Universal just north, of a teeny Spaceship Earth to the distant west, and over Universal Boulevard to the east, of Lockheed Martin's off-limits military weaponry compound. Ironically, its installation in 1957 to serve NASA on the Space Coast set off the chain of events that enabled Orlando to rise as a tourist hub—proving that with the Eye, Orlando comes full circle.

guests chronologically from boarding to the abbreviated voyage to rediscovery, provides a balanced dossier of the sorry tale. There's a little conflation of Hollywood storytelling with history (at the replica of the First Class Grand Staircase, a piano rendition of "My Heart Will Go On" repeats *ad nauseam*), but there's still plenty of meat on this hambone. Join a regular tour, because guides are deeply knowledgeable and truly care; after the tour, you can backtrack for closer looks. The 2-ton slab from her hull, cast in an eerie light, makes for a moving epilogue.

7324 International Dr., Orlando. ✆ **407/248-1166.** www.titanictheexperience.com. $22 adults, $13 kids 3–11. Mar–mid-Apr, August 10am–8pm, mid-Apr–May, Sept–Feb 10am–6pm, June–July 10am–9pm, last admission 1 hr. before closing.

Wet 'n Wild ★★★ WATER SLIDE PARK   The best Orlando water park for pound-for-pound thrills, if not for style, is located smack in the middle of the I-Drive area. It's tough to top this, the world's first water theme park, which was opened in 1977 by George Millay, the same guy who started SeaWorld. This is the purist's paragon—a tightly packed coil of steel framework and get-to-the-point thrills. Most water is heated, RFID bracelets allow cashless purchases, and bigger rafts are hoisted up the ride scaffolds by conveyors. You needn't be an excellent swimmer—lifeguards carefully monitor everything, even if most of them are still on Student Council. Parents tend to sit out the slides by hanging at the 17,000-square-foot **Surf Lagoon** or in the elaborate **Blastaway Beach** soak zone. Unusually, many of the coolest contraptions accommodate families who want to ride together. **The Black Hole** is a two-person raft (sorry, soloists) that whisks blindly through a pitch-black tube, pierced momentarily by disorienting strips of lights. **Brain Wash,** a white-knuckle standout worth waiting for, drops rafts carrying two or four people 53 feet down the wall of a 65-foot-wide funnel that's turned on its side. On **Bomb Bay,** the park's scariest ride, riders step into an enclosed cylinder above a 78-degree chute that drops six stories as close to vertically as physics and lawyers will allow. A sadistic attendant peeks through a window to make sure your arms and legs are crossed, and without warning, hits the release button on a trap door, dropping traumatized riders down the flume below at wedgie speed. But the best ride is **Disco H₂0**, in which cloverleaf-shaped rafts (two to four people) are accelerated in a tube and sent spinning around an enclosed chamber where disco music plays and lights spin; eventually, the raft is washed out a chute. There are 10 more attractions beyond those. The maintenance

SPRING training

Baseball is inextricable from Florida's calendar. Way back in 1923, the Cincinnati Reds began spring training in Orlando at Tinker Field and in the 1930s, the Washington Senators arrived in town and they stayed for the better part of half a century. A few teams in the so-called Grapefruit League (the Arizona trainers are the Cactus League) still call Orlando or its environs their temporary home, and in the preseason you can swing by to watch them practice or play exhibition games with visiting teams. Unlike at season games, players often mingle with fans—in fact, some teams' facilities were built to cozy proportions (you can leave the binoculars at home), with permanent interaction areas where you can collect autographs of the athletes before or after practice. Sometimes it feels like the spirit of old-time baseball, the one supplanted by high-priced players and colossal arenas.

Tickets (usually $15–$25) go on sale in January. Pitchers and catchers report first, in mid-February, and by the end of the month, the whole team is on hand. They play against other teams through March before heading to their home parks by April.

o **Atlanta Braves** (Disney's Wide World of Sports, 700 S. Victory Lane, Lake Buena Vista; ℂ **407/ 939-4263**). Since they took up residence in 1997 at Walt Disney World, the Braves can brag about

having one of the nicest and largest (9,500 seats) training stadiums under the sun. Tickets for the 18-odd games, which are cheapest for the bleachers and the lawn, are sold through Ticketmaster (ℂ **407/839-3900; www.ticketmaster.com**).

o **Houston Astros** (Osceola County Stadium, 1000 Bill Beck Rd., Kissimmee; ℂ **321/697-3200**). The smallest training park in the Grapefruit League (5,200 seats—still hardly tiny) has hosted the Astros since 1985. Team members make themselves available for fan greetings in their Autograph Alley. Tickets are sold through Ticketmaster (ℂ **407/ 839-3900; www.ticketmaster.com**).

o **Detroit Tigers** (Joker Merchant Stadium, Al Kaline Dr., 2301 Lake Hills Rd., Lakeland; ℂ **866/ 668-4437**). Lakeland, between Orlando and Tampa on I-4, has hosted the Tigers since 1934, the longest relations for any major league team, and the team is such a local institution that their so-called "Tiger Town" training complex, built on the site of a World War II flight academy, has grown up with them. For tickets, visit **http://detroit.tigers.mlb.com** or call ℂ **863/686-8075.**

period is September to March, when flumes go out of rotation. **Tip:** It's part of the FlexTicket discount (p. 234).

6200 International Dr., Orlando. ℂ **800/992-9453** or 407/351-1800. www.wetnwildorlando.com. $55 adults, $50 kids 3–9, $10 less online. Hours vary, but it generally opens at 9:30 or 10am and closes at 5pm in winter and as late as 9pm in the summer.

WonderWorks ★ TOURIST MUSEUM You know it's touristy because the facade looks like someone ripped a mansion out of the ground and turned it upside down. But the inverted motif doesn't continue very far into its doors. Instead, you get about 100 hands-on brainteaser exhibits not unlike what you'd find at a science museum or an arcade: an "earthquake simulator" box, a bubble-making area, all swarmed with children. Bring the Purell, because exhibits get smeary, and bring your patience, because some things will be broken. It's all about the children. And small kids love it—but then again, they have no sense of the value of a hard-earned dollar.

9067 International Dr., Orlando. ℂ **407/351-8800.** www.wonderworksonline.com. $25 adults, $20 seniors over 54 and kids 4–12, $7 per game of Laser Tag, $10 ropes course, $10 motion simulator ride. Daily 9am–midnight.

North of Universal & Orlando

Holy Land Experience ★ THEME PARK Here, religion becomes a consumer event for viewers of the televangelists on Trinity Broadcasting Network, which owns this bizarre little park. Shaped by evangelicals seeking their own domain for values-based entertainment (as if Disney was sleazy), this Bible-themed day out has no rides, nor enough attractions to fill the hours, even though performances and special events at the Church of All Nations are spaced out across the clock as though there was. For oddity, there will never be its equal. Will there ever again be a theme park where a major attraction is the Wilderness Tabernacle, which is essentially 20 minutes of an old man miming his custodial duties in a desert temple while a recorded chorus chants Old Testament verses? The day's climax comes when a handsome actor playing Jesus drags himself to the top of a fake mountain to be "crucified" by villainous Romans before an appreciative audience—the act of entertaining audiences with a mock execution is actually more Roman than most guests perceive. While its owners claim they're transporting people back to ancient times, the garish production design is more germaine to '50s Hollywood: Recorded scripture readings are in deep, vaguely James Mason–esque voices and accompanied by a soundtrack of rich strings and timpani intended to stir the devout. If you have been to the real Holy Land, you will quickly grasp that this fantasy version of Israel comes from Charlton Heston movies. Ironically for a park devoted to a great book, there are almost no signs—everything is narrated for you and matched to contemporary Christian power ballads. Its Scriptorium actually contains some impressive specimens of Biblical publishing, although the historical implications they wrought are mostly glossed over in favor of tearjerking.

4655 Vineland Rd., Orlando. ℂ **800/447-7235** or 407/872-2272. www.holylandexperience.com. $45 adults, $30 for children 6–12, $15 for kids 3–5. Tues–Sat 10am–6pm.

Mennello Museum of American Art ★★ MUSEUM The quirkiest selection in Loch Haven Park, the Mennello opened in 1998 as a repository for the luridly vivid paintings of Earl Cunningham, a chicken farmer and folk artist whose conceptions sometimes seem refreshingly naive, and then a moment later declare themselves as brazenly modernist. Cunningham, who died in 1977 while running a curio shop in

Saint Augustine, is now considered so important that the Smithsonian devoted an exhibition to him. The museum also hosts exhibitions of fine American folk art.

900 E. Princeton St., Orlando. ✆ **407/246-4278.** www.mennellomuseum.com. $5 adults, $4 seniors over 59, $1 students, kids 11 and under free. Tues–Sat 10:30am–4:30pm, Sun noon–4:30pm.

Orlando Museum of Art ★ MUSEUM   Although this fixture of local pride is touted as *de rigeur* in much tourist literature, OMA takes less than an hour to see. Most of it is not particularly important, just high atmosphere, but of note are Robert Rauschenberg's "Florida Psalm," a collage paean to the state's fading tourism emblems; Chuck Close's 1982 portrait of his wife done in fingerprints, and John James Audubon's Great Blue Heron. Temporary exhibitions up the par. Expect a pleasant outing, especially if you pair a visit with an amble around the surrounding Loch Haven Park.

2416 N. Mills Ave., Orlando. ✆ **407/896-4231.** www.omart.org. $8 adults, $7 college students and seniors over 64, $5 kids 6–18. Tues–Sat 10am–4pm, Sun noon–4pm.

Orlando Science Center ★ MUSEUM   The center is an excellent (if expensive) example of its type, but it's still just a science museum aimed at children and school groups, and if you have one in your city, you should probably fill your scarce vacation time with other attractions. That's not to slam what it has: an inviting atrium; a dome that doubles as a movie theater; a NatureWorks area stocked with live baby alligators; a miniature KidsTown for kids under 48 inches tall to pretend to do grown-up things; a BeeHive Encounter (don't scientists use spaces between words?) area that feeds outside through a tube; a not-scary dinosaur zone full of reproduction skeletons and sandboxes where kids can dig for simulated fossils.

777 E. Princeton St., Orlando. ✆ **407/514-2000.** www.osc.org. $19 adults, $17 seniors age 55 and over and students with ID, $13 kids 3–11, parking $5. Daily 10am–5pm.

Orange County Regional History Center ★★★ MUSEUM   People who think Central Florida history began with Walt will have their eyes opened in this underrated museum in a handsome 1927 Greek Revival former courthouse. Head first to the **fourth floor,** where the timeline starts 12,000 years in the past and work your way down. In 1981, a high school student rooting through lake muck found a Timacuan dugout canoe from around C.E. 1000, and now it is proudly displayed, as are mastodon teeth, pots from B.C.E. 500, and a 12-foot-tall oyster midden. As you advance through time, artifacts keep coming: saddles used by the forgotten Florida cowmen (the swampy ground made meat chewy, which Cuban customers liked), recipes for Florida Cracker delicacies (Squirrel Soup, Baked Possum), artifacts from the steamship tourist trade (in the 1870s, the St. John's River system was America's busiest one south of the Hudson), and a wall of gorgeous vintage labels from the many citrus companies that once dominated the area. The exhibitions are noticeably conflicted about the growth explosion wrought by the theme parks—the "Building a Kingdom" exhibition was created without Disney funding so it would have the freedom to be frank. An interesting sidelight is the retired Courtroom B, a handsome, wooden chamber out of "Inherit the Wind" silenced by cork floors and emblazoned with the slogan "Equal and Exact Justice to All Men." That was painted over the bench at a time when people were still being lynched here (there's a KKK robe in a nearby gallery), and until as late as 1951 in Orlando, black mothers had to give birth in the boiler room of the hospital. Some justice *was* served here: In 1987, Courtroom B tried the first case in America in which DNA evidence obtained a conviction.

65 E. Central Blvd., Orlando. ✆ **407/836-8500.** www.thehistorycenter.org. $9 adults, $6 kids 3–12, $7 seniors over 59. Mon–Sat 10am–5pm, Sun noon–5pm.

George P. Colby was reared in the Midwest by Baptist parents, but incessant visions (and poor health) compelled him south, where in 1875, he came across land that, he said, appeared exactly as it had been shown to him by his spirit guide, Seneca. Soon after that, Colby enticed a group of refugees from chilly Lily Dale, New York—a town populated by spiritualists that still exists on the **Cassadaga** Lakes outside of Buffalo—to join him in the then-rural wilds of Florida. The winter "camp" of **Cassadaga** ★★★ (exit 114 from I-4; www.cassadaga.org) was born. Nowadays, its residents offer a daily slate of services, laying-on of hands, and readings. The anachronistic town 40 miles northeast of Universal is untouched by development, and only accredited mediums may live among the ramshackle homes and Spanish moss. Tree-shaded, whitewashed, and more than slightly creepy, Cassadaga, on the National Register of Historic Places, is a bastion of metaphysicality in a region otherwise devoted to Christian fundamentalism.

Before setting out, check the town's website for the full list of events and psychics. When you arrive, consult the bulletin board in **Cassadaga Camp Bookstore** (1112 Stevens St., Cassadaga; ✆ **386/228-2880;** Mon–Sat 10am–6pm, Sun 11:30am–5pm) to see which mediums are available to take walk-in clients for readings or healings. Everything in town, including several gift shops for gemstones and talismans, is within

a few blocks, so park and explore. Because the rent's so cheap (the land is owned by the Southern Cassadaga Spiritualist Camp Meeting Association), services go for a fraction of what they cost in the outside world.

Historic walking tours leave from the bookstore twice a week (Tues at 2pm and Sat at 3pm; $15), but the coolest ticket is the **Nighttime Encounter Spirits** tour, on Saturday at 7:30pm ($25) where you bring your digital camera and go hunting for energy orbs. The next morning at 9:30, you can attend Lyceum—that's Sunday School for spiritualists—before Healing Service and church at the Colby Memorial Temple.

Residents shoo away outsiders at 10pm, so the only way to linger past the midnight hour is to stay at the town's old-fashioned inn: the 1928 **Cassadaga Hotel** (355 Cassadaga Rd., Cassadaga; ✆ **386/228-2323;** www.cassadagahotel. net; $55–$65 Sun–Thurs, $70–$80 Fri–Sat, including continental breakfast; no guests under age 21), widely said to be haunted. Rooms (the cheapest ones don't have TVs or phone) are guaranteed to keep you anxiously listening for bump-in-the-night creaks and groans. I asked the owner if I could take some photos of the time-warp lobby. "Sure, you're welcome to," she said, "but most people get a kind of orb or white light instead." I haven't found those, but my shots *did* come out blurry. I'm just saying.

Winter Park & North Orlando

Winter Park has long been a bastion of wealth, particularly from New Money families who failed to find favor among the Old Money of the North. Its expensive tastes are represented by its lakefront mansions, its red-brick streets, and a few wrongly overlooked gems for true masterpieces.

Charles Hosmer Morse Museum of American Art ★★★ MUSEUM   The best museum in the Orlando area, and perhaps the finest in the state, presents an unparalleled cache of works by genius designer Louis Comfort Tiffany, from stained glass to vases to lamps, and even the lavishly decorated Daffodil Terrace and Reception Hall of his lost Long Island mansion, Laurelton Hall, and the bespoke fountains that ran through it. The Morse displays the best collection of Tiffany glass on the planet, including an entire room reconstructing the master's tour de force chapel, made for the World's Columbian Exposition in 1893. Once face-to-face with the uncanny luminescence of Tiffany's best work, even those previously knew nothing about him can't help but come away dazzled. The museum's founders also collected hundreds of other top-quality pieces from the Arts and Crafts movement, including sculpture, but the focus here is definitely Tiffany and his impeccable taste. Set aside an hour or more, though it's easy to combine a visit with a stroll through Winter Park's boutiques, as it sits among them.

445 N. Park Ave., Winter Park. ℰ **407/645-5311.** www.morsemuseum.org. $5 adults, $4 seniors, $1 students, free for kids 11 and under. Tues–Sat 9:30am–4pm, Sun 1–4pm. Free Fri 4–8pm Nov–Apr.

It's Not on the Tourist Maps

The standard tourist literature won't point them out, but pop history happened here:

○ **Disney's Contemporary Resort, Walt Disney World.** On November 17, 1973, President Richard Nixon gave his "I'm not a crook" speech to a convention of Associated Press editors in the ballroom here, throwing gasoline on the fire of Watergate and bestowing him with his catchphrase of infamy.

○ **Disney's Polynesian Resort, Walt Disney World.** While on vacation on December 29, 1974, John Lennon signed the document that officially dissolved The Beatles forever. No one is sure exactly which room he was staying in at the time.

○ **1418½ Clouser Ave., in the College Park area.** In July 1957, 9 months before the publication of "Oh the Road," writer Jack Kerouac moved in with his mother, and he inhabited a 10×10-foot room with just a cot, a desk, and a bare bulb. Here, he wrote "The Dharma Bums," an exploration of personal spiritual renewal through a connection with nature. By the time he moved out in the spring of 1958, he was a literary superstar. The Kerouac Project (www.kerouacproject.org) now owns the home and invites

writers to live rent-free in it for 3-month tenures.

○ **1910 Hotel Plaza Blvd., Lake Buena Vista.** The very first building to be completed on Walt Disney World property was this low-slung glass-and-steel creation, considered painfully modern in January 1970. It was the Walt Disney World Preview Center, on what was then Preview Boulevard. Here, pretty young hostesses guided some one million visitors past artists' renderings, models, and films promoting Phase One of the resort that was being constructed. Naturally, the first souvenir shop at Disney World was also on the premises. The current tenant is a nonprofit organization promoting sports participation.

○ **839 N. Orlando Ave., Winter Park.** In March 1986, the Canadian rock group The Band was in the midst of a disappointing reunion tour. After playing the Cheek to Cheek Lounge at the Villa Nova Restaurant, which stood here, pianist Richard Manuel, 42, returned to his hotel room at the Quality Inn next door and, when his wife briefly left the room, hanged himself in despair. The lounge site is now a CVS drugstore, and the motel is the Best Western Winter Park Inn.

Cornell Fine Arts Museum ★ MUSEUM   Rollins College, whose graduates include Mister Fred Rogers, has long been a university of choice for parents with social aspirations for their children, and so it makes sense that its star exhibition hall would be bequeathed with such a fine collection in such a country-club setting. It's too small to showcase its impressive holdings, so even remarkable pieces (such as Vanessa Bell's portrait of Mary St. John Hutchinson) tend to rotate in and out of storage to make way for changing exhibitions, which spotlight a wide range of arresting works, from Matisse prints to 18th-century European portraits, both planned for 2014. Peaceful, quiet, and usually empty, with a serene backyard gazebo overlooking Winter Park's Lake Virginia, a visit here puts one into a contemplative mood.

100 Holt Ave., Winter Park. ✆ **407/646-2526.** www.rollins.edu/cfam. $5 adults, free for students. Tues–Fri 10am–4pm, Sat–Sun noon–5pm.

South & East of Disney

Diversions get populist as you go south, and their character says more about eccentric Florida than imported wealth; two of Central Florida's most authentic reptile parks are roughly between Disney and the airport.

Bok Tower Gardens ★★★ GARDENS/HISTORIC SITE   About an hour south of Disney, the elegant, 250-acre gardens—designed by Frederick Law Olmsted, Jr., who worked on the National Mall and the Jefferson Memorial—are not often visited, which is too bad, because it's a big reason you're in Orlando at all: It was one of Central Florida's first world-famous attractions. They're genuinely tranquil and among the best surviving remnants of early-20th-century philanthropic privilege. The gardens (don't miss the water lilies, big enough to support a child) and their 205-foot, neo-Gothic Singing Tower were commissioned as a thank-you to the American people by a Dutch-born editor, Edward William Bok, publisher of "The Ladies' Home Journal" and a pioneer in public sex education. Bok was buried at the tower's base in 1930, the year after its completion and dedication by President Calvin Coolidge. The 57-bell carillon on the tower's sixth level sounds concerts at 1 and 3pm daily, and its 1930s Mediterranean-style Pinewood mansion is open for tours. The sanctuary was enshrined in 1993 as a National Historic Landmark.

1151 Tower Blvd., Lake Wales. ✆ **863/676-1408.** www.boksanctuary.org. $12 adults, $3 kids 5–12, half off Sat 8–9am. Daily 8am–6pm, last admission at 5pm.

Dinosaur World ★ TOURIST MUSEUM   An only-in-America roadside attraction, this is not someplace to pass hours—one will do, but it'll be a memorably weird one. Kids like to wander the jungly plot, happening upon more than 100 life-size versions of various dinosaurs, some 80 feet long. A labor of love by a Swedish-born man and his family, it's well kept, even if the foam-and-fiberglass models sometimes look more like aliens than reptiles. It's easy to catch on the drive to Busch Gardens.

5145 Harvey Tew Rd., at I-4's exit 17, Plant City. ✆ **813/717-9865.** www.dinosaurworld.com. $15 adults, $13 seniors over 59, $12 kids 3–12. Daily 9am–5pm.

Fantasy of Flight ★★ MUSEUM   About 20 miles south of Disney on I-4 you can't miss this combination hangar farm/airfield dedicated to restoring obsolete aircraft from the dawn of mechanized flight to the 1950s. More than 100 vintage relics—many rented frequently for Hollywood shoots and all either restored to or destined for flying condition—are on the premises, and guests are shown how they're mended and, if weather's agreeable, there's a daily flying demonstration. For an extra chunk of change, hitch a ride in a barnstorming biplane (one from the 1920s, one from the

1940s), do a ropes course, or fly on a zip line. This elaborate toy shop is a labor of love—its owner, Kermit Weeks, is independently wealthy thanks to a grandfather's oil strike. He just loves planes, it shows, and he even pilots demonstrations, but his play-park has been scaling back its opening hours lately—is he tiring of it?

1400 Broadway Blvd., Polk City. ✆ **863/984-3500.** www.fantasyofflight.com. $30 adults, $16 kids 6–15. Thurs–Sun 10am–5pm.

Fun Spot USA ★ AMUSEMENT PARK   Fun Spot's flagship property is near Universal (p. 136) but this southern outpost delivers the same well-kept carnival-ride playground experience. There's a selection of basic rides that wouldn't be out of place beside a circus (the Hot Seat swings seated riders on the end of a big stick), a new wild mouse-style Rockstar Coaster with spinning cars, and a few multilevel Go-Kart tracks (the Vortex has 32-degree banking, the world's steepest) and racecar simulators. That 300-foot-tall skyline-scarring contraption is **SkyCoaster** ($40 a ride), which harnesses up to three would-be pants-wetters so that they're face-down, hoists them backward, and swings them forward at 80mph like wingless hang gliders.

2850 Florida Plaza Blvd., Kissimmee. ✆ **407/397-2509.** www.funspotattractions.com. Pay-per-ride $6–$9, unlimited ride armband $30–$40 (armband price based on height). Generally daily 10am–midnight.

Gatorland ★★★ ANIMAL PARK   Back in 1949, the reassuringly hokey Gatorland became Orlando's very first mass attraction, featuring Seminole Indians wrestling the animals for tourists, and the house-sized jaw at its entrance was a state landmark for Polaroids and Kodachrome. Back then, Florida was crawling with alligators—you would see them basking by the sides of the roads—but these days, the reptiles have been mostly evicted by development, so sanctuaries like these are the best places to see beasts (such as the newest resident diva, the 15-ft.-long, 1,400-lb. Bonecrusher II) in their ornery glory. Gatorland is rustic in a family-friendly way, as concrete pools have been replaced with natural-looking habitats, a sun-seared layout was molded into a pleasing nature walk, and stuff like a **wading bird rookery,** a **petting zoo,** and **zip line** (not worth the upcharge) were added. At regular showtimes, rangers, buzzed on their own testosterone, wrassle, tickle, and otherwise pester seething gators, and for a few extra bucks, they'll bring your children into the fray—safely, with a wad of rubber bands around the critters' snouts—for snapshots. These guys would be just as comfortable as Broadway actors as gator handlers; every show is staged to contain a near disaster to titillate and thrill tourists. Most of the fun is trawling the 110-acre plot on walkways as the critters teem ominously in murky waters underfoot. **Strategy:** It's easy to get the highlights in 2 or 3 hours, but don't miss the Jumparoo, when gators leap out of the water for suspended chunks of chicken meat. Bring a fistful of cash if you'd like to partake of extras such as being able to feed tamer animals such as tropical birds. And save a few bills for one of its 1960s-era vending machines, which press a miniature alligator out of injected hot wax right before your eyes—it's just one of many unmissable throwbacks here.

14501 S. Orange Blossom Trail, Orlando. ✆ **800/393-5297** or 407/855-5496. www.gatorland.com. $25 adults, $17 kids 3–12. Daily 9am–5pm

Give Kids the World Village ★★★ LANDMARK   You will be surprised to learn that of the annual wishes granted by the Make-A-Wish Foundation and other wish-granting organizations for terminally ill kids, *half* of them are to visit Central Florida. Make-A-Wish turns to this nonprofit to fulfill those dreams, which it does for 196 families at a time and some 7,000 international families a year. No one is refused,

International Drive

MORE ORLANDO ATTRACTIONS

and each family spends an all-expenses-paid week here in their own villa with their parents and siblings, eating as much as they want at the resort premises and playing in a compound that looks like a second Magic Kingdom.

It's the most magical place you never knew existed. The 70-acre, gated operation is its own fantasy world, down to a 6-foot rabbit, Mayor Clayton, who provides nightly tuck-ins. Perkins Restaurants and Boston Market discreetly support the dining pavilion, which looks like a gingerbread house, and there's an Ice Cream Palace where no child is ever refused a scoop. Christmas falls every Thursday, when there's a parade, holiday lighting, and an appearance by Santa, who gives everyone a toy provided by Hasbro. The carousel is the only one in the world that a wheelchair can drive right onto, plus there's horseback riding, a small-gauge train route, miniature golf, and on and on.

As you can imagine, it depends on volunteers—to the tune of 1,200 slots a week. You don't have to commit to anything longer than a few hours; all you must do is apply online about 2 weeks ahead and be at least 12 years old, although exceptions can be made for families who want to volunteer together.

Mornings or evenings are best, because the kids want spend their days at the theme parks, too (something that should fit nicely with your own schedule). The workload is easy. That includes turning person-size cards at the World's Largest Candy Land game, held Sunday nights on a board measuring 14,400 square feet. You could help at Mayor Clayton's surprise birthday party, thrown every Saturday, or at the "dive-in" movies screened weekly. You can spoon hash browns at breakfast (until about 11am), run the carousel or the train, or serve dinner with a smile (from 6–9:30pm)—the opportunities are virtually boundless and the staff is eager to match your talents with the right post.

Your mission is not to lavish pity or love, but to simply run the resort where families escape from hard times. You'll be a host, not a nurse. Not every child is sick—their brothers and sisters come, too, and many of them are starved for attention after their siblings' often long illnesses. You'll find that the village is quite a joyous place as families are, perhaps briefly, liberated from the burden of their lives. A favorite part of Give Kids the World is the Castle of Miracles, where the rafters are covered with thousands of golden stars. Each star is affixed by a child on the last night of his or her stay. Years later, moms and dads sometimes return and ask to see, one last time, the star that their child left behind.

210 S. Bass Rd., Kissimmee. 📞 **800/995-5437** or 407/396-0770. www.gktw.org.

Old Town ★ AMUSEMENT PARK   Walt Disney tried to extinguish honky-tonk, but it lives on, cotton candy and all, at his doorstep. Old Town is the kind of low-rent entertainment center you'd find rusting near a small town somewhere. Built to look like 4 blocks of a Main Street–style town, expect Americana to the extreme: beer-soaked ale halls, Old Glory T-shirts, and a gauntlet of no-name stores peddling impulse buys from baseball cards to puppets to pins to Western gear, plus a variety of special events (Thurs is motorcycle night, Fri and Sat for collector cars, Sun is country music). The area also has about 15 cheap rides, bumper cars, a just-renovated haunted house, and **Windstorm,** a skeletal knot of metal tucked at the back of the park. It must be Orlando's least known roller coaster, which is not an injustice. Old Town may not be posh, and some people may even classify it as trashy, but kids love it, international tourists are fascinated by it, and the truth is that in the right frame of mind, it's a decent place to have a good time for less. You'll probably eat something fried.

5770 W. Irlo Bronson Hwy./U.S. 192, Kissimmee. 📞 **407/396-4888.** www.myoldtownusa.com. Free entry, pay per ride (various), unlimited rides $25. Daily 10am–11pm, rides may remain open later.

Orlando is a world capital for miniature golf. Here, a flat, green fairway just won't do. Here, you play crazy golf under waterfalls, through caves, over motorized ramps, and even into volcanoes that "erupt" if you hit your shot. Putter around with one of these. The coupon booklets print discounts for all but Disney's courses; also check individual course websites for coupons.

○ **Congo River Adventure Golf** (www.congoriver.com): One of the best options, the challenging courses wind through man-made mountains speared with airplane wreckage—and there are live alligators in the pools! Play 18 holes for $12 adults, $10 kids. Two locations: 5901 International Dr., Orlando (© **407/248-9181**); and 4777 W. Hwy. 192, Kissimmee (© **407/396-6900**). Both open daily (Sun–Thurs 10am–11pm; Fri–Sat 10am–midnight).

○ **Disney's Winter Summerland** (outside Blizzard Beach, Walt Disney World; © **407/939-7529;** $12 adults, $10 kids; daily 10am–11pm; 50 percent discount on the second round): Two cute 18-hole courses themed around Christmas. The Winter side, piled with fake snow, has more bells and whistles (love that steaming campfire and that squirting snowman). Combine it with Blizzard Beach without moving your car. Summerland beats the other Disney course, **Disney's Fantasia Gardens** (same rates), themed to the movie "Fantasia," with its two courses: Fairways and Gardens. The Fairways course has challenging shots; Gardens is sillier. Find it by the Swan and Dolphin hotel duo.

○ **Hawaiian Rumble Adventure Golf** (www.hawaiianrumbleorlando.com): These tropical courses are threaded with streams and waterfalls that could use a little upkeep. Play 18 holes for $10; 36 holes for $13. Two locations: 13529 S. Apopka Vineland Rd., Lake Buena Vista (© **407/ 239-8300;** open daily 9am–11pm); and 8969 International Dr., Orlando (© **407/351-7733;** open Sun–Thurs 9am–11:30pm and Fri–Sat 9am– midnight).

○ **Hollywood Drive-In Golf** (CityWalk Orlando, 6000 Universal Blvd., Orlando. © **407/802-4848;** www. hollywooddriveingolf.com; $14 adults, $12 kids 3–9; open daily 9am–2am) The newest (2012) and coolest 36 holes in town, CityWalk's "haunted & sci-fi double feature" is kitted out, hilarious, and always surprising. Spinning vortices! Corkscrew ball elevators! At night, the lighting effects are impeccable. You can even download its own scorecard app and putt with an eyeball.

○ **Putting Edge** (Festival Bay, 5250 International Dr., Orlando; © **407/ 248-0700;** www.puttingedge.com; adults $11, kids 12 and under $8.50; Mon–Thurs 11am–9pm, Fri 11am– 11pm, Sat 10am–11pm, Sun 11am– 8pm). An 18-hole glow-in-the-dark course of fluorescent balls, holes, and decor.

○ **Pirate's Cove** (www.piratescove.net): Navigate wooden ships—a newly installed one is life-size—and falls of blue-ish water. Choose Captain's Adventure or Blackbeard's Challenge. Two locations: 8501 International Dr., Orlando (© **407/352-7378**), and 12545 S.R. 535, behind the Crossroads shopping center, Lake Buena Vista (© 407/827-1242). Rates and hours the same: $12 adults, $11 kids 12 and under; open daily 9am to 11pm.

Reptile World Serpentarium ★★ ANIMAL ATTRACTION   Snake milking! What other enticement do you need? Truthfully, it's more of an unassuming biotoxin supply facility—and venom-collection wonderland—than a zoo. Begun in 1972 to collect poison for medical research and to save the lives of bite victims, its location 20 miles east of Disney tempted its operators into joining the ranks of tourist attractions 4 years later, and daily at noon and 3pm, you can thrill (safely behind glass) as George Van Horn grabs deadly serpents, plant their yawning fangs over the membrane of a venom-collection glass, and get the creatures spitting mad. There are about 50 snakes on display (including an 18-ft. cobra and 11 types of rattlers) at any time, but obviously, this one's about venom spewing. Gotta admit—that's cool.

5705 E. Irlo Bronson Memorial Hwy./U.S. 192, St. Cloud. (© **407/892-6905.** www.reptileworld serpentarium.com. $8.75 adults, $6.75 kids 6–17, $5.75 kids 3–5. Tues–Sat 9am–5pm, Sun 10am–5pm.

KENNEDY SPACE CENTER

In the late 1960s, Central Florida was the most exciting place on Earth, all because of the moon. But the **Kennedy Space Center** ★★★ (© **866/870-8025;** www. kennedyspacecenter.com), which was established in 1958 and ruled the tourist circuit with Disney in the 1970s, has been eclipsed by attractions based on fantasies. Have some pride, America!

Start a full day near opening time. A few miles before reaching the actual visitor center, you'll pass the **United States Astronaut Hall of Fame.** Because they see it first, people make it their first stop, but you're going to be getting plenty of similar information on your tour, so only stop here on the way out if you're still yearning for spacemen. Instead, proceed to the Visitor Center proper. There, many are waylaid by the retired rockets, IMAX films, and simulators, but again, that's not the best stuff. Proceed instantly to the newly opened, $100 million permanent home of the **space shuttle** *Atlantis.* Hanging 26 feet off the ground at an angle of 43.21 degrees (like the numbers in a launch countdown), she's still covered with space dust, and she now tips a wing at everyone who comes to learn about her on the many interactive displays that surround her. This state-of-the-art, hyper-engaging interactive exhibition explaining how she worked can easily consume 2 hours but don't dally too long. Board the can't-miss **bus tour,** which leaves every 15 minutes until about 2:15pm and takes most people around 4 hours—be warned that the last buses don't leave you enough time to browse. Coaches, which are narrated by both video segments and a live person, zip you around NASA's tightly secured compound. Combined with the nature reserve around it, the area (which guides tell visitors is a fifth the size of Rhode Island) is huge but you'll be making three stops not too far away—still, hope for good weather, since you'll be in and out of doors. Each stop allows you to disembark, explore, and then catch the next bus. The system can be slow, but it at least lets you linger where you want. From the first stop, the **LC-39 Observation Gantry,** you'll have a view, across a few miles, of the two launch sites used by the shuttle and by the Apollo moon shots, and you'll receive an intelligent explanation of the preparation that goes into each shuttle launch. Ever wonder why you saw a lot of sparks by the shuttle engines during launch, or why water appeared to be pouring out the bottom? You'll find out why. (If you'd like to get much closer to the launch pads, you have to pay another $25 adult/$19 kids for the Up Close tour; but that's only for die-hards.)

Back on the bus, you'll buzz by eagles' nests, alligator-rich canals, and the absolutely titanic **Vehicle Assembly Building,** or VAB, where the shuttle—which NASA folk call "the orbiter"—was readied; the Statue of Liberty could fit through those doors. The second bus stop, the **Apollo/Saturn V Center,** begins with a full-scale mock-up of the "firing room" in the throes of commanding Apollo 8's launch, in all its window-rattling, fire-lit drama. The adjoining museum contains a Saturn V rocket, which is larger than you can imagine (363 ft. long, or the equivalent of 30 stories), and the chance to touch a small moon rock, which looks like polished metal. The presentation in the **Lunar Theatre,** which recounts the big touchdown, is well produced and even includes a video appearance by the late, reclusive Neil Armstrong.

Once you've completed the standard bus tour, it's up to you whether you want to plumb the sillier, kid-geared business at the Visitor's Complex—it's hard to absorb physics lessons from mewling computerized fowl at **Angry Birds Space Encounter** seriously when you've just heard from Mr. "One Small Step for Man" himself (although that's the point at which some kids engage). By this point, much of it will be redundant, and some of it is pure malarkey, but take the time to check the 42-foot-high black granite slab of the **Astronaut Memorial,** commemorating those lost; **Early Space Exploration,** where you'll see the impossibly low-tech Mission Control for the Mercury missions (they used rotary telephones!), plus some authentic spacesuits from the Gemini, Mercury, and Apollo series. You can also try the $60-million **Shuttle Launch Experience,** in which 44-person motion-simulator pods mimic a 5-minute launch. For an extra fee, you can try truly professional equipment on the **Astronaut Training Experience (ATX),** described on p. 151.

Because the government commandeers the surrounding land as a buffer, there is nowhere else to eat within a 15-minute drive. The center points out that it uses no public funding for its tourist amenities, but I still think charging $15 for two hot dogs and two drinks is gouging. As the stewards of a precious preserve that belongs to all Americans, Kennedy Space Center should provide refreshment at an earthbound price. Good hospitality isn't rocket science, you know.

The center is located on Route 405, east of Titusville. The most direct route from Orlando costs $4.25 in tolls. Admission is $50 adults, $40 kids. It opens daily at 9am and closes between 5 and 7pm, depending on the season. The Astronaut Hall of Fame opens at noon and shares closing times with the center. Bus tours run every 15 minutes but the last one departs at 2:15pm.

Increased Access to NASA Secrets

The closure of the space shuttle program has enabled previously off-limits areas to open for visits. For now, the access is unprecedented: The VAB, opened to the public for the first time in 30 years, can be toured separately on the 3-hour Up-Close Mega Tour ($40 adults, $30 kids 3–11; offered at 10am, noon, and 2pm). You can also visit the shuttle's launch pad, and 350-foot-tall service structure ($25 adults, $19 kids), the Launch Control Center used in the shuttle's last 21 liftoffs ($29 adults, $19 kids), and the Then and Now tour ($25 adults, $19 kids), where you see Launch Complex 34, the site of the 1967 Apollo tragedy, and also get up to speed on NASA's current rocket projects.

Although the Space Shuttle has flown into history, NASA still launches unmanned rockets. Because launches are so often postponed, it would be dangerous to plan a trip to Orlando just to catch one, but then again, if there's a launch when you're in town, it would a shame to miss it. Kennedy Space Center maintains an updated schedule online at **www.kennedyspacecenter.com**. The general public is not permitted to flood NASA turf during the actual events, but Titusville, a town at the eastern end of S.R. 50, is a good place to get a clear, free view, as you'll be across the wide Indian River from the pad. Even if you can't leave Orlando for a launch, you can still easily see the fire of the rockets ascend the eastern sky from anywhere in town. Night launches are even more spectacular.

Kennedy Space Center Special Tours

Lunch with an Astronaut   One of the coolest benefits of visiting the Space Coast in person is the chance to meet a real astronaut, many of whom have retired to the same area where they once worked. At times, you'll have seen headliners such as Jim Lovell and Story Musgrave making the rounds. Typically, these guys (and a very few women) love basking in fandom and in reliving old tales of glory—and unlike out-to-pasture sportsmen, these old-timers really did risk their lives the way heroes are supposed to—so these small-group sessions are geared toward questions.

℗ **866/737-5235.** www.kennedyspacecenter.com. $80 adult, $56 kids 3–11, including admission. Daily at noon.

Astronaut Training Experience ★★★ ACTIVITY   KSC dubs the program ATX, but you could call it Space Daycamp. You'll test a few of the pieces of astronaut equipment, such as the multi-axis trainer (which spins your body within a series of interlinked concentric circles to test your equilibrium), a gravity chair, and a spell in a full-scale mock-up of the shuttle. Nothing is as intense as what astronauts experience, but it's still plenty rigorous for most terrestrials, and the facilitators can answer nearly any question you can launch at them. There's also a milder version, ATX Family, appropriate for younger children. The standard version is called Core.

Astronaut Hall of Fame, 6225 Vectorspace Blvd., Titusville. *℗* **866/737-5235.** www.kennedyspace center.com. $145; minimum age 7; 7 hr.

NIGHTLIFE IN ORLANDO

After nightfall, the exertion of visiting theme parks has turned most visitors into exhausted puddles, and then the resorts mop up the remaining guests at their on-premises nightspots. But these novel nighttime destinations are worth the rally:

Enzian ★★★ CINEMA   This thoughtfully programmed cinema would be the envy of any city in America. Before the movie, you kick back at its Brazilian walnut patio bar, watching the sunset paint the Spanish moss red. Some of the drinks come from the private cellars of the Enzian's founder, the granddaughter of an Austrian princess. The relaxation continues inside at a large single-screen cinema, where a selection of art films and documentaries is shown, plus Hollywood biggies. Unlike multiplexes, there aren't rows of seats, but lollipop-colored levels of tables with cushy seating. Servers take your order (if you have one—eating's not required) before the movie and after the lights dim, your meal arrives surreptitiously and the air fills with the aroma of popcorn and truffled fries. After the show, a 20-minute drive has you back at Disney World.

1300 S. Orlando Ave., Maitland. © **407/629-0054.** www.enzian.org. tickets $10 adult, $8 seniors/students.

Howl at the Moon Saloon ★★ BAR   The 15-strong chain is good fun: a saloon delivered as a theme park experience, where dueling pianists outdo each other for laughs and virtuosity (expect to hear "American Pie"), and the patrons, mostly over 35 and white, clap earnestly to the beat. The theme resorts have their own dueling pianist joints: Jellyrolls at Disney's BoardWalk (p. 153) and Pat O'Brien's at Universal's CityWalk (p. 155).

8815 International Dr., Orlando. © **407/354-5999.** www.howlatthemoon.com. Sun–Thurs 7pm–2am, Fri–Sat 6pm–2am, piano show starts 1 hr. after opening; cover $10.

Icebar ★ BAR   The gimmick: a bar made of 50 tons of ice, from the chairs to the frozen goblets. You're loaned gloves and a cape for warmth. The Arctic cocktailerie is only the size of a hotel room, dotted with ice sculptures, and aglow with cobalt lighting, and when you've had enough, there's a larger, room-temperature lounge where you can continue the party.

8967 International Dr., Orlando. © **407/426-7555.** www.icebarorlando.com. $30 including 2 drinks, $20 without drinks. Sun–Wed 7pm–midnight, Thurs 7pm–1am, Fri–Sat 7pm–2am.

Parliament House Orlando ★★★ BAR/THEATER/DISCO   There's nothing else in America quite like it. In 1975, a dying Johnson-era, 130-room motel was revitalized as an amusement megacenter for gay folks. Its rambling size—10 acres, including a beach on a small lake out back—justifies it as a hangout not only for gay guys, but also for the friends who love them, women who want to dance without being accosted, and open-minded straight guys. Think of it as a fabulous entertainment minimall: There's the Footlight Theater for cabaret and drag hosted by longtime resident mistress Darcel Stevens; a diner; a pool; a disco, which gears up around 9pm; a video bar; and a scuzzy cubby called Western Bar, for leather-and-jeans-wearing guys who play pool and, um, know how to handle a stick. The scene is unexpected when you consider that its operators are a straight couple with six kids and that Orlando politics are still controlled by conservative Christians. It's considered a nucleus of Florida gay life, and when it entered rough financial waters in recent years, some locals advocated for it to be landmarked.

410 N. Orange Blossom Trail, Orlando. © **407/425-7571.** www.parliamenthouse.com. Cover and hours vary.

NIGHTLIFE AT THE RESORTS

After a long day trooping through the parks, you wish list for nightlife may begin and end with a hot bath. But if, once the fireworks fizzle, you're still ready to party, the amusement giants are happy to serve into the wee hours (1 or 2am daily). These playgrounds rock on every night, even if the dance floors happen to be desolate. Their offerings have been concocted by committee to appeal to as wide a spectrum of visitors as possible, and their playlists and decor alike are designed for the masses, but those who surrender to it are bound to have fun.

Walt Disney World

Between the Swan and Dolphin hotels and Epcot, **Disney's BoardWalk** (no admission required) is a lesser entertainment district (p. 94) though it's no match for the **Downtown Disney** area (p. 94). It can be reached from Epcot's International Gateway side entrance, but if you park at Epcot, be careful because once the park closes, you can't cut through to the parking lot. At the very least, BoardWalk is a scrubbed-down idealization of 1930s Atlantic City that makes for a pleasant backdrop for an evening stroll on the water. Most visitors grab an ice cream and stick around for a half-hour or so. Its two clubs thump along, sometimes in lonely desolation, although patronage depends greatly on what conventions are staying at the adjoining hotels and if participants are in a party frame of mind.

Atlantic Dance Hall ★ Appearances to the contrary, it is not a place where they might shoot horses (that concept failed), but an under-patronized DJ dance club for Top 40, '80s, and videos. Its clientele seems to consist of tipsy trade-show attendees from the Swan and Dolphin hotels next door. Hip it's not, and nostalgic it ain't, which is too bad, because its Art Deco interior holds such promise and its spacious wood floor feels good to dance on.

© **407/939-2444.** disneyworld.disney.go.com. No cover, minimum age 21. Tues–Sat 9pm to 2am.

Jellyrolls ★ The brightest entertainment option at BoardWalk is Disney's challenge to the Howl at the Moon Saloon (p. 152): Dueling pianists jam, audiences sing along and try to stump them with requests, and the mood is light. Pianists start at 8pm and the space usually starts to fill up after 9pm, so arrive earlier for a table. There's no food beyond popcorn and the like.

© **407/560-8770.** disneyworld.disney.go.com. $12 cover, minimum age 21. Daily 7pm–2am.

Rix Lounge ★ Far from this planet, in a hotel catering to conventions, you stumble into this misplaced cocktail lounge. An illuminated, amberlike bar and lots of seating nooks make you think you're getting Miami swank, but the action depends entirely on whether a convention is on, when it rollicks with up-for-it partiers. Otherwise it's dead. It's also appalling that any cocktail bar in Florida should serve premixed mojitos by pipe through a tap, as this place does, but at Disney, you greedily lap up whatever nightlife you can get.

Disney's Coronado Springs Resort, 1000 W. Buena Vista Dr., Orlando. © **407/939-3806.** www.rixlounge.com. Sun–Thurs 6pm–midnight, Fri–Sat 6pm–1am.

Universal Orlando & CityWalk

CityWalk ★★ Universal Orlando's 30-acre nightclub mall takes fewer pains than Disney to present a wholesome face to the public. In fact, there's an upscale tattoo parlor. Nights here, in the front yard shared by both Universal theme parks, were designed with jellybean colors and rock-concert panache, to be sure, but they attract locals as well as tourists and therefore have a sharper edge. The drinks are stronger, too, but that might be my imagination. The liveliness is bolstered partly by regular concerts at its Hard Rock Live venue. There is no charge to enter the common area, which is a boon because that allows anyone to tour around before deciding whether they want to pay to enter any clubs. Buying a $12 **CityWalk Party Pass** from any of the kiosks at the complex grants you unlimited admission to any and all of them on a given night; the clubs usually open after 9pm and are otherwise $7 a pop. Some of them serve food during the day and turn into nightspots late, and others open only in the evening. All Universal park tickets with multiday admission automatically come with one Party Pass. The Party Pass also is available with the addition of a movie ticket at the AMC Universal Cineplex (see below), which is part of the complex. That combo costs $15. Finally, there's a package that buys a prix-fixe dinner at eight of CityWalk's restaurants with a ticket to the cineplex for $21. Grab a "Times & Info" guide, which maps the stores and restaurants and lists the current happy hour times and specials. Many clubs only admit patrons 21 or older because drinking is permitted outdoors anywhere in CityWalk.

6000 Universal Blvd., Orlando, exit 75A coming on I-4 from the west, or exit 74B coming from the east. (ℂ) **407/363-8000.** www.citywalkorlando.com. $12 admission to all clubs; daily 11am–2am. parking $15 before 6pm, $5 after 6pm excluding event nights.

Blue Man Group ★★★ Three taciturn, bald, blue guys get into hilarious mischief, play with bizarre homemade toys, and generally make a mess of their custommade theater—get a seat in the first four rows in the so-called "poncho section" (you'll get a plastic cloak) if you think it'd be fun to be splattered with goo. If you've gone to the parks for the day, the Blue Men won't require driving; guests can start drinking cocktails whenever they want and even bring them into the theater, accessible to both CityWalk and Universal Studios (it's practically beneath the Rockit coaster).

(ℂ) **888/340-5476.** www.universalorlando.com. Adults $69–$84, kids from $29. 1 hr. 45 min.

Bob Marley—A Tribute to Freedom ★★ You often get live music for the $7 cover, but mostly it's an easygoing place to kick back, eat, and listen to recorded reggae—an antidote to the high-energy clubs around it.

(ℂ) **407/224-3663.** www.universalorlando.com.

CityWalk's Rising Star ★ This karaoke joint has a spin: You get a band and backup singers. Like all karaoke, the more you drink the more ridiculously fun it gets. Cover is $7, usually charged after 9pm.

(ℂ) **407/224-2189.** www.universalorlando.com.

the groove ★ Sleek and state-of-the-art; this DJ dance club is also middle of the road; music skips from the '70s (Tues) to the '80s (Sat) to recent hits. The cover is $7, and it opens at 9pm.

(ℂ) **407/224-2165.** www.universalorlando.com.

Jimmy Buffett's Margaritaville ★★ Live music nightly in a touristy environment that's first about the cheeseburgers in paradise, secondly about margaritas (there are three bars), and thirdly about island music. Get there before the live music starts at 10pm to avoid the $7 cover charge.

(ℂ) **407/224-2155.** www.universalorlando.com.

Pat O'Brien's ★★　It's "an authentic reproduction of New Orleans' favorite watering hole," which is cool to see, and although its Hurricane rum drinks could make you see double, there are actually dueling pianists playing nightly. O'Brien's serves good food, but if you can't get a seat (or don't want one), you can also grab a drink through a window facing the street. This spot is among the most popular here—the party starts at 4pm—and kids can join in. Cover is $7, usually after 9pm.

📞 **407/224-3663.** www.patobriens.com.

Red Coconut Club ★★　A vanilla version of an ultralounge, it mixes stylish cocktails and cultivates the most intimate atmosphere at Universal Orlando. It's the district's most upscale venture. Tapas are $8.

📞 **407/224-2425.** www.universalorlando.com.

Hard Rock Live ★★　A 3,000-seat, top-of-the-line live-music arena attached to the famous burger joint is one of Orlando's primary concert and comedy venues. The second-floor seating is spacious and has good sightlines; for some concerts, the first floor is converted to a dance floor or to standing room. You can't miss it—it looks like the Roman Coliseum. Check with website to see what'll be on during your visit.

📞 **407/351-5483.** www.hardrock.com/live. Ticket prices vary.

OUTDOOR ORLANDO

Picture an old-fashioned steamship, not unlike the "African Queen," puttering along a narrow river of clear spring-fed water beneath a cool canopy of oak trees. Alongside the vessel swim a few docile manatees that nibble contentedly on the river grass. As the steamship breaks through a curtain of Spanish moss, it enters a wide, warm lake teeming with long-necked birds. The passengers sigh.

It's hard to believe, but that's what Central Florida really is. Well, was. When the area was a nascent vacationland that's how it was observed. Although it was a harsh land with arid soil and mosquitoes in flocks, cypress and oak grew along the lakes and provided welcome shade. Modern-day developers have cleared away everything but the lakes, ripping out the absorbent natural vegetation. (And people wonder why they feel so hot and sinkholes are common.)

When you tire of artificial rocks and loudspeakers hidden in the landscape, remember that Orlando is adored for natural beauty, starting with its year-round warmth, and for wide, blue skies chased by billowy clouds. Central Florida's development explosion only kicked in a generation ago, and some people were smart enough to rope off land from destruction. We're only beginning to understand how important the wetlands are to the ecosystems farther south and how runoff in Orlando affects drinking water downstate.

The tropical conditions mean botanical gardens support a wider array of plants than many others in the country. Look around, and you'll find examples of the land's primacy—natural springs that Ponce de Leon once toured, swamps where alligators lurk beneath bladderwort and spatterdock, and marshy preserves thronged with migrating birds. And should all of that scenery bore, you can speed by it on bracing boat tours or observe from the above in a balloon or hang glider.

Blue Spring State Park ★★ NATURE RESERVE　You stand a fair chance of seeing manatees here, especially in the morning on a cold day. The creatures venture up the St. Johns River from the Atlantic Ocean to seek out the warmth of the springs of this 2,600-acre park, which maintain a constant 72°F temperature even in winter. So from mid-November through March 15, all boating, swimming, and snorkeling are suspended while the big guys (more than 75 some years) are in residence. An exception is made daily at 10am and 1pm, when a **2-hour guided boat tour** (© **407/330-1612;** www.sjrivercruises.com; $22 adults, $20 seniors, $16 kids 3–12) of the St. Johns River is given, and the park also coughs up a few nature trails and canoe rental. Find it 60 miles north of Disney from exit 114 off I-4; go south on U.S. Rte. 17-92 to Orange City, and then make a right onto West French Avenue (there are signs).

2100 W. French Ave., Orange City. © 386/775-3663. www.floridastateparks.org/bluespring. $6 per car. Daily 8am–sundown

De Leon Springs State Park ★★★ NATURE RESERVE   Florida has some 300 springs, and 27 of them discharge more than 60 million gallons of pure water a day. In fact, Florida has more springs than any other American state. With numbers like that, it's easy to conclude that natural springs are more authentically Floridian than pretty much anything else you might see in Orlando, and there's no more enjoyable place to experience them than here. The Spanish, Seminoles, and prepresidential Zachary Taylor all fought over this spot of land, and Audubon saw his first limpkin here. (Remember *your* first time?) It's impossible to overstate the importance of the St. Johns River on the development of Florida—before rail, everybody used it—and, like the Nile, it's one of the few world rivers to flow north, not south. On this segment of the river, there are 18,000 acres of lakes and marshes to canoe (boats can be rented by the hour), a safe concrete-lined area to swim in, and 6 miles of trails to forge as you try to spot black bears, white tail deer, swamp rabbits, and, of course, 'gators. It gets cooler: At its general store–style **Old Spanish Sugar Mill** (© **386/985-5644;** www. planetdeland.com/sugarmill; Mon–Fri 9am–4pm, Fri–Sat and holidays 8am–4pm), you make your own all-you-can-eat pancakes on griddles built into every table ($4.95 per person, but they'll cook you other things, too). Niftier still, the designated swimming area beside the Griddle House, is in a spring-fed boil—30 feet deep in spots—that remains at a constant 72°F, year-round. Bring your swimsuit. To reach it, take I-4 north, exit for Deland, and 6 miles north of Deland on U.S. 17 turn left onto Ponce DeLeon Boulevard for 1 mile. Get there early, because when the weather sizzles, it gets busy.

601 Ponce de Leon Blvd., Deland. ©386/985-4212. www.floridastateparks.org/deleonsprings. $6 per carload. Daily 8am–sundown.

Disney Wilderness Preserve ★ NATURE RESERVE   To gain permission to develop swampland it owns, Disney was required by law to set aside more. Now protected by the Nature Conservancy, the 12,000 marshy acres, once a ranch, constitute part of the headwaters for the Florida Everglades, and they're scarred by barely more than a 2-hour, 3-mile walking trail through scrub and cypress habitats. It's a shame the businesslike hours keep people from enjoying it. Put on your hiking shoes and get Disney's money's worth.

2700 Scrub Jay Trail, Kissimmee. ©407/935-0002. www.nature.org. $3 adults, $2 kids 6–17; Mon–Fri 9am–5pm.

Harry P. Leu Gardens ★ GARDENS   Botanical gardens seem dull on paper, yet once you find yourself within one, inhaling perfume and being warmed by the sun, you're in no hurry to leave. So it is with this 50-acre lakeside escape just north of downtown that gives visitors an inkling of why so many Gilded Age Americans wanted to flee to Florida, where the fresh air and gently rustling trees were a tonic to the

All those golf courses, parking lots, and marinas were built on someone else's home turf.

o **Manatees:** From the surface, they look like 1-ton potatoes. Sweet and docile, the biggest enemy this marine mammal has are the boat propeller, algae, and red tide. Experts estimate that only about 3,200 of them are left. As of mid-2013, 582 had died—more than any year on record.

o **Lizards:** The pigeons of the South. Little kids are fascinated by them, and cats torment them. They can lose a tail and grow it back, but if one dies in your house, it'll stink up the joint and defy discovery.

o **American bald eagles:** Not all of Florida's eagles migrate, so they're here year-round, but the population increases in winter, when the eagles that do migrate show up in "streams," adding to the flock.

o **Alligators:** Poor, misunderstood alligator. We know you'd rather eat small ducks than large people, but sometimes you get hungry and end up in the news. You'll find these reptiles in nearly every body of fresh water, so don't jump into unfamiliar canals. (As if you would.)

o **Florida panthers:** These wily, tawny-colored cats weigh up to 130 pounds and feed on deer and hogs. You're not likely to see one, as fewer than 100 remain.

o **Palmetto bugs:** Maddeningly common, these water-loving brown bugs are about 1½ inches long and eat almost anything. They can fly but prefer to scurry, and came from Africa on slave ships. Don't bawl out your hotel if you see one; they're everywhere. Another of its names: American cockroach.

maladies inflicted by the industrial North. Here you'll find Florida's largest formal rose garden (peaking in Apr); a patch planted with nectar-rich blooms favored by migrating butterflies; a large collection of camellias that bloom in late fall; and the lush Tropical Stream garden, crawling with native lizards and opening onto a dock where freshwater turtles swim and ducks bob.

1920 N. Forest Ave. ✆ **407/246-2620.** www.leugardens.org. $10 adults, $3 kids, free the first Mon of the month. Daily 9am–5pm.

Tibet–Butler Preserve ★ NATURE RESERVE   Located more or less between Disney and SeaWorld (it's incredible it hasn't been turned into a golf course yet), it's the closest to the parks: about 5 miles north of the Lake Buena Vista hotel area. The 438-acre spread is combed by 4 miles of well-maintained boardwalks and trails (which close when flooded) that will give you a soothing respite among the cypress swamps and palmetto groves that once dominated this area.

8777 C.R. 535, Orlando. ✆ **407/876-6696.** Free. Wed–Sun 8am–6pm.

Wekiwa Springs State Park ★★★ NATURE RESERVE   The closest major spring to Orlando (just 20 min. north, off I-4's exit 94) is, despite encroachment by suburbs and malls, one of the prettiest preserves in the area. When you think of Florida, you don't normally picture rambling rivers, but the 42-mile Wekiva (yes, spelled differently than the park's name and pronounced "Wek-*eye*-va") is federally designated as "Wild and Scenic," meaning it hasn't been dammed or otherwise despoiled by development, despite the fact it's just northwest of Orlando's sprawl near Apopka. The

Christmas, Florida, a blip on S.R. 50 between Orlando and Titusville, usually isn't much to write home about: farm supplies, roadkill. Unless, of course, it's the holiday season, when people come from far and wide to give their cards a Christmas postmark from the local post office. You'll find the P.O. at 23580 E. Colonial Dr./S.R. 50 (✆ **407/568-2941;** Mon–Fri 9am–5pm, Sat 9:30am–noon).

springhead, fed by two sources, flows briskly and thrillingly over rock and sand, and some people come to fish, but most agree that its canoeing is among the most spectacular in the state. **Wekiwa Springs State Park Nature Adventures** (✆ **407/884-4311;** www.canoewekiva.com) rents canoes ($17 for 2 hr.). Developers would love to sink their bulldozers' claws into this paradise; in fact, so much water is being siphoned from it that its flow is expected to diminish by 10 percent by 2025.

1800 Wekiwa Circle, Apopka. ✆ **407/884-2008.** www.floridastateparks.org/wekiwasprings. $6 per car. Daily 8am–sundown.

Boat Tours

The real Florida Everglades don't begin in earnest until south of Lake Okeechobee, which is why you'll always hear Central Florida referred to as the *headwaters* of the Florida Everglades. Orlando-area swamps are still home to a wide diversity of life forms, though.

Boggy Creek Airboat Rides ★ TOUR   Airboats use powerful, backward-facing propellers to skip through shallow bogs, and they're a common form of eco-entertainment in Florida, particularly farther south in the Everglades. Though much wildlife is spooked by the din made by boat and plane alike (you'll get ear mufflers), many water snakes and alligators appear too thick-headed to care, so you should see a few on one of the continuously running 30-minute tours—boat skippers will cut the engine and float near the critters. The boats don't operate in the rain. The wildlife spotting is better in South Florida, but this'll is a long-running crowd-pleaser. Coupons are commonly distributed. One-hour night tours ($52 adults, $48 kids 3–12) are also available, but require reservations; check the website for times.

2001 E. Southport Rd., Kissimmee. ✆ **407/344-9550.** www.bcairboats.com. 30-min. tours $27 adults, $21 kids 3–12. Daily 9am–5:30pm.

Scenic Boat Tour ★★★ TOUR   This Winter Park institution has been showing visitors glorious lakeside mansions since 1938, when they were in their heyday of attracting wealthy snowbirds from the North. Three of Winter Park's seven cypress-lined lakes, which are connected by thrillingly narrow, hand-dug canals, are explored in a 1-hour, 12-mile tour narrated by salty old fellas. The lakes are flat and relaxing, with plenty of bird life, and your guide will pay particular attention to the works of James Gamble Rogers II, a virtuosic architect responsible for many of the area's finest homes. Among the high points is a glimpse of the modest condominium where Mamie Eisenhower spent her waning years and 250-year-old live oaks. You'll find this charmer 3 blocks east of the shops on Park Avenue. Bring sunscreen because the pontoons are exposed.

312 E. Morse Blvd., Winter Park. ✆ **407/644-4056.** www.scenicboattours.com. $12 adults, $6 kids 2–11, cash only. Hourly departures 10am–4pm daily.

Golf

Golf courses do great damage to the precarious ecosystem in Central Florida's, but the sport is nonetheless a major draw to the Orlando area. Some of the brightest names in golfing, including Tiger Woods, Annika Sorenstam, Ernie Els, and Nick Faldo, have called Orlando home, as does cable's Golf Channel (which isn't open to visitors). In January, Orlando is home to the annual PGA Merchandise Show (www.pgashow.com), held in January at the Convention Center.

Every self-respecting resort has a course or three, as do luxe condo developments. There are some 170 courses around town, and the competition has caused rates to plummet in recent years. The booking websites **EZLinks.com** and **GolfNow.com** both sell discounted tee times, driving rates down further. Some courses give priority to players who stay in their hotels, either through advantageous tee times, early reservations privileges, or cheaper fees. Prices can be steeper in high season (Jan–Apr), and they may be lowest in the fall and early winter. They usually sink to about half the day's rate for "twilight" tee times, which start around midafternoon. Club rentals cost $40 to $60. Reservations are all but required and most courses have a dress code and even an age minimum, so always ask.

Orlando has plenty of award-winning courses that will cost you more than $150 to play, but if you're willing to pay that much, then you probably won't be hearing about them for the first time here. As you would do before renting a home or a hotel room, go online ahead of time to see what the individual courses are like—whether they're hilly, straightaway, or riddled with sand traps. Most courses post maps online.

DESTINATION COURSES

From pedigrees by well-known designers to clubhouses that operate more like spas, these fashionable courses are the theme parks of the fairway set. Tee time at these pricey greens fill quickly because the courses have national reputations. Count on paying about $10 per hole:

Arnold Palmer's Bay Hill Club & Lodge   Designer: Arnold Palmer, who owns it and also oversees the golf school. This guests-only course regularly receives the most accolades from experts. There's a full map of every hole on its website.

9000 Bay Hill Blvd., Orlando. © **888/422-9445.** www.bayhill.com. 18 holes.

ChampionsGate Golf Resort   Designer: Greg Norman. Headquarters of the **David Leadbetter Golf Academy** (© **888/633-5323,** ext. 112; www.davidleadbetter. com), this resort and handsome high-rise hotel is 10 minutes south of Disney.

1400 Masters Blvd., ChampionsGate. © **407/787-4653.** www.championsgategolf.com. 36 holes.

Mystic Dunes Golf Club   Designer: Gary Koch. Located 2 miles south of Disney, it has steadily won "Golf Digest" praise. Elevation changes up to 80 feet over the course of play.

7600 Mystic Dunes Lane, Celebration. © **407/787-5678.** www.mysticdunesgolf.com. 18 holes.

Reunion Resort & Club   Designers: Jack Nicklaus, Arnold Palmer, Tom Watson. Top designers and a golf school overseen by Annika Sorenstam—all a 10-minute drive south of Disney.

7593 Gathering Dr., Kissimmee. © **407/396-3199.** www.reunionresort.com/golf. 54 holes.

The Ritz-Carlton Golf Club Orlando, Grande Lakes Designer: Greg Norman. This **Golf Digest School** (☎ **800/875-4347**) is taught by PGA and LPGA professionals. Family golf packages are often available.

4040 Central Florida Pkwy., Orlando. ☎ **407/393-4900**. www.grandelakes.com. 18 holes.

Shingle Creek Golf Club Designer: David Harman. Local near the convention center, Shingle Creek is also home to a school overseen by Brad Brewer.

9939 Universal Blvd., Orlando. ☎ **866/996-9933** or 407/996-9933. www.shinglecreekgolf.com. 18 holes.

Villas of Grand Cypress Designer: Jack Nicklaus. In 2012, this club, right next to Disney in Lake Buena Vista, was noted one Orlando's best golf resorts by the readers of "Condé Nast Traveler," who know about such things.

One North Jacaranda, Orlando. ☎ **407/239-1909**. www.grandcypress.com/golf. 45 holes.

Walt Disney World Golf Courses Disney has been closing courses or parceling them to other resorts, but there are currently four left, including the Lake Buena Vista (once a PGA tour host), the just-refurbished Palm, and the Magnolia (the one with the sand bunker shaped like Mickey). Oak Trail (9 holes; $38) is the better choice for family outings. Greens fees include golf cart, when available, and kids under 18 get half off full tee time rates at the 18-hole courses. All courses opened with the resort in 1971.

Walt Disney World. ☎ **407/938-4653**. www.disneyworldgolf.com. 63 holes.

MORE AFFORDABLE COURSES

Unlike the aforementioned courses, these don't have big marketing budgets and they don't always come attached to celebrity names, but they nevertheless are high-quality courses you can enjoy at sensible prices.

Celebration Golf Course In the Disney-built town next door to the Disney-built world, English master designer Robert Trent Jones, Sr. and his son pocked their course with water hazards on 17 of its 18 holes.

701 Golf Park Dr., Celebration. ☎ **407/566-4653**. www.celebrationgolf.com. 18 holes.

Errol Estate Golf & Country Club Golf for $22! The course, mostly through quiet Florida forest with several dogleg-shaped runs and a variety of elevations, is worth more. Its Lake Course is long but easy, while its Grove Course is known for being its trickiest because of dense trees and hills. The club is 20 miles north of Disney in Apopka.

1355 Errol Pkwy, Apopka. ☎ **407/886-5000**. www.errolestatecc.com. 27 holes.

Hawk's Landing Golf Club Because it's part of the Orlando World Center Marriott resort on World Center Drive by Disney, it crawls with convention-goers who keep prices high. Water is in play on 15 of the 18 holes, and the par-71 course carries a slope rating of 131.

8701 World Center Dr., Orlando. ☎ **800/567-2623**. www.golfhawkslanding.com. 18 holes.

Highlands Reserve Golf Club This highly praised public course, with a fair mix of challenges and cakewalks, is a strong value, charging a top rate of $46, and its twilight rates kick in as early as noon. Kids age 15 and under pay $15 to $22. The course is about 10 minutes' drive southwest of Disney.

500 Highlands Reserve Blvd., Davenport. © **863/420-1724.** www.highlandsreserve-golf.com. 18 holes.

Hunter's Creek Orlando   Former cattle-grazing land was transformed into a wavy course with a good gimmick: 13 lakes were created as water hazards for 13 of the holes. The fairways are long, so prepare to drive hard. It's near the airport.

14401 Sports Club Way, Orlando. © **407/240-4653.** www.golfhunterscreek.com. 18 holes.

MetroWest Golf Club ★   This Marriott Golf–managed course is the work of Robert Trent Jones, Sr., famous for tight greens protected on both sides by sand traps, trees, or water. In late 2013, it was "redesigned to make the game faster and more enjoyable for everyday golfers," as Marriott put it. Considering it's one of the city's most popular courses, let's hope that $1.5 million was well spent. It's less than 3 miles north of Universal Orlando.

2100 S. Hiawassee Rd., Orlando. © **407/299-1099.** www.metrowestgolf.com. 18 holes.

Orange County National Golf Center and Lodge   At this wide-open complex (922 acres, unspoiled by houses—atypical around here), fees peak at $65 to $75 for 18 holes, depending on time of year and day of the week (Mon–Thurs are cheapest). Holes have five sets of tees, allowing you to choose a game that ranges between 7,300 yards and a little over 5,000. It's among the developments north of Walt Disney World.

16301 Phil Ritson Way, Winter Garden. © **407/656-2626.** www.ocngolf.com. 45 holes.

Royal St. Cloud Golf Links   Aiming to recall Scotland's great links—there's even a stone bridge that looks like it was built during the days of William Wallace, not in 2001—this modest club, 25 miles east of Disney, charges $18 for fees. Its fairways are noted for being wide, well groomed, and firm, and planners promise you'll use "every club in the bag."

5310 Michigan Ave., St. Cloud. © **877/891-7010** or 407/891-7010. www.stcloudgolfclub.com. 27 holes.

Timacuan Golf and Country Club   There are five sets of tees, adapting this exceptionally well-groomed course from 7,000 to 5,000 yards, and unusually, designers were careful to leave its handsome Old Florida features (undulating fairways, Spanish moss, wetlands) mostly intact. Only 3 holes are riddled with water, which might make it easier for kids. The greens were renovated in 2013. Lake Mary is 10 miles north of downtown.

550 Timacuan Blvd., Lake Mary. © **407/321-0010.** www.golftimacuan.com. 18 holes.

Hot-Air Ballooning & Hang Gliding

Florida is well suited to hot-air ballooning for many of the same reasons that it's ideal for golf: flat, even topography and often placid morning weather. A trip involves a very early start—6am is common. You'll be finished with your hour-long ride by the time the theme parks get cranking.

Magic Sunrise Ballooning   More intimate than its supersized competition, with just 2 to 4 people in the basket with the pilot, this company, flying since 1987, greets landings with a champagne toast.

603.N. Garfield Ave., Deland; © **866/606-7433.** www.magicsunriseballooning.com. $215 per person for 2–4 people, $125 kids under 90 lbs., no kids 5 or under.

Orlando Balloon Rides In business since 1983, its flagship balloon, launched as the world's largest in 2011, is 11 stories tall and its basket fits an incredible 24 people. It meets at a hotel near the main Disney entrance.

407/894-5040. www.orlandoballoonrides.com. $175 adults, $95 kids 10–15, free for 1 child 9 or under with each paying adult, additional kids $95 each, $10 less online.

Wallaby Ranch In flat Central Florida, where there are no mountains that don't contain roller coasters, hang gliders can't soar from cliffs. Instead, they're launched by ultralight "aerotugs," to an altitude of 2,000 feet.

1805 Deen Still Rd., Davenport. *863/424-0070.* www.wallaby.com. Tandem flights $175.

SHOPPING

Orlando is a hotbed for outlet activity, partly because international visitors, with their often-superior currencies, are prone to buying frenzies. Like most modern outlet malls, not all of the items you find for sale here will have come from higher-priced "regular" stores; much of the stock has been specially manufactured for the outlet market (although "Consumer Reports" doesn't think the quality is substantially different from retail). You'll usually find prices between 30 and 50 percent off sales at retail stores, and after the holiday rush, when stores need to ready for the new lines, discounts go deeper. All the best ones are village-style outdoor malls and most stay open for longer-than-usual hours: Monday to Saturday from 10am to 11pm, Sunday 10am to 9pm.

Outlet Malls

Orlando Premium Outlets International Dr. ★★★ OUTLET MALL The most dangerously tempting outlet in town is a stupendous 180-store (give or take) open-air village where it is very unlikely you will come away empty-handed. Many times of year, the place vibrates with 40-percent discounts, luring tourists by the hordes. Nearly every conceivable brand has a presence here, but the chief threats include Neiman Marcus Last Call—a clearance center that sells genuine department store castoffs from its namesake stores, Bergdorf Goodman, and the Horchow catalog—Saks Fifth Avenue Off 5th, Calphalon, Coach, Ann Taylor Factory Store, Puma, Nike Factory Store, Guess? Factory Store, Eddie Bauer Outlet, Kenneth Cole, Fossil, Reebok Outlet Store, Hugo Boss Factory Store, Calvin Klein, Brooks Brothers Factory Store, Kate Spade New York, Tumi, Victoria's Secret, and Juicy Couture. There's a Disney's Character Warehouse to undercut your souvenir bill. Weekdays are quietest, and parking is most ample around back. The website lists sales by store.

4951 International Dr., Orlando. *407/352-9600.* www.premiumoutlets.com.

Orlando Premium Outlets Vineland Ave ★★ OUTLET MALL Being just a mile east of Disney property has its perks—its owners tout it as the most productive outlet center in America, with sales exceeding $1,000 per square foot. That's why at press time, it was about to cut the ribbon on a 110,000-square-foot expansion of a property that already had 550,000 square feet and 150 stores. Among the goods: Armani Outlet, Banana Republic Factory Store, Barney's New York Outlet, Gymboree, and Burberry. One popular shop, because it's so close to the Mouse House, is Disney's Character Premiere, for cast-off official theme park souvenirs. Steel yourself during the weekend; the competition for parking approaches Olympian difficulty. It's 10 minutes from Downtown Disney; the turnoff is just south of I-4's exit 68 on S.R.

535/Apopka Vineland, by Bahama Breeze. The I-Ride Trolley (p. 228) touches down here ostensibly every 20 minutes.

8200 Vineland Ave., Orlando. ☎ **407/238-7787.** www.premiumoutlets.com.

Lake Buena Vista Factory Stores ★ OUTLET MALL   The third-best outlet shopping in town is a strip mall–style collection of about 50 stores, not all of which are owned by famous brands. The offerings here, about 2 miles south of the Downtown Disney gate, are not as shimmering as those at its two rival outlet malls, but they're decent, especially for kids. There are enough names you know (including Tommy Hilfiger Kids, Carter's for Kids, Old Navy Outlet, OshKosh B'Gosh, and Aéropostale) to warrant a quick trip. The Disney Character Outlet has some bargains (half-price mugs, shirts, toys, and some souvenirs dated from a few years ago), and there's a Travelex office for currency exchange. The mall provides a free daily shuttle to and from major hotels around Disney and I-Drive; they leave between 9am and 2:50pm and return in four batches from 12:55 to 7pm (6pm on Sun).

15657 S. Apopka Vineland Rd. (S.R. 535), Orlando. ☎ **407/238-9301.** www.lbvfs.com. Mon–Sat 10am–9 and Sun 10am–7pm.

Downtown Disney

Downtown Disney ★★, Walt Disney World's main free area for restaurants and shopping, ambles along the shore of Village Lake a few miles east of Epcot, in a traffic-clogged zone on the eastern edge of park property. At the easternmost section, the Marketplace section is dominated by stores selling every variety of Disney-themed merchandise you can imagine.

As of this writing, Downtown Disney is receiving a drastic overhaul. By 2016, it will be known as Disney Springs, with more restaurants and shops added and the old Pleasure Island concept extracted like a wart. Disney is known to switch courses, so you have your heart set on anything there, make sure you call ahead to ensure it will be open. Downtown Disney/Disney Springs will remain a place to grab dinner (alas, no cheaper than elsewhere in the World), buy Disney souvenirs, or maybe bowl or catch a Cirque du Soleil show (see p. 94 for its entertainment options and p. 171 for its dining choices). Parking is free but maddening, although a new structure to open by early 2015 will hopefully assuage that. In the meantime, hunting for a space here will be a less-than-magical experience that sometimes requires parking across the street, so consider taking the free Disney bus or ferry from elsewhere in the resort.

The district has three zones; because of the size, it's helpful to know which one you're heading for because the walk between them can be up to 15 minutes. The busiest and easternmost area is called the Marketplace (it's nearest to the DTS bus stop), and it's for shops and restaurants. The westernmost zone is the West Side, and although it has some shops not listed here (such as **Sosa Family Cigars**), it leans toward nightlife and entertainment, with a Cirque du Soleil show, **Splitsville Luxury Lanes** bowling, and a 24-screen cinema (p. 95). Between West Side and Marketplace is the focus of the Disney Springs redevelopment, and it will eventually be divided into The Town Center and The Landing.

Shops at the **Marketplace** (☎ **407/939-3463**) are almost pure Mouse, and nearly all of them sell candy, too. Stores are themed for maximum souvenir sales, including one for toys and games (**Once Upon a Toy**—Mr. Potato Head and toy versions of Disney attractions are huge these days), one for Christmas and holiday decorations (**Disney's**

Days of Christmas), one for high-end collectibles (the Art of Disney), one for kitchen tools (Mickey's Pantry), one for athletic wear (Team Mickey, with a Ridemakerz radio-controlled vehicle store in back), one for urban wear (Tren-D), one for stationery and albums (Disney's Wonderful World of Memories), and Disney's Pin Traders, a hub for collectors of the park's badges. Don't bother looking for a bookstore to browse the range of titles pertaining to Walt and what he accomplished. Disney closed its bookstores.

The Marketplace's tent-pole is the big kahuna of Disney merch: World of Disney, the largest souvenir department store in the resort, crowned by a giant Stitch burping water onto passersby. It's a rambling cathedral-roofed barn stocked from rug to rafter with every conceivable Disney-branded item—a Villains room, a room for men, one for candy, one for the latest branding craze, and so on. You'll find stuff here you won't find at other Disney stores here or at home. Yet sometimes, the same toys and DVDs cost $7 at box stores while Walt Disney World wants $20 or more. Before purchasing, always ask if any item you want is a "park exclusive"—that means it's only available here. Otherwise, you could do a lot better if you got it back home. Despite its status as the chief Mouse mart, World of Disney still may not have what you want. That's because it's the only store that offers annual passholders a discount, which means the most obsessed fans clean the shelves here first. It also may not carry items that might be sold at another store at the Marketplace (tree ornaments, for example, or toys). Disney's merchandise distribution is bureaucratic; shopkeepers virtually beg superiors for restocking, and even then it can take weeks.

Very few stores sell non-Disney plunder. Ghirardelli Soda Fountain & Chocolate Shop is one of the few non–San Francisco locations run by the chocolate-making stalwart. It has a pricey sundae shop and a boutique where $1/12$-oz. samples are freely dispensed. Kids can't be separated from the Lego Imagination Center store (still here despite the fact the toymaker now brands a competing park, p. 133), where children can play with kits for free, or Build-A-Dino which does for reptiles what Build-a-Bear does for teddies. Basin sells bath products for those teeny hotel room tubs. The resort's shopping list has seismically dumbed down since the 1970s, when fascinating international goods were imported for the area then called the Lake Buena Vista Shopping Village.

Bibbidi Bobbidi Boutique ★★★ SALON Little girls bask in the star treatment as they are lavished with glittery, pink makeovers as princesses for $55 (Coach package with hair and a sash; add nails for $5) to over $240 (gown, wand, photos), over seen by a kindly "Fairy Godmother-in-Training." Warning: The dresses are hot and scratchy, so bring a change of clothes if the sun is strong. Boys are steered to the Pirates League in Adventureland, where similar gender roles are ascribed. There's also a salon in the Magic Kingdom in the Castle, but you'll need a park ticket for that and slots are scarcer. World of Disney, Marketplace. ✆ **407/939-7895.** www.disneyworld.com/style. Daily 9am–7pm. Minimum age 3. Reservations required.

Other Interesting Stores

If you feel moved to learn more about Florida history, the book selection isn't massive. The bookstore at the Regional History Center (✆ **407/836-8594**; p. 142), however, is a good start. You'll find a Barnes & Noble (Venezia Plaza, 7900 W. Sand Lake Rd., Orlando; ✆ **407/345-0900**; daily 9am–11pm) among the terrific restaurants of Sand Lake Road west of I-4 and at the Florida Mall (8358 S. Orange Blossom Trail, Orlando; ✆ **407/856-7200**; Sun–Thurs 9am–8pm, Fri–Sat 9am–11pm).

The Pin Culture

One of the most special souvenir traditions on Disney turf is the collection of little enamel and cloisonné pins featuring every known character, ride, movie, and promotional event. When the Haunted Mansion was refurbished, pins were made that contained tiny snippets of Madame Leota's original crystal ball. Sometimes it seems it's easier to get your hands on a pin than it is to find a bottle of water—there's even a pavilion that sells nothing but pins at Downtown Disney. They are usually worn on lanyards, and when cast members clock in for their shifts, they replenish their pin supply at a special window in the backstage area—a dozen to a lanyard at all times. The rule is that if a cast member is wearing almost any pin you want (barring ones commemorating employment milestones), you're allowed to ask them to trade it for one of your own and they're not allowed to refuse if the pin is legit. Universal sells a fair supply, too, but the craze is fiercest at Disney, where the backings are shaped, of course.

Eli's Orange World ★★ SHOP   Agra has the Taj Mahal and Sydney has its opera house—Orlando has a 60-foot-tall orange. Back when most of this land was orange groves, Florida roadsides were full of this kind of souvenir catch-all, stacked high with oranges and grapefruits in their red mesh bags, but the citrus industry cashed out for McMansions. Fruit changes by the season: Fall is for navel and ambersweet oranges, January sees honeybell tangelos, and February through May sees a procession of oranges, honey tangerines, and Valencia oranges; Indian River grapefruit is available year-round. The shelves also teeter with the sort of corny Florida souvenirs that time forgot, including shellacked alligator heads and local jellies. Sure, there are *lots* of schlocky, fluorescent-lit barns selling junky souvenirs on U.S. 192 and I-Drive—but this is *landmark* schlock.

5395 W. U.S. Hwy. 192, Kissimmee. ℰ **800/531-3182** or 407/239-6031. www.orangeworld192.com. daily 8am–9:40pm.

Festival Bay/Artegon Orlando ★ MALL   It's not an outlet mall, but it's a desperate one, so prices are low. Try as it might, this audaciously designed real estate tragedy at the top end of I-Drive hasn't been able to wake from a nightmare that began when it opened in 2001. A stroll down its peppy but depressingly bleak, half-tenanted corridors can feel at times like a trek through a consumerist's tundra, which is why $70 million is being sunk into its reinvention as a space for a farmer's market, beer hall, and bazaar for artisans. No matter what happens inside, the anchor stores remain worthy of attention. The beloved **Ron Jon Surf Shop** from Cocoa Beach, a **Sheplers Western Wear** for honing that proto-American look, and the camping-and-fishing megastore **Bass Pro Shops Outdoor World,** so gargantuan it must be seen to be believed. For minor entertainment, there's the **Putting Edge** glow-in-the-dark minigolf course (p. 148).

5250 International Dr., across from Premium Outlets, Orlando. ℰ **407/351-7718.** Mon–Sat 10am–9pm, Sun 11am–7pm.

CRUISES FROM PORT CANAVERAL

Cruise lines depart from Port Canaveral (www.portcanaveral.com), an hour east of Orlando, so it's easy to combine a cruise of a few days with the theme parks. Parking costs about $20 a day, and there's nothing to do at the port.

As usual, you won't find many discounts from Disney, although MouseSavers.com tells which departures are going cheap. Quotes from specialty agents are often hundreds lower than those the lines themselves offer, and prices of $100 a night or less can be had if you book through a specialist. Check **Cruise Brothers** (© **800/827-7779;** www.cruisebrothers.com), **Cruises Only** (© **800/278-4737;** www.cruisesonly.com), and **Online Vacation Center** (© **800/780-9002;** www.onlinevacationcenter.com). Don't quit before you consult a terrific site called **Cruise Compete** (www.cruisecompete. com), on which multiple cruise sellers jockey for your business by offering low bids.

Carnival Cruise Lines ★ CRUISE   Considered a low-rent line, it's noisy and atwitter with neon, like the inside of a pinball machine. Think "Real Housewives of the Atlantic Ocean." Carnival is popular with families, teens especially like it, and there are few pretensions. Each ship's has a twisting water slide that has also become a line signature. Carnival sails the *Sensation* on 3- and 4-night Bahamas runs, the *Ecstasy* on 3- and 4-day runs to the Bahamas and a 5-day trip for the Bahamas and Key West, and the *Dream,* among the line's largest ships, does 7-night Caribbean cruises, both Eastern and Western. In the spring of 2014, the *Sunshine* and the *Liberty* will replace the two latter ships, making Carnival the largest carrier out of the port.
© **800/764-7419**. www.carnival.com.

Disney Cruise Line ★★★ CRUISE   These high-quality, casino-free ships, the newest of the port's fleet, include character appearances, fireworks at sea, and top-drawer entertainment. The hallmark is the kids' program, and in a brilliant touch, waiters follow you no matter the restaurant you're in (one restaurant, by the way, changes from black and white to full color as you dine). The *Dream,* DCL's largest, ranges 3- to 5-night Bahamas voyages, and the *Fantasy,* just as large, sails for week-long Eastern and Western Caribbean trips. Disney packages trips with theme park stays and provides seamless transitions between the two, although because it's a Disney package it won't give you the best deal on the Walt Disney World portion.
© **800/393-2784.** www.disneycruise.com.

Royal Caribbean International ★ CRUISE   It's the line for young couples and teens, with active diversions such as rock-climbing walls. It hits the sweet spot between the gaudy tackiness of Carnival and the twee branding of Disney. The ship right now is *Enchantment of the Seas,* a Vision-class ship from 1996 (no ice rink, no sheet wave machine) that's among the line's most manageable, at 2,664 passengers. It offers 3- and 4-night Bahamas cruises.
© **866/562-7625.** www.royalcaribbean.com.

DINING
AROUND TOWN

Y ou don't need a guidebook to decide if you want to eat a chain restaurant—and Orlando is crawling with those, in plain view, everywhere. But you might use help locating family-run small businesses or fledgling brands that aren't backed by multimillion-dollar ad campaigns. These are the worthy discoveries you might not otherwise have noticed among the clamor of plastic and neon signage.

That's not to say corporate food can't have local provenance. In Orlando, even supersized brands have a pedigree: Darden, which owns Red Lobster, Olive Garden, and LongHorn Steakhouse, is based here, and so is Hard Rock Cafe. But for those, you already know what you're going to get.

Pretty much every restaurant is open for lunch and dinner. Don't expect places to accept checks—credit cards are Orlando's cash. Also, this is a town where it bears asking for discounts. Turnover is high, so everybody's angling for business.

In addition to the recommendations below, check out **www.scott josephorlando.com**, a food blog, or "flog" by food expert Scott Joseph, once of the "Orlando Sentinel," which highlights Joseph's favorite places to eat, most of them in the "real" Orlando north of the tourist zone. In September, dozens of high-quality area restaurants band together for **Orlando Magical Dining Month** (www.orlandomagicaldining.com), when three-course (appetizer, entree, dessert) prix-fixe dinners cost $33.

In this chapter, prices are classified based on the price range for a main course at dinner:

- Inexpensive: $10 or less
- Moderate: $11 to $16
- Expensive: $17 or over

OUTSIDE THE DISNEY PARKS

These are the restaurants on resort property but not inside a ticketed park. For places inside the parks, plus info on the Disney Dining Plan, see chapter 3. Some of Disney's best restaurants are in its hotels, accessible to anyone. Well, not anyone: folks with deep pockets, soon to be empty. Disney's most affordable hotels don't offer much beyond food courts, but its most expensive hotels usually support a fine restaurant or two.

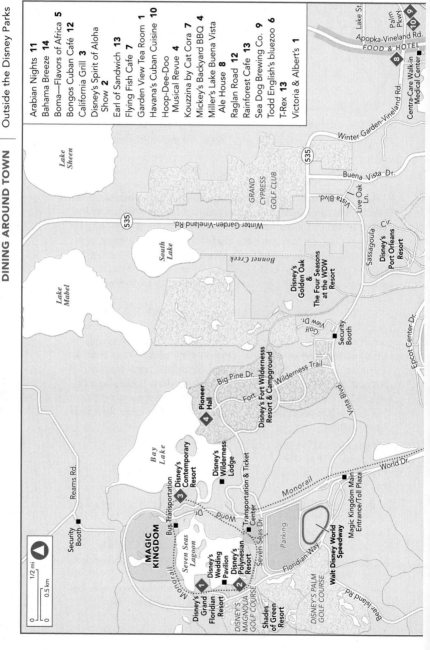

Arabian Nights **11**
Bahama Breeze **14**
Boma—Flavors of Africa **5**
Bongos Cuban Café **12**
California Grill **3**
Disney's Spirit of Aloha Show **2**
Earl of Sandwich **13**
Flying Fish Cafe **7**
Garden View Tea Room **1**
Havana's Cuban Cuisine **10**
Hoop-Dee-Doo Musical Revue **4**
Kouzzina by Cat Cora **7**
Mickey's Backyard BBQ **4**
Miller's Lake Buena Vista Ale House **8**
Raglan Road **12**
Rainforest Cafe **13**
Sea Dog Brewing Co. **9**
Todd English's bluezoo **6**
T-Rex **13**
Victoria & Albert's **1**

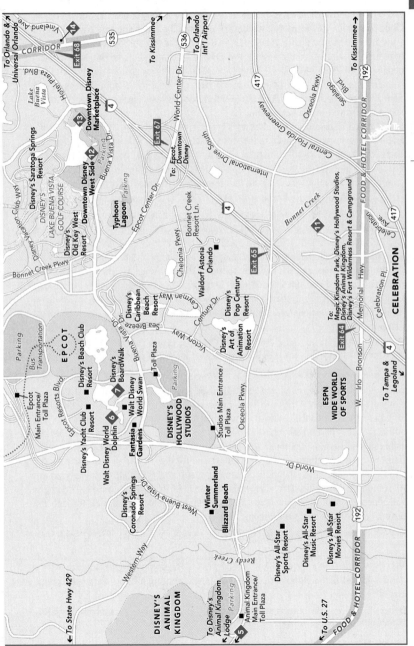

Reservations are pretty much a necessity for Disney's table-service restaurants. Walk-ins are accepted, but you may be turned away. Slots open 180 days in advance, and families throw themselves into it early as if they're Panzer units invading Poland. Obnoxiously, Disney slaps you with a $10 cancellation fee if you fail to show up for your reservation, and taking your credit card details for that purpose can turn a simple booking into an 8-minute dialogue. All Disney's restaurants have the same contact details (✆ **407/939-3463** [DINE]; http://disneyworld.disney.go.com/dining). You can sometimes get around that by making one reservation using its app. Parking is free with a reservation. Reservationists have schedules of events (such as fireworks times) and will help you plan around them.

The nicest restaurants within Disney's hotels generally serve from 5 to 10pm, as it's assumed patrons will eat lunch in the parks. Each resort has at least one quick-service counter and one or two sit-down places to eat. Some are more special than others, and many more have no point of view or phone it in for the convention crowd, so focus your booking attentions on these, all unfortunately in the Expensive category:

Boma—Flavors of Africa ★★★ AFRICAN Make a reservation here and you get a big bonus: a fine excuse to visit Disney's Animal Kingdom Lodge and pay a visit to the animals in its backyard paddocks, floodlit after dark—think of the high price as an admission fee for that. Dinner is a good time, too: A 60-item buffet menu, served in a dramatically vaulted dining room of thatching and bamboo, is not all African. It runs the gamut from roast chicken and beef to such African-themed delights as watermelon rind salad, curried coconut seafood stew, and *bobotie* (a moussaka-like pie of ground beef from South Africa). There's an atmospheric wood fire, with plenty of chefs on hand to answer questions and plenty of options for less adventurous (read: younger) tongues.

Disney's Animal Kingdom Lodge, 2901 Osceola Pkwy., Bay Lake. ✆ **407/939-3463.** www.disney world.com. Adults $39–$43, kids $18–$20. Daily 7–11am and 4:30–9:30pm.

California Grill ★★★ AMERICAN For one blowout night with a view, the best choice is this just-renovated and much-beloved space on the 15th floor of the mod Contemporary Resort. The wine list is extensive (250 by the bottle, 80 by the glass, 10 types of sake), and the fusion-style menu, helmed by Chef Brian Piasecki, is bright and seasonal—the 24-hour braised short rib with truffle-whipped potatoes goes for richness, and sushi is a popular sideline here. Book as soon as you can—the maximum is 180 days before—and get a window seat for the fireworks. The music for the show is even piped in to the outdoor viewing platforms, which are practically on top of Tomorrowland. After dark, Cinderella Castle is lit by a shifting palette of indigos and emeralds. Plus, a dinner here is a fantastic excuse to have a stroll through the atrium of Disney World's most iconic hotel.

Disney's Contemporary Resort, 4600 N. World Dr., Lake Buena Vista. ✆ **407/939-3463.** Main courses about $30.

Garden View Tea Room ★★ HIGH TEA The pseudo-Victorian space with a garden gazebo feel delights little girls with its range of high teas—tea cozies, china, and all.

Disney's Grand Floridian Resort & Spa, 4401 Floridian Way, Lake Buena Vista. ✆ **407/939-3463.** High tea $14–$38. Daily 2–4:30pm.

Jiko—The Cooking Place ★★ AFRICAN The a la carte fine dining room across the hall from Boma is marked by many as one of the resort's most romantic tables. It serves entrees that are very good, too (plus flatbreads—Disney's top restaurants have a love affair with flatbreads), but they often cost what the entire banquet does at Boma. The food coming from the open kitchen is pan-African, but waiters are sometimes too eager to adulterate to pander to American palates. About the filet mignon: "We'll serve it over macaroni and cheese if you want. But if you want something a little more African, the beef short ribs." That said, there are some enlivening twists such as sweet tamarind butter for the bread, frisky amuse-bouches (prosciutto-wrapped pineapple, cucumber sorbet), and crispy beef *bobotie* roll that taste like a Christmasy spring roll. Animal Kingdom Lodge also has one of the largest lists of South African wines in North America. When you're here, you also get to see the animals in the view area at the Lodge.

Disney's Animal Kingdom Lodge, 2901 Osceola Pkwy., Bay Lake. © **407/939-3463.** www.disney world.com. Main courses $28–$44. Daily 7–11am and 4:30–9:30pm.

Todd English's bluezoo ★★★ SEAFOOD A rare Disney restaurant overseen by a true culinary celebrity; in this case, Todd English, known for rich flavors. There's craftsmanship here. Eaten among witty colored-glass baubles that suggest being underwater, the menu changes but the focus is fresh fish. The nightly herb-rubbed "dancing fish" is grilled on a spinning skewer (watch them spin alongside the raw bar); the light clam chowder comes infused with bacon; and the 2-pound "Cantonese" lobster is painted in a sticky soy glaze that must be shared. The Lounge serves a bar menu.

Walt Disney World Dolphin Hotel, 1500 Epcot Resorts Blvd., Lake Buena Vista. © **407/934-1111.** www.swananddolphin.com/bluezoo. Mains $30–$42. Daily 5–11pm.

Victoria & Albert's ★★★ FRENCH Disney's flagship restaurant is the destination for honeymoons, anniversaries, proposals, and gourmands. The company puts much stock in Chef Scott Hunnel, a multiple James Beard nominee who sources ingredients personally and also oversees the top-tier restaurants on Disney Cruise Line. Praised as the only AAA five-diamond restaurant in Central Florida, a citation it has earned since 2000, the 65-seater lays on its indulgent seven-course menu (amuse-bouches, osetra caviar, Iwate Japanese beef with oxtail jus, pheasant consommé) presented to you under cloches like a parade of debutantes. It's so theatrical you just have to swoon. It's like the Very Fancy Restaurant where a character might take a date on a sitcom, which adds to the theater. The resort's most exclusive reservation is here: the four-table Queen Victoria's room, where a private 10-course meal is served behind closed doors for $210 per person before wine. It sells out. Reserve 180 days ahead.

Disney's Grand Floridian Resort & Spa, 4401 Floridian Way. Lake Buena Vista. © **407/939-3463.** www.victoria-alberts.com.com. Prix-fixe from $135, wine pairings from $65. 10-course Chef's Table prix-fixe from $210, wine pairings from $105. 2 nightly seatings, 1 for Chef's Table and Queen Victoria's room. Jacket required for men (loaners available), no children under 10 permitted.

Downtown Disney

In these restaurants, none of the food is as spectacular as the interior decor, and unless you come at lunch when prices drop by a third, you will pay something to the tune of $15 for a burger. Welcome to Disney!

Downtown Disney is full of additional places that charge extreme prices ($30 a plate) but don't give your money back to you in skilled cuisine. Although none serve foul food, most of them coast along by sponging from steady foot traffic. That means you can count these places out, although you will be pressured not to: **Fulton's Crab House,** in a mock riverboat berthed solidly in concrete; the fair-to-average **Portobello**

Country Italian Trattoria, with an Italian theme; and the Asian-fusion **Wolfgang Puck Grand Café** (it also has a walk-up window for quick bites, and there's also a "Bistro" version at Universal's CityWalk), a tired **Planet Hollywood** in need of euthanasia, the quick-service **Pollo Campero** chicken joint; and **House of Blues. Ghirardelli Ice Cream and Chocolate Shop** is a rare offshoot of the San Francisco treasure, but it only does desserts (although its adjoining candy shop always gives away tablet-size free samples).

INEXPENSIVE

Earl of Sandwich ★★ SANDWICHES   The most affordable option at the Downtown Disney Marketplace area, barring McDonald's, is located to its extreme east: a branch of a 26-location franchise based in Orlando. Here, you can easily grab a made-to-order 6-inch sandwich, made with fresh ingredients and toasted on the spot. There are more than a dozen hot and cold selections, from roast beef to turkey with stuffing, plus nine salads, and everything's six bucks. It's hard to believe such good prices exist in Disney World.

Downtown Disney Marketplace. ✆ **407/938-1762.** www.earlofsandwichusa.com. Sandwiches $6. Daily 8:30am–11pm.

EXPENSIVE

Bongos Cuban Café ★ CUBAN   This place proudly reminds you it was co-founded by Gloria and Emilio Estefan, the Cuban-born power couple of Latin music, and that boast is a portent that the focus will be on music and not on food. The dishes (ceviche, plantains, yucca, and lots of grilled or lightly fried fish and meats) are generally unsuccessful, and such inattention to signature Cuban dishes is abrasive when you've paid this much, but there's some festivity in the hypersugary decor, which makes the building look like it's been overtaken by giant, washed-out pineapples, palms, and drums. At night, there's often a (loud) live band, and the upstairs patio is an appealing place to hang out with a rum drink, making it worthy of a gentle recommendation.

Downtown Disney West Side. ✆ **407/828-0999.** www.bongoscubancafe.com. No cover. Mains $17–$25. Free self-parking.

Raglan Road ★★★ IRISH   Downtown Disney's best sit-down choice is run by accessible, contemporary Irish chef Kevin Dundon. Of all the chefs working Downtown Disney, Dundon's got the most imagination. Here, Irish staples are turned into sprightly new visions, including whiskey-glazed steak with basil oil, beef stew infused with Guinness, and good old fish and chips. Although the massive dining area is styled after an Irish pub, it's 20 times noisier. There's free live music most nights, and often step dancers. If you only want fish and chips, get it on the south side of the building for about $8 less at the counter-service **Cookes of Dublin** ★, run by the same people.

Downtown Disney. ✆ **407/938-0300.** www.raglanroad.com. Mains $16–$29. Daily 11am–1:30am.

Rainforest Cafe ★ AMERICAN   Another over-the-top themed doozy where families dine in a faux jungle with lions, pythons, elephants, and other robotic animals that periodically spring to life, interrupting dinner and stoking wild behavior in small children. Think of it as the Jungle Cruise with napkins. Like so much in Orlando, it has no culinary specialization, instead opting to be all things to all eaters: burgers, salads, pizzas, capped by a gift shop with stuffed animals. Because Rainforest exists across America, I'd pick T-Rex. There's a second location at the front gate of Animal Kingdom.

Downtown Disney Marketplace. ✆ **407/827-8500.** www.rainforestcafe.com. Mains $14–$26. 11am–10:35pm.

T-Rex ★ AMERICAN   Nothing would be a more surefire diversion than life-size robotic dinosaurs planted amongst the tables. Every so often, the ceiling (at least, the one outside the simulated ice cave) is the stage for a projected meteor shower while the destruction of all life forms is briefly simulated with cacophony and red lighting. Pass the ketchup. It's so silly it seems like a joke in a movie. You can probably predict the fare: Bronto Burgers, Artifact Stack fried onion rings, and to end it all, the $16 Chocolate Extinction, a fudge cake sundae for two or more people.

Downtown Disney West Side. ✆ **407/828-8739.** www.trexcafe.com. Mains $14–$33. Daily 11am–11pm.

Disney's BoardWalk

BoardWalk is a lakefront promenade that's merely notionally themed to an old-time pier. You'll find a few midway games, occasional buskers, and ice cream and margarita stores—not much, and most of its menus pander with the standard burgers-and-such variety. The **ESPN Club** serves food as an excuse to bask in the blare of countless TV airing live sports while **Big River Grille & Brewing Works** serves food because you have to have something to wash down with its microbrews (and happily, that place doesn't accept reservations, so if other places are jammed you can try there). Postmeal strolls, as ferries serenely cross water and Epcot twitters in the near distance, are pretty, and they're reason enough to come. You can park at the BoardWalk Inn and get your parking validated or you can walk there via Epcot's World Showcase, 10 minutes away, where, it must be said, the dining is more fun. But if you're here. . . .

EXPENSIVE

Flying Fish Cafe ★★★ SEAFOOD   To say this is one of the most underrated restaurants on Disney property is not to say it's a knockout, but that its kitchen is careful to source truly fresh food and deliver a good time in a theme parky-environment. Impeccably prepared seafood (grouper, mahimahi) is its principal domain, but it also does plenty of land-based meats. You can choose between a table or a stool facing the invigorating fire in its open kitchen. The entree of note is the memorable potato-wrapped red snapper, which should tell you about the carbohydrated concessions a fresh-ingredient kitchen must make to keep the booths packed in Orlando.

Disney's BoardWalk. ✆ **407/939-5100.** Mains $20–$35. Daily 5:30–10pm.

Kouzzina by Cat Cora ★ MEDITERRANEAN   The second-best quality of the BoardWalk aspirants, this Greek kitchen by Cora, an Iron Chef, serves calamari that earns raves from just about everyone who eats it. Like all Disney restaurants, it can be a loud, overcrowded machine with distracted service to match, but there are plenty of high spots among the Greek dishes, particularly during a meal's bookends. Get the *avgolemono* (egg-lemon soup) to start and the *loukoumades* (hot donuts with honey and lemon) to finish.

Disney's BoardWalk. ✆ **407/939-5100.** Mains $20–$35. Daily 7:30–11am and 5–10pm.

Parents: I know you came to Orlando to spend some time with your family, but I also understand that you might need to get away from some of them for a few hours. If you're staying in a luxury resort hotel, the management may offer some kind of paid babysitting or supervised kids' club service. If not, there are always these possibilities: **Kid's Nite Out** (✆ **800/696-8105;** www.kidsnite out.com; $16/hr. for the first child, $2.50 for each additional child) and **All About Kids** (✆ **800/728-6506** or 407/812-9300; www.all-about-kids.com; $14/hr. for the first child, $2 for each additional child). Both companies are insured, bonded, and licensed, and both would appreciate a few days' warning for reservations for in-room sitting. Expect $10 to $12 in transportation fees. Five Disney resorts including the Polynesian and Animal Kingdom Lodge operate supervised clubs (✆ **407/939-3463**) for potty-trained kids ages 3 to 12 starting at 4:30pm and ending at midnight. These cost $12 per hour per child, which includes a simple meal during dinnertime and a 10pm snack, and are sometimes open to people who aren't staying in a Disney hotel. I do *not* recommend depositing your offspring at the gates of the Magic Kingdom and speeding off, as actress Tracy Pollan's father once did rather than babysit her.

Universal Orlando

Although **Mythos** (p. 122) is the only restaurant inside the Universal theme parks that's worth a detour, there are worthwhile dining options in Universal Orlando that are outside the parks—ones for which you don't need a park ticket. Universal's three hotels host upscale restaurants, while the CityWalk outdoor party mall, located between the resort's main parking garage and the entrances to the parks, attracts plenty of young local people who have no intention of proceeding to the thrill rides.

After dark, CityWalk has a few windows serving stuff like hot dogs and pizza, plus the slowest Burger King on the crust of the earth. Because they siphon the same post–theme park customers, the ambiance at all of these sit-down restaurants is the same—loud, cavernous, family-friendly, often with faux antiques bolted to the walls. You'll want to arrive before 9pm, because some of these places charge covers after then. Everything closes by 2am. (For CityWalk from the nightlife perspective, see p. 153.)

If you intend to linger at CityWalk for the nightlife (parking is $5 from 6–10pm and free after 10pm unless there's a big event on), there are a few package deals that combine a meal, including a beverage, with a movie and entry to the clubs. The **Meal and Movie Deal** (✆ **407/224-2691;** $22) pairs dinner at one of seven restaurants with a movie at CityWalk's ABC multiplex, and can be purchased at the CityWalk Guest Services window. Conveniently, you don't have to enjoy both meal and movie on the same day.

Entrees cost more than they would outside Universal; they're mostly priced in the teens, with burgers sliding in around $13. So although none of these places are at the top of my list for a value meal, and only one of them is a true gourmet experience, you may find yourself patronizing one after a long day at the parks, so here are some appraisals. Call ✆ **407/224-3663** for more information, unless there's another number listed. You can always eat at **Bubba Gump Shrimp Company** or **NASCAR Sports Grille,** but these are the more interesting choices:

MODERATE

Pat O'Brien's ★★ SOUTHERN   Like its bawdy Nawlins namesake, it does Cajun-style dishes such as shrimp gumbo, étouffée, and jambalaya, optionally served with a fat rum Hurricane cocktail in the hand. The potent drinks account for a clientele with fewer kids, but there is a kids' menu.

CityWalk. ✆ **407/224-2106.** www.patobriens.com. Mains $8–$17. Food daily 4pm–1am.

Pastamoré Ristorante & Market ★ ITALIAN   Family-friendly Italian (wood-oven pizza, pasta, meat dishes), reasonably affordably, but rarely memorably. Most dishes are under $20 and so it tends to be noisy and busy, which lends to the happy mood.

CityWalk. ✆ **407/224-7223.** Dinner mains $9–$24. Daily noon–10pm.

Jimmy Buffett's Margaritaville ★★ AMERICAN   Because it's nearest to Islands of Adventure at the park's closing time, it gets jammed with park-goers clamoring for margaritas and grub like Cheeseburgers in Paradise. In late afternoon, there may be a strummer on the "Porch of Indecision," and after 10pm, the indoor area morphs into a club with a band and that $7 CityWalk cover. Across the way, under a 60-foot Albatross plane, the *Hemisphere Dancer,* is the **Lone Palm Airport** for margaritas and appetizers on the go.

CityWalk. ✆ **407/224-2155.** www.margaritavilleorlando.com. Mains $13–$25. Daily 11:30am–2am.

Hard Rock Cafe ★★ AMERICAN   Hey, look! It's . . . well . . . a Hard Rock Cafe. Granted, the world's largest (600 seats) and possibly the loudest. You've probably already sampled the Hard Rock shtick on offer at 163 of them: a casual tavern done up with music memorabilia (like Madonna's infamous "Like a Virgin" wedding dress and BOY TOY belt buckle, near the gift shop) and out back, a slab from the Berlin Wall. Fun fact: The company's headquarters is just 3½ miles north of here.

CityWalk. ✆ **407/351-7625.** www.hardrock.com. Mains $10–$35. Daily 11am–midnight.

NBA City ★ AMERICAN   The Hard Rock for basketball nuts, with a similarly wide-ranging burgers-and-pasta menu, except there are jerseys instead of Stratocasters on the walls. Turn kids loose in an interactive area to test their jumping and free-throw skills. Rumors persist of an imminent replacement by a WWE theme.

CityWalk. ✆ **407/363-5919.** www.nba.com/nbacity. Mains $11–$34. Sun–Thurs 11am–10:30pm; Fri–Sat 11am–11:30pm.

Bob Marley—A Tribute to Freedom ★ CARIBBEAN   Jamaican food (spicy jerk chicken, fried plantains, even oxtail) done passably, but stick around for when it turns into a reggae nightclub with a dance floor.

CityWalk. ✆ **407/224-3613.** www.universalorlando.com. Mains $9–$17. Daily 4pm–2am.

EXPENSIVE

Emeril's Orlando ★★ CREOLE   The highest standard of fare at CityWalk is a modern New Orleans menu with its heart is in meats, with flavors typified by preparations such as gin and molasses brine (for its pork). The wine list could send you reeling even before you have a single sip—the back wall of this loftlike space displays a 10,000-bottle aboveground cellar built to dazzle. Happily, it offers a kids' menu (including a petite filet mignon), which makes adult pleasures more possible.

CityWalk. ✆ **407/224-2424.** www.emerils.com. Reservations suggested. Mains $11–$26, 3-course lunch menu $22. Daily 11:30am–3pm; Sun–Thurs 5–10pm; Fri–Sat 5–10:30pm. Free valet parking for lunch.

Emeril's Tchoup Chop ★★★ PACIFIC RIM   Should Emeril's be full, Lagasse oversees a second restaurant at the Royal Pacific Resort, a few hundred yards away, that's actually more compelling. Pronounced "chop chop," it serves ostensibly Hawaiian creations, meaning there's a touch of Asian in the meaty offerings including garlic grilled tiger shrimp and banana leaf-wrapped pork loin shoulder. The daffy colors of the high-ceilinged dining room, exuberantly embellished by David Rockwell in rich orange and cobalt glass, are more a nod to Orlando's boundless showmanship than a portent of a saccharine meal.

Royal Pacific Resort, 6300 Hollywood Way, Orlando. ℂ **407/503-2467.** www.emerils.com. Mains $18–$39. Daily 11:30am–2:30pm; Sun–Thurs 5–10pm; Fri–Sat 5–11pm.

U.S. 192 & Lake Buena Vista

If you want truly inexpensive eats and lighter crowds, you *must* depart the theme park turf. Just for a short while—it doesn't hurt. Around Disney, two major zones present every chain restaurant known to familydom. The Disney South zone, U.S. 192, goes both east and west from Disney's southern gate. The eastern zone, Lake Buena Vista, is a mile east of the traffic-snarled Downtown Disney area. The two zones are linked by a few miles of Interstate 4, making it easy to shift from one to the other. But you don't need our help to find chain restaurants. Here are the best places you wouldn't otherwise know about.

INEXPENSIVE

El Tenampa ★★★ MEXICAN   From the outside, you'd swear it was just a grungy mini-mart best avoided, but inside, you discover a family-friendly hideaway of slotted-pot lanterns, hand-carved thrones, and big plastic cups in orange, magenta, and lime. Menus are bilingual but Spanish-first, which tells you about its main clientele, and because Mexican families show up in droves, you also know the food is authentic and good. The fresh *aguas frescas* (rejuvenating sweet water drinks, eight flavors ranging from tamarindo to limon) flow freely, and portions are big and reliable. You'll start with the free salsa and delicate corn chips that are still shiny and hot from the fryer, but don't fill up, because guacamole is a mere $4, whole fish $10, chicken mole with rice and beans only $8, and hefty burritos but $6.50. At its market next door, sample the Mexican popsicles at its *paleteria* and take away homemade pastries for under $1.75. Even Orlando residents, few of whom would dare head to this part of town, are delighted by what they find here.

4565 W. Irlo Bronson Memorial Hwy./U.S. 192, Kissimmee. ℂ **407/397-1981.** Main courses $6.50–$13. www.eltenampamexican.com. Sun–Thurs 10am–9pm; Fri–Sat 9am–10pm.

Jerusalem Restaurant ★★ MIDDLE EASTERN   Unknown to tourists, a growing Muslim immigrant community calls Kissimmee home (you'll see a few halal grocery stores around this area), and this family restaurant is one of the benefits: a friendly choice hidden in an elbow of a quiet strip mall, embellished with bougainvillea, stone walls, and a gurgling fountain. Lunch specials (11am–3pm) get you kebabs for $9, which go for $14 by dinnertime, but wraps (including falafel, shawarma, and—in a nod to the tourists—Philly steak) start at just $6. I love the garlicky hummus ($5.50) and *kibbeh* fritters made of beef, cracked wheat, pine nuts, and seasonings ($6). Couscous dishes start at $13.

2920 Vineland Rd., Kissimmee. ℂ **407/397-2230.** Main courses $6–$17. Daily 11am–11pm.

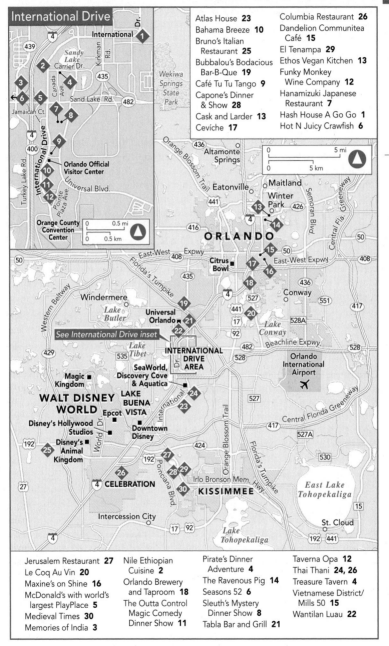

International Drive

439
4
International 1
Sandy Lake
Carrier Dr.
Kirkman Rd.
2
435
3
Canada Ave.
4
6
5
Sand Lake Rd.
482
Jamaican Ct.
7
8
400
9
Orlando Official Visitor Center
10
Universal Blvd.
11
12
Turkey Lake Rd.
International Drive
Pointe Plaza Ave.
Orange County Convention Center
0   0.5 mi
0   0.5 km

Wekiwa Springs State Park

Orange Blossom Trail

Altamonte Springs

Eatonville
Maitland
Winter Park
13
14

0   5 mi
0   5 km

ORLANDO

East-West Expwy 408
Florida's Turnpike
435
Citrus Bowl
17
16
15
East-West Expwy
50
408
18
4
527
Conway
441
20
551
17
Lake Conway
528A
92
Beachline Expwy.
482
528
Orlando International Airport

Windermere
Lake Butler
Western Beltway
429
Universal Orlando
19
21
22
See International Drive inset
Lake Tibet
535
INTERNATIONAL DRIVE AREA
SeaWorld, Discovery Cove & Aquatica
Magic Kingdom
LAKE BUENA VISTA
WALT DISNEY WORLD
Epcot
Disney's Hollywood Studios
Downtown Disney
192
Disney's Animal Kingdom
25
26
CELEBRATION
27
International Dr.
24
23
527
417
Central Florida Greeneway
527A
530
World Dr.
424
Orange Blossom Trail
Florida's Turnpike
27
192
Poinciana Blvd.
27
28
29
30
Irlo Bronson Mem. Hwy.
KISSIMMEE
East Lake Tohopekaliga
15
Intercession City
4
17
92
Lake Tohopekaliga
St. Cloud
192
441

Atlas House **23**
Bahama Breeze **10**
Bruno's Italian Restaurant **25**
Bubbalou's Bodacious Bar-B-Que **19**
Café Tu Tu Tango **9**
Capone's Dinner & Show **28**
Cask and Larder **13**
Ceviche **17**

Columbia Restaurant **26**
Dandelion Communitea Café **15**
El Tenampa **29**
Ethos Vegan Kitchen **13**
Funky Monkey Wine Company **12**
Hanamizuki Japanese Restaurant **7**
Hash House A Go Go **1**
Hot N Juicy Crawfish **6**

Jerusalem Restaurant **27**
Le Coq Au Vin **20**
Maxine's on Shine **16**
McDonald's with world's largest PlayPlace **5**
Medieval Times **30**
Memories of India **3**

Nile Ethiopian Cuisine **2**
Orlando Brewery and Taproom **18**
The Outta Control Magic Comedy Dinner Show **11**

Pirate's Dinner Adventure **4**
The Ravenous Pig **14**
Seasons 52 **6**
Sleuth's Mystery Dinner Show **8**
Tabla Bar and Grill **21**

Taverna Opa **12**
Thai Thani **24, 26**
Treasure Tavern **4**
Vietnamese District/ Mills 50 **15**
Wantilan Luau **22**

177

Miller's Lake Buena Vista Ale House ★ AMERICAN   The Ale House has 65 locations and counting. There are a few locations in town, including on International Drive, but this location attracts Disney cast members who raise 1 of the bar's 75 beers after their shifts are finished. This is the kind of publike sports bar Florida does well— big room, lots of TVs, beers on special by the bucket—with a menu of finger foods like burgers, wings, nachos, and sandwiches. The Ale House's Zingers are boneless chicken wings, a trick of science to be rivaled only by the ones conjured by your future cardiologist.

12371 Winter Garden Vineland Rd., Lake Buena Vista. (℃) **407/239-1800.** www.millersalehouse. com. Main courses $8–$10. Mon–Sat 11am–2am; Sun 11am–midnight.

MODERATE

Atlas House ★★ UZBEK   Not a lot of people know that Orlando hosts a healthy community of folks from Uzbekistan, and this restaurant, owned by two families that recently moved from there, is a rare chance to try the cuisine of the Central Asian nation. Appetizers ($4–$5), large enough to share, include *morkovcha*, a refreshing bird's nest of carrots shaved to angel hair and tossed with garlic, cilantro, coriander, and olive oil; addictive dill-sprinkled *manti* that tastes like beef stroganoff in a dumpling; and the fun *olivie*, a mix of diced egg, peas, pickles that will change the way you make egg salad from now on. Flavors like these are a welcome break from the assembly-line sweetness that pervades this town, plus there are soothing standbys such as kebabs and baklava. It's located in an off-putting, deserted strip mall decorated with life-size Roman statues, a weird setting for an otherwise welcoming place. There's covered outdoor seating.

11901 International Dr. (℃) **407/778-4816.** www.atlashouserestaurant.com. Main courses $9–$13. Tues–Fri 4–10pm, Sat–Sun 4–11pm.

Bahama Breeze ★★ CARIBBEAN   Although this is a smallish corporate chain, it has local provenance: Darden, which owns it (along with Red Lobster, the Olive Garden, and LongHorn Steakhouse), is based in Orlando, a 10-minute drive from this location. This concept is its most Floridian, which you will notice when you hear the live steel drums as you approach. On top of the rum cocktails that you will surely crave as you sit on the outdoor patio, it serves burgers, Cuban sandwiches, rice bowls, Jamaican jerk chicken, coconut shrimp, and other filling quasi-island favorites. I'm all about the fish tacos and the spicy West Indies Chicken Curry made with coconut milk and served with naan and pineapple chutney, but for something mellower, a cup of black bean soup is just $3.

8735 Vineland Ave., Orlando. (℃)**407/938-9010.** www.bahamabreeze.com. Main courses $10–$22. Sun–Thurs 11am–midnight; Fri–Sat 11am–1am. Second location: 8849 International Dr., Orlando. (℃)**407/248-2499.** Sun–Thurs 11am–1am; Fri–Sat 11am–1:30am.

Bruno's Italian Restaurant ★★★ ITALIAN   A true find in every way. A paper sign in the window says, "Don't judge a book by its cover." Boy, is that wise advice here. Your temptation would normally be to drive past this place since it shares a building with dog-ugly gift shop that's garishly painted with killer whales, but inside, it's the food that's killer. There's a lot of junky pasta in the tourist zone, but it's the rare Italian table where the owner is not only cooking with pride, but he's also actually Italian. In this one modest room, Bruno loads his generous plates with garlicky goodness, from his puttanesca to his buttery rolls, and he also does pizzas, calzones, and fresh cannoli. Ask about the daily specials, which include bracciole or a concoction called "eggplant Pavarotti," a rich piling of eggplant, ricotta, spinach, crabmeat, shrimp, and vodka sauce. Kids' meals start at $3, delivery is available to the vacation homes of Disney South.

8556 W. Irlo Bronson Hwy., Kissimmee. ✆ **407/397-7577.** www.brunos192.com. Main courses $9–18. Daily 11:30am–10:30pm.

Havana's Cuban Cuisine ★★ CUBAN It would be a shame to come to Florida without tasting authentic Cuban food. While Downtown Disney is heaving with frustrating crowds for its touristy Cuban, this modest family-run place is hosting more adventurous visitors—and not a few repeat locals—with tender *bistec palomilla* (thin-pounded steak with sautéed onion), aromatic *congri* (red beans and rice), and specials such as red snapper in garlic sauce. For dessert, the milk-soaked *tres leches* cake makes you wish you could start again for another round. It also does pressed sandwiches, a Cuban standard, for $9. Beware the green hot sauce—it'll knock you back. The decor is plain (rust-orange walls, reproduction travel posters), but the heartiness is in the food.

8544 Palm Pkwy., Orlando. ✆ **407/238-5333.** www.havanascubancuisine.com. Main courses $9–$25. Mon 5–10pm; Tues–Sat 11:30am–10pm; Sun noon–9pm.

Sea Dog Brewing Co. ★★ SEAFOOD Hidden in back of a strip mall facing I-4, this new arrival hails from Maine, where seafood matters but decorum doesn't. So expect a kid-friendly, chill joint, airy and relaxed, serving good chowders (Bahamian conch, New England clam), conch fritters, salads, burgers, and dinners ranging from pot roast to broiled cod. If you don't like seafood, the apricot beer-glazed chicken with caramelized onion, gouda, and thyme aioli is more than enough to impress. It's all designed to be served with more than a dozen Sea Dog beers by Shipyard Brewing Company in Maine, which you can also buy here by the case to fill your hotel room's fridge. From 4 to 7pm, the beers are 2-for-1 and oysters cost just 50¢.

8496 Palm Pkwy., Orlando. ✆ **321/329-5306.** www.seadogbrewing.com. Main courses $10–$17. Mon–Thurs 4pm–2am; Fri–Sun 11:30am–2am.

EXPENSIVE

Columbia Restaurant ★★★ CUBAN Not everything in Celebration, the Disney-built town just east of Walt Disney World, is fake. The original location of this palatial restaurant opened in Tampa in 1905, and this 1997 addition bustles as boldly as its daddy. The hot, fresh Cuban bread is so delicious you'll want to fill up on it, but don't, because portions are giant. Tampa was a major arrival city for Cubans, and their tradition holds sway with flavorful grilled steaks and chicken, paella, mojitos and sangrias, and big fish fillets. My favorite, the 1905 Salad ($11) is mixed tableside with ham, cheese, lettuce, olives, greens, and a garlicky wine vinegar dressing that won't help you consummate any courtships but is deservedly on sale by the bottle in the gift shop.

649 Front St., Celebration. ✆ **407/566-1505.** www.columbiarestaurant.com. Tapas plates $10; main courses $20–$27. Daily 11:30am–10:30pm. Reservations recommended.

International Drive & Convention Center

This is a major hotel and entertainment center, so many visitors find themselves here. The stretch of Sand Lake Road west of Interstate 4 is known, somewhat self-deprecatingly, as "Restaurant Row." It's true that some of the city's most popular date-night restaurants are scattered among the shopping centers on this street.

INEXPENSIVE

McDonald's ★ FAST FOOD   You've seen one McDonald's, you've seen them all, right? Not this one—otherwise why mention it? It serves the usual junk food, of course, but there's also a huge array of extra options such as burritos, pastrami sandwiches, chimichangas, tossed pastas, panini, and pizzas. That's odd enough, but it also claims to operate the largest PlayPlace in the world. Looks accurate: You'll find tube slides, a 500-gallon aquarium, and some 100 arcade games with a prize center. It's so big there's an elevator upstairs to still more play areas. Keep kids wowed for the price of fries.

6875 Sand Lake Rd., Orlando. ✆ **407/351-2185.** www.mcfun.com. Main courses $5–$8. Daily 24 hr.

Miller's I-Drive Vista Ale House ★ AMERICAN   There are a few locations of this family-friendly, popular sports bars in town, including at Lake Buena Vista (p. 178), and another at 5573 S. Kirkman Rd. near Universal, but this location is among the largest, with several cavernous rooms that open up to the nightlife on I-Drive. Hang out at a high-top table with a bucket of beers—something is always on special—cheer when your team scores, and dig into family-friendly finger foods like burgers, wings, oysters, pastas, sandwiches. There's even steak and potatoes ($15–$19) and lobster tails ($18 for two) if you're feeling hearty.

8963 International Dr., Orlando. ✆ **407/370-6688.** www.millersalehouse.com. Main courses $8–$10. Daily 11am–2am.

Orlando Brewing and Taproom ★★★ BREWERY   Because it's buried in an industrial area, you have to know about it to find it. There's no food served, either—if you want some, they'll hand you a binder of delivery menus—but that doesn't mean there isn't some delicious cooking happening. At least 20 beers (ales, IPAs, stouts—it changes according to how the brewers experiment) are on tap at 42°F and served at a copper-top bar. The quick rise of the brewery, which has been certified organic, has been remarkable. Orlando's best hotels (including Disney's) and restaurants now serve it. Most days at 6pm, the owners grant a free 30-minute tour of the beerworks, where quaffs are made without pasteurization (like the Old World) for sale within 2 weeks. The bar area is simple but convivial, like a rec room your dad might have slapped up in the basement, and uncluttered by televisions or pool tables, the way a beer snob would have it. Weekend nights, there's easygoing music outside, and Sunday is "Dog's Day," when everyone brings pets.

1301 Atlanta Ave., Orlando (just east of the Kaley Street exit of I-4, exit 81). ✆ **407/872-1117.** www.orlandobrewing.com. No food; beer only. Mon–Thurs 3–10pm; Fri–Sat 11am–midnight; Sun 1–9pm.

MODERATE

Bubbalou's Bodacious Bar-B-Que ★★ BARBECUE   Real barbecue done the way devotees like it, from cornbread stuffed with gooey butter pads to fall-off-the-bone ribs proven to stain shirts. There's no pretense at this tidied-up dive: Order at the counter and eat at picnic-style tables stocked with paper towel rolls and squirt bottles of sauce going from "sweet" to "killer." Get the standards: Texas brisket, pulled pork, ½ chicken, fried catfish, even gizzards. Sandwiches go for $8, but add any 4 sides (like baked beans, black-eye peas, Brunswick stew, or crunchy cole slaw) for $4 more. Or opt for meat by the pound ($11–$14), and take it back to the gang.

5818 Conroy Rd., Orlando. ✆ **407/295-1212.** www.bubbalouscatering.com. Main courses $8–$14. Mon–Thurs 10am–9:30pm; Fri 10am–10:30pm; Sat 10am–9:30pm; Sun 11am–9pm.

Café Tu Tu Tango ★★ INTERNATIONAL   Fun, festive, and noisy in a good way, this casual tapas-style hangout flies high with an artist theme. Actual artists somehow concentrate on painting at easels amid the frolic of group tables, cocktails (like the Leonardo Lemonade or the Michelangelo Mojito), and nightly entertainment of belly dancing, salsa, or flamenco dancing. Their works fill the walls up to the rafters while tables of boisterous diners spill out into the front patio. Despite the gimmick, chef Tiffany L. Sawyer's food is locally sourced from sustainable ingredients and packs flavor. I love the chili-lime marinated chicken skewers with corn pudding and almond pesto and the pork belly Reuben, although the Cajun chicken egg rolls are popular. This may also be one of the only mainstream Orlando restaurants to serve the animal that once owned these parts, the alligator: Try it as spiced gator bites with key lime mustard, or in gator jambalaya; clichés aside, it's kinda like chicken.

8625 International Dr., Orlando. ✆ **407/248-2222.** Tapas $8–$10. www.cafetututango.com. Sun–Thurs 11:30am–11pm; Fri–Sat 11:30am–1am.

Hanamizuki Japanese Restaurant ★ JAPANESE   The theme parks never saw a fish they didn't want to batter-fry. So here, the fresh sushi, chicken and salmon teriyaki, and udon or soba noodle soups make for a refreshing palate-cleanser. The blonde wood and fabric decor conforms neatly to your expectations of a soothing Japanese restaurant—it draws a steady trade of Japanese visitors hungry for a taste of home—and so does the rest, from the greeting when you walk in the door to the deep bowls of flavorsome soup. The fun Ishiyaki Mix Steak allows you to grill meat and vegetables on a hot stone placed on your table. Best of all, because of a tucked-away location in a strip mall near the Kings Bowl Orlando, it's rarely crowded. At lunchtime, it adds ramen to the menu.

8255 International Dr., Ste. 136, Orlando. ✆ **407/363-7200.** www.hanamizuki.us. Main courses $8–$14. Tues–Sat 11:30am–2pm; Tues–Sun 5pm–10:30pm.

Hash House A Go Go ★ AMERICAN   Hash House's claim to fame is shocking immoderation. Dishes are laughably immense, piled as high as Jenga games, and the outcome could be just as messy if you attempt to eat all you are served. Everything on the down-home menu, which the restaurant calls "Twisted Farm Food," sounds like a good idea mostly in retrospect: 1-pound burgers (stuffed with the likes of bacon and cheese, if you dare), towers of fried green tomatoes, a platter of fried chicken and waffles deserving of its own area code. This is destination food. The HH is an import from the casino culture of Vegas, where it began, which makes sense: This is a meal with a high risk-reward ratio. You can bet there'll be lots of leftovers.

5350 International Dr., Orlando. ✆ **407/370-4646.** www.hashhouseagogo.com. Main courses $10–$15. Mon–Thurs 7:30am–10pm; Fri 7:30am–midnight; Sat 7am–midnight; Sun 7am–10pm.

Hot N Juicy Crawfish ★ SEAFOOD   Sometimes when you're in Orlando, you just want to rip your meal apart with your bare hands, and for those times, there's this place, where as soon as you sit down they slap a bib on you and let you loose on the shellfish. Some are market price, but crab usually sells for a pound in the mid-teens, shrimp for $12 a pound, and mussels for $9 a pound. A few accents such as fried calamari, po' boys, and corn fritters are available for further kicks, but don't expect a fork. Vegetarians, give this place wide berth; this is for the vivisectors among us.

7572 W. Sand Lake Rd., Orlando. ✆ **407/370-4655.** www.hotnjuicycrawfish.com. Main courses $9–$15 a pound. Sun–Thurs noon–10pm; Fri–Sat noon–11pm.

Memories of India ★★ INDIAN Overcoming a bland name with flavorful pan-Indian food and a cheerful staff, it has seen its following build. At lunch it prepares *thali,* a platter combining basmati rice, bread, *raita* (yogurt with cucumbers and tomatoes), pickle (relish), a meat dish, a *papadum* (thin wafer) and, at this place, dessert (I like the pulpy mango ice cream)—all for $6.95 to $9.95. The tandoori and naan (a dozen kinds) are made in a clay oven. The Lamb Kada Masala, cooked in ginger, garlic, spring onion, and gravy, is consistently strong. It's a few blocks west of International Drive, in the ignoble Bay Hill shopping plaza, and Universal Orlando staffers often come here for lunch.

7625 Turkey Lake Rd., Orlando. ⓒ **407/370-3277.** www.memoriesofindiacuisine.com. Main courses $11–$16. Mon–Fri 11:30am–2:30pm and 5:30–10pm; Sat 11:30am–2pm and 5:30–10pm; Sun 11:30am–2:30pm and 5:30–9pm.

Nile Ethiopian Cuisine ★★★ ETHIOPIAN When they first opened in a half-empty strip mall behind a Buffalo Wild Wings, I worried about the future for the owners of Nile, but they are so friendly and eager to share their cuisine they have made themselves a devoted fixture on I-Drive. They even offer a few hutlike booths in which you can sit on the ground to eat, East Africa–style. It's a positive experience for families. Everyone tears off a piece of spongy injera bread to scoop up various stews and meats (beef, lamb, chicken, vegetarian) collected on a platter. You can even request a traditional coffee ceremony, in which beans are brewed in a *jabena* pot at your table and the eldest in your party is served first. Ethiopian cuisine is made with infused oil, not butter, so the vegetarian options are truly vegan, and with advance notice, the injera can be made gluten-free. It's memorable and not daunting.

7048 International Dr., Orlando. ⓒ **407/354-0026.** www.nile07.com. Main courses $12–$15. Mon–Fri 5–10pm; Sat–Sun noon–10pm.

Seasons 52 ★★★ AMERICAN This culinary experiment has spread nationwide, but this was its first location. The point of the menu, which changes all the time to make use of seasonal crops, is that no dish clocks in at more than 475 calories (although none will leave you hungry). The servings aren't particularly teeny—the food is just really good, thoughtfully made, and never sees a deep fryer. That's something you'll thank your waiter for after a long week in the theme parks. The desserts come in single-serving shot glasses, but mind they don't catch you licking the glass.

7700 Sand Lake Rd., Orlando. ⓒ **407/354-5212.** www.seasons52.com. Main courses $13–$20. Sun–Thurs 11:30am–10pm; Fri 10am–11pm; Sat 11:30am–11pm.

Tabla Bar and Grill ★★ INDIAN I'm always encouraged when an Indian restaurant is full of young Indians having a good time. Knowing that fact might help entice you inside, because its unappealing location across the hall from the tatty gift shop of an obsolete Days Inn might otherwise deter you. Tabla rises above that. Chef Sajan does the standards (pulling from various traditions like Parsi and Hyderabadi and the dosa of South India), but he also plays around (chocolate samosas and *janat e paan,* a kulfi dessert with glazed *paan*). Start with fresh-made tomato cream soup just like they serve on Indian Railways ($4 for a huge bowl). At lunch (11am–2:45pm), there's an ample all-you-can-eat buffet ($8 weekdays, $13 weekends with champagne), and there's always a full bar where mango-themed drinks are a specialty. Between 5 and 7pm, buy one appetizer, get another free. There's a good feeling here, like being at a club that only you were smart enough to know about, and it's a safe place to try your first Indian food.

5827 Caravan Court, Orlando. ⓒ **407/248-9400.** www.tablabar.com. Main courses $7–$15. Daily 11:30am–3pm and 5–11pm.

Taverna Opa ★★ GREEK It would be hard not to find something to eat, from tapaslike *meze* (hummus with garlic chunks and hot pita bread, *taramosalata, keftedes* meatballs), salads, hearty wood-fired meats and grilled fish, and *moussaka* (an eggplant lasagna with béchamel). There's no resisting the party that starts after 7pm or so—waiters and customers alike toss napkins and dance on the tables as belly dancers and "Zorba" dancers (their term) swirl. Kids really get into it. Lunches are more subdued, and mains are $10 cheaper.

9101 International Dr. at Pointe Orlando, Orlando. ✆ **407/351-8660.** www.opaorlando.com. Meze $5–$12, main courses $15–$27. Sun–Thurs 11am–11pm; Fri–Sat 11am–2am.

Thai Thani ★★ THAI A strip-mall anchor store by SeaWorld channels Chiang Mai with wood carvings, brass, and powerfully romantic private booths. Popular with locals (it recently added a Celebration location near Disney), it serves Thai food suited to newbies—the lemongrass soup is tame, with few chilies, which proves the chef is holding back—but more advanced eaters should choose from the "spicy dishes" section to get the full flair of the cuisine—I like the Thai chili jam stir-fried with veggies and your choice of protein. Finish with Thai Grandma Ice Cream: coconut ice cream with sticky rice and peanuts ($7). Lunch is about $5 less.

11025 S. International Dr. ✆ **407/239-9733.** www.thaithani.net. Main courses $11–$16. Daily 11:30am–11pm. Second location near Disney: 600 Market St., Ste. 100, Celebration. ✆ **407/566-9444.** Sun–Thurs 11:30am–10pm; Fri–Sat 11:30am–11pm.

EXPENSIVE

Funky Monkey Wine Company ★★★ AMERICAN The menu is everchanging at this beloved locally owned eatery that stocks nearly eight dozen types of wine, but count on spry twists such as fries with blue cheese crumbles, salads with rum-soaked pineapple and prosciutto, almond-crusted salmon with brown butter sauce, and a full slate of fresh sushi. It's upscale without taking itself too seriously, a mode that proves itself Fridays at 9pm when a highly amusing drag show entertains diners.

9101 International Dr. at Pointe Orlando, Orlando. ✆ **407/418-9463.** www.funkymonkeywine. com. Sushi rolls $8–$14, main courses $22–$40. Reservations recommended. Second location: 912 N. Mills Ave., north of downtown Orlando, where entrees are about $8 cheaper.

Downtown Orlando

The neighborhood east of downtown, Thornton Park, hosts a few well-publicized bistros and sidewalk cafes, but with prices around $12 a plate for lunch and $20 for dinner, there are no money-saving revelations among them. Instead, try these.

INEXPENSIVE

Dandelion Communitea Cafe ★★★ VEGETARIAN/VEGAN When you hang out at Dandelion, you feel like you're a part of something. That's because it's as much a neighborhood hangout as it is a cafe. Once a private home, hardwood floors and cabinets were left intact, and now diners of all ages roam a multiroom chill zone and front garden where coffee and a huge selection of tea are served with menu items made with local ingredients. The $6 "D.I.Y. Dish" is a great value: Mix and match your base ingredients with toppings and dressings for a big bowl of goodness. There's no meat, and nearly everything is gluten-free. The signature dish is the Giddyup ($9, but only $5 on Mon), a filling nacho bowl of tempeh chili piled with blue corn chips, diced tomatoes, scallions, and cheese. My favorite is Henry's Hearty Chili, the most flavorful veggie chili I've ever had ($4 a cup). Twice a month, on the new and full moon, people gather here to "express your true self with music, rhythm, dance and trance." If you don't travel with your own bongo, they'll lend you one.

618 N. Thornton Ave., Orlando. ℰ **407/362-1864.** www.dandelioncommunitea.com. Main courses $8–$9. Mon–Sat 11am–10pm; Sun 11am–5pm.

Ethos Vegan Kitchen ★★ VEGAN   As one of the only fully vegan restaurants in Central Florida, Ethos garnered such a loyal following it recently moved and expanded. That's because when vegan cuisine is all that you do (even the cheese qualifies), you have to be skilled at making it taste good, too—and Ethos succeeds. Among the favorites are pecan-encrusted eggplant, pumpkin seed pesto penne pasta, and 10-inch pizzas. Kelly and Laina Shockley, who run it, are assiduous about ingredient sourcing and even pay their servers a living wage (not minimum wage). Specials change according to seasonal crops, and there's always a soup of the day. About a third of the menu is gluten-free.

601-B New York Ave., Winter Park. ℰ **407/228-3898** or 407/228-3899. www.ethosvegankitchen. com. Mains $8–$15. Mon–Fri 11am–11pm; Sat–Sun 9am–11pm.

A GASTRONOMIC TOUR OF little vietnam

Just north of Orlando's downtown, along a stretch of 1950s storefronts around Colonial Avenue and Mills Avenue, a thriving Vietnamese area (variously called Little Vietnam, ViMi, and Mills Fifty) is flourishing. Many people fled here upon the fall of Saigon, and Vietnamese dissident Thuong Nguyen Cuc Foshee has been an Orlando resident since the time of the Vietnam conflict. Diners can find cheap meals here, true to Vietnam's reputation for nuanced flavors. Park anywhere (most buildings hide secret lots behind them) and explore on an empty stomach.

The quickest meal is *banh mi*, addictive baguette-style sandwiches stuffed with thinly sliced veggies (cucumbers, daikon, carrots), cilantro, hot peppers, a buttery secret sauce, and meats such as roast pork, pâté, or meatball (or tofu). They're shockingly cheap: $3 to $4, hot, and made-to-order from the counter beside checkout at **Tiên-Hung Market** (1108 E. Colonial Dr.; ℰ **407/422-0067;** daily 9am–6pm). Newcomer **Yum-Mì Sandwiches** (1227 N. Mills Ave.; ℰ **407/ 894-1808;** www.yummisandwiches.com; Mon–Tues and Thurs–Sat 10am–8pm, Sun 10am–6pm) does them for $4 in a

franchise-ready facility (owners are children of Mills Fifty institution Phó 88; see below).

At most of the area's Vietnamese restaurants, where entrees range from about $8 to $10 or $12, menus drone on like a Russian novel, but if you're wise to it, each place has its specialty. **Phó 88** (730 N. Mills Ave.; ℰ **407/897-3488;** www.pho88orlando.com; daily 10am–10pm) excels with *pho* beef noodle soup; bowls seem as large as hot tubs, with many flavors vying for dominance. Its two enormous spring rolls could fill an average stomach for $3.25. The specialty at Ánh Hông (1124 E. Colonial Dr.; ℰ **407/ 999-2656;** daily 9am–9:30pm), on the corner of Mills, is tofu (especially fried), while **Viet Garden** (1237 E. Colonial Dr.; ℰ **407/896-4154;** Sun–Thurs 10am– 9pm, Fri–Sat until 10pm) wows with its crispy noodle dishes. Neophytes prefer the mass appeal of **Little Saigon** (1106 E. Colonial Dr.; ℰ **407/423-8539;** www. littlesaigonrestaurant.com; daily 10am– 9pm), which has several dining areas with yellow walls and red tablecloths that place it as slightly more upscale than its somewhat utilitarian one-room neighbors—but its food is just as good.

MODERATE

Ceviche ★ TAPAS   For a lively night out, head to Church Street Station, a revitalized pedestrian district of red-brick warehouses, gas-lit lamps, and late-night lounges. This rococo dining hall feels like it was plucked off Las Ramblas in Barcelona. The menu, also true to Spain, is piled with more than 100 tapas dishes, most $6 to $10, including daring-for-Orlando meats (quail, crispy chicken livers, oxtail), standard ones (chorizo, veal, lamb chops), and plenty of vegetable and fish choices. And, of course, there's ceviche (I like the tuna, with garlic, lime, onion, and a touch of jalapeño). Because everything's meant to be shared, the energy is social and vibrant. Things get loud when the flamenco band clacks and strums, so enjoy the evening on the front patio.

125 W. Church St., Orlando. ✆ **321/281-8140.** www.ceviche.com. Tapas $8–$11. Sun–Mon 5–10pm; Tues–Thurs 5pm–midnight; Fri–Sat 5pm–2am.

Maxine's on Shine ★★ INTERNATIONAL   If you're not careful, this vibrant neighborhood charmer could make you want to move to Orlando so you could hang out every evening. Hidden in a residential neighborhood (blink and you've passed it), it's a labor of love by its owners, who frequently emerge from the kitchen to party with guests. There's a good wine list plus a tiny stage hosting a roster of entertainment ('70s karaoke one night, classical piano the next). Chicken Maxine blends pan-seared diced chicken with shallots, mushrooms, a Marsala wine cream sauce with penne pasta, but on Sundays at 7pm, I go for the Magical Mystery Meal Tour, when $25 buys three courses, plus a glass of wine, as long as you agree to let the chef serve you whatever inspires him that day. As you depart, a sign thanks you for helping "this little restaurant's dreams come true."

337 N. Shine Ave., Orlando. ✆ **407/674-6841.** www.maxinesoneshine.com. Salads $8, mains $13–$23. Tues–Thurs 5–10pm; Fri–Sat 11:30am–11pm; Sun 10am–10pm.

EXPENSIVE

Cask & Larder ★★ SOUTHERN   Like its sister gastropub restaurant down the street, the Ravenous Pig (p. 186), it's dedicated to ever-changing dishes based on seasonal ingredients. The difference here is that Cask & Larder is less about picking meat off an animal's bones as it is about home-brewed beer by a resident brewmaster and a casual vibe. But you can eat, and comfort food is the thing—from fried chicken (a staple) to an unbelievably addictive potted pimento cheese topped with "ham jam" (ham that's been cooked down with honey). Little touches of richness prevail, such as the vanilla butter slowly melting atop the cornbread, which arrives in its own iron skillet, and the mac and cheese jolted with pickled mustard seeds.

565 W. Fairbanks Ave., Winter Park. ✆ **321/280-4200.** www.caskandlarder.com. Mains $19–$28. Tues–Fri 5:30–10pm; Sat 11:30am–3pm and 5:30–10pm; Sun 10:30am–3pm. Reservations recommended.

Le Coq Au Vin ★★★ FRENCH   Longtime Chef Louis Perrotte hand-picked his protégé Reimund Pitz to take the reins at this classic French romantic restaurant, an Orlando institution since 1976. Diners, many of whom are here celebrating a special occasion, feel more like they're guests in a home than paying patrons, an illusion that's extended by its mostly residential neighborhood. Pitz is classically trained as a French chef, so you get the complicated flavors (a well-marinated coq au vin, beef tenderloin with blue cheese crust, Grand Marnier soufflé) that the prices demand, plus Gallic staples such as frog legs and vichyssoise. Some dishes come in ample half portions that can cost two-thirds what larger servings do. A three-course prix-fixe menu goes for $35.

4800 S. Orange Ave., Orlando. ✆ **407/851-6980.** www.lecoqauvinrestaurant.com. Main courses $23–29. Tues–Sat 5:30–10pm; Sun 5–9pm.

The Ravenous Pig ★★★ SOUTHERN James and Julie Petrakis have won renown for knowing just when to deploy bacon and in what amount, a talent dear to me, and they have been rewarded by operating one of the city's destination dining choices. Expect a beer-friendly yet sophisticated evening where the food is gourmet without pretentiousness. The menu changes seasonally but always features traditional farmhouse meats—in the form of frites, say—and some perennial Southern comfort dishes with an upscale spin, like shrimp and grits with Gruyere biscuits. The Petrakis's cookbook, on sale here, is all about exploiting the best of Florida's ingredients.

1234 N. Orange Ave., Winter Park. ℰ **407/628-2333.** www.theravenouspig.com. Mains $25–$29. Tues–Sat 11:30am–2pm; Tues–Thurs 5:30–9:30pm; Fri–Sat 5:30–11pm. Reservations recommended.

Dinnertainment

Besides "America's Got Talent" and "Dancing with the Stars," there may be no purer form of vaudeville left in America than the Orlando dinner show. Part banquet and part spectacle, most of these guilty pleasures involve stunts, audience participation, and usually, a flimsy excuse to hoist the American flag, even if the plot is set in ancient Mesopotamia. Most of them are mounted in arenas lined with bench seating and long tables, and while the show grinds on, waiters scurry around, distributing plates of banquet food the way Las Vegas dealers deal blackjack cards. These shows are immoderate and tacky to the extreme, but they're an intrinsic part of the Orlando scene. Nowhere else on Earth—at least not since Caligula's Rome—will you find so many stadiums in which to stuff your face while fleets of horses, swordsmen, and crooners labor to amuse you. Dinnertainments aren't top values, but they certainly represent the delight of Orlando's shtick.

Most times of the year, most of these shows kick off daily around 6 or 7pm, but during peak season, there may be two shows scheduled around 6 and 8:30pm. Upon arrival, crowds are corralled into a preshow area where they can buy cocktails and souvenirs, and endure hokey comedy and magic routines—feel free to be slightly tardy, and feel free not to buy anything, as drinks come with dinner. Most shows will be mopping up by around 9:30pm, so schedule a visit on a night when you don't intend to catch theme park fireworks or other evening shows. Most of them also serve kids' standards (chicken fingers, hot dogs, and so on) for picky children. Soft drinks, draft beer, and wine (the cheap stuff, watered down) are unlimited. Bring a sweater if you're sensitive to air-conditioning, and bring enough cash to tip your server because gratuities aren't included. **Money-saving tip:** The free coupon books and discount ticket suppliers should be your go-to for cheap prices on dinner shows. There are so many deals floating around for the banquets held off theme-park property that only a stooge pays full price. The ones thrown by the theme parks, though, generally don't discount. In fact, they tend to sell out, so book those as far ahead as you sensibly can.

IN ORLANDO & KISSIMMEE

Arabian Nights ★★ AMERICAN Horse lovers' hearts swell: The 60 horses and 15 breeds are both beautiful and well trained. The 90-minute show itself, about a girl who learns she's actually the Princess Scheherazade, is preposterously dimwitted, but to be fair, the wish-fulfillment plot is just a ruse for introducing the 20-odd old-fashioned horse acts, including bareback riding, human acrobatics, and not a little waving of the American flag. Expect lots of dry ice, sequins—and food the animals probably wouldn't touch. Another $5 sits you in the first three rows, and another $10 will buy a preshow walk past backstage stables, where kids can pose for photos atop a huge draft horse. A special holiday show, accompanied by pop music, runs at the end of the year.

You'd be crazy to pay full price because most ticket discounters (try Maple Leaf tickets at www.mapleleaftickets.com) sell for far less ($39 adults/$31 kids).

3081 Arabian Nights Blvd., Kissimmee. ℂ **800/553-6116** or 407/239-9223. www.arabian-nights. com. $67 adults, $31 kids 3–11. Nightly.

Capone's Dinner & Show ★ ITALIAN   Kardashian-generation girls pretend to be 1920s flappers and warble to recorded music in this affordable dinnertainment effort. Dinner's a bog-standard steam table buffet of lasagna, spaghetti with meatballs, pizza, nuggets, and a few token nonpasta choices, such as a hot meat carving station. This troupe's own brochures and website promise half-off discounts, which grant the price I list, but I've never seen the so-called full price quoted, let alone charged.

4740 W. Irlo Bronson Hwy., Kissimmee. ℂ **800/220-8428.** www.alcapones.com. $29 adults, $32 kids 4–12. Nightly, some 1pm shows.

Medieval Times ★ AMERICAN   The long-running coach-tour favorite, at which your waitress is called a "wench," is also an attraction in eight other North American cities, qualifying it as the McDonald's of dinnertainment. You eat spare ribs and chicken with your hands while the jousters compete in an arena. For $10 more ($8 online), the Royalty Package gets you front-row seating, a free program, and a souvenir DVD. Its "castle" is located a few miles east of Disney on U.S. 192, in a downtrodden area of Kissimmee. It's also always discounted by brochures to the tune of $15 less.

4510 W. Irlo Bronson Hwy., Kissimmee. ℂ **866/543-9637** or 407/396-2900. www.medievaltimes. com. $60 adult, $36 kids 12 and under. Nightly.

The Outta Control Magic Comedy Dinner Show ★★ PIZZA   More affordable and easygoing than its dinnertainment competition, the show mounted by the WonderWorks science/video playground targets kids—and parents weary of over-produced, overpriced glitz. Unlimited pizza, salad, beer, wine, and soda are distributed while buddy-buddy magicians engage in family-friendly jokes, tricks, mindreading, and improv. Discount coupons get $2 off.

WonderWorks, 9067 International Dr., Orlando. ℂ **407/351-8800.** www.wonderworksonline.com. $25 adults, $17 kids 4–12 and seniors. 6 and 8pm.

Pirate's Dinner Adventure ★★ AMERICAN   For kids who just can't get enough Jack Sparrow–like misbehavior, there's this high-energy eye-popper, set on an 18th-century galleon with a 40-foot-high mast that's amid a 300,000-gallon lagoon—the arena is the most spectacular of all the Orlando dinnertainments. Pirate's is a circus of rapier duels, rope swinging (and lots of it), trampolining, singing, and arrrghing. Although the show provides lots of opportunity for participation (each of six sections roots for its assigned buccaneer, kids get onstage), it treats female characters like sexy livestock. That may account for why its most devoted demographic appears to be 12-year-old boys there for their birthday parties. Production values are fairly high. Buying online yields discounts of $5 a ticket, but many of the free brochures dispensed around town are good for as much as $15 off.

6400 Carrier Dr., Orlando. ℂ **800/866-2469** or 407/248-0590. $64 adult, $40 kids 3–11. www. piratesdinneradventure.com. Nightly.

Sleuth's Mystery Dinner Show ★★★ AMERICAN   After mingling with a few zany characters and watching the show, which takes about an hour and contains at least one murder, you confer over dinner with your tablemates, grill the suspects, and, if you feel confident, accuse a killer. The spectacle-free, low-budget shows change nightly, so you can attend several times without duplicating your experience. Actors seem to be having fun, and they'll even tone down the grown-up jokes if they see young children in the crowd, although the shows are clearly more suited to adults. As for audiences, they appear to be grateful for a rare chance to employ their brains in this town. The food is noticeably better than that of its rivals (although hardly gourmet), possibly because the management only has to cook for a few dozen. Beer and wine are included, too. Lots of brochures discount rates.

8267 International Dr., Orlando. ✆ **800/393-1985** or 407/363-1985. www.sleuths.com. $57 adult, $24 kids 3–11. Nightly.

Treasure Tavern ★★ AMERICAN   The people behind Pirate's Dinner Adventure also put on a 2-hour mix of burlesque, specialty circus and magic tricks, contortionists in garters, and dancing for those 18 years old and over (although if you're older than 14, you can come with a grown-up). The concept is that Gretta, the bawdy proprietor of the Treasure Tavern, has assembled a band of misfits who she puts to work entertaining you. Think "Cabaret" meets "Benny Hill." Because kids are cut out, food is a cut above—the standard meal is beef tenderloin, upgradable to prime rib for $8. The servers are still called "rum girls." I said it was adult, not sophisticated.

6400 Carrier Dr., Orlando. ✆ **877/318-2469.** www.treasuretavern.com. Tickets $64. Tues–Sat nights.

AT THE THEME PARK RESORTS

Disney's Grand Floridian resort does afternoon tea time bookings for little princesses (✆ **407/939-3463**), but these are the parks' dinner shows for the whole family.

Disney's Spirit of Aloha Show ★ POLYNESIAN   The chicken-and-ribs luau presided over by fire twirlers, hula dancers, and the like has been going strong for years in an open-air theater on Seven Seas Lagoon. Bookings begin 6 months ahead, and usually the last people to reserve are shunted to the rear tables, which can feel like they're actually as distant as the Cook Islands; the tables that are farthest away are the least expensive. It bores some kids, but it has its adult adherents (although most of them cite not its educational qualities but its food—pineapple-coconut bread being at the top of their lists, and when it took ribs off the menu, a guest revolt resulted in their reinstatement). It's on the monorail line from the Magic Kingdom, which means it's easy to catch the fireworks after early shows.

Disney's Polynesian Resort. ✆ **407/939-3463.** www.disneyworld.com. $59–$74 adults, $32–$40 kids 3–9. Tues–Sat 5:15 and 8pm.

Gospel Brunch ★ AMERICAN   There is no plot, and it's not sanctified, but the live music is jumping and the cuisine combines Southern and breakfast foods. Tickets are about $2 cheaper if you buy them there, but you run the risk of sellouts (the morning one fills first). Still, because so many House of Blues throw these, you can't say it's very Orlando.

House of Blues, Downtown Disney West Side, 1490 E. Buena Vista Dr., Lake Buena Vista. ✆ **407/934-2583.** www.hob.com. $41 adults, $22 kids 3–9. Sun at 10:30am and 1pm.

Hoop-Dee-Doo Musical Revue ★★ AMERICAN   Book 6 months out, not necessarily because it's the best, but because it's Disney's most kid-friendly dinnertainment, which makes it crazy popular. Six-performer shows put on a hectic and helter-skelter music-hall carnival of olios and gags, which elementary-school age children usually find riveting, and much quarter is given to recognizing birthdays and special events. The headlining menu item is ribs served in pails—enough said? I prefer seats in the balcony, overlooking the stage (the cheapest, anyway).

Pioneer Hall at Fort Wilderness Resort. © **407/939-3463.** www.disneyworld.com. $59–$68 adults, $30–$35 kids 3–9. 3 shows nightly.

Mickey's Backyard BBQ ★ AMERICAN   The dinner show choice for very young children is patronized by rope tricksters and taxi-dancing costumed characters wearing Western-style gear. More informal than the Hoop-Dee-Doo in that it takes place under an open-air pavilion (come dressed for humidity), the event serves passable buffet-style picnic food, but the toddler factor makes it chaotic, and for some cruel reason, seating is first come, first served. You might be less disappointed if you see this as a photo op with Mickey and not as a proper show.

The Outdoor Pavilion at Fort Wilderness Resort. © **407/939-3463.** $57 adults, $33 kids 3–9. www. disneyworld.com. Thurs and Sat Mar–Dec.

Wantilan Luau ★★★ POLYNESIAN   Universal's weekly 2-hour luau is held in a covered pavilion. It, like Disney's Spirit of Aloha Show, has fire dancers and hula girls aplenty, but it trumps the rest for authenticity: Food includes pit-roasted suckling pig, with spiced rum–infused pineapple puree, and a Pacific catch of the day; mai tais are included in the price. Should kids be grossed out by carving meat off the pig, there's a tamer children's menu. The show is more culturally documentary than Disney's, too, as it's attentive to the differences between the various Pacific islanders it represents. You can walk from both Universal parks.

Royal Pacific Resort. © **407/503-3463.** www.universalorlando.com. $63 adults, $35 kids 3–9. Sat at 6pm.

CHARACTER MEALS

A character meal is a Disney rite of passage. Usually all-you-can-eat meal and often buffet, it guarantees face-to-fur time with beloved costumed characters. Always, *always book ahead*—as soon as you can.

Meals are themed by location; at the Cape May Café, characters wear beach outfits, and at Chef Mickey's, they emerge in chef's aprons and do a towel-twirling dance. (Reading that, it sounds a little like a Chippendales show, not a Chip 'n' Dale show, but rest assured it's all preschool-friendly.) The characters (six to eight headliners make appearances) won't actually be eating with you, but they'll circulate, working the room the way a good host does, and signing autographs. This, as kids and grown-ups binge on a smorgasbord that would give Jillian Michaels apoplexy—Mickey-shaped waffles topped with M&Ms and all—comes the day's first sugar crash.

The privilege of dining with characters isn't cheap. Prices vary, but they're a little cheaper at hotels than inside theme parks. When a breakfast is held inside a park, you'll still have to proffer an admission ticket. However, for breakfast, your name will be on a VIP list and you'll be admitted through the gates early (it's fun to walk through an empty park). Try to book the earliest seating available so that by the time you're done, you'll be among the first in line for the rides; you'll also have first crack at the stroller rentals. Tips are not usually included.

Cinderella's Royal Table, inside Magic Kingdom's Cinderella Castle, is the big "get"—there are some intense parents out there with freakishly fast speed-dial fingers, because that place always sells out 180 days early. Also try Chef Mickey's, which is a one-stop monorail ride away from the Magic Kingdom, and the Tusker House, a good start for the early day at Animal Kingdom. Less prestigious addresses, such as the buffet breakfast at the Beach Club near Epcot, can be smart choices, particularly because they tend not to be as crowded and you're likely to have lots more one-on-one time with the stars.

INSIDE DISNEY PARKS

Cinderella's Royal Table
The most difficult reservation (reserve 6 months ahead at 7am Orlando time) features Cinderella, with possible appearances by her Fairy Godmother and other Princesses. Breakfast, lunch, or dinner. Includes five photos.

Cinderella Castle, Fantasyland, The Magic Kingdom. ✆ **407/939-3463.** www.disneyworld.com. Meals $54–$72 adults, $35–$43 kids 3–9, plus park admission. Price includes 5 photos of your party.

Crystal Palace
Appearances by Winnie the Pooh and his friends, three meals per day.

Crystal Palace, Main Street, U.S.A., The Magic Kingdom. ✆ **407/939-3463.** www.disneyworld.com. Meals $25–$44 adults, $14–$21 children kids 3–9, plus park admission.

Dining with an Imagineer
When your kids have outgrown furry friends, there's still this exceptional mealtime meet-and-greet. Over a four-course meal groups no larger than 10 hang out with a longtime Disney Imagineer—an art director, designer, or engineer—and have the chance to ask them anything about the mechanics of the resort. At lunch, you need a ticket to Disney's Hollywood Studios, but at dinner, it takes place at the Flying Fish Cafe (p. 173) at Disney's BoardWalk.

Hollywood Brown Derby, Disney's Hollywood Studios or Flying Fish Cafe, Disney's BoardWalk. ✆ **407/939-3463.** www.disneyworld.com. Lunch adults $61, kids 3–9 $35, plus park admission; dinner $85, kids under 14 not recommended. Lunch Mon, Wed, Fri at 11:30am. Dinner 2nd Tues of the month at 5:30pm.

Garden Grill
Appearances by Mickey, Chip 'n' Dale, and Pluto.

Garden Grill, The Land, Epcot. ✆ **407/939-3463.** www.disneyworld.com. Meals $37–$42 adults, $18–$20 kids 3–9, plus park admission. Dinner.

Princess Storybook Dining
Appearances by the Princesses at breakfast, lunch, or dinner.

Akershus Royal Banquet Hall, Norway, Epcot. ✆ **407/939-3463.** www.disneyworld.com. Meals $41–$55 adults, $25–$30 kids 3–9, plus park admission. Price includes 5 photos of your party.

Playhouse Disney's Play 'N Dine
Appearances by Handy Manny, Jake, Special Agent Oso, Jungle Junction.

Hollywood & Vine, Echo Lake, Disney's Hollywood Studios. ✆ **407/939-3463.** www.disneyworld.com. Breakfast or lunch $27–$35 adults and $15–$19 kids 3–9, plus park admission.

Donald's Safari Breakfast
Appearances by Mickey, Donald, Daisy, and Goofy.

Tusker House Restaurant, Africa, Disney's Animal Kingdom. ✆ **407/939-3463.** www.disneyworld.com. Breakfast $29–$33 adults and $16–$18 kids 3–9, plus park admission.

Donald's Dining Safari
Appearances by Mickey, Goofy, and Chip 'n' Dale.

Tusker House Restaurant, Africa, Disney's Animal Kingdom. ✆ **407/939-3463.** www.disneyworld.com. Lunch $29–$35 adults and $17–$19 kids 3–9, plus park admission.

AT DISNEY HOTELS

Chef Mickey's
Served by Mickey, Goofy, Donald Duck, and Pluto.

Chef Mickey's, Disney's Contemporary Resort. ✆ **407/939-3463.** www.disneyworld.com. Breakfast or dinner $33–$42 adults, $18–$22 kids 3–9.

Cape May Café   Appearances by Goofy, Minnie, and Donald Duck.

Cape May Café, Disney's Beach Club Resort. ☏ **407/939-3463.** www.disneyworld.com. Breakfast $27–$31 adults, $14–$17 kids 3–9.

Supercalifragilistic Breakfast   Appearances by a variety of characters, including Mary Poppins.

1900 Park Fare, Disney's Grand Floridian Resort and Spa. ☏ **407/939-3463.** www.disneyworld. com. Breakfast $22–$27 adults, $13–$15 kids.

Cinderella's Happily Ever After Dinner   Appearances by Cinderella, Prince Charming, Fairy Godmother, and others.

1900 Park Fare, Disney's Grand Floridian Resort and Spa. ☏ **407/939-3463.** www.disneyworld. com. Dinner $38–$43 adults, $19–$21 kids.

'Ohana Character Breakfast   Appearances by Mickey, Pluto, Lilo, and Stitch.

Disney's Polynesian Resort. ☏ **407/939-3463.** www.disneyworld.com. Breakfast $22–27 adults, $13–15 kids.

Garden Grove   Appearances by Goofy, Pluto, and others.

Garden Grove, Walt Disney World Swan. ☏ **407/939-3463.** www.disneyworld.com. Breakfast on weekends, dinner nightly. Breakfast or dinner $21–$36 adults, $13–$17 kids.

UNIVERSAL ORLANDO

Superstar Character Breakfast   Universal's sole meal has SpongeBob and characters from "Hop" and "Despicable Me."

Cafe La Bamba, Universal Studios. ☏ **407/224-7554.** www.universalorlando.com. Breakfast $45 adults, $13 kids, plus park admission.

ORLANDO'S HOTELS

7

Orlando has nearly 118,000 hotel rooms, a staggering figure. Some 57 million visitors come every year for theme parks, conventions, and outdoor recreation, making the city the world's most popular family vacation destination.

As you can imagine, with numbers that large, competition can be fierce, and at some properties, quality can be lax. A little too often, you find yourself shrugging and saying, "Eh, it does the job." Most of Central Florida's monolithic hotel architecture steals and inflates Europe's palatial traditions, often on such a scale that even a Texan would blush. You'll find arcades, frescoes, columns, Spanish tiles, arched windows, and marble . . . but knock on the columns. They're hollow. Get close to the marble. It's often painted on. And the rooms are just rooms. That's why Orlando's resorts, as much as they charge, rarely achieve true opulence. Here, when you pay for a fine hotel, you're mostly paying for mood. I'll help you look beyond the set dressing to find the best value for you—which may not end up being a hotel at all.

Following are a few key questions to ask yourself to help you choose accommodations in Orlando:

How much space would I like to have? If you have kids with you, will a single hotel room supply the elbow room everyone needs? Disney's most affordable hotel rooms, for example, have a maximum occupancy of four people in two double beds, so if your group exceeds that number, you'll have to rent two rooms or upgrade to something more expensive. For most families, renting a home or condo solves the space issue, and usually for less money.

Will I have a car? Unless you're a Disney-only type of person, you should have one. The rival resorts plot to keep you on property, spending inflated rates. Cars can speed you away from their clutches, saving your sanity and your pocketbook. They enable you to see both Disney *and* Harry Potter as well as Orlando's many appealing diversions.

How much time do I plan to spend at my accommodations? If your schedule will be jammed and you're planning to use your room only to hit the sack, then why pay more than you have to? Do you *really* need a fitness center after slogging around the 1.3-mile path of Epcot's World Showcase all day? No, you don't.

Then, grill your hotel about the true value of its enticements: **Is there a resort fee?** It's increasingly common, and they effectively increase the rate. **Is there a parking fee?** It's another way to hide the true cost of a stay. **What's in the breakfast?** It could be just instant coffee and a mound of stale croissants.

GETTING THE BEST RATES

Ask any hotel what it charges, and you're unlikely to get a straight answer. Almost all hotels in Orlando delight in changing their rates according to how full they are, but the emptier the hotel is, the more likely it'll be that rates are at their lowest. As a rule of thumb, prices are lowest when kids are unlikely to be in school (summers, spring break), and followed by the light periods in late January, September, October, and early December. Weekends see slightly higher prices, too, because Florida residents drop by. The prices in this guide represent an average rate.

The good news is that Orlando's average nightly rate is $99, which is $9 cheaper than the national average, so you're already working at an advantage. Primary websites that collect quotes from a variety of sources (whether they be hotel chains or other websites) include **Expedia.com, Hotels.com, Kayak.com, Mobissimo.com, Momondo.com, Orbitz.com,** and **Travelocity.com.** Always canvas multiple sites. The bidding areas on Hotwire.com and Priceline.com are more likely to get you the best rates in the month before you travel; hotels hold out for higher prices until then. Then call the local number of the hotel, not the toll-free one (which may connect to an office far away), to see if they'll do even better. Also check **Hotelcoupons.com** for current discounted rates for some of the cheapest motels in town (no promises about their quality, and that hotels frequently refuse to honor the lowest rates if they hit 75–80 percent occupancy).

Another reliable way to get a cheaper room is to buy your reservation along with an **air/hotel package.** No domestic company operates charter flights to Orlando anymore, but several packagers buy cheap hotel rooms in bulk and sell them with scheduled airfare. Check **Lastminute.com** (© 866/999-8942), **Funjet** (© 888/558-6654; www.funjet.com), as well as some of the vacation wings of major airlines such as **Southwest**

Theme Park Shuttles: Going Your Way?

Almost all of the hotels located off theme park property tout some kind of "free" shuttle service to the major parks (often covered by your resort fee). When they work, they're a dream, but you need to know that most are restrictive. Many run once or twice a day, on their schedule, and you must book ahead. A typical hotel shuttle may leaves for the Magic Kingdom twice a morning and return at, say, 5 and 10pm. Shuttles may provide only one run per direction which drops after the park has opened for the day and returns before it closes, wasting valuable time. Sometimes, hotels will provide shuttles to one area (Disney or Universal/SeaWorld) but not the other. Ask.

Many hotels share shuttles. They can be dirty, worn, and crowded, and you might have to stop at up to a half-dozen other places on your way. If you're hungry, thirsty, tired, or your kids are restless, bring your best Zen face.

Before settling on a hotel based on its advertised rides, ask questions:

1. What time do they leave and return?
2. Which theme parks are not covered?
3. How many other hotels share the same shuttle?
4. Is there a fee? (That $30 for two could have been used to rent a car.)

Vacations (📞 800/243-8372; www.southwestvacations.com), **JetBlue Getaways** (📞 800/538-2583; www.jetblue.com/vacations), **Delta Vacations** (📞 800/800-1504; www.deltavacations.com), and **American Airlines Vacations** (📞 800/321-2121; www.aavacations.com). Internationally, **Virgin Holidays** (www.virginholidays.co.uk) is a huge player, with lots of customer service reps available on the ground should things go wrong. Increasingly, these websites may even sell hotel-only deals using their negotiated rates. Use the properties on its specials page, though, because prices often come out higher in searches.

Few of these players will truly discount a Disney hotel, although they may package Disney products without discounts. If they do, be careful to parse the pricing and compare it to a la carte options—Disney packages are notorious for fees, wasting money, and including more than you could possibly need. Even if you do want a Disney hotel, price be damned, book your Disney hotel separately from tickets or airfare—"room-only", on a separate phone call—because it gives you more scheduling flexibility with Magic Your Way tickets and room-only cancellation rules are far kinder. Don't accept *any* package from a Disney receptionist, even if it's for harmless trinkets, unless you're okay with paying a $200 fee for cancellations made 44 to 2 days ahead; room-only bookings have no penalties for cancellations made 5 to 6 days ahead. When it comes to non-Disney hotels, though, package away, because that's where some great deals live.

Conventions make last-minute bookings risky, but Orlando's **Official Visitor Center** (8723 International Dr.; 📞 **407/363-5872;** www.visitorlando.com; daily 8:30am–6:30pm) will help you find something. You're also likely to find a room (grotty though it may be) on U.S. 192 east of I-4.

ORLANDO'S HOTELS

Every hotel in this book has a swimming pool (because of liability issues, few are much deeper than 5 ft.), Wi-Fi, and air-conditioning, and almost every hotel offers shuttles to at least some theme parks, although fares around $5 to $10 per person may apply. Pretty much every hotel is kid-friendly. In fact, you should expect even the top-end places to be crawling with scampering, shouting children hopped up on a perpetual vacation-permitted sugar buzz. If you crave peace, steer toward a rental home or one of the splurgy resort hotels that lean more toward the convention trade, in which case the rugrats will be replaced by mobile phone-wielding conference-goers in chinos.

How to Save on Lodging

○ **Come during low season.** Hotel prices are trimmed then.

○ **Avoid holidays.** If the kids are out of school, you might pay double.

○ **Make sure the room can fit everyone in your party.** Otherwise you'll have to rent two, doubling costs.

○ **Always get a quote directly from the hotel.** It might be lower.

○ **See what's on offer from a packager.** They have purchasing power.

○ **Plug Kissimmee into Web searches.** It's cheaper than Orlando.

○ **Good locations also save on food.** Are there affordable restaurants nearby?

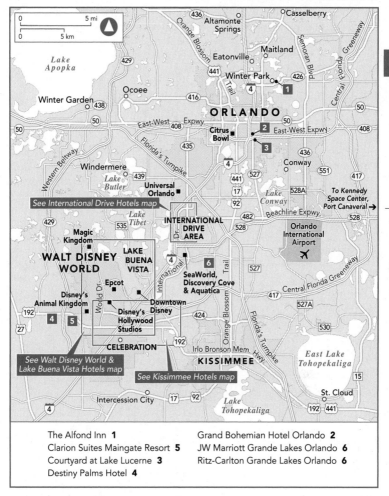

The Alfond Inn **1**	Grand Bohemian Hotel Orlando **2**
Clarion Suites Maingate Resort **5**	JW Marriott Grande Lakes Orlando **6**
Courtyard at Lake Lucerne **3**	Ritz-Carlton Grande Lakes Orlando **6**
Destiny Palms Hotel **4**	

Following are the categories and price ranges for the hotel rooms in this chapter:

- Inexpensive: Up to $95 a night
- Moderate: $96 to $175
- Expensive: $176 and up

Note: Prices in this book don't include taxes, which for hotels add as much as 14.5 percent to your bill depending on the municipality in which you're staying.

Walt Disney World & Lake Buena Vista Hotels

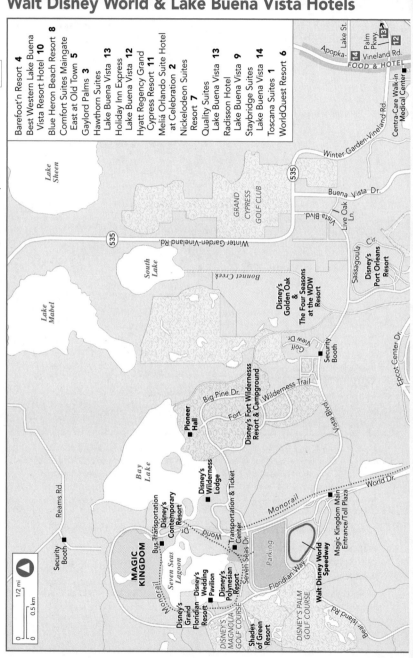

Barefoot'n Resort **4**
Best Western Lake Buena Vista Resort Hotel **10**
Blue Heron Beach Resort **8**
Comfort Suites Maingate East at Old Town **5**
Gaylord Palms **3**
Hawthorn Suites Lake Buena Vista **13**
Holiday Inn Express Lake Buena Vista **12**
Hyatt Regency Grand Cypress Resort **11**
Meliá Orlando Suite Hotel at Celebration **2**
Nickelodeon Suites Resort **7**
Quality Suites Lake Buena Vista **13**
Radisson Hotel Lake Buena Vista **9**
Staybridge Suites Lake Buena Vista **14**
Toscana Suites **1**
WorldQuest Resort **6**

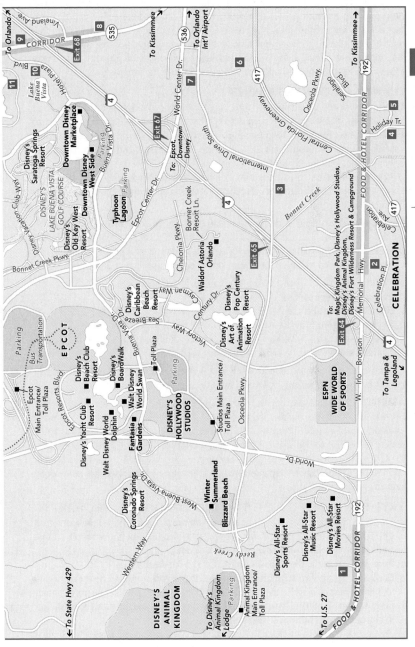

Inside Walt Disney World

Some people don't mind spending twice Orlando's going rate so they can be on Disney property near the resort's storied "magic," but they are hard-pressed to explain what that actually means, though it probably has to do with the sensation of security that well-planned theming elicits. But strictly from a non-pixie-dusted consumer-advice standpoint, there are advantages and disadvantages to saying on property. How many of these considerations are important to you—or justify the expense?

DISNEY PRICING SEASONS

Unlike most hotels, which price dynamically, Walt Disney World's hotel rates are fixed by a calendar. The seasons you need to remember are, in descending order of expense: **Holiday, Peak, Summer, Regular, Fall,** and **Value.** The major price spikes, when charges as much as double, are around spring break, Easter, and the late December holidays—put simple, when school is out.

Likewise, there are three categories of hotel: **Deluxe, Moderate,** and **Value,** plus Disney Vacation Club apartments. Ergo, the get the cheapest room, book a Value resort during a Value period.

SEASONS   The dates for each season shift annually and are tweaked per property, but they follow the same pattern on the calendar. For 2014, the schedule shakes out like this, including the weekday price of a Value hotel room so you'll know the bottom line of the lowest-priced room (on weekends, prices pop up as much as 25 percent):

- **Value season:** Jan 2–Feb 13, Aug 17–Sept 26. Value price: $96
- **Fall season:** Sept 13–Dec 12. Value price: $110.
- **Regular season:** Feb 23–Mar 6, Apr 27–May 29. Value price: $105.
- **Summer season:** May 30–Aug 2. Value price: $150.
- **Peak season:** Feb 13–23, Mar 7–Apr 12, Apr 21–26, Dec 12–18. Value price: $152.
- **Holiday season:** Dec 19–Jan 1. Value price: $190–$198.

MouseSavers.com and **TheMouseForLess.com,** both post codes of all current known discounts. In general, AAA and military service may help cut costs.

AMENITIES   All Disney hotels, regardless of class, have touches that provide relief for families, including shallow kiddie pools at each resort, coin laundries, and playgrounds. Wi-Fi is free. There will always be somewhere to eat, although at Value resorts it will be a food court. Disney Transportation System (DTS) shuttle buses (p. 228) serve all resorts for free, and every property is protected by gated security that checks every visitor against the guest list. And, of course, every resort has at least one souvenir store—usually more.

YAY! THE BENEFITS OF STAYING ON DISNEY PROPERTY

- For those without cars, there's **free bus, monorail, and ferry transportation** throughout the resort. This is the biggest consideration for most people. (Then again, it's free to *everyone* at Disney, guest or not.)
- **Free parking** at the theme parks (normally $15 per day for a car).
- Each day, during **Extra Magic Hours,** one or two parks open an hour early or up to 3 hours past closing for the express use of Disney hotel guests. The major attractions, but not all of them, will be open during this period, and lines tend to be shorter than when general admission takes effect.
- Free coach transfers to Orlando International Airport through **Disney's Magical Express** program. See p. 227 for its drawbacks.

- Every room has a small balcony or patio (except at Value resorts).
- The right to **charge purchases** on your room key card or MagicBand.
- The right to have in-park **shopping delivered to your room.** (The delivery lag time is such that you should be staying for at least 2 more nights.)
- Three or four timed **kids' activities** a day, albeit some at a charge.
- **Wake-up calls** feature Disney characters.
- Sometimes staff (called "Mousekeeping") leaves **towels shaped like animals** (a Disney tradition).
- **Free wheelchair rental.**
- **Guaranteed admission** if parks are full.
- Option to purchase soft drink **mugs** ($16) that you may refill endlessly while at the hotel.

BOO! THESE THINGS ABOUT STAYING WITH DISNEY STINK

- **"Free" resort transportation doesn't mean "fast."** Routes can be circuitous and waits can be aggravating, and you may have to stand.
- **Rates are 40–70 percent higher** than off-property rooms of comparable quality.
- **Stingy occupancy limits.** Most rooms add $10 a night for each person past the limit of two up to the room's stated maximum capacity, so an $105 room will in fact be $125 if four people over 18 stay there. Value and Moderate resorts cap occupancy at four (not including a babe in a crib) and Deluxe cap at five. Families larger than four must rent two units, doubling the expense, but if you have seven or more people to accommodate, it gets ugly.
- **Haphazard room assignment.** In busy times, families with multiple rooms may get split apart. Requests for specific locations may not be honored.
- Disney resorts are so large (often, 2,000 rooms) that **lines,** even for a cup of coffee, are an endless nuisance and **sprawling layouts are confusing** to small children, to say nothing of their parents. Disney has turned the failing into profit: It charges $15 more for "Preferred" rooms nearer the lobby.
- Counterintuitively, the more affordable a room is, they more you could use a rental car. Value rooms are about as **far from the action** as many off-property hotels. The Value resorts, in particular, are a good 15-minute drive from the Magic Kingdom. (No farther than a decent vacation home.)
- **Safes** are tiny (laptops won't fit). In-room cooking is made difficult in that the most affordable rooms lack **microwaves** or **coffeemakers.**
- The most affordable Disney hotels also **don't have restaurants.** They have food courts (burgers, sandwiches, pasta—all at theme park prices of around $10) and the only room service item is pizza. This is less of a problem if you intend to save money by eating off property anyway.

VALUE RESORTS

Although the Mouse pushes you toward its most expensive hotels by making them so cool, Disney, in fact, has more Value rooms, 9,504 of them, more than many midsize cities have in total—available for $106 to $236. The T-shaped building blocks with outdoor corridors can feel at times like thin-walled battery hen hutches, with noisy plumbing and seething with kids who don't realize how sound carries (especially when school groups and cheerleader meets are in town). The walk to each hotel's lobby/food building can be a marathon. There are elevators.

Value-class rooms are for people dying to stay on Disney property but don't want to break the bank doing it and don't mind second-class citizenship.

DISNEY'S "CLUB LEVEL"

For an extra $100 to $150, Disney sells "club-level" concierge-style rooms in a restricted area of certain hotel with a private lounge stocked with free food and beverages. In some hotels, club level entitles you to better views or to buy additional experiences, such as a custom tour of the savannah area at Animal Kingdom Lodge.

FACILITIES   Value rooms are motel-style, often of standard cinder-block construction. They come with two full beds, but a few have kings (request one when you reserve). Rooms fit four (there's a $10 daily charge for each third and fourth adult over 17), plus one child under 3—a full room would be a mighty tight squeeze. If your party is bigger than that, spring for a 6-person Family Suite, which is usually just two rooms with a door banged through and a minikitchen (little fridge, microwave, coffeemaker) added. Those are at the All-Star Music resort and Art of Animation, where the design is more spacious, but at $202 (lowest price at Music) to $252 (lowest price at Animation), you can do *much* better outside the World.

The food court, front desk, and sundries shop are all in the same building by the bus stops to the parks, and some rooms are a 15-minute walk away.

TRANSPORTATION   No Value or Moderate resort is connected to anything by monorail. Roads are your only option, be it a bus or your car.

Disney's All-Star Movies/Disney's All-Star Music/Disney's All-Star Sports ★   Covering the adjoining All-Stars clone cluster a decade ago for "Budget Travel" magazine, I summed them up thusly: "Depending on your point of view, Disney treats you either like a second-class guest or an average American family on vacation." Nothing has changed. The fun is in the outdoor areas, not in the rooms, which are only faintly themed. Their setup is identical—an expanse of concrete-block buildings at the edge of the property enlivened by enormous emblems, as if a giant had spilled the Legos in his toy box. But because they're older (they opened in the late 1990s) and there's no enlivening pond, they are the last-choice Values. At the very least, sinks are outside of the toilet-and-shower room, which eases life for multitasking families. Of the three, I prefer Movies, not just because it's the youngest (opened 1999) and because its decor is laden with Disney-specific iconography while its sisters stick to musical and sports-equipment icons. Disney shuttle buses also tend to stop there last on their circuit of the three, which cuts transportation time. Then again, some choose Sports for the same reason, as it's the first stop and so it's easier to get a seat there. (That concern says a lot about the Value resorts.) The Music is the only one with suites fitting six people.

Buena Vista Dr., Lake Buena Vista. ℭ **407/934-7639.** www.disneyworld.com. 1,920 units each. Standard rooms $96–$198, family suites $249–$445, 3rd and 4th adult $10. Children 17 and younger stay free in parent's room. Free parking. **Amenities:** Food court, lounge, arcade, babysitting, 2 outdoor heated pools, kids' pool, free Wi-Fi.

Disney's Art of Animation Resort ★★★   This attractive 2012 addition benefits from theming more lavish than at other Values, including a spot-on Radiator Springs pool area. Family Suites have two bathrooms, convertible couches, and demikitchens (no stove). Standard "Little Mermaid" rooms are gorgeously and whimsically themed, too—better than at other Values. Other suites draw on "Finding Nemo" (where there's the Big Blue pool, WDW's largest) and "The Lion King." Unfortunately, 6-person suites cost 2½ times more than basic 4-person Value rooms, which is hard to justify.

1850 Century Dr., Lake Buena Vista. ℭ **407/938-7000.** www.disneyworld.com. 1,120 suites, 864 standard units. Standard rooms $100–$191, 6-person family suites $254–$433. Free parking. **Amenities:** 3 pools, food court, kids' pools, arcade, free Wi-Fi.

Disney's Pop Century Resort ★★   The largest Value resort (opened 2002) is a fair choice, with smallish (260 sq. ft.) rooms with one sink and one mirror, and for dining, a heaving central food court with quality akin to the average mall's. As if to counteract such dormlike austerity, the boxy sprawl of T-shaped buildings, some of which face a pleasant lake, is festooned with outsized icons of the late 20th century: gigantic bowling pins, yo-yos, and Rubik's Cubes—which kids think is pretty cool.

1050 Century Dr., Lake Buena Vista. ✆ **407/938-4000.** www.disneyworld.com. 2,880 units. Rooms $96–$198. Free parking. **Amenities:** Food court, 3 pools, kids' pools, arcade, free Wi-Fi

MODERATE RESORTS

The next category up from Value is Moderate, easily $182 to $284 for a double, if not more. Compared to Value, what do you get for the extra dough? Put simply, the main pools have more elaborate themes with slides and there are usually a few additional, simple pools; rooms measure 314 square feet instead of 260 square feet (so: 2 feet wider); most have two sinks instead of one (both outside the shower/toilet room); all rooms have a small balcony or patio with seating (though most have no view to speak of), and you can rent a bike or a boat on the premises. The upgrade doesn't win you the right to fit more people: Rooms mostly fit four, plus one child under 3, same as the Value class.

Moderate properties feel more resortlike when compared to the glorified motels of the Values, but at heart, they're still glorified motels, with exterior corridors (close your drapes) and windowless bathrooms. You'll still be eating mostly in high-priced food courts located at a main building that might be quite distant from your room. Although the bedrooms aren't really much plusher than the Value properties, you will sense more breathing room and personality to the grounds since Disney has been pouring money into glorifying its Moderate pool areas.

Disney's Caribbean Beach Resort ★   Like Coronado Springs (below), this resort is sprawling with a central pond—1.4 miles around!—except there's an island theme. Rooms (mostly full beds) are the Moderate category's largest (by a little) and fresh; Disney spent a ton theming some rooms to "Pirates of the Caribbean" (beds like ships, carpet like decking) that cost $44 to $72 more than a regular room. The main Old Port Royale pool area emulates a waterfront Spanish fort and has a giant tippy bucket, so you can see why families favor this property. The resort's principal drawbacks are a lack of elevators and the fact no other major areas connect to it. At least Port Orleans, for nearly the same money, has boats that go to Downtown Disney; from Caribbean Beach, all connections are by road, so it's strongly recommended to have a car here.

900 Cayman Way, Lake Buena Vista. ✆ **407/934-7639** or 407/934-3400. www.disneyworld.com. 2,112 units. $162–$298 standard double. Extra person $15. Children 17 and younger stay free in parent's room. Free parking. **Amenities:** Restaurant, food court, lounge, arcade, heated pool, 6 smaller pools in the villages, kids' pool, free Wi-Fi.

Disney's Coronado Springs Resort ★★   Built to attract convention crowds with a vibe to match, it nonetheless has fans for its subdued tone. The well-planted grounds, done in a hacienda style around a pond, are far-flung (some rooms are a 15-min. walk from the lobby), and rooms, with kings or queens, have a single sink, as at the Values. The food court is above average, though, as is the pool area (the Dig Site) themed after a Mayan pyramid, and there's a cocktail lounge, Rix, with a semblance of sophistication. The hotel is about 10 minutes' drive from any parks. If you need a room accessible for those with disabilities and the cheaper hotels are out of such units, you can try here, where there is an inventory of 99 rooms.

1000 Buena Vista Dr., Lake Buena Vista. ✆ **407/934-7639** or 407/939-1000. www.disneyworld.com. 1,921 units. $167–$298 double. Extra person $15. Children 17 and younger stay free in parent's room. Free parking. **Amenities:** Restaurant, grill/food court, 2 lounges, arcade, health club and limited spa, 4 outdoor heated pools, kids' pool, free Wi-Fi.

Disney's Fort Wilderness Resort & Campground ★★

Not to be confused with the Wilderness Lodge, an imitation of Yellowstone Lodge, this 780-acre wooded enclave near Magic Kingdom consists of campsites, mobile home–style cabins with decks and grills that sleep six, and RV spots. Camping under the thick pines is far and away the cheapest and most distinctive way to sleep on property, but it's twice the market rate, and without equipment (tents are $30, cots $4, if a group hasn't booked them first). The nightly marshmallow roast and outdoor Disney film screenings are perennial hits.

3520 N. Fort Wilderness Trail, Lake Buena Vista. © **407/934-7639** or 407/824-2900. www.disney world.com. 784 campsites, 408 wilderness cabins. $55–$139 campsite/RV double, $330–$562 wilderness cabin double. Extra person $2 campsites, $5 cabins. Children 17 and younger stay free in parent's room. Pets $5 (full hookup sites only). Free parking. **Amenities:** Restaurant, grill, lounge, babysitting, extensive outdoor activities (archery; fishing; horseback, pony, carriage, and hay rides; campfire programs; and more), 2 outdoor heated pools, kids' pool, 2 lighted tennis courts, free Wi-Fi.

Disney's Port Orleans Riverside and French Quarter ★★

An unwieldy name for an unwieldy property. It's actually two resorts, both built on a canal and awkwardly fused together. The French Quarter (1,000 rooms), built along right angles on simulated streets, purports to sorta imitate the real one in New Orleans. Riverside (2,048 rooms), where buildings are more successful pastiches on magnolia-lined Mississippi-style homes (Magnolia Bend, where princess-themed "Royal Rooms" have touches such as headboards with push-button light shows; $30–$40 surcharge) and rustic cabins (Alligator Bayou, where trundle beds sleep 5), is the nicer of the two, as it has more water for rooms to face (though the privilege will cost you another $30 a night) and is the locale for most activities for the two resorts. The main pool at Riverside is less elaborate than French Quarter's, although it has five pools to French Quarter's one. The properties are far enough apart (about 15 min. walking) that many people choose to use the free boat service linking them. The boats will also take you to Downtown Disney—the trip is one of the most pleasant, least known free rides at Disney World—but the parks are served only by buses.

2201 Orleans Dr., Lake Buena Vista. www.disneyworld.com. © **407/934-7639** or 407/934-5000. 3,048 units. $162–$288 double. Extra person $15. Children 17 and younger stay free in parent's room. Free parking. **Amenities:** 2 restaurants, grill/food court, 2 lounges, 6 heated outdoor pools, 2 kids' pools, free Wi-Fi.

Shades of Green ★★★

Operated as a golf resort for 21 years before being handed to the military as the only Armed Forces Recreation Center (AFRC) located in the continental U.S, it's the best deal on WDW soil if you or your spouse is an active or retired member of the U.S. military (a full list of eligibility requirements is posted online). Standard rooms are among the largest in all of Disney (just over 400 sq. ft.) and suites accommodate up to eight. All rooms have balconies or patios, and pool or golf-course views. Bonus: It's within walking distance of the monorail and the Magic Kingdom.

1950 Magnolia Palm Dr. (across from the Polynesian Resort), Lake Buena Vista. © **888/593-2242** or 407/824-3400. www.shadesofgreen.org. 587 units. $93–$131 double (based on military rank); $250–$275 6- to 8-person suite (regardless of rank). Extra person $15. Children 17 and younger stay free in parent's room. Free parking. **Amenities:** 2 restaurants, cafe, 2 lounges, health club, arcade, 2 heated outdoor pools, kids' pool, 2 lighted tennis courts, free Wi-Fi.

DELUXE RESORTS

No one who has experienced the world's true luxury hotels can seriously say that Disney's quality standards compare. They're 3-star hotels in fancy dress. Sure, they have sit-down restaurants, spas, lounges, and elaborate pools (their main calling card). But they are machines, and rooms are nothing special. What Disney's Deluxe hotels mostly have is uplifting theming—a prevailing mood—that makes a stay memorable, and it's a genuine thrill to be so near a theme park, to get such fantastic views of the Magic Kingdom or African animals—there's just something special about it. Yes, you can certainly pay less than the $239 to $1,018 you pay to sleep in just a standard room. But for many people, they're more than just a place to sleep.

Most Deluxes enable you to dart out of the parks easily. Three are by the Magic Kingdom on the monorail line encircling the Seven Seas Lagoon: the Contemporary (the most iconic), the Grand Floridian (the fanciest), and the Polynesian (the most private and also nearest the stop for Epcot). A fourth, Wilderness Lodge, is linked to the Magic Kingdom by ferry, while the Beach Club, Yacht Club, and BoardWalk are walking distance from Epcot's side door. Only Animal Kingdom Lodge is marooned by roads, but it has other one-of-a-kind perks that counterbalance that.

Disney's Animal Kingdom Lodge ★★★ No grander lodge ever existed on the African veldt, and the higher tariff returns to you in the form of a 24-hour safari. The hotel is built within a system of paddocks, so if you've got a Savannah view (they start at $409—careful that you don't accidentally book a Standard one overlooking the parking lot), when you look out of your window, you'll see whatever genial African animal is loping by at that moment, be it a giraffe, an ostrich, a zebra, or a warthog. You'll find a game-viewing guide beside your room service menu. Because animals tend to be active in the early morning, when families are gearing up for their days, the idea works well. Like the Contemporary, anyone can visit, even if they're not staying here; there's even a public viewing area straight out the back door of the awe-inspiring vaulted lobby. Its principal drawback is its distance from everything except for Animal Kingdom; all connections are by road.

2901 Osceola Pkwy., Bay Lake. ✆ **407/934-7639** or 407/938-3000. www.disneyworld.com. 1,293 units. $319–$652 nonclub double. Extra person $25. Children 17 and younger stay free in parent's room. Free parking. **Amenities:** 2 restaurants, cafe, lounge, babysitting, supervised children's program, club-level rooms, health club and limited spa, heated outdoor pool, kids' pool, room service, free Wi-Fi.

Disney's Beach Club/Disney's Yacht Club ★★★ Both excellent choices, these sisters are on a pond across from the BoardWalk entertainment area and a short stroll out the International Gateway exit of Epcot's World Showcase, which brings the fun close to your room, although you can't watch IllumiNations from it. Their shared 3-acre pool area, Stormalong Bay, has a crazy water slide coming off the mast of a pirate ship, plus sandy shores. (It's easily the best pool on Disney property, and it's restricted to guests.) The difference between them is nearly negligible—so much so that many guests think they're one giant hotel, but the Yacht Club has slightly nicer furnishings, bigger balconies, attracts slightly fewer families with kids, is a tad quieter, and is at 10-minute stroll from Epcot instead of 5. Other than that, it's a toss-up.

1800 Epcot Resorts Blvd., Lake Buena Vista. ✆ **407/934-7639** or 407/934-8000. www.disneyworld.com. Beach: 583 units. Yacht: 630 units. $400–$743 nonclub doubles. Extra person $25. Children 17 and younger stay free in parent's room. Free parking. **Amenities:** 2 restaurants, grill, 4 lounges, babysitting, supervised children's program, health club and small spa, 3-acre pool and play area, 2 outdoor heated pools, kids' pool, room service, 2 lighted tennis courts, free Wi-Fi.

Disney's Contemporary Resort ★★★ Nothing says, "I'm at Disney World" more than the awesome sight of that monorail sweeping dramatically through its glassy Grand Canyon Concourse, which it does every few minutes on its way to and from the Magic Kingdom. The building itself, one of the first two to open in 1971, has transitioned from "dated" to a midcentury architectural treasure, and indicative of the revolutionary methods that Walt Disney World hoped to pioneer: The United States Steel Corporation helped design it; its modular, prefabricated rooms were slotted into place by crane. The brilliant idea was that when rooms required renovation, the capsules could simply be removed like drawers, but in practice, they fused to the steel frame, so renovations are done the old-fashioned way. The current look: soothing putty and slate business-class colors. The best rooms are high up in the coveted A-framed Contemporary Tower, but there are low-level Garden Rooms along Bay Lake, too, by a surprisingly blah pool, that are about $150 cheaper. Rooms on the west of the tower face the Magic Kingdom itself—from the 9th floor, the *ne plus ultra* of Disney views—and every water-view room takes in the nightly electrical parade that floats after dark. Even if you can't stay here, this is the best hotel to tour. Drop by to see the 90-foot-tall, stylized mosaics of children by the visionary Imagineer Mary Blair, which encapsulate the late-'60s futurist optimism out of which the resort was born. If money were no object, this would always be a top choice.

4600 N. World Dr., Lake Buena Vista. ✆ **407/939-6244** or 407/824-1000. www.disneyworld.com. 1,008 units. $378–$801 nonclub double. Extra person $25. Children 17 and younger stay free in parent's room. Free parking. **Amenities:** 3 restaurants, grill, 4 lounges, babysitting, concierge-level rooms, small health club and spa, 2 outdoor heated pools, kids' pool, free Wi-Fi.

Disney's Grand Floridian Resort & Spa ★★ It's strange to spend $600 a night on a hotel room and then have to walk outside in the rain to reach the building it's in, but from a value standpoint, that tells you a lot. This is the Disney hotel with snob appeal, since the whole point is to put on a costume of exclusivity and luxury (two things Walt despised, which is why *his* hotels had populist themes) and brag about it when you get home. So it's encrusted with upper-class affectation, from high tea to a pianist tinkling away in a very pretty lobby (chandeliers, glass dome, wedding-cake balconies). It can't help but strum your imagination of what a white-glove Victorian grande dame hotel might have felt like, but anyone can enjoy that on a day visit without paying insane rates for what amounts to a 3-star room. There *are* vacation-making pluses I'd unreservedly celebrate here if money were no object, such as next-door access to the Magic Kingdom, gourmet restaurants, and an atmosphere more romantic than at any other Disney hotel.

4401 Floridian Way. Lake Buena Vista. ✆ **407/934-7639** or 407/824-3000. www.disneyworld.com. 900 units. $549–$1,018 nonclub double. Extra person $25. Children 17 and younger stay free in parent's room. Free parking. **Amenities:** 5 restaurants, grill, 3 lounges, character meals, babysitting, supervised children's program, club-level rooms, health club and spa, heated outdoor pool, kids' pool, room service, 2 lighted tennis courts, free Wi-Fi.

Disney's Polynesian Resort ★★★ The 25-acre hotel, thickly planted and torch-lit by night, was one of the first two hotels planted here, back when the South Pacific tiki craze was still swinging, and the longhouse-style thatched-roof complex remains one of the most transporting of the Disney resorts. The most expensive rooms glimpse the Magic Kingdom across the Seven Seas Lagoon (there's an on-site monorail station for it), but most have greenery views. Everyone can enjoy the volcano-themed swimming pool with water slide tube and a beach with some of the softest white sand you ever sank your toes into (no swimming in the Lagoon, though). It's a notch better for families, as there's an on-site child-care facility, the Epcot monorail is steps away, and rooms are on the big side, sleeping five. An easy favorite.

1600 Seven Seas Dr., Lake Buena Vista. ℰ **407/939-6244** or 407/824-2000. www.disneyworld.com. 853 units. $482–$981 nonclub double. Extra person $25. Children 17 and younger stay free in parent's room. Free parking. **Amenities:** 3 restaurants, cafe, 2 lounges, on-site babysitting, supervised children's program, club-level rooms, nearby health club and spa (at Grand Floridian), 2 heated outdoor pools, kids' pool, room service, free 7:30pm marshmallow roast, free 9pm outdoor movie, free Wi-Fi.

Disney's Wilderness Lodge ★★ This effective riff on Yellowstone's woody Old Faithful Lodge, swaddled by oaks and pines, is picturesque but disconnected from the rest of the park—the Magic Kingdom, 10 minutes away by ferry, is the only thing easy to reach if you don't have your own car. Most of its tricks are in its dramatic atrium lobby: giant stone hearth, springs that flow to a thronged, geyser-themed pool area out back. Because of the surrounding woods, rooms are a little dark, but they have adorable rustic touches headboards carved with woodland creature finials.

901 W. Timberline Dr., Lake Buena Vista. ℰ **407/934-7639** or 407/938-4300. www.disneyworld.com. 909 units. $325–$609 nonclub room. Children 17 and younger stay free in parent's room. Valet parking $12, free self-parking. **Amenities:** 3 restaurants, 2 lounges, babysitting, club-level rooms, health club and limited spa, 2 spa tubs, 2 heated outdoor pools, kids' pool, room service, free Wi-Fi.

Walt Disney World Swan and Dolphin ★ The only hotels near a theme park where you can use rewards points from the outside world—that's the main appeal to the Starwood-run Swan and Dolphin, which are linked by a footbridge over the lake they share. Former Disney CEO Michael Eisner controversially allowed outside corporations to intrude on resort property and the result was these dated designs distinguished mostly by splashy exterior set pieces—like the 56-foot talk dolphin fish statues. The ceilings are a little bit low, the staff a little bit distracted, but the location never quits: You can walk to Epcot in 15 minutes and Hollywood Studios in 20, avoiding the bus, which is a good thing for Swan guests since sometimes DTS arrives there after having filled up at the Dolphin. The Dolphin is essentially a tarted-up business hotel for conferences, and although it strives to welcome families, too (rooms fit five and its grotto pool is inviting), it's frankly too hard to do both things well and still cast a spell. Rooms are dated, but some rooms in the Dolphin's Center Tower have terrific views right into Epcot. Everything lacks the tonal fantasy at Disney-run hotels, but guests get the same perks as at a Disney-run hotel, except for making park purchases by room key: Separate is not equal.

1500 Epcot Resorts Blvd., Lake Buena Vista. ℰ **407/934-4000.** www.swandolphin.com. 1,509 units. Swan: $239–$505 nonclub double. Dolphin: $219–$579 nonclub double. Extra person $25. Resort fee $17 per night. Children 17 and younger stay free in parent's room. Self-parking $15. **Amenities:** 4 restaurants, cafe, grill, 5 lounges, character meals, babysitting, free domestic phone calls, supervised children's program, club-level rooms, health club and spa, 5 heated outdoor pools, room service, 4 lighted tennis courts, Wi-Fi included with resort fee.

DISNEY VACATION CLUB

Disney sells timeshares, too. Since this isn't a real estate guide, there's no need to go into the fact after you crunch the numbers, **Disney Vacation Club (DVC)** is economical only for people who don't ever want to vacation anywhere that isn't Disney. The company rents its empty villa units to walk-up customers who have no intention of signing any dotted lines. So far there are 10 DVC properties in Orlando (grafted onto the major hotels), plus stand-alone properties including **BoardWalk Villas, Saratoga Springs Resort & Spa,** and **Old Key West,** serving hundreds of thousands of DVC

The "Good Neighbor" Policy

Scattered throughout town as far as the International Drive area are properties Disney has certified as "Good Neighbor" (www.wdwgoodneighborhotels.com). The appellation is mostly meaningless. It means that hotel will have shuttles, can sell Magic Your Way tickets, and screens a mesmerizing 24-hour channel featuring the insanity-inducing Stacey Aswad, the world's most nose-wrinklingly perky Disney fan (she's a Juilliard-trained performer, and to her, everything is "amazing"), and her Top Seven favorites at each park. To be brutally honest, most Good Neighbor hotels are plainly mediocre. Something about the added business that comes with the distinction makes a hotel care a little less about hustling for business. Only the Good Neighbor properties on the west side of Apopka Vineland Road (mostly on Hotel Plaza Blvd.) enjoy half-hourly shuttles; the rest don't. All **"Bed and Brick"** hotels (℅ **800/979-9983**) have shuttles to Legoland. Don't select a hotel just because it's a Good Neighbor hotel. Choose it because it's the hotel for you.

investors. That number is a result of heavy promotion around the resort and even inside the theme parks themselves, which Walt surely would have detested as a fantasy-killer. During value season, the simplest studio with a kitchen costs an insane $327 (at Old Key West, the cheapest) a night, and in high season, it costs $431 a night. Bay Lake Tower ranges $492 to $1,006. Knowing that for that money, you could get week's stay at a condo no farther away than Animal Kingdom, or even 10 rooms on Disney property, I cannot in good conscience suggest you spend your money renting a DVC room.

Inside Universal Orlando

There are four hotels on Universal property, all operated by the Loews hotel group, and they all feel more like true resorts whereas Disney's have a busier, processed feel. There are strong advantages that come with the higher prices. First, you don't need buses because all hotels are within 15 minutes' walk of the parks, and three are connected by a free boat that runs continuously into the wee hours. Rooms have wet bars with coffeemakers, two phones, and turn-down service (rare at Disney). Also, every guest can use their room key to make charges throughout the resort, they get into Harry Potter an hour early, and at three hotels, they can join the Express line at the two parks' best attractions—that perk has the effect of freeing up a vacation schedule. Guests can also drink and dine all night at CityWalk next door without having to drive or wait for a bus. Use the hotels' website to find Hot Deals, which grants discounts of 20 to 30 percent on specified nights; the website also posts floor plans of all room types.

The Universal property is hemmed in by lots of real-world restaurants where prices are realistic, and free shuttles to SeaWorld and Wet 'n' Wild are provided once a day. So unlike cloistered Disney, when you're at Universal, you're linked to the real Orlando, and there's more flexibility. At Easter and during the December holidays, rates are $150 higher than the lowest price.

Cabana Bay Beach Resort ★★★ Universal's fourth hotel, to open in spring 2014, fills a gap for value-priced rooms and family-sized rooms. It was still under construction at press time, but this newcomer, $100 cheaper than its sisters, promises to be much more comfortable than Disney's version of value. Retro to the hilt, it will feature a mod 1950s Miami Beach decor, a Bayliner Diner food court, two zero-entry pools, a lazy river, and a 10-lane bowling alley. Half the rooms will be one-bedroom "family suites" with kitchen areas (microwave, no stove) that sleep six. The lower price has a trade-off: no Express pass privileges like at the other hotels, and to reach the parks, you'll have to either walk 15 minutes or take a shuttle bus.

6550 Adventure Way, Orlando. ✆ **888/464-3617.** www.universalorlando.com. 1,800 units. Standard rooms from $119–$134, family suites $174–$284. Parking $17/day. **Amenities:** Food court, coffee shop, pool bars, 2 pools, water slide, lazy river, Wi-Fi ($10–$15/day).

Hard Rock Hotel ★★★

Besides being the city's most convenient hotel for any theme park—the two parks are both a 10-minute walk away—the Hard Rock has more perks for the money than most of the city's similarly priced hotels. Rooms have genuinely funky furniture, tons of mirrors, two sinks (one in and one out of the bathroom), two big beds, and music systems. The gi-normous pool, which imitates a beach gently descending to depth, has not only a substantial water slide but also underwater speakers through which you can hear the party music. (They really bring out the finger cymbals in "Livin' on a Prayer".) The halls are lined with rock memorabilia (whoa: the gold-lion-head necklace Elvis was wearing when he met Nixon!). The Hard Rock really walks the rock walk: On the last Thursday of the month, the lobby is taken over by the rollicking Velvet Sessions (www.velvetsessions.com) concert series for well-known acts, which have recently included Bret Michaels, Taylor Dayne, and Survivor.

5000 Universal Blvd., Orlando. ✆ **888/273-1311** or 407/503-7625. www.hardrockhotel.com. 650 units. Rooms $254–$259. Parking $17/day. **Amenities:** 3 restaurants, cocktail lounge, Emack & Bolio ice cream shop, babysitting, supervised children's program, club-level rooms, fitness center, pool with activities and bar, Wi-Fi ($10–$15/day).

Portofino Bay Hotel ★★

Universal's priciest and most romantic option faithfully re-creates the famous Italian fishing village, down to the angle of the boat docks and bolted-down Vespas. Beyond that spectacular gimmick (said to have been Steven Spielberg's idea, like much at Universal), rooms are of a particularly high standard—standard ones are a generous 450 square feet, have top-end beds, and were fully renovated in 2013. But because the resort is the farthest of the four from the parks (about 20 min. by boat or foot), it tends to appeal to couples, but a few kids' rooms are decked out in a "Despicable Me" theme.

5601 Universal Blvd., Orlando. ✆ **888/273-1311** or 407/503-1000. www.universalorlando.com. 750 units. Double queen or king rooms $279–$359. Parking $17/day. **Amenities:** 3 restaurants, Mandara spa, 3 pools with activities and bar, nightly opera show, Wi-Fi ($10–$15/day).

Royal Pacific Resort ★★★

The least expensive luxury option at Universal does an apt impression of the South Seas in the 1930s. It's more luxurious yet cheaper than the Disney Polynesian, with a lush pool area (sandy beach, winding garden paths, interactive water play area) and a sophisticated, wood-and-wicker look. The standard is high: very soft robes, cushy beds with fat pillows, and marble-top chests. It's right over the road from Islands of Adventure; many rooms have a panorama of it. In any other city, the Royal Pacific might be everyone's favorite resort. Here, though, its subtler charms get lost in the crowd.

6300 Hollywood Way, Orlando. ✆ **888/273-1311** or 407/503-3000. www.universalorlando.com. 1,000 units. Guest rooms $224–$294. Parking $17/day. **Amenities:** 3 restaurants, sushi bar, cocktail lounge, pool with activities and bars, Wi-Fi ($10–$15/day).

U.S. 192 Area Accommodations

The lowest rung in the Orlando tourist ladder both in class and price, U.S. 192 is where you'll find the most affordable (if often the most tired) motels close to the Disney zoo. Most were built in the 1970s boom and settled into the budget category. These places are technically located in the town of Kissimmee, which posts tourist info at **www. experiencekissimmee.com**—check it for regular deals. In this region, shuttles are often available to Disney, but not always to SeaWorld or Universal.

INEXPENSIVE

Barefoot'n Resort ★ These lemon-colored one-bedroom villas a block off chain restaurant–lined U.S. 192 are everything you need in simple, condo-style accommodation. Rooms come with queen beds, washer and dryer, DVD players, and a sofa sleeper, but you choose between having a fully equipped kitchen with a dishwasher and bar seating or larger bedroom with a spa tub and a partial kitchen. You take care of your own cleaning during your stay. The very sunny pool area has a grill and also faces a pond that's home to brown ducks and a little alligator, Crocky. The tiny resort, which is in good shape and recently renovated, faces the Old Town amusement area, but the drifting music isn't bothersome. If you book by phone, there's no minimum stay requirement.

2754 Florida Plaza, Kissimmee. ℂ **877/978-3314.** www.barefootn.com. 42 units. 1-bedrooms $89–$95. Free parking. **Amenities:** Pool, hot tub, security gate, outdoor barbecue, free Wi-Fi.

Clarion Suites Maingate ★★ A superior-level motel organized around its pool, the Clarion has a quiet, pseudo-resort feel (it's set away from the bustle of U.S. 192 but near enough to its restaurants) that makes it popular with scrimpers, something attentive management has cultivated for years. All rooms come with a small fridge, microwave, and pullout sofa (hence the "suites" distinction of the hotel's name), queen beds, and sleep up to six people. During the week, rooms facing the parking lot usually cost the least, and ones facing the landscaped, free-form courtyard pool cost $10 more. Prices on weekends are about $10 higher, and continental breakfast, with a few plusses such as waffles, is always included. Kids get excited when they look down its driveway and see the summit of Expedition Everest at Disney's Animal Kingdom peeking over the trees nearby.

7888 W. Irlo Bronson Hwy., Kissimmee. ℂ **888/390-9888** or 407/390-9888. www.clarionsuites kissimmee.com. 150 units. $83–$109 doubles. Free parking. **Amenities:** Pool, restaurant, Disney shuttle, free breakfast buffet, game room, barbecue grills, sundries shop, free Wi-Fi.

Comfort Suites Maingate East at Old Town ★★ A good choice for families with kids, it's tucked just off the main drag of U.S. 192, a few miles east of Disney, and both the restaurants and the carnival-style amusements of Old Town are mere steps from the door—but not so near that the noise is truly annoying. The best rates are for "standard rooms" with either a king or queen bed, but you can get a "deluxe" two-bedroom one for about $40 more, and all rooms are on the large side with mini-fridges and microwaves for basic meal preparation. The elevators can be overwhelmed when it's at capacity. Up your occupancy by two by using the pull-out couch that's standard in every unit. AAA membership chops rates slightly.

2775 Florida Plaza Blvd., Kissimmee. ℂ **888/784-8379.** www.comfortsuitesfl.com. 198 units. $79–$169 1-room suites. Free parking. **Amenities:** Pool with poolside bar, 24-hr. fitness center, sundries shop, game room, business center, free park shuttles, free hot breakfast buffet, free Wi-Fi.

WALT DISNEY WORLD

Disney's Hollywood Studios

Blizzard Beach

KISSIMMEE

CELEBRATION

Lake Cecile

ESPN Wide World of Sports

Bonnet Creek

Roads and places:
Vineland Rd.
Poinciana Blvd.
Polynesian Isle Blvd.
World Center Dr.
Continental Gateway Dr.
Central Florida Greeneway
Osceola Parkway
Seralago Blvd.
W. Irlo Bronson Memorial Hwy.
Scott Blvd.
Florida Plaza Blvd.
Holiday Tr.
International Drive South
Arabian Nights Blvd.
Parkway Blvd.
Celebration Ave.
Celebration Pl.
Celebration St.
Campus St.
Celebration Blvd.
Celebration Ave.
Chelonia Pkwy.
Century Dr.
Victory Way
Osceola Pkwy.
World Dr.
W. Buena Vista Dr.
Poinciana Blvd.

To Downtown Kissimmee →

Route markers: 535, 417, 192, 530, 4

Poinciana Blvd.

1 mi
1 km

Barefoot'n Resort **9**
Bohemian Hotel Celebration **7**
Comfort Suites Maingate East at Old Town **10**
Disney's All-Star Movies Resort **3**

Disney's All-Star Music Resort **2**
Disney's All-Star Sports Resort **1**
Disney's Art of Animation Resort **5**
Disney's Pop Century Resort **6**

Holiday Inn Express Hotel & Suites Orlando–Lake Buena Vista East **11**
Meliá Orlando Suite Hotel at Celebration **8**
Palm Lakefront Resort & Hostel **12**
Toscana Suites **4**

Destiny Palms Hotel ★★ Standards are high considering it's at the affordable end of the motel spectrum, and although the decor is less than pristine (it could be classified as "Early '80s Beige"), the staff keeps things spotless, and that's what you want. Rooms, all of which are nonsmoking, come stocked with a toaster oven, mini-fridge, free Wi-Fi, and a continental breakfast upgraded with eggs, oatmeal, pancakes, and waffles. King rooms face the north parking lot and are on the small side while double queen rooms look south on some pleasing old-growth Florida woods. The east-facing pool (it, too, is motel-simple) also faces the trees, which keeps this place from feeling hemmed in. Coupons from the tourist circulars often halve prices to $30 to $40, and its partnership deals with taxi companies and Enterprise Rent-a-Car can halve those rates, too.

8536 W. Irlo Bronson Hiwy./U.S. 192, Kissimmee. ✆ **407/396-1600.** www.destinypalmshotel.com. 104 units. $60–$70 doubles plus $3.50-per-night resort fee. Free parking. **Amenities:** Pool, free continental breakfast, free local calls, free Wi-Fi.

Palm Lakefront Resort & Hostel ★★ Meet the absolute cheapest respectable option in town. The facilities, cinder-block construction, and past-its-prime stretch of U.S. 192 will put pampered types off, but there are major plusses for a budget property, starting with attentive upkeep and a convivial international clientele. It backs up to Lake Cecile with its own dock, and there's also a pool in the giant backyard, where there's also a barbecue pit. You'll find simple private rooms with cable TV, private bathrooms, and twin beds, plus a family room sleeping five ($15 per person). Across the street, there's a Publix supermarket for munitions (the hostel has an equipped kitchen), and the $2 city bus to Disney goes right past the front door. You can't hope for more for rock bottom.

4840 W. Irlo Bronson Hwy./U.S. 192, Kissimmee. ✆ **407/396-1759.** www.orlandohostels.com. $36 doubles $36, $19 dorm beds. Free parking. **Amenities:** Pool, barbecue, shared kitchen.

Toscana Suites ★★ From the outside, it's not much. But this onetime geriatric Ramada Inn has been enjoying some interior TLC and now it's a sleeper hit that few tourists seem to know about. Down a quiet back road, behind doors, motel rooms were joined to make large apartment-style units of approximate luxury (two old motel rooms equal a one-bedroom suite, six rooms make for three-bedroom units for up to eight) where you get sanctuaries of fully equipped full kitchens with eat-in bars, sleigh beds, washers and dryers, spa tubs, and the latest furnishings. Housekeeping is scant, so you'll be left in peace. Even though this is less than a mile west of Disney's entrance on U.S. 192, it's still a well-kept secret, so prices are routinely marked lower than rack rate, sometimes as low as $49 for a one-bedroom suite. Call directly for the best price.

2950 Reedy Creek Blvd., Kissimmee. ✆ **407/465-0234.** www.toscanasuites.com. 60 units. Free parking. Typically $80 1-bedrooms, $120 3-bedrooms. **Amenities:** Pool, fitness center, sundries shop, free Wi-Fi.

MODERATE

Bohemian Hotel Celebration ★★ The Kessler Collection, which operates chic, art-laden boutique hotels in Savannah, Asheville, and other Old South enclaves, also runs this romantic fantasy come true. The civilized, full-service 115-room property evokes funky Florida and gets the pace and look just right. The lakeside setting is soothing and private—there's nothing on the opposite shore but trees and quiet. Furnishings are tropical, almost postcolonial (four-posted beds, wicker-paddle ceiling fans); the halls are filled with slightly skewed artwork that is a hallmark of the Kessler brand; there's a cool martini-style bar; and the restaurant's Kessler Chophouse is

Instead of pecking around Priceline and making blind bids that may waste you money, use one of my three secret-weapon sites, **BiddingTraveler.com, BetterBidding.com,** and **Bidding-ForTravel.com,** to find out what recent bids have been accepted. Then you'll get a sense of how low you can go. Using it one low season, I read about a $40 success story for an off-Disney two-star property. I dared to offer Priceline $29—and got my deal. Next, I shopped for rental cars. Although the major renters were offering around $25 a day on their own sites, Priceline accepted a bid of $16, through Alamo. That made for a total of $35 a day for both hotel *and* car—not bad. Three-star hotels go for $40 to $50, and four-stars for $60 to $70, even in summer.

gourmet and worthy of a date. Right out the front door is Celebration's easygoing waterfront downtown, ripe with nonchain boutiques and restaurants, and Disney is a 5-minute drive away, which is a good thing since there is no provided shuttle (another reason this place isn't suited to kids).

700 Bloom St., Celebration. ✆ **888/249-4007** or 407/566-6000. www.celebrationhotel.com. 115 units. $139–$209 lake-view king or queen. Daily $15 valet parking or $10 self-parking. **Amenities:** Pool, restaurant, fitness center, cocktail lounge, free Wi-Fi.

Holiday Inn Express Hotel & Suites Orlando–Lake Buena Vista East ★★★
Nicer than its price point should permit, this hotel is clean, impeccably run, attractively appointed in a Spanish style, and located 10 minutes from Disney, out of the fray yet close to food options, and offering a very high quality for the price. Family suites are not divided by proper walls, but by waist-high partitions. This hotel, which opened only in 2004 as a La Quinta, has a small arcade with air hockey for kids, and rooms have minifridges and free Internet access. It's enough to make you forget (or resent) all those other worn-down Holiday Inn Expresses. Right outside its driveway, there's a Wal-Mart and, unusual for Florida, a smattering of Halal grocery stores.

3484 Polynesian Isle Blvd., Kissimmee. ✆ **800/423-0908** or 407/997-1700. www.hielbv.com. 148 units. From $98 king, $103 double queen, $111 2-bedrooms with king and 2 twin beds. **Amenities:** Pool, free breakfast, business center, game room, park shuttles, fitness room, free parking, free Wi-Fi.

Meliá Orlando Suite Hotel at Celebration ★★★
Curvy-walled and clois-tered, this 240-room hotel arrived on the scene in 2008 (as the Mona Lisa—her grinning image still greets guests in the lobby) and remains a peaceful, well-kept secret. Fittings are top-notch and modern, with fully equipped kitchens including full-size fridges plus dishwashers. Units also have a little patio, with a queen-size pullout to sleep more people. Protected by the hotel's four curving buildings, a perfectly round vanishing-edge pool ringed with funky red pyramid umbrellas recalls South Beach style, lending the sensation of an upscale resort, so it's not the best choice for rambunctious kids. Getting a pool view adds about $20. The location beside the jungle of U.S. 192 very near Disney is prime, but not a lot of people seem to know about it. The best prices are through its own website.

225 Celebration Place, Celebration. ✆ **888/956-3542.** www.meliaorlando.com. 240 units. $120–$219 1-bedroom suite sleeping 4, 2-bedroom suites sleeping 8 $30 more, $219–$269 family suite sleeping 8. $15-a-day resort fee. Free parking. **Amenities:** Pool, restaurant, park shuttles, shuttles to Celebration village, bottled water, free continental breakfast, free Wi-Fi.

Lake Buena Vista

Roughly speaking, Lake Buena Vista is the area where the eastern end of Walt Disney World around Downtown Disney/Disney Springs meets exit 68 off I-4. LBV, as it's nicknamed, is more compact and higher-class than the comparable cluster of Kissimmee hotels along U.S. 192, a few miles south near Disney's southern gate. One of its magnets is the Crossroads shopping center, walkable from most points, where you'll find plenty of restaurant chains and a high-priced grocery store. For breathing room, the best part of Lake Buena Vista is Palm Parkway, a lightly trafficked, winding, tree-lined avenue of fairly new corporate hotels. It's a secret shortcut that avoids I-4. Drive north on it and you'll pass a turnoff for SeaWorld, a new Wal-Mart, and the restaurants of Sand Lake Road, and eventually you'll hit Universal.

LBV is so compact that those so inclined could walk to Downtown Disney and from there use the free Disney bus system. Or they could even take a taxi to each Disney park (although doing so would not save you much more than getting an inexpensive rental car). Such convenience comes with a trade-off: You'll often pay higher prices than you have to in Kissimmee or on I-Drive, and traffic stinks. Free shuttles around here tend to go to Disney but not to Universal or SeaWorld.

There's a luxury resort boom going on here. In mid-2014, a long-delayed Four Seasons resort is slated to open on a section of Disney property near Lake Buena Vista, following a branch of the Waldorf Astoria, which opened south of Hotel Plaza Boulevard in 2009. The former Royal Plaza Hotel was also undergoing a renovation at press time, to reopen as the B Hotel.

See the map on p. 196 for locations of the properties below.

INEXPENSIVE

Best Western Lake Buena Vista Resort Hotel ★   Another motel-grade tourist machine on Hotel Plaza Boulevard, the congested road leading to Downtown Disney, this 18-story hotel is older and could use a brush-up (you have to request a fridge or microwave, for example, and there are few electrical sockets). But it is distinguished by having a balcony for every room and charging a resort fee of only $10 a day, which is better than the other joints on this strip. It's a fair mid-budget option if you can score a deal online (to pay three digits would be a stretch), and if you're lucky, your room will be high enough to offer fireworks views.

2000 Hotel Plaza Blvd., Lake Buena Vista. ✆ **407/828-2424.** www.lakebuenavistaresorthotel.com. 325 units. $89–$125 2-queen rooms, plus $10 for sleeper sofa. $10 parking with resort fee. **Amenities:** Pool with children's pool, 2 restaurants and a snack bar, frequent Disney shuttle, arcade, fitness center, sundries shop, included Wi-Fi.

Hawthorn Suites Lake Buena Vista ★   The decor is a touch dated (no flatscreen TVs, for example), but the management is attentive and hard-working, so this L-shaped property, arranged around a quiet and uncomplicated kidney-shaped pool, is all you could need for a home base. The special appeal of this place is its full kitchens, standard in all rooms, with dishwashers, stoves, cookware—what you need to cook for yourself and save. All suites are one-bedroom suites, and the cheapest ones have two queen beds. Monday through Thursday afternoons, free cocktails are served, and on Wednesday from 5:30pm to 7:30pm, there's a "Manager's Reception" serving a free hot dog or hamburger.

8303 Palm Pkwy., Orlando. ✆ **866/756-3778** or 407/597-5000. www.hawthornlakebuenavista.com. $79–$159 double. 120 suites. **Amenities:** Pool, hot tub, small fitness center, breakfast buffet, park shuttle, game room, business center, sundries shop, free local calls, free Wi-Fi.

Quality Suites Lake Buena Vista ★★ Fronted by three-story-tall palm trees, these mini-apartments could be called simple but inviting. Probably because it's a pipsqueak among lions, its attentive managers charge a competitively low price and even throw in a cooked breakfast. All rooms, which are larger than the average, have two TVs and fully equipped kitchens with a big fridge, toaster, microwave, dishwasher, and stove—a rarity among hotels that usually make do with microwaves alone, and a lifesaver when it comes to saving money on dining. The hotel is close enough to the Disney parks to make for a realistic lunch break, and the basic pool is open until 11pm, so you can use it for end-of-the-day soaks.

8200 Palm Pkwy., Orlando. ✆ **800/370-9894** or 407/465-8200. www.qualitysuiteslbv.com. 123 units. $79–$139 doubles. $159–$249 2-bedroom units sleeping up to 8. Free parking. **Amenities:** Pool and hot tub, fitness room, Disney shuttle, free buffet breakfast, free local calls, business center, game room, grills, sundries shop, free Wi-Fi.

MODERATE

Blue Heron Beach Resort ★ Ignore the deceptive "beach resort" part; you stay at this mid-priced condo-style property to get above it all. These two high-rise towers overlook Lake Bryan, furnishing the illusion that you're only person in the city and not a mile off Disney property. Units are huge but not artistically furnished, have a private balcony, a washer/dryer, a sleeper sofa, two bathrooms (even in one-bedrooms), and a kitchen so well equipped it even has a blender (margarita time!). There are bunk beds in the hall to increase sleeping capacity for families. The best value is the two-bedroom units, which have perspectives of both the lake to the west and of Disney to the east; from high floors, you can see fireworks.

13428 Blue Heron Beach Dr., Lake Buena Vista. ✆ **407/387-2200.** www.blueheronbeachresort. com. 283 units. $99–$129 1-bedrooms, $129–$199 2-bedrooms. $12 resort fee. Housekeeping $15–$25 per service. **Amenities:** Pool with hot tub and kids' area, Disney shuttle, fitness center, game room, free parking. free Wi-Fi.

Holiday Inn Express Lake Buena Vista ★★ At first, the six-story hotel doesn't look like much more than a concrete box the color of orange sherbet, but it's got a number of advantages over other hotels. First, it's location is near both Disney and plenty of restaurants on the westernmost stretch of quiet Palm Parkway. Rooms are spotless and come with microwaves and fridges, plus balconies made truly private by concrete walls. The pool, found out back where the sounds of frolic at its one-story rock waterfall and short slide won't disturb other guests, is open until midnight—ideal for postpark wind-downs. This old-school hotel comes with no surprises. It's just a reliable value.

8686 Palm Pkwy., Orlando. ✆ **800/465-4329** or 407/239-8400. www.hiexpress.com/lakebuenavista. 200 units. $109–$149 double. Free parking. **Amenities:** Pool, free buffet breakfast, business center, free local calls, free Epcot shuttle, fitness room, kids eat free, free Wi-Fi.

Radisson Hotel Lake Buena Vista ★★★ Gleaming, professionally run, and consistently top-notch for a nonresort hotel. Rooms feel current and are packed with the latest modern conveniences such as HDTVs, iPod docks, free Internet, minifridges, and microwaves. Size is beyond the average, too: Bathrooms are spacious, and in a 2007 gut renovation, old balconies were incorporated as sitting areas with pullout couches, so a superior room can sleep up to five. There are a few downers, such as tricky entry that requires some U-turning, a dull but sunny pool area, and infrequent free shuttles, but those bummers are entirely offset by the quality of the rest and by the fact it's a short, safe walk to the many restaurants of the Crossroads shopping center. Its website often offers the best prices.

12799 Apopka Vineland Rd. ℰ **800/967-9033** or 407/597-3400. www.radisson.com/ lakebuenavistafl. 196 units. Rooms $99–$165. Free parking. **Amenities:** Pool, small fitness center, restaurant, free Wi-Fi.

Staybridge Suites Lake Buena Vista ★★   A little bit north of the Hotel Plaza Boulevard gate to Disney World, and close to lots of restaurants, you'll find these apartment-like quarters (there are two TVs and the kitchens even have dishwashers), which were renovated in recent years. The three-level buildings don't have elevators, but overlook that fact and avoid the ground-floor rooms, which are darker and less private. The full breakfast is free and plentiful, and you can eat it indoors or out. There's also a well-used pool in one of the courtyards. Expect rates along the lines of $140 for a one-bedroom with a king-size bed (sleeps four), or $30 more for a two-bedroom (sleeps six), with prices rising $20 to $40 when it's busy. The Disney shuttle is free. Home or condo rentals are cheaper, but you won't find many of those so close to Disney grounds, and those also come with cleaning fees and minimum stays.

8751 Suiteside Dr., Orlando. ℰ **407/238-0777.** www.sborlando.com. 150 units. $110–$145 1-bedrooms sleeping 4 and $110–$176 2-bedrooms sleeping 8. Free rollaways and cribs. Free parking. **Amenities:** Full breakfast, heated pool, spa tub, business center, sundries shop, free Wi-Fi.

WorldQuest Resort ★★★   A richly appealing facility that looks and feels like a luxury condo complex. Surrounded by nothing but trees and peace, yet only a mile from Disney property, its five-floor buildings gather around a lush, fountained pool area. Each unit is a fresh, contemporary apartment complete with full fridge and freezer, fully equipped kitchens you could bake a cake in, screened-in furnished balconies, DVD player, and a master bathroom that's the size of some hotels rooms elsewhere in town. Here's a major downside: It has no full restaurant and it's too isolated to walk anywhere, so you must use a car. Bookings made on Travelzoo waive the resort fee, and Expedia often packages it for less than you could get directly.

8849 WorldQuest Blvd., Orlando. ℰ **877/987-8378** or 406/387-3800. www.worldquestorlando.com. 238 units. $129–$189 2-bedroom/1-bathroom suites, add $20 for a 3rd bedroom; 3-night minimum stay or a $39 fee; $15-per-night resort fee. Free parking. **Amenities:** Pool with cabana bar, security gate, fitness center, sundries shop, free continental breakfast, free Disney shuttle, free Wi-Fi.

Wyndham Lake Buena Vista ★   Every few years, the brand of this property, across the street from Downtown Disney, changes. At this point in the management square dance, it gets passing, but not flying, marks for not getting complacent despite the fact the place is often full. If you desperately want to be closer to the parks without paying Disney prices, this tourist machine may appeal, and rates bottom out at $84 but are usually in the low $100s for the full hotel enchilada, including an aging fitness center, two big pools, shuttles that depart every 30 minutes, minifridges in the rooms, and the only sanctioned Disney character breakfast on Hotel Plaza Boulevard (3 mornings a week). The polished lobby makes everything seem more luxurious than it really is, but the kid-friendly staff boosts the value even considering its $15 daily resort fee. Ask for a Tower Room on the west side (floors 9–19) for a limited view of Lake Buena Vista.

1850 Hotel Plaza Blvd., Lake Buena Vista. ℰ **407/828-4444.** www.wyndhamlakebuenavista.com. 626 units. $84 doubles with courtyard view, $115 doubles in tower. $15 parking. **Amenities:** Restaurant, 3 lounges, character breakfast (Tues, Thurs, Sat), babysitting, children's activity program, health club, spa tub, 2 outdoor heated pools, 2 lighted tennis courts, complimentary bus service to WDW parks; transportation to non-Disney parks for a fee.

> ## Credit or Debit?
>
> If you use your debit card (instead of a credit card) as collateral against any purchases you may make during your stay, your card may be charged $50 to $250 (or more) *per day*, whether you actually charge anything to your room or not. This policy can seriously deplete your checking account, leaving you with far fewer funds than you might realize—and you won't see a credit back to your account until *up to 10 days after* you have checked out of your resort. Ask about your hotel's policy.

EXPENSIVE

Gaylord Palms ★ The Gaylord, run by Marriott, is geared to meetings, so although its scenery is spectacular, so are its incidental charges. Beneath its mighty glass atrium is a 4.5-acre Florida-themed ecosystem of gator habitats, caves, indoor ponds, sand sculptures, restaurants, and a full-size sailboat—all that makes for an attraction unto itself, and to face it, you'll pay about $20 extra. Rooms, renovated in 2012, sleep five and sport unusually nice granite-lined bathrooms. Even if it weren't nestled against Disney property, you could happily never leave, what with the on-site Cypress Springs mini water park, sports bar with two-story screen, adults-only pool, weekend brunches with Shrek, and the Relâche Spa & Salon. It also schedules family activities and an annual holiday ICE! extravaganza (p. 233). Look on its Web page for last-minute rates that can save $25 or so.

6000 W. Osceola Pkwy., Kissimmee. ℂ **407/586-2000.** www.gaylordhotels.com/gaylord-palms. 1,406 units. $169 king or double-queen rooms. $20 daily resort fee. $24 valet parking; $18 self-parking. **Amenities:** 2 pools, fitness center, spa, 5 restaurants, sports bar, fitness center, arcade, room service, free local phone calls, character breakfast, park shuttles (Disney free), free bottled water, free Wi-Fi.

Hyatt Regency Grand Cypress Resort ★★ Probably the most complete self-contained resort near Disney, the stepped tower packs every conceivable amenity into a lush 1,500-acre campus located practically within Walt Disney World: 45 holes of golf, an unforgettable waterfall-and-cavern studded lagoon pool, trails wrapping around a private lake, horses, and top-floor views of the fireworks at Epcot and the Magic Kingdom, even from the corridor. Better yet, many of its extras (kayaks, paddle-boats, parking close to the building) are free, if you consider free as "included in a high daily resort fee." I've seen $85 Priceline bids accepted. Contrary to its decidedly '80s atrium construction (and a parrot who was allowed to remain in the lobby long after the hotel's previous tropical decor was eliminated), rooms—maximum guests: 4—have an almost Asian sleekness with rain showers, chaise lounges, and adapter panels to play multimedia on the 37-inch HDTV.

1 Grand Cypress Blvd., Lake Buena Vista. ℂ **800/233-1234** or 407/239-1234. www.hyattgrand cypress.com. 815 units. $139–$239 king or double queen. $22 daily resort fee. Valet parking $23, self-parking $13. **Amenities:** Pool, babysitting, kids' club, business center, gift shop, babysitting, 3 year-round restaurants, 3 cocktail bars, coffee bar, game room, golf course, rock climbing wall, fitness center, salon, beach, free park shuttles, included Wi-Fi.

Nickelodeon Suites Resort ★★★ The anima-psychedelic image of the basic-cable staple Nickelodeon is kid heaven, with over-stimulation at every turn. The 777-unit, multimillion-dollar hotel, with one- to three-bedroom suites arranged around two courtyards, is so much fun that kids have been known to forget about going to the theme parks. Not only does it have facilities to make a kid's head explode, but it's also got more activities than Disney's moderate hotels. In the two astounding splashdown areas (the less elaborate one, the Oasis, operates only in high season), water cannons blast, a 400-gallon bucket regularly spills water over squealing kids, and 13 slides and flumes twist. Half the hotel comprises of "premium deluxe" rooms kitted out with eye-popping SpongeBob and Dora decor and cost $25 more than "superior" rooms, which are not. It's acts like a theme park: food court, 3,000-square-foot arcade, character breakfasts with Nick icons, a studio for "Double Dare" live game shows in which parents might get "slimed," a cinema for sensory movies, and a kiddie spa. The three-bedroom suites, which sleep up to eight, come with equipped kitchens (so do one-bedroom kitchen suites), two-bedrooms just have a microwave and mini-fridge, while all KidSuites have a kids' bunk room (doorless) with video games. Everything has a pullout double, too. It's a good choice if you plan to spend recharge time back at base (it's wickedly close to Disney turf) or want to let kids off the leash, as security is superb—it's gated and everyone wears wristbands. As you can imagine, it gets pretty noisy. Its website posts last-minute rates that sometimes halve costs. Don't forget that sky-high $30-a-day resort fee, which bumps this otherwise flawless option into the expensive category.

14500 Continental Gateway, Orlando. ✆ **800/972-2590**. www.nickhotel.com. 777 units. Low-season rooms $109 (1-bedroom) to $350 (3-bedroom), high season rooms $209 (1-bedroom) to $599 (3-bedroom). $30-a-day resort fee. Free parking. **Amenities:** 2 pools with splash playgrounds and slides, cinema, arcade, souvenir shops, kid's spa, adult cocktail lounge, restaurant and food court, basketball court, character breakfasts, character appearances, park shuttle, babysitting, teen lounge, live entertainment, free Wi-Fi.

International Drive, Universal

I-Drive is probably the best place to stay if you don't have a car because it's central, well connected, and full of competing places to eat. It's also the only hotel zone with a semblance of street life. If you stay here, you'll be in the thick of the family-friendly come-ons, amusement halls, minigolf, and theme bars. While you will find good prices, especially at hotels that back up to I-4, you won't find many rambling resort campuses. You'll need wheels to reach Disney (most hotels offer shuttles, but not always to Disney, and not always for free), although Universal is just across I-4 to the north and the dirt-cheap I-Ride Trolley (p. 228) links you with SeaWorld. On many nights around dinnertime, car traffic can clog I-Drive, but there's a workaround: Universal Boulevard, a block east, bypasses the mess. Get ready for change: The new Orlando Eye, open by 2015, has hotels preparing with new coats of paint.

INEXPENSIVE

Fairfield Inn Orlando International Drive/Convention Center ★★★   A newcomer as of March 2013, it's as sparkling clean and pristine, with a terrific location betwixt Universal and I-Drive, which you can walk to. Expect large rooms in yellows and oranges, outlets galore, and large counters and desks to spread out on. On the east, rooms face nothing but greenery. True, the elevators and breakfast buffet can get a tad overwhelmed in the mornings and you have to ask for a room with a mini-fridge or you may not get one, but overall, it's a real find, as bright and as fresh as you could wish for an affordable hotel. Management cares, too; without knowing me, it phoned me 10 minutes after my check-in to ask how I was settling in. Hotwire can bring its rate into the $70s.

8214 Universal Blvd., Orlando. ✆ **407/581-9001**. www.marriott.com. 160 units. $94–$159 doubles. Free parking. **Amenities:** Pool, free breakfast buffet, sundries shop, free Wi-Fi.

International Drive Hotels

Cabana Bay
Beach Resort **5**

Drury Inn Suites **8**

Fairfield Inn Orlando
International Drive/
Convention Center **9**

Four Points by Sheraton
Studio City **6**

Hampton Inn Orlando
Convention Center **13**

Hard Rock Hotel **2**

Hyatt Place Orlando
Universal **3**

Hyatt Place Orlando/
Convention Center **12**

Hyatt Regency
Orlando **15**

La Quinta Inn Inter-
national Drive **10**

Portofino Bay Hotel **1**

Rosen Inn **7**

Rosen Inn at Pointe
Orlando **14**

Royal Pacific Resort **4**

Sonesta ES Suites **11**

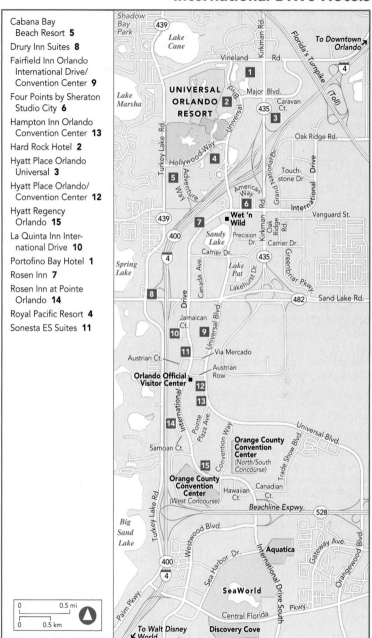

217

Hampton Inn Orlando Convention Center ★★ It may be just like every other Hampton Inn you've ever seen (they must make these buildings from kits), but that doesn't detract from the fact the place is in good shape, there are plenty of restaurants and a multiplex within walking distance, and the cheerful staff runs a tight ship. Stays include a bountiful all-you-can-eat breakfast, including a few hot dishes; there's also a 24-hour lobby booth selling snacks and sundries. I have personally witnessed front-desk clerks offering to beat competitors' prices. Ask for a room on the south side, as these don't face other nearby buildings.

8900 Universal Blvd., Orlando. © **800/426-7866** or 407/354-4447. www.orlandoconventioncenter. hamptoninn.com. 170 units. $79–$160 doubles or rooms with 2 double beds. Free parking. **Amenities:** Pool, free hot breakfast, fitness room, sundries shop, free Wi-Fi.

La Quinta Inn International Drive ★ A veteran four-floor motel with external corridors and the usual minor noise inconveniences of the category, it's not a bad choice if you want a clean, basic place off I-Drive. Windows are on the large side, and most face an interior heated pool cloister instead of the whoosh of Interstate 4. The rooms facing I-4 tend to drive some guests nuts, so request accordingly. Don't believe the rack rate; you can get this place for $49 using the coupon books around town.

8300 Jamaican Ct., Orlando. © **800/753-3757** or 407/351-1660. www.orlandolaquinta.com. 200 units. Doubles from $89. Free parking. **Amenities:** Pool, cocktail lounge, free breakfast, free local calls, free Wi-Fi.

Rosen Inn ★ When you drive up to this concrete tower, you may be concerned. It is, after all, upgraded from what was once the largest Rodeway Inn in America. But fear not: This is value. It's clean and on a lively bend of International Drive near Wet 'n Wild and 2 minutes' drive from Universal, which makes eating cheaply a breeze. The pool is heated when it's cold, security is always around, there's a pub, you can get free Wi-Fi in the lobby ($9 with wires upstairs), and all rooms have a microwave and refrigerator. It's dated, but all you need. The rate sometimes attracts noisy kids on school break, but on balance, you can't do better at this price.

6327 International Dr., Orlando. © **800/999-6327** or 407/996-4444. www.roseninn6327.com. 315 units. Rooms with 2 doubles from $70. Free parking. **Amenities:** Pool, park shuttle, 2 restaurants, pub, park shuttles, business center, game room, free Wi-Fi.

MODERATE

Drury Inn Suites ★★★ A top pick. The popular privately owned Missouri-based hotel group expanded to Orlando in July 2012 on an ideal plot—drive around the corner to Universal, down Palm Parkway to Disney, or go on foot to the restaurants of I-Drive or Sand Lake Road. Design is fresh in rust browns and greens, rooms are wider than the industry average, and there are tons of free extras. So friendly is this brand that every day at 5:30pm, it hosts a "Kickback" with free food, beer, and wine. You could make a dinner out of it, and retire to a room that is newer and cleaner than just about any other budget property in Orlando right now. The king-bed category has only a shower; the others have tubs.

7301 W. Sand Lake Rd., Orlando. © **407/354-1101.** www.druryhotels.com. 238 units. $109–$146 1-king or 2-queen rooms. Free parking. **Amenities:** Indoor/outdoor pool, free hot breakfast, free soda and popcorn, 24-hr. fitness room, business center, free local calls, pets permitted for free, free Wi-Fi.

Four Points by Sheraton Studio City ★ Because it occupies one of those dated cylindrical towers that were briefly in vogue in the early 1970s, the ideally located property has slight novelty that doesn't translate to luxury. It's just an interesting mid-priced choice. Because rooms are carved out of the floors like pie pieces, they're more spacious than the norm, and many have two queen beds. Request a room that doesn't face east, as the floodlights from the minigolf joint next door are blinding. The top floors have spectacular views of I-Drive, Wet 'n Wild (to the west), and Universal (just over I-4 to the north). It's not luxury, but it approximates it, and views in Orlando are rare at any price (particularly the $48 I've seen turn up in blind Hotwire bookings). Breakfast's $10, but there's an IHOP next door.

5905 International Dr., Orlando. ℂ **888/625-4988** or 407/351-2100. www.fourpointsorlando studiocity.com. 301 units. $99–$119 doubles. Free parking. **Amenities:** Pool, pool bar, restaurant, cocktail lounge, business center, park shuttles, free Wi-Fi.

Hyatt Place Orlando Universal ★★★ You check in at a kiosk that spits out your key, and without delay, head to a huge semipartitioned room with giant beds and a sitting area, plus an extra pullout sofa. If you're not familiar with the standardized brand, it has up-to-date design, a 42-inch HDTV you can plug a laptop or a iPod into, granite bathrooms, wet bar, free continental breakfast, Wi-Fi, and plenty of space for five (six if two sleep on the pullout), all from $89. Seriously, why can't they all be like this? A second location at I-Drive isn't within spitting distance of Universal's gates as this one is, but it is nearer to more places to eat (8741 International Dr., Orlando; ℂ **407/370-4720;** http://orlandoconventioncenter.place.hyatt.com; 150 rooms, $127–$209 rooms two double beds). Both underwent 2013 renovations.

5895 Caravan Ct., Orlando. ℂ **407/351-0627.** http://orlandouniversal.place.hyatt.com. 151 units. $87–$179 rooms with 2 double beds, $20 more for king bed. Free parking. **Amenities:** 24-hr. prepared meals, fitness center, free park shuttle, free breakfast, free Wi-Fi.

Rosen Inn at Pointe Orlando ★★ One of the largest budget-priced properties outside of Disney's Value developments (so expect family noise) this former Quality Inn sprawls over 2 well-located city blocks and six Nixon-era buildings (renovated 2010). I-4 runs along the western side, resulting in a constant hum. You'll see rates for as little as $50 a night on sites such as Otel.com, so don't pay three figures. Respectably affordable units, which come with a fridge, microwave, and two double beds, have smoked-glass windows, which helps create privacy given the external corridor construction, but doesn't help illuminate the bathrooms in the back. Rooms in the A building are near the lobby but suffer daytime noise from the sightseeing helicopter pad next door; opt for something in the F building, which is a 10-minute walk/2-minute drive from the lobby and has the most rooms hidden from I-4. Parking is gated but free. You'll feel like you're back on an '80s vacation with Dad just by walking past the three big pools, where kids work off their postpark highs. Many eateries are within walking distance on I-Drive. Universal is 10 minutes north, SeaWorld 5 minutes south.

9000 International Dr., Orlando. ℂ **800/999-8585** or 407/996-8585. www.roseninn9000.com. 1,020 units. $99–$129 rooms with 2 doubles. Free parking. **Amenities:** 2 pools, playground, restaurant, bar, free local calls, free shuttle to Universal and SeaWorld, charged shuttle to Disney, free Wi-Fi.

Sonesta ES Suites ★★ In anticipation of the I-Drive Live project (p. 139), this well-located all-apartment hotel, near plenty of places to eat and arranged around a courtyard pool, is being lavished with a gut renovation, so there are fewer moderate properties that are as current. (Call to ask if it's finished.) All units will have new kitchens with new appliances, just-installed furniture, fresh carpeting, and bedding, a booth for family meals, and lots of added electrical outlets for recharging. Suddenly a dowdy '80s holdover has become a barely-slept-in mid-priced darling. The staff is unusually dedicated, and some have been running this property for years.

8480 International Dr., Orlando. ℂ **407/352-2400.** www.sonesta.com/orlando. 146 units. 1-bedrooms $124–$166, 2-bedroom/2-bath $30–$40 more. Free parking. **Amenities:** Free breakfast, pool, spa tub, bar, sundries shop, small fitness center, free park shuttles (for Disney, connect via Epcot), free Wi-Fi.

EXPENSIVE

Hyatt Regency Orlando ★ Until 2013, it was a spinoff of the famed Memphis Peabody Hotel, complete with the daily "duck parade" of waterfowl, but those party fowl were shipped to the farm and now it's a Hyatt to its conventioneering core. Expect gleaming glass, echoing marble, sculptural waterfalls, luxuriously appointed bathrooms, ankle-level lights that switch on when they sense your movement, and other high-end touches that appeal to business travelers. Walking to I-Drive's restaurants is easy (driving out of the distant parking structure, not so much), and the free-form tropical pool is gorgeous, but the truth is that the staff sometimes has trouble keeping up with all its guests, many of whom are only enjoying these benefits because they are reimbursed by expense accounts.

9801 International Dr., Orlando. ℂ **407/284-1234**. http://orlando.regency.hyatt.com. 1,641 rooms. $185–$425 doubles for up to 4. $17 self-parking, $28 valet, $20 daily resort fee including Wi-Fi. **Amenities:** 3 restaurants, cocktail bar, pool with children's area, spa, babysitting.

JW Marriott Grande Lakes Orlando/Ritz-Carlton Grande Lakes Orlando ★★★ A true resort and a smart choice for a well-rounded vacation, the two luxury towers form a city unto themselves, and indeed, the JW's profile rises like a citadel in a 500-acre plot east of SeaWorld. The JW's 24,000-square-foot pool area, landscaped with fake rocks, jungle greens, and a ¼-mile lazy river, is the poshest outside of the Disney water slide parks, while the Ritz's is formal and refined. The JW's rooms received a 2011 renovation down to tile floors and slots for plugging your MP3 player into the plasma TVs. Yes, like many fancy convention hotels, it's a nickel-and-dime experience—everything costs you, but happily, there's no resort fee at either. As long as you know that in advance, the hotel's upscale amenities (gurgling lobby fountain, echoing bathrooms with separate bathtub and shower, palatial beds, narrow balconies on many rooms) are pleasing, even if the remote location 15 minutes from the parks means you'll have to drive somewhere every time your stomach rumbles if you want to escape resort pricing. At the Ritz-Carlton attached by a corridor, the three-level, 40,000-square foot spa is well reviewed and in the rooms, the pamper factor is yet a notch higher. Both have unobstructed views of a Greg Norman–designed golf course and a nature reserve; west-facing rooms take in sunsets and SeaWorld in the distance. **Primo,** Chef Melissa Kelly's restaurant at the JW, and **Norman's,** Chef Norman Van Aken's ode to Florida flavors at the Ritz, are two top-of-the-line restaurants that use produce grown on the grown and area and would be a credit to any resort.

4040 Central Florida Pkwy., Orlando. www.grandelakes.com. ℂ **800/576-5760** or 407/206-2400 for the Ritz; ℂ **800/576-5750** or 407/206-2300 for the JW Marriott. JW: 1,000 rooms, Ritz: 584 units. $183–$599 double. Valet parking $25; self-parking $18. **Amenities:** 7 restaurants, 3 lounges, babysitting, kids' activities, spa, sundries shops, club-level rooms, health club, golf course, spa tub, 2 outdoor heated pools, kids' pool, 3 tennis courts, transportation to non-Disney parks for a fee, paid Wi-Fi.

Around Downtown Orlando

For years, travel writers have been begging tourists to spend more time in downtown Orlando and Winter Park, just north. There's charm, museums, great food, antiques, ritzy shopping, a student culture, and a relaxed vibe that could make you wish you lived in Florida. Sadly, they've been wasting ink. The theme parks won the war. Because it's a 30-minute ride north of Disney on I-4 (yes, you should have a car for these), a hotel would have to be pretty special to convince a tourist to choose it over one that's nearer. Orlando has a few, where you can find welcome respite from the hurdy-gurdy and plastinated smiles of the tourist zone—and a breather from children.

MODERATE

Courtyard at Lake Lucerne ★★ Despite a name that might have you expecting something corporate, Orlando just doesn't have rooms this individual anymore. South of downtown, near highways that go everywhere, you'll find a rare B&B, and rarer still, it preserves the feeling of Old Florida. There's a reason local couples favor it for weddings: Under Spanish moss, this hideaway of calm preserves four homey buildings of varied historic styles. Top of the line is the city's oldest documented house, 1883's Norment Parry Inn, which believe it or not has the cheapest rates here because not everyone likes sleigh beds and claw-footed tubs; you'll sleep in an elegant four-poster bed among Victorian-era European antiques. I. W. Phillips House recalls Key West because its wooden wrap-around verandah overlooks tropical plantings. Wellborn Suites is Art Deco, less elegant, but with kitchenettes. All rooms have TVs, phones, and private bathrooms.

211 N. Lucerne Circle E., Orlando. ✆ **407/648-5188.** www.orlandohistoricinn.com. 30 units. Doubles $99–$225. Some rooms do not permit kids. Free parking. **Amenities:** Free breakfast, free Wi-Fi.

EXPENSIVE

The Alfond Inn ★★ In August 2013, Rollins College opened the boutique hotel using a $12.5 million donation; its income will endow a scholarship program. That makes it both the newest fine property in town and the one with the biggest incentive to keep quality high. Its haute Southern restaurant and hopping cocktail bar, planted courtyard, and modern rooms striped in teal, wood, and lime are designed to appeal to sophisticated palates. It's too early to render a verdict, but its gleaming new facilities and its enviable location 3 blocks from the shopping of Park Avenue and the Morse Museum (p. 143) have poised this hotel to be a keystone of the Winter Park scene.

E. New England Ave., Winter Park. ✆ **407/998-8090.** www.thealfondinn.com. 112 units. Doubles $159–$249. Valet parking $18. **Amenities:** Pool, restaurant, lounge, fitness center, pets permitted, free Wi-Fi.

Grand Bohemian Hotel Orlando ★★★ Yes, Orlando is sophisticated. Because the hotel's owner, Richard Kessler, is something of a dilettante, its common areas are decorated with eccentric artwork—it's part hunting lodge and part *commedia dell'arte,* including six original drawings by Gustav Klimt, and in the lobby, there's a storefront gallery. An L.A.–style pool terrace keeps sunbathers far above city traffic, and lighting is so muted in its rooms, the dark woods so dark and fabrics so indigo, that a dusky, drowsy atmosphere is created even on days when the Florida sun could blister pavement. By night the Bösendorfer Lounge is a stylish martini nightspot with a following and some epic neo-romantic paintings by William Russell Walker. For a city about fake Spanish country clubs and golf resorts, the Grand Bohemian's urban panache is welcome, and its lounge areas tend to attract local artists (and frequent wedding parties of young professionals) who live more like they're in Manhattan, Chicago, or San Francisco.

325 S. Orange Ave., Orlando. ☎ **866/663-0024** or 407/313-9000. www.grandbohemianhotel.com. 250 units. Standard room $179–$269 for up to 4, weekends $20 more. Extra person $25. Valet parking $22. The garage is 2 blocks west on Jackson St. **Amenities:** Restaurant, 2 lounges, club-level rooms, health club, heated outdoor pool, room service, shuttle to the theme parks for a fee, paid Wi-Fi.

Home Rentals

For value, renting a home is without exception the best way to go. You can stretch out on a leather sofa, watching a TV as big as a lap pool, speaking as loudly you want and firing up the grill beside your screened-in pool—why pay for the battery hen arrangement of a hotel ever again?

The zone pressing up against Walt Disney World's southern border is almost exclusively built with new housing developments. There are dozens of gated communities packed with shiny new two-story McMansions, most owned by people who are here maybe 2 weeks a year. They contract with managing companies who keep them spotless and rent them to visitors. Each management company requires the homes it rents to meet a certain standard, which usually means cable TV in every room, irons, vacuums, fully equipped kitchens, and laundry facilities. And every management company takes care of the nitty-gritty for you, such as making beds before your arrival or wheeling out the trash bins on garbage day. You will also find computers with high-speed Internet, video games, billiard rooms, and heated pools and hot tubs—it's like home, but nicer.

Most rental companies promise their homes are within mere miles of Disney (but do ask, just in case) so they take about as long to reach by car (which you should have) as Disney's cheapest rooms—except for the same price, you get an entire home instead of a single room packed with two double beds. A smaller number of condo-style properties are available near Universal and SeaWorld (the main development there is called Vista Cay).

There are generally two kinds of homes. **Condos** are units that are attached to other units; these may have their own plunge pool, but more often they share a communal, hotel-style pool at a clubhouse. **Houses** are free-standing and are generally about 30 percent more expensive than condos. They will almost always have private full pools, usually screened to keep out insects. Occupancy is governed by law, so be honest about how many people are in your party.

RENTAL AGENCIES

In most destinations, the main way to obtain a vacation rental is to contact the owner directly. This is certainly an option in Orlando, and all the prominent online databases operate here, including **Airbnb.com, FabVillas.com,** TripAdvisor's **FlipKey.com, HomeAway.com, Housetrip.com, Vacation Rentals by Owner** (www.vrbo.com), and **Zonder.com.**

But there are also accredited companies that take the risk out of a rental—ones that actually inspect your potential home and give you support on the ground. In addition to being selected for their reputations, longevity, and inventory, these companies have satisfactory listings with the Better Business Bureau of Central Florida. Check on any company's background for the past 3 years at www.orlando.bbb.org.

A good rental agency will matchmake your needs and budget to the most suitable property. Your credit card will usually be charged a deposit ($200–$300 or 1 night's rent is standard) a month or two ahead of time, and if you cancel, you're unlikely to see that again. You'll also have to pay a one-time fee that goes toward insurance or cleaning; $50 to $80 is normal, which makes stays of a single night less economical. Perks like pool heat or grills may incur a surcharge, which is normal. Also ask your rental agency what it supplies and what you'll need to buy. Typically, you'll be given a roll or two of toilet paper per bathroom, a starter garbage bag, and maybe a packet of detergent, and you'll be expected to buy your own after those run out. Clean bath towels and sheets are supplied, but maid service won't be unless you pay extra. Many rental agencies no longer require you to pick up keys. Instead, front locks are equipped with keypads.

Alexander Holiday Homes   The family-run outfit has been renting since 1981, when the industry was in its infancy. It reps some 250 properties, most of them within 10 miles of Disney. Using its website's Hot Deals, prices go as low as $65 for a two-bedroom condo, and you stay for less than a week. Annoyingly, its website doesn't reveal availability windows; you have to call.

1400 W. Oak St., Ste. H, Kissimmee. ✆ **800/621-7888** or 407/932-3683. www.floridasunshine.com. Wi-Fi $25. Pet-friendly.

All Star Vacation Homes   Frommer's favorite Orlando vacation home renter has an in-house design team that cuts no corners in furnishing each of its 250 homes, with lots of woods, quality fabrics, and dried flowers—the completeness elevates the offerings above the competition. All units, which go up to 9-bedroom mansions, are keyless and have a pool, and most are within 6 miles of Disney. Three-bedroom condo units sleeping up to eight, with a themed kids' room, start at $125 a night, or $75 less than what it costs to squeeze eight into two Disney Value rooms. Or you could have a whole 3-bedroom house for $209. Prices go up as you add treats such as home cinema rooms, arcade rooms, multiple master bedrooms, and so forth. Full six-bedroom houses start at $289—you can split that among 14 people if you've got a full house. Reminder: A standard room at the Disney's Polynesian, sleeping five tightly, can't be had for less than $482.

7822 W. Irlo Bronson Hwy., U.S. 192, Kissimmee. ✆ **800/572-5011** or 321/281-4966. www.allstar vacationhomes.com. No pets.

Award Vacation Homes   Award's inventory is thickest around Hwy. 27, a newly developed corridor 15 minutes west of Walt Disney World via U.S. 192 (via Disney's Western Way back entrance). That distance is a price advantage, as its neighborhoods are serviced by grocery stores that are not as overpriced for tourists as other ones are. For three-bedroom, two-bath places, rates start at $118.

1536 Sunrise Plaza Dr., Clermont. ✆ **800/338-0835** or 352/243-8669. www.awardvacationhomes. com. No pets.

Florida Sun Vacation Homes   Another upfront business, it rents homes ranging from two to seven bedrooms in the Disney area (the Windsor Hills development in particular), with three-bedroom starting prices of $69 in low season and popping to $149 in high season. All of its properties have a pool or a spa (or both). Minimum stays of 3 nights are common, and like many companies, it asks that you reserve and pay at least 6 weeks in advance.

7802 W. Irlo Bronson Hwy./U.S. 192, Kissimmee. ✆ **800/219-1282** or 407/938-0228. www.florida sunvacationhomes.com. No pets.

IPG Florida Vacation Homes   IPG began by serving British vacationers before branching out into Florida, and now its inventor is among the largest, dealing in dozens of home developments south and west of Disney, particularly Bella Piazza, Highlands Reserve, Windsor Hills, and the Villas at Island Club. Two-bedroom condos run from $120 to $160, often less; even something as big as six bedrooms can cost a mere $288.

9550 W. U.S. 192, Clermont. ℂ **800/311-7105** or 863/547-1050. www.ipgflorida.com. Pets with $400 fee.

Lowery's Vacation Homes   Around since 1985, Lowery's reps plenty of inexpensive, tasteful properties in the usual developments, and its website includes 360-degree tours of each property. It's a good fallback in busy seasons. Rates here can be sensational—how about $95 a night for a three-bedroom condo? The largest home available has seven bedrooms.

7864 W. Irlo Bronson Hwy., Kissimmee. ℂ **800/569-3797** or 407/397-0088. www.moremouse.com. Pet-friendly.

VillaDirect   Founded in 1998, it manages some 350 Orlando-area properties in a hodgepodge of styles and quality levels. Condos sleeping six start around $62, although prices in the $80s are more common. Its office is open 7 days, and a majority of its inventory is a few miles southwest of Animal Kingdom, but it also has a few near Sea-World. Helpfully, its website posts videos for each of its vacation home communities.

6129 W. Irlo Bronson Hwy., Kissimmee. ℂ **877/259-9908** or 407/397-9818. www.villadirect.com. No pets.

PLANNING YOUR TRIP TO ORLANDO

Orlando hosts some 55 million people a year, and the people who run the airports, hotels, and theme parks are specialists in moving them from one location to another—the whole system is set up to make it foolproof—so you probably won't get lost in a mire of confusion. You will, however, need to take care of some nitty-gritty details, from flights to transportation.

GETTING THERE

BY PLANE Orlando is served by 44 airlines, so thankfully, competition keeps airfares among the lowest on the East Coast. Nearly 35 million people fly in or out of Orlando International Airport (MCO) each year, or nearly 96,000 a day. Strategies for finding a good airfare include:

Primary websites that collect quotes from a variety of sources (whether they be airlines or other websites) include **CheapOAir.com, Expedia.com, Kayak.com, Lessno.com, Mobissimo.com, Momondo.com, Orbitz.com,** and **Travelocity.com** (which runs Expedia searches). Always canvas multiple sites, because each has odd gaps in its coverage because of the way they obtain their quotes. Then compare your best price with what the airline is offering, because that price might be lowest of all. Some sites have small booking fees of $5 to $10, and many force you to accept non-refundable tickets for the cheapest prices.

Watch for sales. **Airfarewatchdog.com** and the **Trip Watcher** features on **Hotwire** (www.hotwire.com) and Travelocity will send you e-mail alerts when airfare drops below a certain threshold. Airlines also announce sales via Twitter. The "Fare History" link at **Bing.com/travel** tries to predict the ideal time to buy. Sounds odd, but you can often save money by booking between roughly 6 weeks in advance and on a Tuesday or Wednesday. Airline sales are announced on Mondays and matched by competitors on Tuesdays; hitting them right, therefore, helps garner you a lower-priced seat.

The main airport, **Orlando International Airport** (www.orlandoairports.net), is a pleasure. If, on the way home, you realize you neglected to buy any park-related souvenirs, fear not, because Disney, SeaWorld, Kennedy Space Center, and Universal all maintain lavish stores (located *before* the security checkpoint, so budget enough time). The airport, 25 miles east of Walt Disney World, was built during World War II as McCoy Air Force Base, which closed in the early 1970s but bequeathed the airport with its deceptive code, MCO. I don't know how they do it, but the late-departure rate of 19 percent is among the lowest in the country, even though the airport is America's 13th largest (and the 26th largest in the world). Midmornings and midafternoons can be crowded for outgoing passengers, and mid-afternoon summer thunderstorms sometimes create delays.

The main terminal is divided into two sides, A and B, so if you can't find the desk for your airline or transportation service open on one side, it may be on the other side. Several rental car companies are right outside, no shuttles required.

Rental car companies at MCO:

Alamo ℭ 800/327-9633; www.alamo.com

Avis ℭ 800/831-2847; www.avis.com

Budget ℭ 800/527-0700; www.budget.com

Dollar ℭ 800/800-4000 (U.S.), 800/800/6000 (international); www.dollar.com

Enterprise ℭ 800/325-8007; www.enterprise.com

E-Z Rent-A-Car ℭ 800/266-5171; www.e-zrentacar.com

Hertz ℭ 800/654-3131; www.hertz.com

L & M Car Rental ℭ 407/888-0515; www.lmcarrental.net

National ℭ 800/227-7368; www.nationalcar.com

Thrifty ℭ 800/367-2277; www.thrifty.com

Also keep in mind Hertz-owned **Firefly** (ℭ 888/296-9135; www.fireflycarrental.com), which can offer lower prices than most of its competitors because its vehicles are older and well used.

Very few airlines (Allegiant, Icelandair) use **Orlando Sanford International Airport** (www.orlandosanfordairport.com), or SFB, 42 miles northeast of Disney. It's connected to the Disney area by the Central Florida GreeneWay, or S.R. 417—the trip takes about 40 minutes and there are tolls, so new arrivals should have U.S. dollars. European visitors might fly into **Tampa International Airport** (www.tampaairport.com), or TPA, 90 minutes southwest.

BY TRAIN Amtrak's (ℭ **800/872-7245;** www.amtrak.com) Silver Service/Palmetto route serves Orlando and Kissimmee. Trains go direct between New York City, Washington, D.C., Charleston, and Savannah.

Transportation to & from MCO

BY RENTAL CAR If you intend to experience any of Orlando's "real" personality or its rich natural wonders, get it car. If you want to save huge amounts of money on meals, if you ever want to take a breather from the theme parks' relentless plastic personalities—get a car.

Economy rental cars start around $25 a day. Test the waters at a site such as Kayak, Orbit, or Travelocity, which compare multiple renters with one click. Priceline and Hotwire have been known to rent for as little as $15 a day.

If you rent a car from the airport be alert as you **exit the airport**—you must decide whether to use the south exit (marked for Walt Disney World) or the north exit (for SeaWorld, Universal, the Convention Center, and downtown Orlando). Whichever route you take, you will pay a few dollars in tolls, so have loose change. Whichever path you choose, stay to the right, where the cash toll booths are.

If you're staying on Disney turf, a budget-saving solution is to rent a car for only the days you'd like to venture off property. To that end, **Alamo** (ℭ **800/462-5266;** www.alamo.com) operates satellite agencies within the Walt Disney World Resort: one at the Car Care Center near the parking lot of the Magic Kingdom, and one at the

Buena Vista Palace Hotel east of Downtown Disney. Renting away from the airport incurs taxes of around half of those charged by renting (or even merely returning) a car at the airport, where they're over 20 percent. Always fill up *before* driving back to the airport. Gas stations near the airport's entrance have been nabbed for gouging. The stations inside Walt Disney World charge a competitive price. Prices are best, though, well away from the tourist zone.

The legal age minimum in Florida for a rental driver is 21. Agencies will usually slap those aged 21 to 25 with a surcharge. **Continental Rent-a-Car** (7948 Narcoossee Blvd.; ☎ **800/221-4085;** www.continentalcar.com), a privately owned outfit located 4 miles from the airport by shuttle bus, also charges $15 a day. Most companies won't rent to anyone older than 85.

BY SHUTTLE Mears Transportation (☎ 407/423-5566; www.mearstransportation. com) is the 800-pound gorilla of shuttles and taxis; it sends air-conditioned vans bouncing to hotels every 15 to 20 minutes. Round-trip fares for adults are $30 ($24 for kids 4–11, kids 3 and under free) to the International Drive area, or $34 per adult ($27 for kids) to Walt Disney World/U.S. 192/Lake Buena Vista. You'll probably make several stops because the vans are shared by other passengers.

If you have more than four or five people, it's more economical to reserve a car service (do it at least 24 hr. ahead) and split the lump fee; an SUV for 5 would be about $135. Try Mears, **Tiffany Towncar** (☎ **888/838-2161** or 407/370-2196; www. tiffanytowncar.com), or **Quicksilver Tours** (☎ **888/468-6939** or 407/299-1434; www.quicksilver-tours.com), which for round-trips tosses in a free 30-minute stop at a grocery store so you can stock up on supplies.

If you have a reservation at a Disney-owned hotel, you have the right to take the company's airport motorcoaches (also known as **Disney's Magical Express,** run by Mears). By offering the perk, the Mouse makes it seem simple by sending you tags for your luggage, which you affix before leaving home, and telling you everything will be taken care of from there. By the time you board the bus to the resort, you'll already have waited in two long lines—the first of many, many lines you'll endure, so get used to it—and then you'll stop at up to five other hotels first. Your bags may not meet up with you again for 6 to 8 hours, so hitting a park right away may be difficult. When you depart for home, you must be ready 3 to 4 hours before your flight. Magical Express is free, but it costs you. It lulls you into not renting a car, which means you'll probably never leave Disney property again and you'll have to rely on the park's slow buses for your entire vacation.

BY TAXI Taxis are not the best bargain. The going rate is $2.40 for the first ¼ of a mile or the first 80 seconds of waiting time, followed by 60¢ for each ¼ of a mile. Taxis carry five passengers. It'll be about $70 to the Disney hotels, $60 to Universal, not including a tip, which is cheaper than a town car but not a rental.

GETTING AROUND

BY CAR Probably 90 percent of what a tourist wants to do lies within a 10-minute drive of Interstate 4, or I-4, as it's called. That free highway runs diagonally from southwest to northeast, connecting Walt Disney World, SeaWorld, the Convention Center, Universal Orlando, and downtown Orlando. I-4 is technically an east-west road linking Florida's coasts, so directions are listed as either west (toward Tampa and the Gulf of Mexico) or east (toward Daytona Beach and the Atlantic Ocean). Once you've got that down, you'll be set. Exits are numbered according to the mile marker at which they're found. Therefore, the Disney World exits (62, 64, 65, and 67) are roughly 10 miles from Universal Orlando's (74 and 75), which are about 9 miles from downtown (83). If you know the exit number, you can figure out distance.

If you stray much onto minor roads, it's a good idea to carry a map. Roads can go by several names and be confusing. Disney World is a particular disaster, since its signage is intentionally incomplete. Don't rely on free maps; laughably, some maps provided by Universal don't acknowledge that Disney exists at all. The **Visit Orlando** (www.visitorlando.com/mapexplorer) has free maps.

SHUTTLES   Universal is easy: You walk or take a free boat everywhere. At Disney, though, hoofing it is simply impossible. It's so big as to require a fleet of more than 270 buses, the **Disney Transportation System (DTS),** which anyone may use for free. Curiously, DTS qualifies as the third-largest bus system in the state, after Miami and Jacksonville's public services. Taking DTS to a theme park eliminates the parking tram rigmarole, and during the Magic Kingdom's operating hours, the bus stops at its doorstep, eliminating the need to take either the monorail or ferry. However, once you add waiting time, which can be 20 to 45 minutes, plus the commute itself, which can be just as long and require a transfer, you'll find that in almost every conceivable instance, having a car of your own is worth the expense.

DTS is particularly overwhelmed during the opening and closing of the theme parks, but dispatchers run extra buses around those times and keep routes rolling for about 2 extra hours before opening and after closing. If you're staying at a Disney resort that offers another kind of transportation—say, the monorail to the Magic Kingdom—then a bus won't be available for the same route. Also, since the system has a hub-and-spoke design centered on the theme parks and Downtown Disney, *you will often have to transfer if you're going between two other points,* like two different hotels or a hotel and a water park.

On balance, DTS can save you from having to rent a car *if* you only plan to go to Disney attractions and nothing else (which would be a shame for you—thumb through the rest of this book) and *if* you're a patient soul who can face a potential 1-hour-plus commute, possibly standing the whole way, after spending 11 hours swimming upstream in the parks.

The second shuttle variety is the **hotel theme park shuttle,** which are often free. The upswing is that, yes, you can save a lot of money by using them, but there are strong downsides, including wildly inadequate scheduling and rambling routes. These also only go to the parks' gates, keeping you away from inexpensive restaurants, shopping, and all natural and historic attractions.

A third option is the **I-Ride Trolley** (© **407/354-5656;** www.iridetrolley.com; adults over 12 $1.50 per ride, seniors 25¢, kids age 12 and under free; day pass $5, 3-day pass $7, 5-day pass $9; daily 8am–10:30pm), an excellent shuttle bus with plenty of clearly marked and well-maintained stops, benches to wait on, and genuinely useful routes—except it doesn't go to Disney. Its **Red Line** (every 20 min.) plies International Drive from the shops and restaurants just north of I-4's exit 75 all the way to Orlando Premium Outlets, near Disney; along the way it touches down at SeaWorld and Wet 'n Wild. The second route, the **Green Line** (every 30 min.), takes in Wet 'n Wild and SeaWorld, too, but heads down Universal Boulevard, making it more of an express route, and turns around at Orlando Premium Outlets. It comes within a long block of the entrance to Universal Orlando. Visitors without cars may find it feasible to stay on

I-Drive, use this dirt-cheap shuttle to see nearly everything, and then tack on the hated hotel shuttle or a city bus for Disney days.

BY CITY BUS There's not a lot to love about public transit in Florida. Buses are infrequent (usually one or two an hour), and shelters inadequate (often nonexistent), and when the sun's strong, the combination is dangerous. Distances are also fairly great, so journeys can take a while. The Central Florida Regional Transportation Authority runs the **LYNX system** (www.golynx.com), on which one-way fares are $2, day passes cost $4.50, week passes are $16, and transfers between lines are free. Up to three kids 6 and under ride with adults free, and you have to pay with exact change. In downtown Orlando, there's the free **LYMMO** (www.golynx.com; Mon–Thurs 6am–10pm, Fri 6am–midnight, Sat 10am–midnight, Sun 10am–10pm) bus service, which makes a loop between City Hall and the Controlled (including Church Street Station and the Orange County Regional History Center) every 5 to 15 minutes.

For tourists, here are the most convenient routes, many of which stop at Downtown Disney where you can transfer to Disney's free bus system:

o **Route 56** heads down U.S. 192 from the Osceola Square Mall in Kissimmee and straight to the front gates of the Magic Kingdom, where you can catch DTS to the other parks. This makes U.S. 192 east of Disney the only major hotel zone that provides transfer-free bus access to Walt Disney World. Buses run every 30 minutes, but the last one leaves at 10:53pm.

o **Route 8** does most of International Drive, including the Convention Center and SeaWorld. It duplicates the service offered by the I-Ride Trolley (p. 228).

o **Route 50** goes from the central LYNX station in downtown Orlando, down Interstate 4, to Downtown Disney, and to the gates of the Magic Kingdom. It stops at SeaWorld where passengers can connect to I-Drive by on Route 8.

o The lesser Disney areas are served by the 300-series lines. Number **300** goes to Hotel Plaza Boulevard from downtown; **301** to Epcot and Disney's Animal Kingdom from Pine Hills; **302** to the Magic Kingdom from Rosemont; and **303** to Hollywood Studios from the Washington Shores area. Bus **304** is the only one that connects with another tourist zone; it trawls Sand Lake Road, which bisects I-Drive. Once they're off I-4, 301 and 302 pass within a few blocks of Universal Orlando, on Kirkman Road, so if you toss in about 15 minutes of walking, they could technically be used for Universal, too, but it wouldn't be fun.

o **Route 21** goes up Turkey Lake Road from Sand Lake Road to the Universal Orlando park and links with the downtown depot.

o **Route 42** starts at the Convention Center on International Drive, and 75 minutes later, reaches the airport.

BY TAXI Given so many alternatives, taxis are not a natural choice. You will, however, almost always find a cluster waiting outside of the major theme parks' gates, waiting to take fares to their hotels. If you spend more than $30 a day on taxis (a one-way ride from the Magic Kingdom to the hotel stretch on U.S. 192 east of Disney would cost about $25), smack your forehead, because you could have rented a car for that amount.

Many companies accept major credit cards, but ask when you summon a ride, because your payment may need to be processed by phone. Companies are not carefully monitored, so only choose a recommended carrier. Call your own:

o **Diamond Cab Company:** ℂ 407/523-3333
o **Transtar:** ℂ 407/857-9999
o **Yellow:** ℂ 407/422-2222

TRAVELING FROM ORLANDO TO OTHER PARTS OF AMERICA

Orlando, while not an important air hub, is well connected to the cities that are, particularly New York, Atlanta, and Chicago. For advice on how to find cheap airfare, see "Getting There," p. 228.

The **USA Rail Pass** is the American equivalent of the Eurail Pass in Europe—although our national rail system, **Amtrak** (© 800/872-7245 or 215/856-7953; www.amtrak.com), hardly compares to the European system. The pass allows travel within the U.S. The cheapest pass is a 15-day pass, which grants eight trips ($439); the most expensive offers 45 days of travel over 18 trips ($859). Those on a grand tour of America may benefit from those rates compared to flying.

From late April through June, many car renters redistribute inventory by offering **"drive-out"** deals for one-way rentals that originate in Florida and drop off elsewhere in the country. Rates can be as low as $10/day, so look for those.

For bus travel, Orlando is served by **Greyhound** (© 800/231-2222; www.greyhound.com) and **Megabus** (© 877/462-6342; www.megabus.com). Long-distance bus travel in the United States is a purgatorial experience. Don't.

WHEN TO GO

The main consideration when it comes to selecting a date for your visit is balancing good weather with thin crowds. Crowds keep you from seeing everything. In the peak season (such as spring break or the week after Christmas), the Magic Kingdom's turnstiles spin like propellers. None of the theme parks close on **public holidays.** In fact, they do better business then. On December 27, 2006, three Disney parks reached capacity and briefly sealed gates. But come September, you can do nearly everything in a day.

Mouse Clickers: The Best Planning Websites

If you really want to be intense about your planning (for your sanity and relaxation, I don't recommend it), there are obsessive resources online that go into granular detail. You'll find that the official park websites mostly furnish doctored photographs, meaningless homilies, bandwidth-hogging animation, and a near-total lack of cogent information. Thank goodness, then, for rabid followings.

○ **AllEarsNetcom** & **WDWFans.com** offer encyclopedic compendiums of everything Disney, down to the menus, what's under renovation, and which rooms are best.

○ **OrlandoInformer.com** comprehensively reports Universal, including deals.

○ **WDWmagic.com** and **WDWinfo.com** (and its **DISBoards.com**) host some of the most active message forums for news and Q&As.

○ The independently run **PartyThroughTheParks.com** rates drinking and nightlife and **DisneyFoodBlog.com** keeps track of meals.

○ **MouseSavers.com** and **TheMouseForLess.com** post current Disney deals.

○ **Jim Hill Media** (www.jimhillmedia.com). No one's better at insider gossip.

Which Day of the Week?

The busiest days at all parks are generally Saturday and Sunday. Seven-day guests are often traveling on these days, and weekends are when locals come to play. Beyond that: Tuesday and Thursday see an uptick in the Magic Kingdom; Tuesday and Friday (and evenings) at Epcot; Wednesday is a tad busier Disney's Hollywood Studios; and Monday, Tuesday, and Wednesday can be a zoo (forgive the pun) at the Animal Kingdom. Crowds tend to thin later in the day.

So when are the **peak seasons?** Put simply: when American kids are out of school. That means midspring, summer, and the holidays. Hotel rates rise then, too. If you want to **save cash,** early January, early May, late August, all of September, and the first half of December are prime. The flipside of low season is that the theme parks trim services when it's quieter. January is a particularly tough month for missing out on rides due to rehabs. And especially in the winter months, you may find it too chilly to enjoy the rides that get you wet, which is a shame since Orlando has some of the best water rides in the world.

CLIMATE June to September is the heaviest season for rain. It seems like every afternoon, like clockwork, another heavy storm rolls in and shuts rides temporarily. Those storms usually roll out within an hour, just as reliably, but in the meantime, you'll see torrents and lightning. Central Florida suffers more lightning strikes than any other American locale. During those tropical seasons, bring along a cheap poncho from home.

Orlando Average Temperature & Rainfall

	JAN	FEB	MAR	APR	MAY	JUNE	JULY	AUG	SEPT	OCT	NOV	DEC
HI/LOW DAILY TEMPS (°F)	72/49	73/50	78/55	84/60	88/66	91/71	92/73	92/73	90/73	84/65	78/57	73/51
HI/LOW DAILY TEMPS (°C)	22/10	23/10	26/13	29/16	31/19	33/22	33/23	33/23	32/23	29/19	26/14	23/11
INCHES OF PRECIPITATION	2.25	2.82	3.32	2.43	3.30	7.13	7.27	6.88	6.53	3.16	1.98	2.25

Orlando's Calendar of Events

Check the special events pages at the theme park websites to see if any themed weekends or smaller events are in the works. In addition, the events listings at **Visit Orlando** (www.visitorlando.com), **"Orlando Weekly"** (www.orlandoweekly.com), and the **"Orlando Sentinel"** (www.orlandosentinel.com) are comprehensive. You will also find a few listings at **"Orlando" magazine** (www.orlandomagazine.com).

JANUARY

Capital One Bowl. It used to be called the Citrus Bowl—can *anyone* keep track of the square-dancing corporate naming rights anymore? Held New Year's Day at the Florida Citrus Bowl Stadium, it pits the second-ranked teams from the Big Ten and SEC conferences against one another. www.floridacitrussports.com.

ZORA! Festival. The great folklorist and writer (1891–1960) was from Eatonville (a 30-min. drive north of Orlando), the country's oldest incorporated African-American town. This weeklong event includes lectures and a 2-day public art fair. ☏ **407/647-3307.** www.zorafestival.com.

Harry Potter Celebration. In late January 2014, Universal began trying out a weekend party for Potterheads including Q&As and film tributes. www.universalorlando.com.

FEBRUARY

Winter Park Bach Festival. This annual event at Rollins College began in 1935 and has evolved into one of the country's better choral fests. Although it has stretched to include other composers and guest artists (Handel, P.D.Q. Bach), at least one concert is devoted to Johann. It takes place mid-February to early March, with scattered one-off guest performances throughout the year. ✆ **407/646-2182.** www.bachfestivalflorida.org.

Silver Spurs Rodeo. Lest you doubt Central Florida is far removed from the American Deep South, it hosts the largest rodeo east of the Mississippi (with bareback broncs, racing barrel horses, rodeo clowns, and athletes drawn from the cowboy circuit) over 3 days in mid-February in an indoor arena off U.S. 192. 1875 Silver Spur Lane, Kissimmee. ✆ **407/677-6336.** www.silverspursrodeo.com.

Mardi Gras at Universal Studios. On Saturday nights, Universal books major acts (Bonnie Raitt, Hall & Oates, LL Cool J) and mounts a parade complete with stilt-walkers, jazz bands, Louisiana-made floats, and bead tossing—although here, what it takes to win a set of beads is considerably less risqué than it is in the Big Easy. It's included with admission. ✆ **407/224-2691.** www.universalorlando.com/mardigras.

Spring Training. See p. 228 for a rundown of which Major League Baseball teams play where. Mid-February through March.

MARCH

Epcot's International Flower & Garden Festival. This spring event, which lasts from March to May, transforms the park with some 30 million flowers, some 70 topiaries, a screened-in butterfly garden, presentations by noted horticulturalists, and a steady lineup of "Flower Power" concerts (Chubby Checker, Petula Clark). It's free with standard entry. ✆ **407/934-7639.** www.disneyworld.com.

Florida Film Festival. This respected event showcases films by Florida artists and has featured past appearances by the likes of Oliver Stone, William H. Macy, Christopher

Walken, and Cary Elwes. ✆ **407/644-5625.** www.floridafilmfestival.com.

APRIL

Epcot's International Flower & Garden Festival. See March for full listing, above.

MAY

Orlando International Fringe Festival. This theatrical smorgasbord, the longest-running fringe fest in America, spends 14 days mounting some 100 newly written, experimental performances in Loch Haven Park. ✆ **407/648-0077.** www.orlandofringe.org.

Florida Music Festival. Some 250 bands over 4 days give exposure to up-and-coming musicians—at a pace of 50 per night, all over town. www.floridamusicfestival.com.

Epcot's International Flower & Garden Festival. See March for full listing, above.

JUNE

Gay Days. What started as a single day for gay and lesbian visitors has mushroomed into a full week of some 40 events managed by a host of promoters. It's said that attendance goes as high as 135,000, and it's become one of the biggest annual events in Florida. Held around the first Saturday in June, Gay Days are a blowout party with unofficial group visits to each of Disney's parks, plus an ongoing pool bash at the host hotel. Dance events—including Magic Journeys, an all-night, after-hours dance party at Arabian Nights—are sold through www.onemightyweekend.com.

Star Wars Weekends. Hollywood Studios' major annual do, held over 3 weeks late spring, sees actors from the franchise arrive for signings, parades, and Q&As. Warwick Davis, who once squeezed into an Ewok costume, has made a career out of these events. It's not just for kids—the finer points of the Lucas catechism are discussed. A regular ticket gets you in. www.disneyworld.com/starwars.

SEPTEMBER

Night of Joy. It's actually a long-running pair of nights of outdoor Contemporary Christian concerts—eight or nine acts—spread throughout the Magic Kingdom, which stays open late for the occasion. Rides run all night, and it's separately ticketed. ✆ **877/ 648-3569.** www.nightofjoy.com.

Rock the Universe. Universal's festival of top-flight Christian rock bands who perform on stages around Universal Studios. Rides and performances continue past midnight, after regular patrons have gone home. It's separately ticketed. www.rocktheuniverse.com.

OCTOBER

Epcot's International Food & Wine Festival. The World Showcase makes amends with the countries it ignores by installing temporary booths selling tapas-size servings of foods and wines from many nations. That's supplemented with chef demonstrations and seminars, and in "Eat to the Beat" concerts by known acts (Hanson, the Go-Gos), and tastings by at least 100 wineries. A few of the more extravagant events are charged, but most talks are free. The festival lasts from late September to mid-November and the hotly awaited details are posted by Disney in the summer. ✆ **407/939-3378.** www.disney world.com/foodandwine.

Mickey's Not-So-Scary Halloween Party. The best of the Magic Kingdom's separately ticketed evening events, this one mounts a special Halloween-themed parade with fiendishly catchy theme song, a few special shows, a fireworks display that surpasses the usual one, and stations where you can pick up free candy. Lots of kids even show up in costume, although it's not required. The event happens on scattered evenings from mid-September through the end of October. Unfortunately, it's so oversold that you will barely be able to move. Halloween sells out early. Target audience: people who like lollipops. ✆ **407/934-7639.** www.disneyworld.com.

Halloween Horror Nights. Unquestionably Universal's biggest event, HHN is the equivalent of a whole new theme park that's designed for a year but only lasts a month. After dark, the Studios are overtaken by grotesque "scareactors" who terrorize crowds with chain saws, gross-out shows, and eight big, walk-through haunted houses that are made from scratch each year. The mayhem lasts into the wee hours. Wimps need not apply; children are discouraged by the absence of kids' ticket prices. A bawdy revue based on the Bill and Ted movie characters skewers the year in pop culture and draws huge, enthusiastic crowds of tipsy young people. On top of all this, most of the rides remain open. HHN has legions of fans. Target audience: people who like to poop themselves in fright. (Busch Gardens' Howl-o-Scream event's scariness is somewhere between Universal's and Disney's.) www.halloweenhorrornights.com.

SeaWorld's Halloween Spooktacular. SeaWorld throws a sweet, toddler-approved weekend Halloween event of its own, with trick-or-treating (kids dress up), a few encounters with sea fairies and bubbles, and show starring Count von Count from "Sesame Street." Target audience: people who have a naptime. It's included in admission.

Orlando Film Festival. Like all festivals worth their salt, this one presents mostly mainstream and independent films in advance of their wider release dates. It lasts only a few days in mid-October or early November, screening at various downtown venues. ✆ **407/843-0801.** www.orlando filmfest.com.

NOVEMBER

ICE! It debuted in 2003 at the Gaylord Palms hotel and has quickly become a holiday perennial. The hotel brings in nearly 2 million pounds of ice, sculpts it into a walk-through city, keeps it chilled to 9°F, and issues winter coats to visitors. Add Christmas and synchronized light shows and you've got an event that charges $29 for entry—and sells out. ✆ **407/586-0000.** www.gaylord palms.com/ice.

The Osborne Family Spectacle of Dancing Lights. No, not Ozzy and Sharon, but Jennings, Paul, Mitzi, and Breezy (I swear I'm not making this up), whose preposterously overdone Christmas display at their Little Rock house was deemed so vulgar that neighbors went to the Arkansas Supreme Court to shut it down. Enter Disney's Hollywood Studios. Every 15 minutes, it twitters and "dances" to Christmas carols, all as foam "snow" gently wafts from above. It lasts until the first week of January.

Mickey's Very Merry Christmas Party. This crowded Christmas event, which occurs on various nights starting even before Thanksgiving, is probably Disney's most popular special annual event. It requires a separate ticket from regular admission. What you get is a tree-lighting ceremony, a few special holiday-themed shows, a special fireworks display (very green and red), an appearance by Santa Claus, a special parade, and *huge* crowds. Meanwhile, Disney's warehouse for holiday decorations (it exists) empties out and its hotels deck the halls: The Grand Floridian erects a life-size house made of gingerbread in its lobby. © **407/934-7639.** www.disneyworld.com.

Holidays Around the World at Epcot. This one features a holiday customs of many nations and a host of costumed storytellers, but its real showpiece is the daily, 40-minute candlelight processional, a retelling of the Christmas Nativity story by a celebrity narrator (recent names have included Sigourney Weaver, Whoopi Goldberg, Trace Adkins, and Neil Patrick Harris) accompanied by a 50-piece orchestra and a full Mass choir. The processional is a WDW tradition going back to its earliest days—Cary Grant did it! www.disneyworld.com.

Grinchmas & The Macy's Holiday Parade. Usual holiday traditions include a musical version of "How the Grinch Stole Christmas" and daily parades by Macy's, which brings balloons and floats to Universal when Thanksgiving is over. That's included in the ticket price. www.universalorlando.com.

Russell Athletic Bowl. An ACC team battles a Big Ten team, usually a few days before New Year's and always at the Florida Citrus Bowl Stadium. www.russellathleticbowl.com.

New Year's Eve. Yahoo.com reports that Orlando regularly makes its list of top five most-searched New Year's Eve destinations. There's no shortage of places to party. At the parks: **CityWalk** lures top acts such as Cyndi Lauper. Three **Disney parks,** minus Animal Kingdom, stay open until the wee hours. **SeaWorld** brings in big-band music or jazz, plus fireworks.

Getting Attraction Discounts

For a full breakdown of Disney's ticketing system, how it works, and how to ward against overspending, see p. 228.

One of the true discounted programs is the **FlexTicket.** For admission to five parks (Universal's pair, SeaWorld, Aquatica, Wet 'n Wild), you want the Orlando FlexTicket ($305 adults, $385 kids 3–9), which grants unlimited admission to all of the parks for a full 2 weeks. Tack on Busch Gardens for $40 adults or kids. Considering 1-day admission to Busch Gardens alone is $89 adults and $81 kids, you don't have to get near a calculator to see the savings, but you do have to go to as many parks as possible. Once you've paid for parking at your first theme park ($15 is the going rate), you can keep your ticket and avoid paying it again. Many hotel closed-circuit TV programs promise $10 off, so when you're buying a FlexTicket in person, claim you learned about it from your in-room programming and ask for the deal. FlexTickets are sold online, too (http://tickets.visitorlando.com, the area's official tourism bureau, gives small discounts on it).

Universal and SeaWorld discount the gate price if you book online, and all the parks discount per-day entry if you buy multiple days. SeaWorld and Busch Gardens also offer courtesy admission for members of the military and their families. Check www.herosalute.com to see if you are eligible. **Orlando Magicard** (www.visitorlando.com/magicard) grants discounts to heaps of attractions, meals, home rentals, and hotels. The participants are members of the local tourism bureau. Its discounts aren't much different from what the free coupon circulars promise, but they're still good deals. You

Before Magic Your Way made ticket expiration standard, pretty much every Disney ticket was good forever. That means there are a lot of unused days floating around. It's illegal to sell them, but that doesn't stop people. When you see a sign on the side of U.S. 192 promising discounted tickets, guess what may be for sale? Buying a ticket like this is a gamble, particularly if you don't have the expertise to recognize a fake or a spent ticket. Often, only a Disney computer scan can tell for sure.

Other organizations, such as time-share developers, do offer legit tickets to theme parks and dinner shows, but to get them, you will have to endure heavy-duty sales presentations that last several hours. The requirements for attendance can be tight: Married couples must attend together (gay couples are often excluded—that's legal in Florida), you both must swear your combined annual income is above a certain amount ($50,000, for example, for Westgate branded resorts—yes, run by the time-share baron in "The Queen of Versailles"), that you are in a given age range (23–65 is common), and that you commit to staying for at least 90 minutes, although being pitched for long as 4 hours is also common. Even if you're fearless, an entire morning of your hard-earned vacation time is worth a lot more than whatever discount is being provided. After all, how many days of working did it take for you to accrue those 4 or 5 hours? You also may not arrive at the parks until lunchtime, missing (in some cases) a third of the opening hours. Don't be so cheap and discount-obsessed that you throw away your time.

will also find coupons through **OrlandoCoupons.com** and the discount circular **HotelCoupons.com.**

A few outfits such sell faintly discounted tickets. **Maple Leaf Tickets** (✆ **800/841-2837;** www.mapleleaftickets.com) and **the Official Ticket Center** (✆ **877/406-4836;** www.officialticketcenter.com) **Undercover Tourist** (✆ **800/846-1302;** www.undercovertourist.com) and **Ticket Momma** (✆ **866/996-7508;** www.ticketmomma.com) are all accredited by the Better Business Bureau. No Disney deals are ever deep enough to offset shipping fees or the hassle of picking up your tickets at some third-party office; however, multiple purchases and third-tier diversions such as dinner shows ($10–$15 off) may work out for you. Tickets are nontransferable. A desk at the Orlando Official Visitor Center (p. 244) furnishes similar discounts on tickets you can trust.

One to be wary of is the **Go Orlando Card** (✆ **866/628-9036;** www.goorlandocard.com), which offers admission to many secondary attractions. The catch is you get an obscenely short time to use it. Rare is the person who can visit enough places to make the price (a 2-day card is $145 for adults) pay off.

[FastFACTS] ORLANDO

Accessible Travel
Hotels and theme parks have their acts together. Nearly everything is accessible. This excellent customer service predates the Americans with Disabilities Act of 1990; as multigenerational attractions, the parks have always worked to be inclusive, and in response, guests with mobility issues have long embraced them in return.

There was a time when guests in **wheelchairs** and **ECVs** were given special treatment and ushered to the front of lines, but now, with so many guests on wheels for reasons including obesity, Disney (with the exception of Make-A-Wish Foundation kids and other special groups, by prior arrangement) feeds everyone into the same attraction queues. You might have to transfer to a manual wheelchair. Once you're near the end, there will usually be a place for you to wait for the special wheelchair-ready ride vehicle to come around. Often, this translates into longer waits, as special ride vehicles can be in high demand. The park maps carefully indicate which rides will require you to leave your personal vehicle. A very few, pre-ADA attractions, such as Tom Sawyer Island and the Swiss Family Treehouse, require you to be ambulatory. Those are marked, too.

For off-property stays, consider renting a house, which provides much more room; most home-rental companies also comply with ADA requirements.

All the parks have a full range of in-park services for guests of every need. Disney maintains a Special Services hotline to answer all accessibility needs, including full arrangements for the blind and captioning for the hearing-impaired: ℃ **407/824-4321** and TTY ℃ 407/827-5141. Universal Orlando can be reached at

℃ **800/447-0672** [TTY] or 407/224-4233 [voice] (www.universalorlando.com); SeaWorld Orlando's number is ℃ **407/363-2400** (www.seaworld.com); Kennedy Space Center is at ℃ **321/449-4443** (www.kennedyspacecenter.com). Most parks can arrange sign language interpreters with a few weeks' notice; all furnish assisted listening devices or scripts for some, but not all, of the biggest attractions.

Medical Travel, Inc. (℃ **800/308-2503** or 407/438-8010; www.medicaltravel.org) specializes in the rental of mobility equipment, ramp vans, and supplies such as oxygen tanks (be aware that many rides do not allow tanks). Electric scooters and wheelchairs can be delivered to your accommodation through these established companies: **Buena Vista Scooters** (℃ **866/484-4797** or 407/938-0349; www.buenavistascooters.com), **Scootaround** (℃ **888/441-7575**; www.scootaround.com), **CARE Medical Equipment** (℃ **800/741-2282** or 407/856-2273; www.caremedicalequipment.com), and **Walker Medical & Mobility Products** (℃ **888/726-6837** or 407/518-6000; www.walkermobility.com). All the theme parks, except the water parks, rent ECVs for about $50 a day and wheelchairs for about $12 a day. If your own wheelchair is wider than 25 inches, think about switching to the park model, as it is

guaranteed to navigate tight squeezes such as hairpin queue turns.

Organizations that offer assistance to travelers with disabilities include the **American Federation for the Blind** (℃ **800/232-5463**; www.afb.org) and **Society for Accessible Travel & Hospitality** (℃ **212/447-7284**; www.sath.org).

Area Codes The area code for the Orlando area is **407** (if you're dialing locally, a preceding 1 is not necessary, but the 407 is), although you may encounter the less common **321** code, which is also used on the Atlantic Coast. The **863** area code governs the land between Orlando and Tampa, and the Tampa area uses **813** and **727**. The region west of Orlando uses **352**.

ATMs/Banks See "Money," in this section.

Business Hours Offices are generally open weekdays between 9am and 5pm, while banks tend to close at 4pm. Typically, stores open between 9 and 10am and close between 6 and 7pm Monday through Saturday, except malls, which stay open until 9pm. On Sunday, stores generally open at 11am and close by 7pm.

Cellphones See "Mobile Phones," later in this section.

Car Rentals This topic is perhaps the most hotly debated issue in all of Disneydom. But the bottom line is there's only one reason to do without a car: You never intend to leave Disney.Quite simply, this should be a part of your budget.

Disney guests often justify forgoing a car by saying they can't afford one. This is a fallacy. Disney hotels charge as much as twice what you'll pay to stay at a hotel of similar quality off-site. If you stay at a non-Disney property, you can afford a car and *still* pay less. A large inventory means rentals are cheaper here than in other American cities: $26 a day is common for a compact car.

One caveat is that **parking charges** can add up. Valet is often free in town, but the theme parks charge $14 to $15 a day for a space (Universal is $5 after 6pm). If you stay at a Disney resort, it is free. However, if you pay for parking once at any Disney park, you won't have to pay again for another park on the same day. In the rest of Orlando, parking is free, plentiful, and off the street.

Get a car that locks by remote control fob; those are handy for making your vehicle honk and locating it in those expansive theme park parking lots.

Crime Disney may advertise itself as "the Happiest Place on Earth," but it's still on Earth. That means bad things happen. Never open your hotel room door to a stranger, and never give your personal details or credit card number to anyone who calls your room, even if they claim to work for the hotel. **Pickpockets** are virtually unheard of, but that doesn't mean they don't exist. Be vigilant about bags; you're going to be bumped and jostled many times—one of those bumps could be a nimble-fingered thief taking your cash.

Customs Rules change. For details regarding current regulations, consult **U.S. Customs and Border Protection** (📞 **202/927-1770;** www.cbp.gov).

Doctors There are first-aid centers in all of the theme parks. There's also a 24-hour, toll-free number for the **Poison Control Center** (📞 **800/282-3171**). To find a dentist, contact the **Dental Referral Service** (📞 **800/235-4111;** www.dentalreferral.com). **Doctors on Call Service** (📞 **407/399-3627**) makes house and room calls in most of the Orlando area. **Centra Care** has several walk-in clinics, including ones at 2301 Sand Lake Rd., near Universal (📞 **407/851-6478**); at 12500 S. Apopka Vineland Rd. in Lake Buena Vista, near Disney (📞 **407/934-2273**); and at 8201 W. U.S. 192 (W. Irlo Bronson Hwy.), in the Formosa Gardens shopping center (📞 **407/397-7032**). The **Medical Concierge** (📞 **855/326-5252;** www.themedicalconcierge.com) makes "hotel house calls," arranges dental appointments, and rents equipment.

Drinking Laws The legal drinking age is 21. Proof of age is always requested, even if you look older, so carry photo ID. It's illegal to carry open containers of alcohol in any car or public area that isn't zoned for alcohol consumption (as CityWalk is), and the police may ticket you on the spot.

Driving Rules Americans drive on the right. In Florida, you may turn right on red after making a full stop. Many intersections are equipped with traffic cameras that will take a photo of your license plate, and rental car companies pass on fines along with hefty fees. If your plans take you outside the Orlando area, some toll roads (in Miami and Tampa, for example) are cashless and can only be paid by a SunPass sensor that must be rented, for an extra daily fee, from your rental agency, otherwise you will incur large penalties. Last, Florida is full of visitors who don't know where they're going. These lost souls will halt, cross three lanes of traffic, and get in the wrong lane without thinking. Keep a safe distance from the car in front of you.

Electricity The United States uses 110 to 120 volts AC (60 cycles), compared to the 220 to 240 volts AC (50 cycles) that is standard in Europe, Australia, and New Zealand. If your small appliances use 220 to 240 volts, buy an adaptor and voltage converter before you leave home, as these are difficult to come by in Orlando.

Embassies & Consulates The nearest embassies are located in the nation's capital, Washington, D.C. Some consulates are located in major U.S. cities, and most nations have a mission to the United Nations in New York City. If your country isn't listed below, call for directory information in Washington, D.C. (✆ **202/555-1212**), or log on to **www.embassy. org/embassies**.

The embassy of **Australia** is at 1601 Massachusetts Ave. NW, Washington, DC 20036 (✆ **202/797-3000;** www.austemb.org). There are consulates in New York, Honolulu, Houston, Los Angeles, and San Francisco.

The embassy of **Canada** is at 501 Pennsylvania Ave. NW, Washington, DC 20001 (✆ **202/682-1740;** www. canadianembassy.org). Other Canadian consulates are in Buffalo, Detroit, Los Angeles, New York, and Seattle.

The embassy of **Ireland** is at 2234 Massachusetts Ave. NW, Washington, DC 20008 (✆ **202/462-3939;** www.irelandemb.org). Irish consulates are in Boston, Chicago, New York, San Francisco, and other cities.

The embassy of **New Zealand** is at 37 Observatory Circle NW, Washington, DC 20008 (✆ **202/328-4800;** www.nzembassy. com). New Zealand consulates are in Los Angeles, Salt Lake City, San Francisco, and Seattle.

The embassy of the **United Kingdom** is at 3100 Massachusetts Ave. NW, Washington, DC 20008 (✆ **202/588-7800;** www. britainusa.com). Other British consulates are in Atlanta, Boston, Chicago, Cleveland, Houston, Los Angeles, New York, San Francisco, and Seattle.

Emergencies Call ✆ **911** for the police, to report a fire, or to get an ambulance. If you have a medical emergency that does not require an ambulance, you should be able to walk into the nearest hospital emergency room (see "Hospitals," below).

Family Travel All parks have a **baby care center** for heating formula, nursing, and so on. But think carefully about whether your child is ready for the theme parks. Too many parents consider an Orlando vacation such a rite of passage that they rush into it too early without considering whether their child will find the experience overwhelming, or even if they'll *remember* it. I agree with many parenting experts who say that about 3 years old is the minimum age. It's not just that many younger children get wigged out when they see their first costume character, but also because it's no fun for a kid to get turned away from a ride they have their heart set on.

Some experts say kids are not truly ready for the rigors of theme parks until they can walk on their own all day. Whether or not very young children are *advisable,* they are *possible:* Scarier rides have what's called a **child swap.** That provides an area where one adult can wait with a child while their partner rides and then switch off so the other gets a chance. Many rides also have a bypass corridor where chickens can do their chicken-out thing.

Let kids take an active role in planning their vacation. Their excitement will make the going easier. The Walt Disney World website (http://customizedmaps. disney.go.com) provides online maps of its parks, which you can use to highlight a must-see list according to your tastes. With 3 weeks' notice, the resort will print your maps and mail them ahead for free.

Strollers will not be allowed inside most attractions, and they will not be attended in parking sections, so never leave anything valuable in them. Come prepared with a system for unloading valuables. Also have something that covers the seat; like in parked cars, they get sizzling hot in the Florida sun. Finally, tie some identifying marker (like a white flag, as in surrender) to yours so you can identify it amidst the sea of clones.

○ **Familiarize yourself with the height restrictions for all rides,** which are posted at the parks' websites and listed on the maps. Universal also keeps physical gauges in front of both its parks. Everything is measured in inches, so if your child is usually measured in centimeters, multiply by 0.393.

○ **Bring supplies to kid-proof your hotel room.**

○ **Slather your kids in sun lotion.** Florida sun is stronger than you think.

○ **Dress kids in bright colors.** You'll spot them faster if you're separated. Some parents even put their phone number on their kids with child safety temporary tattoos (yes, they exist).

○ **Dress kids to get wet.** There are water playgrounds, plus frequent rains.

○ **Hotels offer "kids eat free" programs**—you pay, they don't. Ask.

○ **Theme park strollers are easy, but basic;** they don't recline, and they won't secure kids younger than toddlers. Folding "umbrella" strollers have distinct advantages. They make getting onto trams, monorails, and into other tight spaces easier (not just for you—also for people waiting for you).

○ **Bring a picture of your child** or keep one on your mobile phone.

○ **Use a walkie-talkie app** such as Voxer or WhatsApp to communicate with your party; the phone carriers are often overwhelmed by the volume at the parks and text messages sometimes arrive with long delays.

Health Your biggest concern is the **sun,** which can burn you even through grey skies on cloudy days. You will be spending a lot more time outdoors than you might suspect—rides take 3 minutes, but some of their lines will have you waiting outside for an hour. Hats are your friends.

Holidays Banks close on the following holidays: January 1 (New Year's), the third Monday in January (Martin Luther King, Jr., Day), the third Monday in February (Presidents' Day), the last Monday in May (Memorial Day), July 4 (Independence Day), the first Monday in September (Labor Day), the second Monday in October (Veterans Day), the fourth Thursday in November (Thanksgiving Day), and December 25. The theme parks are open every day of the year.

Hospitals **Dr. P Phillips Hospital** (9400 Turkey Lake Rd., Orlando; ✆ **407/351-8500**) is a short drive north up Palm Parkway from Lake Buena Vista.

To get to **Florida Hospital Celebration Health** (400 Celebration Place, Celebration; ✆ **407/303-4000**), from I-4, take the U.S. 192 exit; then at the first traffic light, turn right onto Celebration Avenue, and at the first stop sign, make another right. Clinics: **Centra Care Walk-In Urgent Care** in Lake Buena Vista (12500 Apopka-Vineland Rd., ✆ **407/934-2273;** Mon–Fri 8am–midnight, Sat–Sun 8am–8pm); near the vacation homes south of Disney (7848 W. U.S. 192, Kissimmee; ✆ **407/397-7032;** Mon–Fri 8am–8pm, Sat–Sun 8am–5pm); and by Universal (6001 Vineland Rd.; ✆ **407/351-6682;** Mon–Fri 7am–7pm, Sat–Sun 8am–6pm). In addition, each theme park has its own infirmary capable of handling a range of medical emergencies. If you don't have a car, **East-Coast Medical Network** (✆ **407-648-5252;** www.themedicalconcierge.com) makes house calls to area resorts for $150 to $275 for most ailments. It's available at all hours and brings a portable pharmacy, although prescriptions cost more.

Insurance Among many options, you could try **MEDEX** (www.medexassist.com; ✆ **800/732-5309**) or **Travel Assistance International** (www.travelassistance.com; ✆ **800/821-2828**) for overseas medical insurance cover. **Canadians** should check with their provincial health plan offices or call

Health Canada (www.hc-sc. gc.ca; ℂ **866/225-0709**) to find out the extent of their coverage and what documentation and receipts they must take home.

So what else may you want to insure? You may want special coverage for **apartment stays,** especially if you've plunked down a deposit, and any **valuables,** since airlines are only required to pay up to $2,500 for lost luggage domestically, less for foreign travel.

If you do decide on insurance, compare policies at **InsureMyTrip.com** (ℂ 800/487-4722). Or contact one of the following reputable companies: **Allianz** (ℂ 866/884-3556; www.allianztravelinsurance. com); **CSA Travel Protection** (ℂ 877/243-4135; www. csatravelprotection.com); **MEDEX** (ℂ 800/732-5309; www.medexassist.com; **Travel Guard International** (ℂ 800/826-4919; www. travelguard.com); **Travelex** (ℂ 800/228-9792; www. travelex-insurance.com)

Internet & Wi-Fi Getting online isn't hard. Wi-Fi is now considered an essential amenity, like running water. Most hotels will have free access—sometimes in common areas, sometimes in guest rooms, and sometimes in both places. Walt Disney World's hotels have free Wi-Fi, and so do its theme parks (although the connection can fail intermittently). Hotel connections aren't always fast enough to stream movies, but they're

usually more than enough for standard uses. Nearly all home rentals also come with Internet-connected computers and Wi-Fi, too. Many restaurants have signals, too.

Language English is the primary tongue, plus some Spanish.

LGBT Travelers Orlando still has a conservative streak, but like most cities, it has come to realize that America welcomes every kind of person. The parks also employ thousands of gay people. As a consequence of all this mainstream visibility, gay visitors to Orlando simply won't need special resources or assistance. Most hotels aren't troubled in the least by gay couples, and gay people can be themselves anyplace. The most intolerant attitudes will come from other guests at the theme parks, who, of course, mostly aren't from Orlando—public displays of affection there are not likely to be attacked, but don't expect a warm reception, either. Sexual affection by gay people and straight people alike is not celebrated in the parks. Use your intuition—and your common sense.

Mail At press time, domestic postage rates were 33¢ for a postcard and 46¢ for a letter. For international mail, a first-class letter of up to 1 ounce costs $1.10; a first-class international postcard costs the same as a letter. The

post office most convenient to Disney and Universal is at 10450 Turkey Lake Rd. (ℂ **407/351-2492;** Mon–Fri 9am–7pm, Sat 9am–5pm). A smaller location, closer to Disney, is at 8536 Palm Pkwy., in Lake Buena Vista, just up the road from Hotel Plaza Boulevard (ℂ **407/ 238-0223**). If all you need is to buy stamps and mail letters, you can do that at most hotels. For more information, including locations nearest you, go to **www. usps.com** and click on "Calculate a Price." Ask at the theme park Guest Relations desks if mailing your items there will entitle you to a themed postmark.

Medical Requirements No inoculations or vaccinations are required to enter the United States unless you're arriving from an area that is suffering from an epidemic (cholera or yellow fever, in particular). A valid, signed prescription is required for those travelers in need of **syringe-administered medications** or medical treatment that involves **narcotics.** It is extremely important to obtain the correct documentation in these cases, as your medications could be confiscated; and if you are found to be carrying an illegal substance, officials tend to lock you up first and ask questions later.

Mobile Phones If you're not from the U.S., you'll be appalled at the poor reach of the **GSM (Global System for Mobile**

Communications) wireless network, which is used by much of the rest of the world. Your phone will probably work in Orlando; it may not work in rural areas. To see where GSM phones work in the U.S., check out www.t-mobile.com/coverage. Phones can be rented from **InTouch USA** (✆ **800/872-7626;** www.intouchusa.com); some car rental outlets do it, too. If you have Web access while traveling, consider a broadband-based telephone service (in technical terms, **Voice over Internet Protocol,** or **VoIP**), such as **Skype** (www.skype.com) or **Vonage** (www.vonage.com), which allows you to make free international calls from your laptop.

Money   This town exists to rake in money. Consequently it places few obstacles between you and the loss of it. Most ATMs that you'll find are run by third parties, not your bank, which means that you'll be slapped with fees of around $2.50 per withdrawal (around $5 for international visitors). Machines accept pretty much anything you can stick into them. Citibank customers can avoid the usage fee by using the fancy Citibank machines located at most 7-Eleven convenience stores in the area. International visitors should make advance arrangements with their banks to ensure their cards will function in the United States. Also ask your bank if it has reciprocal agreements for free withdrawals

anywhere. One institution known to charge international usage fees that are below the industry standard is **Everbank** (✆ **888/882-3837;** www.everbank.com); another is **Charles Schwab** (✆ **866/855-9102;** www.schwab.com), which reimburses ATM fees.

Credit cards are nearly universally accepted. You could strut off the plane with just plastic and live in style for your entire trip. In fact, you *must* have one to rent a car without a hassle. The majority of places accept the Big Four: American Express, MasterCard, Visa, and Discover. A few places add Diners Club to the mix, and some smaller family-owned businesses subtract American Express because of the pain of dealing with the company.

Before you leave home, let your credit card issuer know that you're about to go on vacation. Many of them get antsy when they see unexpectedly large charges start appearing so far from your home, and sometimes they freeze your account in response.

Not only will Orlando clerks almost always neglect to check the purchaser's identification, but also, in the high-volume world of the theme parks, they don't even require signatures. You just swipe and go. That means you need to be doubly sure to keep your cards safe.

Try not to use credit cards to withdraw cash. You'll be charged interest

from the moment your money leaves the slot. **Tip:** There is an exception that the resorts don't sanction, but I certainly do: Instead of using your credit card to draw cash from an ATM, use it to buy Disney Dollars (✆ **407/566-4985,** option 5). They're private scrip (sold at big shops and most guest services desks), valued precisely like U.S. dollars. But they are charged as a purchase, *not* as a cash withdrawal, so there are no additional fees. You can spend them like cash within the respective resorts. Pretty sneaky, sis!

Now that ATMs are common, traveler's checks are nearly dead. Using them, you run the risk of most places declining them. Creditors have come up with **traveler's check cards,** also called **prepaid cards,** which are essentially debit cards loaded with the amount of money you elect to put on them. They're not coded with your personal information, they work in ATMs, and should you lose one, you can get your cash back in a matter of hours. If you spend all the money on them, you can call a number or visit a website and reload the card using your bank account information. **Travelex Cash Passport** (✆ **877/465-0085;** www.cashpassport.com; $2 per ATM transaction) works anywhere MasterCard does; also try **NetSpend** (✆ **866/387-7363;** www.netspend.com; $1 per purchase, $5 per ATM transaction). That one costs $4.

Like traveler's checks, exchanging cash is on the outs, and good riddance, as exchange rates are usurious. Because ATM withdrawals give better deals, old-fashioned exchange desks are few and far between, although you'll still find a few at the airport, at large hotels, at the **Travelex** at Lake Buena Vista Factory Stores (p. 163). If you need to change money, better rates come from banks during regular banking hours (Mon–Fri 9:30am–4pm).

Finding a bank isn't difficult in the "real" world of Orlando around SeaWorld and Universal, but at Walt Disney World, you could use a hand. The nearest bank is the **SunTrust** (1675 Buena Vista Dr., across from Downtown Disney Marketplace; ☎ **407/828-6103;** Mon–Fri 9am–4pm, until 5pm on Fri).

Newspapers & Magazines

Business hotels distribute that shallow McNewspaper, "USA Today," to use as your morning doormat. The local paper, the "Orlando Sentinel" (www.orlandosentinel.com) is less widely available but much better for discovering local happenings. "Orlando Magazine" (www.orlando-magazine.com) is a glossy that covers trends and upscale restaurants. Also see the box on amateur-run websites covering the theme parks on p. 230; those are better for park goings-on.

Packing

For the latest rules on how to pack and what you will be permitted

to bring as a carry-on, consult your airline or the **Transportation Security Administration** (www.tsa. gov). Also be sure to find out from your airline what your checked-baggage weight limits will be; maximums of around 50 pounds per suitcase are standard. Anything heavier will incur a fee. Paying for the luggage at the airport is often more expensive than online.

If you forget something, there's nothing you can't buy in Orlando. It's hardly Timbuktu. But bring the basics for sunshine (lotion of at least 30 SPF, wide-brimmed hat, bathing suit, sunglasses), for rain (a compact umbrella or a plastic poncho, which costs $8 inside the parks), for walking (good shoes, sandals for wet days), and for memories (camera, storage cards, chargers).

Pets

None of the Disney resorts allows animals (except service dogs) to stay on the (the only exception being Disney's Fort Wilderness Campground, where you can have your pet at the full-hook-up campsites). The major theme parks offer animal boarding, usually for about $12 to $15 per day. Disney offers a single facility, **Best Friends Pet Care,** on the Bonnet Creek Parkway (☎ **877/493-9738**). Universal Orlando and SeaWorld will board small pets during the day only, not overnight.

Universal's three Loews-run resorts allow pets on the property. So do Drury Hotels (p. 218). To find

more pet-friendly hotels, two solid resources are **www.petswelcome.com** and **www.dogfriendly.com**.

Pharmacies

The tourist area hosts mostly national chains. **Walgreens** (7650 W. Sand Lake Rd. at Dr. Phillips Blvd., Orlando; ☎ **407/370-6742**), which has a round-the-clock pharmacy, could, at a stretch, be deemed an outfit with local roots; back in the day, Mr. Walgreen spent the cold months in Winter Park. **Turner Drugs** (12500 Apopka Vineland Rd., Lake Buena Vista; ☎ **407/828-8125**) is not a 24-hour pharmacy, but it delivers prescriptions to most Disney-area accommodations.

Police

Call ☎ **911** from any phone in an emergency.

Safety

Train kids to approach the nearest park employee in case of **separation.** Never dress kids in clothing that reveals their name, address, or hometown, and unless it's a travel day, remove any luggage tags where this information will be visible. If people can read your address off a tag while you're in line at Jurassic Park, they they'll know you're not at home. Don't leave valuables visible when you park your car. Also, please keep your arms and legs inside the vehicle at all times. Thank you.

Senior Travel

Just about every secondary attraction offers a special price for seniors, but the theme parks offer precious little. If you're over 50, you can join **AARP**

Besides the usual toiletries, recharging cords, and drugs, you might not have thought of these good ideas, too:

- **Earplugs.** Orlando flights are jumping with kids going insane with excitement.
- **Hand purifier.** Turnstiles. Safety bars. Handrails. Furry mice. You're going to be handling a lot of dirty things.
- **Dark-colored shorts or pants.** On almost all flume rides, the seating doubles as a step, so you're bound to stain your butt with a slightly muddy footprint.
- **Sandals that fasten.** Water-based rides soak regular shoes and cause pruning. Flip-flops won't always do because they're not hardy and they won't stay on.
- **Skin-tight underwear.** Hot, moist days can cause chafing even in

people who rarely experience it. Under Armour or nonpadded bike shorts preempt that.

- **Sunscreen, a hat, and sunglasses.** Okay, so you probably thought of these, but it bears repeating.
- **A mobile phone battery recharger.** Between Wi-Fi, photos, social media updating, and the My Disney Experience app, you could use a battery for top-ups.
- **A superabsorbent shammy.** For lenses and wet children.
- **Pocket-size games.** People talk about rides, but they neglect to mention the hour in line before those exciting 3 minutes. Orlando *is* lines. Bring diversions.

(601 E. Street NW, Washington, DC 24009; © **888/687-2277;** www.aarp.org) to find out what's being offered in terms of discounts for hotels, airfare, and car rentals. Before you bite, be sure that the AARP discount you are offered actually undercuts others that are out there. Elderhostel's well-respected **Road Scholar** (© **800/454-5768;** www.elderhostel.org) runs classes and programs, both inside the theme parks and around the Orlando area, designed to delve into literature, history, the arts, and music. Packages last from a day to a week and include lodging, tours, and meals. Most are multigenerational; bring the grandkids.

Smoking Smoking is prohibited in public indoor spaces, including offices, restaurants, hotel lobbies, and most shops. Some bars permit it. In general, if you need to smoke, you must go outside into the open air, and in the theme parks there are strictly enforced designated areas.

Taxes A 6.5 to 7 percent sales tax is charged on all goods with the exception of most edible grocery items and medicines. Hotels add another 2 to 5 percent in a resort tax, so the total tax on accommodations can run up to 12 percent. The United States has no VAT, but the custom is to not list prices with tax, so the final amount that you pay will be

slightly higher than the posted price.

Telephones Generally, hotel surcharges on long-distance and local calls are astronomical, so you're better off using your **cellphone** or a **public pay telephone.** Many convenience groceries and packaging services sell **prepaid calling cards** in denominations from $10 to $50; for international visitors these can be the least expensive way to call home. Many public phones at airports now accept American Express, MasterCard, and Visa credit cards. **Local calls** made from public pay phones in most locales cost either 35¢ or 50¢. Pay phones do not accept pennies, and few will take anything larger than a quarter. Make sure you have roaming turned on for your cellphone account.

If you will have high-speed Internet access in your room, save on calls by using **Skype** (www.skype.com) or another Web-based calling program.

For calls within the United States and to Canada, dial 1 followed by the area code and the seven-digit number. **For other international calls,** first dial 011, then the country code, and then proceed with the number, dropping any leading zeroes.

Calls to area codes **800, 888, 877,** and **866** are toll-free. However, calls to area codes **700** and **900** can be very expensive—usually a charge of 95¢ to $3 or more per minute, and they sometimes have minimum charges that can run as high as $15 or more.

For **reversed-charge or collect calls,** and for person-to-person calls, dial the number 0, then the area code and number. If your operator-assisted call is international, ask for the overseas operator.

For **local directory assistance** ("information"), dial *Ⓒ* **411;** for long-distance information, dial 1, then the appropriate area code and 555-1212.

Time The continental United States is divided into four time zones: Eastern Standard Time (EST), Central Standard Time (CST), Mountain Standard Time (MST), and Pacific Standard Time

(PST). Orlando is on Eastern Standard Time, so when it's noon in Orlando, it's 11am in Chicago (CST), 10am in Denver (MST), and 9am in Los Angeles (PST). Daylight saving moves the clock 1 hour ahead of standard time. Clocks change the second Sunday in March and the first Sunday in November.

Tipping Tips are customary and should be factored into your budget. Waiters should receive 15 to 20 percent of the cost of the meal (depending on the quality of the service), bellhops get $1 per bag, bartenders get $1 per drink, chambermaids get $1 to $2 per day for straightening your room (although many people don't do this), and cab drivers should get 15 percent of the fare. The Disney Dining Plan automatically includes gratuity. Elsewhere, don't be offended if you are reminded about tipping—wait staff are used to dealing with international visitors who don't participate in the custom back home.

Toilets Each theme park has dozens of clean restrooms. Outside of the parks, every fast-food place—and there are hundreds—should have a restroom you can use. Large hotel lobbies also have some.

Visas Citizens of western and central Europe, Australia, New Zealand, and Singapore need only a valid machine-readable passport and a round-trip air ticket or cruise ticket to enter the

United States for stays of up to 90 days. Canadian citizens may enter without a visa with proof of residence.

Citizens of all other countries will need to obtain a tourist visa from the U.S. consulate. Depending on your country of origin, there may or may not be a charge attached (and you may or may not have to apply in person). You'll need to complete an application and submit a photo, and your passport must be valid for at least 6 months past the scheduled end of your U.S. visit. If an interview isn't mandated, it's usually possible to obtain a visa within 24 hours, except during holiday periods or the summer rush. Be sure to check with your local U.S. embassy or consulate for the very latest in entry requirements, as these continue to shift. Full information can be found at the **U.S. State Department**'s website, www.travel.state.gov.

Visitor Information Orlando has one of the most responsive and question-friendly visitors' bureaus in America and it operates a storefront, **Orlando Official Visitor Center** (8723 International Dr.; *Ⓒ* **407/363-5872;** www.orlandoinfo.com; daily 8:30am–6:30pm), in a strip mall on the western side of I-Drive not far north of the Pointe Orlando shopping mall, that's stocked from carpet to rafter with free brochures. Although many, many other places in town (souvenir stands, mostly) claim to offer "official" tourist information, this is the only *truly* official place. Staff is on hand to answer any questions, and its ticket desk has the inside line on discounts.

Kissimmee, the town closest to Walt Disney World, maintains its own tourist office, the **Kissimmee** **Convention and Visitors Bureau** (1925 E. Irlo Bronson Memorial Hwy./U.S. 192; Kissimmee; ✆ **407/944-2400;** www.floridakiss.com; Mon–Fri 8am–5pm). Its website also lists current discounts. The Kissimmee CVB works with the Orlando bureau, so you won't have to make two trips.

Water Tap water has a distinct mineral taste. Your hotel's pipes are not to blame. Rather, think of Orlando as an island floating over a cushion of water. Most of the city's lakes started, in fact, as sinkholes. The drinking water is drawn from the aquifer, hence the specific flavor and odor. It's safe.

Index

See also Accommodations and Restaurant indexes, below.

General Index

A

Accessible travel, 235–236
Accommodations, 5, 192–224.
    See also Accommodations
    Index; and specific parks
    and areas
        home rentals, 222–224
Adventureland, 34–37
Adventurers Outpost, 82
The Affection, 84
Africa, Animal Kingdom, 83–84
Air travel, 225–226
Alexander Holiday Homes, 223
All Star Vacation Homes, 223
Alligators, 157
A'Lure: The Call of the Ocean, 127
The Amazing Adventures of
    Spider-Man, 114
American Idol Experience, 73
Anaheim Produce, 78
Angry Birds Space Encounter, 150
Animal Actors on Location!, 109
Antarctica, 128–129
Apollo/Saturn V Center, 150
Aquatica, 2, 124, 132
Area codes, 236
Ariel's Grotto, 44
Arnold Palmer's Bay Hill Club &
    Lodge, 159
Asia, 84–85
Astro Orbiter, 45–46
Astronaut Hall of Fame, 149
Astronaut Memorial, 150
Astronaut Training Experience
    (ATX), 150, 151
Atlanta Braves, 140
Atlantic Dance Hall, 153
ATMs, 241
Attractions+ plan, 25
Award Vacation Homes, 223

B

Baby care, 238–239
Backstage Magic tour, 96–97
Backstage Safari tour, 97
Backwater Bar, 121
Banks, 242
Barnes & Noble, 165
The Barnstormer, 44
Baseball, 140, 232
Basin, 164
Beaches, 50
Beauty and the Beast—Live on
    Stage, 74
Beetlejuice's Graveyard Revue,
    106
Behind the Seeds tour, 97
Beluga Interaction Program, 131

BetterBidding.com, 211
Bhaktapur Market, 84
Bibbidi Bobbidi Boutique, 164
Big Thunder Mountain Railroad, 38
The Black Hole, 139–140
Blastaway Beach, 139
Blizzard Beach, 2, 9, 90–91
Blue Horizons, 126
Blue Man Group, 154
Blue Spring State Park, 4, 156
The Blues Brothers, 105
Boardwalk Baseball, 134
Boat tours and cruises, 156,
    158–159, 166
Bob Marley—A Tribute to
    Freedom, 154
Body Wars, 57
Boggy Creek Airboat Rides, 158
Bok Tower Gardens, 4, 145
Bomb Bay, 140
The Boneyard, 87
Boop Oop A Doop, 115
Brain Wash, 140
Bruce's Sub House, 58
Build-A-Dino, 164
Bus travel, 229, 230
Busch Gardens Tampa, 135
Business hours, 236
Butterbeer, 117–118
Buzz Lightyear's AstroBlaster,
    92–93
Buzz Lightyear's Space Ranger
    Spin, 45

C

Calendar of events, 231–234
Camp Jurassic, 116
Camp Minnie-Mickey, 87–88
Campfire sing-alongs, 50
Canada, 65
Capital One Bowl, 231
Captain EO, 59
Captain Jack Sparrow's Pirate
    Tutorial, 37
Car rentals, 226–228, 236–237
Caro-Seuss-el, 120
Casey Jr. Splash 'N' Soak
    Station, 44
Cassadaga, 143
Castaway Creek, 92
The Cat in the Hat, 120
Celebration, 12
Celebration Golf Course, 160
Cellphones, 240–241, 243
Center Street, 27
ChampionsGate Golf Resort, 159
Character Greeting Trails, 88
Character meals, 49, 93, 189–191
Characters, 39
Characters in Flight, 94
Charles Hosmer Morse Museum
    of American Art, 143–144
Chase Disney Rewards Visa, 22
Chester & Hester's Dino-Rama, 87
Child swap, 238
China, 61–62
Christmas, Florida, 159

Cinderella Castle, 33–34, 46
Cinematic Spectacular, 102
The Circle of Life, 59
Circus World, 134
City Hall, 32
CityWalk, 153–154, 234
Club 626 Character Dance
    Party, 44
Clyde & Seamore Take Pirate
    Island, 126
Coastersaurus, 134
Colonial Town, 14
Condos, 222
Congo River Adventure Golf, 148
Conservation Station, 84
Consulates, 238
Cornell Fine Arts Museum, 145
Country Bear Jamboree, 39
Cranium Command, 57
Credit cards, 241
Cretaceous Trail, 87
Cross Country Creek, 91
Crush 'n' Gusher, 92
Crystal Arts Shop, 27
CSI: The Experience, 136
Curious George Goes to
    Town, 110
Customs, 237
Cyberspace Mountain, 92
Cypress Gardens, 133, 135

D

Dapper Dans, 27, 32
David Leadbetter Golf Academy,
    159
A Day in the Park with Barney,
    109
Days of the week, 231
De Leon Springs State Park,
    4, 156
Debit cards, 215
Delancey Street Preview Center,
    106
DeLeon Springs, 9
Delta Vacations, 194
Despicable Me Minion Mayhem,
    104
Detroit Tigers, 140
Devish and Banges, 117
Dinnertainment, 186–188
DinoLand U.S.A., 85, 87
DINOSAUR, 87
Dinosaur World, 145
Dino-Sue, 87
Disabled travelers, 235–236
Disaster!, 106
DISBoards.com, 22
Disco H$_2$O, 140
Disco Yeti, 85
Discounts and money-saving tips,
    20–21, 234–235
Discovery Cove, 2, 124
Discovery Cove Marine Mammal
    Keeper Experience, 132
Discovery Island, 80–83
Discovery Island Trails, 82
Disney, Roy, 32

Disney Cruise Line, 166
Disney Dining Plan, 22–24
Disney Dollars, 25, 241
Disney Junior—Live on Stage!, 76
Disney Transportation System
  (DTS), 228
Disney Vacation Club (DVC),
  205–206
Disney Wilderness Preserve,
  156–157
DisneyQuest, 92
Disney's Animal Kingdom, 2, 8, 9,
  79–89
Disney's BoardWalk, 153,
  173–174
Disney's Dolphins in Depth, 97
Disney's Fantasia Gardens, 148
Disney's Hollywood Studios, 2, 8,
  69–79
Disney's Keys to the Kingdom, 97
Disney's Magical Express, 227
Disney's Winter Summerland, 148
Doctors, 237
Dolphins, 58, 126, 127, 132, 133
Donkey's Photo Finish, 105
Double strollers, 26
Downhill Double Dipper, 91
Downtown Disney, 94–95, 153,
  163–165, 171–173
Downtown Orlando, 13–14
  accommodations, 221–222
  restaurants, 183–186
Dr. Doom's Fearfall, 114
Dragon Challenge, 118–119
Dream Along with Mickey, 34
Drinking laws, 237
Driving rules, 237
Driving School, 134–135
Drugstores, 242
Dudley Do-Right's Ripsaw Falls,
  115
Duff Brewery, 107–108

E

"E" tickets, 45
Early Space Exploration, 150
Echo Lake, 70
ECVs (electric convenience
  vehicles), 26, 236
839 N. Orlando Ave., Winter
  Park, 144
The Eighth Voyage of Sindbad
  Stunt Show, 119
Electrical Boat Parade, 93
Electrical Water Pageant, 50
Electricity, 237–238
Eli's Orange World, 165
Embassies and consulates, 238
Emergencies, 238
Emporium, 27
Enzian, 151–152
Epcot, 2, 4, 7, 8, 52–69
Epcot DiveQuest, 97
Epcot Seas Aqua Tour, 98
Epcot's International Flower &
  Garden Festival, 232

Epcot's International Food &
  Wine Festival, 233
Errol Estate Golf & Country Club,
  160
ESPN Wide World of Sports, 94
E.T. Adventure, 109
Exits, secret, 12
Expedition Everest, 84–85
Explorer's Aviary, 132
Express Pass, 100–101
Express Plus, 100
EZLinks.com, 159

F

Family travel, 238
Fantasmic!, 74–75
Fantasy of Flight, 145–146
FASTPASS, 25, 42, 43
FASTPASS+, 35
Fear Factor Live, 107
Ferries, 26, 50
Festival Bay/Artegon Orlando,
  165–166
Festival of the Lion King, 87–88
Fievel's Playland, 109
Finding Nemo—The Musical,
  85, 87
Fingerprints, scanning, 24
Fire Station, 33
Fireworks, Magic Kingdom,
  46, 93
Fireworks Dessert Party, 46
Flag retreat ceremony, 32
FlexTicket, 100, 234
Flight of the Hippogriff, 119
Flights of Wonder, 85
Florida Film Festival, 232
Florida Music Festival, 232
Florida Sun Vacation Homes, 223
Flying Fiddler, 130
Food, 49, 90. See also
  Restaurants
Fort Wilderness, hiking, 50
Fossil Fun Games, 87
1418 ½ Clouser Ave., College
  Park area, 144
France, 64–65
Freedom Flyer, 138
Freshwater Oasis, 132
Frontierland, 37–39
Frontierland Shootin' Arcade, 39
Fun Spot America, 136, 138
Fun Spot USA, 146
Funjet, 194
Future World, 52, 54–59

G

Gangplank Falls, 92
Gatorland, 2, 4, 146
Gay Days, 232
Gays and lesbians, 240
Germany, 62
Ghirardelli Soda Fountain &
  Chocolate Shop, 164
Gibson, Blaine, 34

Give Kids the World Village, 3–4,
  146–147
Go Orlando Card, 235
Golf, 148, 159–161
Gran Fiesta Tour Starring the
  Three Caballeros, 60
The Grand Reef, 132
The Great Movie Ride, 70, 73
Grinchmas & The Macy's Holiday
  Parade, 234
The groove, 155
Guest Relations, 24
Guest Services, 24
"Guidemap," 24

H

Habit Heroes, 55
Habitat Habit!, 84
Halloween Horror Nights, 233
Hang gliding, 162
Hard Rock Live, 155
Harmony Barber Shop, 33
Harry P. Leu Gardens, 4, 157
Harry Potter, 117–119, 231–232
The Haunted Mansion, 39–40
Hawaiian Rumble Adventure Golf,
  148
Hawk's Landing Golf Club, 161
Health concerns, 239
Health insurance, 239–240
Height restrictions, 24, 238
Hidden Mickeys, 78
High in the Sky Seuss Trolley Train
  Ride!, 120
High Octane Refreshments, 78
Highlands Reserve Golf Club, 161
Hog's Head Pub, 122
Holidays, 239
Holidays Around the World at
  Epcot, 234
Hollywood, 108–109
Hollywood Boulevard, 70, 73
Hollywood Drive-In Golf, 148
Hollywood Rip Ride Rockit, 104
Holy Land Experience, 141
Home rentals, 222–224
Honey, I Shrunk the Kids Movie
  Set Adventure, 75
Honeydukes, 117
Hospitals, 239
Hot days, 9
Hot-air ballooning, 162
House of Blues, 94
Houston Astros, 140
Howl at the Moon Saloon, 152
Hunter's Creek Orlando, 161

I

ICE!, 233
Icebar, 152
I-Drive Live, 139
If I Ran the Zoo, 120
IFly, 138
ImageWorks, 59
Imagination Zone, 135

Incredible Hulk Coaster, 113–114
Indiana Jones Epic Stunt
    Spectacular, 73
Innoventions, 55–56
Insurance, 239–240
International Drive
International Drive (I-Drive), 13
    accommodations, 216–220
    attractions around, 136–149
    restaurants, 179–183
Internet and Wi-Fi, 240–241
IPG Florida Vacation Homes, 224
I-Ride Trolley, 228
Island in the Sky, 134
Islands of Adventure (IOA), 2, 7,
    8, 112–122
Italy (Epcot), 62
Itineraries, suggested, 6–15
It's Tough to Be a Bug!, 82–83

J

Japan, 63–64
Jazzy Jellies, 130
Jedi Training Academy, 73
Jellyrolls, 153
JetBlue Getaways, 194
Jimmy Buffett's Margaritaville,
    155
Journey into Imagination with
    Figment, 59
Journey to Atlantis, 128
Jungle Cruise, 35–36
JungleLand Zoo, 134
Jurassic Park, 116–117

K

Kali River Rapids, 85
Kang & Kodos' Twirl 'n' Hurl, 108
Kennedy Space Center, 3, 9,
    149–151
Ketchakiddee Creek, 92
Key West at SeaWorld, 127
Kidcot Fun Stops, 58
Kilimanjaro Safaris, 83–84
Kiss Goodnight, 46
Kissimmee, 12–13, 245
Kraken, 128
Kwik-E-Mart, 107

L

La Nouba, 94–95
Lake Buena Vista, 13, 176,
    178–179, 212–216
Lake Buena Vista Factory Stores,
    163
Last Chance Fruit Stand, 121
LC-39 Observation Gantry, 149
Le Chapeau, 27
Lego Imagination Center, 164
Legoland Florida, 2, 4, 133–135
LGBT travelers, 240
Liberty Square, 39–40
Lights, Motors, Action! Extreme
    Stunt Show, 75
Living with the Land, 59

Lizards, 157
Loch Haven Park, 14
Loggerhead Lane, 132
The Lost Continent, 119
Lost Kingdom Adventure, 134
Lowery's Vacation Homes, 224
Lucy: A Tribute, 108–109
Lunar Theatre, 150
Lunch with an Astronaut, 151
LYMMO, 229
LYNX system, 229

M

Macy's Holiday Parade, 234
Madame Tussauds, 139
Magic Carpets of Aladdin, 36
Magic Kingdom, 2, 26–52
The Magic Neep, 118
The Magic of Disney Animation, 77
Magic Sunrise Ballooning, 162
Magic Your Way, 17, 20, 21
Magical Midway, 138
MagicBand bracelet, 35
Maharajah Jungle Trek, 85
Mail, 240
Main Street, U.S.A., 27–34
Main Street Electrical Parade, 46
Malls, outlet, 162–163
Manatees, 58, 157
Manta, 128
Mardi Gras at Universal, 232
Marketplace, 164
Marvel Super Hero Island,
    112–115
Mayday Falls, 92
Me Ship, the Olive, 116
Medical requirements, 240
Melt Away Bay, 91
Men in Black: Alien Attack,
    106–107
Mennello Museum of American
    Art, 141–142
MetroWest Golf Club, 161
Mexican Folk Art Gallery, 60
Mexico, 60
Mickey's Jammin' Jungle
    Parade, 83
Mickey's Not-So-Scary Halloween
    Party, 233
Mickey's Very Merry Christmas
    Party, 234
Mills 50, 14
Miniature golf, 148
Miniland, 135
Mission: SPACE, 56–57
Mobile phones, 240–241, 243
Money, 241–242
Monorail, 26, 50
Monsters Inc. Laugh Floor, 47
Moose Juice Goose Juice, 122
Morocco, 64
Muppet*Vision 3-D, 75
My Disney Experience, 35
MyMagic+, 35
Mystic Dunes Golf Club, 160
Mystic Fountain, 119

N

Neighborhoods in brief, 10–15
New Year's Eve, 234
New York, 105–106
Newspapers and magazines, 242
Night of Joy, 232–233
Nightlife, 93, 151–155
Nighttime Encounter Spirits, 143
1910 Hotel Plaza Blvd., 144
No Expiration option, 20
Norway, 61

O

Ocean Commotion, 130
Official Visitor Center, 194
Old Spanish Sugar Mill, 156
Old Town, 147
Ollivanders, 118
One Fish, Two Fish, Red Fish,
    Blue Fish, 120
One Ocean, 125
Online Vacation Center, 166
Orange County National Golf
    Center and Lodge, 161
Orange County Regional History
    Center, 142
Orlando Balloon Rides, 162
Orlando Eye, 139
Orlando Film Festival, 233
Orlando International Airport
    (MCO), 225–227
Orlando International Fringe
    Festival, 232
Orlando Magical Dining Month,
    167
Orlando Magicard, 234
Orlando Museum of Art, 142
Orlando Premium Outlets
    International Dr., 162
Orlando Premium Outlets
    Vineland Ave, 163
Orlando Sanford International
    Airport, 226
Orlando Science Center, 142
The Osborne Family Spectacle of
    Dancing Lights, 233
Outdoor activities, 155–162
Outlet malls, 162–163
Outpost, 62

P

Pacific Point Preserve, 129
Package deals, 21–22, 194
Package Pickup, 60
Packing tips, 242
Palmetto bugs, 157
Pangani Forest Exploration
    Trail, 84
Panthers, 157
Parades, Magic Kingdom, 37, 93
Park Hopper option, 17, 20, 22
Parking, 23–24, 26, 237
Parliament House Orlando, 152
"Partners" (statue), 34
Pat O'Brien's, 155

The Peabody Orlando, 154
Pete's Silly Sideshow, 44
Pets, 242
Pets Ahoy!, 126
Pharmacies, 242
Photographers, Universal, 101
PhotoPass, 25
Pins, 165
A Pirate's Adventure: Treasures of the Seven Seas, 37
Pirate's Cove, 148
Pirates' Cover Live Water Ski Show, 135
The Pirates League salon, 37
Pirates of the Caribbean: Battle for Buccaneer Gold, 37, 92
Pixar Place & Animation Courtyard, 75–78
Popeye & Bluto's Bilge-Rat Barges, 115–116
Port Canaveral, cruises from, 166
Port of Entry, 112
Poseidon's Fury, 119
Priceline, 211
Primeval Whirl, 87
Production Central, 102–105
Project X, 135
Pteranodon Flyers, 116
Pumpkin Juice, 118
Push the Talking Trash Can, 44
Putting Edge, 148, 166

Q

Quick Service restaurants, 22–24, 47. See also Restaurants Index

R

Rafiki's Planet, 84
Rail travel, 226, 230
Rainfall, 231
Rainy day activities, 9
Red Coconut Club, 155
Redmond, Dorothea, 34
Reedy Creek Improvement District (RCID), 12
Regional History Center, 165
Rental agencies, 222–224
Reptile World Serpentarium, 149
Reservations, Advance Dining Reservations (ADRs), 24
Restaurants, 5, 167–191. See also Restaurants Index
    character meals, 189–191
    dinnertainment, 186–188
    Disney's BoardWalk, 173–174
    Downtown Disney, 171–173
    downtown Orlando, 183–186
    International Drive area, 179–183
    Islands of Adventure, 120–122
    outside the Disney parks, 167, 170–171
    SeaWorld Orlando, 130–131
    theme park resorts, 188–189
    Universal Orlando, 174–176
    Universal Studios, 110–112

U.S. 192 & Lake Buena Vista, 176, 178–179
Walt Disney World, 22–24, 47–52, 65–69, 78–79, 88–89, 189–191
Reunion Resort & Club, 160
Revenge of the Mummy, 105
Richard Petty Driving Experience, 94
Ripley's Believe It or Not! Odditorium, 138
The Ritz-Carlton Golf Club Orlando, Grande Lakes, 160
River Country, 134
Rix Lounge, 153
Roa's Rapids, 132
Rock [']n' Roller Coaster Starring Aerosmith, 74
Rock the Universe, 233
Routes, 229
Royal Anandapur Tea Company, 88
Royal Caribbean International, 166
Royal Joust, 135
Royal St. Cloud Golf Links, 161
Runoff Rapids, 91
Russell Athletic Bowl, 234

S

Safari Trek, 135
Safety, 242
San Francisco, 106
Scenic Boat Tour, 158–159
Scooters, 236
Sea Carousel, 130
SEA LIFE Aquarium, 139
The Seas with Nemo & Friends, 58
Seasons, 198, 230–231
SeaVenture, 133
SeaWorld Orlando, 2, 3, 8, 122–133, 234
SeaWorld's Halloween Spooktacular, 233
Security, Walt Disney World, 24
Senior travel, 242–243
Serenity Bay, 132
Seuss Landing, 119–120
Shamu Express, 130
Shamu Stadium, 129
Shamu's Happy Harbor, 129–130
Shark Encounter, 129
Shark Reef, 92
Sherbeth Road, 12
Shingle Creek Golf Club, 160
Shopping, 60–62, 112, 162–166
Shrek 4-D, 104–105
Shuttle Launch Experience, 150
Shuttles, 193, 227, 228
Sid Cahuenga's One-of-a-Kind Antiques and Curios, 77
Silver Spurs Rodeo, 232
The Simpsons Ride, 108
Ski Patrol, 91
Sky Tower, 129
SkyCoaster, 146
Sleeping Beauty Castle, 34

Slingshot, 138
Slush Gusher, 91
Smoking, 243
Snow Stormers, 91
Soarin', 58–59
Sorcerer Mickey Hat, 70
Sorcerers of the Magic Kingdom, 33
Southwest Vacations, 194
Souvenirs, 25
Space Mountain, 45
Spaceship Earth, 55
Spider-Man, 112
Splash Mountain, 27, 38
Splendid China, 134
Splitsville Luxury Lanes, 95
SpongeBob StorePants, 109
Spring training, 232
Springfield, 107–108
Star Flyer, 138
Star Tours—The Adventure Continues, 73
Star Wars Weekends, 232
Stingray Lagoon, 127
Stitch's Great Escape!, 47
Storm Force Accelatron, 114
Storm Slides, 92
Storm Struck, 55
Street of the Lifted Lorax, 120
Streets of America, 75
Strollers, 26, 101, 238, 239
The Studio Backlot Tour, 76
Sum of All Thrills, 55
Summit Plummet, 90–91
Sunset Boulevard, 74–75
Surf Lagoon, 139
Surf Pool, 91
Sweet Spells, 78
Swishy Fishies, 130
Swiss Family Treehouse, 34

T

Taxes, 243
Taxis, 227, 229
Teamboat Springs, 91
Telephones, 243–244
Temperatures, 231
Terminator 2: 3-D, 108
Test Track, 57
"The Making of Me" (film), 57
Theme parks, best, 2
TheMouseForLess.com, 22
Thornton Park, 14
Tibet-Butler Preserve, 157–158
Tickets, 17–22, 25, 100–101, 235
Tike's Peak, 91
Timacuan Golf and Country Club, 161
Time zones, 244
"Times Guide," 24, 39
Tinker Bell's Magical Nook, 34
Tip boards, 24, 55
Tipping, 244
Titanic The Experience, 139
Titusville, 151
Toboggan Racers, 91
Toilets, 244

Toluca Legs Turkey Company, 78
Tom Sawyer Island, 38–39
Tomorrowland, 44–46
Tomorrowland Speedway, 45
Tomorrowland Transit Authority PeopleMover, 46
Toon Lagoon, 115–116
Tours, Walt Disney World, 95–98
Town Square Theater, 33
Toy Closet, 109
Toy Story Midway Mania!, 75–76
Train travel, 226, 230
Transformers: The Ride—3D, 105
Transportation, 227–229
Traveling to/from Orlando, 225–230
The Tree of Life, 80
TriceraTop Spin, 87
Tune-In Lounge, 79
Turkey legs, 49
Turnstiles, Walt Disney World, 24
Turtle Talk with Crush, 58
TurtleTrek, 127–128
The Twilight Zone Tower of Terror, 74
Twister . . . Ride It Out, 105
Typhoon Lagoon, 2, 9, 91–92

U

Under the Sea—Journey of the Little Mermaid, 44
United Kingdom, 65
United States Astronaut Hall of Fame, 149
Universal Express Pass, 100
Universal Horror Make-Up Show, 108
Universal Meal Deal, 111
Universal Orlando, 2, 3, 99–122
Universal Studios Florida, 2, 101–112
U.S. 192 area, 12–13, 176, 178–179, 208–211
U.S.A., 63
Utilidor system, 95

V

Vehicle Assembly Building, 150
VillaDirect, 224
Villas of Grand Cypress, 160
Virgin Holidays, 194
Virtual Jungle Cruise, 92
Visas, 244
VISION House, 55
Visitor information, 244–245
The Voyage of the Little Mermaid, 76

W

Wahoo Two, 130
Wallaby Ranch, 162
Walt Disney: One Man's Dream, 77–78
Walt Disney's Carousel of Progress, 46–47

Walt Disney's Enchanted Tiki Room, 36
Walt Disney World, 2, 3, 16–98. See also specific parks and attractions
Walt Disney World Golf Courses, 160
Walt Disney World Railroad, 32, 38, 44
Walt Disney World Tours, 95–98
Water, drinking, 245
Water Park Fun & More (WPF&M), 17, 20
Waterfront at SeaWorld, 129–130
The Watering Hole, 122
Weather, 231
Websites, 230
Weinkeller, 62
Wekiwa Springs State Park, 4, 158
Western Way, 12
Wet [']n Wild, 2, 9, 139
Wheelchairs, 26, 101, 236
Where's the Fire?, 55
White Lightning, 138
Wi-Fi, 240–241
Wild Africa Trek, 98
Wild Arctic, 130
Wildlife Express Train, 84
Wind-Away River, 132–133
Windstorm, 147
Winter Park & North Orlando, 14, 143–145
Winter Park Bach Festival, 232
Wishes, 46
The Wizarding World of Harry Potter, 107, 117–119
Wonders of Life, 57
WonderWorks, 141
Woody Woodpecker's Kidzone, 109–110
Woody Woodpecker's Nuthouse Coaster, 110
World Expo, 106–107
World of Disney, 164
World Showcase, 52, 60–65
Wreck-It Ralph, 93

X

Xanadu, 134

Z

Zonko's Joke Shop, 117
ZORA! Festival, 231

Accommodations

The Alfond Inn, 221
Barefoot'n Resort, 208
Best Western Lake Buena Vista Resort Hotel, 212
Blue Heron Beach Resort, 213
Bohemian Hotel Celebration, 210–211
Cabana Bay Beach Resort, 206–207

Cassadaga Hotel, 143
Clarion Suites Maingate Resort, 208
Comfort Suites Maingate East at Old Town, 208
Courtyard at Lake Lucerne, 221
Destiny Palms Hotel, 210
Disney's All-Star Movies/Disney's All-Star Music/Disney's All-Star Sports, 200
Disney's Animal Kingdom Lodge, 203
Disney's Art of Animation Resort, 200
Disney's Beach Club/Disney's Yacht Club, 203
Disney's Caribbean Beach Resort, 201
Disney's Contemporary Resort, 144, 204
Disney's Coronado Springs Resort, 201–202
Disney's Fort Wilderness Resort & Campground, 202
Disney's Grand Floridian Resort & Spa, 204
Disney's Polynesian Resort, 144, 204–205
Disney's Pop Century Resort, 201
Disney's Port Orleans Riverside and French Quarter, 202
Disney's Wilderness Lodge, 205
Drury Inn Suites, 218
Fairfield Inn Orlando International Drive/Convention Center, 216
Four Points by Sheraton Studio City, 218–219
Gaylord Palms, 215
Grand Bohemian Hotel Orlando, 221–222
Hampton Inn Orlando Convention Center, 218
Hard Rock Hotel, 207
Hawthorn Suites Lake Buena Vista, 212
Holiday Inn Express Hotel & Suites Orlando Lake Buena Vista East, 211
Holiday Inn Express Lake Buena Vista, 213
Hyatt Place Orlando Universal, 219
Hyatt Regency Grand Cypress Resort, 215
JW Marriott Grande Lakes Orlando/Ritz-Carlton Grande Lakes Orlando, 220
La Quinta Inn International Drive, 218
Meliá Orlando Suite Hotel at Celebration, 211
Nickelodeon Suites Resort, 215–216
Palm Lakefront Resort & Hostel, 210
The Peabody Orlando, 220
Portofino Bay Hotel, 207

Quality Suites Lake Buena Vista, 213
Radisson Hotel Lake Buena Vista, 213–214
Rosen Inn Pointe Orlando, 218, 219
Royal Pacific Resort, 207
Shades of Green, 202
Sonesta ES Suites, 219–220
Staybridge Suites Lake Buena Vista, 214
Toscana Suites, 210
Walt Disney World Swan and Dolphin, 205
WorldQuest Resort, 214
Wyndham Lake Buena Vista, 214

Restaurants

ABC Commissary, 78
Aloha Isle, 48
Arabian Nights, 186–187
Atlas House Miller's Lake Buena Vista Ale House, 178
Bahama Breeze, 178
Be Our Guest Restaurant, 51–52
Beverly Hills Boulangerie, 112
Biergarten Restaurant, 68
Blondie's, 121
Boulangerie Pâtisserie, 66
Bruno's Italian Restaurant, 178–179
Bumblebee Man's Taco Truck, 111
The Burger Digs, 121
Cafe 4, 121
Café La Bamba, 112
Cape May Café, 191
Capone's Dinner & Show, 187
Casey's Corner, 48
Catalina Eddie's, 78
Chef Mickey's, 190
Chefs de France, 68–69
Cinderella's Happily Ever After Dinner, 191
Cinderella's Royal Table, 34, 51, 189, 190
Circus McGurkus Cafe Stoo-pendous, 121
Classic Monsters Café, 110
Cletus' Chicken Shack, 111
Columbia Harbour House, 48
Comic Strip Cafe, 121
Confisco Grille, 121
Coral Reef Restaurant, 67
Cosmic Ray's Starlight Cafe, 48–49
Croissant Moon Bakery, 121
Crystal Palace, 190
The Crystal Palace, A Buffet with Character, 51
Cypress Bakery, 131
Dine with Shamu, 130

Dining with an Imagineer, 190
Disney Junior Play 'n Dine at Hollywood & Vine, 79
Disney's Spirit of Aloha Show, 188
Donald's Dining Safari, 190
Donald's Safari Breakfast, 190
El Tenampa, 176
Electric Umbrella, 66
Expedition Café, 131
Fairfax Fare, 78
Fast Food Boulevard, 111
Finnegan's Bar & Grill, 110
Flame Tree Barbecue, 88
The Friar's Nook, 48
The Frying Dutchman, 111
Garden Grill, 190
The Garden Grill, 67
Garden Grove, 191
Gaston's Tavern, 48
Gospel Brunch, 188
Green Eggs & Ham Café, 122
Hollywood & Vine, 79
The Hollywood Brown Derby, 79
Hoop-Dee-Doo Musical Revue, 188–189
Islands of Adventure Fire-Eaters' Grill, 122
Islands of Adventure Islands of Adventure Captain America Diner, 121
Jerusalem Restaurant, 176
Kringla Bakeri Og Kafé, 66
Krusty Burger, 111
La Cantina De San Angel, 66
La Hacienda de San Angel, 67
Le Cellier Steakhouse, 69
Liberty Inn, 66
Liberty Tree Tavern, 51
Lisa's Teahouse of Horror, 111
Lombard's Seafood Grille, 110–111
Lotus Blossom Café, 66
Louie's Italian Restaurant, 110
Luigi's Pizza, 111
Mama Melrose's Ristorante Italiano, 79
Mango Joe's Cafe, 131
Medieval Times, 187
Mel's Drive-In, 112
Mickey's Backyard BBQ, 189
Moe's Tavern, 111
Monsieur Paul, 69
Mythos Restaurant, 122
Nine Dragons Restaurant, 68
'Ohana Character Breakfast, 191
The Outta Control Magic Comedy Dinner Show, 187
Pecos Bill Tall Tale Inn and Cafe, 48
Pinocchio's Village Haus, 48
Pirate's Dinner Adventure, 187
Pizza Planet Arcade, 79
Pizza Predattoria, 121

Pizzafari, 88
Playhouse Disney's Play 'N Dine, 190
Plaza Ice Cream Parlor, 48
The Plaza Restaurant, 51
Princess Storybook Dining, 190
Princess Storybook Dining at Akershus Royal Banquet Hall, 67
Rainforest Cafe, 89
Restaurant Marrakesh, 68
Restaurantosaurus, 88
Richter's Burger Co., 111
Rose & Crown Pub & Dining Room, 69
Rosie's All-American Cafe, 78
50's Prime Time Café, 79
San Angel Inn Restaurante, 67
San Francisco Pastry Company, 110
Sci-Fi Dine-In Theater Restaurant, 79
The Seafire Inn, 131
Sharks Underwater Grill, 131
Sleuth's Mystery Dinner Show, 187–188
Sommerfest, 66
Spice Mill Cafe, 131
Spice Road Table, 68
Starring Rolls Café, 78
Studio Catering Co., 78
Sunshine Seasons, 66
Sunshine Tree Terrace, 48
Supercalifragilistic Breakfast, 191
Superstar Character Breakfast, 191
Tamu Tamu Eats & Refreshment, 88
Tangierine Café, 66
Teppan Edo, 68
Terrace Garden Buffet, 131
Three Broomsticks, 122
Thunder Falls Terrace, 121
Tokyo Dining, 68
Tomorrowland Terrace, 49
Tony's Town Square Restaurant, 51
Tortuga Tavern, 48
Treasure Tavern, 188
Trilo-Bites, 88
Turkey Leg Cart, 48
Tusker House Restaurant, 89
Tutto Gusto, 66
Tutto Italia Ristorante, 68
Universal Studios Kid Zone Pizza Company, 111
Via Napoli Ristorante E Pizzeria, 68
Voyagers Smokehouse, 131
Wantilan Luau, 189
Wimpy's, 121
Yak & Yeti Local Food Cafes, 88
Yak & Yeti Restaurant, 89
Yakitori House, 66
Yorkshire County Fish Shop, 67

DATE DUE

PRINTED IN U.S.A.